VESTAVIA HILLS LIBRARY

VESTAVIA HILLS ALABAMA

TO THE ENDS
OF THE EARTH

MICHAEL TALBOT

TO THE ENDS OF THE EARTH

ALFRED A. KNOPF

New York 1986

THIS IS A BORZOI BOOK
PUBLISHED BY ALFRED A. KNOPF, INC.

Copyright © 1986 by Michael Talbot
All rights reserved under International and Pan-American Copyright Conventions.
Published in the United States by Alfred A. Knopf, Inc., New York,
and simultaneously in Canada by Random House of Canada Limited, Toronto.
Distributed by Random House, Inc., New York.

Library of Congress Cataloging-in-Publication Data
Talbot, Michael
To the ends of the earth.
I. Title.
PR9619.3.T257T6   1986   823   85-45604
ISBN 0-394-53376-3

Manufactured in the United States of America
FIRST EDITION

For my wife, Val,
and my friend Howard Gotlieb.
Thank you . . .

TO THE ENDS OF THE EARTH

1

"WHERE YE SHALL be gibbetted at the place of common execution and your body burned by the public hangman—"

"N—no!'

"And may the Lord have mercy upon ye thereafter." Mr. Justice Spivey touched the black cap on his wig and nodded at the waiting tipstaffs. "Take her down."

"No!" the woman was still screaming, dress ripping on the court's spiked barricade, manacles flailing. "Not me sir! I never done nothing—!" The men were closing from behind, one wrenched her hair into a short rope, his mate folded her knees with a kick. Old Bailey's iron trap slammed over her raging as the public gallery began jostling to get at a pieman's tray before the next prisoner came up for judgment.

Only the clerk kept his peace, back hunched to the jury bench, eyes squinting in the wintry daylight as his quill closed another life in copperplate. "Kemp, Mrs. Mary. 17.x.1785. Death & Burning for treason in the second degree. Viz: coining and uttering base halfpence to the value of £491.11.2½d." He strewed grey sand across the paper and flexed aching fingers while the ink dried, then folded the sheet and tapped most of the sand grains into their wooden caster: the rest he blew across the courtroom floor.

Mr. Justice Spivey had stopped trying to get a legal opinion from London's lord mayor, almost unconscious since their midday meal together, and was now leaning across him to beckon a court usher. The man trotted up, wiped nose with sleeve and nodded at the justice's commands before going to find a window which might ventilate the public gallery without, at the same time, blowing the court's papers into even greater muddle.

Tired seams creased Spivey's face as he settled back in his high seat beneath its gilded G III R cypher. The first week of this legal year—which, since the Middle Ages, began in October—had already threatened to be no less of a burden than any other in the past, serving the Crown and defending society in this thankless task.

Spivey sighed. His bushy eyebrows, nutcracker profile and pleated cheeks had again been held up to public ridicule by the cartoonist Gillray, and it hurt him. It hurt him deeply. Edmund Spivey knew that he was a sensitive, cultivated, scholarly man. The sort who never could, never would get more than a few moments of pleasure from this stern duty of sentencing whores to be flogged naked at Newgate wall, or branding army deserters on the cheek, or sending saucy pamphleteers to be pelted to death in the pillory, or despatching grand larceny to the gallows. Only a truly Roman sense of honour could hold him steadfast for so long, he liked to announce with gloomy relish.

The chamber pot clenched between his knees was brimming again. It often did these cold days. He grimaced into its murky mirror and twitched his ermine robes against a new draught from the rainy streets outside. "Let us now proceed to the final process for this afternoon, Mr. Grimwade."

The prosecuting attorney got to his feet, brushed pie crumbs off his lap and bobbed a short bow to the Bench. "May it please the court, m'lord, it is the matter of *Rex versus Joseph Cribb*, delivered to trial on a special warrant entered by Mr. Alderman Gurney." Grimwade paused as the usher began thumping the floor stones with his staff of office. "Call Joseph Cri-ibb!"

The iron door banged open under the prisoners' dock and a sharp kick from behind started the day's last defendant up its worn steps, fetters clinking, breath rasping, face the colour of dead mullet after a season in Kings Bench Prison where an outbreak of gaol fever freed one man in seven before trial. Only the ragged greatcoat came anywhere near fitting him, unlike the pair of wet breeches which slapped around bare, spindly legs. The oddly matched shoes also squelched cold vinegar from the bath which each prisoner was thrown into before coming to judgment. A sensible precaution. A few years earlier a judge of common pleas, a baron of the exchequer, a lord mayor of London, together with forty of the barristers and jurymen had died after fever crept into Old Bailey on a similar batch of prisoners.

Cribb stumbled over the last step into the dock and aimed a feeble kick at the nearest tipstaff. "Keep your bleedin' maulers to yourself, pig ears! 'Ere's a cove what can still stand on 'is own two feet!" On cue, the public gallery replied with delighted whistles and cheers: a prime die-hard was worth every shilling of the ushers' tip for a good view of the fun.

Spivey was not amused. He scowled across the courtroom while the constables restored order with their truncheons. This Cribb item promised to be one of a type far too common these days on the streets of London—

the broken soldier. The reckless flaunting of that filthy red coat was worth minutes of sworn testimony to Spivey's trained eye.

Although it was now three years since the army had failed to hold down the American colonists, it was still almost impossible for decent citizens to pass through the streets of the capital without being abused by ragged hordes of discharged soldiers and sailors, baring their wounds and chancres for a penny, twopence to cover them again. Dirty, insolent, dangerous men. More of a threat to their betters than ever they had been to the king's rebel subjects.

Spivey's scowl hardened as he trapped and held Cribb's darting glare from the dock. Very dirty. Very dangerous. A typical dark beast from that underclass whose uprising back in '80 had collapsed Spivey's Thames-side residence into a hillock of blazing timbers, along with much else of value in the city. It had been hard to flog Gordon's rioters back into their kennels after their week of looting, and then only after infantry and dragoons had swept the streets with musket fire. But, Spivey and many others now wondered, what would it be like next time when many of the rioters would themselves be veterans? Nobody knew, but most in authority doubted if a few rounds of ball and a display of force would be enough to reduce the Cribbs to due subordination: next summer it might indeed be necessary to order up the horse artillery as well, recapturing London block by block with grape and canister shot.

Spivey was still scowling as the constables finished their work. The prosecutor rubbed chilblained fingers, bowed again to the Bench and began summarising the Crown's case in a flat, bored voice, breath puffing small wisps of cloud in front of his plump, well-scrubbed face. "Joseph Cribb. It has been stated that, on the tenth day of February, this year of our Lord 1785, you were properly and lawfully apprehended by officers of the Phoenix Fire Assurance Company as you did run from the burning manufactory of James Watkins and Sons, Feather Lane. Furthermore, it is charged that, when properly and lawfully challenged by them, you did have a roll of saddlers' leather, sworn value six pounds, nine shillings and threepence farthing, concealed about your person. Thereafter you were given in custody to the City Watch House where you did cause a grievous affray and disturbance to the prejudice of public order and the peace of our gracious sovereign, King George, whom God ever preserve and protect, amen."

The prosecutor glanced up from his sheaf of papers. "How then do you plead? Guilty? Or not guilty?"

Cribb blinked. This was the first official statement of the indictment he would have to answer for his life in the next few minutes and, for a moment, he was relieved that it had stopped short at simple arson and robbery, though either charge would be enough to bounce him into eternity at the end of a rope. He blinked again, winning time to plan his counter-attack, reading the court's moods and undercurrents—

"*Well?*"

Cribb chose an old and trusted opening tactic, the Timid Smile, adding for good measure a convincing catch in the throat as he spread both hands as far as their manacles would allow. "Ho no, sir, that's not the way at all! I mean to say—!"

"Confine yourself to answering the charge, my man!" Mr. Justice Spivey snapped, crouching forward again. "Are you or are you not guilty as stated?"

Cribb flinched respectfully. "Me, *guilty?* Def'nitely not, Your Honour-ship, sir!"

The gallery murmured appreciation at such a polished performer and shrewd judges of form began laying off bets on the probable verdict and for how long the jury would need to retire: the odds against Cribb's acquittal shortened slightly.

The prosecutor pursed lips and began flicking through his papers. "May it please the court, call Mr. Abel Pope to the stand."

There was a sudden silence as the usher's iron-shod staff thumped and a stocky, medium-height man in plain brown Hackney coat with deep pistol pockets, his red choker neatly tied, marched into the witness box. He gripped the Bible while one of the clerks hurried him through a binding oath. Abel Pope was equally brisk with the reply. The Crown's prosecutor nodded approvingly: a jury picked off the limited roll of businessmen would know whom to trust when told to weigh the evidence of Cribb against that of this substantial, well-fed man. Grimwade began strengthening the impression. "Mr. Pope? Describe your employment."

Abel Pope squared shoulders, well rehearsed in courtroom procedure after a lifetime of bounty hunting and thief trapping across the capital's central mile. He was a man of power, he could afford a lazy smile at Cribb's glare. "Well, sir, most times I nabs burny prigs for the Phoenix Fire Assurance Company o' Leadenhall Street." The voice was gruffly confident with just the right depth of respect for his questioner's higher profession and social class.

" 'Nabs burning pigs'?" Mr. Justice Spivey interjected.

The prosecutor bowed low. "*Prigs*, m'lord. Mr. Pope is saying that he is a well-regarded thief catcher, one whose services are in great demand tracking down 'fire priggers,' those depraved ruffians who first raise fires, then steal goods by pretending to save them from the burning warehouse, shop or dwelling place."

"Ah. Quite. Proceed."

The prosecutor read the hardening set of his jurors' mouths. "Mr. Pope? Outline your recent experiences in this your, ah, avocation."

"Uh?"

The smile cooled. "What have you done for a living these past several months? Let us say, since the beginning of January?"

Abel Pope studied scarred knuckles. Business was slack now that the winter rains had wet London, and there were too many unpaid bounties waiting to be claimed from Bow Street after their executions had been carried out. Meanwhile a citywide network of spies still had to be paid, regardless of his own income.

He glanced up uneasily. "Well, sir, it was me what nabbed the Whitechapel Crew when they torched Brudenell's place across in Southwark. An' I got Mother 'umphries necked for the raisin' o' that blaze in Pudding Lane. I also done for Jem Scruby, but 'e went an' croaked first, so it's not worth a brass farthing now. Then I—"

"Quite so." The prosecutor flicked a hand. "I shall rephrase my question. In your capacity as a trusted and experienced officer, employed by a most respected city assurance company, do you perhaps recognise anyone in this courtroom today? Someone whom you may have encountered earlier this year in the course of your profession?"

The thief catcher's face cleared. "Indeed I do, sir."

"Oh?" The prosecutor arched eyebrows for effect. "And where might that be?"

"Why, a-standing in the dock, Phossy Joe Cribb, sir."

"Phossy?"

"Yessir, Phossy, sir, 'is flash name. From phos'phrus, sir. A flammable stuff used by such fly coves to torch their burns."

The prosecutor let Pope's words torch the imaginations of a jury whose own warehouses, shops and dwellings were—if they'd survived the inferno of '80—highly flammable shells of wood and soft brick. He smiled. "And this, ah, 'Phossy' is the accused's flash name among his criminal associates and colleagues?"

"Yessir."

"Hoy! That's enough o' that! I'm a proper respect'ble—!"

"Silence!" Mr. Justice Spivey aimed a deadly finger across his courtroom. "The accused will speak only when spoken to!"

Grimwade cocked a knowing eye at the jury foreman, then warmed another smile for the thief catcher to encourage him along the same fruitful track. "Mr. Pope. Describe to the court how and where you last saw, ah, Phossy Cribb."

Abel Pope was also determined to nail down this conviction as he retold in brief, simple sentences how he and his team of human bulldogs had gone with the company's water pump and ladder to a major blaze in Feather Lane, where a bucket chain of neighbours was losing its fight with the roaring flames. A justice of the peace had already sent to the Tower armoury for gunpowder and troops in case a fire lane had to be blasted through the downwind tenement block. Meanwhile, bales of leather and finished harness were being pitched into the street and guarded by two overseers and Mr. Watkins himself.

"There being nothin' out of the ordinary yet 'appening that side o' the incident, I then proceeded to the back yard, where I expected we might find a familiar face or two. . . ." Abel Pope paused, enjoying the jury's attentive silence. "I was right. 'Beef the pigs!' their spyman shouted as I coshed 'im cold and straightway the whole pack o' rotten mongrels began leggin' it back to Ratters' Castle, followed close by my men."

"And?"

"Why, sir, I then turned back an' stood by an open door. 'If there be any o' that priggy crew still inside,' I said to meself, 'they'll soon smoke out an' nab sweetly.' "

"And were there any more thieves hiding inside the blazing premises of James Watkins and Sons?" Grimwade prompted.

"Oh, def'nitely, sir! In my experience o' the trade, there's always some cully cove what thinks I'm grassy enough to toddle after the kiddykins while 'e rumbles off with the boodle bag."

"Mr. Grimwade?" Justice Spivey interrupted again. "Would your witness kindly confine his evidence to the king's English?"

The prosecutor bowed. "May it please the court, but there is a species of canting talk used by the lowest orders which defies exact translation. However, I am sure Mr. Pope will oblige us most handsomely." He turned, glanced at his jury to see how well he was being received, then began pacing the short distance between them and the witness box. "Mr. Pope. Describe what happened next."

The thief catcher was brief. A shape had dashed from the boiling smoke, still clutching a roll of leather, tangled his feet with Pope's cudgel and gone sprawling across the cobblestones. Pope had sapped him over the head and bundled him off to the watch house with the luckless spyman. "Kicked up regular bad when 'e awoke, so I'm told."

"You refer to Phossy Cribb, of course?"

"Yessir. Of course."

Grimwade stopped his pacing and suddenly appeared thoughtful, as if noticing something for the first time. "Mr. Pope. From the tenor of your evidence it would seem you already had considerable previous experience of this—individual?"

"Yessir. Def'nitely considerable."

"Can you be more explicit?"

"It'll be a regular pleasure." Pope's mouth tightened at the damp shape between a pair of tipstaffs in the dock. "I long 'ad me eyes on Phossy Joe, sir. A regular cunning cove, sir, a regular bad lot. Very flash. Long ripe for the short drop. Said as what nobody 'ad yet made the rope what'd choke 'im." Pope's imperfectly genteel accent was crumbling fast. "For what reason 'e always worked alone or with them other bloody-backed redcoat shits, reckoning as what the law would never lay a finger on 'im while 'e kept outside o' regular family." The thief catcher glared across the courtroom. "What goes to show 'ow wrong you can be!"

"Balls!" the prisoner replied.

"Yours or mine!"

"Mr. Grimwade! Control your witness!"

The prosecutor's wig bobbed urgently. "May it please the court! I shall direct Mr. Pope to confine his comments strictly to the matters under consideration—!"

"Please do!"

Abel Pope was venomous as Grimwade brought him to heel again and began leading him through a detailed history of Cribb's street life since the Seventh Regiment of Foot, City of London Fusileers broke four of its six companies after the peace of '82. "Let a cove like Phoss 'ave enough rope an' it'll 'ang 'im for sure," the thief catcher went on, gathering speed again. "Not that 'e was always on the burny prig, o' course. Before that 'e footpadded round Covent Garden with a crew o' other masterless soldiers an' suchlike, calling 'imself 'Captain Gun,' as nasty a bill o' goods as ever slit your pocket or cut your throat," Pope added, with loathing for the many thousands of defeated men who had limped home to live off city streets which, by right and custom, already belonged to established families of beggars and pickpockets, dog snatchers and cloak snitchers.

The delicate and profitable balance between thief and catcher had been thrown out of joint by an invading army of broken soldiers whose only saleable skill was murder in hot blood to the beat of drum. A truce had been declared between the two halves of London's underclass as both combined to hunt down this threat to their ancient way of life.

Pope's mouth twisted. "An' if ever a gent wanted a knuckle job doin', or some cove pushed off early, an' if the price was right, you can bet your sweet life Captain Gun would soon be a-splashin' of 'is money around the Saracen's 'Ead like the fleet was in port!"

"Mr. Grimwade? Translate."

The prosecutor bowed. "May it please the court, m'lord, what Mr. Pope is endeavouring to say is that the accused already has a most unsavoury reputation—"

The judge's finger lifted. "That may be so, but today he stands indicted upon a charge of stealing from the scene of a fire. In matters larcenous, such as we now address ourselves to, it is the *animus furandi*—the intention to steal—which must first be established. Mr. Pope's evidence thus far, interesting though it may be, does not in my opinion bear much upon the question to hand." He turned again to the lord mayor, still slumped along the judicial bench, mouth ajar. "Isn't that so, Sir Samuel?"

"Uwhazzat?"

Spivey sighed. "I said, the proof of *animus furandi* as a causative factor in establishing matters larcenous was clearly defined by our learned predecessor, Mr. Justice Molineaux, sitting on the Kings Bench in 1473."

"Ab—ab'slutely!" The lord mayor's face was clearing as he struggled upright again, hand over hand, peering at the darkening courtroom. "By God, Spivey, you're right! Damned rogues the lot of 'em!"

Spivey looked away. "Mr. Grimwade? Allow *me* to direct your attention to the fact that it is the intention which constitutes a felony. This principle was clearly incorporated into common law well over three centuries ago when the then king's attorney said, 'Felony is to defraud him in whom the property is, that is to say, *animus furandi*.' To which the chief justice replied, 'It is the intent of a man which is triable at robbery.' Clearly, then, these are fundamental factors in the determination of justice." Spivey's frown deepened. "It ought not to be necessary for me to bring such basic rules to your attention, Mr. Grimwade."

The Crown prosecutor made a bow which bordered on the impudent. "May it please the court, but the present circumstances are such that the prior intent of the prisoner must be quite obvious. That a fellow of his reputation, with a flash name based upon phosphorus, is taken at the scene of a major blaze carrying stolen goods—"

" 'Goods alleged to be stolen,' " Mr. Justice Spivey corrected.

Grimwade bowed again. "As m'lord directs. Let us then say the prisoner was apprehended with goods, ah, alleged to be stolen at the scene of a fire. Surely this combination of factors is more than adequately covered by the equally fundamental principle of *Qui peccat inscienter scienter emendat?*"

The judge steepled fingertips at twelve baffled jurymen. "My learned colleague is drawing your attention to a legal maxim of King Henry the First, namely, 'He who sins unwittingly shall, upon knowledge thereof, make due reparation.' "

Spivey looked back at the prosecutor with wary respect. "Mr. Grimwade. While concurring in general terms, for the moment the sole concern of this court is the proven intent of the prisoner at the bar. Can your witness so do? Or has he completed his deposition of the facts, the *facts* as he knows them to be?"

Grimwade hesitated, then flicked a hand for Abel Pope to clear the witness box.

"As I thought," Spivey observed. "Very well, let the accused now give an account of himself."

Cribb left a puddle of vinegar on the wooden planks and awkwardly clutched the Bible with fettered hands while the clerk recited the oath. Then Cribb clenched spiked rails to steady his knees while trying to place every cough, shuffle and grunt in the two rows of shadowy faces behind the lawyer.

Grimwade was pacing floor again, soles crushing loose grit and old egg shells, hands tucked under his black gown for warmth and dramatic effect. Cribb swallowed, steadying his breath, shoulders bunching to break the enemy's attack at bayonet-point in his imagination. Grimwade shipped round, finger jutting over the rails. "You are Phossy Joe Cribb! Alias Mr. Gun! Alias——!"

And just as suddenly Cribb's mind was moving freely again after months of nagging uncertainties. "*Me*, sir? Ho no, sir! I'm *Joe* Cribb, sir! A poor ostler what's fallen on 'ard times and newly come down from Birming'am for to look for honest work! *Joshy* Cribb's my big brother, sir, oh, a regular bad lot 'e is! 'You not like your brother Joshua,' that's what me wife—sweetest Meg, the angels guard 'er—used to say. Many's the time she told me: 'You're as sober as the day is long, Joe dearest. You're a 'ardworking and decent 'usband, not like your brother Joshy. 'E'll come to a bad end, 'e will, just you mark my words——!' "

As planned, Grimwade lunged after Cribb's decoy story. "Then what were you doing in Feather Lane, at two of the night of February the tenth, fleeing from a conflagration with a roll of leather under your arm?"

"Shoulders, sir," Cribb corrected timidly, wiping his nose on his palm. To flatly deny the charge would back him against a wall with no further room to manoeuvre, the trial would be over almost as quickly as if he had told the truth, for once, and said how Pope had bought a rat in Cribb's gang, set an ambush behind the Saracen's Head, pinioned Cribb in a sheet of sailcloth and planted him at the blaze in Feather Lane for his rope money. And to settle old scores.

Grimwade blinked.

"Shoulders, sir," Cribb repeated humbly. "I 'ad the leather slung across my shoulders, sir. It's easier to carry that way. Terrible 'ard stuff to carry, leather. That's why I took it: I 'oped the reward for saving such a big 'un would be enough to get me a bite to eat while I found work in a stable——"

"You lyin' bastard!"

"Mr. Grimwade!" Spivey warned from the bench. "I shall not tell you to control your witness again!"

"As m'lord directs!" the prosecutor promised, eagerly bobbing head up and down. He glared at Pope—now sinking back into his place—then at Cribb's timid, vacant smile. Either this was just a lucky simpleton, or here was a particularly slippery cove.

Grimwade was learning to be careful, slowly pacing in front of the jurors. "So, my man, you claim you took the leather hoping it would get you food?" He spun, finger jabbing. "Instead it earned you lodging in gaol!"

"A terrible mistake, sir," Cribb replied with another simple-minded smile. "Shouldn't 'appen to a Christian, sir, but times is terrible 'ard up Birming'am way so I walked down to see if any of my cousins might 'elp out, like."

"*Cousins?*"

"Yessir, cousins, sir, lots o' Cribbses, sir. We're a particular close lot."

Grimwade's lip curled. "And I suppose you all look particularly alike?"

"Many say as what we do."

"*So* alike that an experienced thief catcher would imagine you were someone else by the light of a blazing warehouse?"

"That's what they say," Cribb agreed with an empty grin at the jurors. "Times is terrible 'ard up Birming'am way so I walked down to London for to earn honest bread. The very day I got in, there's this terrible fire and lots of people shifting stuff out the back." Cribb read the prosecutor's sarcastic yawn and deftly switched his attack, gripping the iron spikes in front with sudden passion. "'Ow was I to know they wasn't on the straight? 'Ow was I to know when I joined in to get a reward I'd be bashed on the 'ead and chucked in clink! Now you all saying as I gone and stole things what wasn't mine—!" Tears began trickling down his cheeks. "It's not p-p-proper Christian right!"

Grimwade thought fast: this case was proving bothersome. "What an incredible fabrication," he sneered. "You have, of course, character witnesses who will testify on your behalf?"

"Birming'am is a terrible long walk for the likes o' me, sir," Cribb sobbed, manfully trying to hide the tears. "No money in looking after 'orses these days, there isn't."

Grimwade brushed this nonsense aside and went for the kill. "You cannot be serious when you pretend that a rogue of your reputation cannot afford to buy a strawman . . . ?" A sly reference to the professional witnesses who were, even now, loitering outside with wisps of hay in the heels of their shoes, touting for hire.

"Never learned much about drawmen," Cribb mumbled, floating out of range, foiling Grimwade's clumsy thrusts. "I done nothing wrong, nor ever will, sir, 'cause it's *Joshy* Cribb you want and I'm only—"

"Mr. Grimwade?" Spivey interrupted testily.

"M'lord?"

"The hour grows late. Unless you have any further questions to put, or unless the defendant has anything else which is strictly pertinent to the matter in hand, I propose to instruct the jury."

The Crown's prosecutor bowed. "May it please the court, I have nothing more to add. The accused's intent and motive are self-evident and, unless one can believe this absurd confection of 'cousins' and 'walking down from Birmingham,' ample proof of grand larceny has been presented. In any event I consider the charge to be proven beyond any shadow of doubt by the sworn testimony of Mr. Pope when he drew our attention to the accused's previous record." He bowed again and sat down.

Mr. Justice Spivey cleared throat and peered across the darkening courtroom. "Members of the jury. You will confine your deliberations strictly to the evidence presented to you by Mr. Pope and the defendant, Cribb. You will weigh their words and answers carefully before deciding whether or not an adequate *animus furandi* has been established, without which no felony can be said to have happened at law. If so established you must then, as a consequence, bring down the only verdict for aggravated felonies—death." He paused, frowning. "You may now retire to consider your verdict."

Cribb watched from the plank between his two keepers as the jurors filed away to their left. A door slammed behind them and Cribb began flipping links of his fetters over the dock's iron spikes in a kind of solitaire quoits, humming a flat, nervous marching tune while he held up a shaky front of indifference.

Not that many in the public gallery were bothered during the interval; most were concerned with doing their own business or throwing apple cores at a pair of ushers as they carried a long stepladder, lighting the lamps which swung overhead.

Cribb was still flipping iron when the jurors began returning in single file. The Old Bailey was brought to order by the head usher as the king's judges also returned to their bench a few minutes later. Mr. Justice Spivey settled with a contented burp, refreshed from the sideboard in his chambers, and eyed the standing jury foreman. "You have reached a verdict?"

"We have, my lord."

"And what is your verdict?"

"Guilty as charged, my lord."

Spivey nodded and steepled fingertips again. At six pounds, nine and threepence farthing value, the accused's felony was well over twice the legal minimum for a capital conviction and, as such, an offence just as serious as sacrilege, and rape, and sodomy, and stealing an heiress, and concealing a bankrupt's effects, and impersonating a Chelsea pensioner, and chipping stone off Westminster Bridge. There were other, many other capital crimes on the statute books, and he had tried most of them, he remembered, wearily looking up as the usher's staff began striking floor in time with the man's nasal whine: "Oyez! Oyez! My lord, the king's justice, doth strictly charge and command all manner of persons to keep respectful silence while sentence of death is passed on the prisoner at the bar!"

Spivey fitted his black cap for the second time that afternoon, then sat bolt upright to complete the necessary ritual. "Joseph Cribb. You have been tried and found guilty as charged. From evidence given in court it is quite plain this has been a melancholy conclusion toward which you have long tended, combining as you do the glib tongue of an habitual liar with the reckless cunning of an incendiary and murderer.

"Not that it could always have been so: as a soldier in His Majesty's service you ought to have been taught the virtue of due subordination to your betters. But, instead, you have wilfully chosen to set yourself in defiance of all order and the laws of this realm. That was truly rash. Happily those same laws provide for full repayment and all here today may rest assured that you will soon be quit of your debt to a society which you have disgraced for so long.

"However, you may also take some crumb of comfort from the knowledge that your life will not have been altogether without purpose if, as you pass from this world into the next to answer your summons at that higher seat of judgment, you also give timely warning to others similarly tempted by delusions of dishonest gain. Because England's laws are not unjust, nor are they vengeful. Quite the reverse. We seek by the terror of their implacable example to save the lives of many by the merciful sacrifice of a few. Remember: the law is at her most merciful when she shows no pity for those who defy her reasonable burden."

Spivey studied the dark, sweaty, staring face, the unremarkable face of many a tinker, or poacher, or gypsy brought to judgment over the years. He sighed: only their names seemed to change. "Joseph Cribb. It is the verdict of this court that ye shall be returned hence to the place whence ye came, and thence at a time to be stated, to the place of common execution where ye shall be hanged by the neck until the body be dead, dead, dead. And may the Lord have mercy on ye thereafter." He touched the black cap. "Take him down."

The cramping words. Cribb swayed, grabbing the dock's spikes, fighting to stand up, to show pluck, to go game. "Them Indians! Them Frogs! Them Rebels never croaked me! Nor will—!"

The tipstaffs struck, felling him from behind, dragging Cribb feet first into the prisoners' hold. The iron trapdoor slammed for the last time that afternoon and they completed their duty by driving him around the floor with boots to the belly, back, balls. Cribb writhed, arms protecting his exposed neck, waiting for their hobnailed soles to tramp away for the day's committal warrants.

He took a shuddering breath and flopped over. Nine other convicts lolled against the walls, most watching with happy detachment now that it was someone else's turn to suffer. Only the woman condemned before Cribb—Mrs. Kemp the coiner—was still lost in her own hysterical misery. " 'Ere! You! What they give *you*, eh? What's yours, soldier?"

Cribb ignored her and crawled over to an unclaimed piece of stonework where he could lean his own troubles.

"Well?!"

Cribb shut both eyes. "The neck job."

"Huh! I got to be burned! Me! What never done nothin' but 'elp me 'usband! 'E gets off, an' I gets b-b-burned!"

"Ar, shut yer face, Granny," a red-nosed man commanded, eyes fixed on the pair of dice he was shooting with one of the turnkeys and a young boy who had just begun seven years for stealing brass doorknockers on Sundays. "If you'd both 'ad more sense you'd 'ave stayed with a nice little larceny like queer divin'. Nobody's never got jerked to Jesus for jumpin' in the river to claim a Humane Society guinea. Three months from now I'll be out on the job again, free as air. Dead easy."

"Hn!" Cribb winced, trying to sit upright against the cold wall. "One yellow george to split three ways? Muggins to jump in the drink while the others drag 'im out again? That's not *my* style!"

The queer diver shrugged, collecting a shilling off the turnkey. "Like they say, there's old ones an' there's bold ones, but I ain't never seen an old bold one."

"Joe Cribb's not stiff by a long day's march!"

"Ain't it wonderful 'e can still think so?" the man said with a knowing wink at the other prisoners. "I just 'eard as what the next wry neck day's been set for the end o' this month. . . ."

Cribb bared teeth at the circle of grinning faces, all from established London families, all without any time to waste on outsiders. "Not for me it ain't! 'You'll croak in your bed like a ge'man,' an old 'Gyptian woman told me once. 'In a room full of golden sunshine, with a bag o' gold under your pillow like a regular swell'!"

The red-nosed man was happier with a silver shilling now. "I s'pose them what sleeps in their clothes always dies in their beds, no matter when Mr. Grim calls."

Cribb started jerking a stiff middle finger in the air between them as the other hold door banged open and London's marshal stooped through with a roll of warrants signed by the Bench. "On your feet!"

The convicted prisoners listlessly stood in line while another pair of guards looped chain round each set of wrist irons and padlocked it round the last man's neck.

"Move!"

Cribb stumbled through the door after the queer diver, tugging enough slack on his own length of chain to flick a hand over the man's pocket in the short, dark passageway. But the shilling stayed tantalisingly out of reach as they jerked to a halt in Old Bailey's despatch yard. An escort of javelin men stood in the night, black tricorne hats tugged low against the drizzle, fists gripping wooden spear shafts.

The city marshal puffed up a mounting block's step and got across his saddle. He slapped loose rein and horseshoes crunched over the cobbles. London's sheriff was waiting in an archway, cloak buttoned to chin. "Any the mob wants to spring or scrag?" the senior law officer asked, jabbing a thumb at the locked gates and rising surge of noise where the crowd was gathering outside.

"Nah. Just the usual."

The sheriff raised his whip. The escort closed ranks round their prisoners. Iron baskets of rope pickings and Stockholm tar blazed above poultry and vegetable stalls in the street as Old Bailey's gates rumbled on metal rollers and armed men tramped through. Someone at the back of the waiting crowd lofted a turnip over the heads in front, missing the sheriff by a whisker and splattering two prisoners instead. The javelin men took it as their order to bunch closer and start clubbing a path through hostile jeers, whistles and running volleys of refuse.

2

NEWGATE GAOL had spanned the far side of the market place for the past six centuries. Set due east and west along the line of an old Roman wall, its stonework had been manured by the countless generations of sparrows and pigeons which nested among its pilasters and statues. One, a badly streaked "Liberty" with Dick Whittington's cat coiled round her feet, still balanced in a niche above the city gallows which had recently been moved into London from the open fields of Tyburn. She was lucky to have survived this long; almost everything else had been smashed during the torrid summer of 1780 when Lord George Gordon's Protestant Association detonated its week of bigotry, looting and house-to-house fighting.

The capital's main prison was as old and, if possible, more hated than the Bastille which still served Paris. Its gates had been battered off their hinges, bales of hay soaked with gin from the nearby Langdale's Distillery had been pitched inside and a torch thrown after them. Only when most of the prisoners had been sprung and the buildings well ablaze had the mob then turned on the private chapels and embassies of those Catholic powers who supported the American rebels.

Cribb clinked nearer Newgate's fire-bleached walls. It had only been months after others had finished their seven days and nights of plunder and rape that a garbled version of the good news had reached the ranks of the British army in Carolina—after Cribb's troop of mounted rangers had ambushed a mail cart carrying captured London newspapers, behind enemy lines. He snapped back to the present and crossed fingers as the line of ironed prisoners stumbled past the gallows and was counted through Newgate's small wicket. "Seven. Eight. Nine. Ten's yer lot!"

The rebuilt gate heaved shut. Heavy bolts dropped into granite paving slabs. A yellow torch flame tugged and snatched in the icy wind which slashed across the open press yard. Sleet rattled off the roof tiles, spraying the crouching prisoners. The city marshal slid off his horse and advanced to Newgate's head keeper.

Mr. Arthur Bambridge paced forward to greet him halfway, paunchy and thin-lipped, wig powdered and curled, cane tucked under one arm. Recently promoted from the Fleet Prison, where he had ruled as deputy, Bambridge was now in effect the general manager for a syndicate of City grocers who had leased the Crown's privilege of selling bread, bed and water to the destitute. Keeper and marshal formally raised hats to each other and the warrants changed hands. "Three debtors, Mr. Bambridge. Two lagged for fourteen years. Two for seven. One at three months. And a couple o' ropedancers."

Bambridge checked the wax seals and beckoned his turnkeys to separate the latest batch of inmates. Cribb and Mrs. Kemp, under sentence of death, were the last to be moved. For a few moments they were free to hunch alone in the bleak yard where, until a year ago, confessions had been crushed from witnesses: the press yard's stone weights and oak boards were still piled to one side, ready.

Cribb watched the escort hurry out of the weather and start cadging drams of spirits from the gaol's taproom, then went back to worrying an ulcer inside his cheek while imagination tried clambering up the sheer walls on every side of the yard. "Shit."

The nearest turnkey stopped valuing Cribb's tattered greatcoat and began valuing its wearer instead. His face twitched. "You not been through the finishin' school afore?"

"Hn!"

"Didn't think we'd seen you," the turnkey replied. "Won't be seein' you again," he added. "You know 'ow things is done in the academy?"

"I been told."

"Right. So you knows you'll need someone to run errands an' do things. Right?"

Cribb brushed melting sleet off his bare head and face. "Maybe."

The turnkey's face twitched faster. "I can always get things Outside, good price, all fair an' square!"

Cribb shrugged. "Prove it. Nick off to the Saracen's 'Ead for pease pudding, a pair of sausages with plenty of fried mash, and a noggin o' blue ruin."

The turnkey's eyelids ticked slower now that he had gaffed a paying catch. "It'll cost. . . ."

"You think they're necking me for springing a poor-box lid?" Cribb sneered, flicking the shilling which he'd dipped going through Newgate's wicket. He watched the turnkey trap it midair, then bite the coin to see if it was legal silver before hiding it inside his own coat.

"Right-o, chum, I'll let you go up to five guineas on the slate, but not a penny more," Twitch said. "Or else. . . ."

"Or else *what?*" Cribb replied, measuring the shortest distance between his fingertips and the turnkey's pocket.

"Never—you—mind!" It was the other man's turn to sneer, prodding Cribb with the leather cosh worn like a badge of office on its wrist loop. "Just remember as what the cove who comes to twist you off can make it tolerable easy, or terrible 'ard if you don't clean your slate afore 'e knots you up!" The cosh jabbed again. "An' if you're the sort o' flash cove what thinks 'e can take the short drop an' the long choke, don't forget as what the barbers is always lookin' for stiffs to otamise. A wink from us an' they'll all come a-runnin' to cut you down an' settle the bill."

Cribb rolled a gob and spat to prove to the world that his mouth hadn't dried with fright. But it had. The Honourable Company of Barbers & Surgeons of London never had enough fresh subjects for their apprentices' anatomy lessons, a ready market which had earned Cribb's gang many a gold pound defending resurrectionists' wheelbarrows in running fights from Bunhill Fields burial ground to the lanes behind Surgeons' Hall. And not only with demented relatives; established street families were as determined to snatch bodies for resale. It had been the first trade Cribb had mastered after leaving his regimental depot one rainy afternoon with little more than the coat, two body wounds and seven years' hard service to live upon, just one of tens of thousands of broken soldiers who had been shipped home in disgrace from America.

He had chewed up with a Grenadier, a couple of Empire Loyalists— New Jersey militiamen who had fought for King George and chosen exile in London rather than Canada—and a shell-shocked Welshman in the blue tunic of the Royal Artillery. Cribb then shopped around until he'd bought a contract for their services, to be ready up a side alley the following morning when the *Nottingham Rocket* made an unscheduled stop to drop off a pair of infants rolled in old matting, addressed to a rival gang in Cripplegate.

The street battle had opened with a barrage of brickbats to stampede the coach and horses as men clashed over the two small cadavers. Cribb had almost lost his left eye to a swung saw blade early in the brawl. Moments later and the sawyer lost his jaw and a piece of skull to the ounce bullet which Cribb fired point-blank from a cavalry pistol. Before nightfall London's newest firm had been approached by two more upright men— gang lords and street chieftains—who also needed steady workers for contract jobs.

Bambridge was striding back, gesturing for the last prisoners to be led away. Cribb and the sobbing woman shuffled in close order through the gaol's lodge, across its taproom where the night guard were puffing clay pipes, and sipping from mugs of porter, and riffling cards in hands of piquet round the blazing fire. A rivetted grating covered most of the opposite wall from rock floor to stone ceiling, the holding cage for those men and women whom the law would kill every sixth Monday morning unless hanging day fell on an Easter or Christmas, in which case the date would be moved forward by twenty-four hours.

The latest batch shambled to a halt and waited. Their chains were loosened and a key fitted in the barred iron gate. Cribb's tongue worried its ulcer as he peered ahead. About two dozen faces stared back; some old, some older; some young, some younger; and none who owed him any favours. He was alone again. His eyes darted. A single lantern swung in the draught from a small grille set high in the south wall of the condemned cell. No escape there. And none up the barred chimney where a meagre fire smouldered for the night. The key squealed. Twitch gave a shove and Cribb stumbled after Mrs. Kemp as the gate slammed shut.

"Garnish—!"

"Strip or pay, you buggers!"

Crowded fingers snatched, groping, plucking the newcomers for anything saleable. Cribb pitched against the grating, covering himself against flank attacks, clenching fists, clubbing his manacles at the nearest shape. The iron smashed teeth, spraying blood as someone writhed over dung and sawdust. The other condemned fell back to a safe distance. Cribb mastered his breath. None of the inmates spoke or moved as he shoved past and trod to the fire where a plump, quite dapper cove sat in shirtsleeves, toasting fresh cheese and new white bread over the hearth. Cribb gave him a sharp nudge in the back. "You the upright?"

Any softness stopped far short of this man's colourless eyes. He glanced up from his supper. "Yes, I am. And the next time you dare touch me I shall have you killed."

Cribb nodded at this proper show of spirit. "Try." Then, "What's the prime lurk?"

The death cell's chief had returned to toasting his cheese. "So far as I am concerned you may strip, you may garnish, or you may go Nancy Jane. Otherwise, find your own heat and light in the corner."

Cribb peered through the gloom at a small huddle of outcasts who would soon be leaving the world as naked and defenceless as they'd entered it. Cut off from Outside friends and money, they were unable to buy even a small share of the cell's comforts except by trading their clothes, "strip," or their bodies, "Nancy Jane." Cribb sucked a tooth and weighed the options. Survive one gaol or prison camp and a cove's learned to survive them all: he reached down and slipped off one of his shoes to peel a guinea from between first and second toes. "Garnish."

The upright nodded at the rest of Newgate's aristocrats, those under sentence of death who could still afford food and fire. "Shove over."

Cribb accepted the invitation and flexed fingers by the warm coals. Mrs. Kemp had not been so prepared for her future. For all the thousands of counterfeit halfpence in her past, she would still have to trade her only asset until her man sent a lifeline from Outside. "You can never tell!" she bantered with a cracked giggle, trying to coquette by recalling other women who had won nine months' reprieve in here until their babies were born. "I might cop a belly plea yet!"

"It'll be a bleedin' miracle if you do fall now, deary," a husky voice quipped from the other, darker side of the cell. "I mean, at *your* age? An' the end o' the month bein' so near, so to speak—"

"You cow's twat!"

"Bitch!"

"Pig's tit!"

"Oooo!"

The upright glanced over his shoulder at a shape near the fire corner. "Bosun."

"Uh?"

"Stop the ladies."

"Aye aye!" And one of the biggest men Cribb had ever imagined unfolded from the floor, yard by yard, hair dragged back and braided with tarred string, face cratered by gunpowder grains.

"Belay there—!" Bosun's voice had grown to manhood fighting the ocean in all weathers, like the fist he was readying to swing. The two women cowered and waited for a belting, but this time they were in luck. Twitch was fronting up to the gate with a wooden bowl and spoon, a pennyworth of cindery grey bread and a leather mug knotted inside a rag. He coughed mockingly. "Dinner's served for Mr. Phossy Joe!"

Cribb elbowed to the bars and laid claim to his evening meal before anyone else did. The turnkey pushed it through, slopping some of the blue ruin—gin spiked with oil of vitriol and coriander seed. Cribb cursed. Twitch smiled loftily. "Tch! Tch! Is that a proper way to speak when someone's just 'elped a Christian soul?"

Cribb ignored him. " 'Ow much?"

"Enough."

"I said, 'ow much!"

Twitch counted fingers. "For a feast like that? I'd say three shillin's, not includin' me boy's tip."

"You bleedin' robbers."

"Not us, soldier, not *us*. It's *you* as we'll be a-measurin' for a wooden eternity suit a week next Monday."

"Don't believe in wastin' no time, do you?" Cribb said, crooking a finger through the rag to wriggle a warm sausage between its soggy folds.

"Neither ought you," Twitch replied with a yawn. "Now, is there anythin' else you'll be needin' tonight? The nypper's waitin' outside an' 'e can run a message on 'is way 'ome to Mum."

Cribb lopped the tip off the sausage and gnawed slowly to get full value for money, then he shifted the plug of meat under one cheek until later and moved nearer the gate, bashing a stray hand from his bowl. "You got paper and things to letter with?"

"It'll cost."

" 'Ow much?"

"Sixpence'll do for starters—"

"*Sixpence?*"

"Take it or leave it, chum, it's your funeral." The turnkey had no fear of competition depressing Newgate's economy. Petitioning a member of Parliament or a city alderman for a lifelong sinecure in one of London's gaols was neither easy nor cheap; everyone in the taproom had the same incentive to support private enterprise. Cribb gritted teeth and nodded. Twitch strolled away to find a quill, an ink horn and a page ripped from the back of the watch book.

"Don't you move!" Cribb ordered, snatching the writing materials through the bars. He cleared a piece of floor inside the lantern's cone of light, dragged over a stool to be a desk, then glared round the circle of faces. "Any of you know 'ow to do the necessary with these?"

Someone at the back sniggered but that still didn't stop a shabby youth in quite good waistcoat and breeches from lounging forward. "What's it worth?"

"I'll go sippers," Cribb replied, tapping the mug of blue ruin.

"Not enough."

Cribb used the wooden spoon to scrape a little of the pease and mash to one side of his bowl. The youth's fingers prodded the remaining sausage. Cribb winced. "You'd rob your own mother."

"So I did."

The older man made a rare grin. "Then, my bene cove, you'd better write good or I'll shove a fist down your guts and pull back my share."

"There is no risk of that," the clerk drawled, making himself comfortable at paper and quill. "For a while there was no one in London better than I at altering wills or powers of attorney." His wrist chains made him awkward as he reshaped the goose feather's point with a blunt thumbnail. Satisfied, he glanced up again. "Now, the addressee and destination."

"Uh?"

"Where do you wish this letter to go?"

Cribb scooped pease with a plug of sausage and popped it in his mouth. "Mr. Nathaniel Fields." Chew. "Gent." Chew. "Tweezers Lane."

The quill began its stately hooking and dotting across the paper, then paused. "And what is it you wish to communicate to this Mr. Fields?"

Cribb licked fingers. "Tell 'im Mr. Cribb's been jugged for the neck job. Tell 'im it's worth 'is while getting over 'ere, quick smart."

The youth frowned, translating into English. "Is that all?"

"It'd better be."

The quill scratched softly and the clerk blew the paper dry before handing it over for Cribb to inspect while he gobbled the other sausage and fingered cold mash into his mouth.

Cribb twisted the paper from side to side under the lantern, stringing together shapes and squiggles to make sounds inside his head. Then he reached for the quill himself and proudly drew his name at the bottom of the sheet, another skill which a Rebel deserter had taught him during the New England winter when they'd shared the same underground cage at Copper Hill prison camp. He eyed his handiwork and passed the letter with a flourish for Twitch to grab between the bars. " 'Ow much?"

"For a regular scholar like you?" the turnkey sneered, " 'Alf a crown."

"Two shillin's an' sixpence to run one message!"

"Take it or leave it."

"I'll be picked clean before breakfast!"

"That'll cost you, too."

"Don't I bloody well know it!" Cribb yelled as Twitch sauntered away.

A hunk of chaff bread, a paring of cold mutton and a pint of watered beer from the taproom reduced Cribb's credit by another eighteen pence after the next day's orders had been served. He cut his breakfast into equal rations, one to be chewed slowly, the other to be buttoned inside his greatcoat for a later meal, or trade. He grunted: bellies are surly neighbours, never remembering how well they were treated yesterday, ever ready to grumble about tomorrow. And the wintry dawn which seeped between the window bars was doing nothing to raise his spirits: now he could see as well as feel the damp which slicked like snail tracks down the walls.

He scowled: the death cell's fire, in which he had invested a sizeable part of his winnings from the card school in Kings Bench Prison, was being re-laid with green twigs by a debtor from the gaol's main yard. The cunning little maggot must have pull with the keepers to land such a plum job: even the cell's upright man was having to sweetheart the smirking little sod with a pat of beef dripping just to get some dry sticks. Cribb considered striding across to work some of the grips which had interrogated Rebel traitors and British turncoats in the Carolinas, but for the moment he decided against meddling with another leader—unless their shared fire stayed cold for much longer. Instead, he joined the morning parade which was shuffling backward and forward across the taproom's line of sight.

Backward. And forward. Ten paces to the right of the iron gate, fifteen to the left. Halt. About face. Slow march. Heel. And toe. Like so many other freezing dawns in Quebec and New York Colony, both hands shoved up opposite sleeves to fight off the frostbite, only this time he was cradling thirty inches of chain, not the long, cold weight of Brown Bess. Cribb pulled a face at the memory: he'd live forever if he could win a day's reprieve from the gallows for every minute he'd schemed to chuck his Tower musket on the march south from Canada; felling trees; adzing planks and beams; wading across swamps; pioneering the log road for waggons and coaches to roll where squirrels had hardly dared to skip before; battling leeches and flies for every hungry yard of General Burgoyne's advance on Saratoga. Cribb had stopped dead at the blank wall. He turned away and began limping back to the death cell's fireplace. Rummy how a cove don't always know what he's seeing with his own two eyes till months, till years later, when old Mr. Grim has him cornered again. Like now. And like then, Over There. Only difference was, in Americky a cove generally had good mates when the going got hot.

Cribb sighed. It had all seemed so different then. Things had seemed so good at fifteen when, for the first time ever, he had not been just a gypsy outcast's half-bred nypper, fair game for any man on any street. Then, Over There, he had been accepted, as a part of something bigger, something stronger, something he needed and which had needed him once the call went out for fusileer marksmen to volunteer for the line regiments' pioneer companies and forward scouts. And it had not been just his regained freedom to hunt in the forest for extra rations; or the new boots and shirt; it had not even been that second shilling a week for baccy and grog. It had been the something he could never name, the eery tingle which still had the power to lift his chin, to straighten his back, to square his shoulders as he had often done during the years after escaping Old Grim's clutches at Saratoga Springs, and now when he must soon struggle for life on Newgate drop.

Cribb shuddered and turned from the blank wall again. There would be no honour to be won on the gallows, nothing but a man's final duty to go game, as they had after winter began encircling Burgoyne's army and the Rebels blocked the only road to New York and safety.

Ghostly regiments of other ragged shapes were starting to parade across the death cell floor with him, officers at the front, their swords drawn; sergeants to the flank, their halberds level; corporals in the rear, their canes raised. Newgate's walls were blowing away like powder smoke as regimental colour parties marched forward, fifers shrilling, drummers pounding the beat, and five thousand bayonets rattled inside Cribb's skull. His breech hole was once more plugged with wet moss to dam the watery fire of dysentry. He was barelegged, stripped to undershirt, tunic and cartridge pouches, and the hour had come to test his year of foot drill, his months of travel, his weeks of waiting. Cribb was again knotting a sweat rag over his eyes and biting his thumb for good luck as four ranks of the Sixty-second Wiltshires launched their attack on the Rebel strong point, straight uphill, without artillery and without support.

Cribb was now stumbling from fire to wall and back, drenched with sweat as a blizzard of grape, case, shot and shell gnashed through the British ranks around him. The West Country shepherds and ploughboys had begun to cheer, to run, to pant, to gasp, scythed like ripe barley at a hidden rip-gut fence along Bemis Heights. The American gunners and their womenfolk were standing fast! Fighting back with sponging mops and rammers! Killing, being killed, stopping a bayonet charge—! The British advance faltered and drained away downhill.

"Steady there, m'lads!" A phantom sergeant was bashing together three ranks of dazed survivors with his halberd shaft while a five-gallon jug was snatched from hand to hand. Almost ten years later, Cribb could still taste the rum's wonderful power as he nuzzled the open bung, and the buglers sounded, and the silent lines of redcoats began their slog into the cannon fog.

"Them Yankee Doodlers've got new boots! An' tons o' grub!" a hysterical corporal was pleading, trying to stop his men rolling away to the river line. Cribb tottered past and hunched behind a clump of bushes, propped on his musket, eyes squeezed shut against a world gone mad as squalls of dysentry tore his empty belly and sliding whistles of shot skipped grit and dust around him.

Whole regiments were collapsing as their men also left the war. Another young private was on hands and knees behind the same bush, puking green and pink slime. A second had slumped against a nearby tree, staring at what had just happened to his leg, twisted like a dish rag, its heel now where the toes should be, smiling with bewilderment even as he went grey from the chest upward. A third lad was cowering behind a log, arms thrown over his head to protect it while he convulsively stroked his neck. A fourth was—

"Time us got back to work, son." An elderly private of the Sixty-second had finished climbing out of his tattered and foul breeches. Half-naked, the blond bullock gave Cribb's shoulder another heavy poke. "Us got to go now."

Struggling and cursing, Cribb found himself being hauled to his feet again and steadied back to the start line where a third attack was being paraded by junior officers. Cribb never remembered the bugler as two ranks of infantry moved up the bullet-swept scarp, breaking into a shambling jog, charging as the enemy gunners fired point-blank with nails, pebbles and sacks of pistol balls from behind their rampart of corpses.

The Sixty-second Wiltshire Regiment had destroyed itself in twenty minutes; entire battalions were now little more than platoons as they regrouped at the river line. Cribb was sleepwalking the nightmare of Saratoga. He had never understood why he'd let himself be drawn into that single rank of bacon chewers and country yokels. Nor would he ever understand the sudden, the frightening silence as two armies held their fire and stared into the valley while private soldiers put themselves through the drill manual.

Somewhere to Cribb's left a hoarse voice began croaking one of Mr. Wesley's hymns. Another took it up on the right, jumping verses from throat to throat, quickening the trudge to a walk, to a clumsy trot, to a vaulting gallop, storming the gun pits with fists, and knives, and chunks of rock, winning back their regiment's colours and—for a few moments— even planting them atop the American breastworks. But already General Arnold was rallying his Massachusetts Militia, one knee shot through, roped to a horse, cursing the British and damning King George to hell as he counterattacked and drove Burgoyne's army from the field.

Cribb had fled after them with a mate from the Seventh Fusileers—also attached to the Sixty-second as a pioneer—stumbling downhill, sniper fire splashing ricochets between their legs. Years later, he was panting again, fighting to escape, to break into open country, to live. It was something which others like Mrs. Kemp would never have time to learn—or practise.

Cribb squashed his forehead against the blank wall and wept. Behind him, on the other half of the death cell's floor, was the last privacy which anyone would know before the grave; Mary Kemp had not yet given up hope of falling pregnant while paying for her garnish. Younger and prettier, she might have invested her remaining hours to earn stronger beer and better meals by entertaining gentlemen who relished coupling, in Mr. Bambridge's spare bedchamber, with a technically dead woman. Instead she had to be grateful for whatever came her way on the straw.

"You'd 'ave more luck if you was more like that there Brandon bitch!" a rival jeered, staring down at her, hands on hips.

"Ooo!" Mary Kemp was struggling to her feet, tugging skirts and drawers together. "An' I suppose you'd be the one what knows all about it, Miss Lardy-da Hoity-toit! Bitch? *Witch* more bleedin' likely!" She tossed her head. "I got more self-respect than to sink as low as what *she* done!"

"Nyah!" her rival sneered. "If you got ol' Kitty's chances, you'd 'ave grabbed 'em years ago—!"

"That I never would!" Mrs. Kemp screeched back. "I'll 'ave yous all to know I'm a proper respect'ble woman I am! I'm no bleedin' *murderess* like that there painted 'arlot Kitty Brandon I'm not!"

"Nyah—!"

The death cell was springing back to life after its morning glooms as factions warmed up with private brawls while the more nimble-witted held bets on which of the two women would best the other. Everyone had an interest in stirring up a good fight, just as almost everyone had an opinion about the remarkable woman who still featured in many of London's broadsheets. It was to be expected: Mrs. Brandon's reputed style and obvious cunning at cheating the gallows for so long had captured the minds of England's readers, just as her original crime—engraved on wood blocks and hawked around country fairgrounds for one halfpenny apiece—had captured the hearts of a nation's illiterates.

The faded yellow prints which survive in the British Museum's collection differ in many details, but all agree on one point: a wild-eyed tragic actress must be staring across a vast stage, a dripping sword in one fist, a severed head in the other while her terrified audience stampedes for the doors. As in most things the truth is different.

Told very briefly, a gentleman admirer had gone too far one summer evening in Winchester. Mrs. Katharine Brandon, actress, had been about to step aboard the waggon which her undermanned troupe of players had pushed behind the Woolsack tavern while she produced a night of *Virtue Deceiv'd, or, A Maiden Undone*, the play in which she had created the starring role of Lady Lucinda Lively at the Theatre Royal, Drury Lane. As the oil lamps glimmering cheerily, the hired oboe player had struck up a jaunty air in the orchestra pit between the waggon shafts as Mrs. Brandon set her face in a bright smile behind the draped blankets, and collided with the tipsy son of a local baronet who was now staggering across the planks to find her. He lurched forward and began groping up her skirts: the audience howled with laughter when he also puckered up for a kiss. Even then his luck might have held if only the leading lady hadn't been armed with a sword for the comedy scene with Toby Buttock, Lord Lively's stuttering manservant. The tent's capacity crowd whooped with delight as Lady Lively gave the drunken oaf a withering glare, drew back a pace, then lunged like a fencing master.

So far, so bad. If only she had been content to let matters drop with him at that point she might have escaped with a conviction for aggravated manslaughter. But Kitty Brandon had never managed to do anything by half-measures in all her life. One foot planted on the man's belly, she had jerked the blade clear again and given him the lusty back-hander which had lopped off his head. At which point she swooned, so there can be no question of her picking up the head and waving it around. Nor would such a seasoned audience have run for the doors after such a topping show. Jumping on benches and upturned barrels, they gave Mrs. Brandon three rousing cheers as the peace officers came to take her away and, at last, she was a national celebrity.

She was also the murderess who had killed the son of a local magnate whose tenants were the jurors and whose friends sat on the bench of quarter sessions. The facts that her face and figure were said to be worth far more than a second look, that she was red haired in an Irish sort of way and very sharp tongued with the judge, none of these had weighted the scales of justice in her favour when sentence of death was passed. But it did mean that every window and shop front on Winchester market was booked long before her execution day and that telescopes were fetching two shillings a peep as the cart rumbled to a halt under the county gallows.

The crowd turned ugly when it saw that Mrs. Brandon was not being roped to the crossbar with the other half dozen or so felons: there had been a late appeal to a higher court on an obscure point of law, following replies to a pair of brief notes to General the Honourable John Burgoyne and Mr. Richard Sheridan, both members of Parliament and both intimately connected with the stage. The anxious M.P.s' letters had also included cash drafts, exactly as instructed by her, and a few days later a London barrister had stepped off the *Winchester Flyer* to announce that Mrs. Brandon's appeal to the Privy Council would now be handled by him. Since when, hanging days had come and gone without Kitty Brandon making her final public appearance, much to the delight of England's pamphleteers and the envy of others less well connected in Newgate's death cell.

"A red-'aired whore, that's what she is!" Mary Kemp screeched again, veins standing out like whipcord on her neck, daring the other woman to shout louder as Cribb punched his way through the crowd and one open palm exploded across the woman's face, piling her backward across the floor.

"Oy! Turn it up!" someone yelled above the riot as the fun was spoiled and all bets cancelled. "Get your fuckin' nose out of where it ain't—!"

Cribb was suddenly inches away, staring up at the other man's confident jeer. "Button your lip."

"Uh?"

"There's many a cove, better'n what you'll ever know 'ow to be, only got 'ome again because of what that lady done for us in Americky."

"*Uh?*"

Cribb gave the man plenty of time to take up the challenge and put up his fists, then turned and shoved away to reclaim his small patch of warmth near the fire. He squatted and gobbed at the smouldering twigs: too much was happening inside his head, too many words and names were reminding him again of the unroofed barn on Schuyler's Farm where a regimental surgeon had burned out the pocket of maggoty gangrene on Cribb's hip with a red-hot bayonet. The rum jar had been sucked dry long before it had been Cribb's turn for treatment. That night he had been kept awake by the hoarfrost, listening to wolves padding down from the forest to feast in a nearby pit of legs and arms.

Saratoga had been Cribb's first and last battle as a foot soldier. Yet, although it was now further away in time than, say, Charleston, or Chickamauga Creek, or Guildford Courthouse, or Yorktown, Saratoga remained the Nightmare, the smothering horror which could repeatedly jerk him awake, screaming and struggling for breath.

His face glistened as he stared back at the death cell's fire. Queer how a cove can't forget some things, can't remember others. . . . Not that anyone who'd limped with him from that battlefield and into the enemy's prison camps would ever forget how few of the officers' women had left their coaches to see how their men's men were taking defeat. Only one, the general's fancy woman no less, only one had come down after the cease-fire to tonguelash the corps of sluts and dram sellers who had followed the army south.

Before evening new latrines had been dug, fresh water drawn from the river and kettles of boiled horse meat sent to the dressing stations while Katharine Brandon patrolled the lines, wrapped in Gentleman Johnny's scarlet cloak, swinging a blackthorn cudgel at marauding dogs and grave robbers alike. One rainy night, crouched under the wreckage of Schuyler's chicken coop, the general's young lady had raised her lantern on the end of that legendary shillelagh and had personally wished each man of the three dozen wounded a speedy recovery and a safe homecoming.

Cribb's eyes blurred with tears again.

3

A PRISONER'S friends and family could pay their shillings at Newgate's wicket any time between dawn and dusk, then come inside to chat through the grating for as long as they liked. Or, if they wanted it and could afford the fee, a condemned felon could be released to host a private dinner in the taproom, stamping his feet to the flute, fiddle and song also provided by the grocers.

Newgate Gaol offered many other delights. Every fortnight a privileged ring in the debtors' division clubbed together to have a dozen fighting birds sent across the Thames from Southwark cockpits. Matched pairs were force-fed black pepper to sharpen their tempers, had brass spurs strapped to their legs, were then pitched into the ring for a fight to the death. Meanwhile, the rest of the prison and many of its extra visitors would have begged, borrowed and stolen enough to buy a seat around the press yard and, perhaps, a lucky number in the turnkeys' sweepstake.

The new head keeper was determined to add to the attractions. One which appealed to him most was bare-knuckle combat between selected prisoners every summer afternoon, weather permitting. As he had recently urged in a memorandum to his masters, the sight and sound of two bruisers squaring off would give the casuals another incentive to stay until the evening meal was ready for sale near the death cell. Casual visitors— tourists up from the country, with a good sprinkling of gentlemen from abroad—were also welcome to sample Newgate's entertainments on the same footing as prisoners' relatives. Most came for the fun, of course, but some also came for moral uplift, and hardly a day passed without some child being given a good spanking in front of the gallows before its worried parents bought one of Arthur Bambridge's lectures at the death cell's bars.

Which happened this afternoon when Cribb won the bank at primero. He immediately covered all bets with both palms while a knot of visitors trooped into the taproom, following Bambridge and a pair of turnkeys, oak staves at the ready. The head keeper removed his tricorne hat, flakes of starch sifting from the grey horsehair wig underneath, and busied himself by taking snuff as the hat passed from hand to hand, coins chinking softly inside its crown.

Satisfied with the take, he trapped a sneeze, tucked the cambric handkerchief up his sleeve and folded both hands round the knob of a walking cane. "And now, dear friends, we come to that last dismal abode of the damned which the law has set aside for all such malefactors as we have spoken of today." His phrasing was an uncanny imitation of a clergyman's chant, each sentence worn smooth as a pebble by frequent rehearsal.

A mother at the back of the small crowd tweaked her son's ear and started rocking his head from side to side. Bambridge smiled. "Be assured, madam, none have ever escaped from Newgate's condemned cell—except one—and even then his respite from justice was only brief. I refer, of course, to Jack Shephard!"

There was a sudden buzz of attention at the name of a man who was still a popular hero in parts of London, though few now would have been alive when he flourished as a footpad and gaol breaker earlier in the century. Bambridge's smile ripened. "Justly condemned, Idle Jack was cast into this same place to await his doom. And yet, something of the former impudence still remained to him. Only hours before his appointment with death, this notorious rogue somehow contrived to bend apart the bars in that very chimney while all others slept around him." The visitors moved forward to get a better look. "Minutes later he emerged in the chapel above this floor, broke his way through the locked doorway and so ran onto the roof, whence he lowered himself to the street and, as he thought, sweet liberty. . . .

"But the gallows, England's sovereign cure for all who trouble the king's peace, are not so easily cheated!" Bambridge wagged a finger at the snivelling boy. "A civic-minded accomplice of young Jack Shephard was persuaded to return the escaped felon to justice and, this time, to make doubly sure, he was chained to the ground in that very corner—" The visitors pushed forward a second time.

Bambridge swung his cane to keep the condemned at a respectful distance. "The awful hour approached! There would be no respite for reckless Jack this time, or so't was believed!" The head warder's voice throbbed. "No living soul knows what happpened next. Some do say the devil himself entered this very room and made a blood pact with Jack Shephard, as his imps and demons have made one with those who now lodge behind these bars." The boy had begun to sob wildly, trying to shake off his mother's grip.

"Ah, dear friends, I have my suspicions but, alas and alack, my lips are forever sealed by a most solemn oath. But, surely, only infernal power could have allowed the condemned wretch to break his leg irons a *second* time? To force the chimney again? And once more to retrace his steps to the delusion of safety?" There was a sound like a pistol shot as the boy's father slapped his face.

Bambridge was gathering speed. "Never would there be a third time. Surrendered to the officers of the peace by another public-spirited citizen, bold Jack Shephard the thief was brought low at last by that same stubborn pride and greed which ensnared the deluded souls you see before you today! And, as they must soon be, he was launched into eternity as a dreadful warning to all idle apprentices and masterless men!"

Bambridge shook head in sombre reflection. "Ah, what may we say on such noble occasions? When you return in eight days to see *them* mount the scaffold and pay for their wasted lives, only recall that, in every case, these wicked and wilful beings have, at last, exhausted man's justice and God's mercy!" His cane swept along the bars. "Regard them now! Thieves! Murderers! Whores! Fornicators! Sodomites! Fire raisers! Cheats, crimps, flash men and wastrels of every degree and debauchment! But, from this place onward, united in deepest sin and most shameful death!" The boy was screaming again.

It was mother's turn to silence him as the head keeper's voice tumbled to a dramatic groan. "Draw nearer, gentle friends. See for yourselves the bitter fruits of reckless spending. Yea, draw nearer! Learn from them before 'tis too late! Learn from them where the paths of lewd living must end! And, as you do, good people all, spare a mite of Christian charity for these, our lost brethren. . . . ."

Exhausted, Bambridge bowed left and right, then stood back to empty his hat in private while visitors and condemned exchanged stares along the grating. Most of the outsiders held their breath and moved closer to the death cell. The boy was being lifted by one of the turnkeys to get a better view over the adults' heads while another turnkey limped past, thwacking his stave between the bars. "Back, scum! Let the ladies an' ge'men see yous proper!"

Cribb had closed the card bank. Someone else had already begun leading the stampede for good places at the bars. Cribb quickened his pace. Then he charged, head down, biting and kicking to get to the front and cling to a bar, breaking a desperate grin at the nearest pair of tourists—by the cut of the man's grey smock and canvas gaiters an elderly farmer down from the Midlands to sell a flock at the nearby Smithfield slaughter yards.

"Be kind, sir! Missus!" he bellowed above the other screams and entreaties. "Take pity on a poor soldier what gave all for king and country a-fighting of them dirty Rebels!"

The farmer and his wife glanced uneasily at Cribb's supporting scabs, then, with more interest, at his red coat under its crust of filth and age.

Cribb stopped smashing a nailed heel into the melee behind and began fitting another, more winsome smile. "Charity! For a luckless soldier! For pity's sake, sir! Missus! Just 'alf a guinea for the poor wretch what lost all a-fighting for King George!" The farmer and his wife were drawing away, disturbed. "Five bob then! Just five shillings to make a poor bloke's last hours 'appy!"

The farmer's wife was giving her husband's sleeve gentle, anxious tugs. "Dearest 'eart, do be a-lettin' 'im 'ave somethin' now. For Billy's sake."

The elderly man scratched an ear and looked as if he might still offer to buy Cribb for fattening up. "Ar. Mother an' me, we 'ad a boy what took the king's shillin' when work were bad. 'Listed in the Fifty-third Regiment o' Foot, 'e did."

"The Shropshires!" Cribb gasped, kicking even harder behind him.

"Tha's right. Private Billy Parkin by name 'e were. Did ever meet 'im?"

"No!"

"Well, ought've," the farmer muttered. "Went to Americky too, 'e did. Only our boy weren't so lucky. 'Ere!"

Cribb snatched the half crown before anyone else did and surrendered his grip on the bars as others swarmed over his shoulders to get at the day's charity.

Taproom prices doubled immediately the last of that afternoon's visitors had trooped across the press yard and returned to the world of the living, Outside.

Cribb's temper was none too sweet as he nursed a mug of fourpenny ale and returned to study the chimney bars where others had long ago picked away every scrap of mortar which anchored them to the stonework. Problem was, after Jack Shephard's two victories, someone had poured molten lead into the cracks, setting the bars as firm and solid as the surrounding granite.

A tricky job, but not impossible once a cove got the right mates with him. Not seven years back—Over There—a stick of dying men had crouched up a far smaller shaft than this one, listening to the boozy smash of bottles in a guardroom overhead, waiting for an inch of broken saw blade to finish stroking the trapdoor's last hinge. . . .

Cribb had been the third shape to erupt from the old mine shaft, armed with a copper nail from the workshops where men had been chained to anvils since General Washington named Copper Hill to be his special punishment camp for the Continental Army's hardest cases and the worst of the British escapers. A handful had made it through the stockade's gateway and scattered across the surrounding heathland. Most had been recaptured or bayonetted by Connecticut militiamen sent up from Simsbury to put down the mutiny, but Cribb had not been among the survivors executed by firing squad in the prison yard the following noon.

Very frightened, very alone now, young Cribb had begun to reverse his first escape route from Saratoga by trudging northwest, following the sun and stars across the Berkshire wilderness to ford the headwaters of the Housatonic on the Mohawk frontier. Only this time he didn't make the mistake of being in too great a hurry to cover ground. Night after night he had foraged the summer landscape like a *phuri dai* Romany, remembering lessons taught with many a clip to the ear whenever he'd failed to lift a hen from her roost without waking the farmer's watchdog. Slowly, gently, mile by mile and meal by meal, the escaping soldier had ghosted southward down the Hudson Valley until, on his last night alone, he'd crawled into a British outpost on Bronx Heights.

"No bastard could stop me then," Cribb muttered to himself, staring up the death cell's chimney at a small square of wintry sky. "No bugger's going to start now."

"You'll find another lot o' bars 'alfway up there," Twitch advised from the grating, bored by every prisoner's daydream of freedom after hearing Bambridge's story. Cribb spun round, slopping some of the beer. "Any case, sunshine, you're wanted. By a swell ge'man lawyer, no less. Come special to talk."

Cribb shoved nearer the gate. "Where?"

"In the lodge."

"I can see 'im there?"

The turnkey shook his head. "Against the rules. I brings 'im to *you*."

"But it'll cost me."

"You learn quick."

Cribb ignored the man's tone. " 'Ow much this time?"

"A tanner."

"Shi-i-it! All right, slap it on the slate—"

"*Cash.*"

Cribb stalled, then shoved a handful of small coppers through the bars. Twitch counted the halfpence and farthings, collected another penny-worth to make up the sixpence, then shook his bunch of keys to unlock the gate. Cribb stooped through and walked free for the first time since being committed at Old Bailey. Twitch gave him a shove in the back, turning him toward a plain pinewood table and two hard chairs which served for interviews.

A minute later and Nathaniel Fields bustled down the steps from the keeper's lodge, still dusting melted snow off his cloak. He flicked it aside to display a gorgeous dark blue frock coat with silver-gilt buttons, nankeen breeches and ivory silk stockings. Twitch humbly collected the gentle-man's cloak, hat, gloves and ebony cane. Fields nodded distantly at this trifling service and waited for Twitch to stop flapping a rag at a piece of chewed bacon rind.

"Much obliged." Fields arranged his coat tails and sat down with as much attention to detail as he paid to the choice of lip rouge, pomade and henna rinse for the one glory that now remained—his own hair—waved and tied at the nape with a sky blue ribbon in the latest French style. He smiled impersonally at the filthy object sitting just across the table from him. "You do not seem to be your normal, cheerful self today, Joe. I don't understand: you're as pretty as a picture, well framed and ready to be hung. Nothing worrying you, I trust?"

Cribb shrugged. "You know 'ow it is, Nat? Up one day, down the next."

"True, but in your particular case I very much doubt if you'll be 'up' anywhere after you go 'down.' Mm?"

"That's what they're sayin' round the Saracen's 'Ead?" Cribb replied. "Tch, tch, some coves' in a regular 'urry to fill the 'ole before they've filled the coffin."

Fields ignored him and levered a thumbnail under the lid of an enamel snuffbox which had recently changed pockets in the Theatre Royal, then found its way over a number of fences into the lawyer's personal collection. He tapped the sides to settle the powder, laid a large pinch along the back of his wrist, inhaled deeply and muffled the sneeze in a starched linen belcher. "There! Now I can hear you more clearly. Did you not mention something about it being 'worth my time' visiting you, Joe? Your note— and congratulations upon the much improved handwriting—your note gave me a distinct impression that we might still have something of value to discuss."

Cribb also took his time and managed an equally relaxed murmur over the narrow table. "Nat, my cully cove, I want *out*."

Fields' pencilled eyebrows arched in amazement. "So, I imagine, does everyone else in here! Alas, for most if not all of your unhappy band of pilgrims, frogs will grow feathers and fly before you do, so what makes your case exceptional?"

Cribb damped lips. "A good lawyer always knows where to go at times like these. Right?"

Fields nodded thoughtfully. "Ye-es, and I thank you for the compliment. However, you are overlooking one detail: justice is never cheap."

"So we buy some!"

"*We?*" Fields peered round Cribb's head and looked at the other dozen or so faces staring through the bars, pressed against the rusty iron and mouldering stonework, trying to overhear. He glanced at his client. "Joe. For a man of substance you are sleeping uncommon rough tonight."

Cribb stopped gnawing the ulcer. "Nat, stop pissing around. I always been good to you, I 'ave. Never let you down once. I always done the right thing by you when you wanted a rush job doing special—"

"And we always paid you the contract price, promptly," Fields interrupted, not impressed.

Cribb shrugged impatiently. "So once I'm Outside again we can pick up where we left off. A cove what was in the Gunners told me this new way to mix resin, sulphur and stuff like they fill shells. You'll be needing it soon, right?"

"Wrong." Fields studied his fingernails, then looked back across the table. "Let us assume for one moment that you somehow avoid grinning from a noose in the sheriff's picture frame with your charming companions, you will still be marked for life by every thief catcher in Bow Street. Meanwhile, all I have to do is snap my fingers on any street for a dozen items of your background and talent to come running, all eager to work for our Organisation, all unknown to the world at large. You see, Joe, I am very much afraid that you are finished, ended. We simply do not need you any more, dead or alive."

"Pig's arse you do!" Cribb's wrists were white under their irons. "I know too much!"

"Really?" Fields murmured. "Please don't make any rash statements you won't live to regret. And, please, restrain your voice like a good chap or I shall have to leave even more quickly than I intend doing."

Cribb shook his head. "You'll stay right there! It's not too late to turn king's evidence."

The eyebrows arched again. "Is that so? Dear me! I am beginning to wish you tucked up with a spade inside your little wooden cot."

Cribb dragged rusty fetters across the table as he crouched forward, voice hoarse and low. "There's a list of names. And dates. All written down, just ready for a time like now."

Fields patted a yawn and consulted a choice Venetian fob watch, the one with a pair of masked cherubs under its crystal, bobbing backward and forward, teasing each other's nudity with the ticking seconds. "Two more minutes, that's all I can spare. Sorry."

"You maggot! I'll blow the works on your 'Organisation' if it's the last thing I do!"

"Which it most certainly will be," Fields replied without ill-feeling. "Be serious, Joe, who on earth will ever believe the written word—delivered *post mortem*—of a necked felon like yourself? Do talk sense, there's a good fellow."

Cribb's threats subsided as Fields began studying the pale fleck under his fingernail again. "As we used to say up at Cambridge, 'Gather ye rose-buds while ye may, Old Time is still a-flying. And this same flower that smiles today, tomorrow will be dying.' Not that you have much reason to smile today, Joe, but I hope it makes the point?" Cribb's face never moved. "So, let us summarise our progress thus far. You have tried touching my conscience: a flattering notion but quite pointless. Logically, you next tried the approach threatening. Also futile but, of course, you were bound to try. Shall we now consider the third—and final—possibility?"

"Like what?"

Fields smiled. "That, like the cunning little squirrel which you so closely resemble, there *may* be just enough golden acorns put away for such a bleak winter as you now face. Mm?"

Cribb sucked a tooth. "You're a fly cove, Nat. Regular brainy."

"Thank you for the testimonial, but we waste time, a commodity which—for you—is strictly limited." It was Fields' turn to lean across the table, no longer sparring with words. "How much? Where is it?"

Cribb traced a thumbnail along the grain of a table plank. Then, defeated, he slowly looked up again. "About fifty."

"*About?*"

"Pox your eyes! Fifty-six!"

"Guineas or pounds?"

"Yellow boys."

Fields eased back in his chair, smiling sadly. "Only fifty-six pounds set aside for a rainy day after all the eventful times we've had together, Joe? That was not very provident of you or really very much for me once the necessary expenses are paid."

Cribb's fingers were meshing and tangling on the table top. "Nat! 'Alf a 'undred quid's not to be sneezed at!"

"True, in some minor cases you may be right, because then there would remain a useful margin to show for my clerks' labour. However, you are overlooking another detail: your trial papers make particular reference to your skill at fire raising—"

"What of it?"

"What of it?" Fields snapped. "My dear Joe, if this matter has even the ghost of a chance of reaching the Privy Council—and that is the level at which reprieves from death must be sought these days—then we should have to somehow erase all reference to arson."

"Why? What's wrong with it?"

Fields breathed out, under control again. "Joe, sometimes I wonder at the state of your mind, I really do. Look. Whereas simple murder, say, is generally a misunderstanding between a Mr. A. and a Mr. B., both of whom know each other sufficiently well to heartily wish the other dead. And whereas theft is usually a private business transaction between non-contracting parties, once our little Phosphorus Demon and his secret mixtures go to work on an overinsured warehouse or manufactory, then half London becomes a party of the second part if the wind changes direction." He paused, enjoying the sight of Cribb's clumsy mind being baffled by legal subtleties.

"Now," Fields continued, "it must follow that buying a royal pardon for murder or theft is not altogether out of the question if the right persons are approached in the right spirit, at the right time and at the right place. But arson remains, I fear, a vastly more difficult subject to prepare for His Majesty's boundless mercy after so much of His Majesty's capital city has been repeatedly threatened by our little firebugger."

Cribb looked haggard. "Nat, *please*, I want to go free!"

"So you insist in telling me, but I am trying to explain to you why it cannot be done. Just get that simple fact into your stupid head."

"Nat!"

Fields scowled at the raised voice. "Be silent! Your request is absurd."

Cribb muffled choking sobs in the crook of his arm, face squeezed against the table's greasy boards. "Oh, Nat! 'Elp me, 'elp me!"

The lawyer looked down with disgust at the scabby scalp and signalled for his own hat and cloak to be brought. Cribb slowly dragged himself together again. "That's—your last word! You—won't 'elp old Phossy?"

Fields was more concerned with the slushy yard he must cross to reach his waiting sedan chair. "Nobody can help you, my good man. You have made your bed, now you must sleep in it." He turned away and reached for his cane.

"Then get your arse back on that chair!"

Fields spun as if someone had just laid a whip across his shoulders. "*What* was that you said?"

Cribb's eyes were bright and dry. "I said, get back on that chair." He glanced past the stunned lawyer and jerked a thumb at Twitch, hovering nearby, waiting for his tips. "Piss off, you. *I'll* say when the ge'man's going 'ome."

Fields' mouth clapped shut and he began fumbling with coat tails as he sat with as much dignity as he could muster. "Well! Have we perhaps remembered the location of another eight or nine hundred pounds?"

Cribb cupped his chin with ironed wrists, elbows on table. "No. I got somethin' much, much better'n that, chum." He made a dreamy smile. "I've just remembered the location of some little things what's worth every quid you'll ever earn."

Fields did not like the twist this conversation was starting to take. He damped lips. "Explain yourself."

"All in good time, Nat, all in good time." Cribb's smile never wavered as he dipped a friendly wink. "Before we start, you ever been skint?"

"Of course not!"

"I didn't think you 'ad," Cribb agreed in a murmur that could be heard only by the lawyer. "It sort of shows when you been poor, like it shows when you always got money. Money sort of changes the way a cove looks, and it's more'n the warm clothes, and the lashings of 'ot grub on the table, and the way every swell wants to shake 'is 'ands." Cribb was smiling. "But when you got no money, nobody even remembers your name, let alone wants to shake your 'and. I tell you straight, Nat, a dead dog on a shit 'eap 'as more friends than a poor cove in London."

Fields made an elaborate yawn, but Cribb didn't seem to notice as he went on chatting. "O' course, some of us will always get by—we was born with the knack, so to speak—but for every one of us naturals, there's a 'undred what slips off the seat and vanishes. And nobody will even care they was there once the shit closes over their 'eads. . . ."

The lawyer stared bleakly into the middle distance. "Come to the point."

"You in a 'urry to go 'ome?"

"Yes!"

"So'm I."

"Come to the point!"

"Nat, *please*, not so loud, there's a good fellow," Cribb soothed, laying one hand on the other man's wrist. Fields jerked it away. "Tch, tch! No need to get on your 'igh 'orse, Nat, I'm only trying to 'elp. Oh, I can see we're not listening too good today, because I been talking about the point all along."

"Which is?" Fields was icy.

"Why, just 'ow alone a cove can feel on the streets of London town once 'e got no money, nor no job to get 'im some." Cribb snapped fingers as if a sudden thought had just hit him. "*You* remember old Percy Green?"

"Uh?"

"Old Perce, your 'ead clerk. Surely you've not forgotten a good and faithful servant like old Mr. Green?" Cribb asked anxiously. "Strewth! You sent 'im on enough errands when your Organisation didn't want to get its 'ands dirty a-passing of messages to the likes of me!"

"The Mr. Green you speak of absconded from his place of work without ever giving a reason!" Fields snapped back. "I would hardly ever call that the action of a good and faithful servant!"

Cribb nodded soberly. "Dead right, Nat, dead right: disgusting bad manners. But let's be fair to the poor old bugger, 'ow was 'e to know that 'e was due to leave so soon? Like, 'ow was *you* to know old Perce's eyes was giving 'im whack?" Cribb sighed. "Must be desperate 'ard being a quill driver once the old peepers start pegging out. Perce used to talk about it a lot when 'e come round to my place with jobs, almost as much as we used to talk about 'the Interest. . . .' " Cribb paused lightly, watching the name impact on Fields like a musket ball. "Oh, I can tell you straight, your 'ead clerk was terrible worried about 'is peepers and the way they was going downhill fast. Just another year or two working for you, then— pffft!—kicked out onto them streets we been talking about, with no job and no money, because it's a bit tricky saving golden acorns for rainy days on the sort of brass you splash around. But ol' Percy was no fool, regular brainy in 'is own little way was your Mr. Green. Know what 'e done? Got 'imself an insurance policy, I think that's the way 'e said it."

"How very provident!" Fields sneered. "Meanwhile how much longer am I to sit here and listen to your impudent comments?"

"Nearly done, Nat, we're nearly done," Cribb soothed again. "So there 'e was, terrible worried about what would 'appen to 'im and Mrs. Green once 'is peepers shut for good—"

"So you keep saying!"

"Then, one loverly day, as you'll remember better'n me, I being Over There in Americky still, every burny prig on the game decided to go for the big 'un and torch London—lucky sods. Anyways, a whole lot of swell coves legged it, leaving their shops, and dwelling places, and—are you listening careful, Mr. Fields, sir?—their *offices* pretty much as per usual for their good and faithful servants to do sentry. Now, old Perce wanted to do the right thing by you, so 'e just checked you'd left nothing behind in the bedroom before the place next door burned through the walls, and what 'e found under them floorboards was indeed a sight for sore eyes. . . ."

Fields missed the joke: there was an oddly fixed stare around his own. Cribb smiled. "It seems 'e found this box crammed full of the rummiest things 'e'd ever seen—blue cardboard wheels, and sheets of numbers, and a little bottle of stuff what looked like water but worked like ink once some other cove warmed it over a candle. Oh, I can tell you, old Perce was fair stumped—"

Fields' rouge had begun to glisten.

"Months an' months passed while 'e puzzled 'imself silly over that box and all the things you'd left inside it. Then, just as 'e was about to chuck it as a bad job, who should you send 'im to meet but yours truly, fresh 'ome from being sergeant major of Colonel Tarleton's Rangers, the ones they used to call for when there was a special despatch to be got somewhere in a 'urry—"

Streaks of crimson dye were running down the lawyer's raddled face.

"So it didn't take me more'n ten ticks to work out them code wheels and message slips. Then Perce and me, we got our 'eads together one night while I done what I seen the colonel do tons of times in Americky, and your 'ead clerk copied down pages and pages and pages of ships, and troops, and secret Parliament stuff about the Prince of Wales, and—"

"You lie!" Fields' spittle splashed the condemned man's face. "This cannot be true!"

"I do 'ope you're wrong," Cribb replied, "because I'm betting my neck on this. Anyway, to cut a long story short, old Perce shook my 'and like I was a long lost brother, and said as what I'd just saved 'im from being kicked on the streets when 'e couldn't write for you no more. Then 'e toddled off to give 'is missus the good news. Only, I suppose, 'is peepers must've started giving 'im more trouble as 'e got near the Thames. Lonely there at night, and desperate slippery round Dung Wharf. Still, lucky for us 'e wasn't 'olding your box when 'e tripped."

"You lie!" Fields repeated in falsetto.

Cribb shook his head slowly.

Fields was having trouble coming out of his trance, unable to credit that a filthy little illiterate could break the French diplomatic cypher and, with it, read most of Fields' secret traffic to Paris during the recent war. If it were true, if it were even remotely possible that certain papers had not burned during the riots of '80, then—no! It was impossible. Fields shuddered, he needed time to think, to plan, to get out of a dreadful trap which this unlettered, unwashed knuckle man had just sprung. "Well! We can't sit here all night, you know!"

"I can," Cribb corrected, getting closer to Fields' perfumed ear. "Like I said, you're a brainy cove, brainy enough to see that your stuff to the Frogs is only safe while I am. Remember: the minute *I* drop, *you* start coming down with me." Cribb straightened. "We're wasting time, a commodity which—for both of us—is strictly limited. You'd better start gathering them rosebuds while your fine friends still want to know the shit'ouse rat what sold 'is mates to the French."

4

FIELDS NO LONGER cared about the slush in Newgate's yard, or the sedan chair's rolling plod across London to his chambers in Tweezers Lane near Middle Temple. Instead, he crouched against the stuffed leather padding, head jolting from side to side in the darkness, weeping with self-pity while he tried to come to terms with the impossible. Within eight days, within less than two hundred hours, a notorious firebug had to earn a royal pardon from the Privy Council. If not, if he failed, if Cribb were still among the two dozen or so felons whose fetters would be struck off in that yard back there before being herded onto the gallows outside, then he—Nathaniel Fields, M.A., Gent.—would have at best a few more hours to settle his affairs and gallop for Dover to begin a dishonoured exile in Calais.

The chair had halted. Fields crouched out, slammed the door behind him and threw a coin at its two porters. His manservant could also read the signs of a gathering storm and trembled at the top of the street steps with a branch of candles to light his master home from work. Fields elbowed past and went upstairs two at a time. "Bath! Food! Now!"

"But sir!"

"Don't you 'But sir' me!" Fields screamed from the first floor landing, finger aimed like a pistol.

His temper simmered throughout the quick sponge bath of eau de cologne and the equally hurried snack of cold jugged hare, a pork pie, salmon tart, some egg pudding with nutmeg, all washed down by a pint of mulled claret.

The manservant tried hard to dress hair with gum arabic and powdered orris root while his master paced the carpets in front of an open fire grate, glaring into the mirrors at every turn. "Dolt!" Fields yelled at the second attempt to tie the black velvet ribbon, and delivered a vicious kick in the breech. "Get out!" The man yipped and fled downstairs to abuse the cook, who slapped the scullery girl's face, who cried herself asleep in the coal hole.

Upstairs, the master finished tying his own bow before matching silk brocade coats and stockings which his tailor had sent from Paris in a Dieppe fishing smack, duty free. Meanwhile, limping through the slop and rainy slush of nearby Milford Lane, the servant managed to corner a vacant sedan chair and ordered it up Tweezers Lane for hire to the Pineapple Tree, Covent Garden.

Within a few years the Pineapple Tree would have established itself in the very front rank of London's many casinos and sporting houses but, for the moment, it still had to build its reputation by offering generous credit to selected members, usually the younger sons of older gentry whose passion for fast living outstripped their slow livelihood from land or joint-stock dividends. Fields' part, as the managing syndicate's financial director, was brutally simple: to secure watertight mortgages on properties and annuities pledged for gaming debts and then to rack every penny at compound interest.

Fields had a natural flair for the work and had developed a taste for power, the power to move freely behind the scenes of England's social and political world, enjoying an unrestricted entrée to the closed circle around Westminster. Fields had also developed a keen nose for approaching disaster, he reminded himself between clenched teeth as two porters strapped themselves between the sedan's shafts and set a brisk pace into Maltravers Street, following a link boy's smoky torch.

Fields' face reflected its latest worries in the chair's small glass window. The directors of sure-fire gaming houses were subject to the same fickle laws of risk and chance once alone in the streets of London, another reason why he had always worked through networks of subcontractors like Cribb whenever it became necessary for the syndicate to burn down or beat up its enemies. But the real risk, he was starting to learn, lay much closer to home than the shadowy streets. It lurked among the servile, the meek, the cringing, the lickspittle Percy Greens of this earth! Ungrateful swine, devoid of principle or honour, no better than the loathesome rabble which had spewed from St. Giles and Cripplegate back in '80, defying all law and authority!

Central London had burned for a week and so had his old chambers in Tweezers Lane. Fields had often regretted the loss of many treasures that summer, but never once the small box hidden under his bedroom floor, or the cyphers and invisible inks which had paid for another's silence. Fields' face was dragging into hard, vertical creases at the memory of such weapons now in the hands of a brainless clod like Cribb——!

The sedan chair lurched, stopping dead at the unlit corner of Arundel Street and the Strand. Fields jammed his cane across the chair's door, barricading it from the inside, tugging a double-barrelled pistol from his waistcoat, locking up the spike bayonet, knocking back hammer flints with one stroke of the palm. "Sorry, guv'nor!" A false alarm. The glimjack hired to walk ahead of the chairmen had only stumbled into a pot hole and dropped his link of burning rope and tar. "I'm reely sorry, guv!" The sedan chair was tilting upward again, unevenly rocking from side to side as it got under way. Fields released his breath. Then, just as slowly, eased the pistol's hammers and folded its spike.

The Strand's west end had become London's pride and the wonder of all Europe after the local parish council increased the window tax to replace their old fire cressets with modern lamps. It was possible now to actually see a newspaper's page at midnight by the glare of whale oil wicks hung overhead every thirty paces.

Fields tensed again as the sedan chair swung into darkness at Burleigh Street, following a night soil cart. Fortunately there was also a convoy of costermongers up ahead, joking and shouting as they hurried with their baskets and lanterns to the vegetable market in Covent Garden. And for once Fields was glad of such low company, composing himself to wait till his chairmen could overtake the costers at Bedford Gardens and turn left along the south side of the broad piazza into Henrietta Street.

The chair's rocking steadied once the men's shoes began hurrying across gravel past the small grotto of trees—once a convent garden—where fruits, herbs and flowers were being traded in another welcoming blaze of light. Fields managed a smile for the first time in several hours as he got ready to dismount: Tweezers Lane might be perfect for quiet rest and discreet dealings, but Covent Garden was the only place for a man of taste to come alive and *live*.

The chair had stopped and was being lowered to the ground opposite St. Peter's Hospital and St. Paul's Church. Fields had picked the Pineapple Tree's address with his usual flair: on one side two apostles, on the other Maiden Lane. It had been a good omen, Fields reminded himself with a confident lift of the chin, climbing out and stretching cramped knees in the three-storey glow of candlelit windows.

"Er, guv?" Fields turned at the coarse voice and tossed a florin. "Thank 'ee!" the outline mumbled back, scooping up the two-shilling piece from a puddle and biting the silver to prove it.

"An' don't fergit me, guv'nor!" Fields peered for a moment at the young link boy's face, going over it point by point, imagining its cheeks scrubbed clean, its hair combed and trim. "I lit the way—!"

"Now and then," Fields had to admit, losing interest. "But you also dropped your light and nearly upset my chair, so let my reply be a valuable lesson, you will thank me for it later," he added, starting to turn away.

"Remember: without a proper attitude to labour, no man can ever hope to rise to the top of his chosen career. That is all."

One of the Pineapple's liveried bouncers was hurrying down the portico steps, burly and long armed with the splayed nostrils and thickened forehead of a bareknuckle pug. " 'Aving a spot o' trouble Mr. Fields, sir?"

"Nothing I cannot handle for myself, Lucas, but I thank you for being observant," Fields replied, striding past, sensing rather than hearing a fist dismiss the impertinent brat. The club's resident manager was waiting just inside the foyer door. Fields nodded distantly as the man straightened. "Capital weather for the season, Driscoll."

"Yes indeed, sir, splendid weather for the time of year," the manager agreed with a wary smile.

"The sky is clearing," Fields observed, letting a footman take his cloak, gloves, hat and cane. "I should not wonder if we pulled quite a decent crowd tonight."

"Neither would I, sir, neither would I."

"Then how are we doing?"

The other, younger man made a lightning estimate of the clients already inside and their likely purses, the same nimble arithmetic which had advanced him from towel boy in a Vigo Street bagnio to a position of trust in the syndicate. Fields nodded at the figures but said nothing: two more footmen were hurrying across the parquet floor, a rich veneer of Honduras mahogany glued over the cheapest Baltic pine. They positioned themselves at the lowest step of a double sweep of stairs which came together again on the first floor near the cut glass chandelier which Driscoll was promoting as the most expensive crystal in Europe.

Fields' spirits soared again as he strode between more footmen bowing like clock ornaments and inhaled the salon's rich fog of male sweat, brandy fumes and cigar smoke. "Not bad, Driscoll, not bad at all!" The manager gratefully bobbed head. It was true, hardly a seat remained to be filled at his faro banks and the night had barely started. Not that Driscoll could claim all the credit. It was unlikely that a single faro table in all Europe wasn't packed that evening. Polite society had lost its wits to faro during the past few years and casinos were mushrooming from St. Petersburg to Lisbon to feed the demand for ever faster action.

Fields stopped at the nearest bank, where a liveried croupier was flipping cards, win-lose-win-lose, as men crowded round, hurling bets on the layout—a table painted with a full deck from ace to king—each certain his card must be drawn the winner. Fields glanced at his manager, voice rising above the guffaws and groans. "How's our margin?" Driscoll had these figures ready, too. "Well, don't let it drop any further." Fields was moving again. "And I trust that our roly poly is performing better than last week?"

Driscoll's head bobbed. "Mother Jordan has been told to predict a big
'un soon."

Fields smiled bleakly. London's most popular clairvoyante was protected by the Interest and knew how to repay the service. One of her private consultations, like a copy of her *Dreambook & Almanack*, was as
necessary as a deep pocket to the modern English sportsman. Fields
glanced across the excitement and made a sudden wave, playfully crossing
fingers at several acquaintances who were also going into the next salon.
"They say there's going to be a big win soon!" he called after them.
"Good luck!"

Good luck? They'd need it! Fields knew that the problem with roly poly
was that it was no longer the fashionable vice which had funded the French
national debt when Louis XIV sold licences to run the game as *hoca*. Recently renamed odd-even, it would take all of Mother Jordan's predictions
to keep the wheels spinning much longer in London. Fields sombrely
watched one rattling round and round with its forty evenly spaced letters—twenty O's and twenty E's—while the banker flicked a small white
ball against its hollow rim and everyone craned forward to see where it
would finally land, on odds or evens.

Fields turned away with a contemptuous shrug. "What an absolute
bore."

"People still like playing it, sir."

"*People* still like tossing ha'pence over a piece of string or betting on
cockroaches!" Fields snapped. "We, however, are not in the business of
amusing *people*. Our sole task is to excite men of quality and breeding.
Understand?"

"Yes, sir."

Fields glanced in at the hazard salon, where a promising crowd was gathering round the clicking dice. He looked back at his manager. "Remember, Driscoll, I shall never be content until we have a club at least equal
to the one that thieving wine merchant Brooks built upon the ruins of
Almacks."

"Yes, sir."

"That mountebank had almost sixty thousand pounds on the table last
night, with the Prince of Wales, Charlie Fox and George Brummell whif-
fling round it like demons to turn the right card." Fields was scowling.
"When were they last at the Pineapple?"

The younger man damped lips. "Well, sir, His Royal Highness did call
a week ago last Friday and plunge two thousand—"

"Bird seed." Fields spoke quietly but Driscoll's face burned. "Your
'plunge two thousand' is not nearly enough, nor is your 'last Friday' frequent enough."

"Yes, sir."

"And another matter, Mr. Driscoll, order your men to stoke these damned fires till the bars melt! A pennyworth of coal returns me a poundsworth of sweat. And I want those buffets loaded, *loaded*, Mr. Driscoll, loaded to overflowing with spiced meats, hot pickles and salted biscuit! Never forget: I have three hundred dozen of champagne lying idle in your cellars and I intend to be deafened by the thunder of popping corks! And Driscoll—!"

The manager spun. "Yes, sir?"

"When you've attended to that chore, make ready the debtors' ledger."

"Yes, sir!"

Fields dismissed him and moved closer to one of the fireplaces, luxuriating in its fierce heat as he scanned the passing crowd. "Damn," he muttered, "any other night of the year and I would never escape the whining wretch. Now, just when he's needed—pffft!—nowhere to be seen." Fields snapped fingers at one of the club waiters. "You."

"Sir?"

"General Burgoyne. Where the hell is he skulking tonight?"

"Er, indeed I cannot say, sir!"

"Find him. Search under every table and behind every door, he can't be far. Then give him my compliments."

"Yes, sir. Immediately, sir!"

Fields turned his back on that problem for a moment and began a fresh smile as another familiar figure lurched away from a packed table, still munching a wedge of tongue and mustard between two thin slices of buttered bread. "Good evenin', Nathaniel!" Duncan Campbell coughed, blowing chewed crumbs over his friend. "I'd better rest m'luck." Munch. "Been tryin' yon' damned martingale system o' Mother J.'s." Swallow. "Trouble is, no matter how I double, then double again, I don't seem to be gettin' anywhere tonight."

Fields looked genuinely distressed by Campbell's story. One of the new breed of Scottish businessmen who had trooped south of the border when the Earl of Bute came down to London as King George's first prime minister, Duncan Campbell had bought his way onto the board of the West India Company and become a principal shipping contractor to the government. Both posts had given him valuable leverage when farming his slave compounds in Senegal, Fields knew, starting to frown. "I'm most awfully sorry to hear that, Duncan, it must be the old law of averages working against you for once. . . ."

Campbell grunted and swallowed. "The trouble is, I seem to be a bit short o' the ready cash this evening, but I don't want to leave the club just yet."

"*Leave?* Great heavens, man, the place would never be the same! Here, allow me to sign you for another two, three? Just to carry you over till tomorrow?"

"Better make it five."

"Just as you wish." Fields busied himself with notebook and silver pencil, Campbell scrawled his signature and two more club waiters began moving closer with an ebony coffer piled high with rolls of newly minted guineas. Fields' eyebrow warned them to keep their distance as he smiled again at Campbell and tucked the pencil back in his waistcoat. "There! Ever happy to oblige. But before you go, Duncan, informed rumour has it that you'll soon be getting a plump Admiralty contract, one for rather remote shores. . . ."

"Ohhh?" Campbell's bloodshot eyes narrowed. "An' I would say that informed fact is that someone will get the most horrible earache if he continues pressing that close to official keyholes."

Fields' genial smile never wavered. "There's no need. My Lord Sydney's nephew—who is, as you know, his under secretary at the Home Office—also happens to share our interest in the sporting life. He and I often chat. Speaking of which, how much is it worth to clear the prison hulks?"

Campbell shrugged. "Something like eighteen shillings a month, per ship ton, for the transports out to New South Wales. Ten shillings a ton while they chuck off the cargo. And an open-ended licence from the Honourable Company to back-load tea from Canton. I should also clear about seventeen quid a nose for every felon's rations on the voyage."

Fields pulled a respectful face at this commercial coup. "You certainly have the Midas touch, Duncan!"

"Aye, it's a gift ye either have or have not," Campbell had to agree, sucking mustard off fingers and thumb. "But lagging crims around the world will not be so profitable as booting niggers across the Atlantic."

"True, true."

"Still," Campbell continued with a fair-minded burp, "at least I'll not have Billy Wilberforce creeping around Westminster behind m'back, calling me nasty names." The Scot grinned. "Why, if ye can believe some opinions, I am now almost a public benefactor! No more gaol fever and no more crime on the streets o' London, and all because o' your humble servant, Duncan Campbell, Esquire. Meantime, o' course, our glorious monarch continues to take all the ri-i-isks."

"Really?"

The grin deepened. "Really. Yon' English clerks are as soft as lard when it comes to writing business paper. Why, the whole Botany Bay expedition is no more than a blank cheque in the right hands."

"Which, I suppose, yours are?" Fields asked with open admiration. "May a mere mortal enquire what is the secret this time?"

"Simple, I'm only astonished that nobody else thought o' it afore me." Campbell reached for a bottle and glass as they passed on their way to another club member. He made a mocking salute, upended the drink and smacked his lips. "Anyway, as I was saying, this contract expressly omits to say *anything* about the goods being fit and ready for plantation labour when finally they land in New Holland. Can ye imagine that?"

"Incredible."

"Isn't it? So, for aught I care my shipmasters can feed every last man to the fishes once they're below the horizon." The Admiralty contractor was pouring a generous reload from the bottle, hand rock steady. "The seventeen pounds will remain in *my* pockets whether or not its subject ever reaches the end o' his journey, alive or dead."

Fields appeared breathless with envy. "A master stroke, Duncan, there's no other name for it. Indeed, I think I can even see how you will *save* money on fodder without it affecting saleable condition, unlike that old problem of running niggers to Kingston—"

"Precisely, for yon English trash has no saleable value in the first place! Indeed, as I was saying to m'head factor only the other forenoon, 'Mr. Monro!' I said—"

"Oh, if only we had your nation's financial genius," Fields interrupted with a charmingly modest smile as he glimpsed the burly shape of General Burgoyne being shoved through the crowd by a waiter. "Anyhow, Duncan, don't allow me to keep you any more from the pleasures of the night. As ever, the Pineapple Tree is honoured to extend you another five thousand credit, secured by your interest in the Botany Bay venture. And do convey my devoted regards to dear Mrs. Campbell when next you meet her!" Fields added brightly, turning away and preparing himself to suffer another attack of threadbare lying about an obscure jungle fort, or farm, or something, called Saratoga: all the shabby, down-at-heel dramatics Burgoyne had been playing since coming home on an American parole to tell Britain why he had left her army behind in Rebel prison camps. God give me patience. "My dear general! So indescribable to see you again!"

"Ah! You too, Fields, you too. Damn' decent of you to say so, damn' decent, what?" Burgoyne wheezed, blotchy cheeks flapping in and out like a punctured bellows. "Ah! Don't seem to be having much luck recently at this place of yours, not much luck. Deuced nuisance, what? Must be on a losing streak, ha!"

No reply was expected. The Burgoyne family had been on losing streaks ever since the late Captain John died a pauper in the Kings Bench

Prison and his only son, the future General John, had eloped with the Earl of Derby's daughter to blaze away her fortune in three astonishing years. "Ah, damned inconvenient, damned inconvenient, what? Um. I don't suppose you could see your way clear to obliging an old theatrical colleague with a small personal advance? Got a new play coming along! Looks good. What?"

Fields wrinkled his nose as the aging cadger pressed too close for comfort. Gentleman Johnny? Feh! No one in London knew more than Fields about Burgoyne's gaming debts and his scribbling for the stage which barely covered the interest bill. It was a total mystery how such a fellow could still remain connected with the Derby interest in Parliament, and connected with that flashy young contralto in the Theatre Royal by whom he was now breeding up a sizeable kennel of bastards despite advancing years.

The actress' name jogged Fields' memory of another woman in the same profession. He fixed a smile. "Then allow me to be the first to congratulate you, general. Indeed, I'm glad you told me, for I was about to ask your opinion of a rather similar matter."

"Damn me, you were, what?" Burgoyne wheezed, puzzled.

"Yes, for it is always my policy to approach informed men whenever I desire information."

"Deuced decent of you to say so, Fields, deuced decent, ha!"

"Therefore, and speaking now as a senior member of our legal fraternity rather than an old and—dare I hope?—trusted friend, I have to confess that I am utterly consumed by curiosity to learn how you are progressing with your, ah, appeal to the Privy Council on behalf of that Mrs. Brandon person?"

"Kitty?" Burgoyne bared his teeth as if the name were a bad apple. "By God, Fields, that whore! That damned slut! That ungrateful gutter bitch! And after all *I* did to get her launched on the stage! Ha! Don't you go listening to those others, no, just you listen to *me*—!"

The lawyer smothered a sigh and began nodding mechanically as General the Right Honourable John Burgoyne launched himself upon a rambling tirade against this latest canker to blight his life. Luckily for Fields, Dicky Sheridan had already spilled a sizeable part of the story during a moment of rash confidence, after he'd found himself being exquisitely blackmailed by one of the most notorious women in the land.

Unluckily for Sheridan, he had originally forgotten that La Belle Brandon, though of a vastly inferior station in life, had begun her climb in the world from the fleapit playhouses of Dublin's fair city—his own home until he was sent across the Irish Sea to school in England. Sheridan had been out of luck in other ways, too. Any well-bred, decent girl would never have stooped to collect the letters and gaming receipts of a rising young playwright and politician, but Katharine Brandon had proved to be neither well-bred nor English.

There had been none of his usual lilting charm the night he hurried round to Tweezers Lane for advice on the quickest way to silence a woman who was now threatening to Tell All unless large sums of money and a royal pardon were delivered to Winchester Gaol. That had been rather before Cribb had sprung a similar trap, so Fields had been brief: let the hag hang. Sheridan's reply had been even more curt: if she swung, then his personal reputation swung with her, along with those of many others of honour and breeding. Men like Jack Burgoyne were also in it, up to his neck in every sense of the expression.

It was common gossip that Gentleman Johnny had been as thick as thieves with the woman in America, but what everyone did not know was just how much of Burgoyne's secret correspondence with the Rebel general Lee   with whom he had served in the British expedition to Portugal, back in '62—had survived intact after the disaster of Saratoga. The British general had destroyed them, he thought, but the young Katharine Brandon knew differently. Even now, years later, once the pamphlet writers on Pitt's payroll got hold of what she could prove about events leading up to the surrender, then Burgoyne might indeed wish he'd gone before a firing squad when he returned home, Sheridan concluded.

Since then, Fields had discovered, matters had gone from worse to worst for the Brandon woman and her desperate victims. A powerful bloc of the Hampshire interest at Westminster was implacably opposed to any reprieve for the woman: she would pay for the murder of Sir Warren Hardwicke's son and be twisted off the back of a cart in Winchester market. Meanwhile Sheridan, Burgoyne and other concerned members of Parliament were lobbying to get their numbers in the Privy Council to outweigh the Hampshire gentry's considerable hold on His Majesty's goodwill. And there, for the moment at least, the case rested while both gangs of gentlemen fought a deadly tug o' war inside Farmer George's misty mind.

Fields' hand abruptly stopped Burgoyne's monologue. "Quite so. Now, strictly between ourselves, I cannot believe that men of *real* standing in the community—such as yourself and Dicky—could encounter resistance obtaining the royal clemency for that Brandon trollop. Oh, I know what the gossips are saying, but it is inconceivable that His Majesty's health is not—how shall we say?—as robust as ever it was . . . ?"

The conversation was aging Burgoyne. His pleated chins slowly crumpled over his cravat. "What a wretched mess, what a wretched, wretched mess it all is."

"Oh? Then it is true?"

Burgoyne looked at the floor. "I—I can't say. By God, Fields, you'll never know how lucky you've been to stay clear of such a rotten business as this has become. It's so bad, so damned bad."

"Or is it damned *mad*?" Fields snapped, boring into his cross-examination, starting to sweat himself, far from clear of an equally wretched mess if Cribb's name were not soon on a stay of execution.

Burgoyne obstinately shook his head. "Can't say. Sorry I spoke, what? Forget I said anything. My lips are sealed."

Fields' lips were compressed. "General. Attend me closely. I am an attorney at law. My chambers are as sacrosanct as the confessional. In my profession no secrets of the heart remain untold for long, and few secrets of state. Therefore, rest assured that everything you have said, or are about to say, will go with me to the grave, a sacred trust for which I must one day answer at that higher seat of justice which awaits us all. Now, I say again, is it or is it not *true* that nobody can shove a reprieve through the Council for that woman? And is it or is it not true that His Majesty's mental health is the real stumbling block until an Act of Regency can be shoved through in Parliament?"

"I—I cannot say."

"Dammit, I can infer!" Fields snarled, sensing the ground quake under his own feet as Cribb's execution ticked ever closer, and hopes for a quick pardon began fading at an alarming speed.

Burgoyne's chins flicked up and, for a brief moment, the face above them was that of the shrewd young brigadier who had won back the fortress of Alcántara for Portugal. "Nothing troubling you personally, I suppose . . . ?"

"Of course not! It's, well, just that in my profession one needs to stay abreast of certain administrative details, that's all."

"Administrative details?"

"Procedures. Pettifogging nonsense. Yes."

Burgoyne's bushy white eyebrows shot up. "By God, Fields, *I* would never describe winning a reprieve from a deadlocked Privy Council, when His Majesty is all but certifiably insane, as 'pettifogging nonsense'!"

"A figure of speech," Fields muttered, stifling the urge to scream. The fire grate behind him was roasting his rump: he barely noticed as he worked up another blandly confidential smile. "Look, Jack, I know that I can trust your judgment absolutely—"

"Oh, absolutely, absolutely."

"Because it's really like this. I have a client, an elderly country gentleman, the very backbone of our nation, you know the sort. A decent and honourable man who was very nearly in tears when he came down from Durham to plead for an only son who's fallen to the law. Oh, it's nothing serious, but a hanging matter nonetheless," Fields added, spreading his hands eloquently.

"Of course, in the normal run of events nothing would be easier to prepare for His Majesty's boundless mercy, but times are no longer normal, are they? So, where else can I turn for this necessary act of clemency, Jack? The poor old devil—my client, that is—does so want his son to inherit the family name and title. *You* understand. . . ."

"Why should that concern me?"

Fields' face was aching but he dare not relax his smile yet. "My dear old friend, it's really very simple. As I understand matters, you are dealing with a very similar problem vis-à-vis that Brandon wretch. Now, it would seem the most perfectly natural thing if we agreed to pool our resources and, somehow, secured *two* royal pardons instead of merely one."

"Hmm. Deuced sticky problem. Deuced sticky, what?"

"My sentiments exactly."

"Trouble is," Burgoyne went on, "I am but one cog in a mighty engine. Much grander wheels and springs would break me to pieces if I now overloaded the mechanism by asking it to deliver two, rather than one, of the necessary papers, what?"

"Jack, please!"

"Sorry, old son, no can do. If your client's boy swings, too bad." Burgoyne's attention was starting to wander as he looked around the salon for a waiter; it must be almost half an hour since he last downed a decent drink. "But if that infernal bitch gets necked, it will overwhelm far more than just one old country gent. Ah! Over here! *Toot sweet*—!"

5

FIELDS' TEMPER was only marginally better when he awoke late the following morning and hurled a shoe at his manservant for not being ready with a bowl of hot tea while the blinds were drawn to let in London's bleak daylight. His aim was practised. The fellow yelped and ran down three flights of steps to the basement scullery to resume screaming at the cook while his master punched the pillows into a comfortable throne and sat up in bed, nightcap askew, wire-framed spectacles on nose, to check the documents and briefs which his head clerk brought in from the copy room.

That day's work done, Fields finished sipping another bitter, laxative tea and swung bare legs out of bed while his manservant held open the commode's teak lid and bowed. He then adjusted his master's enema tube. Fields grunted at the ivory nozzle's chilly poking but stoically endured the pain of easing himself like a gentleman of quality. He grimaced at the servant's impassive face. "And lay out—my—street clothes!"

"Yes, sir."

"The best grey," his master wheezed, "and matching—breeeeches. With thick, flannel waistcoat—ouch!—and muffler."

"Yes, sir."

Barely an hour later and Fields was ready to address the rest of his day to purging Cribb from his life. He stood unsteadily in front of the mirrors, buttoning into a sober suit of clothing which, apart from its superior cut, would let him pass unnoticed among the functionaries at Westminster. Satisfied with the disguise, Fields buckled on a rapier, checked that it flicked from its scabbard and reached for a beaver hat, one of the new consignment from Amsterdam with red silk lining around the daringly narrow brim—next year's fashion, now.

Thirty minutes later he had paid off his hackney carriage in lower Whitehall. The lawyer elbowed across the crowded wooden pavement outside the Home Office in King Charles Street. A government pensioner parked an opened bottle under the counter of his small alcove by the main entrance. Fields waited impatiently while the fellow tried reading the *carte de visite* upside down, then flipped the half-guinea which the doorman used to rap on an interior glass window. A young page, possibly his grandson, trotted out in reasonably clean livery and smart brown wig. Fields eyed the lad's splendid calf muscles from both sides as he led the gentleman upstairs to the home secretary's antechamber. Fields spread a linen handkerchief on the chair which the page had found in another room and sat down while the boy minced off with Fields' card on his brass tray and Fields' two shillings in his pocket.

The lawyer's smile died as he glanced round the packed, noisy, squalid chamber, its windows nailed shut at the start of winter, paper strips glued along the edges to keep out unhealthy draughts. In the far corner a countryman and his woman seemed as if they had taken up permanent lodgings. Place seekers, Fields judged, probably hoping to catch a glimpse of the home secretary, Lord Sydney, if only they waited humbly enough, long enough. Perhaps they wanted to press a petition for some relative condemned by law, Fields wondered idly, or maybe beg for a sinecure on the government payroll? Fields damped lips as he studied his rivals for Lord Sydney's favour. Some snoozed like the country couple, heads lolling, wigs awry. Others shot dice against the wainscoting in quick runs of hazard. While others just stood, dumbly staring through the windows at the Palace of Westminster's rainy rooftops. An immediate neighbour was a late-middle-aged naval officer, darker and shorter than the average, the lawyer's practised mind noticed, with heavy eyelids, thin features and a hooked, Levantine nose. The comic little mannikin sat bolt upright in his chair, heels barely touching the floor, glaring ahead like a bantam cock, as if presiding over an invisible court martial. Fields took comfort from the man's faded blue frock coat with its musty smell of Chinese camphor, probably from being stowed in a sea chest while its luckless owner eked out a threadbare living ashore on half-pay. The gold lace on his cocked hat, perched across both skinny knees, was equally dull with age, while the regulation white kersey stockings could do nothing to smooth the shaped cork inserts which fleshed out his spidery legs.

Heartened, Fields lost interest in his neighbour as the young messenger hurried back and halted in front of him with a cheeky bow. "M'lord's compliments, sir! 'E says you are to wait upon 'im presently. This way, *h*if you please."

Fields' spirits continued soaring at the buzz of envy behind his back, so he took his time folding the handkerchief before strolling through a pair of varnished wooden doors and down a short passage to the home secretary's cabinet. A second pair of doors swung open. Fields paused on the threshold, made an affable bow, then continued toward the shirt-sleeved man who sat profiled at an escritoire, back to the blazing fire, a pair of candlesticks pooling light round his scratching quill. The home secretary glanced up—"Ah! One moment—" and finished sprinkling sand across a sheet of paper.

Although he had graduated from Clare College, Cambridge, a few years ahead of Fields and then entered Parliament as plain Thomas Townshend, Lord Sydney had continued to share old friends and enemies with the younger man. Indeed, Sydney's later appointment as army paymaster general had presented him with many reasons to request discreet advice from the rising lawyer.

Then, for almost ten years, Townshend's star set as his opposition to Lord North and the American War cost him a place in every successive government. Yet in the end patience and planning triumphed. The war party steadily lost favour with the king as Britain bankrupted herself in America, and Townshend's speeches urging peace with the colonists eventually earned him a grudging peerage and a place in the younger Pitt's administration as secretary of state for the Home Department. The lean years were over for Townshend, and now he was enjoying a rich banquet of political prestige, power and pay-back. But not against Fields, even if he was in the Pineapple with North, for theirs was a relationship mellowed over time by a tolerant understanding of each other's human frailties. Besides, the lawyer was too useful whenever certain actions demanded speed and silence beyond the law's creaky cogs and wheels.

Sydney finished blowing sand grains and skimmed the document aside, then turned again, smiling briskly. "Now. To what do we owe this pleasure?"

Fields had loosened coat and muffler and made himself comfortable near the fire. He smiled back. "Purely a personal call, m'lord, nothing particularly urgent today."

"Damned glad to hear somebody say that for once," Sydney grunted, stretching himself to let the fire toast his cramped shoulders. "Everyone else who creeps through that door is either begging a favour or trying to sell a secret patent once the government pays him to build the damned thing in the first place."

"Really?"

"Yes, really." Sydney was sitting comfortably again. "But enough of my chitchat for the moment, what of yourself?"

Fields chose his words. "You knew I'd taken the liberty of keeping an eye on young George's interests at the Pineapple Tree?" he asked, referring to Sydney's nephew and under secretary, George Selwyn.

The fond uncle chuckled, glancing slyly at his visitor. "And *now* what's the young blade been doing? Overdrawn at the bank, as usual?"

Fields pulled a wry face. "Yes. And no. Yes, he is in debt: no, it is not as usual." Sydney was no longer chuckling as Fields went on in the same measured voice. "I happened to be at the club last night and found a special entry for George—"

"So?"

"He's post-obitted you for a twelve."

"The devil he has!"

"Indeed, m'lord, the devil he has." Fields reached inside his coat and pulled out a stiff sheet of paper, sealed with red wax and Selwyn's personal signet. He passed it across without comment and waited.

Sydney's eyebrows crept together as he picked through the bramble thicket of legal terms and binding clauses, any one of which could land the signatory inside Marshalsea debtors' prison for life. But it was not young Selwyn's gaming expenses which troubled his uncle. After all, in a town where an even younger Lord Fowley could, for example, blaze through an inheritance of two hundred thousand pounds in less than a Newmarket racing season, or the Prince of Wales beg his prime minister for a quarter of a million off next year's budget to settle this year's creditors, George Selwyn's twelve thousand was little more than pocket money. But once he began raising loans at giddy rates of interest by anticipating a relative's death and the subsequent inheritance—well!—that was a different matter and unlikely to amuse the post-obitted relative. Especially if he also happened to be the home secretary.

Sydney looked up very slowly. "And what do you propose doing with this matter, Fields?"

"Do? Why, nothing, m'lord. The moment I discovered it, the syndicate arranged for the bond's redemption and its conversion to a simple loan, instalments payable as they become convenient to the young scapegrace."

"Damned decent of you. Damned decent."

Fields shrugged modestly. "It was the very least we could do for him.

However," he went on, "what really troubles me is the thought that young George may try papering another post-obit, perhaps at Brooks, and so fall in the jaws of the sharks political as well as the predators financial—"

"Hm."

"And I doubt if your government's enemies, at home or abroad, will scruple to take advantage of such youthful folly—"

"Hn!"

"I therefore felt it my duty to acquaint you with this matter and to suggest that an uncle's kindly advice may succeed where that of a concerned friend would not." Fields paused lightly. "You may, of course, keep the bond if you wish to bring it to his attention in private."

Lord Sydney folded the paper and pocketed it. "I don't know what the young set's coming to, deuced if I do, Fields." He glanced up, a tired old man. "Dammit. Taking a post-obituary loan is, well, too much like betting on the date someone else will die and then losing when they refuse to oblige."

Fields nodded. "True, m'lord, very true. I can only agree there is a certain lack of decorum these days." He smiled sadly. "Do you think *we* would have done such a thing?"

"Of course not!" The home secretary was gathering speed again. "*We* had breeding. We could hold our liquor an' always knew what was the right and proper thing to do. However, sufficient to say that it's devilish good of you to keep such a close eye on George. Much obliged."

"My pleasure, m'lord," Fields replied, reaching for his hat again. "Only, don't be too hard on him. The world is so full of these young colts nowadays, prancing around, feeling their oats, it's only natural—as I was so vividly reminded yesterday afternoon."

"Oh?"

Fields reluctantly obeyed Sydney's glance and let the hat fall back to the floor. His head shook at a painful memory. "A sad case, m'lord, a bad case. The poor wretch had spent almost his last penny, of which he had very few anyway, coming up from Devon to see a young son who had fallen to the law."

Sydney laid a pinch of snuff along his wrist. "Nothing too serious, I hope?"

"Serious enough, I fear."

Sydney sniffed, snorted, put his belcher away. "So serious you'd plead his case with me—?"

Fields smiled coyly. "We-ell, let us say that in my professional work I have always maintained that it would be an uncharitable world if Justice could not show a human face now and then, to concern herself with the condition of those less fortunate, as it were."

"Noblesse oblige?"

"Exactly so, m'lord, the responsibilities as well as the privileges of supe-rior birth."

Sydney's eyes were shrewd. "Are you suggesting that Justice concern herself with this particular case of yours?"

Fields shrugged. "It could do no harm if something were done to ease the young lad's predicament."

" 'To err is human, to forgive divine'?"

"Precisely so, m'lord," Fields chuckled. "Though, truth to tell, I doubt if anyone has ever detected much of the divine spark in young Joseph Cribb—"

"Cribb?"

"Er, yes. Cribb." Fields was immediately alert.

"No relation to 'Iron Man Cribb,' the pug who went sixty-two rounds with Nigger Spinks at Newmarket last May?"

"Er, I think there is a strong family connexion. On the father's side."

"Glad to hear it. Iron Man carried five hundred for me at seven-to-one." Sydney sneezed again, into the fireplace this time, then glanced up, wiping fingers on his shirt. "So what's the young boy doing inside clink?"

Fields apologetically spread both hands. "They called it 'theft at the scene of a fire,' but *you* know how it is? A moment's temptation, an impul-sive act, then regret forevermore."

"Sounds more like a hanging matter to me."

"Alas, it is."

Sydney frowned irritably. "Oh, well, send a note round and we'll see what can be done."

"I very much fear that will be too late." Fields was groping inside his coat again. "Young Joe is due to meet his Maker next week. Knowing which I have taken the liberty of preparing a petition in advance." He tugged out a copy of Old Bailey's transcript, modified by his head clerk in the early hours of the morning, and laid it on the home secretary's desk. "Any further delay in this matter could be fatal. And not only for young Cribb."

"Oh?"

Fields chose his next words with extreme care. "Shall we say that, al-though of a class in which nobody will inherit a penny by post-obitting him, this is one occasion when a good deed now could reap a good deal later on?"

"Ah, one of that sort." Sydney lightly touched the packet of documents and stirred it around with his fingertips. "And you recommend this ought to be brought to His Majesty's attention?"

"Immediately. Indeed, many other interests will be handsomely served by a prompt display of royal clemency at this time."

"Whose interests?"

"Ours. The Interest."

Sydney kept silent for several moments. "Next week, you say?"

"Yes. Monday morning."

The home secretary looked troubled. "Deuced if I know what you really hope to gain for the poor fellow. Even allowing that His Majesty is still able to recall what his signature looks like, what would we have done for your luckless client?" Sydney pulled a long face. "Instead of letting the law take its course, admittedly with some brief discomfort for the person in question, we should have consigned him to a lifetime aboard one of the hulks off Woolwich, slaving with shovel and barrow on those dockyards."

He looked up, still troubled. "Have you any idea how short, brutish and nasty that lifetime would be? I don't know of anyone who has gone for more than three years at hard labour, whereas, kicking his heels outside Newgate, it's all over in about three minutes. Frankly, I'm damned if I know why anyone in his right mind would ever want to be reprieved to a floating pesthouse from which the only release is sweating fever or the pox."

" 'Hope springs eternal in the human breast'?" Fields quipped, hurrying to divert the home secretary's mind into less morbid channels.

"Among *humans*, maybe!" Sydney was annoyed at the interruption. "But aren't you overlooking the fact that we are dealing with a different category of item when we speak of condemned criminals?"

"I stand corrected, m'lord," Fields murmured, backing off an obviously sensitive topic. "However, have I not heard that you are soon to begin emptying them at Botany Bay in New Holland?"

"Of course you have," the home secretary snorted, starting to pace the floor between hearth and desk. "So, I hope, has everyone else. Now, for the first time since we lost the American colonies a sentence of transportation is going to mean exactly what I say it means! I tell you this, Fields, the criminal class will soon have every reason to think again before they disobey their betters." Sydney paused abruptly, finger punctuating his words as it often did on the floor in Parliament. "I shall go further: Botany Bay might have been especially designed by nature for the purposes for which we intend it. Now, instead of cavorting recklessly on the scaffold, hurling defiance at authority, the lawbreaker faces the certain prospect of a dismal journey to distant shores, a dreadful example to all others of like stripe." Sydney paused abruptly, studying the effect of these words on his listener.

Fields smiled disarmingly. "Well, then, m'lord, surely this is our answer? Do but let Iron Man's wayward nephew go to Botany Bay—"

"And the devil take all others like him!" The home secretary plunged on, flicking the question aside. "It is the government's intention that every one of those floating cesspits be emptied before any further damage can be done." He paused, wondering how much he could count on this being gossiped around London. "In the strictest confidence, Fields, the capital was damned lucky to avoid an outbreak of the putrid fever this summer. Damned lucky. It was touch and go with the water supplies at one point. And the mere existence of such concentrations of the criminal class is the gravest possible threat to society's health and morals. I tell you this, it is the firmest resolve of His Majesty's government to remove that twin threat by every means possible, as far as possible, to Botany Bay."

"Most relieved to hear it, m'lord," Fields said, puzzled by Sydney's unprompted lecture on the obvious. After all, informed London opinion—from the lord mayor, Sir Samuel Wainwright, downward—had been clamouring for months, demanding stronger government action to find a solution to the overcrowded prison hulks which threatened their city's air and water. "Now, this question of young Joe Cribb . . . ?"

"What of him?"

Fields assembled another disarming smile from his dwindling stock of parts. "Well, m'lord, surely he could be reprieved to a lifetime of useful labour in a new world, far removed from temptation?"

Sydney scowled; even the mention of transportation seemed to irritate him. He knocked the petition aside with annoyance. "Leave it here. I won't promise anything."

Fields hid his panic with another desperate smile. "Of course, m'lord, nobody expects miracles, however I am confident that if anyone can find a mitigating circumstance which can snatch this young brand from the fire, it will be *you*, my lord! And, as you have so correctly observed, if error is human, then forgiveness must be the most divine of emotions, the one noble title which cannot dim with age or become—!"

The home secretary was tugging a fine steel wire which ran up from his desk, across hooks in the ceiling and through the opposite wall. A bell jangled faintly. A few moments later and a second, smaller door opened into the cabinet. "Uncle?"

"Oh. It's you. We have something to discuss. In private. Meanwhile, kindly escort Mr. Fields out and show in our next petitioner."

"Immediately, m'lord."

"Who the hell is it?"

George Selwyn paused at the door, frowning. "A Captain Arthur Phillips, I think—"

"*Phillip?*"

"Er, yes, m'lord."

"Then why the devil didn't you tell me earlier!"

Fields shared a puzzled smile with Selwyn as the door shut behind him.

Alone in the room now, Sydney scowled and poured a generous measure of port from one of several decanters on the sideboard. He also took the opportunity to rummage inside a mahogany canister for a handful of his favourite cinnamon wafers, then paced across to the cabinet's main table, sipping the tumbler of wine. Every chart, every docketted file, almost every letter to Parliament on the subject of convict transportation now stretched before him, rank upon rank, heap upon heap, the end product of years of committee work and evasion. "Order. Counterorder. Disorder."

For almost a century every home secretary had needed to do little more than initial papers which offered batches of convicted prisoners to merchant syndicates for resale across the Atlantic. Once ashore in Maryland, or Virginia, or the Carolinas, and still being fed at the contractors' expense, felons had been sold to plantations for the balance of their sentence—usually a minimum of seven years at hard labour—in a private alternative to public execution. The transportation system had been, as London's newspapers and gentlemen's magazines never failed to remind Parliament, a benevolent and enlightened policy from which everyone gained something of value: the Treasury's agents sold lucrative contracts to the shipping magnates, local councils saved themselves the cost of building larger gaols, the colonial empire gained robust labour to grow more cotton and tobacco for the mother country. It had been an elegant solution to an ugly problem, the alchemy of transportation had changed human dross into gold, and there had been no reason to think it would not continue doing so indefinitely but for the disturbances of 1776.

The home secretary snapped a wafer and eyed a stack of files with outlandish names: a few enterprising German companies had tried to continue the system by sailing under the independent flags of Bremen and Hamburg to load cargoes in Ireland for the Spanish wholesalers of Florida, the short-lived White Guinea Trade. But even this expedient had tapered off once the Royal Navy's blockade began choking the American Rebels' economy. Meanwhile, in the English courts, transportation continued to be the only alternative to death for theft of goods valued at more than a shilling, breaking down a fishpond wall, stealing shrouds from graves and much else that Sydney could never remember.

He sipped wine. In practise all that a sentence of transportation now meant was confinement aboard a hulk or floating prison cage, one of many dismasted men o' war which contractors towed round the coast whenever forced labour was needed to excavate a dockyard or build a new breakwater. Sydney studied the ruby distortion of a candle flame through his glass, then looked back at the inch-high piles of petitions which his committee had noted, each urging this or that favourite scheme to replace the lost American colonies.

Five years earlier, while the war was still dragging to its end, nearly eight hundred assorted convicts had been offered pardons if they would enlist in the Royal African Regiment and sail to the Gold Coast to fight the Dutch, dirt, disease and tropical death.

Two years later and George Moore, a Bristol merchant with sound connexions inside government, had decided to revive the old trade with Maryland. Sydney had not been the only one to be annoyed when His Majesty's former subjects declined the overflow from his gaols, no matter how attractive the credit terms. Moore's captain had been told to ship them south, much further south to the logwood camps of British Hondu-ras, but even here the venture was out of luck. The settlers refused to bid at auction in Belize, claiming that London's convicts would only corrupt the morals and discipline of their black slaves. In the end yellow fever took his cargo and Moore lost heavily.

Sydney tasted wine and sadly turned over another sheaf of documents: fortunately for Parliament and its Committee on Transportation, the president of the Royal Society—Sir Joseph Banks—had then remembered naming Botany Bay, an impressively remote speck halfway round the globe on the Pacific Coast of New Holland.

Seventeen years earlier the then young scientist had spent a pleasant week camping on the beach, collecting plants while his captain, James Cook, refilled HMS *Endeavour*'s water barrels. After some deft prompting from the committee and home secretary, Sir Joseph had clearly remembered how fertile the soil had been, how attractive and lush the vegetation, how mild this New Holland place was.

Sydney skimmed the maps aside and looked up as George Selwyn appeared in the cabinet's main doorway again. "Captain Phillips, m'lord."

The under secretary eased himself aside, just enough to let the small, dark-featured naval officer march past, cocked hat and sword gathered tightly under one arm, heels rapping together as he halted, head inclining sharply. "Your servant, m'lord."

Sydney gestured for Selwyn to leave and shut the door as he walked across to greet his visitor. "I trust you had an agreeable journey up from Hampshire, captain?"

"Most agreeable, m'lord." Phillip's voice, like his manner, was trained to be obeyed on a warship's quarterdeck. However, Sydney's English ear noted the subtle undertones of another class, of another language in the accent, and he smiled at the secret knowledge as he escorted Phillip nearer the fire, hand on elbow. "I imagine it must be rather chilly at Lyndhurst? It always was, though I have the most pleasant memories of the time I sat for your county in the Commons. You are to be congratulated upon your choice of home, captain."

"Thank you, m'lord."

Sydney sat at the escritoire again and nodded for Phillip to be seated. "You've had, ah, sufficient time to study our proposals?"

"Yes, m'lord."

"And what do you think?"

Phillip sat bolt upright in the chair Fields had warmed for him, frowning into the firelight. Then he glanced up, eyes heavy after the long ride to London. "Botany Bay can be done."

"In time . . . ?"

"Yes, if I have the right vessels, well found and provisioned."

"Have no fear on that account, captain. The Admiralty has already located six ships which the contractors say are most excellent for your task."

"I am relieved to hear it," Phillip replied in a neutral voice.

"Indeed, there is no reason why the first transport should not be loading on the Thames before Christmas, ready for your flagship to join her at Portsmouth early in the new year. They say that will get you away in time to catch the next summer in the southern latitudes."

"As m'lord directs."

Sydney smiled ironically. "Correction, captain, as Our Lord directs, He still sets the pattern of winds and rainfall, I'm told. Moreover, Sir Joseph assures me the southern winter is quite unlike ours, being always mild and kindly." Sydney paused, just the hint of a frown on his pink, solid face. "You do not appear altogether convinced by my words, captain."

Phillip hesitated. "No, m'lord, I am not."

"Oh? And why, may I ask?"

Phillip hesitated again. "Because, for a number of years between sea appointments, I have had to manage my properties for a living."

"So?"

Phillip no longer hesitated. "My personal observations of agriculture are that even with the best soils, the most lush vegetation, the mildest climate, things rarely run the course we steer."

"Meaning?"

Phillip could not miss the gathering frost in the home secretary's voice, but he had never flinched from doing his duty or speaking his mind, and he would not start learning the courtier's trade now. "I mean, m'lord, that weather can turn freezing cold, or scorching hot, or send down a hailstorm to destroy in a few minutes all that the labourers have toiled for months to grow."

"Captain. The empire has not reached its present extent just because we were discouraged by sudden hailstorms!"

"I'm aware of that, m'lord, but the key factor in your plans for establishing our presence at Botany Bay would seem to be the harvesting of flax."

"Quite so," Sydney snapped back, "for as sugar is to the Caribbean, and indigo is to Bengal, so must flax be to this new colony. And not only to weave sailcloth," he went on, softening his voice slightly. "God alone knows it's costing us a fortune just to underwrite this venture. Without some worthwhile production to underwrite your expenses, I very much fear that London's enthusiasm for transportation will die even faster than we gave it life."

"I'm also aware of that, m'lord, for which reason I raise this matter of climate and for which reason I must again urge that you first send out a reconnaissance vessel. We know absolutely nothing about this Botany Bay place. Nobody does. I consider it most imprudent to chance everything on it being exactly as we hope."

Sydney's frown deepened. "Sir Joseph assures me that New South Wales is, if possible, even more blessed than Tahiti."

"With respect, m'lord, he was last there almost twenty years ago. No matter how accurate his impressions then, are they accurate now?" Phillip replied. "No one is more aware than I of the compelling need to establish a base in the Pacific before His Majesty of France beats us to it. After all," he went on with an expressive shrug, "it was I who watched frigate after frigate being laid down at the Chantier du Roi, Toulon."

The home secretary fiddled with one of the quills on his desk, absentmindedly swishing the feather to and fro, shooting loose sand grains across the parquet floor. Plain speech was not a thing he tolerated from middling naval officers of obscure origin and with no connexion among the Interest—England's unseen rulers, the old landed families, her political kingmakers who filled the House of Commons with friends and relatives—but he would this time, for Arthur Phillip's personal dossier was also lying among the papers on the table behind him.

The son of a Jewish refugee from Frankfurt who had settled in London to eke out a living by teaching languages, Arthur Phillip had been sent to sea from the Poor Boys' Establishment, Greenwich, finally winning a lieutenant's commission at the capture of Havana in '63. Thereafter he had retired on half-pay to marry and farm in Hampshire until volunteering for service with the Portuguese in their war against Spain. His papers from the Ministro do Marinha, Lisbon, were also in the dossier and showed that Phillip had rapidly risen to the independent command of a cruiser and had served with courage off the Rio de la Plata. At the end of three years the Portuguese crown had requested London to extend his term of service, an almost unheard of compliment for an Englishman and nominal Protestant in a proudly Portuguese and fiercely Catholic navy.

Sydney also knew more than would ever be told about Phillip's lonely months in the south of France, now an eccentric German gentleman of private means with his barbarous French and absentminded pottering after flowers and beetles on the hills around Toulon, France's main naval base after Brest. And the same dossier made only passing reference to the year which Phillip spent at a drawing board in the Admiralty's Charts &

Surveys Office while transcribing his sketchbooks into a penetrating analysis of the French Mediterranean fleet.

It was while in the Office, and by now promoted from commander to captain over the heads of others with more seagoing experience, that Arthur Phillip's name had been advanced as a candidate for the first governorship of Botany Bay. His neighbour at Lyndhurst, Secretary of the Treasury George Rose, had endorsed the proposal in a conversation with the prime minister and a self-effacing little naval officer found himself sharing state secrets with fewer than six men outside the Cabinet.

Sydney flicked the last sand grain and looked up. "I'm sorry, captain, a reconnaissance is out of the question; there is simply no more time. It is absolutely imperative that your fleet sail for the Pacific at the earliest possible moment. Admiral de La Pérouse is already out there and God knows what he might not have already claimed or done: I don't have to remind anyone what it means if he pips you to the post and establishes France at Botany Bay first."

Phillip remained silent. The memoranda he had been studying for the past weeks at Lyndhurst had said everything that could be said about London's need for a source of mast timber and sailcloth in the Western Pacific to refit the Chinamen when war broke out again, and both were said to grow in New Holland. The same plans had chosen Botany Bay to be the empire's victualling base on a great circle route, south about Africa and Van Dieman's Land to Canton when the French or Dutch next threatened to shut the Cape of Good Hope and the Malacca Straits to British convoys.

Phillip had also glimpsed a confidential estimate from Pitt to Treasury, totalling the funds needed to buy pamphlet writers and city aldermen in the campaign to make public opinion demand a return of convict transportation, regardless of cost, regardless of distance. And regardless of common logic, Phillip had judged at Lyndhurst, calculating that hulks moored five miles downstream off Woolwich and Blackwall presented no threat to water supplies piped from springs on Finchley Common or drawn from the Thames above London Bridge.

He had not been smiling when he reached for his own pen to underscore one of the prime minister's paragraphs, noting in the margin that this new Pacific strategy would depend on simple gardening: without an urgent and popular reason, like convicts, to send an armed squadron into the South Seas, Pitt's enemies in Parliament—Fox and Sheridan, egged on by the Prince of Wales, who was desperate for pliable servants in Treasury—would make another coalition as they had done against Lord North and bring down the present government on charges of financial mismanagement unless there was immediate production of saleable timber and vegetables in the colony.

The plain truth was that, five years after the loss of thirteen in America, colonies were known to be costly to found, troublesome to defend and ruinously expensive to keep once they had decided to go their own ways. Colonial adventures were no longer fashionable in London. Fortunately for Phillip's personal ambitions, distant convict camps most certainly were, at least while the *Gentlemen's Magazine* and *London Courant* did as they were told.

Sydney coughed sharply, bringing Phillip's attention back to the present. "M'lord?"

"I said, do you consider seven hundred felons to be a sufficient labour force to build a base and establish gardens?"

Phillip shrugged wearily. "I shall know that only when I get there. All I can say at the moment is that we threaten to burst at the seams once we add their guards and civil administrators and men to work the transports, together with supplies for a minimum of two years. To be frank, m'lord, this is a tall order—"

"But one we are—confident you will—discharge most handsomely," a third voice interrupted. Both Sydney and Phillip spun round. Selwyn was respectfully holding open the second door while an equally young, sharply featured man strode into the cabinet, erect and energetic, dressed in crumpled worsted, auburn hair tugged back in a careless bob. The home secretary immediately bowed. "An unexpected pleasure, prime minister."

Phillip timed his bow exactly, glancing to see when Sydney straightened again, then stood to attention himself, looking up as William Pitt approached him directly—a full head and shoulders taller—returning the prime minister's unexpected handshake. Then Pitt strode past to the fireplace, flapping sodden coat tails in front of the blaze: the afternoon drizzle had turned to a downpour while he'd walked around the corner from Downing Street. "Sir Charles Middleton dropped in from Admiralty," Pitt said over one shoulder. "Told me Captain Phillip was in town. Like George Rose, he speaks well of his work for us in France." Then, at Phillip, "High praise indeed, captain."

And high praise from such a naturally aloof man, Sydney judged, glancing at this Phillip with renewed interest as the small naval officer rapped heels and inclined his head in that oddly foreign way of his. Pitt had turned again, warming his rump, stockinged legs wide apart in front of the hearth. "Townshend? Can you spare Captain Phillip for a few minutes? There are certain matters you and I need to discuss."

"Of course, of course. Captain? Would you excuse us, please?" The distant bell jangled and Selwyn escorted Phillip back to the antechamber.

Pitt watched the door click shut, then lifted an eyebrow at Sydney. "Interesting enough fellow, but rather old for the job, isn't he?"

Sydney grimaced. "He's not really that much older than I am, y'know."

"Quite." Pitt made another rare smile. "Would *you* volunteer to go to the ends of the earth at his age?"

"Hardly!" Sydney returned the smile, stoppering a decanter and walking across to the younger man again. His own daughter had recently married the prime minister's elder brother, the second Earl of Chatham, cementing the already close ties of class and politics. "Here."

"Thank you."

"To your health?"

"To ours."

Two glasses clinked in the intimate silence. A knob of blazing coal rattled against the iron fire basket. Pitt breathed out, relishing the wine's explosive glow in his stomach as much as he did the coal's heat on his legs. "I am not entirely sold on him, Townshend, not entirely."

Sydney frowned. "Just because he is a little older than you expected?"

"Yes. But that is not all. He looks as if the first decent puff of wind would blow him out of sight if not out of mind, and then where would we be? But seriously," Pitt went on, draining his glass and signalling for a refill, "surely we have someone younger? With more breeding? Someone more suited to a colonial governorship?"

Sydney tilted the decanter. "I'm not sure we have."

"And why not?"

"Two reasons," Sydney replied, handing the glass back and lifting his own. "Firstly: time has run out. Mr. Cummings bought a reliable source in Paris, someone close to their minister of marine, we're being kept posted on La Pérouse's secret instructions."

"I told him to." Pitt was neutral.

"Oh. Well, secondly: I suspect that our little captain's lack of suitable background may, in an odd manner, prove of value."

"How?"

Sydney made a slight grimace. "Because of the very nature of his cargo. Masterless felons and whores they may be now, but once landed at the other end they will be our white niggers until a trade can be established with the kings of the black 'uns in New Holland, for local recruits. It will be brutally hard work, I do not doubt, hewing stone and wood. A gentleman would scruple to apply the necessary stimulants to labour under such harsh circumstances. Fortunately for us, Captain Phillip is not a gentleman."

"Hm."

"In addition, we have Rose's word that the man is always cold sober, industrious, generally obedient, knows how to keep his mouth shut and doesn't seem to chase after skirts, five unusual qualities which ought to ensure a minimum of friction with his garrison officers once the novelty of their isolation wears off and they start duelling among themselves."

"Another sound point," Pitt was forced to agree, moving nearer the cabinet table and a large globe which stood in an alcove by the rain-streaked windows. He spun the heavy ball inside its brass gimbal rings, tilting the revolving map to let a fingertip trace its lonely track around Africa, down to the polar ice, then north again past Van Dieman's Land into the blank which wrapped one-third of the world from Cape Town to Spain's outposts in Chile. "How remote and unimportant it all seems, Townshend," Pitt said, frowning at the globe, "but will it still be so ten, twenty, thirty years from now? That is the question we have to address ourselves to and pray that we choose the right path." He hesitated, withdrawn. "It is claimed that nature abhors a vacuum: so do men of affairs. London or Paris, never Paris *and* London, will finally decide whose voice is obeyed in those South Seas."

"Then we had better make damn sure the Frogs don't jump us first," Sydney commented, joining his chief at the window.

The prime minister was now alone with his memories. "London or Paris? Nothing has changed. Our national objectives are still the same as they were in 'fifty-six. Whether or not we patch up this treaty with France, the fundamental equation of England's foreign policy remains what it has always been—never London and Paris acting together—for what one of us needs the other cannot afford to surrender. So it was in the beginning, is, and ever more will be until one or another of us is annihilated."

Sydney looked uneasily among the candlelit shadows and then back at the younger Pitt. "Surely you're laying it on a bit thick?"

"No," the same flat voice replied. "I fear we shall yet live to see the storm break again over Europe. This week or this year? Next year? The one after? Who knows? One thing only is certain: the fleets and armies are already moving into their predestined positions on the board. Neither you nor I, nor His Majesty of France and all his many conflicting advisers will be able to prevent a veritable battle of the titans once they are in place. This will be a war to the death, Townshend."

Pitt read the globe. "There is not enough space in the whole universe for both our empires to exist in peace. Yet, for the moment, we are both equally bankrupt after decades of bid and counterbid. They have lost Canada and India from their hand, while we have lost the American colonies. The only worthwhile card which now remains for either of us to draw is here—" the finger slowly traced north, through Luzon Strait to Canton—"the East. Whoever controls the China trade will trump all others and sweep the table clear."

Sydney smiled at hearing sporting talk from such a normally straight-laced young man. "I must say, Pitt, now you *are* beginning to remind me of your father. I well remember the day he said—"

It was a poorly timed jibe. "Is that such a reprehensible or comic thing, Townshend?"

"Er, no, I really meant—"

"Kindly remember, for whatever time I wish you to remain in my administration, that while other children were still whipping their tops, or chasing a hoop, or netting minnows, *I* was being taught to form letters by copying my father's despatches to the four corners of a world at war." The scowl deepened. "I was cutting my teeth on Chatham's cabinet papers while others older than I were still lisping their alphabets at Mama's knee. Such a schooling and such a schoolmaster leave one with a singular understanding of history and its workings. Remember that."

Sydney shuffled his feet, still learning his limits with a man who had brought down a budget as chancellor of the exchequer at twenty-three and formed a cabinet as prime minister barely a year later. Pitt's finger was stabbing the globe. "When I say that our nation's very survival hinges upon an eastern policy, then it is so. China, Townshend, *China* and its natural complement, India. We must control both or we lose all." The finger continued its relentless tattoo. "There are countless millions of industrious and obedient subjects here, in the Celestial Empire. If one in every ten bought a pocket handkerchief apiece from us, all the spinning mills of Lancashire would never be able to keep up with orders for thread. It is a situation which highly commends itself to me."

"Yes, but—"

"For another of my father's maxims was 'Rule the rulers and let the rulers rule the ruled,' something I imagine his father learned the hard way as governor of Madras." Pitt's look had not softened. "I cannot afford any more rebellion, Townshend. The future of the empire lies with quiet trade and the modest expense of an ambassador to enlighten our local despot, not funding armies of occupation."

"I hope you're right," Sydney observed, swirling his glass and emptying it. "It's costing a fortune just to send a modest embassy to the cannibal kings of New Holland."

"And worth every penny." The finger thrust southward across the Spice Islands. "As Gibraltar is the key which opens or shuts the Mediterranean for us, so are Botany Bay's forts and dockyards the key to the world's last great unknown, the Pacific." Pitt's voice was harsh. "New Holland will be the lynch pin of our future trade with China, and the French know it. The world will belong to whoever occupies that remote and unappetising coastline."

Sydney was shaking his head at the prospect. "You have the happy knack of making it all sound so easy—halfway round the world of which you speak—but all our fine plans will not be worth a row of peas if the Dutch business boils over and the Frogs order their fleet into the Narrow Seas to support their clique in Amsterdam."

Pitt straightened. "I know. Every night I pray to God that we can settle this present dispute with soft words and promises, anything to buy time to recover our strength. Only a little more time, that's all we need. Middleton has promised me twenty-five new men o' war off the private yards and about sixty under repair, but for the next year or so it will be a close-run race if we have to mobilise the fleet and go to war. A close-run race."

6

"AND I STILL SAYS that if old Jack Shepard could've got up 'ere, so can we!" Cribb snapped, forcing his shoulders into the death cell's fireplace and twisting around to stare at the tantalising square of sky. The second iron grating was now within reach of his fingertips: it was also still warm and anchored rock solid to Newgate's outer wall. Someone with a longer arm and far greater strength had once filed a small nick in the end of one bar. Coughing, Cribb dragged himself out backward over the hot hearth and smeared sooty snow off his face while Bosun slapped a smouldering patch on the greatcoat.

The old sailor grinned vacantly. " 'Appier now, chummy?"

Cribb gobbed at the ashes where he'd lain while the other man covered him from curious turnkeys in the taproom. Not that any of the other condemned had taken much interest in him: this was the last afternoon they would ever know and the hours which remained were too precious to squander on daydreams.

Only Cribb, and Bosun, and a young nypper who had attached himself to the old tar while he spun yarns of war at sea now remained in the death cell. Several prisoners had clubbed their pennies together and bought two gallons of gin to kill time in the taproom corner. Others with more to spend were gorging hot meat pies and roasts with their friends and families while the grocers' blind hum-strum player sat astride a barrel, sawing jigs on his mop stick, pig's bladder and pack-thread fiddle.

Cribb took aim and gobbed harder while Bosun made another cracked grin. "Didn't I tell you it was no use frettin'? Didn't they ever learn you that in the army? If you gets croaked today, why, you're safe tomorrow. . . ."

"And didn't I tell *you* as what they've not made the rope yet what can choke me!" Cribb replied, finger jabbing hard. "It's writ on my face, an old 'Gyptian woman told me so! 'You'll croak in your bed, in a roomful o' sunshine, with a bag o' georges under the pillow, like a regular gent.' That's what she said, so I got to get out——!"

The older man's grip was surprisingly gentle on Cribb's flailing fist. "So you will, chum." He made a wet giggle. "Tomorrow mornin'. We walks through that there door, steps up the ladder, an'——"

"Pig's arse!" Cribb made Bosun flinch. "Know what I got learned in the king's army, mate? I learned that a regular cove ain't croaked till some other prick is up there, a-shovelling dirt on top, and even then I wouldn't bet on 'im staying in the ditch for long!" Cribb drew breath. "Jack Tar might think 'e's safe tomorrow if 'e croaks today, but that ain't *my* style. If it 'ad of been, I'd be a maggot's granddad long before now."

Bosun made an empty smile and began scrubbing at the powder burns on his face and chest. "I got a good story about maggots. It all 'appened while we aboard the ol' *Retribution*——"

"*I* got an even better story!" Cribb snarled, getting closer, dropping his voice to a penetrating hiss. "It all 'appened to the gamest crew of coves you'll ever meet, Over There, when we bolted from Copper 'Ill camp. . . ." Bosun giggled and began picking his toes. Cribb gritted his teeth and wondered if this was worth the effort.

Within a day of being slammed in the death cell he had cut the rest of the prisoners as being hopeless, without hope. Only the shell-shocked old tar, Bosun, might still have enough nerve and discipline for an assault on the taproom later that evening when the parting feast was at its height, working together to heave a crock pot of rum into the open fireplace before grabbing a broomstick apiece and bayonetting through the panic and flames. Once clear in the press yard, they'd have only moments to snatch up a heavy oak plank and rush the gatekeeper's lodge before he dropped the bar inside. If they beat him to it, Bosun could barricade the press yard's door while Cribb broke the keeper's arm to get the wicket gate's keys and break out, into the market place.

It was not foolproof—the war had taught him that few plans ever are—but it was far better to go game in a suicide attack than to squat in a boozy stupor, waiting for the hangman to come and twist their necks. But Cribb knew he could never execute it alone: there had to be at least one other dependable man with him to make a fighting chance.

He crouched, tapping Bosun again. "Listen careful, I won't say this more'n once." His voice dropped even lower. "We got clear of that devil's trap, Copper 'Ill, alongside which this place is nothing more'n a paper bag. 'Ow did we crack it? Simple. We stuck together. Like we learned in the king's service. . . ."

Bosun grinned uncertainly at another's war story, one disturbingly different from the high adventures he told the nypper. "You been told about the king?"

"Pin your ears on straight!" Cribb snarled. "I'm telling you we still got a fighting chance if, *if* we stick together and do things right! *Savvyvoo? Fair stainsy?*"

But not even these scraps of the international shorthand which British veterans had brought home after fighting the French and the American rebels alongside German allies could jolt Bosun into action. The old sailor was scratching his powder pocks again. "Must be terrible 'ard bein' the king. An' now they say 'e ain't feelin' too good. That's bad on the queen, eh?"

Cribb no longer bothered to comment. There was not a soul in Newgate who didn't suspect the true state of the royal mind once the turnkeys began grumbling about having to fit twenty-four on a gallows made for ten.

Officially, His Majesty was indisposed. Only essential government papers were being considered by the weekly councils at Windsor: reprieves from death were not essential paperwork. Now the gaol's carpenter was having to raise another beam along the market-place wall, three feet in front of the first. When the enlarged trap crashed away tomorrow morning, an entire batch of felons would tumble through in one gala hanging as a curtain raiser to Mrs. Kemp's burning at the gibbet. Bambridge had promised the grocers a handsome return from such a unique attraction, London's grandest public execution since the Scottish rebels had been hanged, drawn and quartered at Tyburn forty years earlier. The *Gentlemen's Magazine* thought so too when it urged readers to reserve seats overlooking the market, either for their own parties or to take a quick profit once all tickets were sold and demand pushed up the resale price.

Bosun settled down on the floor beside Cribb and stretched his legs, fetters clinking among the sawdust and straw. He pulled a short twist of baccy from his patched canvas jacket and made an offer. Cribb knocked it away and went back to glowering at the trampled bedding between his heels, so Bosun chewed the plug tobacco for himself as he leaned against the wall for a lazy yarn. "You afraid o' dyin', chum?"

"Hn!"

Bosun squirted juice and hit the fireplace smack in the middle. Satisfied that his aim was as true as ever, he glanced at the younger man again. "I once 'ad a shipmate like you, on the ol' *Endeavour*. Every night, regular as clockwork, 'e prayed to go straight to 'Eaven when 'is bell struck; but you can bet 'e was quick to add that 'e didn't want to go just yet!"

Bosun stopped chuckling at his own joke and went on, as if yarning from one hammock to the next after an easy watch aloft. "I've 'ad a good run. I seen things you'd never believe in a thousan' years, unless you'd been there with us." He paused, chewing slowly. "I been round the world!

Not many as can say that, eh? I spent three months on Tar-heaty in the South Seas, I did. Fort Venus they called it. Blimey, they got the right name that time! Loverly young girls as you'd only dream about back 'ome." He sighed contentedly. "But even *that* weren't nothin' to what we seen in New 'Olland, at what they call Bottommy Bay. There, them black cannibals *eat* the biggest rats you ever did see!"

The young nypper was wriggling closer, chin on knees, mouth ajar. Bosun chuckled. "I thought that'd surprise you, son. God's truth, in New 'Olland the Indians run after jumpin' rats bigger'n what I am, chuckin' bits o' bent wood at 'em."

"Go on, mister!"

"Well, it all started like this," Bosun said, taking another gnaw from the tobacco plug. "Mr. Cook an' me decided the best thing we could do was—"

Cribb dragged himself off the straw. The Quaker visitor, kneeling by the gateway, smiled brightly and beckoned him to come and join her small prayer circle, but Cribb shoved past and leaned his throbbing forehead against the barred ventilation chute instead. He was still cursing Fields, somewhere out there in the icy darkness, when Twitch flung open the gates to let in the turnkeys' paying visitors, more tourists and gentlemen who liked to join the condemned and share their fun. "Spend up! Can't take it with you!"

The taproom was starting to fill and those prisoners who had nothing left in their pockets, or who still had bills to settle, were being encouraged to take every last chance to raise the necessary funds. For example, dentures were now fashionable and some well-connected false teeth had begun their second youth in Newgate after Mr. Edward Lilly and his assistants had paid their respects to the keeper. Arthur Bambridge pocketted his tip and snapped fingers for a pair of trusties to carry the dentist's tool kit into the taproom, trampling down steps where friends and relatives were tippling from leather jugs. Lilly followed and ran a practised eye over the evening's prospects while his men cleared a good pitch under the lantern.

Smiling broadly, the dentist jumped on the table and spilled a purseful of guineas over his tambourine's parchment to make music that never failed to charm an audience. His message was always simple, always welcome in the death cell: two gold pieces for the first sound tooth pulled, a guinea for every other, and the first volunteer was not slow to edge forward, urged on by thirsty friends from Outside.

Lilly was not the only one to be hunting spare parts. Every six weeks a heavily cloaked Mother Jordan was driven by carriage to Newgate where she sipped port in the lodge while her footmen scouted the crowd, dropping hints and nodding at the half-open door. It was risky work. The statutes against sorcery were merciless and by no means forgotten: judges who condemned coiners to burning after death could just as easily burn witches alive. Even Arthur Bambridge had drawn a line at taking a percentage from what amounted to black magic, but a gentleman representing the Interest had changed his mind and now Newgate's head keeper looked the other way whenever Mother Jordan came to buy her "Hands of Glory."

But first the executed criminal's right hand had to be chopped from the hanged corpse and wrapped in a piece of used shroud to drain. Then it had to be pickled for a moonphase in peppercorns, saltpetre, rum and balsam. Afterward, the Hand was dried in the heat of the rising sun and turned at every dawn before a final smoking over damp mandrake root and hemlock. At this point, any drops of fat which ran from the wrist had to be blended with virgin bees' wax to make the candle which Mother Jordan stitched between her Hand's fingers and thumb. When properly made and lit, everyone knew that the candle's pale glimmer would keep any householder unconscious in bed while his or her rooms were burgled. Such powerful magic was never cheap and never lacked clients.

One of Mother's men sidled past Cribb, whispering a price for hands which, by tomorrow, would be of no value to anyone but the surgeons. "Ten yellow boys," the footman muttered. "Mark the paper an' tell the 'angman it's the lady to collect. . . ." Cribb nearly gave the man a clout round the ear, remembered who employed him and turned away instead, pocketting a bottle he'd won at primero earlier that day. "Pox yer eyes, soldier! Twelve then!"

Cribb jerked a stiff middle finger behind his back and pushed away to a corner near the chimney, where he'd hidden a few twigs, and got the fire going again. He squatted, almost alone in the death cell now that it was open house in the taproom. There was serious work to be done. But first he tilted the bottle and dropped a dose of overproof rum, filched for the previous owner by friends in the bond stores at Custom House Quay. Its thick, syrupy fire landed on target under his heart and Cribb began to mellow: along with much else, the army had taught him that only grog has the power to keep a cove's chin up, whether storming a gun pit against hopeless odds, or marching onto a scaffold with dry legs.

He was going to need the support of other rituals, too. He poked out the wooden pegs which held his wrist fetters—it had cost him many hours with a wet leather bootlace and fine grit to saw through their iron rivets in the Kings Bench—and slipped both arms from his red greatcoat. The time had come to spit on a piece of rag, dip it in the fire's ash, and polish buttons. Cribb took another disciplined pull from the bottle and began to hum quietly, working on his kit for his last public parade. "O, 'ere comes yankee doodle dandy, yankee doodle's got t'die," he crooned, cutting back the buttons' tarnish and letting their brass shine through as he twisted them from side to side in the lantern light. "Across the field with steady tread or mounted on a pony, up lads! Aim straight! Right in 'is eye!"

His whistle faded: a fresh argument had broken out in the taproom, where a plump draper, condemned to death for retailing cotton goods with forged duty stamps, was being comforted by his benevolent club. The other tradesmen were shouting that, with nearly thirty pounds to his credit on the club books, it ought to be easy for him to buy a plain, decent funeral and *still* host several pounds' worth of fun with friends who had given up their valuable time to visit him in his hour of need. But the draper was being stubborn, he was determined to have nothing less than a full church service with coaches, polished coffin, brass handles and a silver nameplate on his lid. The condemned man jabbed a finger down the club's list of rules. "I know my rights, I do! That's what I paid for, *that's* what I'm goin' to get or I'll have the law on you!"

Cribb went back to his buttons. Varnished coffin or an open ditch on a battlefield, in the end it all came down to the same thing. He tilted the bottle again and squinted round its stubby neck at Bosun's young nypper, also sitting alone by the fire, his grimy little face pinched between knees, staring into the dying embers. "Oy! Pecker up!"

The boy glanced Cribb's way. "Whassat, mister?"

"I said, pecker up. Strewth, you look like you lost a george and found a dud penny." The child's mouth trembled but he said nothing as Cribb finished corking his bottle again and made room in the corner. "Come on, son, squat over 'ere."

The boy crept closer, keeping a wary distance. "Wha'you want?"

"The same as you, I'd bet," Cribb replied with a wink. "To get out fast and to grow old slow. You et today?"

"Nn."

"Well, then! Stands to reason we can't expect you to be more chipper. Come on, work the gnashers round some of this grub." Cribb had felt inside his coat and was tugging out a rag which held cold chops, several boiled potatoes, two sausages and a hunk of cheese. Like the rum, they were profits from games with turnkeys who had never lost their pay to the cardsharps and fur traders of Montreal's Little Barbary.

The nypper's hand swooped, hovered for a moment over the rich spread, then fluttered backward while he searched the older man's dark, beaky face with its thin but not entirely cruel mouth. "Wha' you want me to do for it?"

"*Do* for it? Why, eat up and cheer up, that's what I want! But before you do, I didn't quite get your 'andle. . . ."

The tiny face peered over both palms, now clutching a cold potato. "Darkee."

"Darkee, eh?" Cribb commented with a respectful nod. "That's a good 'andle. Many an upright cove's got started by working as a darkee. Why, I done it myself! I used to slip into flash places just when it was getting dark and tuck away in a cupboard till the swells upstairs was asleep. Then, quick as mouse—I'd jimmy the door lock from inside for my dad and 'is mates to turn the place over. . . ." Cribb smiled dreamily, hefting the rum bottle from hand to hand, basking in the sunny memories of childhood.

There had never been any lack of grog around the Royal Oak tavern where Mum had worked in the kitchen and where young Joe had picked up the ostler's trade as soon as he could pick up a full water bucket. Hard work. Dirty work. Thankless work, slapped awake before dawn to clean out stalls and make the horses ready for gentlemen travellers to cross Hampstead Heath and reach London. Risky work, too. Many a sprig had run into a darkened stable with his lantern, stopped a flying hoof on the head or chest, then been walked out again inside a wheelbarrow.

Young Joe had been hungry for his dad's occasional visits with exciting tales of adventures in far-off Shrewsbury and Norwich, Exeter and Devizes. He'd taken the road himself just as soon as he was old enough to sprint for cover but still young enough to squeeze convincing tears if a housewife nabbed him with a bit of her linen under his arm. That had been the first of several glorious seasons, tramping the secret byways of England to team up with other crews of horse copers and pot menders, bear dancers and jugglers, fortune tellers and wandering actors. It had also been the first of several bitter years, brawling around hidden encampments, slugging it out with fists and bare feet, spitting snot and blood at any *mush* who dared call him a *didikai*—a half-bred gypsy—and being bashed back for his insolence.

Looking back on it now, that had been the best start a cove needed to make a regular go of life, Cribb reasoned fairmindedly, dabbing more charcoal on his buttons. Darkee was watching him closely. Cribb glanced up and winked, then held out one of the shiny brass discs for the young boy to finger. "See that 'seven' in there? That means the Seventh Regiment of Foot, that does. The Royal Fusileers, London's Pride. . . ."

The young lad squinted at the numeral inside its crowned laurel wreath as Cribb returned to his duties. "You been a soldier, mister?"

Cribb nodded, breathing on the next button. Darkee's face was starting to come alive again as he sensed more untold tales of high adventure in the war. "I bet you see lots o' battles an' things."

Cribb spat on his rag to make a fresh paste. "Some."

Darkee's eyes glittered. "So 'ow many Frogs did you stick through the guts?"

Cribb quietly folded the rag. "Too many."

"I'll bet it's fun!"

Cribb studied the rag for a long time. "You just lost."

Darkee pouted. "Er, you *sure* you been a proper soldier?"

"Uh huh."

"Then where was you, then?"

Cribb looked up. "Americky."

"Gor!" Darkee hunched forward. "You been in Americky?! 'Ow long was you there?"

"Seven years," Cribb replied, going back to work. "I couldn't get back 'ome quick enough."

"Go on."

"What's there to go on with?" Cribb shrugged, starting to buff another button. "Once I did get back, and they kicked us off the payroll, all I 'ad to show for it was three quid and a fistful of coppers. Want to know what I done then?" An excited Darkee grinned and nodded. "I blew the bleeding lot on a slap-up feed to prove to my guts that we was still alive and kicking. Then I 'opped across the river to Vaux'all Gardens to see if I could free a pocket or two. . . ." Cribb's polishing slowed to a halt. "There was fireworks that night; I'd not seen as good since we torched a powder dump at Rich Man in Ginya. There was a band, too, playing tunes—free. And there was fountains with pretty little lights, like fireflies in a swamp. But you know what topped it all for me?" Darkee grinned and shook his head. Cribb smiled. "Getting inside the Pavilion same as any gent, even if the cove on the gate didn't like the look of my coat, and paying four bob to stand at the back. Worth every shilling it was, because *she* was there again, up on the stage thing, large as life and twice as loverly, a-singing away fit to burst my 'eart."

" 'Oo was?" Darkee prompted excitedly.

"Why, Mrs. Brandon, o' course!" Cribb was shocked that it wasn't common knowledge which particular actress had been making her London comeback at Vauxhall Gardens, one autumn evening three years ago.

"Gorr! Not ol' Kiss an' Kill Kate?!"

"I mean *Mrs.* Brandon," Cribb corrected with sudden coolness, "and don't you forget it, m'lad."

"Huh!"

"Go huh yerself," Cribb replied. "There's many a good man only breathing today because of what that lady done for us, Over There, when things got bad." Cribb took another pull at the bottle and unsteadily thumped its cork down again. "With my own two eyes I seen growed men, raving mad on the sawbones' cart, go quiet as little lambs when she told 'em to."

"Gor!" Darkee chortled, hugging his knees at this novel twist in the tale. "You seen lots o' coves bein' sawed up?!"

"Uh?"

"I'll bet you seen lots o' coves bein' sawed up in them battles: I 'ope they let me be a soldier!"

Cribb breathed out, slowly. "And I 'ope they don't, because it seems to me you've been fed some bloody queer ideas about what it's like."

Darkee began to pout. "Look 'ere, I 'eard tons o' soldiers say what they done in Americky!"

Cribb wasn't listening. Suddenly he was very old and very tired, tired of remembering things which can never be forgotten. "Son, *I've* 'eard a roomful of tavern grenadiers telling me what it was like Over There, but if you wants my opinion most would've catched round-eye fever and shat their drawers off if they'd so much as 'eard a gun go pop."

He stopped, wondering if anything he could say would ever make sense to the young boy. "You see, it's not always like they say; stepping down the road to fife and drum; smart as new paint for all the pretty girls to run after and kiss." He groped for better words. "It's *different,* but you've got to been there to know 'ow different it is, there's no other bugger can ever tell you. Trouble is, once you find out, you'll wish you didn't. See?"

Darkee had begun to sulk. "Well, I 'eard tons o' real soldiers countin' 'ow many Frogs they stuck, and 'ow good it was, so there."

Cribb's eyes were squeezing shut, fists clenching against the yielding rip! of blue and white tunics as he lunged again, tugged again, crossed his butt again. And again. And again. The spasm passed.

Cribb tried aiming a gob at the fireplace, and missed. " 'Ave it your own way, but it still seems to me you've got a terrible lot to learn." Darkee was disappointed with what had promised to be such an exciting story. Cribb wiped his face and read the look: he made a sad smile. "And now I suppose you'd like me to tell you 'ow good it really was?"

"Not 'alf!" Darkee's face brightened as he wriggled closer, chin on knees, looking up as Cribb patted pockets for the clay pipe and black shag which had come with his rum and rations. He finished tamping baccy and nodded for fire. "Chuck us a light. Thanks," he added, sucking heat off the twig and getting his thoughts in order.

Cribb whiffed smoke and coughed. "I s'pose it wasn't all bad, not all the time. I mean, 'ow could it be when a cove 'ad good mates, and sometimes there was 'ot beef and suet pudding to share with them? And it felt good when you could see the whole regiment on parade, with every cove from the colonel 'imself down to the littlest drummer boy, all working together. That's a *good* feeling, the sort them dipshits will never know," Cribb added, jerking a thumb toward the crowded taproom.

"What about the battles, mister?" Darkee pleaded.

Cribb grimaced. "All right, but only if it'll make you feel any 'appier." He paused again, still sorting his memories. "Well, I suppose it all begun the first time I was nabbed by them Yankee Doodlers. Bad time that, after we come down from Canada. Anyway, once I could stand on me own two pins again, I legged it with a mate, but 'e got croaked by some Indians and I got nabbed a second time. The Doodlers said they didn't like the look of my face, so they shoved me in Copper 'Ill camp—what you *don't* want to 'ear about—so I bolted again and made it back to the town they calls New Ork. Right?

"Now, there's not many coves ever done what I done, so the general 'imself—*Sir* 'Enry Clinton, no less—the general asks to see me. First 'e gives me five guineas, what they call the escape bounty, and then 'e asks me, very civil-like, what regiment I wanted to rejoin, as a corporal. Well! By then I'd 'ad a bellyful of foot-slogging, so I told 'im the next time I fed smoke to the Doodlers it'd be from an 'orse, like a gent."

Cribb's eyes creased at their corners. "It's not easy gettin' into the cavalry, son; cavalry's not the sort of job any cove can pick up in a couple of months on the parade ground. But me and the general 'ad a chinwag while 'e asked me about dosing 'orses for worms, and trimming 'ooves, all the stuff a *phuri dai* Romany gets learned before 'e can walk. Then Sir 'Enry picks up 'is pen and writes a special order to Major Tarleton—as 'e still was then—saying that maybe 'e might like the look of my face for the Rangers. . . ."

Cribb hung a lazy smoke ring round the death cell's lantern and winked at Darkee. "Now I seen some officers in my time, but Colonel Tarleton— as 'e later become—Colonel Tarleton was always special. There was only one other I seen like 'im, and that was the Rebel bigwig what pushed us off at Saratoga, Bene Dick Arnold. Like 'im, Mr. Tarleton was a prime shitfire. With my own two eyes I seen *three* mounts shot out from under 'im, and still 'e was game to get back in the saddle and finish the job." Cribb paused dramatically. "And *that* was after we'd just covered one 'undred miles, flat strap, to cut off Jacky Reb's retreat at Allemance Creek."

"Gorr!"

Cribb nodded. "Anyway, to cut a long story short, it would've been about June or July the year after we took Charley's town, only now we was up north in Virginya. Shortly after sunup, though I'll swear it was already 'ot enough to grill an egg on a shovel, what do I see but a messenger an' escort from general 'eadquarters, galloping past like the devil on wings was after 'em! A couple o' ticks later and the colonel 'imself was shouting for yours truly: 'Sarn't major! On the double!' "

"Go on, mister!' "

Cribb grinned. "Now, at first sight the Green Dragoons might not 'ave *looked* so flash as some of your more regular 'proper soldiers,' but it's all London to a brick you'd never 'ave seen better fighters as we set off to nab the Rebels' king, Mr. Jefferson, no less. Riding all that day and all that night, we got through the Doodlers' lines till we was hid in some trees, just a river away from the town they call 'Arlotville. So there we was, just about to slip across and circle round Mr. Jefferson's palace when, suddenly, some Royal Welch shitwits we 'ad along as mounted infantry, took off to attack by the front! Oh, the cat was out of the bag now, make no mistake! So over we galloped after 'em, straight up the main street, barkers banging left an' right, sabres splitting 'eads like turnips, catching the Rebs with their drawers down!"

"Go on, mister!"

Cribb finished reloading his pipe and nodded for another smouldering twig before the hearth went cold. "There's not much to go on with, son. We got to the top of the 'ill and turned over Jefferson's palace all right, but the cunning bastard 'ad up and bolted when 'e seen the Green Devils was paying a visit. Can't say I blame 'im much," Cribb added, cupping his pipe and staring at the dying fire. "Loverly place though, Montècello. It was all so big, and fancy, and things like that inside. But outside? Outside there was the biggest green paddocks you ever did see, with white fences, and blood stallions, and brood mares, and foals, all shiny, and clean, and well fed. . . ." He swallowed hard. "I—I always reckoned I'd like a palace one day." He glanced up sharply as Darkee began to sniffle. "Oy, I only said—"

"I-I-I never seen a real palace!" Darkee bawled, all bravado gone now. "An', an' when they neck me I ain't never goin' to see one!"

"Oh, shit." Cribb flapped his food rag and tossed it for the boy to try and catch. "Wipe your nose."

The farewell parties were starting to peak in the taproom, outside. One of the condemned men was now getting howls of drunken applause as he capered about on the table, bottle in one fist, a woman's frock clutched over his bare knees with the other while he piped in a mock-treble: "Oh, Tom runs from his wife to get rid o' his troubles, taran-taree-tara! He drinks an' he drinks till he sees double, taran-tara-taree! But when he ceases the wine with brandy to mingle, Oh what he'd give to see himself single!"

Cribb's teeth tugged the cork from his own bottle. Darkee sniffed miserably and watched Cribb swill a mouthful of raw spirit before flinging back his head to drown the other singer: "I'm a Romany *rai*! I live 'neath the sky! I've got a tent so I don't pay no rent, that's why I'm a Romany *rai*!" He shoved his bottle for the snivelling nypper to share. "Now the first chorus: *Kakka chavvi, dik akai!* Dad sold a *mush* the *kushtigai*!" Cribb's black eyes glowed as the rum took hold. "Get that chin off the ground, young lad! Smarten yourself up! Show them tavern grenadiers what they'll never be!"

7

DAYLIGHT.

Cribb shuddered, groping for the coat to pull on again, but Darkee was still fast asleep, breath whistling softly, curled under the borrowed scarlet broadcloth. The child whimpered as Cribb snatched collar, furious with himself for volunteering for a night's shallow doze in the freezing darkness. The nypper twitched a hand to keep the coat where it was. Cribb swore, bunched knuckles, took aim. Then, against his better judgment, the collar slowly fell back. "You poor little bleeder. . . ."

The other condemned were also stirring as a pair of turnkeys tramped in. One accidentally kicked a small blue medicine vial across the floor, past Mrs. Kemp's cold yawn. "Get the doin's ready!" the other yelled back to the taproom. He spun again. "Rat stuff?"

The second turnkey was sniffing hard at the vial. "Nah! Poppy juice! We might get 'er back!"

The first keeper dropped to his knees, lifting, dragging, hurrying the suicide to the taproom. Cribb heard her body thud along the table. A jug rattled over a funnel in her mouth, head pulled back, cold salt water sluicing her gullet. Sometimes they revived, sometimes they drowned on the table, sometimes they had already cheated the hangman of his fee.

Cribb heard a weak retch and the turnkey's mumbles of relief, then went back to studying the contents of his own private bottle. He shook it miserably against the window's pale square: splitting down the middle with Darkee had not been such a good deed, after all. Though only small and underweight the nypper had mopped up as much grog as a grown man before collapsing under Cribb's coat. He, by contrast, was still cold sober.

Cribb sighted the bottle, guessing there was barely enough for three small nips spaced over the last hour, or one decent jolt just before they went over the top. He could have bought more on credit from the taproom but, so far, he had kept his garnish strictly from winnings. Even Twitch's five guineas' credit had been repaid in full from primero. Cribb's affairs were in order.

He scowled across the taproom: a Quaker woman was cautiously treading down the slippery steps from the yard, grey skirts rustling, basket over one arm. She stopped to speak a moment with Twitch. The gate hinges squealed and she quietly walked into the death cell, bonnet dipping as she reached into her basket for hot loaves with salt herrings folded inside.

" 'Ere lady! What about '*is* rations?" Cribb demanded, stuffing his own under one arm and pointing at Darkee. "'E's my mate, I'll see 'e gets 'em!"

The Quaker woman never doubted that Cribb would keep his promise as he went back to gnawing his own last meal and she finished her round of the cell by the gateway, kneeling on the straw, silently folding hands in her lap.

Hurrying footsteps, laughter and whistles began echoing up the ventilation chute, stronger and louder as all London turned out to enjoy another Newgate holiday and a line of javelin men escorted a load of plain coffins and firewood across the snowy market place.

They halted round the scaffold, weapons crossed, knocking back the crowd to jeers and slow handclaps while the waggoners dropped off twenty-three coffins before helping the hangman stack his wood under an iron tripod and chain.

The London sheriff and his marshal were riding up from the watch house with a batch of petty felons, three common whores and five lapsed beggars, stripped to the waist for a summary flogging as an appetiser for the day's main attraction.

Only the first few hundred in front of the crowd had any hope of seeing justice done after the law officers dismounted at Newgate wall. However, the rest—backing away along Holborn—were already being entertained by the Punch and Judy tent on St. Sepulchre's steps. Children were squealing with delight as the comic Mr. Punch murdered his baby on the tiny stage. "Away, nasty creature! There you go, over!" the jolly showman squawked through a brass swozzle tube at his rapt audience. "Thy mammy's a trollop! Thy daddy's a rover!" And it was worth every penny of the parents' money to stand tippy-toe and watch Mr. Punch battering Mrs. Judy to death in rhyming couplet: "Who'd be plagued by a wife that could set himself free? With a rope, or a knife, or a cudgel—like me!" Finally outwitting the puppet hangman and seeing him choke in his own toy noose. "I'm out! I've done the trick! Jack Ketch is dead and Punch runs free!"

Hot gingerbread sellers were also doing well on such a wintry day, jostling through the crowd, covered trays on their heads, handbells ringing as they shouted their wares. At least one had baked several dozen little pastry women the night before: "Fresh Mary Kempses! Smokin' 'ot Mary Kempses! Get your Mary Kempses 'ere!"

Meanwhile, at the scaffold, the sheriff was ordering an end to the beggars' punishment. The flogger untied their wrists and the petty rogues huddled under the drop, mopping their wounds, waiting to be set free again. The senior law officer read his pocket watch and squinted up at the tower of St. Sepulchre's as its passing bell tolled, the clapper buffered with rag. "Bit early, aren't they?"

"Sooner started, sooner ended," his marshal replied, more worried by the way that London's principal hangman was still fumbling with twenty-four ropes on two horizontal beams, trying to offset them so that the back row could be seen by the crowd. It should have been a simple enough task, but the public executioner was drunk in public, again.

"Hurry up!"

The hangman probably couldn't hear. He staggered almost to the end of the scaffold, grabbed the upright post with one hand and groped around his hood with the other, trying to get its slit over his eyes, not his ears. His assistant was more steady on his feet. He was soaping most of the knots to let them shut neatly: only one cove had ratted on his debt to the turnkeys and been booked for the surgeons after a slow choke. Soap also let the knots open easily when their work was done. Used rope was a valuable perk in the hangman's profession. Priced at sixpence the inch, it was the most powerful talisman against quinsy and other throat infections.

The crowd was now a lake of faces stretching away beyond Turnagain Lane. At this point in the ceremony it was traditional to boo the execution-ers as rotten vegetables shied up the market place at Newgate's walls and scaffold. The under-hangman ducked a skimming roof tile. His master blundered after him to more guffaws and both hangmen fell in the snow. They limped after the law officers, through the gaol gate. Bambridge paced across the press yard to greet them and solemnly raised his hat. "Ready?"

"Ready."

Newgate's curate was also ready, white surplice flapping over his long coat and tall boots, thumb marking a page in the Book of Common Prayer while he shared a hot rum toddy with some visitors. He sensed the quick-ening pace and downed the rest of his drink, bowed to the ladies and took up his position by the lodge door as the first of the condemned filed past, flinching at the icy wind. Only Mrs. Kemp had needed to be roped to a chair and carried out.

The blacksmith was ready with his anvil and rivet punch. Bosun's fet-ters dropped. He drifted away, blinking uncertainly, then stared around. " 'Ere! What's goin' on?" The smith grunted something under his breath and went on punching rivets, shoving felons to get their ration of watered gin. Cribb tugged his coat closer and straddled the anvil block. His ankle irons fell. Then, before the smith could raise his hammer again, so did the loosened wrist irons.

The visitors began nudging each other and pointing his way. Cribb stared back, hands on hips. Then he turned and strolled along a row of leather mugs on a nearby trestle table: St. Giles' Cup, the first and last free drink anyone ever had in Newgate. He sipped one thoughtfully, grimaced and spat on the snow. "Dog piss."

"Good on you, Phoss!" a hoarse voice bellowed through the general yard's gateway, now packed with the gazing faces of lesser prisoners. "You show them bastards the proper army way!"

Cribb grinned. "That you, Tom Bunce?"

"Blood oath it is!"

The grin wobbled. "What they got *you* slammed for this time?"

"The duffin' sneak!"

"Bene game!" Cribb shouted back. "Sink a dram for me at the Saracen's when you get sprung!"

"That I will! Good luck, mate! See you in 'ell!"

"See you soon!" Cribb was turning away, steadying his hands again, knowing that his voice was also shaking. The delighted visitors were still nudging and smiling his way. He pulled his private bottle from the coat. The cork squeaked as his teeth tugged it out. He spat it away. Darkee stopped walking from the anvil. Cribb ignored the boy's thirsty look. He tilted the bottle. He shut his eyes. He hesitated. He opened his eyes again. "All right son." The nypper's hands wobbled as he sucked the bottle. "Better?"

"Yuss!"

Cribb shook the last few drops into his own mouth, then wiped a finger round the neck and sniffed its mellow fumes. He flicked the empty bottle into a snowdrift and glanced at the boy again. "Cold?"

A shuddering nod.

"That makes two of us. Still, it don't matter for me, but when the ladies and ge'men out there see you shaking, they'll reckon a darkee don't know 'ow to go game." The fusileer's red coat was coming off with effort, leaving Cribb's shirt tail flapping over his breeches as he crouched to the boy's level. "Best put this on."

The masked executioners were starting to tug grey flour bags onto dazed heads, pinioning arms with leather straps. Cribb shifted himself so that the young lad couldn't see and hurried with clumsy fingers to close these buttons for the last time.

"There we are!" He winked, fighting to smile. "I reckon the king 'imself don't 'ave a gamer cove in 'is Guards than what you look now. Just keep your peepers on the colours, stick close to Uncle Joe as we go over the top, and we'll—!"

" 'Urry up! I've not go', got all bleedin' day!"

Cribb straightened in his own time, one arm thrown across Darkee's shoulders. "The name's Cribb. Sergeant major. Two wounds. Seven battle honours. Stand to attention when you look at me."

The hangman was sober enough to make sure this set of straps dragged tight, burying their buckles in Cribb's arm. Then his assistant pulled a flour bag over the condemned head and slammed his knee into the smaller man's groin.

Cribb straightened again, more slowly. "I'll be waiting for *you* in 'ell, too."

"Move along!" the sheriff shouted, checking his watch again. "Right face!"

The gate squealed open. A roar of cheers greeted Mary Kemp as she led the bedraggled procession between two files of city constables. Her head lolled from side to side while they pushed her chair up the ladder and dragged it along the drop. The other twenty-three prisoners were prodded aloft and shoved into place, facing the crowd through open nooses which swayed in the wintry sun.

The chaplain was still chanting from his prayer book. He halted on the scaffold, back to the market place. "Then shall appear the wrath of God in the day of vengeance, which obstinate sinners, through the stubbornness of their hearts, have heaped unto themselves—!"

The sheriff began treading along the rows of trussed shapes, reading death warrants to every man, woman and child while the hangmen followed, pulling down the bags and tightening knots. He halted. "Name?"

"Joseph Cribb."

The law officer riffled through a sheaf of papers in his gloved hands. "Then be it known that His Most Excellent Majesty George the Third, King of England, Ireland and Scotland, Duke of Hanover, is graciously pleased to extend the royal mercy by commuting your sentence of death to one of transportation beyond the seas for the term of your natural life."

Cribb was freezing hot, sweating ice, ears roaring as the scaffold's planks crashed up, sideways.

The under-hangman's boot revived him in time for the nearest constable to drag him past the chaplain and off the drop. "As we brought nothing into this world, it is certain we can carry nothing out! The Lord gave, and the Lord hath taken away; blessed be the name of the Lord—!"

The principal hangman fell down the ladder. The marshal gave his orders. The man wavered upright and tried pushing the bolt's lever. Nothing happened. He pushed harder, lost his balance and pulled. A thunder of yells and catcalls smashed against Newgate's walls as the drop banged open. Dead legs tramped air level with Cribb's face.

The under-hangman had been cheated of a fee. He dragged the flour bag off the reprieved man's head and twisted the leather straps to jerk their buckles open. The marshal gave Cribb a shove toward the main gate. The smith hammered back another set of fetters. The inner gate crashed shut behind him as Cribb pitched forward among the general felons. All around him hands were waving, snatching, trying to slap his back and ruffle his hair to win some of his luck.

A familiar face was punching its way through the laughing crowd of inmates. Tom Bunce gripped Cribb's shoulders to help him stand and to steady the shakes. "Strewth! I reckoned you was gone that time, Phoss!"

"You and me both, mate," Cribb replied, wiping an unsteady hand around his neck. "Didn't I tell you, though? They still ain't made the rope what'll croak me. Ar, piss off!" Cribb smacked another's hand from inside his empty pockets and looked at Bunce again. "Where's a cove to get some peace round 'ere?"

Bunce dipped a wink and turned, jabbing a clear path across the yard. "Shove over! Make room for Mr. Phossy Joe Cribb 'imself!"

The applauding crowd fell back to a respectful distance and Cribb braced himself, waving right and left, blowing kisses at Newgate's Queens of the Three Ins—In debt, In jail, In danger of staying there forever unless gentlemen friends took a fancy and bought their release—whose barred windows overlooked the general yard. A tattered posy dropped in the slush. Cribb scooped it up as he went through the archway below, sniffing its faded lavender with a gallant flourish, and tucked it in a shirt buttonhole.

Bunce escorted him across the general felons' ward, its stone floor roughly divided into territories where gangs of messmates ate morning and evening, their wooden benches doubling for tables or barricades at night. Down in the cellars, felons of the second rank lay ten to a cell, while those of the third degree—now too weak or too old to fight—spent their days on the stairs, battling the rats and each other. There was an unending underground warfare to win a place in the general ward where only the strongest, the best-connected Outside could hope to win a seat near the cooking hearth.

Bunce led Cribb to a heavily defended corner about sixty feet from the fire and introduced him to nine other veterans, also clinked since their discharge from the war, who now formed a small clan of their own among the larger Newgate families. Some he knew by name, others by reputation, and all returned a brother's handgrip for the cove who had just cheated the gallows.

Bunce nodded for Cribb to step into the darkest angle of the corner where their bedding and food reserves were guarded. Cribb slumped on a chaff-bag mattress and tried easing his cold fingers, cursing the impulse which had given the hangman a decent coat to strip off Darkee and sell later today. Bunce loaned him a threadbare blanket and squatted himself. "You et?"

"Only what Loaves and Fishes brought in."

Bunce snapped fingers at one of the nyppers who hung around the yard, waiting for jobs. The boy sauntered up and took the tin pannikin of cold stew which Bunce passed him. A minute or so later he came back from the cooking fire, still holding the pannikin. "They says as if Mr. Cribb wants it warmed free, 'e can stuff it up 'is arse. Today's price is thruppence."

Cribb sucked a tooth. "Nice mates, Tom."

"You ain't seen the start, yet," Bunce replied, digging into his breeches for the three pennies. "I could tell tales about this 'ole what not even you would believe."

"Like?"

Bunce finished giving the nypper a cooking fee and nodded after him as he trotted past the fire's guards. "See the tall one? With a kind o' lump on 'is back?"

"Uh huh."

"That's Black Teague. The last cove 'e stiffed was cooked and mostly finished, right over there."

Cribb blinked, suspecting a ritual leg-pull for newcomers. "You joking?"

"The buggery I am. Things 'appen in this trap what no turnkey wants to know."

"Of course," Cribb agreed. "But *eating* a cove? Shit, we never done that, not even in Copper 'Ill camp!"

"That was Over There, mate, things was different."

"But what about roll call?" Cribb persisted.

"What roll call? There's coves slammed for debt so long ago, they've forgot their own names. There's nobody Outside to buy 'em out, and Inside they can earn garnish, so what's the worry? And when they snuff it, the screws'll sell 'em to the sawbones. I tell you straight, Phoss, you bastards 'ad it easy in the death cell. I'll tell you this, once my number comes up I'll be out that gate like a cannon ball's brother."

"Hm. Meantime we pay for Tiggy's crew to warm their toes?"

"That's what they reckon."

Cribb's eyes swivelled. "You planning a push . . . ?"

"All depends," Bunce murmured back, lips barely ajar.

"On what?"

" 'Aving knuckle to do the job right. . . ." Bunce's whisper trailed away as two of Teague's crew strolled past, warm and well fed, escorting one of their trusties to collect firewood at the main gate.

"We've got iron?" Cribb muttered as the convoy passed.

"Shivs."

Cribb caught a glimpse of the homemade sheathknife up Bunce's shirt-sleeve. "What've Tiggy's lot got?"

"Shivs. And numbers."

Cribb watched the nypper come back through enemy lines with his rations. He borrowed Bunce's spoon and dipped into the lukewarm mess of boiled turnip and mutton. "Thanks." He chewed slowly, watching the trusty and escorts come back with the heavy bundles of branchwood. "They do that often?" he asked between mouthfuls.

"Twice a day. Why?"

"Just curious." Cribb licked his spoon clean and dipped again, letting the warm food go to work on his knotted belly muscles. "Speaking of other things, Tom, being nabbed for the duffing sneak is a bit out of your class, isn't it?"

Bunce studied broken nails. Until marrying and settling down, he had made a steady living by killing for subcontractors like Phossy Cribb. But an opportunity had come along to better himself and go into business on his own account, so he had rented a pitch on the Strand where visitors liked to stroll at night, admiring the shop fronts and London's blazing lights. Many had spot cash in their pockets and most were in the mood to buy something special to take home and brag to the neighbours, an irresistible combination. Cheap lace, ribbons and notions snatched from shop counters or warehouse fires were ideal baits, pinned inside a long coat and urgently flashed as choice goods smuggled across the Channel. As he stood under a streetlamp at the mouth of a black alley, and sniffed an illegal bargain which might run away unless the deal was closed quickly, human nature triumphed again and again in the duffing sneak.

Bunce looked up and shrugged modestly. "Oh, I reckon I done all right."

"Hm. Well, the sneak might work Outside, mate, but I can't see much elbow room for it in 'ere. What's the lurk?"

Bunce clenched his fist. "This. There's no end o' bacon chewers slammed for passin' dud shillings, or standin' bail for a fly cove what's legged it." He paused. "Life's desperate 'ard for a bloke with no big brother. . . ."

"We spunge 'em?"

"Right."

Cribb nodded. Squeezing was the logical trade Inside. He finished the pannikin, licked it spotless and returned the spoon with a grateful burp. "Thanks. Nothing beats a ration of belly timber to bring a cove back to life."

"I reckon you'd know all about *that,* too," Bunce commented, stowing the utensils. He glanced over one shoulder. "You was due to piss yourself in the picture frame, but you didn't. Can't all be luck. I mean, you was due for the 'igh jump this time, make no mistake, so 'ow did you duck it?"

Cribb shrugged. "Always put something aside for a rainy day, that's my motto, Tom. Besides, the devil looks after 'is own."

Bunce looked sceptical. "I'd 'ave thought the old bugger 'ad plans for you to report 'ome today."

"Not yet." Cribb was stretching into a yawn, his body strangely exhausted, his mind unnaturally alert. "Better get some shut-eye. Give us a shake when it's my turn to do sentry."

He struggled and muttered through a doze until sometime after midday, then took the post of an ex-private in the Fifty-seventh Middlesex, gamely hopping along on one pin since the other was shot off defending Brooklyn. Cribb wrapped himself in a blanket and settled down to guard the crew's territory while the rest circulated yards and wards, protecting old clients and poaching new ones. He tried to seem asleep as the afternoon's firewood convoy passed, returning to the warmth and laughter of Teague's territory, but he was still setting up an imaginary ambush when one of the nyppers hurried across to Tom Bunce and pointed his way.

Bunce frowned and walked over. "There's a ge'man waitin' to see you special, Phoss."

"Ge'man?"

"A swell lawyer cove, no less."

"Oh, shit." Cribb hesitated, then returned the blanket.

"Good luck."

Twitch was waiting to unlock the gate and let him into the darkening taproom. "Come for a second go?" he grumbled, jerking a thumb at the empty death cell, its gate wedged open, fresh straw and sawdust laid for the next batch to start assembling from Old Bailey.

Cribb ignored the question. He paced across the almost deserted room and snatched one of the turnkeys' chairs, twisting it round at the interview table and sitting, fettered arms along the back.

Fields stopped picking at a scab of candlewax and looked up from the table, his face impassive as he noted the wilted nosegay on Cribb's shirtfront. "You took your time."

"So did you, this morning. Another two ticks and I'd 'ave been necked!"

Fields wasn't interested. He flicked the wax away and leaned closer. "You will recall that we made a certain bargain. I have kept my part."

"The bloody 'ell you 'ave." It was Cribb's turn to lean across the table. "I said I wanted *out*, remember? So what do I get? A lifetime in the slammer, spunging pennies off country bumpkins what don't know their arse from their elbow! Call that keeping a bargain?"

Fields appeared to consider the question. "No. I do not."

"Well, then—!"

"However," the lawyer went on in the same flat voice, "I would suggest you first get your facts straight, even if you cannot be expected to show a little common gratitude for what has been a very, very difficult case to plead."

"What facts?"

"You might indeed be getting 'out' as you term it."

"Why didn't you say so first!" Cribb's voice shook with the sudden release from tension. "When?"

"It could be a week or two. Perhaps before Christmas."

"That's the ticket!"

"Now. That property of mine which you acquired a few years ago and which you promised to return intact. Whom shall I ask for it?"

"Whoa! There's no 'urry, Nat." Cribb's eyes narrowed. "It'll keep a bit longer. Let's say, till I get clear . . . ?"

Fields' face stayed blank. "I said: whom shall I ask for those articles of mine?"

Cribb smiled. "All in good time, all in good time."

"You wouldn't be thinking of reneging on your promise, by any chance?"

"Break a promise? *Me?*"

"Yes. You."

Cribb's smile spread. "Tch, tch, Mr. Fields, sir, the very idea never entered my 'ead, cross my 'eart and 'ope to die."

"You very nearly did, this morning." Fields' hands were flat on the table and there was a quality of stillness about the man which Cribb had never noticed before. "Now. Whom shall I approach for those articles of mine?"

"Nobody. Not till I get clear."

Fields was, if possible, even more still. "Has it never entered your head to wonder by whom you were being employed to perform certain chores?"

Cribb frowned. "Why, you." Fields remained silent. "All right, who then?"

The lawyer chose his words with care. "There is a small group of private gentlemen in England. Their names could not mean anything to such as yourself. But when they whisper, King George strains to listen. Now. Is it likely that such masters would employ only one item of your class? Or would they have several? Or even many hundreds?"

Cribb shifted uneasily in his seat. "Oh, I suppose they'd need a few, now and again."

"Wrong. They need many hundreds, all the time. And they are everywhere. There is no escape from them, especially where you will be when—or if—you leave the security of this gaol."

"Uh?"

"I speak of the hulks."

"*Uh?!*"

"The hulks."

"You can't do this to me!"

"*I* cannot do anything for you," Fields replied neutrally. "Everything has been decided, elsewhere."

Cribb was crouching, his finger jabbing the other man's chest. "You 'aven't 'eard the last of this! If you think you can shove *me* down the river to one of them, them 'ells afloat, you got another think coming!"

Fields flicked the finger aside. "It's a free country, the choice is yours. Meanwhile, where is my stolen property?"

Cribb's jaw clamped under its crust of stubble and dirt. "So that's the size of it. I tip you my bundle and stay 'ere for the rest of my natural, or I keep my mouth shut and take the 'ulks?"

"Correct. Lucky, aren't you? Your former companions in distress, now of Surgeons' Hall, would have been more grateful if offered such a choice."

"Well, I'm not!" Cribb exploded, making Twitch jump as he hovered nearby. "I'm not staying 'ere, and I'm *not* going down the river! I'm getting out and you're getting me out!"

Fields was standing. He snapped his fingers for Twitch to bring the cloak, the hat, the gloves, the cane.

"Where do you think you're going?!"

"Home."

"Er, what about the stuff?"

"It can wait. I'm sure it is being well looked after."

"Now look 'ere—!"

"Goodbye, Joe."

8

ABOUT TWO HOURS after dawn, the day before Christmas Eve, a platoon of City militia straggled up Eastcheap from their armoury and marched into Newgate behind beating drum and the deputy sheriff's horse. The volunteer soldiers piled muskets in the snow and hurried after their corporal into the taproom while the law officer dismounted and raised his hat to the keeper. "Mornin', Mr. Bambridge. Compliments o' the season."

"And a very good morning to you, Mr. Henty. Thank you."

"Got many this batch?"

"Three dozen, I think. A typically bad lot." The keeper escorted Henty through the general yard's gate and stood to one side with the still unissued buckets of ha'penny bread and skilly, thirty-five rations lighter than yesterday's breakfast of bread and skilly.

Cribb was bandaging split knuckles after the desperate battle which had finally cut Teague's supply route across the army veterans' territory, forcing an uneasy truce and free cooking in exchange for free passage of firewood while both gangs probed each other's defences and called up fresh allies. He stopped as Bunce skidded into the ward, scant yards ahead of the first turnkeys. "Phoss! It's laggin' day!"

Squads of Bambridge's men were storming through the cellars, up the stairs, across the yard, booting felons into line as the keeper read names. "Cribb, Joseph—!"

"Good luck!"

The turnkeys were closing in fast, cudgels ready, grabbing Cribb, dragging him toward the others lagged for transportation. Only when they were separated from the permanent inmates were the breakfast buckets issued and the transportees jabbed away into the press yard. The gates crashed shut.

The smith and his striker had been called in again to check fetters and marry the prisoners in pairs by stapling their right and left ankles together as the two lines inched past their anvil. Fresh blood slicked one broken shoe as Cribb found himself being shackled to a despised bacon chewer, a Suffolk ploughboy with a tangled thatch of straw-coloured hair and the guileless face of a baby: now neither man could dodge a musket volley. And if either jumped in the Thames to escape, both would drown. Cribb ignored his unwelcome neighbour and again cursed the impulse which had given his greatcoat to Darkee. Winter had started to bite London, and if it wasn't snowing then it had just stopped, or was about to start again: no weather to be outside in a flannel shirt, split breeches and odd shoes. Not that many of the others bound for the hulks were in better shape as the smith finished his work.

Although there were no paying visitors to impress, Bambridge felt the occasion should not pass without a few uplifting words to the academy's latest graduates. The frown hardened. "God's mercy is infinite! Indolent and incorrigible rogues you may be, but even now in the eleventh hour you have been granted another chance to redeem yourselves by honest sweat and labour! Even now, by sober industry and due subordination to your betters, you may yet be dragged back from the yawning pit and so make amends to society!"

One of the women mumbled something and wiped a streaming nose on the piece of blanket which wrapped her baby. Cribb was far away in a warm daydream, conning the boots and thick coat off a nearby militiaman. Only the Suffolk boy seemed to be listening to the keeper, his homely face amazed by all the long words. He nodded vigorously several times, finally catching Bambridge's attention. "You be right, master! Honest labour's all us need!"

Bambridge was delighted to see that he had the gift of touching stony hearts. "All Heaven is uplifted to hear you say so, my good man!" he beamed back. "And, pray, what is your name?"

"Ben Thorpe they call me, master," the ploughboy replied, still nodding in agreement. "An' Oi thank you for this 'ere chance to redeem. An' Oi promise to work 'arder for my betters more'n Oi've worked afore. In fact, mister, Oi'm a-goin' to be 'appy a-workin'! 'Appy an' glad, master!"

Bambridge's smile was radiant. He shared his pleasure with the deputy sheriff, now pocketing the removal warrants and getting ready to remount. He even shared some of it with Thorpe as he faced the man again. "See that you keep firm in that resolve, my good fellow! Never forget, Heaven forgives a contrite heart. Er, before you go, just what is your accustomed labour?"

The ploughboy's blue eyes never once wavered in their innocence. "Gravedigger!"

There was a stunned silence, then a gale of laughter and jeers swept around the yard, as much from the militiamen as from their lagged prisoners. Only Newgate's turnkeys missed the joke, closing fast, cudgels swinging at the grinning yokel, catching Cribb too.

The deputy sheriff had more urgent business waiting at Guildhall later that morning. Tight-lipped, he climbed the mounting block and pulled himself across the saddle, raising his whip in reply to the corporal's salute.

"Fi-i-ix bay'nets!" The muskets' long, triangular blades rattled. "Ta-ake position!" Nailed boots shuffled and stamped on the packed snow. "For-ward *march*!"

Newgate's main doors squealed back on their hinges and two files of redcoats crunched into the market place again, pairs of prisoners hopping along between them, turning sharp left in front of the empty gallows. A slim crowd had braved the weather to hoot and whistle but there was never any real threat and the militia had no reason to clear the street. By the time they had tramped across Ludgate Hill and swung right into Playhouse Lane, they were alone except for the normal shoppers and tradesmen, all guarding their pockets, their goods and their doors as King George's Hard Bargains stumbled past.

There was a short stop at the Bridewell where women under sentence of transportation could fill in the years of waiting by picking rags to make lint shoddy. The deputy finished handing over papers, women and babies to a new set of keepers and remounted to lead his remaining twenty or so prisoners across Blackfriars Fields to Dung Wharf.

A cruel wind was blowing off the Thames. The deputy's nose wrinkled and he groped around for a handkerchief: London's night soil was ripening in long mounts before being shovelled aboard lighters for sale to the orchards round Battersea. Dense flocks of gulls fought over the steaming heaps, shrieking away downwind as the drummer boy tapped closer. The deputy twisted in his saddle, glaring at a fight which seemed to have broken out when one of his prisoners, a stocky, blond, peasant type, had tried stealing a vegetable from the frostbound market gardens which stretched along Thamesbank to the lawyers' chambers of King's Bench Walk. He turned away as a pair of redcoats restored order, bashing the man into line with their muskets. Cribb had to cover the back of his head, again, soaking up the blows which missed while he dragged Ben Thorpe along by one leg. "You dozy shitwit!"

"But Oi'm 'ungry!"

"Tell me something new!"

A flurry of sleet hissed across the river, cooling everyone's temper as they slogged the last hundred yards to Dung Wharf, the southern boundary of London's ancient privilege to guard herself and the start of the sovereign's right to station his own armed troops.

A detachment of regular marines was sheltering between two huge urine vats, the textile industry's only source of ammonia and the first step in making cudbear, a scarlet dye boiled from rock moss treated with strong alkali. Government clothing contractors now loyally demanded the British product in preference to the more expensive cochineal imported from Spain, even though British army uniforms tended to fall apart within months. The marines probably did not know and almost certainly did not care where their clothing came from as their corporal jabbed with his rattan cane to get them standing. "Move! Up, up, up! Show them City ge'men what real soldiers look like!"

The two groups of redcoats stared curiously at each other across the dock's slippery planks while the deputy sheriff dismounted. On one side of him, the chubby militiamen, muskets shouldered like broomsticks: on the other, lean, foxy veterans wearing the scars and sores from every campaign of the last twenty years in India, Canada and the Colonies. Their muskets were clenched across chests, black tricorne hats pulled down hard against the arctic wind, pipe-clayed crossbelts and cartridge boxes smudging damp coats. Subjected to iron discipline at sea or ashore, these guards had even less reason than City troops to waste pity on the convicted criminals who huddled between them, eyes dull, coughing whenever the wind creamed spume off the open vats.

London's deputy sheriff handed his papers to the senior marine and remounted, the militiamen faced left and set off at a brisk double march behind their gagging drummer boy. The corporal watched them retreat, then inspected his new charges before clearing throat and spitting. "Yous lot. One cheep, one whisper, one *thought* o' doin' what you shouldn't, an' you gets this." He reached sideways to play with the tip of the nearest bayonet. "Jus' two inches o' cold steel in the brisket an' it's deady bones. Ain't that so, Marine 'Odge?" he added, glancing at the man who gripped the bayonet's musket. The weatherbeaten fox cracked a kind of smile. His corporal shared it and looked back at the lags. "We don't do things by 'alf measures in the Corps o' Marines. Not us. The first one o' you what so much as farts without my permission gets the whole sixteen inches in one side and out the other! What did I say?!" His finger jabbed at one of the older transportees.

The man blinked, trying to cup an ear with a manacled hand. "Er, whuzzat? You said? If I fart, I'll get a sixteen-inch hole?"

The corporal's smile faded. "Marine 'Odge. Kindly demonstrate what we mean for our little comedian."

Marine Hodge advanced with a light, springing step, clubbing his butt smartly from side to side, sprawling the shackled man. He then steadied one boot on a flailing arm, took aim with the bayonet and spiked the hand to a wharf plank. He rested a moment, grunted, tugged the blade free again and returned to his place in the ranks.

"The next one gets it straight through the tripes!" the corporal screamed. "Because you're nothin' but trouble! Because if you live or die don't matter to nobody no more! Because you're no better'n that 'eap o' shit!" He pointed at the high compost heaps, then glanced along his men's faces. "Right, lads, shovel 'em aboard."

Two open barges were waiting at the foot of the steps, manned by sailors on light duties from the Greenwich hospital, tarpaulin jackets and hats wet with melted snow. They sat easy, yarning quietly, sweeps shipped, watching the awkward convicts stumble up the centre thwarts while marine guards crouched in the stern, bayonets levelled.

The leading barge's coxswain parked his quid of baccy under one cheek and put over the helm to catch a falling tide. "Brightly now!" The sweeps dipped together, creaking against their rowlocks as tarpaulin jackets bent and stretched, dropping their craft down King's Reach.

Brash ice and small floes jogged past them between the piers of London Bridge, spreading out again and falling astern as the barges stroked downstream past Custom House Quay, where the Thames was packed spar-to-spar with shipping. Past whalers from the South Seas, their blackened sails furled, their blubber pots and chasers secured on deck; fruit schooners from Portugal and Italy, unloading baskets of Christmas oranges and lemons; tall East Indiamen, their gilded sterns the equal of any on the king's sixty-four-gun ships. Past much smaller craft, too. Brigs, hoys, ketches and lighters; Dutch bilanders, Baltic galliots, Hamburg snows and East Anglian brick wherries.

The marines gripped their weapons, ready to fight off a barrage of ballast stones if they got too close to the gangs of mudlarks and scuffle hunters who preyed on the moored merchantmen; but the coxswain held his course, following the river's curve north past Bermondsey's cow pastures, letting the tide pull him south again between Rotherhithe village and the Isle of Dogs.

Flurries of sleet blanketed the royal palace of Greenwich and the observatory on its hill behind, even if Cribb had cared to look ashore and had known that he was now crossing the meridian between east and west. Something more real was waiting for him just around the next bend in the river, the invisible frontier between the normal world and existence aboard a hulk, and Cribb was frightened. He had once sheltered a cove on the run after bolting from one of the floating prison camps off Woolwich. Even allowing for a dying man's delirium it had been a terrible tale of bashings, buggery and back-breaking slavery.

Cribb gnawed his lip and hunched lower, letting Thorpe catch more of the weather. What he did not yet know was that several hulks had been towed upstream to Blackwall and anchored at the mouth of the River Lea to work on the new dockyard. In winter.

The brief days of peace were fast running out. The highest priority had been given to rebuilding the Royal Navy, and contracts had been let for a new squadron of frigates to be laid down at Blackwall once roads had been cut across open marshland and fitting-out basins dug from mud. The hulks had been moved upstream to moor an additional two thousand workers on Blackwall Marsh, where time and money could be saved by letting winter firm the mud while chain gangs swung their pickaxes below water level.

The Admiralty was pleased with the new spirit of co-operation and expected, if the present quota could be maintained, to lay the first keel next spring. The contractors were more realistic, knowing the risks they ran by relying on convict labour. The prisoners aboard one hulk in Portsmouth harbour had dared to demand a ration of warm food and clothing. The ship's commandant had noted the delegation's complaint and sent ashore for a company of infantry to restore order. In the end only eight mutineers had been shot before the rest returned to cracking rock on an icy breakwater.

The Blackwall contractors were taking no chances with their workers. Military convicts from the army's own punishment hulk, *Savoy,* were being offered pardons if they would enlist in a special guard battalion until the shipyard was finished. Issued with a musket, a bayonet and twenty rounds of cartridge, they were clothed in cast-off blue uniforms from the Royal Artillery to distinguish them from regular infantry, and then ordered to wear white armbands to keep them apart from the gunners.

Every morning, regardless of the weather, they paraded on *Savoy's* upper deck at first light while regulations were read to them. The rules were simple to remember. Any convict who appeared to be running, not walking, was to be shot on sight. Any convict who strayed near the line of sentry boxes and chained dogs which surrounded the dockyard was to be shot without challenge. Any convict who disobeyed any order was to be shot. The guards were also reminded every morning that several of their own number had been executed by firing squad behind the sea wall.

Cribb looked grim as a driving nor'easterly wrapped *Savoy* with snow cloud. The two barges were now swinging inshore, letting the current drift them down a line of three old battleships, warped close to Blackwall bank. Iron gangs of convicts were trudging home up long drawbridges as visibility fell below musket range.

All three hulks were identical in shape and outline, their top decks boxed with planks, their poops roofed to make living quarters for the commandant, his deputies and their standing guard. Three lines of frozen washing jerked from mast stumps which jutted above their rooflines. Open latrine chutes draped long brown icicles over anchor chains from three sets of heads. A windmill apiece churned in the blizzard which now swept off Newham Marsh, cranking the hulks' bilge pumps, spurting grey water over their sides and into the Thames for another cycle through the old warships' spongey timbers.

Cribb tried steadying his courage as the barge shipped oars and drifted past the first hulk's chains. A rotting figurehead of a pop-eyed Greek god in laurel wreath, sword over one shoulder, stared ahead under the jib boom. The little that remained of HMS *Retribution*'s glory was streaked with rust and crumbling away in the weather. The coxswain swung his hook and caught a mooring line, hauling the barge alongside an embarcation stage which rose and fell with the tides. Four marines went over the bows and climbed the companionway, weapons covering the convicts who were now being jabbed off the barge. Fettered ankle to ankle, Cribb and Thorpe learned to swing in step and help each other stagger up the ice-glazed planks. "You been 'ere before?"

"No, Oi—!"

"Not so loud!" Cribb hissed. "I've lived through worse. Act thick, and keep that bloody mouth shut."

They limped on deck. A gun butt knocked them into line on the poop, facing a shut door. Cribb shambled to a halt, silent, shoulders slumped. "You too!" he whispered to Thorpe as the door opened and a midshipman shuffled through, his cheeks fallen over missing teeth, skin blotched, grey with stubble.

The marine corporal ignored the gilt button and white flash on the cocked hat of *Retribution*'s commandant. "Twenty-one. Nine pairs, one trice, none gone over." He tossed an oilskin wallet of papers for the other man to try and catch, then signalled his own troops to clamber down to the barge and return to barracks on *Savoy*, where they guarded the guards.

The hulk's commandant gave a tubercular cough and spat after the redcoats. More than thirty years a candidate for commissioned rank, he had risen steadily from boy, to man, to naval pensioner without finishing the most important part of his lieutenant's examination—winning the good opinion of any five flag officers convened as a naval board.

Once he must have dreamed of flying his pennant aboard a man o' war like *Retribution,* bravely steering her through banks of hot cannon smoke to a knighthood, to Parliament's thanks, to a mansion in the country. In those days he would never have believed that when the call to command finally came, she would be awaiting her turn to be beached and cremated for recoverable ironwork and copper nails. For somewhere an Admiralty clerk had lost his file, a patron had lost political influence, and he had lost the promotion race. True, he had lived to walk the quarterdeck of a battle-ship, but now it was a walk unsteady with drink, a walk that needed two convict trusties—unfettered, lengths of oak battens under their arms—to stiffen his authority while surly bluecoats stood behind spiked barricades, fore and aft.

He cleared throat again and spat, upwind, then wiped his face and stag-gered away to quarters, leaving the trusties to do his duty. The two men swapped smirks behind his back and began strolling along the latest intake of workers, playfully pinching flesh. They halted at Cribb. The tallest of the pair smiled. " 'Ello Joe. We was told you was comin' today." They moved on, still pinching and stroking until they reached an undersized youth, shaking with ague as much as fear and cold. They faced him, one either side, and swung cudgels, smashing him to his knees, to the deck, into silence.

Nobody else moved.

Cribb's chest tightened. Fields had kept his word. The tallest trusty was not even breathing hard as he absentmindedly played with a ripe pimple on his cheek and smiled at the rest of the day's arrivals. "The next cove we don't like gets done over proper an' chucked down the black 'ole to mill with rats as big as cats. Right?"

Nobody moved.

"That's the spirit. I'm your best friend from now on. Any worries, ask me, because I'm the captain o' the upper deck. Your upright man. An' Shorty, 'ere, 'e's your best chum on the lower deck. We're Number One. Say 'ello captains all."

Cribb kept silent while one or two others led a mumbled chorus.

"Louder."

" 'Ello captings all!"

Pimple smiled. "That's the spirit, because we do like you to be 'appy in your work." He looked troubled for a moment. "You *are* 'appy, aren't you?"

"Yes."

"Louder."

"Yes!"

Pimple smiled. "That's the spirit. In a couple o' ticks the smith is goin' to split you up. Then I'm goin' to take some o' you lucky people— 'specially you, Joe—'ome to the upper deck. Shorty'll take the rest to meet their new mates below. Ain't that nice o' us?"

"Yes."

"Louder!"

"Yes!"

Cribb was parched. Nothing in the Kings Bench Prison, or Newgate's death cell, or even Copper Hill prison camp had prepared him for life aboard this floating slave colony with its trusty overlords.

Pimple's genial smile never changed. He eased aside while the smith moved his anvil, punch and hammer down the line, unshackling pairs of ankles. Pimple eased back and started poking selected bellies with his oak stave. Cribb flinched and faced left. The first newcomer stumbled toward an open grating in the deck.

Cribb followed Thorpe and straightened at the bottom of the ladder, almost ripping his scalp as his head bumped the roof of what had once been *Retribution*'s midgundeck. Now it was a black hole choked with the stench of rancid mutton, muddy clothing and human dung. Without moving his face, Cribb scanned left right, right left. Bodies were crammed in hammocks a bare fourteen inches apart, three deep. Eyes, masked with drying yellow mud from the dockyard, stared back as other trusties—fat and sleek as Pimple—stood guard.

Pimple thwacked his new followers into line under a smoky lantern. "Say 'ello, mates."

" 'Ello, mates!"

" 'Appy to meet you."

" 'Appy to meet you!"

Pimple smiled. "Now, before any o' you lot can properly call yourselfs lags, it's strip, garnish, or go Nancy Jane." He turned on the first man in line. "What's it goin' to be, curlylocks?"

The offered guinea was snatched and its former owner kicked toward the slaves.

Cribb's tongue shifted two silver florins between teeth and cheeks, his dividend from the primero bank which Bunce's veterans protected in Newgate.

The second convict stripped off a pair of stockings which Pimple contemptuously valued at half a crown.

Cribb was next. Pimple smiled. " 'Ello Joe. There's a ge'man said as what you'd be joinin' us today. 'E wants us to ask you a few questions, private like. . . ." A moment of sadness clouded his sunny humour.

"Trouble is, 'e didn't say nothin' about payin' your garnish. Still, 'e said as what you was a regular little gamecock, so I'll bet you're not short o' georges for your new mates."

Cribb's lip trembled. Then his shoulders quaked. He knuckled both eyes, fighting manfully not to show the hot tears as they splashed off his chin. "M-mister? W-what's all this Joe stuff? You, you sure you got the right bloke?"

"Very sure. We got Phossy Joe Cribb."

The tears trickled faster. "N-not me, mister! I'm Joshy Cribb, 'is little brother! The one you want is *Joe*, 'Iron Man Cribb,' ask any in the sporting fancy, they'll tell you!" The newcomer was staring hopelessly, blubbering without shame, shaking with fright. "Before Joe got started in the fight game up Newmarket way, 'e used to mill me! Honest!"

Pimple tweaked finger and thumb around Cribb's chin to study the snotty mess. "Phossy Joe Cribb."

"N-no! *Joshy* Cribb! Iron Man's little brother!"

"Joe Cribb."

"N-no! If you don't believe me, get your maulies up! Mill me! See!"

Pimple's smile leached away. The little man was serious, squaring off, bare fists doubled under filthy rags, fetters slowing him as he tried puffing his chest like a regular pug. "Garn! Get 'em up! Mill me!"

Pimple tossed his stave for another grinning trusty to catch. Then he peeled off a brand-new sailors' fearnaught jacket, rolled the thick flannel shirt-sleeves underneath, and spun, spearing a wicked right, crossing with a left, dumping Cribb into a heap against the mainmast.

The little battler swayed upright and aimed a swipe at Pimple, took another stinging right to the shoulder and went down again. Up once more, slowly. A second wild loop, this time connecting and bouncing off Pimple's jaw like a flat stone off water. Another savage left to the brisket in reply and Cribb was out of the fight, rolling over and over and over his agony. "Ah! Ahh! Ahhh!"

Pimple was roaring with laughter as Cribb flopped to a halt on the deck at his feet, and, "Gotcha!" Both iron shoe heels crunched into the upright man's golden archway. Pimple's eyeballs popped, fingers darting mindlessly over his crotch. He was collapsing like a brick wall as Cribb jerked clear, ten pounds of loose wrist chain axing across the falling man's skull, following through, smashing back the nearest trusty's kneecaps, one against all, going game, dying hard.

Pimple's men stamped out the first spark of resistance anyone had ever dared strike against their rule. "Not yet! The Big Cove needs 'im!" someone yelled from the back, punching and kicking to reach the middle before it was too late.

They peeled Cribb off the deck and flung him against the mainmast, arms hammer-locked. "Get that bleedin' light nearer!" the same voice shouted.

Someone else obeyed and held it over the bloody pulp of Cribb's face. A bucket of slops threw it back and a third trusty squinted to pull up an eyelid. "That's the ticket! We don't want to slip your anchor yet, do we?" A fourth trusty was urgently tugging at his sleeve. Squint turned. "Wha's up?"

" 'E done Slim! The littler bleeder's croaked Slim!"

Squint whirled, fists bunching. "You 'eard that?! *You* just croaked our upright!"

" 'Old it!" the first voice commanded again, shoving forward. "Remember the Big Cove's questions!"

"Yeah? Well, *I'm* the kiddy to ask 'em!" Squint sneered. He peeled Cribb's eyelid again to check that he was still conscious and able to hear. "So you croaked Slim. Cheeky. That means we got to croak *you*. But not yet. First we got to show the rest what 'appens to saucy little sods, because we don't want 'em to make the same mistake, do we?" He smiled, like the late Pimple. "First we're goin' to 'ave some fun by feedin' you to yourself."

Cribb jolted. Squint nodded. "That's right, we're goin' to chop off your bollocks an' watch you chew 'em. Then, with the same shiv, we're goin' to make a little 'ole—*'ere!*—an' pull out your tripes like wet sausage. Then we're goin' to knot 'em round your neck to swing you off that." He smiled at the lantern hook, bolted to an overhead deck beam.

"You're goin' to look regular comic up there, dancin' for us in your birthday suit. Not that you'll be seein' the joke o' course. You won't be seein' nothin', because the very first thing I'm feedin' you is *these!*" He ripped at the eyelid again, swooping a sharpened thumbnail as if he were about to scoop an oyster from its shell—

Cribb's stare saw the top of Squint's head implode like a softboiled egg, splashing brains around Ben Thorpe's fetters. The ploughboy was a howling berserk, trampling over Squint, his chain ripping away the man on Cribb's left arm.

"Rat 'unt!" someone yelled, leading the London mob's battle cry, chains, knees, fingers, teeth, rat hunting Pimple's men in the almost total darkness.

The nearest slaves watched their world being destroyed by the men from Newgate. One of the surviving trusties ran straight into a bulkhead, shrieking as he bounced off, his face flapping where a broken bottle had got him. The spell broke. Yellow claws grabbed him, tearing, dragging, struggling over the nearest latrine bucket, shoving his face under while another sobbing trusty was kicked to death, trying to escape up the ladder.

"Cock! Level! Fire!" Muzzle flashes exploded round the hatchway, rolling thunder, lead balls blowing away meat and bone, point-blank.

"Slip the dogs!" A pack of mastiffs hurled themselves down the ladder.

"Bayonet!" The bluecoats charged, stabbing, clubbing anyone who had not hit the deck and surrendered to the dogs. And some who had. The riot died, except for the gurgling sobs of the wounded, the harsh breath of the guards, and the whirring snarl of the mastiffs.

Cribb panted, face just off the deck, watching a lanky shape clambering from *Retribution*'s lazaretto on her orlop deck, a sailor's bag slung over one shoulder. The nearest mastiff bared its fangs and lunged. The silhouette cracked a piece of rag bandage across its slobbering snarl. "*Shlumpfer drek!*" The dog yelped backward, as demoralised by the shock of raw courage as the wolves of Saratoga when they fled Mrs. Brandon's shillelagh.

"Leafy!"

" 'Elp me, 'elp me. . . ."

"*Leafy!*"

"Wait! Am I with ten hands?" the stooping shape yelled back as the hulk's commandant slipped off a ladder rung, waving an unsteady cutlass. "What! What's going on!" Then, as the powder smoke cleared and he saw the carnage, "God's teeth. . . ."

"Shoot the fuckin' lot," one of the bluecoats suggested, using the break to ram a fresh cartridge and prime his firelock.

"S-silence! Let me think!"

A snug sinecure on the Thames was in open rebellion, and yet, regardless, *Retribution*'s quota of prisoners had to be wheeling barrows and hacking mud at first light or else his own head would roll. Ordering a general massacre now would not only irritate Whitehall but draw the fury of civilian contractors who had been offered cash bonuses for finishing this dockyard on time, and either party had the power to kick him over the side into poverty before appointing a stronger commandant who could keep the peace and maintain the pace.

He dug a hand round his sweaty collar, grappling with problems which would have frightened men far younger, more sober, with greater self-confidence. "W-where's my upright!"

One of the grumbling bluecoats began searching from mainmast to bulkhead, untangling arms and legs where the blast of musketry had struck. " 'Ere! I think."

Retribution's commandant winced: Pimple would never help him again. "This is intolerable! Intolerable!" Smouldering panic was beginning to flare out of control. "Who did it! Who did it! Who did it!"

Cribb heard the symptoms of cannon fever in the other man's voice: several of his teen-age officers had caught a dose and fouled their breeches before their first battle in the Colonies. A few more moments of this and the commandant's shabby authority would collapse in a bloodbath as the bluecoats ran amok. But, just as surely, Cribb had glimpsed a way out as he dragged himself off the deck, staggering to attention. "I done it, sir!"

"Uh?"

"Me sir! For the showing of disrespect to an officer!"

The commandant's cutlass wavered at the butcher's yard around him. "*You?* Did that?"

"Yessir!" Cribb fought off another wave of pain to stay on his feet. "I 'ad to, sir! No other way!"

"N-no other way?"

"Yessir. They said as what they was the captains of this ship," Cribb replied, with the whipcrack of real authority in his voice. "Said as what they was Number One and could do what they liked. But I know what's proper and I told 'em so. Told 'em as what only *you* was the captain, and that I'd only take orders from you," Cribb added, taking aim at the elderly man's wobbly confidence. "So they tried striking me for the doing of my duty to you, and King George, God bless and keep 'im safe."

The cutlass dug its point into the deck as the commandant leaned against it to get his bearings. Pimple would never again terrify anyone into submission. His sun had set, but the need to keep strict order on a deck of three hundred animals still remained. A taskmaster would still be needed down here while *Retribution*'s manager drank away his troubles in the poop cabin.

He looked up, eyes bleary, trying to focus them on the shape in front of him. "W-what's your name?"

"Cribb. Sergeant major. Two wounds. Seven battle honours."

"Y-you were in the king's service, then?"

"Yessir. Canada and Americky."

"A-and you did all this?" the elderly midshipman persisted, still not quite believing the evidence heaped around him.

"Yessir. Me and a few mates, that is."

The hulk's commandant tried bracing his shoulders, too, his mind lurching down a new track. "Th-then you know what needs to be done to keep order."

"Yessir." Cribb made an awkward salute with his chained wrists. "And these . . . ?"

"C-cut them off."

Cribb sagged against the mast as bluecoats and dogs continued their advance, kicking prisoners back into the hammocks. Ben Thorpe was wriggling from under one of the dead trusties. Cribb reached down and gave him an arm to climb. Then he frowned. "Why did you stoush that sod? 'E was none of your business."

Thorpe looked confused. "Oi don't know! Just, sometimes, it 'appens." Like once it happened when other Saxon peasants stormed Bemis Heights with their bare fists.

Cribb understood. His grip eased. "Most coves call me Phossy. Only special mates know it's Joe. What's yours?"

Thorpe grinned unsteadily. "Ur, Ben. Oi'm Ben."

"Good on you, mate, you've got regular style. Now, rattle off and get that smith. We'd better slip the darbies before boozer changes 'is mind." He spun as someone else tugged at his shirt tail. "And what's your trouble, sunshine?"

"The 'andle's Dipper!" One of the former trusties was also gripping the lanky man's wrist. "I brung Leafy to look after you!"

"Uh?"

"Dipper! I dips pockets! An' don't forget it was me what got Leafy!" The little helper let go and stood by to run more errands while the stooping shape cursed them both in a tongue neither could follow.

Cribb scowled back at the angry face with its heavy eyelids, hooked nose, flaming red hair. "Leafy? Not Leafy Levi, that Yid what——?"

"Shut your mouth," Levi commanded, shoving Cribb's chest backward, nearer the lantern light.

"Leafy's safe, really!" Dipper promised, eagerly peering over one shoulder as *Retribution*'s self-appointed wardman, apothecary and surgeon went to work on the new upright's battered face. Cribb squirmed, forced to sit still as a blunt needle and cotton puckered the open wounds, trusting himself to a murdering Jew's hands, want it or not.

London had nearly enjoyed a repeat of the Gordon riots when Abraham Levi, a quack doctor and herb seller of Cripplegate, had answered a charge of poisoning Bessie Jarvis, a servant girl with a titled family in Grosvenor Street. His rambling defence at Old Bailey, reported verbatim in the press—complete with comic pronunciation and outlandish words—had claimed that young Bessie had come to his Magnetic Consultorium late one evening to rid herself of a stomach growth.

Innocently, or so he had alleged, Levi had then sold her an envelope of his special "leaf tea" and explained its use. But the girl had been impatient for results. She had douched the entire hot infusion at one draught, aborted in front of her mistress, and bled to death on the carpet—but not before moaning Levi's name. Evidence had then been given by the Public Office, Bow Street, that many other girls and women sought this foreign quack's help, and that his reputation extended far beyond the mere servant class. This last remark was struck from the record and the Jew was sentenced to hang for murder.

The trial and execution of Lazarus Zellick, or Blind Fagin, had recently taken place, and the London mob was up and waiting to do its patriotic

duty as Levi stepped from the court. At one point the mob almost suc-
ceeded outside St. Sepulchre's, but the javelin men and city marshal had
fought back to back round their prisoner until a militia company advanced
along Eastcheap, firing volleys as they came.

Levi had escaped to the safety of Newgate's death cell. The mob,
cheated and disappointed, drained away into Houndsditch, where Manas-
seh Ben Israel had endowed London's first synagogue of recent times, to
loot the shops and ragpicking yards where more refugees from Germany
and Poland had settled since the wars of '68.

Cribb won himself a box of hats during the second riot, the one after
Levi was reprieved to transportation for life. The *Gentlemen's Magazine* of
that week had hinted darkly at disloyal rumours of a highly placed interest
in the Levi case, and then proved to its readers that such malicious gossip
was impossible:

> For Jews are of the very lowest order of cheating coves. They are to be
> found lurking in every street, lane and alley, pretending to buy old clothes,
> glass, rabbit skins and metal, but their real object is to corrupt servants to
> pilfer from their masters. Rarely paying the thief more than one-third its
> true value, they circulate base money by every possible trick and fraud. By
> denying the divinity of Christ, such depraved rufflers never scruple to utter
> false oaths in courts of law (unlike true born Englishmen), hence the ex-
> pression "Cheap as Jews' Bail."

Cribb flinched as this notorious villain stopped working on his face and
blew powdered chalk into the raw wounds. "Will live," Levi commented,
shouldering his bag and stooping away to find others with greater need of
his skills as the smith knelt to free the latest man to rise to power below
decks.

Flexing his fingers and rubbing his wrists, Cribb limped over to Pimple.
He kicked away two other looters and helped himself to the boots, the
breeches, the flannel shirt and the fearnaught jacket.

9

"WEATHER GLASS risin', sir," Arthur Phillip's manservant announced,
shutting the door. "Looks like it'll be a nice day for a change," he added,
setting down the can of hot water, the towel, razor and soap before crossing to open the inn's pair of shutters.

"Thank you, Bryant." Phillip snuffed the candle on his desk. He capped
inkwell and started gathering together sheets of paper, folded several and

licked a sealing wafer to close the bulky packet before dropping it into an Admiralty despatch box. He paused, listening to hooves below his window where ostlers were slapping fresh horses across the Bower Anchor's stable-yard, backing them into the *London Mail*'s traces, then turned both keys and handed the box to Bryant. "Please see the guard gets this personally."

"Aye aye, sir."

"And ask the kitchenmaid if my uniform is yet dry: I shall need it imme-diately after breakfast."

"Aye, sir. Speakin' of which, an' beggin' pardon, they want to know what you'd like, the fish or the 'am?"

Phillip tugged an earlobe. "The fish. And a brace of eggs, hardboiled."

"With bread an' flip?"

"Please."

His servant touched fore and middle fingers to brow, turned and clat-tered away downstairs while Phillip walked over to the can of water. He wedged a pocket mirror in the window frame above it and glanced outside. Bryant was not exaggerating, the weather glass must be moving up at last: for the first time in nearly a fortnight he could now see the green hills of Wight, sharp and bold across Spithead's crowded anchorage. Phillip craned his neck further round the window, cocking an eye to windward: but the fine weather wouldn't hold for long, the year was still too young for more than a few hours of wintry sunshine between squalls and advanc-ing westerlies.

Humming quietly, Phillip began stropping razor on palm while studying the face in his mirror, turning first one profile, then the other, as if it were still being sat for its portrait. All things considered, that artist had made several tactful improvements on nature's handiwork, Phillip thought to himself, but the plain truth was that no amount of oil colour and smooth brushing would ever rebuild him another twelve inches in his shoes, or refit him as a bluff, ruddy-faced John Bull Englishman. Phillip grimaced and began working a lather in his shaving mug.

Yet, to be fair, there had been a time in life when such heavy noses and dark complexions had been the rule, had indeed been fashionable—among the *fidalgo* officers of Portugal's navy where a talent for languages had earned the English lieutenant a captain's commission and warm testimoni-als from Lisbon. Reassured, he went on scraping whiskers, wiping the blade clean with a square of newspaper as his servant crossed behind, bal-ancing the breakfast tray, a dry uniform over the other arm. "Oh, Bryant?" he asked the reflection.

"Sir?"

"My compliments to Mr. King. I shall be going out to *Alexander* on the cutter and won't be back till much later."

"Aye aye, sir."

"I also expect a Mr. Bligh and a Mr. Vancouver to share my table this evening. If they should happen to arrive before I return, please see they lack for nothing."

"Sir."

Phillip turned, dabbing the nick on his chin while looking across Spithead again. The first of his convict transports had, at long last, beaten down Channel from Deptford and dropped anchor on the Motherbank. By squinting hard against the water's dazzle, Phillip could just make *Alexander*'s three-masted rig among the thicket of spars and timber which dotted the Solent. There should have been five more transports assembled around her by now, but slapdash administration in London and contrary winds up the Channel had scattered them from North Foreland to Plymouth and put the Botany Bay expedition far behind schedule. That morning's despatch to the Admiralty included the latest of several tightly controlled requests for news of his three supply ships—*Borrowdale, Fishburn* and *Golden Grove*—wherever they were.

Phillip snapped his razor shut, turned away from the window and began pulling on white breeches before modestly dropping the long dressing robe. Bryant had finished brushing the nap on his master's blue serge cutaway and was now using teeth to snip a loose cotton left by the sewing woman who had recently tacked a wide double row of commodore's gold lace around its high collar. He made a dry spit from the corner of his mouth and shook the coat open, holding it wide as Phillip finished buttoning a long grey underjacket and turned again, pushing both arms down the sleeves. "And make certain mine host downstairs remembers this evening's dinner: I don't want another of his impromptu cold picnics."

"Aye aye, sir."

Phillip nodded a dismissal and began his usual quick, lonely breakfast, perched by the window with plate and fork on his knee while enjoying again the first real evidence that he was now a governor and captain general—*Alexander*'s distant outline. The half pint of flip—with its odors of warmed ale, honey, nutmeg and brandy—also lifted his spirits. A stiff breeze was blowing; it would be a wet haul to the transport.

He trod downstairs a few minutes later, cocked hat under one arm, clipping his boat cloak with a brass chain as he stepped from the Bower Anchor's front door and set a brisk pace along High Street, following a drayload of kegs and cordage from a nearby contractor's yard. He brushed past the permanent crowd of half-pay officers loitering outside the port admiral's office, opposite the Fountain where he had also stayed when only a lieutenant on two shillings a day, before shaping a course for the shanties and brothels of Portsmouth Point where *Alexander*'s victualling cutter was stowed and waiting at the sea stairs.

A squad of marines was clambering aboard, piling knapsacks, blanket rolls and weapons among the barrels of pork and flour. A young officer had been detailed to oversee his men's embarcation. He turned and saluted as Phillip approached through the crowd. "Major Ross' compliments, sir. He begs leave to wait upon you at the earliest convenience."

Phillip hesitated only a fraction, then smiled distantly. "My compliments to Mr. Ross. I shall, of course, be happy to receive him at the earliest possible moment. Shall we say, nine tomorrow morning?"

"Sir?"

"Please inform him that I shall be fully engaged for today and cannot say what I'll be doing after returning from inspection."

"Sir."

"Thank you, Mr. Tench." Phillip politely touched hatbrim to the young man, gathered his cloak together at the skirt and stepped aboard the cutter as its coxswain snapped fingers to brow. "Whenever you're ready, Evans."

"Aye aye, sir!"

The mooring lines splashed and the cutter's jib shook, tightening its gaff, helm over, bows slicing through grey chop between Haslar Naval Hospital and Portsmouth Castle. Phillip settled into the stern sheets and pulled his cloak tighter, watching the ten redcoats hunch amidships against the same drenching spray. He knew them well, if not by name then by their reputation.

These men, and those before them, had been every seagoing commander's sure bulwark against mutiny since the time of Charles II, standing sentry on officers' quarters, ships' waterbutts, the spirit lockers and powder magazines, without fear, without favour. Fanatically loyal to a regiment which most openly called the family, marine marksmen, grenade throwers and boarding parties had fought in every naval engagement of the past century. But Phillip also knew the risk he ran by relying on two hundred of these same men to sail with him halfway round the world to secure a deserted beach last seen half a lifetime ago. Only the most optimistic of them could imagine there would be fresh laurels to be won at Botany Bay, or even a penny in prize money to be earned guarding England's human refuse against Indian spears from the surrounding forest. Indeed, their only reasonable hope of glory would come if Admiral, Count de La Pérouse, had already built a Fort St. Louis at Botany Bay and diplomacy failed to dislodge him.

Phillip scowled at that likely prospect and looked at the marines amidships, taciturn beneath their black tricornes: whatever the outcome, they would do their duty and die hard, obeying the tasks their officers had set the sergeants to execute. But whether those officers would obey their naval governor's requests was, he already suspected, a rather less certain matter.

Irritated, he peered over one shoulder at the receding shoreline as his cutter luffed, beating to windward from a three-decker, HMS *Intrepid,* one of the new construction, then shielded eyes as her gilded figurehead drew abeam. Dense flocks of gulls were perching among her nine miles of cable, rope, line and cord, the intricately precise maze of rigging and spars which could drive her sixty thousand square feet of canvas from pole to tropics, night and day, month after month. She was the most powerful weapon ever built, designed to carry Britain's orders across the world. One word of command from her quarterdeck could run out batteries of ninety cannon, opening broadside after broadside from the forty tons of powder in her magazines, and all the soldiers of Europe could stand to arms and watch, helpless, as she went past under a cloud of sails.

Phillip looked over *Intrepid*'s proud lines: *this* was his navy. The smile altered. Other gulls were squealing for scraps round the warship's blood-red gunlids, swung open along bulging black timbers where trots of bum-boats hung on the tide, their traders jiggling ribbons and fancies for the several hundred girls already aboard, either brought by the same boats or permanently quartered in the orlop as the ship's supercargoes and swab-bers. And yet, as Phillip also knew from personal experience, her captain would sleep well tonight, knowing that no pressed man would bribe his way ashore while marine sentries paced the decks.

His hand dropped. *Alexander* was closing over the last few hundred yards. Only the gulls and the sentries were the same. Any bumboat within musket range of this transport took an ounce ball across the bows, as the first two had already found out. The naval coxswain also sensed a differ-ence in standing between king's and merchant service, setting his jib aback as he came alongside in spanking style. Phillip's nose also twitched, puz-zled by a smell that was neither tar, nor salt, nor even the green weed which grew like a garden on *Alexander*'s timbers, swaying under the suck and smack of running waves.

"Er, ready, sir?"

"Oh, thank you, Evans." Phillip gathered cloak under one arm, stead-ied himself a moment, then scrambled up the barque's flaky yellow sides. He straightened at the head of the ladder while the marine corporal stamped boots and brought his guard to attention. Phillip touched hatbrim and glanced round for a ship's officer to receive him among the knot of lounging merchant seamen. "Corporal?"

"Sir!"

"Has the master been informed that I would soon be coming aboard?"

"Yessir!"

"Then where the devil is he?"

"Gettin' dressed, sir!"

"Oh." Phillip looked up at the sun's altitude, read the hour, then wrinkled nose again. The smell was more noticeable now and too strong to be just from the hen coop or even the flock of goats tethered to *Alexander*'s mainmast. "Corporal?"

"Sir?"

"That stink."

"Stink, sir?"

"Yes, stink. What is it and where does it come from?"

The marine looked baffled. "It must be them, down there. Gets a bit 'igh at times, sir."

"High?" Phillip queried. "Good God, man! It reeks more like an open cesspit than a ship on His Majesty's service!"

"Yes, sir." The corporal fell silent, then cleared throat. "Beggin' pardon, sir, we only guards 'em. It's the other lot what does the rest. . . ."

Phillip said nothing as a scuttle fell open and someone clambered on deck, blinking around at the daylight, still fumbling with his wig. A bull-necked man, bandy-legged and dressed in a striped flannel jacket of antique cut; seaman's galligaskins or petticoat breeches waterproofed with tar; grey worsted stockings and large, tarnished silver buckles which hid three-quarters of his shoes. He also wore a hanger and pistols strapped round his belly and, to make sure, carried a cudgel under one arm.

Both men advanced to meet at the spiked wooden barricade which guarded *Alexander*'s poop and wheel from the open waist. Phillip touched hat again. "Captain Sinclair?"

"Aye?" the civilian master replied in broad Lowland Scots, blinking down at his visitor. "Ye must be—Commander Phillips?"

"Phillip. No 's.' Commodore. Royal Navy." A pause. "Now, shall we repair to your quarters? I wish to become acquainted with the manifest."

"Oh, aye, 'course, o' course." Sinclair made vague gestures at the open scuttle. "Ye must excuse the present state o' things, we had a very busy time last night. There's still a lot o' work to be done."

Phillip ducked his head and climbed down to *Alexander*'s great cabin, squeezing past a small chart table to put the stern windows and their light behind him.

"The manifest, ye said?" Sinclair asked, starting to rummage over his cot.

"Yes. Please."

"It must be up here, somewhere. I stowed it last night. Och shiiiit!" He stumbled. "Then p'raps it's down here, eh?" After a time he straightened and dropped a black metal box on the table. Phillip tried to be helpful, pushing a parade of empties to one side, hoping to make some room, but one fell, toppling the others like ninepins. "Mind out, ye clumsy—!" Sinclair trapped his tongue just in time, caught one of the rolling bottles instead and shied it straight past his guest. Fortunately that particular window was open. Phillip sat motionless as the other dozen plopped astern and slowly jingled away on a falling tide. "Er, the manifest, ye say?"

"Yes."

Sinclair found the right key among many by stuffing them all in the lock, one after the other, till one turned and he could shove back the lid. "The manifest?"

"Yes, Mr. Sinclair, the manifest!"

Packets of owner's instructions hit the table with bank drafts for Canton traders of the *Ko-Hong*, some Admiralty paperwork, several old dockets and miscellaneous provedores' receipts. "The manifest."

Phillip took the clip of papers and quickly ran his finger down the columns of copperplate names. It seemed that *Alexander* had embarked two hundred and eleven sound male convicts at Blackwall, ex HMS *Retribution*, per account Messrs. Duncan Campbell & Partners, or roughly one passenger for every six inches of her registered length of one hundred and fourteen feet. Phillip's finger stopped, then went back to the top of the first page. The men's term of transportation—seven years, fourteen, life—had been penned beside their names, with occupations and place of trial. The finger moved again, more and more slowly as he read down the column. "Fellmonger? Vinegar casker? Ostler? Wig maker? Sturdy beggar? Catgut spinner? Herb seller . . . ?" Phillip's voice shook as he glanced up and found Sinclair's wandering eye. "Are these facts true?"

"I s'pose so," *Alexander*'s master was not too concerned, twisting head to peer over Phillip's shoulder.

"And do I really have three coal heavers, a ragpicker and two snuff grinders aboard your ship?"

"Why?"

"Why, Mr. Sinclair?" Phillip's voice began to rise. "I shall tell you why, Mr. Sinclair. Because it is the intention of His Majesty's government to establish a new base in the South Seas, Mr. Sinclair! A base able to support itself by its own exertions and not become a charge upon the public purse! To which end express orders have been given to send out only those prisoners who are experienced husbandmen and farm labourers!"

Sinclair wiped sandy eyebrows and shook his head with amusement. "Oh, Commodore Phillips, sir, I wonder who's been feeding ye that blether?"

"The Admiralty."

"Very well, yon admirals ought've been at Blackwall when I started kicking this lot aboard. D'ye think for one moment that any contractor in his right mind would part wi' useable 'husbandmen and labourers'? Well, *do* ye?"

Phillip won the struggle and beat his temper into submission. "How do you mean?"

Sinclair grinned. "I mean that it stands to reason, that's what I mean. When yon *Retribution* was told to supply lags for overseas, they made bluidy sure each one was either a troublemaker or could dig no more—"

"Say again?"

"All right, commodore, sir, I will say again. *Retribution* swept out their hard cases and those too knackered to work any more on the dockyard. And if ye think this lot's rough, just wait till ye clap eyes on the surprise packet Captain Sever shipped from Woolwich aboard *Lady Penrhyn!*"

Phillip drummed fingers on the table. "So, there are no labourers? And no husbandmen for agriculture? Just ostlers, sturdy beggars and cinder sifters? Is that it?"

Sinclair shrugged, puzzled by the little man's attitude. "Come, come sir, let's be frank wi' each other, who would expect anything else to happen? Don't tell me *you* haven't worked it in yon other navy when someone's asked for volunteer replacements off your ship?"

Phillip said nothing. He looked back at the manifest. "These red lines. What do they signify?"

Sinclair glanced again. "They're no longer on the strength. Lost to the ship."

"Lost? How?"

Sinclair made a slow diving movement with both hands. "Splash."

"You mean, they escaped?"

"In a manner o' speaking. They're fish dinners."

"But you can't have had eight deaths just between here and the Thames!"

"Who says I can't?" Sinclair replied with dignity. "The only surprise is that I have not launched more, considering the state they were in when first they came aboard! Nasty, and I've seen a thing or two on nigger boats atween Senegal and Kingston Town."

Phillip was beyond rational comment. He shut the manifest and gave it back to Sinclair. "I would be much obliged if you would now show me over your vessel, captain."

Sinclair's eyes narrowed. "Why?"

"Why?" Phillip was increasingly remote. "Because it is normal for a colonial governor to show some passing interest in the condition of his future subjects—"

" 'Condition'?" Sinclair's bushy eyebrows were inching closer together. " 'Condition' is the sort o' word a hasty writer may use in an unconsidered letter to this or that department when making untrue claims about the state o' another's private property. O' course," Sinclair went on, "it would not be polite for a simple mariner to say any more to a commodore o' the Royal Navy, but one hears, in roundabout ways, that our Mr. Campbell has many friends. And they also have friends. And lesser friends have greater friends, and so *ad infinitum*. . . ."

Phillip's face was rigid. "Nor would it be polite for a commodore of His Majesty's navy to draw certain matters to the attention of a simple mariner, Mr. Sinclair, but if it has to be done, rest assured that at least one officer of your acquaintance will never swerve from his duty." The voice stung, hard. "Now. You may accompany me on a tour of the guards' quarters and their adjacent areas. Marines, Mr. Sinclair, are not private property."

"Hn!" The shipmaster kicked open his cabin door and stepped into a narrow companionway where *Alexander*'s other officers slept in two over-sized cupboards. He banged a fist on one lid. "Show a leg there!"

The cupboard door fell open after a tussle inside and the first mate rolled off his shelf to join the ship's rounds. Phillip ducked head and followed both men into a narrow curve of wooden space, thirty feet at its widest and no more than eight from the back to front where a solid wall of oak, pierced with loopholes, had been built at Deptford. The ten marines were changing places with the outgoing men, chatting and joking as they slung hammocks among the stowed casks and bales. Their corporal saw Phillip's gold braid behind Sinclair's back and slapped gaitered legs together. "Stan' fast the guard!"

"Carry on," Phillip replied. "Everything in order?"

"Yessir!"

Phillip's nose was wrinkling again. "The ventilation, Mr. Sinclair. Who normally attends to it?"

Alexander's master looked at his mate in mock surprise. "The ventilation, Mr. Olsen. Who normally attends to it?"

"Yoh? Er, vatch officer!"

Phillip coughed. "That wouldn't happen to be you by any chance?"

"Er? Yoh! Is me!"

"Then concerning the ventilation, Mr. Olsen, ought not something to be done about this stench?"

"Stinch?"

"Yes, stench! The disgusting, foul, repulsive stench which I can detect all around me at this very moment, in a space occupied by government property, to whit, ten soldiers of the Maritime Regiment of Foot! Kindly investigate it!"

Sinclair made a sigh of exaggerated patience as his mate patted pockets and found a teaspoon. Olsen made a thorough job of burnishing its silver with his shirt then held the spoon upright at eye level for several moments. He smiled with relief and looked back at the naval visitor. "No tarnishings!"

"Kindly bring it over here." Phillip was standing by one of the loopholes. He held breath and blinked through it again, eyes watering, more accustomed now to the near-darkness. Shapes were creeping about on the other side, chains lagged with strips of canvas or bagging. He pulled away and pointed as Olsen stood close. "Place the indicator there." They waited for exactly a minute by Phillip's pocket watch as a dull draught blew through the loophole, past the spoon and into the marines' quarters. The watch lid snapped shut. "Now let us see."

Olsen shifted feet and twisted the spoon around in a narrow chink of sunlight from above. "It seeming a bit misty, perhaps?"

Phillip turned. "Mr. Sinclair. Would you also agree that your mate's indicator seems a bit misty?"

"It would all depend on how ye care to define the word 'misty,'" *Alexander*'s captain grunted. "Speaking for m'self, I've seen silver tarnish a lot worse on the Gambia River and it never hurt anyone—"

"I am not speaking of 'anyone,' Mr. Sinclair. *I* am speaking about Crown property, viz, ten of His Majesty's marines. Kindly have those holes shut tight, forthwith."

Sinclair's already high colour flushed to the roots of his wig. "That's not possible!"

"Why?"

"Dammit all to hell! Yon' holes are there for your precious bloody backs to fire through when the niggers get saucy! I'll not have them shut, that's final!"

"In which case make the necessary adjustments elsewhere in your command." Phillip looked through the loophole again. "When next I have the pleasure of inspecting these quarters I shall find a marked improvement in their ventilation. Limewash, oil of tar and sulphur will be an excellent start." He looked away. "I shall inform the fleet quartermaster of your ship's needs when I go ashore. They will be ready for purchase within a few days." The marine corporal wiped a sly grin off his face as Phillip glanced across at him, too. "And see that your men employ them in here."

10

THE WIND HAD backed westerly and strengthened by the time Phillip was ready to go ashore again. *Alexander* was pitching heavily at her cables as he jumped the last four or five feet into the cutter where the outgoing guard was huddled for'ard, empty ration barrels stowed around them for a weather shield. The cutter's jib snapped taut as the coxswain put up helm and began tacking into grey curtains of rain. Phillip was soaked to the ribs long before they beat past Haslar and ran alongside the sea stairs. He jumped again, managed to keep his footing on the greasy weed and trudged up to the quay, where he stood, wiping bitter salt spray from mouth and nose, before turning his back on the Bower Anchor and walking through the rain to the fleet quartermaster's office.

Much earlier, as the downpour began sluicing across Portsmouth's rooftops, Bryant had wheedled a bucket of coals and some dry sticks from the inn's kitchenmaid. He chipped flint and steel when Phillip at last plodded upstairs, and blew the tinder to heat while his master dropped cloak, tunic, jacket and undershirt in a sodden heap on the floor. Phillip took the offered towel and wearily rubbed chest and arms before kicking off his shoes and peeling away the wet breeches, too. Bryant had flapped the dressing robe in front of the smoky fire and was now holding it open for his master. "L'tenant King's compliments, sir. The *Mail* come early, for once. He's taken the liberty o' opening some routine packets an' put the rest on your desk."

"Uh huh," Phillip replied, bending to massage fingertips over the sticks' feeble warmth as they began to crackle. "Is this evening's meal attended to?"

"Ready aye ready, sir."

"Very well, inform me when either Mr. Bligh or Mr. Vancouver arrives."

"Aye, sir." Bryant gathered together the pieces of wet uniform as Phillip stood again with a twist of burning paper and walked across to his desk to touch the candle. "Er, beggin' pardon, sir, what will you be needin' to wear for dinner?"

Phillip shrugged. "Anything. Anything at all so long as it is dry, it is warm, and it is not navy blue in colour."

"Sir?"

"My street clothes."

"Aye aye, sir."

Phillip went back to fitting keys in the despatch box as Bryant left for the kitchens. Hardly a day passed without some fresh order from the Admiralty and Home Office. The same afternoon coach could bring down letters urging even greater prudence and economy, while others in the same box demanded to know why convict labourers were not already building fine avenues and palaces in New Holland, and all too often they had been written in the same department of state, on the same day, by the same clerks. Phillip counted himself very fortunate that his former executive officer aboard the sixty-four–gun *Europa,* Gidley King, had again volunteered to work with him. As such he had permission to winnow the routine and the tedious, leaving his chief to find answers for the more puzzling, or delicate, or diplomatic, such as today's lengthy demand from the Royal Society.

Phillip reached for his wire-framed spectacles and brought the candle closer. It seemed that Sir Joseph Banks now wanted him to devote his time ashore in New Holland to the collection of unusual plants. Two reams of absorbent paper, some flat boards and leather straps were being sent down from London by special messenger, together with a detailed set of instructions on how to press flowers. The Royal Society also needed more skins of a very large jumping rat, called by the Indians "canguru," which, Sir Joseph assured Phillip, was very easy to salt and dry. These pelts should be rolled and sewn in canvas, then despatched to Sir Joseph's private address in Soho Square by the earliest available ship. He also wanted artifacts traded from the natives and detailed accounts of their habits, customs and religion. Finally, his collection needed a feathered chieftain's cloak, similar to the ones found in New Zealand, failing which the skin and plumage of a large, flightless bird called "imu" should be sent to the same address, post-haste.

Phillip flicked away the Royal Society's revised shopping list and ran his thumbnail under the seal of the Admiralty's latest despatch. It was blunt to the point of offence: nobody in London knew anything about the current state of his chartered transports. They knew nothing about the expedition's flagship, HMS *Sirius*. Nor would they consider replacing the totally inadequate—as only Phillip thought—170-ton sloop HMS *Supply* with a more roomy despatch boat. Finally, the Lords Commissioner of the Admiralty had disallowed his urgent requests for an extra issue of rum for the marines while guarding convicts, pointing out that it would cost an extra three pounds seven shillings and sixpence a week, and Treasury could not issue a cash voucher unless the Naval Board of Lunacy, Sick & Hurt first countersigned that spirits were needed for specific medicinal purposes.

Phillip swore quietly and let the matter drop for a moment as he began studying a petition from the parish clerk of Whitby, Yorkshire, begging for the speedy return to civilian life of an Able Seaman William Benthall, believed to be serving aboard HMS *Sirius.* Pressed into the Royal Navy while unloading a collier at London Pool, Benthall had left a wife and seven children for the parish to feed. Her husband's prompt release was humbly begged to save his neighbours this extra burden on the local poor rate. Failing which, could AB Benthall's fourpence a day be sent to the undersigned without delay? Whitby's clerk looked forward with humble confidence to an early and favourable reply to this humble petition, while promising ever to remain Phillip's sincerely humble and obedient servant, Jas. Ackroyd.

Phillip watched Mr. Ackroyd's humble ball of paper flare on the fire's coals; then began reading the state of his own finances with Drummonds'

Bank, Whitehall: he was now thirty pounds overdrawn on a salary of five hundred pounds per annum since refitting his sea chest at the tailor's and an early settlement was expected.

Bryant pushed his head round the door frame. "Mr. Bligh, sir."

Phillip was grateful for any excuse to fold the remaining papers and lock them away. Bryant brushed and laid out his master's street clothes, a comfortably worn brown coat and buff breeches which made Phillip both look and feel like a gentleman farmer again.

Downstairs, the Bower Anchor's landlord had taken William Bligh's hat and cloak before limping ahead into the front parlour, out of sight if not out of sound of the public bar, and kicking the fire alive with the blackened toe of his wooden leg. He winked at the naval officer. "It's an ill wind what blows no good, sir!" and thumped away again, pocketing sixpence.

Bligh turned, warming knees while examining the landlord's collection of curios: a pair of swordfish bills nailed to the wall above several triton shells, a fully rigged Spanish corvette in a bottle, an engraved whale's tooth and a carved coconut tobacco jar. He turned again, stiffening as footsteps tramped down the wooden steps and Phillip walked into the parlour. The older man made a brief smile. "Mr. Bligh? So happy to meet you at last. No, please, stand easy. Let informality be our rule this evening."

"As you say, sir."

Phillip moved away from the doorway as the landlord thumped in again, eight bottles racked like powder charges down his pair of crutches. He swung to a halt and nimbly planted them along the dinner table. "Port. Madeira. Burgundy. Rhine. Malaga. Cognac. Jamaica rum. 'Ollands gin. All nations, so where's the voyage startin' tonight, ge'men?"

Amused, Phillip glanced at Bligh. "Shall we weigh anchor in Portugal? Later, when Lieutenant Vancouver arrives, we may care to ship for Madeira, then go round Gib' and up the coast to Málaga?"

"Capital idea."

The landlord twitched a piece of twine on one of his crutches, flicking a corkscrew from its leather scabbard. Phillip waited till the man had polished three glasses on his apron and filled two. He nodded the landlord's dismissal and raised one of the glasses. "To your good health, Bligh."

"To yours."

Phillip tasted the wine, then set the glass on the mantelshelf. "May I say how grateful I am that you could accept my invitation?"

"I'm honoured."

"It was only by the best of fortune that I heard from Sir Joseph Banks that you had recently returned from Trinidad and would be in Portsmouth for a few days."

"Yes. There are important matters I must attend to before reporting to Deptford."

Phillip nodded, still tuning his ear to this young man's abrupt style of speech. "They tell me you are being offered an independent command."

"Better than offered, I've got it. On paper. One of the Campbell boats, *Bethia*. They're recommissioning her as an armed transport, *Bounty*. I knew her on the West India run. Should do well."

"Indeed?" Phillip smiled wryly. "I could only wish I might say the same about my flagship. However, are you not also bound for the same general area, Tahiti . . . ?"

"Yes. Round the Horn. Directly to Matavai Bay. Then west—about Java and the Cape to Jamaica and home. Three years."

"*Really?* Around the globe? I must congratulate you in advance!" Phillip saluted his guest over the glass rim. "And did not Sir Joseph also say you would be doing some botanising in Tahiti . . . ?"

"He did?"

"That is the impression he gave me. Indeed, he seems quite elated by the thought of you collecting breadfruit—that is the proper name?—seedlings."

"Nigger fodder," Bligh replied, remembering to give the correct, the public reason for his voyage. The Admiralty's secret orders were different: not only would HMS *Bounty* back-load a useful food for the West Indian slave plantations and defray some of the government's expense with Messrs. Campbell & Partners, she would also test a sailing vessel's endurance to the limits.

This armed transport was to sail farther and longer than almost any other ship before her—Portsmouth to Tahiti via Teneriffe and Cape Horn—with only one charge of naval rations, malt, soup blocks and water to carry her into the central Pacific. Nobody was sure if it could be done, but *Bounty*'s men and rigging were to be stretched to breaking point to determine if a warship could half-circle the globe while escorting Indiamen into the South Seas when the next war shut the Cape of Good Hope and the Straits of Malacca to British flags.

"Beg pardon?" Phillip repeated with another discreet cough.

Bligh snapped back to the present. "Cheap nigger fodder. Breadfruit. Grows about the height of a crab apple tree. I told the planters it would shoot up like a weed in the Caribbean. Fruit's shaped rather like a pig's bladder. The Indians of Tahiti scorch it black in the fire and then scrape off the rind. They eat it."

"Interesting," Phillip commented drily, finding it hard to adjust to Bligh's distinctive voice and tone. Not that he didn't have every reason for self-assurance, Phillip thought, watching him drain his glass and stride over to the table for a refill.

Barely fifteen years after joining the navy as a seven-year-old boy, this evening's guest had been appointed master of HMS *Resolution* on Cook's third and last voyage to the South Seas when James Cook had already set a level of performance that had become the standard for others to equal, if they could. It had also been common knowledge that Cook never suffered fools gladly or ever accepted near enough as good enough, an impatient attitude to normal humans and their work which an impressionable young man might try and improve upon after promotion by a commander like James Cook. . . .

Phillip smiled quickly: he had been daydreaming again in the fire's warmth while his guest spoke. "Beg pardon?"

"I said, d'you want that glass filled?"

"Er, yes, please." Phillip held it out for the other man to top up. "Thank you, that's enough for the moment." He sipped. "Actually, I was just thinking about Jimmy Cook—"

Bligh's hand stopped tipping another refill for himself. "The captain? By God! *He* stood no nonsense from anyone, dead or alive!"

"Really?" Phillip enquired, unsure of Bligh's exact meaning. "Well, perhaps we shall have an opportunity to discuss his work over dinner?"

And for the first time that evening Bligh's face relaxed into a kind of smile. "You'll wish you hadn't. George Vancouver and I both served under him. Once started, we probably shan't speak of anyone else."

Phillip encouraged the smile. "That is a risk I am eager to run. I shall be, as they say, 'all ears,' because my own experience of the world east of Madras is precisely nil. Therefore—"

"L'tenant Van Couver, ge'men!" The landlord thumped aside, holding himself to attention as a square-set naval officer marched past, younger than Bligh by a few years, younger than Phillip by almost half a lifetime. He halted, heels rapping together as he bowed. "Your servant, sir!"

"Mr. Vancouver?" Phillip returned the bow with another smile. "So very happy to make your acquaintance, and so glad you could spare me one of your last evenings ashore. I do believe you already know my other guest . . . ?"

Vancouver turned, then suddenly grinned, hand darting out and gripping tight. "I'll be damned, Billy Bligh! Last I heard you were still slaving for your wife's uncle on the Trinidad run. What on earth are you doing back home, and in uniform too?"

Bligh winked knowingly. "Still working for the Campbell Interest, you may be sure, but with a big difference. He's just palmed *Bethia* onto the government payroll, and m'self with it. She's my independent command. It's back to Tahiti again."

"Lucky devil."

"Oh, well, your turn may come. Now, tell me what are you doing with yourself these days?"

Vancouver shrugged apologetically. "Much the same as usual. I'm still with Gardner on *Europa,* patrolling the Sugar Islands. Every hurricane season we pull back to Kingston and I pick up a bit of survey work: the Port Royal charts are being revised." He grimaced. "Nothing like taking your own command into the Pacific."

"Ah well, that's the luck of the draw, but you *still* haven't told me what you're doing in Portsmouth?"

Phillip coughed. "Shall we be seated, gentlemen? We can continue this conversation at leisure. Besides, mine host is anxious to display an example of his inn's famous cuisine, isn't that so, Clarke?"

"Yessir!" the landlord bobbed chins. "Nothin' fancy, o' course, I don't allow none o' them Froggy fal-lals 'ere. But it's always 'ot, it's always English, an' there's always plenty."

"Relieved to hear it," Phillip observed, spreading coat tails and sitting at the head of the table. "Mr. Vancouver? Your glass, please."

"Thank you."

"My pleasure." Phillip settled back in his chair, letting the fireglow play across his neck and shoulders. "A few moments ago you were saying that you are surveying Port Royal. I may be wrong, but I gather from the tone of your voice that you would rather be doing something else?"

"Yes. At times I would," Vancouver replied.

Phillip smiled kindly. "May an older, if not much wiser, man say how much he envies your opportunity?"

"Sir?"

"It's true, I envy you. How many officers of the king's service can boast they have completed one—or is it two?—Pacific explorations as you have? And how many can say they learned their craft from James Cook? For there was a man who would not tolerate a dullard on one voyage, let alone a second. Neither, I fancy, does Commodore Gardner, whom I remember from my own command of *Europa,*" Phillip added simply. "The fact that he entrusts you with such vitally important work as the revision of his charts is, surely, a mark of especial favour? A sure sign that you are bound to go far in the service."

Vancouver fiddled with his glass stem and said nothing as Phillip glanced at Bligh's haughty, weatherbeaten face, scarred by the hatchet which his father threw at him just before the boy went to sea. "And while we are bestowing bouquets, may I include you? I am often reminded that, with any luck, most of us will live to wear an ounce or two of gold lace around our collars, and a few of us may even contrive to pin a jewelled star and length of coloured silk to our tunics, but I know of only one individual in all history who will ever have the honour of saying, '*I* was Cook's sailing master in the Pacific. . . .' "

Phillip paused while the landlord led his tapster and kitchenmaid into the parlour with steaming platters of boiled mutton, spinach pudding and mashed turnip. Another pair of corks were drawn and Phillip could hear their squeaks turning shillings into guineas on his bill. "Thank you, Clarke, that will be all."

He looked back at his guests as the staff returned to their kitchen. "Having said which, gentlemen, you now know the reason why I am so grateful you could accept my invitation to dine." Vancouver coughed and was about to say something, but Phillip's finger lifted. "You see, I also have been given orders to sail into the Pacific. However, mine do not restrict me to a tight little ship with permission to wander hither and thither in search of Heaven knows what." He paused, studying his guests' reactions.

"On the contrary, I have been given a sizeable convoy of independently minded merchantmen to escort into distant waters where few have ever navigated. I then have to make landfall on a coast where even fewer have set foot. And, finally, I have to establish a major naval base where none have ever thought to live before. Thereafter," he added with an ironic grimace, "I must somehow feed everyone on the efforts of derelict ostlers, return a profit from the labour of convicted catgut spinners, and build a prosperous community upon failed pickpockets." Phillip paused to help himself to vegetables.

"And yet I am confident it can be done. Despite our somewhat lack-lustre material Botany Bay will succeed and flourish where others have not. So it is not that which troubles me, gentlemen, rather it is our sheer lack of factual information: what I know about New Holland could easily be written on the back of a playing card. It is therefore prudent I enquire where I can, while I can, and from whom I can. Will you help me?"

Bligh nodded with rare, for him, understanding of another's problems. "Damned glad I have only *Bounty* to kick along. I've seen enough ships like that *Alexander* on the slave run. And they've dumped—what?—five of 'em in your lap."

"Six."

"Half a dozen too many. Such tubs are rotten loaded with niggers. God alone knows what they'll be like stuffed with gallows' fodder." Bligh insisted in shaping his words as if they were a bosun's cob to be slashed round a slow crewman's bare legs.

Not so Vancouver. He put down his mutton bone and frowned harder. "I can't agree with you, Bill."

"Uh?"

"I can't agree. Too many well-connected people in the capital are speaking about this Botany Bay venture. It's going to save us a lot of trouble, more moral and hygienic, and personally I think it makes excellent sense to plant a colony in the Pacific before the Frogs do. I mean, such a base in New Holland will be an ideal point to launch an attack on Peru or Manila once we have to heat iron for the Dons again."

"Now just look here—!"

Vancouver's hand silenced his friend. "Surely you can remember those islands round Nootka, swarming with sea otters? And what were the Chinamen paying the Russkies for pelts at Unalaska, two hundred Spanish dollars apiece?"

"Hn!" Bligh was unmoved. "All I remember is fog, and ice, and snow, and a damned treacherous coastline to chart. While you were tucked up in your cosy cot, Mr. Midshipman, I was rowing ahead in the jolly boat with a sounding line, and let me assure you that was no time to be swooning over the wonders of nature!"

"Bilge!" Vancouver replied with a grin.

"Gentlemen?" Phillip interrupted. "May I return our attention to the question of New South Wales? I have been told that neither of you served on *Endeavour* when she surveyed that coast, but does that mean that neither of you has actually been to New Holland?"

Bligh frowned. "Afraid so. The nearest either of us ever came to your Botany Bay was when *Resolution* took on refreshment at Van Dieman's Land before setting course for whatever lay north of Canada."

"Could you describe it?"

"Van Dieman's Land?"

"Yes."

Bligh puffed cheeks and shrugged. "Well timbered. Excellent spars and planks, I'd say. Good supply of firewood. Plenty of water, wouldn't you say, George?"

Vancouver nodded. "Yes. And the Indians were incredibly docile, rather like deer running away between the trees: we didn't have to pepper them with birdshot once. Primitive beyond belief, with not a stitch of clothing except a bit of rat skin round the shoulders. An odd lot. No one placed any value on the things we offered, not even the hatchets, nails and beads. Really very odd."

"And the soil?" Phillip prompted. "Is it fertile?"

"Oh, I suppose so, judging from the way trees seem to thrive," Bligh replied. "Seemed a bit like brown tobacco."

"Hmmm." Phillip sucked a chop and spat a lump of gristle into his palm before flicking it at the fire. "Let me frame my question another way. Imagine for one moment that you had been given a task similar to mine, but already had your experience of Pacific navigation, what preparations would you be taking now?"

"Health, health, and again health," Vancouver answered without hesitation.

"How do you mean?"

The young man shrugged, unable to describe what he felt to be so obvious a truth. " 'Scurvy will sink you as surely as an enemy broadside,' Mr. Cook used to say and I never knew him to be wrong."

Phillip said nothing. Figures published in the *Public Record* at the end of his own war, back in '63, had shown that just under fifteen hundred sailors had been killed in battle during seven years of war: sickness had wasted another one hundred thousand men. He looked up. "How would you apply this experience?"

"Simple," Vancouver replied. "Do as Mr. Cook did. I would take on less salt horse. I would demand blocks of fruit soup equivalent to seven man rations per week. Lemon juice sufficient for one half pint, per diem, per man. And three pounds per week of that pickled cabbage they call sour, er, sour—?"

"*Sauerkraut.*"

"That's the stuff. You've tried it?"

Phillip smiled. "My father used to insist we eat it at home. But to continue, what about ship's hygiene and ventilation?"

"Utterly essential," Vancouver continued. "The ratings will resist, arguing that they get enough fresh air on deck and that nobody can sleep unless there's a 'snug yellow fug' down below. That's rubbish. Every week, without fail, Mr. Cook used to order us to rig windscoops and burn gunpowder damped with vinegar to sweeten the air atween decks. We also stowed large quantities of tar oil, limewash and sulphur—"

"George, for God's sake get off that hobby horse of yours!" Bligh interrupted, reaching for the bottle. "All the whitewash in the world won't be worth a gypsy's shit if your standing tackle is unsound, right?" He looked back at Phillip, hand gripping the bottle's neck as he tried jabbing a finger at his host, slopping wine on the table. "You want to learn about navigating the Pacific? Very well, I shall teach you all about navigating the bloody Pacific, and quite free from vinegar, lemon juice or cabbage. Lesson one: the Pacific is rarely pacific. On the contrary it is exceedingly large and, in the latitudes by which you will approach it around Van Dieman's Land, exceedingly violent. And very frightening," he added with untypical humility, propping the bottle neck on his glass and watching it fill to the brim.

He sipped, wiped mouth along his wrist, looked up again. "The southern ocean is quite unlike anything you have ever seen in the Baltic, or the Med', or even the Atlantic at its worst. You're going to be hunted for days on end by bloody great mountains of green water, running high, running fast, every one with a smoke cloud of white foam as it circles the globe from Cape Horn to Cape Horn."

Bligh pushed the bottle aside, and caught it. "Those are the good days.

Wait till the weather glass starts to fall and it'll be all hands to the storm-yards, believe me. Within minutes you'll be plunging close-hauled through sleet and snow as black as a church roof." He look up from the table, far more emotional and sensitive than Phillip had first thought. "When that happens, as happen it will, you'll be bloody glad your master double-checked every stitch of canvas that even smelled like a contractor had bought it cheap to sell for poor sailors' shrouds."

He eased back in his chair. "Lesson two: that most unpacific of all oceans is damned big. Madras is our last port going east and Batavia is the very end of the world for those skinflint Dutch bastards—er, sorry, George," he added with surprising tact. "It'll be no use discovering shoddy lines and tacky cloth when you're three thousand miles further on. Which means you'll have to stow everything you'll ever need, from hanks of marline to spar timbers, all personally accounted for before you weigh anchor back here. And don't count on those cheeseparing sons of whores at the Cape of No Hope for anything decent. And mind your standing tackle at all times, that's the lesson I learned aboard *Resolution,*" Bligh added with a sideways glance at Vancouver as he swigged his glass dry and reached for the bottle again. "I'll tell you a story, a true story, right? If it hadn't been for *me,* back at Deptford, we'd still be playing with the sea otters on George's precious coastline—as bits of driftwood."

Phillip smiled politely. "How do you mean?"

Bligh muffled a belch. "The glass was falling fast. Damned near seventy-one degrees north we were, about as far as anyone will ever sail through Bering's Strait. Right up against the pack ice, growling white floes smashing together all around, when suddenly she starts to snow! Right off the North Pole. Christ, our entire suit of storm canvas was shot to buggery and blown halfway to Siberia before you could bless yourself. And every inch had been stamped 'sound' with the king's mark by those rotten, bastardly, vile, poxy, pigshit civilian contractors. But we survived, ask George, and after some desp'rate hard work on our part we got off the ice. Know why?"

"No."

"*Resolution*'s fore rig and standing brace held. And you know why they didn't fly after the rest and drown the lot of us?"

"No."

"Because they were still her original tackle, stitched for merchant use in the North Sea, God knows how many years earlier, but they were *sound.* For which reason they had been tossed out at Deptford since a naval contractor couldn't make another penny by keeping 'em aboard. So out they went to make room for his filthy junk." Bligh's finger jabbed at Phillip's face. "But I didn't let 'em stay ashore for long. Soon as the land sharks weren't looking, I ripped down all their slovenly handwork and rigged materials I knew would hold fast when our yards were stiff with hoarfrost and the ratlines solid with icicles as long as your leg."

Phillip coughed drily. "Very interesting and graphic, I'm sure, but isn't Alaska some distance from New Holland?"

Bligh's scowl hardened. "Your end of the Pacific is going to be as cold, and violent, and deep as any other. You asked me for my frank opinion, sir, well here it is: keep a weather eye cocked for money-sucking civilian leeches who won't give a fart when you and all your men dock at a thousand fathoms to await Judgment Day."

Phillip was about to ask him something else when the landlord thumped into his parlour again, chest puffing mightily. "Major Ross, ge'men!"

"Omigod."

Phillip opened eyes to see his marine commandant and the recently appointed lieutenant governor of New South Wales marching through the doorway, face slightly paler than his tunic's scarlet cloth. Ross' heels whacked floorboards and raised dust as he halted. "Goo' evenin', sir!"

Phillip forced a smile. "Good evening, Mr. Ross. How very pleasant to see you so soon. Allow me to introduce my guests for the evening, George Vancouver, William Bligh. . . ."

"Ross! Robert! Major, His Majesty's Maritime Regiment o' Foot!" the elderly soldier barked out in an accent painfully like Sinclair's aboard *Alexander,* Phillip realised, watching Ross' flushed cheeks and wet eyes.

He tried another smile. "Would you care for a small drop of something light?"

"Port when I'm in port, sir!"

Phillip measured a modest dose and passed it across the table. "Er, won't you sit down a moment?" he asked, just stopping himself from adding, "Before you fall down?" Ross obeyed, sword clenched between knees, one fist wedging it to his chest like a tripod leg. "Now, to what do we owe the pleasure of this visit? Did not Lieutenant Tench inform you of my message this morning?"

Ross drained the glass and smacked lips. "He said I could not see you till nine o'clock."

"That is true, I told him so, so this must indeed be a matter of the greatest urgency if you must bring it forward by some twelve hours."

"It is. Where's yon rum ration for my men?"

Phillip's smile was beginning to wear thin. "It is curious you should happen to mention that—"

"Why?"

"Because only this afternoon I received a despatch from Treasury—"

"And?"

"Your extra spirit ration would cost another three pounds a week and the empire cannot afford it. In plain terms, unless the Lunacy and Sick board can certify that an extra measure of grog is justified, your troops will simply have to moderate their habits."

Ross' eyebrows clamped together. "That's not to be done! My men have earned this extra consideration and I am determined they shall get it! The cream o' mankind sent out to nursemaid the scum o' the earth? I'll not have it, I tell you!"

Phillip studied his toothpick. "Commendable sentiments, but neither will your men have that extra grog unless the Lunacy is first convinced of their need."

"O' course they need it!" Ross spluttered. "And I shall make bluidy certain they get it!"

Phillip sheathed the pick in its pocket case. "Delighted to hear you say so, now the problem is in safe hands. When you have found the means of justifying it to Treasury, please tell me and I shall forward it to them. Meanwhile, gentlemen all, it is getting late."

He stood. "No, please, continue here for as long as you like." He smiled distantly, wondering just how long it would be before Bligh's tongue lashed Ross into a tantrum and made sleep impossible in the small upstairs room. "I am sure Major Ross will relish telling you about his adventures in the American colonies. I have heard them before and tomorrow promises to be another long day for me. Mr. Vancouver?" Phillip bowed slightly. "So glad to have met you. A speedy return to Kingston and, please, give Commodore Gardner my best regards." He shifted slightly. "Mr. Bligh? I shall carefully consider everything you have told me and apply it where possible. A prosperous voyage on *Bounty* and a safe homecoming to England. Gentlemen all—" Phillip bowed again—"Good night."

11

"WEATHER GLASS 'igh an' steady again, sir!" Bryant announced, heeling the door shut. "Looks like it's goin' to be another scorcher," he added, setting down the can of water near its towel, razor and soap mug.

Phillip licked fingertips and pinched the candle dead before sweeping together his papers and tossing them at an open despatch box on the floor. Bryant had turned away from opening the shutters and was now collecting his master's shoes, uniform coat and sword, intending to give them a thorough overhaul and sponge while Phillip was away from Portsmouth. He paused in the open doorway. "Er, beggin' pardon, sir, but you did tell me to remind you about Mr. King. . . ."

"I did?" Phillip asked, pinching the bridge of his nose, eyes squeezed shut. "Oh. Very well, send him up when he arrives."

Bryant touched forefinger to head and clattered away while Phillip capped the inkwell and stifled a yawn. He stood and trod across the small room, stripping off his dressing gown and flopping it over the back of a chair while he wedged the mirror on its usual part of the window frame. Phillip grimaced: he'd been lodging at the Bower Anchor so long the looking glass had started rubbing away a small patch of paintwork, here, in the corner. He sighed and began stropping his razor on his belt while he looked across Spithead.

A convoy of East Indiamen was slowly dropping away on the morning tide, nimble dots crouching along the high yards, shaking out the great courses of tan sailcloth which bellied taut and hard on the freshening breeze. A sudden grey puff spurted from an open gunlid as the first merchantman drew abreast of Portsmouth Castle, breaking out her ensign. The tavern window rattled a few moments later as the signal gun's thud rippled past.

Phillip sighed again and went back to working lather round his chin while he read today's weather from the colour of Wight's hills, still arched with early summer cloud as they had been for the past week. Beneath them, without looking, he sensed rather than saw the coppice of black spars which belonged to him—kept well apart from the forest of masts which always crowded this anchorage. Finally, after months of wheedling and threatening, bluffing and plain hard work, England's thief fleet was almost ready to follow the Indiamen onto deep waters. Unit by unit, Phillip's command had been beating its way down Channel since midwinter, hauling to on the Motherbank until the remaining five convict transports and their three store ships had taken moorings round *Alexander*, watched by armed picket boats from HMS *Sirius* and her tender, HMS *Supply*.

Phillip frowned back at his reflected face: the eight months since taking his governor's commission had left their mark, and Botany Bay was still sixteen thousand sea miles into the future. His razor stopped midstroke as someone tapped on the chamber's door. "Come in!"

A stocky naval officer stepped through, leather despatch bag under one arm, a cocked hat under the other. "Good morning, sir."

" 'Morning," Phillip commented, finishing the stroke and watching Lieutenant Gidley King's reflection as the younger man dropped his bag on the desk. Bryant set down a tray of coffee and toast, shutting the door again as Phillip began on the other side of his face. "You checked those figures? The ones from the Winchester justices?"

"Yes, sir, I did, and no matter how I juggle 'em I'm afraid there'll still be another mixed consignment to berth before we weigh anchor," King replied. "Speaking of which, I was thinking we could quarter the women aboard *Friendship*—"

"No." Phillip wiped razor, rolled the ball of newspaper between fingertips, and flicked it straight through the window into the yard. "Can't be done. They're bursting at the seams already."

King frowned respectfully. "Oh, I wouldn't say that, sir. Surely we could squash another half dozen or so into her hold without risking an explosion, and any surplus could always be stuffed aboard *Alexander*?"

"The devil it could!" Phillip snapped, dabbing chin to stop the bleeding. "That fellow Sinclair still has—what?—one hundred and ninety-eight effectives below decks."

"One ninety-seven," King corrected. "He put another over the side yesterday evening."

"Hn!" Phillip had begun trimming eyebrows with a small pair of nail scissors. "This is becoming a habit with our Mr. Sinclair. Continue at this rate and we'll be spared the need to leave England at all."

"Sir?"

Phillip ignored the question, changed hands and trimmed the other eyebrow before turning, his annoyance under control again. "So, thanks to the good Captain Sinclair, we now have another berth to offer our prospective passengers. But how in hell does that affect our basic problem, victuals, if the batch from Winchester gets here before we leave?"

King unbuckled his despatch bag and checked a pencilled list. He glanced up. "The Ordnance Board says she embarked stores for two hundred and twelve at Blackwall. Now, assuming she slips another dozen or so before we drop moorings, that will leave us with a margin of about twenty empty spots to fill aboard *Alexander*. Such being the case—"

"Such being the case Sinclair will go on feeding the fishes at government expense," Phillip interrupted, "meanwhile netting a handsome seventeen pounds nine shillings apiece in unconsumed rations. Thank you, no, I would rather our late arrivals took their chances aboard *Prince of Wales*."

"Whatever you say, of course," King replied slowly, "but I think they'll be very uncomfortable squatting on each other's shoulders. I'm sorry, sir, but *Alexander*'s spare stowage is still our best hope. Besides," he added with a shrug, "let's be fair, Sinclair has started cleaning her up, well, a bit. Once the old and doddery have been thinned, why, she ought to be quite spruce again."

"Piffle." Phillip turned away from his mirror and began buttoning into grey breeches and plain brown stockings. "Now, during the time that I am away, you are to keep hounding those masters. Understand? I intend to *smell* a far higher standard of cleanliness below decks when I return. And get onto those surgeons' mates." He reached for a shirt and punched arms along its sleeves. "Bestir them how you will, I simply do not care." He turned, pushing shirt tails under his belt. "These ships of mine are going to look, smell and behave as if they were upon the king's service, understand?"

"Oh, I understand, I understand perfectly," King replied wearily, "but all too often there's a bottomless quagmire between one person understanding a need, and someone else undertaking the task—"

"Then bridge it." Phillip had gone back to the mirror and was knotting his cravat. "You have my heartiest approval to kick *Sitzfleisch*. You can kick it hard, you can kick it as often as you like, and you can kick it from breakfast to suppertime," he added, glancing over one shoulder, "because I intend unloading sound limbs and wind at the other end of our journey, able if not actually willing to work, and I don't give a damn how we do it! Never forget: those depraved items moored out there, those sifters of cinders and spinners of catgut, are the rosy-cheeked farm boys of our immediate future, the hands who will be growing the bread you and I must eat or go hungry." He scowled into the mirror again. "So, if for no other reason than self-interest, let us endeavour to keep those caskers of vinegar and makers of wigs in a reasonable state of health."

King had learned to interpret Phillip's many complex moods in the West Indies, aboard *Europa*. "Sir, I *am* doing the very best I can."

His chief said nothing, pulling on a plain buff waistcoat and leaving it hung open while he began pouring cups of coffee. "One sugar?"

"Two, please."

Phillip used the spoon to flick away some floating grains of scorched barley before handing the cup to his friend. "I know you're doing your best, Pip. Would I have ever asked you to accept this thankless position if I hadn't known that you would always exceed my greatest hopes?" The older man sat on the end of the wooden bedframe and began stirring his own cup, spoon clicking from side to side. "It's not in either of our natures to accept near enough as good enough, is it? And ought we not to draw some comfort from the fact that what you and I have been toiling at these last several months is the master plan of something never before attempted in the entire history of the world? Have you considered that?"

"Since when have you ever given me time?" King replied, reaching for two slices of toasted bread.

"Never have, never shall," Phillip answered with a sudden grin. "But, to be serious for a moment, please don't lose sight of the fact that you and I have been chosen to plant the first colony—of any nation—on a wholly new continent. Perhaps the world's last, who knows? Just think about that." He paused to sip coffee. "Almost certainly this will be the last such chance history offers anyone, the chance to establish a more energetic, a more enlightened people upon the ruins of God alone knows how many decayed civilisations."

"Sir?"

Phillip finished another sip and made a lopsided smile. "Y'know, sometimes at night, while we were patrolling the Gulf of Campeche, I used to order my cot be brought on deck for the cool. Remember? Well, that's what everyone was supposed to think, but the truth was I used to stare back at the stars and see which of us blinked first. And if the breeze lay from the right quarter, to drink in the damp, spicy odours of the jungle only a few miles away. A strange sensation. . . ."

"Sir?"

"Quite odd in fact," Phillip went on, almost speaking with himself now. "I often used to wonder if the early dons who sailed that same course ever suspected that, in the mountains of Mexico, far above the naked Indians and squawking parrots they'd found on the seashore, were cities quite the equal of anything they'd left behind in Europe? I doubt it. And I doubt if Senhor Cabral ever imagined the boundless wealth of Brazil when he first made landfall and faced those impenetrable forests, too." Phillip's smile altered. "But you and I are wiser, aren't we? We know better than Christopher Columbus or any of 'em. We know that, although there was not a scrap of evidence among the swamps of Yucatán to suggest a rich civilisation beyond those cloudy mountains, history tells us that the Aztecs were there all the time."

King stayed silent as Phillip took another sip of coffee and went on thinking aloud, as he often did in private. "So, who can say what marvellous sights we shall not see behind some antipodean hill, or hidden deep in some mountain valley, or built upon the banks of a river greater even than the Amazon? Indeed, who can say how many of the Seven Cities of Gold remain to be discovered in New Holland as they were in New Spain only two or three hundred years ago?"

He glanced at the younger man, eyes focussing again, unusually relaxed and content. "Perhaps it won't happen in our time, Pip, but of one thing we may be sure, those who finally discover a new Peru or Mexico in *Terra Australis Incognita* will be building upon the firm foundations which you, and I, even Major Ross have laid for them. Thief colony it may be for many; diplomatic gaming token for the few in the know; but for all of us—including those luckless wretches out there," he added, nodding toward the open window and Spithead, "this Botany Bay is our very last chance to wipe the slate clean and begin again in a truly New World."

King finished folding a slice of pressed tongue between the pieces of toast. He bit and swallowed. "Speaking of Major Ross, how would you suggest I handle him if he tries another scene like the last one?"

"With extreme tact," Phillip answered, also helping himself to the cold breakfast. "Despite every provocation we must never forget that Ross and his men will be our only defence against mutiny once the convoy is under way and, God knows, they're few enough considering the size of our task." Phillip paused to spread mustard. "However, with any reasonable luck he'll be too busy embarking his own stores to bother us about that damned rum. And by the time he's finished I hope to be back on deck."

King nodded, leafing more papers. "And the females' clothing? The last batch came down to us in rags, an absolute disgrace, even for women of that class."

"I've penned another stiff memorandum to Ordnance: let's see what effect it has."

Only partly satisfied, King ticked that item off his list. "And Mr. Balmain's request for wine and cordials to give the sick? Do we allow it?"

"Yes."

"And the extra eight ounces of beef?"

Phillip hesitated. "Yes. Buy stock on the hoof and find someone who can butcher it for us. Above all, tell Millar not to broach any more ration casks without direct orders. He will grumble but a twelvemonth from now he'll see the point and be thankful he obeyed."

King's pencil jotted as Phillip stood to pack the razor and nightshirt in his portmanteau. "Oh. One other thing, sir. The parson and his wife are, and these are his words, 'not entirely happy with the standard of accommodation being offered by Captain Sinclair.'"

"That name again!" Phillip finished tugging the straps tight and began threading brass buckles. "Very well, return my compliments to the reverend gentleman. Tell Mr. Johnson that I most strongly urge him to get off his bunk and take a short walk for'ard to the marines' quarters, whence he can peep into the accommodation being offered by Captain Sinclair to his future parishioners. If Mr. Johnson still feels inadequate after that experience, let him call upon me when I return and we shall have a little chat."

King grinned slightly and ticked that item as well. "And when ought that to be, sir?"

Phillip had gone to the door to call down for Bryant. He glanced back. "Beg pardon?"

"When are you planning to return?"

"That will depend upon what I find waiting for me at home, but I hope to be finished by Friday or Saturday. If anything of especial importance happens, something which cannot wait and which cannot be dealt with by yourself or Ross, then send a courier posthaste to Lyndhurst."

"I hope that won't be necessary."

"So indeed do I!" Phillip stepped aside and let Bryant tramp past with the luggage and a folded civilian topcoat, then checked his pocket watch. "Well, I suppose I'd better be moving, don't want to keep the *Rocket* waiting."

"A safe journey, sir."

"Thank you." The older man turned and followed his lieutenant downstairs, out into the street, where a porter was warming himself in a patch of sunlight under the Bower Anchor's signboard.

"My good man. Pray convey the commodore's equipage to Gosport Steps," Bryant ordered, as if awarding a rare honour instead of dropping a scuffed leather bag and a small trunk onto the wheelbarrow.

"Aye aye, ge'men!" The naval pensioner saluted unsteadily and began adjusting the barrow's straps across his shoulders.

Phillip nodded his manservant's dismissal and followed the porter, now limping away up Gunwharf Road toward the Royal Dockyard. Phillip's step quickened, taking its time from the hustle and energy of a workday ashore in the empire's main naval base. All around him men were running or tumbling drunkenly into one another, raising their fists and voices, and now and again the splintering crash of bottle glass through the open windows of pot houses. And all the while in the background, the rumble of iron-shod wheels as waggons of cordage and bales of sailcloth plodded in from the flax mills at Fordingbridge, a few miles west of his own home.

Phillip was smiling again, looking up at the sunshine and wheeling flocks of gulls as he drank in the clean reek of seaweed and listened to the growl of waves breaking on nearby shingle. Even a whip fight between two drayloads of charcoal, probably from the New Forest, and now jammed on a corner where only one could pass, did not spoil his sense of well-being. Or the cursing midshipmen who darted past him from brothel to brothel, hunting up their boats' crews while bosuns dragged bleary men into the daylight, clothing askew, kicking them all the way back to the landing, ready to pull an oar when their captains returned from duty at the port admiral's office.

The porter leaned into the handles of his pension, a government licence to push wheelbarrows for hire, and tried keeping pace with a jaunty little naval officer in mufti. Phillip didn't notice, quite happy with the anonymity of civilian clothes among the blue and scarlet which eddied with him along the wharfs near the Mast House where hundreds of new "sticks" from Canada and the Baltic were pickling in scummy black creosote; and the long ropewalks; and the broad sail lofts; and the workshops, the magazines, the building slips and forges with their man-high coils of anchor chain. A gang of dockyard mateys was slowly mixing a vat of red lead, linseed oil and turpentine paint in front of high tiers of tar barrels. Phillip glanced above them; high against the sunlight a haze of smoke was wisping from the bakehouse chimneys: down below, in the dark tunnel ovens, thousands of ration biscuits were being hardened for sea service.

The porter slowed as six high waggons, with stout wooden bars across their tops, ground past behind sweating horse teams. Two files of infantry from Hilsea Barracks were tramping alongside, easing the pace now they were almost at the end of their surprise raid on the fishermen's villages between Chichester and Itchenor. A few women were still plodding in the dust behind, but most had long before given up shouting encouragement to their menfolk or hurling abuse at a squad from the Impressment Service atop the waggons' slats, cudgels ready to crush groping fingers.

"Looks like it's been an 'ot press, sir," the pensioner commented, watching the waggons rumble past. "Never used to see the like o' it in peacetime. If you asks me, sir, we mean to drub them Frogs again—"

"Quite so, quite so," Phillip interrupted shortly, glancing at his watch again. "Now hurry along, there's a coach waiting for me!"

"Aye aye."

Lighters and ferries were also waiting down by Gosport Steps. The soldiers had already arrived and drawn themselves into a hollow square around the waggons, bayonets fixed, watching the latest naval recruits being roped together for the last part of their journey, out by barge to a receiving hulk where they would be held until issued to a man o' war.

Phillip waited impatiently as the pensioner passed down his luggage to a skiff, then shut his purse and dropped a sixpence into the man's hat.

"Thank'ee sir! Long life an' honour!"

Phillip nodded and climbed down the steps. The waterman held a mooring line till his passenger had settled amidships, then let go and stood in the stern; leaning against his long sweep, then drawing back again; sculling across the narrow deck of Portsmouth harbour. He shipped sweep at Gosport landing as Phillip climbed the weedy steps, rushed by more porters, jostling and shouting for hire. Phillip cursed them all, cuffing away the nearest and fittest while he looked for another naval pensioner, but there were none to be had at the moment, so he pointed to the youngest instead. "You!"

"Aye aye, your honour, sir!" the boy piped, running to haul his client's trunk ashore. He crouched, nimbly working it onto his back and then secured the load with a strap looped around his forehead. The lad straightened with a grunt and plodded after Phillip, now carrying the coat and portmanteau himself, covering the short distance which remained to reach the Admiral Benbow where a coach was being readied, the royal mail cypher stencilled in yellow paint on her battered red doors.

Phillip stood aside as another pair of horses backed past him into their traces, sparrows hopping among iron-shod hooves, pecking undigested grain in the steaming new dung. Swearing ostlers were running with buckets yoked over their shoulders, slopping water while the other men stuffed oatbags and tightened harness. The *Southampton Rocket*'s driver also kept apart from the crowd, green coat open to the knees, toddy glass in one hand, timekeeper in the other, king o' the road while his guard ticked passengers from the list and stowed their luggage.

"Mr. Phillips, sir?"

"Phillip."

"Better 'urry up, sir, we're jus' about done. Er, seat num'er two, kept it special for you, the others'll get the sun in their eyes."

"Much obliged." Phillip tipped the man a half crown and climbed aboard the swaying bodywork, its leather suspension straps creaking as the guard heaved his trunk and bag onto the roof and lashed them down.

Phillip was the last. He nodded civilly at the five other travellers and was still making himself comfortable on a haybag which doubled as a cushion and reserve horse fodder when four dragoons took up positions, sabres and carbines jingling, ready to escort the royal mail for its fifteen-mile run across the waste of Lock Heath to Southampton. The guard flourished post horn and his driver cracked reins along the team's backs—"Giddyapp, y'bastards!"—wheeling the *Rocket* onto Gosport's cobbled High Street before whipping up a brisk rumble inland.

Phillip found he still had the sailor's knack of being able to doze anywhere, no matter how rough the road, only awakening again as the coach passed under Southampton's walls and the post horn clanged, rebounding off overhanging tenements as the *Rocket* slowed to a halt at the terminus in Castle Street. Stiff and weary, he stepped down as ostlers from the Golden Tun hurried to change teams while onward passengers and mail transferred to the *Winchester Lightning,* another of England's modern, high-speed diligences connecting her major towns and cities.

Phillip turned, watching his trunk and bag being thrown off the coach as a tall, elderly man with grizzled side whiskers pushed through the crowd, his homespun linen smock, buttoned leggings and green hide shoes of a neater cut than most others lounging outside the inn. " 'Marnin', cap'n."

Phillip returned the salute by touching his own hatbrim. "Good morning, Mathew."

"The boy did bring over your message, master. Said as 'ow you'd be on the ol' *Rocket,* so where be the things?" Phillip's farm steward stared around suspiciously at all the hurrying city folk.

"Over there."

"Ah. Well, just keep a close eye on'm while I gets Jess." Mathew Godwin shouldered a plain fowling piece and tramped back toward a string of mounts hitched to iron rings on the tavern wall. He tramped back leading a pair of saddle horses and a pack pony. "Right. Now, keep a-hold o' them while I loads 'er up."

Phillip held their heads while his steward embraced the trunk, lifting it without strain and lashing it to one pannier on the pony before balancing it with the portmanteau. Then he took one of the horses and waited until Phillip had shortened stirrup leathers, tied down his rolled coat over the crupper and pulled himself across the saddle. Godwin fell in behind, towing the laden Jess as Phillip led their way through Southampton's old Jews' Quarter and out along West Road.

They halted again while Godwin shouted for the ferryman to row across Blackwater. Phillip was glad of the chance to dismount and enjoy the herons which flapped across the lonely skies of Totton Marsh, almost as grey as the clouds which were starting to gather farther inland, beyond the wilderness of bog myrtle and asphodel.

"Ready, cap'n?" Godwin asked again, worried by his master's frequent lapses of attention. Phillip nodded and helped lead their horses aboard the ferry's worn planks, standing hock-deep in water as the ferryman cast off and leaned into his ponderous sweep, eyes squinting, aiming between the tide mill and a line of salmon nets. "You'm a-goin' far, ge'men?" he panted, words snatched from his mouth by the breeze as they neared midstream.

"Aye!" Godwin replied. "Up along by Lyndhurst way!"

"Far 'nough!" the ferryman shouted back from the stern. "Keep your eyes peeled! Said as what—there's some masterless men—on the road! Gypsies! Stole a goose this marnin', they did!"

Godwin muttered and got ready to lead their horses onto dry land again while Phillip shut his purse and checked the pair of pistols in his waistcoat pockets. They remounted and clipped along the track past Eling about half a mile to their left, a sleepy little port where ships had been laid down from New Forest oak since the Norman Conquest.

Like most things, and places, and people in this closed and enclosed part of old England, Eling showed another face on moonlit nights when darkened French luggers brought in bales of lace and cambric, velvet and silk, to load up with duty-free English wool for French weavers. Rumour said that more gold *louis* were buried under the hearthstones of Eling and the surrounding forest than in any comparable part of the kingdom of France. Phillip could believe it: once he had found a newly minted *écu* in a handful of change, a piece of silver which had not come back to England in his own pocket. He had said nothing, of course, and to that extent he had become accepted as a New Forester.

Godwin drew abreast again as they began the long plod up to Colbury Common and a dark rampart of trees where a work party of local tenants was shovelling gravel from a bullock cart, tamping it over a bed of furze branches cut from the nearby heath. The women shuffled aside, staring as horsemen plodded over their gravel and twigs. Phillip touched hat in reply and glanced across at Godwin. "They seem to be making a good job of it, Mathew! Who's the waywarden this year?"

"Billy Buskett."

Phillip kept silent for several paces, riding to an easy rhythm as the horse picked its own way between unmade ruts and gullies. "That must be Dave Buskett's boy?"

"Aye, that it be, ol' Dave's boy, Billy."

"Nothing like keeping it in the family, eh? Being the waywarden is quite a Buskett tradition," Phillip added, smiling at nearly a decade of memories of life in Lyndhurst, some good, the rest he would rather forget. "So what's become of the father? Still grazing Clayhill?"

"Ol' Dave? Not 'im, master. Got the flux an' died nigh on a year ago come next Michaelmas."

"Oh." Phillip fell silent again, letting the horse plod their last few miles down the Lyndhurst track. Old Dave had once been Young Dave Buskett, a neighbouring farmer, elected parish waywarden the year Phillip had become its overseer of the poor. The new waywarden had also taken his duties seriously, Phillip remembered, surveying parish roads and assigning labour for those families which could not pay the highway rate in cash—as the women behind were now doing. Phillip had often sat alongside him at vestry meetings in his own capacity of overseer, which included auditing the annual rate books, and tythingman or village constable.

Phillip hunched shoulders and rode on, lost in thought. For a brief while, after coming ashore in '62 as a half-pay junior officer and moving down to Hampshire with his new wife, Phillip had felt part of a civilised community again. For that short summer, until the endless bickering over her money began to corrode his sense of well-being, Phillip had given a naval officer's standards of efficiency to overseeing the local poor, collecting rates and passing judgment with the brisk impartiality of a battleship's quarterdeck. True, he may have irritated some villagers, happier with the muddle of a thousand-year tradition, but despite their moans and grumbles he felt that Lyndhurst's accounts had been kept in order with the mathematical precision of a logbook.

A pair of fallow deer stopped grazing as the horses and pony came into sight, then sprang across the track to disappear among the beech trees which arched overhead. Phillip didn't notice though once he had spent many hours alone with his telescope on Clayhill, re-educating himself by studying land animals and memorising the names of new birds as they came to winter behind his property at Vernalls.

And not only winter, for never once in all their years together had Charlotte declared a close season on her nagging that he strive harder, higher, longer so that she could lord it over this or that lesser neighbour's wife. Thinking back now, Phillip could only shake his head at so many lonely hours, watching mallard and teal glide over his secret pond while she exhausted her temper on the servants. And then, not one day too soon, they agreed to part. It had been almost the only thing they ever agreed upon, he to serve in the Portuguese navy, she to live in Cheltenham Spa where, no doubt, she still drank endless cups of tea with her cronies while brewing endless mischief behind their backs.

Phillip winced as the trees began to close around him, trying hard not to imagine the tales she would be telling now that her ne'er-do-well husband's name and title had been published in the *Government Gazette* for all to see. The wince eased into a lopsided grimace: to be fair to the bitch, without her money he would never have won himself a secure place in this England of tradition and established values. There was no hiding the fact that her annuity had bought the broad green acres which had raised them to the gentry, just as his naval commission had secured them a modest rung on the ladder of privilege. At the time it had seemed a fair basis for a lifetime partnership: Charlotte had got what she wanted, and so had he.

Almost his earliest memory was of his father telling and retelling how hard life had been in foreign lands with their prince archbishops and margraves, their counts palatine and exclusive orders ruled by Graf von This or Herzog zu That. But this England? Oi! Here anything is possible once a man enters that all-powerful but untitled middle order of country gentlemen. . . . And the years since then had proved him right, for England's social order really was like a suit of used clothes, able to fit anyone with only a tuck here, a nip there.

For in England there were none of the insuperable barriers of caste which Phillip had experienced in France. There, the able and ambitious son of a Bordeaux merchant, with a sugar fleet of his own, could never serve above petty officer rank in Louis' aristocratic navy. As for the puny son of Jakob Philipp, late of the Judengasse, Frankfurt-am-Main, ever being commissioned a royal governor of the French Crown—! Arthur Phillip could hardly keep his face straight at the absurd thought.

But over here, on this side of the Channel, what a difference to the air one breathed! Here, in England, not only was it possible to dream of better things, the able and ambitious could live to make them happen—as he was proving at this very moment with only a nip of conscience here, a tuck of custom there, drop one letter in the old name, add another to the new. Phillip was living proof that if anyone but work hard enough at being an Englishman, most English country gentlemen would accept the newcomer with a tolerance far removed from the official *Tolerenz* of German princes for their Jewish subjects which had driven Jakob to hunt his fortune beyond the seas.

Phillip's horse plodded along the woodland track, hooves muffled by leaf loam, while he smiled around at this England he knew, this England he trusted, this England where he felt accepted. For this was a good land, peopled by good, solid men and women, mellowed over the centuries until all was ripe for it to be transplanted to the empty coasts of New South

Wales, there to begin another cycle of growth; nurturing countless generations of other tolerant, affable English gentlemen from all lands and backgrounds; encouraging them to dream of glory in their turn, allowing them to make it happen. Yes—

"I said, we be nearly there, cap'n!" Godwin announced again, tapping his master's arm and pointing forward. They were now crossing the log bridge which spanned the headwaters of Beaulieu River. Around them the forest was starting to thin while, ahead, the familiar spire of St. Michael & All Angels was slowly rising above the treeline.

Not before time. Under the dense canopy of leaves he had not noticed more grey clouds in the west, reaching up to meet the day as it dipped into evening. A chill wind flicked off White Moor, spiked with raindrops. Phillip unbuckled his topcoat and tugged it on as he kicked his horse into a lumbering trot. Godwin pulled his own shapeless hat further down and kept going. A few yards ahead, where the forked tracks from Beaulieu and Southampton met, the local gallows still framed Lyndhurst's only street. Someone had been gibbeted quite recently, Phillip noted, passing well to windward and glancing at the antlers which the Court of Verderers had ordered be nailed to the beam overhead, a warning to other deer poachers just as they had been since Norman game laws began protecting royal property.

Phillip had more pressing matters on his mind as the rain began to fall steadily and he clipped down the lane to his own farm gate, still protected by a tall bay tree to scare off the devil and protect the animals from harm. Godwin leaned from the saddle and held it open as his master rode past and dismounted in the yard of a gabled house which the past two centuries had treated kindly. The steward's wife—Phillip's housekeeper—stood waiting at the door, wiping floury hands on her apron, a woman as dark as her husband had once been blond. She checked that her cap was on straight, then bobbed a curtsey as the master strode up his steps out of the weather. "Welcome 'ome, cap'n, I got it just the way you like it to be."

Phillip smiled, shaking his coat tails dry. "I'm sure you have."

"An' the water's a-heatin' for your tub, sir, an' Mr. Rose did send over a brace o' hares when he knowed you was a-comin'. An' I've aired the bolster in your bedchamber, an' put on fresh sheets, an'—"

"Mrs. Godwin." Phillip smiled again, pausing inside the doorway while her husband led the horses round to their stable. "Wherever should I be without you to fuss over me?"

" 'Deed I don't know, sir!"

"Neither do I," he confessed amiably, walking ahead of her to run a finger along the mantelshelf above a crackling fire, weaving it between a sailor's curios from India and Brazil, America and the Caribbean. No dust.

And none under them, he noted, lifting a brass Benares candlestick for a moment. Satisfied that everything else in the small farmhouse parlour remained exactly as he required, Phillip turned to warm his legs as Mrs. Godwin bustled back from the pantry with one of the wooden salvers he'd bought in Cuba, inlaid with chips of coloured shell and now balancing a bottle of Madeira. "Compliments o' Mr. Rose, sir. Sent it over special this marnin'. Remembered as 'ow you liked it."

"Thank you. Put it down there, please, I'll do the honours." But she insisted on polishing the tumbler with her skirt hem before hurrying back to the kitchen to scold the maid for something. Her master moved nearer the firelight and broke a dab of wax which stuck Rose's note to the bottle. He read the address with quiet satisfaction: "To His Excellency Govr. Arthur Phillip Esq." The hand was as welcome as the wine, the elegant script of an educated man who had risen to the very top of his profession, becoming secretary of the Treasury in the years since they had both left the navy as penniless junior officers.

Phillip was still smiling at his friend's instinctive courtesy as he thumbnailed the sealing wafer and smoothed stiff paper. "My Dear Arthur," he read, squinting in the firelight. "Pray drink your health and mine before retiring tonight. I know how limited your time must be now, and how much remains to be done both here and at Portsmouth, yet Theodora and I would esteem it the greatest honour if you would be our dinner guest before departing upon your travels. Shall we say tomorrow? As ever, I remain yr. afft. friend, George Rose."

Phillip folded the letter and carefully put it away in his pocketbook as Mrs. Godwin bobbed another curtsey. "Will you be a wantin' of your tub afore or after eatin', sir?"

"Before. Please."

Phillip was beginning to ache and feel chilled after the long day's journey. He loosened cravat and kicked off shoes as Mrs. Godwin rolled a wooden tub in front of the fire, and signalled for the maid to start ferrying jugs of hot water from the kitchen boiler.

"Thank you."

Both women curtseyed again and left as their master finished undressing and folded knees into the bath—an old naval rummer sawn across the middle—with a contented sigh. Mathew Godwin tramped through a side door and stood hat in hand till Phillip gave him permission to come closer. "The bags've been took up to your room. Be there anythin' more you'll be a-wantin'?"

"Not tonight, Mathew, however I shall be making an early start tomorrow morning. Have the accounts ready for me to sign. I shall also want to discuss our cropping for the next three or four years."

"Next *four* years?"

"Perhaps longer, I cannot yet say," Phillip replied, sponging water over his bony shoulders and reaching for a cake of homemade tallow soap.

Godwin looked down at his hat, then looked up again. "Er, they do say as what you're bound for foreign parts again. But *four* years is a wonderful long time for to be away from 'ome. . . ."

"It's also rather a long way," Phillip said, scrubbing vigorously. "Cheer up! Heavens, man, it's no different from the time when I served the king of Portugal, is it?"

Godwin looked uncertain. "I dunno 'bout that. It's not *right* at your time o' life to be a-runnin' off like this. It ain't *natural,* that's what it's not."

"Mathew, some men like travelling."

"Oh, so do I, master, so do I! Been up to London once, I 'ave, but not for no *four* years it weren't!" His finger jabbed at the ground beneath the parlour's stone floor. "'Ere's where I belong, like me dad an' 'is dad afore 'im, an' 'is dad's dad afore '*im.* An' I thank God I got a good boy what'll think the same way about me—"

"Then you—are indeed more fortunate—than you will ever know."

"Master?"

"That will be all."

The outer door shut quietly behind the steward.

After a long while Phillip pulled himself up by the tub brim and slowly turned in front of the fire while he rubbed his shanks dry with a rough towel. The bottle of Madeira also promised warmth and comfort of a sort. He tugged its cork and splashed a full measure into the tumbler while his maidservant bailed out the bath water and Mrs. Godwin laid a single place at the parlour table. Phillip curtly ordered her away, finished knotting his robe and escorted the bottle to dinner.

12

SOON AFTER first light, while he still snored overhead in the great bed-chamber, Mrs. Godwin swept up the splinters of green glass where Phillip's empty bottle had smashed against the parlour wall. Her tureen of braised hare and carrots had hardly been touched, and the raspberry tart had been mutilated by knife slashes.

She was still kneading bread and scolding the maidservant when he finally trod downstairs to the kitchen, hair tied back neatly, shaved and dressed for the day's work. She eyed him warily. " 'Marnin', master."

"Good morning, Mrs. Godwin."

" 'Marnin', master!" the young girl piped, busy with holding her curtsey, watching to see when the housekeeper would straighten again.

"Good morning, Sally."

"I've a-set out the cheese, an' fish, an' a nice bit o' pickled beef in the parlour, master."

Phillip's eyes squeezed shut, head throbbing in time with the kitchen clock. "Thank you, no, I'd rather not. Just toast. And egg flip." The eyes opened again. "And Sally? Find Mr. Godwin. Inform him that I am now waiting in my bureau."

"Master?"

Phillip sighed. "The small chamber which used to be our sewing room." The maid ducked another curtsey and ran away from the kitchen, skirts held awkwardly, an eleven-year-old happy to be free of the day's drudgery for even a short while.

Phillip crossed the parlour and pushed open a plain oaken door which had probably creaked like this since the time of the Armada, no matter how much warm mutton fat one dripped on the hinges. Inside, the room was warm and still, its mullioned windows facing south to catch the sun across an English garden of hollyhocks and wild roses. This had always been the cosiest room in the house, which is why his wife had laid claim to it to incubate grudges and propagate new varieties of complaint against any neighbour who seemed to be rising above her station in life.

Phillip paused and leaned against the door frame. The woman was still as much a part of him as she had once been a part of this room. Indeed, if he shut his eyes he could almost smell her acrid imprint on the air, like burned gunpowder. Phillip felt the ghosts crowding round and, not for the first time, realised that Charlotte had been a thorough snob even before they married. But after serving in a navy where a man might easily be at sea for two years without touching land, and after living in a world where the only girls one ever met usually had a queue of sailors waiting outside a blanket screen, *any* woman who didn't spit tobacco juice on the carpet was bound to impress an eager and lonely young naval officer. The more so if she knew how to dress in fashion, could play a few simple airs on the harpsichord and was an experienced widow with sixteen thousand pounds in secure government bonds.

Phillip straightened and stepped into the room which was now used only to store farm records and correspondence. He blew dust off a set of ledgers, laid them along the table and was still grinding dried ink in a horn of water when his steward's shoenails crunched to a halt outside. "Come in, Mathew!"

Phillip glanced past him and nodded to Mrs. Godwin, waiting in the background with a tray. "Come in, come in, set it over there." He went back to mixing ink to the right texture before reaching for a sheaf of goose feathers. "Sit down, Mathew."

"If it's all the same, an' beggin' pardon, master, I'd rather stand. It wouldn't be proper," he added simply.

"As you wish, as you wish." Phillip was more concerned with shaping a new quill, paring away the feather with his penknife. He sat back on the stool and glanced up. "Now, let us begin with our fleece and hide receipts."

Godwin dipped into his leather dinner satchel and pulled out a bundle of hazel twigs tied up with rawhide string and notched in different patterns. Phillip said nothing and began sorting the tally sticks into separate heaps along the table, relying on Godwin's memory to name which dealer or fellmonger had made which payment to Vernalls in the past twelvemonth. The notches were tallied in groups of three—pounds, shillings and pence—and their totals entered in the farm ledgers. About halfway through the annual audit Phillip slipped off his glasses and eased back on the high stool while he finished breakfast. "Mathew?"

"Master?"

"How much do I pay you?"

The steward scratched his head. "Er, a pound ev'ry quarter day. Tha's on top o' firin', pannage for us porkers, cow forage, five yards o' wool, a Chris'mas cheese, a—"

"I thought so, I thought so," Phillip interrupted wearily. "Now, what would you say to an extra ten shillings every quarter day?"

Godwin scratched harder, trying to find the hidden catch. "Why, that'd be right 'andy, master. But what'd I 'ave to do for it?"

"Very little, really. Just present yourself to the Reverend Mr. Tancred next Sunday after Communion and give him my compliments. Ask if he would kindly show you how to make your letters and cypher accurately to ten—" Godwin was already shaking his head—"then, when you can dispense with these bits of twig and show me a simple daybook, clearly written in English, I shall raise your wages yet another ten shillings." Phillip looked across at the slightly older man, now awkwardly shuffling hands round the front of his smock. "I would seriously ponder upon it, Mathew. Remember, this could mean almost another guinea a quarter. . . ."

The man's white head shook again. "It wouldn't be proper, master, not at my time an' station o' life."

Phillip controlled his annoyance and brushed individual crumbs off the open ledger with his quill. "Mathew. How old are you?"

The steward scratched even hard, more puzzled than ever. "Well, let me reckon a-right. Young Lucy died o' the spots the year o' them big

troubles up London way, an' she were eight then. Betty an' me we'd been
wed nigh on six afore *that*." He looked up triumphantly from his fingers.
"Two-an'-fifty come next Swithun's Eve!"

Phillip nodded, glancing at his own figures jotted in the margin of
Vernalls' petty cashbook. "You are barely three years ahead of me."
He glanced up again, exasperated. "Good heavens, man, that's no age at
all to be improving your mind!"

"Beggin' pardon, master, but you can't never teach ol' dogs new
tricks."

"Please do not interrupt me." The quill struck air, underscoring Phillip's words as he looked up at his steward's whiskery face. "Dogs, young
or old, big or small, black, white or brindle, *dogs* have nothing to do with
the case in question, understand?"

"Master?"

"I say again: no man—unless he is naturally stupid, in which case he has
no right to be holding a position of great trust, or one so decrepit that he
must soon be consigned to the poor house—no *man* is ever too old to learn
new skills if he but sets his heart upon it."

"But master!"

"But nothing." Phillip was quietly severe. "Attend very carefully to
what I say. I shall be abroad upon the king's business for several years.
You, together with Mr. Rose's bailiff and a Mr. Hayes of Drummonds'
Bank, will be responsible for every penny which enters or leaves my estate.
It will be extremely vexing if, after I return from overseeing some thousands of men and very considerable sums of money, if I am presented with
these bits of firewood!" The quill dipped and ran over the heaps of tally
sticks. "Do I make myself clear?" Godwin nodded, fingers knotting and
pulling apart again round his hatbrim. "Are you *quite* sure you understand
what I am telling you?"

"Master."

"Then I would most earnestly suggest you speak with the Reverend
Mr. Tancred next Sunday," Phillip concluded, turning back to the cashbook. "Because you seem neither stupid nor, I hope, about to be put out of
your cottage and onto the parish. Now, what's this little piece of nonsense
here?" he asked, impatiently flicking at more sticks.

"Birds' beaks, master. Finches an' nutchatters mostly."

"What of them?"

"I pays the village boys to get shot o' such vermin from us corn an'
barley stooks. They brings the beaks an' I gives 'em a penny the dozen.
Cost us nigh on a pound last year, it did."

It was late morning before Phillip finished his accounts and could take
off his glasses for the last time. Godwin was equally glad to escape out-

doors and start saddling horses while Vernalls' master shut his ledgers and completed a few written instructions. Then Phillip slipped into the old naval stormcoat which he wore around the farm, picked up a salt-bleached black tricorne and hurried down the front steps to the mounting block.

Godwin held the yard gate open and shut it again as Phillip trotted through and began cantering across his meadowlands. The steward caught up at a shambling gallop and paced his master down to the creek which drained his estate from Foxlease Pond, eastward to White Moor. Phillip reined up short, exhilarated by even a few hours away from Admiralty despatch boxes and contractors' Oriental plots. He pulled out his notebook and steadied pencil for a moment. "I want that ditch taking down another two feet before the next rains, and have those rushes cut right back." The pencil jotted quickly. "Get Barney Wild to bring over his waggon and team, I want the muck spread on our top paddock. He can cart the rushes for thatch as his repayment. And attend to that hedge—" he pointed riding whip—"I noticed it last night by Shagg's Meadow, sheep could easily break through at several points."

It was early afternoon before Phillip had completed the tour of inspection and had decided upon the next four years' farm work at Vernalls. Both men plodded back to the house and Phillip dismounted again, leaving his steward to ride round to the stables. "Ease the saddle and give her a rubdown! I'll be riding over to Mr. Rose's presently."

"Right, master!"

Phillip strode indoors and went up to the great bedchamber. He threw his hat and whip between the four-poster's curtains and walked to his clothespress, turning over the contents, trying to imagine what the climate might be at Botany Bay and which shirts would be suitable for the seasons. In the end he gave up guessing and took thick flannel for winter, thinner wool for summer, and half a dozen of the finest cambric for public ceremonial and visiting the Indian kings. He checked them for moth holes, replaced the sticks of Chinese camphor and began packing his small sea chest, stowing a set of oilskins under its curved lid, anticipating the shambles once heavy seas broke over *Sirius'* stern and began washing out his cabin.

It was soon done. For a moment he hesitated, then peeled off the old stormcoat and squashed it over his breeches and a bag of stockings: there might be a need for workclothes among the flax plantations of New Holland. The lid slammed and he hefted one side of the chest for weight, lifting on a rope becket decorated with Turks' heads and Portuguese sennit work.

Satisfied, Phillip changed back into yesterday's clothes—still smoky after a night over the kitchen fire—and took a last look around, checking that nothing of use had been left behind. Then he turned and left without regret, hurrying downstairs to where Mrs. Godwin was waiting at the parlour door. "Oh, master! I've put some nice pickled brisket in soak. 'Ow d'you like it done up for dinner?"

She probably did not understand Phillip's grimace which turned to a quick smile. "Thank you, Mrs. Godwin, but I shall have my fill of salt beef during the next year or two. In any case," he added, twitching a riding cloak over his shoulders and reaching for a better hat, "I shall be dining at Cuffnells tonight."

Phillip crossed the stable yard, tightened his mare's girth straps again and pulled himself aboard, turning her head out of the main gate. He skirted the triangular patch of rough grazing which was Goose Green and set off at a jog up Chapel Lane, keeping Lyndhurst's roofline on his right hand. The fitful sun was starting to wester behind Emery Down and the encircling forest seemed to draw closer. Phillip gave a touch of spur and urged his mare into a canter as he turned her up Pinkney Lane, searching for a familiar break in the boundary hedge. He slowed, dismounting to drop the sliprail, and led his horse into Cuffnells Park.

"Halloa—!" Phillip looked up as he replaced the barrier: someone was walloping a small pony between the widely spaced trees, elbows and knees flying. "Wait for me!"

Phillip's smile deepened. He mounted, trotting to meet the young boy, and returned his salute as they reined alongside each other to raise hats.

"Father said you might be coming over tonight!"

"Might?" Phillip asked, still smiling. "How could I do otherwise, Billy? Or is it William now?"

The young boy frowned earnestly. "William sounds more grown up, don't you think?"

"I couldn't have put it better myself," Phillip agreed, slapping his mare into a quick walk. "Sir William Rose? Dr. William Rose? The Reverend William Rose? Mr. William Rose?" Phillip tasted the words with care. "They're all good. No matter how things turn out for you it's a good name, quite as fine and upstanding as, well, 'Mr. William Pitt,' and look where that's taken him, eh?"

"Father says that Mr. Pitt is the greatest man in England!"

Phillip made a judicious nod. "Then I can only agree: your father is a fine judge of character. Now, young William, what's our handicap to be this time? Remember, I'm only a simple sailorman, more nimble aloft among the yards than charting a course around all this green stuff."

"Thirty?"

"Twenty!"

"Five-and-twenty?"

"Done!" Phillip laughed.

"Starting from, now—!" William Rose shouted over one shoulder, crouching like a Newmarket jockey and tanning his pony across the open parkland toward Cuffnells House while Phillip stood, counting slowly. He was still chuckling as he reached twenty-five and eased into a loping canter so that the boy could lead most of the way with a few yards to spare. They pulled up together under the marble balustrade—shipped back from Italy when the park's previous owner had finished his grand tour to debauch the rest of his fortune in London—and Phillip dismounted with a comic show of fatigue, puffing and blowing hard as he threw the reins to a waiting gardener and lightly followed the boy onto the terrace. "I beat him, Father!"

George Rose was leaning against the marble, smoking and watching the evening settle across his estate. He straightened, scratching the pipe stem under his bob wig and looked properly puzzled. "Dashed if I know how you manage to do it, Billy. The way you can fly her along, we must've put Pegasus over that little creature's dam and never known it." He patted the boy's shoulder as he stepped forward, hand outstretched. "Arthur. So very good to see you again."

"You too, George," Phillip replied, returning the grip of another man who had risen from obscurity by talent alone. For although George Rose laboured hard and long to seem a Tory squire, to the manor born, there was still a noticeable Scots burr in his voice whenever he forgot the education which a merchant uncle in London had provided for his young adopted son.

Rose's smile deepened. "And now, my friend, may I be the first to congratulate you upon the much enlarged scope of your governor's commission?"

"Then it *has* been approved?"

"Yes."

"How on earth did we swing it?" Phillip asked, smiling uncertainly. "The last I'd heard, Dundas and M'Lord Howe were still dead set against any further revision of my powers."

Rose's eyelids drooped. "Oh, one shouldn't pay too much attention to gossip. What are a few tantrums around the Cabinet table? Nothing of any lasting consequence: nobody takes them seriously. Besides, *you* know how these things work, a dip from the left pocket, a slip into the right, the speed of the hand deceives the eye, mm?"

Phillip was shaking his head. "Not in this case it didn't, George."

"True," Rose had to agree. "But by the most incredible coincidence your name happened to be on the agenda the day we discussed M'Lord Cornwallis' reply to our request that he proceed with the utmost despatch to Bengal, before the French repeat their American meddling and align themselves with the more restless of our Indian princes."

"And?"

Rose smiled enigmatically. "A very wise and experienced man of the world, M'Lord Cornwallis. He said that he had no intention of being pitched from the saddle into the same thornbush which made Mr. Hastings' governorship such a vale of tears—the need to rule through a council of gentlemen whose only interest is to return home to England in the minimum possible time with the maximum personal profit. Can't say I blame him," Rose added. "And so matters rested. We would either squabble over details while what was left of the empire was hosed away down the gutter of time by the French, or we could agree to his lordship's terms."

"The full viceroy's commission."

"Correct. There was no other way we could budge him out of England. He simply would not move another inch unless he also took with him the absolute power to be a governor in fact, as well as a governor in name." Rose shrugged. "It wasn't easy, as you can imagine, but in the end he got everything he needed and almost everything he wanted."

"Hm. And what did Cabinet say when my letter came up for discussion?"

Rose pulled a weary face. "You have exactly the same plenipotentiary status, with a slightly different title, that's all. India and New Holland now share equal rank in our future plans. How can it be otherwise? With China they are the three legs of the same tripod: if one falls or is swept away, the other two will surely collapse and drag down our nation with them. It's that simple."

"Hm, well, I still think—"

Rose touched his friend's elbow. "Come along, Arthur, let's go inside, it's growing rather chilly out here."

Both men left the broad east terrace and stepped into one of Cuffnells' withdrawing rooms. A fire of last year's apple prunings had been lit under the marble mantelshelf above which hung a panorama of St. Mark's, Venice, a spread of painted canvas only a few inches smaller than many a warship's topgallant sail.

"You'll be staying the night, of course?" Rose asked.

Phillip glanced up, still warming his fingers at the blaze. "I would prefer to."

"We thought you might. Your room is always ready." Rose turned as another pair of doors swung apart and his wife entered, powdered hair piled high like Marie Antoinette's to emphasise an imagined resemblance to the reigning queen of France.

Phillip pointed a leg and bowed, remembering the hours when he had practised in front of a mirror while an anxious father hovered in the background, praying for the miracle that would strengthen his boy's singing voice until it could subsidise a language teacher's meagre tips and fees. *"Enchanté, madame. Aujourd'hui vous êtes vraiment 'La Vie en Rose.'"*

Theodora Rose also remembered life's earliest lessons, drilled into her by a Creole governess on her father's sugar plantation. Her curtsey was full but restrained as she smiled at the *galant* pleasantry. *"Pas de rien, m'sieur le capitaine."*

Her husband finished another scratch under his wig. *"Qu'est-ce que de seulement 'capitaine'?"* he queried, also lapsing into Europe's only language for higher diplomacy and statecraft. *"Alors, ma chère Dora, n'sais-tu que notre ami est maintenant le gouverneur et capitaine général du Botany Bay?"*

"Oui, maman!" young William interrupted, slapping his boot with a tiny riding whip. *"Oncle Arthur est aussi gouverneur d'une colonie absolument nouvelle!"*

"The Reverend Mr. Tancred," one of Cuffnells' footmen intoned from the doorway behind them. "And Mrs. Tancred."

Rose turned sharply. "Oh? How splendid. I didn't expect them quite yet, but no matter, no matter, we never stand on ceremony when we're at home, do we, my dear?" Rose looked for confirmation from his wife; then, to Phillip, "I do hope you won't mind it too much, but I took the liberty of inviting them over this evening. You see, I'm considering his appointment to the Commission of Justices, despite his unfortunate connexion with the Wilberforce Interest. I tell you, Arthur, after this latest scandal we're going to need as many sound J.P.s as possible on the bench."

"Scandal?"

"That's putting it mildly." Rose sniffed. "The very fabric of society is in peril once spiders like Burgoyne and Sheridan can openly manipulate Parliament to the advantage of such trollops as that—that Brandon woman. You've heard about it, of course?"

Phillip found it hard to remember anything but Admiralty paperwork these days. "Heard what, George?"

"How that Brandon bitch made complete monkeys of us all." Rose was still furious. "First she murders poor old Hardwicke's boy in cold blood, in front of a common playhouse audience, and then she perverts the course of justice to escape the consequences! By God, there have been some very angry gentlemen in the county since *she* got off the cart." Rose clenched his fist. "We must never allow such monstrous injustice again, or else the rabble will think we've gone soft, handing 'em a licence to pillage and plunder. Damned woman. Made monkeys of us all."

"Hm. I remember now," Phillip said. "A bad business."

"Is that the best you can say?" Rose snapped. "By God, your blood would've boiled to see the way she flaunted herself in court!"

Phillip's interest quickened. "Then you saw her tried?"

"Of course. I went up to Winchester especially for the assize. It was my duty to support the Hampshire Interest. Damned saucy bitch. Cool as you please. Blood on her hands, yet putting on airs as if *we* were only there at her command! By God, I've seen some hardened rogues in my time on the bench, but that harlot Brandon would beat 'em all for sheer effrontery." Rose scowled. "D'you know what she had the nerve to tell Parry, the presiding justice?"

"No."

The scowl darkened. "She told him to his face that, far from regretting her action, she would happily slay ten more Harry Hardwickes if they gave her occasion, and that if any gentleman now present in court gave her reason and a sword, she would prove it, promptly and with despatch!"

"Did she, by God!"

"Damned right she did."

Phillip carefully phrased the next question. "Is she as, oh, *interesting* as the gazette claimed?"

Rose shrugged irritably. "That class of woman has never been to my taste. Too flashy and pert by far, with too much to say for herself. She is only an actress, you know. And Irish to boot! Need I say more?"

"No-o, but they did say that her speech, before sentence was passed, was extraordinarily powerful and moving."

"Hm! I'll wager she wouldn't have been so glib delivering it from the back of a cart, with a halter round her neck. Insolent bitch. But enough of her, I don't wish to spoil dinner," Rose grunted, limping forward to greet Lyndhurst's vicar while Theodora lightly buffed rouge, cheek to cheek with the clergyman's wife.

The Reverend Mr Tancred disengaged himself from Rose and stalked forward, peering around for the guest of honour. "Ah, dear Captain Phillips, there you are. Such a delightful surprise. They tell me you are about to go upon your peregrinations again. Not Brazil this time, but the antipodes. '*Anti*,' or 'against,' and '*podes*,' or feet. You'll be standing upside down. That is why dear Dean Swift chose them to situate Brobdingnag and Lilliput when he reported Dr. Gulliver's travels."

Phillip made a puzzled smile. "Really?"

Tancred nodded. "Really. Do tell me what you're doing with yourself these days. Do you remember the altar cloth you brought back from South America? We have it still. Delightful stitchery. Such clever fingers they must all have—for papists. But no matter, Our Lord's ministry is worldwide. And now you've been called to labour in His vineyard at Botany Bay? An enchanting town—"

Theodora Rose laughingly gripped the clergyman's arm with fingers like a blacksmith's tongs. "Dear Mr. Tancred, please! Do allow His Excellency the governor to get in at least *one* word edgewise!"

Tancred blinked. "But I thought we were having such a marvellous conversation?"

Phillip smiled and made a bow. "There will be other opportunities to discuss the matters you've raised, as the evening wears on. Meanwhile, would you excuse me? I should like to rinse my hands before we dine." He turned and bowed again. "Theodora? Mrs. Tancred?"

Phillip's riding boots clicked on the Florentine tilework as he strode upstairs to the guest quarters, where, as Rose had promised, his room was always ready. Now there was a coal fire glowing in the hearth and an ewer of water on the wash stand by the windows. He stood by them, forehead pressing against a cool pane, feeling the months, the years, a lifetime of tension slowly dissolve away.

Crows were cawing down the night in a beech grove which surrounded Cuffnells' private lake with its cunningly aged ruins and hermit's grotto. Sunset was fading behind Emery Down, the sky erupting with volcanic reds and golds above the dark forest. There were few other estates so beautiful in all England, a fact which not only attracted guests like Phillip, but continued to delight the king. Lyndhurst was a royal manor, held by the Duke of Gloucester for his elder brother, and for at least two weeks of every year, life at Cuffnells was the heartbeat of the empire while His Majesty rode with deer hounds during the day and discussed Cabinet memoranda with Mr. Secretary Rose at night.

Phillip had been presented to His Majesty on many occasions over the years, and once, on an evening not unlike this one, both men had exchanged greetings on Lyndhurst hill, where Phillip had often gone alone to look across the New Forest and wistfully count sails on the Solent. The half-pay naval officer had scrambled to his feet and uncovered his head as the familiar, plump, slightly pop-eyed "Farmer George" dismounted and very civilly asked if he could borrow the spyglass for a few moments. A few moments which stretched into a quarter of an hour as the king peered through someone else's telescope and made penetrating remarks about the true state of his warships in the far distance. But no sea appointment had ever followed this chance encounter and, in the end, Phillip had returned to active service under Portuguese colours to fight a foreigner's war and to win a stranger's battles.

He sighed. Night was filling the room. He straightened away from the pane, lit a spill of twisted paper at the fire, touched a branch of candles and poured water.

13

"WHAT'LL IT BE, Arthur?" Rose beckoned him over to the sideboard as he returned to the blaze of light downstairs. "I've recently uncovered some capital Malaga in the cellars."

"Thank you." Phillip took the glass and saluted his friend across the rim. The Reverend Mr. Tancred had been cornered by Theodora Rose, leaving her husband free to speak of more weighty matters than altar cloths.

Rose also sipped wine, no longer the bluff country squire but now the most powerful government servant in Britain, master of the nation's wealth, answerable only to the first lord of the Treasury—William Pitt. He looked Phillip straight in the face. "Why the delay?"

"With the convoy?"

"What else?"

Phillip hesitated. "George, we are proceeding as fast as humanly possible, but hardly a thing has changed for the better since you left the navy. It is still the most dreadful muddle, really it is."

"Surely to God there must be *some* discernible improvement? I've booked two million for the Admiralty this year—virtually our entire tea revenue—and Sir Charles Middleton has been working like a hundred horses at the Navy Office to reform the dockyards since we got into power!"

"It's not that simple," Phillip replied. "Dockyard mateys and their lackadaisical civilian habits are only a trifling part of the overall problem. There remains the Board of Ordnance. Frankly, I doubt if anyone has told them which reign we're in, yet. And as if that weren't enough, I am at the beck and call of every puddle-hopping justice of the peace with a pack of whores his parish no longer needs." Phillip took another mouthful of the rich brown wine and warmed to his theme. "I tell you, that last batch of women had been on the road for nearly three weeks, marching down from Manchester in all weathers. Their sheer wretchedness must've made the stones weep as they passed over."

"Look, if we—"

"One moment, George," Phillip continued earnestly. "I am by no means finished. On top of all that I have to placate marine officers who resent being sent abroad to serve as gaolers, and conciliate merchant masters who defy any suggestions which might limit their private trading profits."

"One of whom is Duncan Sinclair," Rose warned.

"Yes. You know him?"

"Watch your back. He's as thick as thieves with Campbell o' the Sugar Interest. Need I say more?"

"Hardly!"

Phillip held out his glass for a refill, but Rose ignored him as he went on. "And need I say that we are both skating for our lives on extremely thin ice, vis-à-vis the whole question of transportation to New Holland?"

"Oh? How's that?"

Rose scowled at something unseen, something unwelcome. "As you are fully aware, there is a clique at Westminster which could cheerfully sink this whole enterprise at its moorings, blame our administration for its inability to float, then slit a few chosen throats upon the altar of Public Good."

Rose sipped wine. "Tommy Townshend's bought enough votes off the boroughmongers to dish them for the moment if it comes to a brawl in the Commons, but after this latest uproar over the Prince of Wales' debts and his light of love, Mrs. Fitzherbert, who knows how much longer we can control 'em?"

Rose drained his glass. "I still remember what it felt like when Shelburne took power and sold out to the Rebels in 'eighty-two: my rump hit the pavement in Whitehall so hard I couldn't sit down for months thereafter. I tell you this, if those Whig dogs can crucify Warren Hastings because of what they allege he did in India twenty years ago, where the devil does that put you and me in the here and now?"

Rose refilled his glass. "I never dreamed I'd live to see a day when the governor of Bengal—only the empire's financial keystone now that we've lost the American colonies!—when a nabob like Hastings could be put on public trial by swine like Fox, Burke and Sheridan." Rose's mouth tightened. "Such being the present state of affairs, my friend, neither of us can afford to relax our defences until *I* can go up that hill one morning and watch *you* disappearing into the Channel mists, out of sight if not out of mind, and far beyond the power of anyone to order you back. Understand?"

"Come now, George, surely matters have not reached that pitch yet?"

"Surely they're worse, if possible!"

Phillip reached for the decanter. "Well, barring a freak hurricane, or the pox, or simple war, I ought to get out of port within the next week."

"See that you do." Rose upended his own glass and signalled Phillip to leave the decanter stopper where it was. "Incidentally, I would never discount that last eventuality."

"Which? War?"

"Yes."

Phillip frowned. "How do you mean?"

Rose touched a finger to his lips. "*Mon ami,* whatever you hear or suspect tonight must forever be strictly *entre nous,*" he cautioned, reverting to French again as a footman walked past with a tray of predinner aperitifs for the ladies.

"*Mais naturellement,*" Phillip replied. "But I did not think we were ready for war yet?"

"Neither more are we, despite everything Middleton can do to launch more ships for us. But Paris can see that we are crowding on all sail to close the construction gap—particularly those new frigates off the Thames yards—and M. de Castries is said to be inflexibly determined to recapture Bengal for France before we reach parity at sea again."

"I know." Phillip sighed quietly. "A pity. In most other things *monsieur le maréchal* appears to be a reasonable enough man, but he does have this blind hatred of Britain and of all things British which tends to colour his judgment. He assured me of the fact himself, in so many words."

Rose blinked. "Did you actually meet him, over there?"

Phillip nodded. "Once. We exchanged a few words during a levee at their Admiralty office. Nothing more."

"And . . . ?"

Phillip shrugged. "Let us just say that he was rather more open, airing his opinions with Herr Doktor Mahler, an obscure German savant who happened to be applying for permission to collect fungi inside a naval base, than he would have been if he had known that I was also a British officer?"

Rose began chuckling. "If only I'd been there at your elbow! It would've been better than a seat at the opera to watch you hobnobbing with the Frogs' *ministre de la marine*!" He made a wry smile. "Unfortunately, those are pleasures which I am forever condemned to enjoy at second hand. Still, my friend, from what you've said and from what our other sources have reported, one can only sympathise with M. de Vergennes' impatience at having such a fire-eater as de Castries shaping policy from the same Cabinet table.

"For once I am in complete agreement with my opposite number on the other side of the Channel: both our nations are utterly bankrupt. But of the two, France has lost more by winning the American war than we have by losing it. Indeed, according to one well-placed informant, the French economy is in absolute tatters unless the Compagnie des Indes can show some profit for the nation's foreign creditors." Rose paused. "You heard, of course, that their bonds dropped another six points on the Frankfurt bourse last week?"

"No."

"Well, they have. And there's also talk of alloying more copper in this year's mintage of *louis*. As a gold piece it already looks uncommon queer and liable to turn green in damp weather," Rose added, swirling the wine in his glass. "God alone knows what the repercussions could be if they further debase the coinage. They could have trouble over there unless someone gets a grip on the public debt.

"Anyhow, it is Cabinet's opinion that everything now points to the French being in an extremely dangerous frame of mind for such a proud and volatile people. Regardless of how much Vergennes may personally urge peace until his treasury is replenished, I very much fear that de Castries' faction must soon carry the day and begin shipping matériel to the rajahs' armies, if only as a foreign circus to distract the bread rioters at home. And once *that* happens we're as good as finished." Rose tasted his wine and grimaced. "I suppose you know how much cable and canvas we now hold in store at Bombay to refit the Indian Squadron?"

"No, but I can guess."

"I'll bet you can't!" Rose replied. "Halve your first estimate, then halve it again. There is not enough sailcloth to resuit a single seventy-four. Neither are there more than twelve sticks suitable for bowsprits or main yards," Rose went on. "Goa teak may work for planks and frames, but only Baltic fir will ever do for a mast. Yet apart from the dozen or so I've just mentioned, India's replacements are still pickling in creosote at Gibraltar, ten thousand miles away."

"Good God."

"And that's not the worst of it, Arthur. Only this morning I got another express despatch from London: France has revived her wartime alliance with Holland. Three days ago they signed a 'defensive pact' with the republican faction in Amsterdam——"

"Surely not!"

"Surely so," Rose replied quietly. "By some means or another the *comptoir général* has scraped up a subsidy to buy those elements in Dutch public life who oppose the legitimate principle of monarchy. Once they succeed in toppling the crown of Holland, the Dutch fleet in Java will be ordered to join forces with the French squadron based on Mauritius to drive us from the Bay of Bengal. And when they do, they'll have rolled back the calendar to 'fifty-seven."

"But——!"

"Meanwhile," Rose continued in the same sombre tone, "France has been offered a twenty-five-year lease on the anchorage at Walcheren as security for their 'loan.' Once that is ratified we shall be in the unenviable position of a gentleman on the streets who finds himself with a loaded pistol aimed at his brains while a footpad relieves him of his watch, seals and pocketbook."

Phillip said nothing. This was one lesson in strategy which every British naval officer had to learn from his first day afloat: the same winds which bottled the Royal Navy at the mouth of the Thames would also drive an enemy across the Narrow Seas in a single night, cleared for action and holding the weather gauge.

Rose read Phillip's face. He swirled wine again. "Europe, the entire world, will change hands in only a few hours if we allow Paris to establish that naval base on the Schelde Estuary. We must never allow it. That will be the one battle our nation can never afford to lose, no matter what price we must pay. France? Yes, she can take another thrashing—as before— and rise again; for if we sank every ship she had, she would still remain a formidable land power on the Continent. But if the dice fell the other way and, God forbid, our battle line broke for only one-quarter of an hour off the Thames, then it would be all over. There will be no second chance for us. The empire's trade with the East would be lost forever, and with it any hope of ever rebuilding a navy greater than a mere coast guard directed by M. de Castries at his *ministère de la marine*. . . ."

Rose gnawed his lip, lost in thought. He looked up again. "Our culture would vanish within a generation. Our language would become a minor European dialect, a curiosity like Irish or Icelandic which others might study for their amusement. It would be the second Battle of Hastings."

Phillip cleared his throat. "So what are we doing?"

"Everything possible," Rose replied, still distracted by the future. "Even as we are standing here tonight, a courier is on his way to Berlin via Hamburg: Cabinet is offering half a million in gold once the Prussian army stops the Austrians from linking arms with their Bourbon cousins of France. Meanwhile, we shall blockade the Channel ports and stake everything on another victory like Quiberon Bay."

"Can we mobilise the fleet that quickly?"

"Middleton thinks so."

"In which case I shall lose *Sirius* and *Supply*."

"Yes, for the moment. However, I shall make certain you get a seventy-four to command."

"And the governorship of Botany Bay?"

Rose shrugged his shoulders. "One of Dame History's many stillborn infants. Speaking of which, and harking back to our opponents in Paris, I seriously doubt the mental stability of Louis' current advisers."

Phillip frowned, trying to see the connexion with Botany Bay and the defence of Britain's eastern empire. "Why?"

Rose shrugged again. "Twice in the same decade they have urged him to commit *l'armée royale* to win victories for a republican rabble. First he did it in the American colonies, now in Holland; where next, I wonder? For the life of me I cannot see what the king of France hopes to gain by chopping away the rungs of a ladder which bears him aloft as much as it supports every other crowned head in Europe."

"Hm. A good point. Do you think it could ever amount to anything more serious than bread riots?"

Rose's shoulders slumped. "Who can tell? You are much better acquainted with life across the Channel than I, but in *my* opinion the scene is being set for incalculable mischief unless the hotter heads in their government are quickly cooled. Speaking for ourselves, Arthur, let us hope that France outgrows her current enthusiasm for novel forms of government; there are sufficient jokers in this shuffle without anyone cutting more to further stack the odds against us. But enough of such gloomy matters for the moment; we are about to be called to dine." Rose finished his drink, bowed to the vicar's wife and reverted to English again. "Mrs. Tancred. Permit me the honour."

Her husband leaned on Theodora Rose's arm and fell in behind the first couple. Phillip exchanged bows with William Rose, now being groomed in adult courtesies before being sent to Westminster School like his father before him, then up to Oxford, like his elder brother. The young boy matched paces with Phillip and they followed into Cuffnells' dining hall.

Dinner had been laid in front of the open hearth. Rose stood behind his chair, smiling round with satisfaction, proud of the style he could now afford. "Vicar? Would you favour us with Grace?"

Tancred beamed back. "Deeply honoured! Such simple words are, of course, a living token of our Dear Saviour's Last Supper in which He broke bread and gave blessing to His—"

"*Grace.*"

"Oh. Ah. Look down upon this humble board with loving care, dear Lord—"

"Amen."

Rose adjusted the chair for Mrs. Tancred and sat down, signalling the servants to move forward with a large game pie, dressed with hardboiled eggs round the upper crust, and a side of fresh salmon from Rose's other estate, on the coast at Christchurch. He glanced at Phillip. "What'll it be, Arthur? Claret? Burgundy? Médoc?"

"Claret."

"A sound choice: it has an impeccable pedigree." Rose turned, snapping his fingers. "Two of Mr. Pitt's bottles for Governor Phillip and myself. And something for the vicar."

Phillip had seated himself next to young William, now watching the adults and copying them exactly. Rose passed over a generous bumper of his own claret for the boy to practise upon. William cleared his throat and looked up at Phillip's profile. "Mr. Tancred declares that you may indeed discover a tiny empire with soldiers no taller than a handspan."

Phillip looked down. "I beg pardon?"

William rephrased his question. "Mr. Tancred says that it is highly probable an island such as Lilliput really exists off the coast of Van Demons Land, just as Dr. Gulliver's map shows, and that you must pass close by on your way to the an—, an—, oh, damn."

"Antipodes?"

"Yes."

Phillip also chose his words with care as he reached for a serving of salmon. "I've heard tell of the book to which you refer, though I cannot say I've had an opportunity to study it yet. However, ought we to believe anything just because it is printed? Remember, the proof of the pudding is in its eating. And so it is with stories of midget soldiers on South Sea islands."

Phillip licked his fingers and genteelly wiped them on the tablecloth, watching the boy's troubled frown. "Let me put it another way. I shall believe what I've been told about New Holland after I've seen it, not before. That way I shan't build up my expectations too high, only to tumble down thereafter."

But the boy was still troubled by something. "Mr. Tancred says there are scores and scores and scores of islands, and cities, and peoples in the world, all awaiting civilisation's discovery. Surely that is not impossible, is it?"

Phillip smiled kindly. "Now we are debating a fresh problem, young William. Your six-inch warriors belong to one class of items: islands and unknown peoples are in an altogether different category."

"Then it is possible?"

"Ye-es, in the unknown anything within reason is possible; but are such discoveries likely? I really don't know. Of course, I shall be keeping a sharp lookout for evidence of civilisation among the antipodean Indians. After all, the Caribs whom the Spaniards first saw were mere naked savages too. Yet all the while, only a hundred leagues inland, beyond the mountains, were great cities of gold. That must've been a wonderful sight, don't you think?"

"Mmm!"

"Thus might it be for our expedition," Phillip added, reaching for his bottle of claret. "Meanwhile, since Botany Bay appears to be on nearly the same line of latitude as Tahiti—described by travellers as an 'earthly paradise'—we might yet find a second Eden in New Holland and have no further need for Dr. Gulliver's marvellous little men. What do you think of that?"

"I—I must confess that I really do not know," William replied, copying Phillip exactly by toying with his own glass stem. "And yet you *did* say there could be undiscovered islands off Van Demons Land, just a little bit like Lilliput?"

Phillip smiled. "I give you my word of honour that I'll keep my weather eye cocked and let you know when—or if—I ever see Lilliput."

The vicar's wife had been leaning her bosom across the table, trying to distract Phillip's attention her way. "*Dear* Captain Phillips!"

"Your servant, ma'am?"

"I could not help overhearing something of your remarks concerning the possibility of the discovery of civilisation among the naked savages of New Holland—"

"You couldn't?"

"And I must confess that it troubles our conscience, too!" she galloped on. "But can one really speak of *civilisation* being found in any part of the globe which has, hitherto, been denied the Light of the Gospel's message?"

"Ma'am?"

Mrs. Tancred damped her lips. "Surely, captain, such peoples—no matter how cunningly they shape their wicked idols and build their blood-stained temples—surely they remain heathen, don't they?"

"I must confess that I really haven't given much thought to it recently, ma'am."

Dorcas Tancred looked baffled. "But isn't that the reason why dear Reverend Mr. Johnson is accompanying you as bishop designate of New Holland? To gather in Our Lord's harvest of souls among the lost tribes of Indians?"

Phillip studied his wineglass. He looked up again. "I have heard Mr. Johnson being called many things in the past few months, but this is the first time anyone has promoted him to the rank of bishop."

"Oh. But Mr. Wilberforce has so described him to one of our most devoted friends and colleagues. I thought—?"

Phillip's finger silenced her. "Ma'am, you must remember that I am only a simple sailorman and so cannot presume to speak for Mr. Wilberforce or any other of your Society for Promoting Christian Knowledge. However—please allow me to finish—I was under the impression that only His Majesty could appoint bishops."

"Damn' right, Arthur!"

The vicar's wife looked perplexed. "But at our very last meeting, after giving prayers that the black slaves might yet throw off their shackles, we offered up joyful hearts that our Mr. Johnson should have been called to till the Lord's Vineyard as bishop of New Holland."

"I'm sure he must appreciate the compliment," Phillip observed. "But for the moment he remains a plain naval chaplain with my permission to weed God's garden among seven hundred souls aboard the convoy."

"How many, Arthur?"

Phillip glanced across the table. "About seven hundred effectives, with yet more on the road, I'm told. Doubtless a few will also be departing to claim their eternal reward before we make sail."

"That's not very many, is it?" George Rose asked, absentmindedly scratching under his wig, then laying the fork down while he reached for his glass again. "I mean, considering the labour which awaits them at the other end . . . ?"

Phillip pulled a face. "Please don't remind me! But if you think that's all, remember that our figures double when we add civil officers, guards and ships' crews. We'll be damned lucky to clear the Channel with fewer than fourteen hundred mouths to feed. All of which means that, at three man-rations *per diem per caput,* I shall have to supply better than four thousand issues of sustenance every twenty-four hours.

"Now," he added, warming to the giddy arithmetic of provisioning a sailing fleet, "assuming one hundred and fifty days at sea, not counting time at Rio and the Cape, that comes to—" Phillip wrote imaginary sums on his plate with the knife point, then looked back across the table. "That comes to something over half a million rations, not including spoilage, and we shall only just have arrived at Botany Bay. True, I am assured by Sir Joseph that we shall find fertile soil, but not even he can promise me any edible vegetation awaiting our first dinner."

"Meaning?"

"Meaning that I shall then have to fill those same fourteen hundred empty bellies from government stores until the first harvest, which, almost certainly, will *not* be our first year of settlement." Phillip looked down at his knife point, then up again at Rose. "Two million, eight hundred thousand."

"Beg pardon?"

"I said, in addition to all our other impedimenta, the animals, their feeds, the guns and ammunition, our spare rigging and six hundred thousand sea rations, we also have casked another three million meal equivalents for our time ashore. The human cargo is being stowed wherever it will fit."

"By God, I haven't considered it that way before."

"Believe me, George, I have. Often."

Rose might be smiling, but the Reverend Mr. Tancred most certainly was not. "Gentlemen. I fear we depart from the subject of our conversation, which is the current state of moral darkness in New Holland." He frowned severely at Phillip. "Am I to interpret your foregoing remarks as indicating a certain, ah, laxity on the question of bringing the Gospel light to native peoples?"

Phillip liked to pretend that he was rather hazy about landmen's affairs: in fact, he had never underestimated the evangelical cobweb which certain members of Parliament were casting over Westminster, or their power to unmake appointments which displeased certain merchant interests. He smiled distantly at a vicar who was on first-name terms with the M.P. for Hull, William Wilberforce. "Dear Mr. Tancred, please do not misunderstand my meaning. In God's good time we shall attend to the Indians, but first of all I must obey my instructions from His Majesty."

"Which are?"

"Why, the establishment of a self-supporting penal colony in New

South Wales, one which will not only cleanse our towns of all moral filth and physical danger, but also be capable of clothing, feeding, defending and in all other ways providing for itself while performing the task of reformation among the insubordinate and rebellious. And with a minimum of cost to Treasury," he added, for Rose's benefit.

Tancred's frown had not eased. "Of course, we understand all that, but does this indicate that you have given no thought to the welfare of the native peoples?"

"On the contrary! I am most concerned that we establish our authority without any ill-feelings from the indigenes." Phillip looked around at the others, who had now fallen silent and were listening intently. "I really am, you know. I am absolutely determined that we not repeat the errors which Spain, for example, made when she colonised her new world of Mexico and Peru—"

"Papists!"

"Er, true," Phillip agreed. "But cannot we learn from another's mistakes after reflecting upon them over an interval of some two hundred years? I believe we can. And I believe we can make Britain's civilising mission a model of tolerance and mutual understanding, as it ought to be between gentlemen." He paused, waiting for contradiction, but there was none. "I shall give orders that no native Indian is to be molested in any way. If any of our number do, or steal the Indians' property, then he will hang just as swiftly as if it had been an Englishman's home he had violated. Remember: the law is at her most merciful when she appears to be merciless."

"That's the way, Arthur."

Phillip nodded. "I shall do everything possible to give the Indians the highest possible opinion of their guests. I am informed that hatchets and beads are highly esteemed. Sir Joseph has also told me that when they use a light, they hold it in their hands, so small tin lamps ought to be very welcome." Phillip sipped wine. "I repeat, the Indians must have the highest opinion of us, for which purpose it will be necessary to limit the transports' crews from having intercourse with the natives. The convicts, it need hardly be said, must have none at all. For if they do—which God forbid —the women will be abused and their husbands' weapons turned against us."

"That's a pretty tall order you've set yourself," Rose commented. "I mean, keeping the women and men from getting up to any, well, *you* know—hanky-panky."

"Agreed. It will not be easy, but it must be done," Phillip replied briskly. "Once ashore in New Holland I shall order an earthwork to be thrown up at some convenient location, as a defence against any disaffected Indians and to secure our stores against the convicts." He sipped more wine and judged his audience, now sitting forward on their chairs, eager to hear everything possible about this expedition to the far side of the planet.

"I shall then emplace some of *Sirius'* cannon, here," Phillip went on, setting down his glass inside a small square of forks and spoons, borrowing from William to finish the diagram and clearing the table for everyone else to see.

"Here, here and here will be ramparts, facing inland. Here is the beach where we shall build a stone landing jetty and another breastwork against the French. These corks are eighteen-pounders and here is the magazine, the first stage of the fortress which we shall build to guard the harbour mouth.

"Meanwhile, here, here and here I shall plant maize fields, perhaps with yams and sweet potatoes similar to those which feed your labour in the West Indies," he added, glancing at Theodora Rose. "Over here, by the salt cellar, will be the first trial plantation of flax. When grown and harvested, it will be dressed at a mill on this river, here, and woven up into sailcloth, here, close to the timber mill, which manufactures spars and planks from the trees being floated downstream, here, for the dockyard and careening beach, here."

"Hm. Ingenious, Arthur," Rose had to admit. "But I am deuced if I can see how any of this will protect the native women from the more depraved of our, ah, 'colonists.'"

Phillip smiled as he sat back in his chair. "I thought you'd ask that, George. However, I do have an answer, for it is necessary to have the matter settled before we go ashore."

"Agreed."

"Now, you must first remember that we shall have about two hundred women of our own kind—"

"Fourteen, take away two." Rose glanced up from his own knife point. "That still leaves you with twelve hundred men and a ratio of six-to-one against the fair sex. Pushing our luck a bit hard, aren't we?"

"You mean squabbles over who gets which and when?" Phillip enquired delicately, sensitive to others' ears around the table.

"I mean bloody murder!"

"Oh, I think not, George, I think not. Indeed, it will be best if the most abandoned of our women—all of whom are sluts and whores of the most disgusting class—if these women were set apart and allowed to receive the visits of such as need their favours, at certain hours and under certain conditions, the way they do at the Bridewell. Meanwhile," he added, "the rest of the women, those of a better temper and of a more submissive disposition, could be kept in another place and, by allowing the men to be in their company when not actually at work, they ought, I suppose, to marry."

"You *seriously* think so, Arthur?"

"Of course. The Reverend Mr. Johnson will have my approval to join together all of the convict class who ask for the blessed sacrament of marriage. Indeed, I feel I ought to encourage marriage as a stabilising influence upon the colony and as a cure for certain, ah, human depravities."

"And these other women?" Rose enquired, pointing to Phillip's plan among the silverware. "The ones too abandoned, etcetera, etcetera?"

Young William had been following the adults' conversation, as he was intended to. It was his turn to nod and point like his father. "But surely, captain, aren't we discussing the establishment of a bordello?"

"Ohh!"

Phillip glanced at Dorcas Tancred's heaving bosom, then back at his young neighbour again. "Yes, we are, but only in a manner of speaking. It will be a temporary expedient which will, as time passes, become less necessary. For we must always face facts, no matter how disagreeable they may be. Transporting thieves from England to New Holland will, I hope, reform them into useful artisans, but some human failings cannot be reformed by distance alone."

"Quite so," the young boy agreed.

"Such being the case," Phillip continued, "I think it probable, if we proceed cautiously and win their confidence, that we might persuade the Indian kings to trade their surplus women with us, to come and live with our men after a certain time. As for the soldiers of the garrison, Sir Joseph suggests that we try recruiting women in Brazil, but I think that somewhat ambitious for the moment—"

"Popery?" Mr. Tancred queried.

"Er, yes, among other things," Phillip agreed. "I rather imagine we ought to look at Tahiti in the Friendly Islands, establish some kind of commerce, and bring back such women as are willing to come. They could be supported on government rations for a while until they've learned our customs and language, then they could be given a plot of ground and be allowed to marry—but only after being examined for signs of the clap, of course."

"Ohh!"

"Hm," Rose observed, following his friend's plan among the jumble of cutlery and corks. "I must admit you've covered most of the points, Arthur. A brilliant scheme."

Phillip made a modest smile. "Thank you, George. The simple fact of the matter is that the laws of this country, this England of ours, become effective in New South Wales the moment my commission is read and our formal possession taken of the colony. Consequently, as there can be no slavery in a free land such as ours, there cannot be any illegal coercion of the individual or introduction of slaves from outside. It will be a new world."

"Then who the deuce will labour?" Theodora Rose asked, with a grate of irritation in her voice.

"Initially? The transportees, ma'am."

His friend's wife was far from convinced. "Really? And do you seriously think that people of that class are *able*, let alone willing, to work?"

Phillip smiled. "Privation is an amazing schoolmaster. People may only pay lip service to the nation's laws, but they will always obey the pangs of hunger."

"How do you mean?"

"I control the commissary and stores," Phillip replied quietly. "Rations will be drawn only for those who show the proper spirit of labour and sub-ordination. The rest may shift for themselves on an alien landscape. I'll wager that within a fortnight of landing, we shall have them eating from our hands in every sense of the phrase."

Theodora Rose was far from convinced by his argument. "I do not doubt that hunger will reduce them without delay, but what of their crude animal capacity to work in the first place?"

"I'm not sure I quite understand you, ma'am?"

"It's really quite elementary, you know," Theodora Rose replied. "Many are the times I've ridden around my father's property on Antigua. I imagine that the climate is similar to yours in Botany Bay, and, I assure you, it can be rather fatiguing. Yet it is nothing to see three or four hundred blacks cheerfully cutting cane while another two or three score boil the syrup in temperatures which would make an Englishman—of whatever class—swoon."

"Slaves!" the vicar's wife snapped, forgetting herself in the heat of the moment.

"Not entirely," the squire's wife corrected. "For if that were the case, then so are the mules and oxen which are also working components of a plantation's economy. And I have yet to hear anyone seriously suggesting that we in England now throw away our whips, leap between the shafts and pull our 'freed' horses whither they will us to go."

She looked back at Phillip's amused smile. "Arthur. You have been to the West Indies. Can you really see the likes of, oh, that Dan Patchett—"

"I necked him for poaching the other week," her husband explained. "A bad lot."

Theodora Rose began again. "Arthur. In your experience of the world as it *is*, not as we would like it to be, can you imagine seven hundred Dan

Patchetts labouring day in, day out, growing anything but indolent beneath a tropic sun?"

Phillip toyed with his wineglass stem. "Frankly, I don't know."

"*Don't know?*" she repeated softly. "Then does not your enterprise resemble a dunce hat set upside down in the classroom corner, a paper cone wobbling upon its apex? For every fine plan you have described thus far is contingent upon you at least managing to feed your infant colony by its own sweat and toil, without aid from anyone else."

Phillip looked up from the wineglass. "You're right."

"Of course I'm right," Theodora Rose said and smiled, pursuing this friendly discussion with all the ruthless energy which had advanced her husband to the Board of Treasury during their escape from a debt-ridden plantation on the dark shadowline of empire. "Such being the case, do you seriously consider that seven hundred Dan Patchetts are able, let alone willing, to work that hard for their masters?"

"Oh, Dora! For Heaven's sake, what a question!" Rose snapped.

Phillip raised his hand to silence him. "On the contrary, George, I couldn't have said it better myself. However, we must never lose sight of the fact that all this is only a temporary expedient, a draft or two of white niggers to get us started in the colony until regular trade can be opened with the black kings of New Holland for their surplus.

"I mean," he went on fairmindedly, "it makes more sense to ship out a cargo of, oh, musket flints and tinplate to buy a thousand field hands in prime condition than to go to all this expense of transporting a handful of surly white derelicts halfway around the world. They're hardly the most robust specimens now: God only knows what shape they'll be in after another eight or nine months at sea."

"You'll still need to apply the necessary stimulants, whatever their skin colour," Theodora Rose observed.

"Sticks and carrots, ma'am, sticks and carrots," Phillip countered. "I shall have an open hand for those who show the proper spirit. Let any man prove that he can reform himself by work, and remain sober, and I shall wipe the slate clean so that he can begin again, far from the temptations which brought him low in the first place. He shall have rations, his freedom within reason and sufficient land to till."

"But what if he does not?" Theodora Rose enquired drily.

Phillip's mouth tightened. "The same hand will close around the stick. It is a principle we understand well in the navy, ma'am." He glanced around the table. "Such a remark may seem heartless to us while we sit here in peace and security, but all such fine feelings blow away when a gale is bearing down and great seas are bursting across our bows.

"It is then a commander must order his men onto the topmost yards, often in pitch darkness and blinding snow, shortening sail as the masts pitch and yaw like mad things. Even the stoutest heart feels naked terror at such a time, but we must fear our captain's wrath even more, or else all is lost.

"Seen from the quarterdeck of a man o' war, one's opinions of mankind are much simplified: we either learn to haul together, or we sink together, and anyone who thinks otherwise is swiftly brought to reason. But there I go, preaching again!" Phillip added with a deprecating smile as he reached for his glass.

"On the contrary, Arthur," Rose said, reaching across the table to top up his son's drink. "I'd rather Billy learned about the real world from you than imbibed the pious piffle which nowadays passes for knowledge."

He sat back. "Now, concerning your earlier statements. I fancy you'll have plenty of opportunity to perfect this natural philosophy at Botany Bay; however, *entre nous,* though sticks and carrots may work well enough among shellbacked sailormen, can you see them working among the sort of items I've had paraded before the Bench?" Rose shook his head. "Some are very intractable, the kind who, had they been stallions, we should have gelded long ago. But of course we can't, not any more. But neither can we permit 'em to rampage upon decent society without curb or rein. Such being the case, do you *really* see any number of carrots placating such animals?"

Phillip considered the question. "Yes, I do. If we persevere I am sure it will. Remember, we shall be in novel surroundings, quite unlike those of our own country. I—I hope that a sentence of death will never be necessary in New Holland. The dreadful isolation, coupled with the fact that I control the supply of drink and victuals, ought to bring all but a raving lunatic to his senses."

"Hm. I wish you luck," Rose said. "But my experience of dispensing justice cautions me against placing too much faith upon novel forms of punishment. As you said only a moment ago, when it's haul together or sink together, a coil of hemp is wonderfully effective!"

Phillip smiled. "Point taken, George, but let us at least *try* to devise new incentives for a new land?"

Theodora Rose had finished wiping her toothpick on the tablecloth. "This may be all very well in theory, gentlemen, but what of the facts o' the matter? Aren't we forgetting the vital pinch of salt which must go with our, ah, carrots?"

"Ma'am?"

"I speak of the need to anticipate disobedience and then disarm it," she replied. "Believe me, on Antigua we never underestimate the field hands' capacity for mischief once returned to their barracoons for the night.

These are the times when one needs intelligencers, men and women who will, for their own profit and the general good, report secret oathings and combinations against their masters."

"Spies, ma'am?"

"Call 'em what you will, Arthur; *I* say that rebellion is like fire, best stamped out before it gets too great a hold."

Phillip filled his glass and looked up again. "You see spies as a proper part of any regime of rewards and incentives?"

"Of course. Pick at least one person from each work gang—better you pick two or three so that they can watch each other—and let them know that their reward—and their punishment—will be in direct proportion to their loyalty and powers of observation."

"Hm. An interesting concept, ma'am."

"Arthur?" Theodora Rose went on. "When you have been keeping labour docile for as long as we have, you will also discover that the only reliable methods are the proven methods. Remember, back home we are often outnumbered by hundreds to one, and our estates generally stand isolated from the island's main garrison. Not one of us has ever forgotten what happened on San Domingue when their field hands combined in revolt."

"Oh, Dora!" her husband snapped again. "Not in New South Wales, not in a British colony!"

"No-o?" she replied, emptying her glass and clicking her fingers for a servant to refill it. "We shall see who's right after Arthur has tried putting seven hundred Dan Patchetts to work, all items of very dubious pedigree. I doubt if many days will elapse before he does as we all do."

Phillip made a tired face. "Well, ma'am, let us hope you are mistaken about New Holland, though I do see the point you are making."

The mantel clock began chiming behind the Tancreds, still wrapped in a frosty silence, and Theodora Rose drained her glass. "I'm for bed. No doubt you and Arthur will want to share a pipe while you discuss affairs of state: I'll see that our guests are lit to their quarters for the night."

She turned from her husband and sank a deep curtsey. *"Bonne nuit, m'sieur le gouverneur et capitaine général de la Nouvelle Hollande."*

Phillip also stood and smiled back, hand on heart, as he bowed. *"Avec tout mon coeur, ma chère madame."*

His friend's wife straightened and, in English this time, made a loud stage whisper. "So why don't you marry again? Silly goose! 'Od's blood, I could name half a dozen *very* eligible consorts for a colonial governor." She smile archly. "Think about it. . . ."

14

PHILLIP'S CHUCKLE faded as she swept from the hall and both doors were closed behind her. "Never stops trying, does she?"

Rose had limped over to a sideboard. He glanced round, holding a crystal decanter in one hand, two cut-glass goblets in the other. "You ought to know my Dora by now: she'll never stop matchmaking until she sees you as happy as I am."

"Ah, if only it were that easy. . . ." Phillip had gone round the table and was kicking a fresh log into the hearth, watching sparks fountain up the chimney breast.

"Why not, in Heaven's name?"

Phillip said nothing for a moment. "Because they don't make many like Theodora in any one generation and I'm getting too old to wait for the next batch to pop from the oven."

"But if they did, would you . . . ?"

Phillip looked up. "What was it I read recently: 'a second marriage is the victory of hope over experience'?"

" 'Triumph,' " Rose corrected, limping back to pour a reserved vintage which shimmered like liquid rubies in the warm firelight. " 'Second marriage is the triumph of hope over experience.' But you evade the question, *would* you marry again if Dora did the necessary?"

"Perhaps." Phillip took the glass and savoured it. "Perhaps, if she were still young enough to bear us children. And if she had a gentle voice. And a mild temper." He hesitated. "And if there weren't always the shadow of Lotte between us."

"Oh, that's no problem," Rose announced, eyes shut, sipping his port, relaxed and at ease with the world. "We can easily arrange for something to happen that will turn your separation into a more permanent condition."

Phillip shook his head. "It wouldn't be fair, George. We can't ask her to rake over cold ashes in court. Besides, I'm told she's not in very good health these days." Phillip kicked the log again and began kicking off his riding boots as well, letting stockinged feet toast near the blaze, toes wriggling. "What a mess it all was, George, what an utter mess. Still, it's been over for a long time."

"Eighteen years."

"That long?" Phillip stared into the flames. "I suppose it must be. Eighteen years? God, how time flies. I might have been a grandfather by now. But Lotte could not, or would not, and whenever I raised the matter she'd have an attack of the vapours and vanish for another couple of months to purge her spleen by taking the waters at Cheltenham." Phillip paused. "You're a lucky devil, George: two fine sons to bear your name and plenty of time yet to see grandchildren. They're a credit to both of you."

"Oh, fair to middlin', fair to middlin'," Rose had to agree with quiet pride. "George seems to be doing well for himself up at Oxford; mark my words, there's a good head on his shoulders. But young Billy is a bit harder to fathom, takes after Dora's father, too dreamy at times for his own good. Don't misunderstand me," Rose added quickly. "The boy doesn't have a slate loose, nothing like that, but he does tend to daydream rather a lot."

"Is that really such a bad thing?" Phillip asked.

Rose scratched, thinking it over. "I suppose it will all depend on what he plans doing with himself. As a man of affairs, following me into the Treasury, it could be a deuced handicap."

"So perhaps he'll steer some different course through life? Perhaps we're all fated to disappoint our parents?" Phillip added with a wry smile. "My father always wanted me to be a *Kantor*, a singer as his father had been, and not become a teacher as he was. So what happens? I am a British sailor!"

Rose nodded gloomily. "You're probably right, Arthur, so few things ever go according to plan. Damned if I can see where it will lead Billy. True," he added, rallying to defend the boy, "he don't write a bad fist and he seems to have a bit of a knack with languages, but it's damned hard to see what a gentleman can do with those skills alone."

"Time will tell." Phillip smiled. "As the dons like to say, '*En cien años todos serán calvos,*' 'One hundred years from now we'll all be bald.' "

"Nicely put!" Rose chuckled. "Now, how about a pipe . . . ?"

"Why not?" Phillip stood to save his friend's leg and fetched a sheaf of pipes and a tobacco jar from the sideboard. Rose took one, tamped leaf into the clay bowl and snapped off an inch of mouthpiece to make a clean stem, then tweezed a hot coal from the hearth.

He eased back in his chair and drew fragrant warmth, fondling the jar, letting his fingers trace round the stiff outline of a Shawmut Indian incised on the pottery lid. "Seems like yesterday when I bought this in Boston, Arthur; the shopkeeper wanted three shillings for it, but I got him down to a couple of bob in the end. Had to." Rose drew smoke and shut eyes. "I was only a middie and couldn't afford one penny more. 'What a cheap little curio! Chuck it out!' I suppose the boys will say one day as they divide the inheritance, but during my life I wouldn't have swapped it for the Garter and a seat in the House of Lords. . . ." Rose fell silent for several moments before continuing, "They were good times, Arthur, the best. We'll not see their like again. D'you remember how we used to keep it up at that tavern on the corner of King Street and Mackrell Lane, near 'Mount Whoredom'?"

"The Bunch of Grapes?" Phillip chuckled around his pipe stem.

"Aye, the Grapes! God knows where the landlord found such tearaways for serving maids! I mean, all *that* and a sixpenny bowl of punch big enough to float a frigate. . . ." Rose slowly puffed smoke. "What was the chorus they used to belt out? 'Let sailors come, let sailors go, and carry home belief, that Boston Gals are ever served, by a yard o' Yankee Beef!' "

Phillip nodded quietly. "We'll not see their like again, either."

Rose went on fondling the tobacco jar. "It's a long time ago, my friend; this little thing must've been with me since, oh, 'fifty-nine?"

Phillip wafted smoke at the fireplace. "And so has that knee. You ought to rest it more."

Rose grimaced. The truth was there had been no peace in his right leg since the day it stopped a shell splinter aboard the bomb ketch HMS *Infernal,* duelling with a French shore battery north of Quiberon Bay. It had been just enough war service to make him a veteran and one of the Royal Navy's elect—like his friend, now sitting across the warm firelight, eyes shut—one of Hawke's squadron when it annihilated the French Atlantic fleet as night fell and a November gale bore down the Breton coast.

His career at sea had stopped dead that wintry afternoon. There would be no more racing up the ratlines to the foretop. And no more nimble stepping along the airy yards with his men. There would be nothing. Only dry papers. And a scratching quill. And the sombre tock-tick-tock of the Cabinet room clock at three in the morning. And the halting echo of his limp along empty corridors as dawn broke over London.

Phillip had reached for the coal tongs and was drawing on his pipe again. "You"— puff—"are quite serious about the risk"—puff—"of war this time round?"

"Yes. Dammit. Why?"

Phillip glanced sideways. "Because I already have enough uncertainties aimed at my head without any more joining the crowd."

Rose tasted the rich Virginia flake, held it for several seconds, then let it escape. "Something worrying you?"

Phillip studied pipe bowl, then nodded. "Yes. The alleged state of His Majesty's health."

"Oh? And why should that concern us now?"

Phillip watched the brown splotches of age on the backs of his hands. "As you said earlier this evening, the Prince of Wales' friends are baying for one colonial governor's head: where else might they turn for their sport if he becomes prince regent, too?"

"Hmm, a reasonable concern," Rose conceded from the depths of his chair, eyes hooded again. "However, point one: if Fox's pack of dogs make government, then *I* am the one whose arse hits the pavement first and goes bouncing all the way down Whitehall, not you. Point two: I don't consider His Majesty to be as sick as some would like us to believe."

"No? But I thought he'd been seen talking to the trees?"

Rose examined his pipe. "Have you never discussed the pros and cons of this and that with yourself whenever you thought nobody else was looking? I have." Phillip kept silent as Rose went on. "Besides, our Farmer George is much tougher in his body and mind than is generally supposed."

"You should know."

"Yes, I suppose I should. I have seen H.M. tire three horses in the chase and still be game for more while men half his age were reeling with fatigue." Rose glanced up. "Oh, I know there's still a lot of carping about the American business: 'Why didn't General Clinton do this?' And, 'Why didn't M'Lord North do that?' And, 'Why didn't His Majesty do everything for everybody at the same time?' But crying over spilt milk never ran it back into the jug.

"Thus, as a nation, we must now brace ourselves to brave whatever the future may bring," Rose went on. "It will be the next few months, not the last ten years, which will decide if we are to continue our descent into the valley of the shadow or, by our own exertions and courage, regain the sunlit uplands of empire. God alone in His wisdom knows what lies in wait for us this time. History alone will tell what manner of men we were when all the world worked for our destruction. But of one thing I am certain: we shall fight. We shall fight them at sea, we shall fight them on land, we shall fight them to our last cartridge, we shall fight them to our last shilling, we shall never surrender."

"And His Majesty?" Phillip prompted quietly.

Rose's frown had not eased. "Those are his sentiments as much as they are Mr. Pitt's words, which is why I shall never be ashamed to say that I like the man as much as I respect the king." Phillip's head had cocked to one side. "That ought not to surprise you, Arthur, for close up he is much as we are. He breathes, he sweats, and to judge from the size of his family—eleven children—he enjoys life with huge gusto.

"His Majesty is also a man of sound character, despite all the petty gossip you may hear, for he is a man of his word," Rose went on, staring into the firelight. "Let him but say he will do a thing and you may be sure he will or burst in the attempt. I have always found him constant and true in his friendship, something which I personally esteem and strive to return in fullest measure. In brief, I have always found His Majesty to be an English gentleman, and one can say no more than that of anyone."

Phillip nodded thoughtfully. "But what of the Prince of Wales . . . ?"

Rose glanced up and hung a smoke ring overhead. "Now, concerning the French. You ought to keep them in mind at all times, of course, but if the fleet is mobilised and as a consequence you lose *Sirius* and *Supply,* we'll see you get a seventy-four to command. Let the war run for any time and thin the Captains' List and you'll be in line for a squadron. Just think of the prize money in that, eh? It will be infinitely more than anyone will ever win at Botany Bay and there could easily be a knighthood in the box with your name on it. . . ."

Phillip smiled but slowly shook head. "I want New South Wales, New Holland, Botany Bay, whatever we finally agree to call the place, nothing else."

"Uh? Even more than your own squadron?"

Phillip hesitated, then nodded. "Yes. I need that governorship even more than a line of battleships crowding on sail behind me, my broad pennant flying aloft and the entire enemy fleet trapped on a lee shore."

Rose pulled a very long face. "May an old friend ask why?"

Phillip made time to think by reloading his pipe. "Shall we just say that I know my limitations?"

"What limitations?"

Phillip looked up sharply. "George, I have spent more time ashore, daydreaming of glory, than I ever put into sea work. There are others, many others, far more experienced than I in the evolutions of gunnery, of patrolling a blockade, the basic skills of higher command. No, please, don't interrupt," he went on, raising a finger.

"Some while ago I met a couple of young chaps—both still lieutenants—yet both had already sailed around the globe since they joined the service as boys. One is about to do so again while the other has actually been at sea for twenty of his thirty years. What they don't know about seamanship would not cover my fingernail. Compared with such men I am nothing more than an old fossil with the rather eccentric habit of joining navies for short periods of his life."

"Don't be hard on yourself," Rose grunted. "People who matter know what you've been doing behind the scenes."

"I am not being hard on myself," Phillip insisted, "just honest. Events have passed me by for some reason. Somewhere, somehow, I've taken the wrong turning while others of our generation continued the other way, climbing to those sunlit uplands of yours where men win glory and a secure reputation—something else I was reminded of the other day when I consulted James Cook's journals."

"Don't be so damned pessimistic," Rose advised gruffly.

"I am not, George. For once I am being frank with myself," Phillip corrected. "I know that I shall probably never command a British man o' war in battle, much as I would like to have done. And, although I hope to reach flag rank by the normal advancements, that flag will never lead a fleet to victory."

"I still think you're being unduly pessimistic about your prospects."

"Not pessimistic, realistic," Phillip insisted gently, "which is why I need Botany Bay so much, don't you see?"

"No, I do not see." Rose hung another smoke ring in the space between them. "What in hell is so damned attractive about a place at the arse end of nowhere? A place hardly anyone has seen, a place which hardly anyone in his right mind—yourself excepted—even wants to see?"

Phillip smiled. "Perhaps that is the attraction?"

Rose's eyebrows drooped again. "How do you mean?"

Phillip shrugged. "Very simply, I mean that it's untouched. Virgin. I shall be the first to know. I also mean that, just because nobody else much cares for Botany Bay, I think that I ought. Does that sound odd?"

"Yes, but do carry on."

Phillip shrugged again. "That's all there is to say. For the first time I am going to be first: this time I shall not be picking up another's crumbs. Therefore I would take it very hard if, for any reason, my commission were cancelled at this last moment."

"There's little chance of that."

"*While* we have peace," Phillip corrected. "For truth to tell I've grown to like the sound of 'governor' and 'captain general.' Now my name has substance, it has weight and value, now I mean something. All I need is 'admiral of the ocean sea' and my collection would be complete," Phillip added with another ironic smile.

"Uh? What's this admiral nonsense?" Rose enquired sharply.

"Oh, just a title the dons awarded Christopher Columbus when he discovered the Americas for them. Sounds rather grand, doesn't it?"

"S'pose so," Mr. Secretary Rose observed. "But keep your mind on the matter in hand, there's a good fellow."

"Have no fear, George, I know what I'm about."

"You do?" Rose's eyebrows shot up. "Thank God someone does! The Admiralty and the Home Office are running around each other like headless roosters, trying to see what they are to do with Botany Bay; Cabinet is spending a fortune on pamphlet writers and hacks to promote transportation for the most absurd reasons; simultaneously we're trying to dish Charlie Fox and Sheridan, hold the lid on the Dutch crisis, rebuild a navy and secretly establish a Pacific empire!" He ran to a halt. "I am much relieved to discover one man in England who actually knows what the devil *is* going on!"

Phillip's smile deepened. "It's really not that difficult, George. I am going to put down roots. This time I am going to build something solid and worthwhile, and not only for myself but for countless others in the years ahead."

"Uh?"

"It's true, George, that is what I am about to do." Phillip studied his pipe for a moment. "The convicts won't last forever—nothing ever does—they are at best a quick solution to our labour problems until more regular supplies can be developed closer to the plantations. Then, in due course, free settlers will come to build their tomorrows upon all our yesterdays. And they will, you know. I see this present convoy as little more than England's *verloren hoop,* the storming party which a general must order into the breach to take the enemy's first fire before he follows up with grenadiers."

"For once I'll agree with you there!" Rose coughed round his pipe stem. "That little flock of lost lambs at Portsmouth must be the most forlorn hope which ever left any shore. My God, Arthur, I have to admire your pluck. But," he added quickly, "don't count too heavily upon the long-term prospects for New South Wales, I wouldn't want you to take another tumble if it came to nothing. For truth to tell, we have a pretty dismal record of planting overseas colonies—you remember the Gambia?—and those which do take root against all the odds eventually want to go their independent ways. Just concentrate on the present and let the future take care of itself," Rose concluded, reaming his pipe bowl with the pickwick from a nearby candleholder.

Phillip stubbornly shook his head. "I tell you we shall not fail. Botany Bay *will* amount to something far more than a refuse tip for broken ostlers and hopeless herb sellers."

"Damned glad to hear that someone still believes in the miraculous," Rose mouthed, tweezing another hot coal over his pipe. He leaned back. "Just you capture a bridgehead in the South Seas with your *verloren hoop,* that's all we require. Let us handle our problems and leave the rest to muddle along with theirs." He whiffed smoke and watched it disperse. "You knew, of course, that your opposite number—M. le Comte de La Pérouse—has taken an armed flotilla into distant waters, officially to press pretty flowers and to sketch bosky scenes of Indian campfires?"

"Of course."

"What I'll bet you don't know is that he also picked nearly seventy condemned items from the Bicêtre prison and embarked them under the strictest secrecy at Brest—"

"Good God!"

"Don't worry, it shook us too after Ministre de Castries sank deeper than normal into his cups last month and began boasting to a colleague's wife how *la belle France* was about to teach the barbarians a lesson in colonisation they would never forget. . . ."

"I'll be damned."

"Not yet you won't." Rose's pipe stem suddenly jabbed air. "Time is of the essense, time, speed and accuracy. *Nothing* must stop you being in such a position that, by this season next year, we can defend our interests in the East, especially now that Holland has fallen under the French spell. Once war breaks out they will promptly put a stopper on our revictualling at the Cape until we capture the place from 'em.

"Once the guns start firing again, our Indiamen will be under constant threat from the French on Mauritius and the Ile de Réunion, and from the Dutch off Sumatra and Java. It will be in that desperate hour that we shall most need every stick of timber and yard of canvas your dockyards can supply in the South Seas as our ships close-haul off Brazil and round the Cape, catch a wind down to the high Forties, then beat past Van Dieman's Land for the Manila Straits and Canton. Remember: you will be their only safe haven after untold thousands of miles of shipwreck and gale. You *must* be ready for them. Understand?"

Phillip nodded but said nothing.

Rose savoured his port wine again and also fell silent. A log slipped in the hearth and more sparks fountained away behind the mantelshelf. Somewhere in the parkland beyond the tall windows a hunting owl called across the waning moon. Another replied from the roof of Cuffnells' ice-house, much closer to the mansion.

Rose continued studying Phillip's sleepy profile, then cleared his throat. "Arthur, attend me very carefully. As we have often said, the next war will be the last, there can be no repeat of the past forty years of ebb and flow, win and loss. It is 'either Paris or London, not Paris and London,' and yet both our nations have virtually drowned in red ink on the world's financial ledgers."

"Oh?"

Rose nodded sombrely. "Have you any idea how much Britain now owes her creditors after that business in the American colonies?"

"No. I haven't."

"Guess."

"I can't. It must be several million."

"Would that it were!" Rose snorted. "No, my friend, currently our nation's debt totals two hundred and forty-three million pounds."

"Good G—!"

"Furthermore," Rose went on unemotionally, "there are some fourteen million pounds' worth of navy and ordnance debentures due for redemption when I return to London. At eight million pounds per annum, our interest bill alone is well over half the total revenue from all sources. If I were to divert every farthing of our current budget into paying these debts we would not be clear again until—" the Treasury secretary ticked finger-tips—"until about the year 1910.

"It is no exaggeration to say that Britain is now bankrupt and the coming war with France—the decisive one—may last for even longer than seven years, compounding our debt to a figure unheard of in all history. And yet, if we are to win, as I said we must, it will not be by blood and iron alone—though the general run of people think that is the way of the world."

"How, then?" Phillip asked, increasingly puzzled by this brooding monologue.

"By gold." Rose was withdrawing further into himself. "As I said earlier this evening, we have a courier riding posthaste to Potsdam for a secret audience with His Majesty of Prussia." Rose glanced up at Cuffnells' calendar clock, an exact copy of the one in the Cabinet room, Downing Street. "He should get there the day after tomorrow. He will not be delivering a large box filled with guineas, though many also think that is the way we order our affairs."

"Oh?"

"Our man is carrying a plain oilskin packet sewn inside his boot. Inside that is a simple sheet of paper, written by me and closed by the Great Seal. It is about this big—" Rose was adjusting his fingers until they were a few inches apart. "If our ambassador has followed his instructions, King Friedrich will assent to our proposal and that piece of paper will then depart Prussia altogether, hurrying south to Rhine-Hesse, to Frankfurt-am-Main, to the counting house of our agent, Herr Meyer Rothschild.

"Now, as you know, Herr Rothschild is a very cultivated and shrewd business gentlemen whose acquaintance I esteem highly and whose opinions I would ignore at my peril, but sentiment has never been any part of his character. He will treat my draft like any other. He will call for certain books and ledgers. He will scrutinise the reports of his intelligencers here in London, and Paris, and Madrid, and Amsterdam. He will add and he will subtract, multiply and divide figures which you and I will never see. Finally, he will write an equally brief note to his Berlin agent. Soon after it is decyphered, one half million in *Reichsthaler* will be delivered to the army paymaster and France will again find herself threatened by a Prussian Guard on one hand, Jack Tar on the other, always a fatal prospect for her. . . ." Rose looked up. "But why am I so confident that our Herr Rothschild will continue to underwrite Britain's bond issues to his continental investors and will continue to honour my drafts to buy fresh allies even if the next war lasts twice seven years?"

"Deuced if I know, George, this is way above my head."

"Not any more it isn't," Rose replied. "In metaphor if not in fact it *is* your head we are discussing. But to continue a moment, Herr Rothschild will invest his clients' savings in our two percent perpetual consols only while he knows that London is a sound risk. Every year, without fail, he must have tangible evidence of a kind which my opposite number in Paris does not have," Rose added. "But what is this cast-iron, copper-bottomed asset of ours which Herr Rothschild so values?"

"I—I don't know."

"Then I shall tell you," Rose went on in the same withdrawn voice. "It is the China and India Customs, four little words around which the future will hinge, either to let us pass, or to slam shut in our nation's face. For while we have those receipts we have almost limitless credit to draw upon to buy others' blood and iron—as we did in America. And to win—unlike America. But if ever we lost control of the Customs, or if it ever seemed they were in danger from any quarter, then our Treasury notes would be discounted on the money market like those pathetic bits of scrip which Spain must now hawk around at ruinous rates of interest."

Rose looked up from the fire's glowing embers. "But we are not going to lose the China and India Customs, are we, Arthur? You said that we were not going to fail this time, didn't you? Your convicts are going to be hewing stone and cutting timber at Botany Bay as they've never worked before, aren't they? And every year, come hell or high water, three hundred Indiamen will be going down the Channel, outward bound to the four quarters of the globe with our manufactures. And every year, come gale or tempest, France or the devil, three hundred more will return laden with tea and silk, lacquer and drugs, dyestuffs and cotton. They will work their way up the Channel to London Pool, no matter what the French may try, and they will break their cargoes. Our customs will be taken *ad valorem* and the treasures of the East will be re-exported for our greater profit and Herr Rothschild's peace of mind. And do you know why?"

"Er, no, not exactly," Phillip replied.

Rose sipped wine and stared at the fire in its reflection. "The other Mr. R. will continue to service my paper because he also knows that your arsenal and sail lofts, ropewalks and vegetable gardens are out there in the South Pacific, ready and able to bring home those storm-battered merchantmen whose very survival *is* Britain's survival."

Phillip had never seen his friend so grim before.

"Botany Bay has nothing to do with sweeping assorted riffraff off London's streets," Rose went on quietly. "Botany Bay has nothing to do with putting the niggers in britches and teaching 'em hymns. Botany Bay has *everything* to do with George Rose being able to write a brief note to Frankfurt, and for my colleagues in Cabinet to know that His Majesty of France will awaken the following morning to find his worst nightmare a stark reality—that he must now fight a two-front war. One pen. One piece of paper. The Customs. And you at Botany Bay. That is all I need to put another's army on the road to Paris any time I like."

Rose began tamping more flake into his pipe and then tweezed another hot coal. He drew hard, eyes slit. "Just apply your mind to that and leave the daydreaming after glory to others with less experience of the real world."

Phillip's mouth tightened. "Is it really so reprehensible for a man to want his life to have amounted to something when old Mr. Bone finally taps on the bedchamber window?"

"No-o," Rose was forced to concede, "I suppose it's a poor sort of man who doesn't feed the hungry worms of ambition. But there is always a danger of losing sight of the here and now for what we fancy awaits us 'way out yonder under bluer skies—"

"George, I'm damned near fifty years old!"

"That makes you different?" Rose grunted, sucking pipe stem.

Phillip ignored his friend's tone. "I shall soon be fifty. With any luck I might make another five or ten good years. There's little time left and only twice have I felt that I had the right to belong anywhere, just twice, in fifty years!"

"Uh?"

Phillip steadied himself again. "The first was here, in Lyndhurst, just after we married."

"And the second?"

Phillip hesitated a moment. "Rio."

"*Brazil?*" Rose looked puzzled. "Why?"

Phillip spread his hands with some embarrassment. "Let's just say that for once I was among people who thought, who behaved, who even looked a bit like me."

Rose studied pipe bowl. "What else?"

"That's all," Phillip said. "There's nothing more to say, unless, if it's true that third time round pays for all losses, I'm ready to gamble my last penny and my last hour on that remote bay which Sir Joseph has described in such glowing terms."

Rose looked up and coughed. "Then may a friend hope, for your sake as much as mine, that it exceeds your expectations? I think it will, just as you will exceed those critics of our government who say, 'Phillip? Phillip who? Never heard o' the man!' Figuratively speaking, of course," Rose added, a little too quickly.

There was a long silence before Phillip spoke again. "George?"

"Yes?"

"Why did you nominate me for this task?"

Rose fiddled with his pipe stem. "Frankly, I could not think of anyone else so suitable or with such a driving ambition to mount over obstacles and win."

"Suitable? *Me?*"

"Yes. Suitable. *You,*" Rose replied. "So don't go casting yourself down without reason, there's a good chap."

"I'm not!"

"Glad to hear it," Rose commented. "You're going to need all your energies for the work ahead."

"You still haven't said why you nominated and supported me even when others—figuratively speaking, of course!—were saying 'Phillip? Phillip who?' "

"Look here, Arthur, don't go fretting yourself over nothing!"

"*Nothing!* Is my personal honour nothing?"

"Steady on!" Rose snapped, wagging a finger. "You know what you're worth, so do I or I would not have battled so hard and long with M'Lord Howe to get your name on the commission, rather than his nephew's!" The finger crooked round its pipe stem again. "Cabinet shares my opinion, Botany Bay requires your kind of skills—"

"Skills!"

"Yes! God-dammit-all-to-hell-an'-back-again, *skills!*" Rose roared, pipe flying across the hall in a dozen pieces. "Get this into your thick skull and off your thin skin if you forget all else I have told you tonight! I am not, repeat *not*, in the business of advancing the interests of nincompoops! My own, and Dora's, young George's and Billy's too—my whole family's future very much depends upon my continuing to offer sound advice to our rulers! When I kept on pushing your name forward to Cabinet it was not because I owe you any debts of affection or gratitude!"

Rose sat back angrily. "There is a list of available captains and commodores as long as my arm in the Navy Office. We could have picked any name but yours from that, but most of them have—as you so accurately noted—more than half a lifetime at sea. They may be all very fine when they're flogging the hide off shellbacks in a howling gale, but we shall need a vastly different touch when dealing with civilians and merchant officers, marines and cannibal kings in the simple day-to-day business of running a small town beyond the edge of the known world!"

"Is that all?"

Rose grimaced. "If it were, then it would still be far more than most have to offer us. But no, it is not all." He paused, searching for exactly the right words. "Prickly and damned Continental you may be at times, Arthur, but I also know you to be an officer who will not shirk the unpleasant options. If some luckless wretch has to be necked at Botany Bay, I know you will see that it is promptly carried through."

He paused again, voice softening a fraction. "I have also lived long enough beside your farm to know that you have a practical grasp of husbandry and to know that this town was never so smartly run as when you were its tythingman. Moreover," he added, "you've served under a foreign flag—no easy thing, I'd imagine—escorting just the sort of item we must now send out to construct a naval base. Lisbon said you did very well with their white niggers and handled that dose of plague like a hero—their words, not mine," Rose added, stiffening his friend's brittle self-confidence.

"But most of all, Cabinet knows you can be depended upon to keep cool in emergencies, to administer justice with an even hand and not to become drunk with power—something of paramount importance when the home government is at least a year's sailing time there and back." Rose paused; then, quietly: "Believe me, Arthur, if they hadn't known you were as steady and reliable as M'Lord Cornwallis they would *never* have given you a viceroy's commission, with sweeping authority to rule by decree without a council. In theory you are answerable only to His Majesty for whatever you do: in fact we shall be watching every move you make, very closely indeed." He reached for the decanter again. "Now, what about a nightcap?"

"No. Thank you, George." Phillip smiled uncertainly. "But many thanks for the reassurance. There are moments when I sometimes need, well, you know. . . ."

"Oh I know all right!" Rose said with genuine feeling. "Don't imagine that life has always been a featherbed for Dora and me."

"I don't," Phillip replied, reaching for his boots near the hearth. "However, it is getting late and I must be away early in the morning or else Lieutenant King will begin to wonder if he is to take out the whole convoy by himself."

Rose muffled a yawn and began standing too. "That's another emotion I am familiar with." He stretched. "Anyhow, sleep in a bit longer if you like, I've put my carriage at your disposal: we can't have the king's viceroy bumping shoulders along his royal highway with Mrs. Boobs and Jack Nasty Face, can we? Besides, I fancy it will save some fatigue, thus leaving you with even more energy to be up and off within the week. You did say it could be done within the week, didn't you, Arthur?"

"Yes."

15

PHILLIP STRETCHED full length across both seats of the coach and watched the New Forest falling astern. Mathew Godwin had insisted on riding escort for Rose's maroon and black carriage, at least as far as the ferry, and Phillip could see his shadow trotting along behind with fowling piece slung across one shoulder, guarding his master's sea chest, which was now lashed above the berlin's rear axle. Two hampers of cold meats, potted preserves and a dozen of champagne had also been loaded aboard as refreshments for the journey to Portsmouth. Then, just as the liveried coachmen were about to whip up their team and leave Cuffnells Park, young William had run across the gravel with a personal gift, a very patched book in half-bound calf.

Phillip gently leafed backward through its dog-eared pages to the title plate: *Travels into Several Remote Nations of the World,* by Lemuel Gulliver. An earlier and shakier "Bily his boke" had been inked out and a new dedication quilled underneath in a very fair hand: "For His Excellency the Govr. & Capt. General Arthur Phillip, Esq., trusting this small token of my esteem may yet prove of service in the land of Golbasto Momarem Evlame Gurdilo Shefin Mully Ully Gue. Very respectfully, Wm. Rose." The clue lay, as Phillip had discovered, on page twenty opposite an engraved map which placed Lilliput, an island said to be ruled over by the Emperor Golbasto Momarem, about two points nor'west of Van Dieman's Land.

Smiling, Phillip shut the shabby volume and put it away until he could read it at leisure, then glanced back at his own faint reflection in the window and pulled a wry face: "Well, I don't suppose it's any more fanciful than most else that's been written about New Holland. Six-inch soldiers? Or the seven cities of gold? Or what?"

Phillip shrugged and reached for the nearest wicker hamper, lifted its lid and began choosing between a large venison pasty and a roast chicken wrapped in crisp white linen.

The mud-streaked berlin rolled into Portsmouth well after dusk, oil lamps glimmering on wet cobbles as Rose's leading coachman reined back in the Bower Anchor's yard. Phillip shook himself awake and climbed down into the knifing wind. Gone were the soft brown smells of Forest mould: he had left home again for the hard blue stab of blown salt. And it felt good. His face tingled as he peered up at the drivers' muffled silhouettes.

"Thank you! I shall arrange a bed for you both. Meanwhile, take this for your trouble."

"Thank'ee, sir!" The coachmen clutched gold and knuckled salutes. "A pros'prous voyage an' a safe return, your honour!"

Phillip briefly touched hat and turned, pulling the cloak tighter as he hurried into the tavern's welcoming fug of shag smoke, raw spirits and plain cooking. Its landlord tucked up his wooden crutch and drew himself to attention as Phillip passed the bar. "Dinner, cap'n, sir?"

"Please. In my chamber. And a bed for the coachmen."

"Aye aye!"

Phillip trod upstairs after the maid and let her candle touch flame for his before he dismissed her. Bryant had not been idle, he noticed, running his finger over his number one uniform, its navy blue nap raised almost like new. Indeed the gilt buttons were new, matching the rich gold lace round its collar. His dress sword had also been brought to a mirror finish with brick dust and light oil, Phillip saw with pride, never tiring of reading the ornate inscription engraved along its Toledo blade: "*Al Honor del Excelentísimo Señor Don Rafael Escudero y Guzmán, Duque de Valencia, Capitán General de Buenos Aires, Año 1770.*"

While only an unknown English lieutenant, Jakob Philipp's son had taken this sword with the surrender of a grandee of Spain on the bloody shambles of a quarterdeck, and with it the thunderous cheers of Portuguese who had forgotten what it meant to win a slugging match, gunport to gunport, with a once-invincible enemy.

Phillip's spine stiffened as he snapped hilt and scabbard together and laid the sword on his cot, alongside his white breeches and rolled stockings. He looked around. His flag lieutenant had been hard at work, too. Invoices, receipts, copied memoranda, correspondence out, replies in, all were neatly arranged along his desk and weighted with stones against the eddying draughts.

Phillip was still leafing through one of Sir Joseph Banks' orders for more plants and Indian curios when someone rapped door. He glanced up as King entered, cloak stained and sodden, draped over the leather satchel which never seemed to leave his side these days. "Good evening, sir."

" 'Evening. How are we proceeding?"

King turned at the small fire and dropped his cloak over the nearest chair back. "As well as may be expected."

Phillip skimmed some of the cargo manifests. "Our provisioning appears to be well advanced."

"Yes, once I drove a toecap up the victualling mateys."

"Uh huh. And Major Ross?"

"Embarked. All numbers at their posts. All equipment secure and accounted for."

"Not before time. And *Alexander*?"

"Down another three."

Phillip began absentmindedly doodling with his quill, drawing interlocking ovals round and round a scrap of paper, like chain links. "Then the sooner we are at sea, the better." He glanced up sharply, mind set. "I fly my broad pennant tomorrow morning."

"Sir?"

"I am moving my command aboard *Sirius:* speed is now the essence of this contract."

"But *Hyaena* hasn't even arrived on station yet," King insisted with more than a touch of worry.

Phillip frowned. "Where was she last sighted?"

"Off the Downs. Beating our way, but very slowly."

"Damn. That could mean she'll arrive tomorrow, or next month. Very well, we shall be ready to weigh anchor and proceed to sea the moment our escort arrives." Phillip nodded at King's despatch case. "More returns?"

"Yes, but none from Winchester yet."

"Good. I shan't lose any sleep if that batch of whores misses the boat. Put your bag over there, I shall attend to it presently."

There was another rap on the door and one of the kitchen maids bobbed her way into the room with a tray. "Your dinner, sir!"

"Thank you." Phillip looked at King again. "Have you eaten yet?"

"Yes, thank you. Earlier."

"Very well," the older man said, more to himself. "Then I had better accustom myself to dining in lonely state again."

King paused in the doorway and turned to face Phillip at the table. "I—I know it won't be proper to say this after tomorrow, so I'll say it now: we're glad it's your command, sir."

"Oh?"

King groped for the right words. "It's that, well, if anyone can keep this ragtag lot from each other's throats and start them hauling together, sailor-style, we know you're the man to do it."

Phillip examined his knife minutely and made a careful job of scraping a thumbnail between the fork prongs before looking up again. "Thank you, Pip."

"Thank you, sir."

"Good night."

The rain and wind eased just before dawn. Phillip could now see the hills of Wight again below scudding cloud. He sniffed outside the open window and looked up at the sky: with any luck the weather would blow out later in the day and back a few points east.

"Er, weather glass low to middlin', sir," Bryant announced behind him, heeling the door shut again and setting down the can of hot water with its towel, razor and soap.

Phillip pulled his head inside and shut the window to adjust the pocket mirror on its nail for the last time. He began stropping steel as he watched Bryant's reflection gathering together his few remaining things and stowing them in the other sea chest. His manservant was changing, too. Bryant's walk was more jaunty and alert than it had been for many months past. The blue fearnaught and striped vest were store-new, and his pigtail had just been braided with fresh marline for the occasion. And he was talking far less.

The gap between Phillip and almost fifteen hundred men was widening by the minute, just as it had already opened between Bryant—the commodore's manservant—and every other tar in the convoy. It was inevitable, Phillip knew, starting to lather his sombre reflection. The moments when he would be, indeed could be, just like another man were slipping away like a sounding line through the fingers of time.

Bryant had taken up the blue serge officer's coat and was checking each button's anchor for exact alignment with the one below. Something about that coat's cut and gold lace reminded Phillip of the rich vestments which he had often seen naval chaplains wear at Mass aboard the king of Portugal's warships. Years later it was now his turn to assume something of their awful powers over life and death by a simple outstretching of arms. Phillip shivered and attended more closely to his toilet.

As commodore, as captain of all the captains, he would soon not only be their commander in chief but also their judge and jury and court of last appeal. His viceroy's commission would come into effect at Botany Bay, but long before that he would have been answerable only to his sovereign for whatever he chose to do. Once he was aboard his flagship, every man, regardless of birth or rank, would be his subject. His nod at a court-martial could send any one of them to the yardarm or have him flogged senseless at the gratings. His power to give, his right to take, was unlimited.

Phillip knew he would spend the next months, the coming years, isolated from everyone by the great cabin's bulkhead and whatever passed for Government House at Botany Bay. There would always be an armed sentry at the door, and whenever the commodore passed to walk the quarterdeck his captain and lieutenants would shift to leeward until he cared to notice them. No man who valued his hide would dare to speak to him directly unless upon some point of duty, and then only with head uncovered, hat in hand, at a respectful distance. The Portuguese chaplains had served only God: fourteen hundred souls aboard the transports to Botany Bay were about to learn that Phillip *was* God.

He pulled himself together and wiped the razor. Bryant marched forward and packed it while his master pulled on white breeches and stockings before tightening the gilt-buckled shoes. Then he stood, arms outstretched, ready to receive the burden that would never leave him until he returned to England or died at his post. Bryant slipped the heavy blue coat over Phillip's shoulders, smoothing its collar as his master turned again, tightening the sword belt at his waist. Bryant stood back, taking up the cocked hat and ankle-length cloak which he would carry until the commodore needed them outside.

Phillip didn't move. Instead, he slowly looked round the cramped attic which had been his bedroom and office for so many nights. It was little enough, really, for his pay had not allowed for more than thrifty comfort, but remembered from a man o' war running before a gale in the South Atlantic it would become the stuff of dreams. He pulled himself together: two of the inn's stablemen were waiting to lift his sea chests. He glanced at Bryant's weathered face. "All squared away?"

"Aye ready, sir!"

Phillip began pacing downstairs, where the entire domestic staff of the Bower Anchor were standing in line at the street door. The landlord hopped forward, wooden leg hitting the flagstones as he halted. "Beggin' leave sir, it would *honour* us 'normously if you'd accept this 'ere small token o' you being wi' us for so long, like." He held out a small leather pouch. "It's a knife. For pens."

Phillip's face relaxed into a smile, perhaps for the last time ever: someone had remembered the trouble he had once had in the small hours when he couldn't find a sharp blade to point a quill. He let his fingertips stroke the small gift. "Thank you. Everyone."

"A pros'prous voyage an' safe return, sir!"

Phillip was moving down the line, awarding small envelopes which chinked with coin as their new owners bobbed a curtsey or bowed awkwardly over their tips. And then he stepped onto the crowded pavement, pausing to close his cloak's neck chain and wait for his chests to be loaded aboard their barrows. Then he set his hat square and, without once looking back, began the last half mile he might ever walk on dry land.

It could have been his imagination after Rose's warning, but there did appear to be more men on Portsmouth's streets than he had seen for many months, linking arm in arm, reeling from tavern to tavern. One ship's mess table had clubbed together and hired a coach for the morning: a gunner's mate was now hanging over the side, whistling after every skirt as the horses clattered past, urging her to jump up for a quick adventure in the furze bushes of Southsea Common.

The coach was being slowed by the advance company of a regiment embarking for overseas, shoving through its bow wave of wives and children, hucksters and mountebanks, fortune tellers and pickpockets. The colonel was mounted behind his colour party and drummers. Phillip stood aside, removing his hat as the army officer's sword flashed, saluting him from the saddle, only replacing it when the last infantry had crunched past in their scarlet regimentals, muskets shouldered, greatcoats, camp kettles and spare boots lashed across leather knapsacks.

Sirius' gig was manned and ready at the sea stairs. Phillip settled himself in the stern sheets as his chests came aboard with Bryant. He knew from long experience that every man was watching his every move without apparently seeing a thing. There would not be a tar below decks who would not know, within five minutes of him coming aboard the flagship, that he had nicked his chin again. And that he only stood waist high to a water butt. And that the new commodore had a great bowsprit of a nose which jutted for'ard of a tarry face. Phillip also knew from experience that he would need all the isolation of his cabin long before this voyage was done.

The coxswain was the only one permitted to look directly at him. He coughed warily. "Ready aye ready, sir!"

"Give way."

"Aye aye, sir!" The scrubbed pine oar blades swept back, paused, dipped together as the painter splashed. "Lively now, m'lads! Heeeave—!"

Haslar slowly fell astern and the gig began taking the Solent's choppy water. Phillip ignored the spray trickling down his neck while others, less protected, bent to the oars. It wasn't his imagination: there were more warships at Spithead than there had been even a few days earlier. An outward-bound convoy of levanters had come under the shore batteries and were anchored while their escorts assembled for the run down an almost certainly hostile coastline to Gibraltar and the Mediterranean. Phillip steadied his pulse and concentrated on the job to hand: taking out the six convict transports, their three store ships and the three naval escorts the moment *Hyaena* reported for duty.

The gig was closing round his flagship's stern with her newly gilded name carved above the full stretch of windows. For some reason he had yet to fathom, the Navy Office had insisted in renaming the twenty-four-gun *Berwick* as HMS *Sirius,* claiming that it was "that great Dog Star, brightest of all the southern heavens," a romantic whimsy that Phillip could well do without: his men already had enough to worry them without some damnfool clerk in London breaking one of the sea's ironbound superstitions.

He purged his own imagination again and got ready to go aboard as the gig eased under *Sirius'* wasp-striped tumblehome. Phillip crouched, balancing with the roll for a moment, then sprang for the fixed companion ladder, gripping tight while a surprise wave drenched him, and began climbing for the entry port.

A marine lieutenant's sword rasped scabbard as Phillip's gold lace drew level with the deck's rim. "Honour guard! A-ten-shun!" Pause. "Pree-sent arms!" And twenty open palms slapped musket slings while bosuns' mates and sideboys stiffened, pipes trilling.

Their commodore stepped aboard, doffing hat to the quarterdeck, sensing rather than hearing the crack of his broad red and white pennant breaking at the mainmast peak.

Sirius' officers had formed the third side of the hollow square which faced the entry. Her captain stepped forward and halted, hat off, his own silvery hair blowing around. "Welcome aboard, sir."

"Thank you, Mr. Hunter." Phillip completed his inspection of the marine guard, then looked at Hunter again. "Make to all ships: captains and masters will assemble aboard the commodore."

"Aye aye, sir."

Phillip walked aft to the poop deck, cloak swirling round wet shoe-marks. Behind him bare feet were pattering to the signal halliards, bending on flags as the midshipman of the watch read aloud from *Sirius'* signal book. Phillip smelled the cannon's recoil, alerting the convoy to a stick of coloured bunting as it spilled into the wind overhead. Two further charges of powder had to be fired before all the convoy's transports noted *Sirius'* orders by flying their reply pennants. The midshipman reported to his lieutenant, who reported to Hunter, who alone could approach Phillip and doff hat again. "Acknowledged, sir."

"Thank you, Mr. Hunter." Phillip turned. "Have them attend me in the great cabin."

"Aye aye, sir."

Phillip touched hatbrim and went below, ducking his head up the short passage between the captain's and first lieutenant's cubbies. The marine sentry clicked to attention as the commodore passed and the door shut behind him.

The great cabin was only large relative to everything else aboard a five-hundred-ton man o' war, Phillip knew, pausing to let his eyes accustom themselves to the gloom, but at least someone had recently had the initiative to give the bare timbers a lick of canary yellow paint—except, of course, for the regulation crimson daubed over the long nines' gunlids. A pair of thirty-two-pounders also shared the cramped space with him, their carriages and ammunition trunks roped to ringbolts in the deck.

On his right, behind a blanket screen, was his cot. Astern, opposite the door, was the full sweep of square windows and a panorama of Spithead inching past as *Sirius* swung at her moorings. To his left, the small desk where King had laid the documents he would soon need. Phillip unclasped his cloak and stowed it inside the cupboard which could, at a pinch, serve as the coffin for his pickled body if he should die at sea and ask not to be put over the side, sewn in sailcloth. Then he unclipped his sword and hung it on a peg behind the door: his hat would have to stay on the cot until its tin box came aboard.

Phillip squeezed round a bare table that would serve for most things in the years ahead, be it laying a new course off an unknown coast, or entertaining a foreign ruler to dinner, or court-martialling some luckless sailor, or sawing off limbs if *Sirius'* cockpit began to take water in battle. But today it would serve at his first conference, though by the nature of things there would be precious little conferring by anyone once the commodore had spoken, he knew, sorting the documents and arranging his chair to put his shoulders to the windows and get the best light from the poop deck's scuttle overhead. Lieutenant King had remembered to write up the key points in a larger hand than usual: Phillip would not have to wear spectacles for his first public appearance.

Satisfied that everything was now shipshape, he eased back, permitting himself the luxury of a quiet moment by himself. It felt good. It felt very good to be a part of the navy's timeless world of ritual again, an ordered world where every man and boy learned his place and where everyone had a place to learn, hauling together for the common good. Phillip sighed: if only those other worlds, the ones ashore, could learn to work in the same brisk way it would indeed be a better world for everyone, not just the few.

Phillip considered this thought: he was right. True, the Royal Navy doled out a small ration of privilege according to rank—like the coffin-cupboard over there on his left—but they could be earned only by experience, not the accident of birth. That colonel on his fine horse had bought his rank outright, if born well connected, or hawked shares in his future winnings like a joint stock company to raise the price of a commission if he were not. In either case he would then have to learn his trade as he went along.

But not so in His Majesty's navy. Any man aboard *Sirius* today—if he applied himself hard enough and long enough to astronomy, algebra and arithmetic—could hope to present himself to a naval board for advancement. Once over that hurdle he could reasonably hope to climb the Lieutenants' List, the Commanders', the Captains', and finally sit in a cabin like this, assured one day of wearing an admiral's golden epaulettes and—perhaps—even the red sash of knighthood. Phillip knew. He was proof that, in the greater world of entrenched privilege, the Royal Navy's small universe was astonishingly open to talent, for only natural ability counted at sea: a duke's son would drown just as readily as anyone else if he but once miscalculated the bearing off a rocky headland.

This discovery put Phillip at ease with himself again as he rang the hand bell to call Bryant from stowing cabin plate in the small pantry outside. "Coffee."

"Aye aye, sir. Beggin' leave, when would you like me to stow your chests in 'ere?"

Phillip listened to the first longboat drawing under *Sirius'* entry port: it would be some time before all the captains and masters were assembled on deck and Hunter could bring them down. "Now."

Almost an hour passed before *Alexander*'s longboat made fast to the boom and hung on a falling tide. Phillip had dictated a despatch to the port admiral and given instructions to his clerk by the time Hunter appeared in the doorway. "All captains and masters await your commands, sir." Although it was many years since he had lived in Edinburgh, Hunter still tended to roll his final r's.

The bell tinkled and Bryant cleared the coffee cup. Phillip nodded. "Show them in, Mr. Hunter."

"Aye aye, sir."

Phillip sat easy behind the table and waited as Hunter led in Lieutenant Ball of HMS *Supply*; the marine commandant, Ross; and nine civilian masters, their heads ducking under the transverse beams where the thirty-two-pounders' rammers, sponges and worming hooks were stowed with boarding hatchets, cutlasses and cases of pistols. The men shuffled into line, facing aft, hats tucked under arms or gripped tightly in both hands. Only the king's officers were in uniform, the rest wore a medley of styles which went back to the japanned trousers, fighting coats with rolled cuffs, and hair clubbed with tarred line which Phillip remembered from his own apprentice years in the merchant service.

He nodded at the master of *Scarborough*, a vessel recently off the Yorkshire yards. "Mr. Marshall?" Then to *Charlotte*'s, a Thames barque, "Mr. Gilbert?" Then to the *Prince of Wales*', a new three-master from the Blackwall yards, "Mr. Mason?" *Lady Penrhyn*, another Blackwall construction. "Mr. Sever?" The *Friendship*, from *Charlotte*'s home yard. "Mr. Walton?" And, finally, *Alexander*, a Hull barque and, at 445 tons, his largest ship after *Sirius*; she was registered by another Walton but operated like everyone else for the far-reaching Campbell Interest. "Ah, Mr. Sinclair." The masters of his three store ships, *Borrowdale*, *Fishburn* and *Golden Grove*, were acknowledged before he gave permission for them to be seated.

The twelve men shifted around, finding whatever came to hand in the cabin, ammunition trunks, gun carriages or Phillip's sea chests. Sinclair cut out and boarded one of the few chairs, lashed behind netting on the wall, and sat with legs comfortably outstretched, hands over an ample belly.

"I shall begin by reading my instructions from the Lords Commissioner of the Admiralty," Phillip announced without haste or preamble. He squinted slightly at the papers in front of him. " 'Whereas His Majesty,

George the Third, by the Grace of God Defender of the Faith, King of Great Britain and Ireland, etc., has been graciously pleased to receive certain petitions concerning the insalubrious state of certain houses of correction, and ever mindful of our nation's need to establish a presence in the South Seas, His Majesty has commanded that all due steps be taken to resume the practice of transportation as was hitherto the case before the recent conflict in America.' " Phillip's voice carried a surprising weight from such a small man.

" 'Accordingly you are hereby charged to assemble the requisite transport vessels, to attend to their readiness, and when victualled and fit for His Majesty's service, to assume the rights, privileges and duties of Commodore. Thereafter, in pursuance of His Majesty's pleasure, signified to us by Lord Sydney, one of the principal officers of state, you are hereby commanded to put to sea at the first favourable opportunity of wind and weather, proceeding with your squadron as expeditiously as possible by way of Teneriffe, Rio de Janeiro, the Cape of Good Hope, to Botany Bay situated at thirty-four degrees South, one hundred fifty-two degrees East in the territory of New South Wales upon the coast of New Holland.

" 'Having arrived at your destination you will then take all necessary measures to establish His Majesty's possession of the above-mentioned territory, for which purpose you will then assume the rank, style and privileges of Governor and Captain General.

" 'Given under my hand and the Great Seal of Admiralty, Second May 1787. Howe.' "

Phillip folded the document again and put it aside: his authority was now above challenge. He noted Sinclair's shut eyes and heavy breathing, but everyone else present seemed to be reasonably impressed by the occasion. "I shall now draw your attention to the current state of uncertainty between our country and France. The possibility of war is very real—" Sinclair's eyes flicked open. "Accordingly, all vessels will proceed in convoy, paying especial attention to keeping station by night as well as by day." Phillip paused to let his words take effect before adding, almost as an afterthought to nobody in particular, "French prisons are most uncomfortable and their method of ransoming prizes long and expensive, so we shall all do well not to lose contact with our escorts. *Sirius* will be commanding the windward division, *Hyaena* the lee, *Supply* will be our acting frigate and despatch boat. Your vessels will be given their stations in my orders, which you will receive presently.

"I now direct your attention to the internal economy of our convoy, in particular the matter of discipline." He paused again, studying the other men's faces. "I need hardly say that the maintenance of good order is of paramount importance while transporting the items you have embarked below decks. Therefore, point one: it is my firm opinion that the only way to keep large bodies of men in order is by dividing and subdividing them, with officers and petty officers to regulate their conduct.

"Every ship's company will therefore be divided into as many companies as there are lieutenants. Or mates," Phillip added for the civilian masters. "These companies will be reviewed every day by their officers, who will ensure that the men appear tight and clean in every respect. The officers will see that defaulters are promptly punished. They will also see that their men are daily exercised at arms, at the sails and in the rigging. I expect each master or captain to review them personally at least once a week."

Sinclair's face was turning a bright crimson and he was no longer slouching in his chair, but Phillip wasn't noticing as he went on in the same calm, distant voice. "When it can be done the men will have full time for their meals and rest, and certain portions of the week will be allotted for washing and mending their clothes. But, and here I must stress the point, at all other times they will be kept constantly employed. And whatever they are about, let your mates be sure it is done with cheerful attention. Your petty officers will allow nothing that is sloppy or half-hearted in this convoy. Remember, the old adage that 'the devil finds work for idle hands to do' applies as much to sailors—and marines—as to any other class of men." Phillip paused again, his frown fixed and aloof.

"Fortunately you are well placed to encourage this ideal behaviour, being confined within narrow limits, without any brothels, tippling shops or playhouses to debauch your men while at sea. But notwithstanding all this, if two or three hundred men are herded together aboard ship and left without proper division as I have instructed, and your officers only shout their orders from the quarterdecks or gangways, then such a crew is surely hell-bent to become a disorderly mob, and if that happens all work will be done—if done at all—in a shoddy and careless way. Worse, not being closely overseen by their officers, your people will become sottish, lazy, slovenly, dirty and bored, trifling with cabals and imaginary grievances, rotten ready for mutiny."

Sinclair was beginning to shake, but Phillip continued studying a point in space above the table. "I repeat: 'the devil finds work for idle hands,' so ensure he finds no lodging aboard your ships by setting the men to work before he can stow his sea chest. Remember, you are now upon His Majesty's service, and whatever you may have done previously is of no account now you are under Admiralty orders. As a consequence you will be guided by fighting regulations at all times, and if anyone think otherwise," Phillip added, "let him remember that a French prize-master will not make the slightest distinction between a captured merchantman or a warship, except to sell the former at a much better price when it is towed into port and its crew thrown into a fortress."

"But—!"

Phillip's eyes moved slightly. "I may ask your opinion later, Mr. Sinclair. Meanwhile I shall now direct everyone's attention to the question of convict discipline." He waited for the coughs and mutterings to die away. "In their particular case the devil has already found ample work for them to do, but here again we must labour cheerfully to defeat his plans. Adequate rations and ventilation will do much to raise their spirits and remove, for the majority, reasonable grounds for grumbling. Once we are clear of land and any hope of swimming ashore, I shall give orders for their irons to be struck off and—"

"But—!"

Phillip's mouth tightened. "Once we are clear of land I shall give orders for their irons to be struck off and they will be allowed on deck in small parties, under close guard, of course, to exercise themselves. Appropriate tasks can be given: the convicted women can make and mend, while the males can be set to holystoning decks, polishing brightwork, picking oakum, whatever seems of most benefit to you. It is my firm belief that by so doing ninety percent of all troublemakers will simply disappear."

Phillip paused to gauge how the masters were taking this lecture. "There remain, however, those hardened ruffians for whom reason is thought to be weakness, something to be exploited: how are they to be subordinated and controlled? I would suggest you begin by discovering their plans and forestalling them, for which purpose I am instructing you to take a good look at your, ah, passengers and select two or three who will keep you informed of what is being discussed at night in the convict lines. There will be no dangerous oathings and combinations in *my* squadron, gentlemen. None.

"You may offer suitable rewards for the moment—without giving the other convicts any reason to suspect that your intelligencers are getting special privileges—and hold out the more distant hope of lenient treatment when we reach Botany Bay." Phillip could sense the unspoken reaction to this order. "There are, I know, some ill-informed persons who equate spies with traitors, and vice versa, but I suggest you revise your opinion unless you wish to be pitched over the side and your vessel sailed into Montevideo or somewhere equally unpleasant."

Phillip left them to adjust to that thought while he studied his pencilled agenda. He sat back. "I shall now direct your attention to the matter of my inspections." There was a sudden murmuring as everyone shifted uneasily on their seats. "From now until we weigh anchor—which will be just as soon as *Hyaena* is with us—I shall make it my particular duty to inspect every transport and assure myself that they are fit for the king's work. You will recall that during the past several months I have often spoken about hygiene and ventilation, so this is no time to raise the matter again.

However, no master will be judged severely if he delivers a *full* complement of labourers at Botany Bay, sound of wind and limb, ready to work as they have never worked before." Phillip glanced round unemotionally. "Such being the case, I shall commence tomorrow morning with *Alexander*. Mr. Sinclair . . . ?"

Alexander's master was hauling himself upright, wig askew, finger shaking angrily. "Am I to understand that we, *we* are to reorganise our crews just to conform wi' navy 'regulations' and suchlike?"

"Yes."

"But—!"

"No more 'buts,' Mr. Sinclair," Phillip advised calmly. "While bearing members of His Majesty's armed force—to whit, soldiers of the Maritime Regiment—all ships will attend closely to their commodore's instructions. And if that is not a sufficiently compelling reason," he added, "remember that the king of France commands one half of the Channel coastline and all the land under our lee between here and Spain."

"This is intolerable!"

"So, I am informed, is being kept a prisoner of war."

Sinclair glowered round at the other merchant captains, found little support for the moment, and sat down with a sullen grunt.

Phillip nodded at *Friendship*'s master. "Mr. Walton?"

"Er, beggin' pardon, sir, but I got this 'ere twenty-odd females an' eighty-somethin' males locked down alow."

"Go on. . . ."

"Well, sir, I put 'em asunder with bars an' all, but if they're to be let on deck together, there'll be some rare ol' rantum-tantum, make no mistake."

"Go on. . . ."

Walton awkwardly shifted his weight to the other leg. "Well, in short, sir, what punishments can I serve 'em for that sort o' thing?"

Phillip breathed out quietly: this question had been a long time coming, but now it had arrived, a decision had to be made, for there was no shirking the fact that three of his transports had mixed batches of convicts crammed into the same tight, dark spaces below. He looked up from his pencilled notes and made a brief smile. "Happily we can all trust in the discipline and good sense of Major Ross' men, Mr. Walton. The marines can be depended upon to do their duty. There will be no, ah, rantum-tantum while they stand to their posts. However," Phillip added, "in the event of there being a disturbance which needs summary punishment, make a signal and they will be brought aboard *Sirius* for a little romp with the bosun's nine-tailed pet. Does that answer your question?"

"Well, sort of, I s'pose," Walton conceded. "But can't *we* flog 'em too?"

"No. In extreme cases, hand them over to the corporal of marines for a caning and enter it in your ship's punishment log."

"But the *women,* sir!"

"What of them?"

"Sorry sir, an' still beggin' pardon, but some o' them's worse'n the men!"

Phillip began to frown slightly. "Explain yourself."

"Well, sir, an' I know I speaks for Cap'n Gilbert with nigh on the same number aboard *Charlotte*—" He glanced round for support from the leathery face of another merchant captain with much the same collar of white chin whiskers, then back at the dapper little naval officer again. "Well, sir, I never seen the like o' what them females get up to, God's truth, an' I'm not one o' your Bible bangers sir. Done my time on the Slave Coast an' West India run, I 'ave, but I never seen the like o' them doxies. They got to be seen to be believed! The things they say an' do would make the devil blush, an' that's a fact."

Phillip laid his pencil aside. "Thank you, Mr. Walton. I appreciate your concern and candour. I shall, indeed, be seeing them very soon. In the meantime, strive to be impartial, and if any of your men show the least signs of indiscipline, lay to with the lash, there must be no promiscuity between crew and cargo."

"Sir?"

"Rantum-tantum," Phillip explained civilly. "Speaking of which, it might be a good idea if you passed the word that all females have come through the Bridewell and are, therefore, poxed. It's not entirely true, so far as our surgeons can tell, but I judge it a pardonable lie under the circumstance."

Phillip began gathering his papers together. "Very well, gentlemen, that is all. You may return to your commands and be ready to make sail the moment wind, weather and *Hyaena* are with us." Phillip looked up, conscious of the shadow falling across his table as the merchant captains began leaving. "Ah, Major Ross."

"About my men's rum ration."

Phillip eased back in his chair; this dour, stubborn, pigheaded redcoat had fought alongside Admiral the Earl Howe on the American station and, not altogether by coincidence, would soon be lieutenant governor of New South Wales. Phillip picked up the pencil again and ticked something on his agenda. "Thank you for reminding me. Your concern for the welfare of your men is most commendable, an example to the rest of us. They are an outstanding body of troops: I have rarely seen their equal and never met better. You and your officers are to be sincerely congratulated—"

"And the extra grog issue?" Ross rasped in an irritating echo of Sinclair's voice.

Phillip smiled tightly. "Depend upon it, major, just as soon as the Lunacy Board has signalled its approval, your men shall have an extra half pint apiece, per diem. Now, Mr. King assures me that you have everything stowed and squared away for our voyage?"

"Aye."

"Splendid. Then that's one less worry for both of us, isn't it?" Phillip concluded with another tight smile. "May I ask you to shut the door quietly as you go out? I have to attend to others who are not so well organised."

16

FIRST LIGHT. Phillip slowly awoke and enjoyed the gurgle of waves running along *Sirius'* timbers, almost level with his ear. After months ashore he could relish the lazy creak of cordage aloft and the thump of swaying blocks. A bell struck. Bare feet slapped overhead in double time as the watch turned out. Phillip tugged the blankets over his chin, glad that such bells now struck for others as another roller passed under the flagship; the bows dropped and she slid down the trough, coming up hard against her mooring hawser. The compass, fixed upside down in its brass gimbal rings above his cot, jolted and swayed, its card inching round as *Sirius* took a new heading: there was also a matching compass over the captain's end of the great cabin table, as the helmsmen and their watch officers well knew.

Reluctantly, Phillip let the blankets fall back and swung his legs over the cot side. Yawning, he pushed through the curtain and padded across to stand at the stern windows in his nightshirt, watching the convoy's riding lamps snuff out one by one as dawn swelled over Spithead. He squinted at the scudding cloud, then across at the wind pennant atop a nearby three-decker. "Wes' sou'west? Damn." He turned and rang the hand bell.

Bryant uncoiled from his berth under the pantry bench and rubbed sleep from his eyes as he brushed past the sentry. "Sir?"

"Coffee."

"Aye aye."

Phillip continued rummaging around for his sea clothing and was buttoning into the heavy, serviceable breeches when Bryant came back from a small spirit kettle, anchored securely to its bed of wet sand—like every other open flame aboard this floating shell of dry wood, hemp, tar, paint and explosives. He laid the tray and pewter coffeepot on the table and stood, waiting for more orders while his master finished shaving with a handful of cold water. Phillip shut his razor and stowed it in one of the table's drawers. "Who's on deck?"

"L'tenant Bradley, sir."

"My compliments to Mr. Bradley. Request him to step below."

"Aye aye, sir."

Phillip had poured himself a warm drink by the time the young duty officer ducked under the door frame and doffed hat. "How stands the wind, Mr. Bradley?"

"Wes' sou'west half a point west, sir."

"Your watch book, if you please." Phillip took the salt-stained record of everything that had happened aboard in the past twenty-four hours, indeed every hour since *Sirius* had been commissioned at Deptford. He sipped coffee and read the weather, trying to divine its pattern at this time of year, then glanced up again, letting the book fall shut. "I doubt we shall see *Hyaena* today."

"No, sir?"

"I shall require the jolly boat. See the men get an early breakfast, then inform me when all is ready. I wish to be aboard *Alexander* without delay."

"Aye aye, sir!"

The crew had finished breakfast within ten minutes and the ship's jolly boat was brought round to her entry port. Phillip gathered his cloak across one arm as he went over the side to the squeal of pipes and settled himself in the stern sheets. "*Alexander*."

"Aye aye, sir! Give way, m'lads, heeeave—!"

Phillip made the most of the brief passage to compose more notes and instructions in his mind before the boat came alongside the convict transport. An armed sideparty stood to order as their commodore swung up the companion ladder. "A-ten-shun!"

"Thank you, corporal. Has the master been informed?"

"Sir!"

"Still getting dressed?"

"Sir!"

"Very well, I shall take a short turn around deck. Dismiss your men to their duties."

"Sir!"

Phillip touched hatbrim and began strolling for'ard. *Alexander* was improving, though she still remained far short of being a man o' war, he added to himself, stepping across a coiled brace which would have earned someone two dozen at the gratings in the other navy. But improving, yes, definitely improving and with rather less stench coming through the barred hatchway.

He paused a moment at the pigpen, built in an angle between the foremast and the ship's heads, abaft the spiked barricade, and cast an eye over the sow and her litter as they nuzzled her teats. The last piglet would be banged on the skull just in time for replacements to come aboard at Teneriffe. The two milking goats were booked for the galley, too, when they ran dry. So was the coop of hens once they stopped laying eggs for the officers' table. Phillip leaned elbows on the pen railing and scratched the sow's back with the tip of his sword scabbard. "Never mind, old lady. . . ."

He turned abruptly as footsteps hurried closer, expecting to see Sinclair, but it was Richard Johnson, the chaplain, still buttoning a coat to his chin. A young man with far to go, also well connected with the Wilberforce Interest, Phillip reminded himself as Johnson ran to a halt, his pale hair blowing everywhere. "Ah, Captain Phillips! Such a delightful morning, isn't it? Divine Providence would seem to be favouring our enterprise!"

"Yes. Isn't it?" Phillip wondered if ordination also meant the ritual loosening of a man's tongue-strings as he nodded up at the chaplain's rather meaty face, then gestured into the pigpen. "I was just taking stock."

"Aren't they dear little creatures? I've reserved two for our own table!"

"A wise move," Phillip agreed drily, nodding aft to the padlocked tub where the day's ration of salt beef was being softened in sea water for the crew. "Some of the things cooky dredges from the harness cask lack a certain zest." He smiled distantly at the hills of Wight. "Settling in all right, Mr. Johnson?"

The young man bit lips and composed a frown. "Well, captain, I was rather hoping we might speak upon that very subject. You see, dearest Mary and I have been assigned this space—I would never call it a cabin—this *cupboard* by Captain Sinclair. Now, far be it from me to criticise his running of this magnificent ship, but the space is really most inadequate."

"Hardly enough room to swing a cat?"

"Cat?" The Reverend Johnson was genuinely puzzled by such an odd remark as he looked around deck for the animal. "What cat?"

"The bosun's pet." Phillip was laconic. "But please continue. Am I to understand that there is not enough living space for your wife and yourself?"

"Precisely so." The young man groped around for the right phrase and lowered his voice. "You see, my wife and I have only just entered into the blessed state of matrimony and, well, we are finding it very difficult to be, well, um, *alone?*"

"Heavens! It must be cramped if you can't even dance the blanket hornpipe."

"Hornpipe?"

"Just a nautical term," the much older man commented with a distant smile at the horizon. "Anyhow, it would seem you find it hard to be alone."

"Exactly so. It is very difficult."

"So what do you expect me to do about it?"

Johnson bit lip again. "Well, seeing that you are in charge, I thought you might order our transfer to a bigger boat. . . ."

"A *bigger* boat, eh?"

"Quite. A bigger boat."

Phillip counted up to five, slowly. "Mr. Johnson: *Alexander* is my biggest transport. At about four hundred fifty registered tons she's damned near the equal of HMS *Sirius* and more than twice the size of *Friendship* out there!" He paused, watching the young man's face for a flicker of understanding, then went on even more slowly. "My brig, *Supply*, would fit into this ship three times over: I could almost winch her aboard at this moment and condemn *Alexander*'s launch for firewood."

"But Captain Phillips—!"

"Mr. Johnson, enough. None of us is living in the lap of luxury, but if we learn to haul together and remain cheerful I'm sure we shall all make a safe landfall in God's good time."

"But Mary says—!"

"My compliments to Mrs. Johnson. I can appreciate her feelings in the matter. Please inform her that, if during my rounds of inspection I find accommodation larger than *Alexander*'s, I'll have your things sent over. All right?"

"Um, yes."

"Good." Phillip sucked a tooth reflectively. "Lieutenant King assures me you have all your equipment stowed and squared away . . . ?"

"What?"

"I am told you have all your hymn books and things, ready to go to work."

Richard Johnson's worries rarely lasted for long and he was already looking much brighter as he nodded. "Definitely. Dear Mr. Wilberforce used his very best offices to obtain a full supply of suitable reading materials for the voyage, and afterward too."

"Did he, by God? That was damned decent of him."

"Indeed, very decent of him," Johnson corrected tactfully. "We have enough books to allow each convicted felon to borrow six at any one time."

"Incredible."

"Yes, isn't it? As well as testaments, catechisms and prayers, there are also two hundred copies of *Exercises Against Lying*, fifty copies of *Dr. Woodward's Caution to Swearers*—I can lend you one—and no less than a hundred *Exhortations to Chastity*. There are also five score of *Dissuasions from Stealing* and a dozen *Wilson's Instructions to the Indians*."

Phillip minutely studied the hills of Wight while the chaplain held an expectant smile. Then the commodore glanced sideways again. "How many convicts can read?"

"Read?"

"Letter the English alphabet."

"Er, I'm not altogether sure of the exact figure—"

"Then I suggest we begin by finding out this morning. Please don't run away just yet! We shall continue this conversation when I've had a few words with Captain Sinclair." Johnson stared down at the surprisingly tough little fingers which now pinioned his own wrist as *Alexander*'s master tramped from behind the poop barricade with its swivel gun of grapeshot permanently trained on the ship's waist. Phillip touched hatbrim with the other hand. "Good morning, Mr. Sinclair."

" 'Morning. Commodore."

"Indeed, as I was only saying to myself a few moments ago, *Alexander* is a credit to you and Mr. Campbell's Interest. You and your officers are to be congratulated. Please inform the men when you parade your divisions later this morning."

"Er? Oh, aye."

"Now, would you be so kind as to rouse your carpenter? I am about to inspect the prisoners' accommodation."

"Inspect the *what*—!"

"Government property, Mr. Sinclair," Phillip interrupted mildly. "They are under Admiralty contract now. M'Lord Howe has made me personally responsible for every tick, nit, flea and louse aboard this convoy. The carpenter, if you please."

Sinclair turned uncertainly and aimed his mouth into the fo'c'sle hatch. "Aloft the chippy!"

Within moments a dried-up prune of a man had climbed on deck and stood, bandy legs astride, waiting for orders. Phillip nodded at him. "You have your awl?"

"Ready aye ready!" the carpenter replied, touching the long steel probe which he wore on his belt with the hammer and toolpouch of his office.

"Good. We are going into the hold. You too, Mr. Johnson." They walked to the main grating. A marine snapped to attention, musket tucked against his side, as Sinclair searched around his key chain and began wrestling with the padlocks. The marine swung musket to hip and aimed at the square opening as its bars crashed back against the deck. Phillip checked that his service sword was easy in its scabbard, took a deep breath and led the way into foetid darkness, hand over hand down the ladder.

He stepped off the bottom rung and stood in a narrow space between the for'ard stowage, with its tiers of kegs, and a timber bulkhead pierced with the same loopholes as the one astern by the marines' quarters. An empty cage of four-inch-square oak battens had been rigged on the starboard side of the entry and its gate padlocked. "Mr. Sinclair!" Phillip coughed. "That space, in there! What's it being used for now?"

"We-ell, seeing as we have fewer mouths to feed than formerly, it has tended to fall into disuse. . . ."

"I hardly imagine your employer will allow you to sail on to Canton with so much cargo capacity left empty," Phillip mused aloud.

"Oh, ye may depend I've certain ideas how it might be used. . . ."

"So have I." Phillip looked at the carpenter again. "In a few moments we shall be going inside. I would suggest you take only the awl and leave your other tools outside: we mustn't put temptation in the way of our weaker brethren. And remember, I require you to carry out a thorough examination of all standing timbers, particularly probing into dark joins and down under the bilge."

The carpenter checked the candle flame inside his glim and shut its glass door. "Lookin' for somethin' special like?"

"That will very much depend on how enterprising your passengers have been. Now, shall we go inside?"

Sinclair sniggered and drew the iron bolts, holding the gate open with exaggerated courtesy for Phillip to make the first move. "After *you*. . . ."

With almost two hundred men packed into a space forty feet long by thirty wide and at most eight feet high in the centre, Phillip realised that accommodation was bound to be a little cramped. He stooped through the gateway and slowly looked around at the slatted wooden racks which served for sleeping shelves. Johnson shuddered beside him: the near silence unnerved Phillip, too. Just the wet, tubercular hacking of someone dying in darkness abaft the mainmast's foot, and the impersonal clink of fetters as someone shifted a hand or leg. No one else moved even an eyelid along the tiers of blank faces that stared off the racks at the unwelcome strangers from Outside.

Phillip reminded himself that, if *Alexander* had been shipping African labour to Kingston, then almost twice the number would have been stowed here, so the discomfort was really only relative. He cleared his throat and tried ignoring the acrid stench of thickened spew, dung and piss round the nearest open bucket. "The spoon, Mr. Sinclair."

Alexander's master finished polishing his indicator and handed it over for the other man to study before returning it with a nod. "Much better," Phillip said. "Keep up the good work." Then he gathered his cloak and gingerly stepped past the bucket to reach the centre of the aisle which ran the full length between bulkheads.

"My name is Phillip," he began. "I am commodore of this convoy and will be governor of the colony when we arrive at Botany Bay in New Holland." There was a sudden rattle of interest up and down the hold as the cargo had its first official notice that it was going anywhere at all. "As such you will have many opportunities to learn my methods. You will find them very simple: work hard, stay out of trouble, and I shall wipe the slate clean for a new start in life. If, on the other hand, some of you wish to remain idle and tempt your fate, you will surely find that all the laws and punishments of England have been sent ashore with me, sharp, bright and ready to strike down without pity. The choice will be yours. Think well upon it."

He looked round at the unblinking masks of caked dirt and scabs. "Now, are there any reasonable requests you wish to bring to my attention?" Nobody moved. Only the dying man continued to wheeze and cough. Nobody else did or said anything and Phillip was struck by the thought that he had slipped into a foreign language by mistake, or that his labourers were all deaf mutes. "Come, come! Surely your quarters are not so generous that you lack for nothing!" Someone tittered at the back. "What? Nothing?" Phillip insisted, wearing down their stubborn silence. "*Nothing . . . ?*"

Nobody moved. Nobody spoke. Then, uncertainly, a shape crouched into the aisle and inched closer like a spider, holding its shirt tight against theft. It stopped short at a safe distance, watching Sinclair's fist tighten round a pistol butt. "*Excellenz!* Listen me. These are with the *Skorbut.* All needing the greens." Phillip started at the guttural accent. "Soon, more *kaput,* dead! I know. Green leafs. Quick!" The shape turned and scuttled away, not daring to loiter any longer and be marked down for punishment.

Phillip wrenched himself back to the present and glowered at Sinclair's lofty sneer. "Make to the victualling cutter. Cabbage and carrots, ad libitum, daily issue. You may use the tops and stems to boil soup."

"Soup!"

"Or broth. Never forget," Phillip snarled, shaken by his own fury. "When you have finished conveying these scurvied items to New Holland, I shall have only begun!" He looked at Johnson's sweaty face. "Now, you want to say a few words?"

"Oh, I don't think——"

Phillip scowled along the aisle. "Mr. Johnson is your chaplain, come today to bring you spiritual comfort. But first he requires to know how many of you can read." Nobody moved, nobody spoke, perhaps nobody understood their governor. "What? Not even a few letters?"

Someone broke wind in the shadows, low and slow.

Phillip pursed his lips and looked at Johnson. "Evidently Mr. Wilberforce is better acquainted with the needs of Africans, but don't give up yet. Meanwhile, is there anything else you'd like to ask before we go aloft?"

Johnson damped his lips and took the plunge. He stood on tiptoe and peered round the foetid gloom. "How many of you are communicating members of the Church of England?"

Another mocking fart rumbled away among the packed shelves. "*That* t'yez an' yez England church," a County Kerry man threatened from the darkness. "We wants us own Father!"

Johnson's face sagged as a ripple of agreement echoed round the hold. He stared down at Phillip. "There are papists in here!"

"How fortunate. Now at least you'll have a topic of conversation with some of your parishioners; I imagine the rest might as well be Hottentots." The older man's tight smile never wavered. "Ah, let's see what curiosities our carpenter has found. . . ."

Phillip returned the boarding axe to Sinclair without comment, along with a pair of files, several sharp lumps of bottle glass, a broken knife blade, ten yards of new rope and almost a hatful of iron nails prised from *Alexander*'s timbers. Then he glanced round and pitched his voice for everyone to hear. "Think carefully about what I have told you! And think very, very carefully before you try dismantling any more of your ship." Phillip returned their unblinking stares and turned away.

The gate slammed behind him. Its bolts shot home and the padlocks clacked. The tension eased and life returned to normal as the hatchway crashed shut. Cribb shoved his head over the end of his shelf, voice at the usual penetrating hiss since the marines had made home only a few yards away, behind the after bulkhead: "You dozy bugger, Leafy." Levi didn't seem to notice or care, too busy with something else. Cribb's voice hardened: "Oi! Buggerlugs! I said, keep that mouth shut or I'll shut it for you!"

Levi took his time finishing what he was doing. Then he straightened and pushed closer, sticking his face within inches of the other man's. "So you don't like what I say, heh? You shut my mouth, you say? Try it." Both lips were rolling back to bare gums, then Levi's tongue wiggled one of the yellowing teeth. "What you see, heh?"

Reluctantly, Cribb's fist relaxed. He grimaced at the rotten breath as he peered into Levi's mouth. "What's special?"

Levi wiggled harder and fresh blood wept from the pulpy root tissue. The mouth shut. "Is *der Skorbut*—you call skurfee? I seen plenty times in Po Land and Turk Land. When comes winter and the poor has only potatoes and salt fish, then comes *Skorbut* also to the table. But not to the stable for cowses and horses. I ask myself, 'Why?' I answer myself, 'Cowses and horses don't eat potatoes and salt fish and zhit we eat now. Cowses and horses eat greens—' "

"Chrissakes."

"Is not winter down here but I got *Skorbut* coming soon," Levi went on relentlessly, ignoring Cribb's annoyance. "So has your Crystal Prig and the Slyboots, they got it coming. Maybe *you* got it coming? Who cares?! I only know the sureness of such a dying is reason to risk the unsureness of getting a whip for talking out. What I got to lose? Soon we all upside down in the *Kuckteppel*—what you say?—zhitpot."

"Hn!"

"Go 'hn' yourself. I know what I know, and what I know is green leafs."

Cribb had been struggling to follow the other man's mishmash of languages and accents while, not for the first time, wondering how to silence this stubborn, opinionated, contrary challenge to his authority. The other two hundred or so men below decks had long since divided into two unequal halves: the smallest, Cribb's family, those others from Newgate and some survivors of Pimple's trusties, who had embarked with him from *Retribution* at Blackwall after consolidating their power by fist and boot; and the majority, those too weak or broken to shovel the hulk's quota of mud and fit only for transportation to the future dockyards of Botany Bay. Typically, Levi had refused to be part of this natural order.

"Well?" the condemned quack doctor rasped. "What *you* going to do about the skurfee if *I* don't order the green leafs?"

Cribb's scowl deepened. "You and your green leafs! That's all you can talk about, leafs, leafs, leafs! You oughter been born a bird so's you could spend your time up a tree talking with the leafs!" Cribb's finger was jabbing at Levi's thin, razor sharp nose. "You listen to me! I don't give a stuff for your Po Land and your Turk Land, because *I* been around too. Right? You ain't the only bugger down 'ere what's seen the world, not by a long shot! I been to Canada. And Americky—"

"*Ach, Klainkeit.*"

"Seven years of it, a-fighting for the king—"

"*Shmok!*"

"I seen scurvy, *real* scurvy, in the boats and in Copper 'ill camp, scurvy so real the meat drops off a cove's legs like bits o' bacon. Wobbly teeth's *nothing,* see?"

Levi was far from impressed by the story, but, luckily, another shape was crouching near the upright man's shelf to whisper something in Cribb's ear: the cook's paddle had just begun stirring burgoo on deck, knocking against the copper boiler and gently vibrating through *Alexander*'s timbers to the family's "crow"—or lookout—ear pressed flat against a main rib: the first breakfast bucket would soon be dropping through a narrow hatchway between the marines' bulkhead and the mainmast.

Cribb swung his legs off the shelf and elbowed into the aisle, then banged his bowl and spoon like a wooden gong. "Brother Ben's crew is first in line today! What don't mean *you*, nicknacks!" he added with a lunge, the spoon cracking back an impatient hand which had been first yesterday as well. "Next, Brother Dipper's crew, then Brother Scrag's!" Cribb had tamed hungry recruits: the same glare now tamed a hunger riot. "Brother Mangler sends up the slops today—"

Cribb helped discipline the first division of convicts, commanded by Ben

Thorpe, as buckets of burgoo—biscuit crumb, oatmeal and beef water from last night's boiling—were doled into wooden bowls and the shuffling line kept moving with random kicks. It was the law on *Alexander* that the dozen or so members of the family were served last: any scrap of meat or lump of oatmeal would have settled on the bottom of the buckets by then.

Cribb made himself comfortable on their improvised mess table, the one nearest the gate's meagre ventilation, and began polishing his spoon while the other six men watched, waiting for him to be first. Then, just as deliberately, he snapped a tile of ration bread which had also been thrown through the hatch and began breakfast, chewing slowly, taking an austere pride in controlling his own stomach as well as everyone else's.

"Lip-oo darkums covees," he announced in mumbled cant, inaudible beyond the family's line of sentries, now watching the other hundred and seventy-odd lags slurping burgoo. Eyes flickered and paid attention when the upright spoke. "Two little friends got called up to 'elp cooky last night. Never 'appened before. They was away a long time. Why?"

Nobody spoke.

"Second point. What was Sparrow Legs doing at the cage before 'e come in?"

Dipper flicked an eyebrow. "Reckon 'e knows somethin' 'e oughtn't . . . ?"

"If 'e does, we'll bloody soon find out," Cribb replied in the same buzzing murmur. " 'Ow's Tommo's lurk coming on?"

Dipper's mouth stayed the same thin, motionless slit. " 'E needs more time."

Cribb spooned beef water and sipped. "Better nudge 'im along: we're sailing to 'Olland soon."

"Be you sure?" Ben Thorpe muttered anxiously.

"All London to a brick, mate. Sparrow Legs as good as told us so. Besides, I been on boats, to Americky and suchlike. A fly cove learns what's what. . . ."

"I'd better 'urry 'im," Dipper interrupted quietly.

"Right," Cribb agreed. "Tommo was dead lucky this time: Chippy didn't look 'ard enough in the right place."

"We stash the boodle in 'nother dump quickums?" the Scragger murmured.

"Right. After snoozer tonight," Cribb ordered, licking his bowl clean, inside and out. "Cooky's little mice could easy forget who their regular mates is for a nibble of cheese. Nasty."

Ben Thorpe was gnawing a white bone, more for the memories it brought back than with any hope of finding a scrap of marrow or sinew. "You want me to squeeze their knackers and find out, Joe?"

"Not just yet, Ben," Cribb replied softly, restraining the baby-faced yokel, who was now his private enforcer and personal bodyguard. "Better the cove what you know's bent than the one you think's straight. Besides, we got tons of time to squeeze squealers. . . ."

17

EVERY DAY Phillip returned from another tour of inspection and controlled his temper by pacing *Sirius*' poop deck, glaring aloft at the wind pennant which was still fixed in the sou'westerly quarter. Then, early on May 12, the breeze began to back easterly and freshen. Phillip immediately cancelled Saturday's inspection of *Borrowdale* and gave orders that he was not to be disturbed until *Hyaena* beat between Selsey and Wight.

He was still working on his final draft of masters' standing regulations in the great cabin when, shortly before midmorning, Hunter rapped on the door and ducked through. Phillip looked up, steadying his quill. "*Hyaena*?"

"I'm afraid not, sir. Not yet. It's the Winchester trollops."

Phillip laid his work aside and knit fingers together. "Where?"

Hunter showed no emotion. "They're already embarked: the port admiral's command."

Phillip's jaw muscles began to work. "Make to Mr. King: have him come aboard immediately."

"It was he who informed me, sir," Hunter replied. "He's waiting outside now."

"Then get him here!"

Lieutenant King trotted from the companionway, despatch bag clasped under one arm along with his hat, and joined Captain Hunter in front of the commodore. Phillip fixed him with a bleak stare. "How many?"

"Eleven, sir."

"Then *dis*embark 'em without delay. Inform the local Bridewell to collect. We are about to make sail. They are not—"

"It can't be done, sir."

"Uh?"

"Admiral Muir's express command, sir. Also, the M'Gee infant's papers have arrived from the Home Office. The child, and its licence to proceed with the mother, have been signed for. There'll be the very devil to pay if we refuse them a berth now."

"Damn. Damn, damn, damn."

"Sorry, sir. Another twelve hours and we'd probably have slipped them."

Phillip brushed away King's sympathy and scowled at the despatch bag instead. "Where do we stow them? *Friendship*? Or *Alexander*?"

King knew which one his chief wanted to hear; instead he gave a truthful opinion. "*Alexander*."

"Hn!"

"Sinclair still has that extra dunnage where he intends shipping a personal cargo from Teneriffe to Canton," King persisted.

"Don't be ridiculous! That birdcage wouldn't take eleven adults and one child even if we pushed them in sideways like firewood!"

King shrugged. "He's already buried twelve or thirteen males; it'd be a direct swap and his ration manifest need not be altered in any way."

Phillip fell silent. Then, after a struggle with himself, he looked up again. "Not *Friendship*?"

"No, sir. It's *Alexander* or nothing."

"And neither the Home Office nor the port admiral will allow 'nothing,' damn them." Phillip stood and leaned by the stern windows, wistfully looking out at the dancing waters and the high skies of early summer. "The threat of those damned whores has been hanging over my head since I can't remember when. Now, just as we're about to slip our moorings—" He stopped and turned sharply. "*Where* did you say they were?"

King looked uncomfortable. "Alongside. In the cutter. It was Admiral Muir's orders that I personally went out with them and made certain they never came back."

"Holy stones!" Phillip grabbed his sword and hat as he ran through the door, up the companion ladder and ducked on deck. The whistling and hoots stopped dead at the first flash of gold braid, and about two dozen tars scattered back to their work. "Officer of the watch—!"

"Mr. Midshipman Giles, sir!" a bosun's mate panted, running aft and halting in his tracks.

"Mr. Giles to my cabin, on the double! Mr. Thomas: assume deck duties!"

"Aye aye, sir!"

Phillip halted at the entry port and stared down at the Winchester justices' contribution to his many problems: women. Convicted women. Women of all shapes and ages, penned at wavering bayonet point by a guard of marines. The cutter's crew struggled to keep straight faces as their commodore recoiled from the brazen jeer. "Oooooo!"

"Only a lit'le shrimp, aren't 'e, girls?"

"Garn! I'll bet it's a regular whopper—!"

"Get 'em off, sailor boy! Show us yer stuff!"

"Aaaah!"

Phillip fell back another two paces. "Mr. King! Consign-those-items-as-directed! Mr. Hunter! Make to *Alexander*: eleven supernumeraries coming aboard forthwith!"

Reluctantly, King touched hatbrim and went over the side, stamped on several groping fingers and slumped in the stern sheets again. "*Alexander*. God damn you all."

The cutter's jib tightened, slicing her bows across the last half mile of anchorage as *Sirius*' gun boomed behind him and signal flags streamed. The coxswain still had a dreamy look on his face as he swung up the helm and settled alongside the transport, picturing the next scene. It wasn't long in coming. The women crossed fetters and wouldn't budge from their places, enjoying every succulent moment as King began to flush, then lose his temper. "Get up that side this instant!"

"Oooo, what a way t'talk t'ladies—!"

"Don't 'ave no manners, 'e don't, 'is mum'd be *ashamed*!"

King whacked the nearest man's musket. "Prod 'em with your bayo-net!" An unfortunate choice of words: the gale of laughs had every crew-man aboard *Alexander* lining her rails within moments, bawling en-couragement. "The *bayonet*, damn your eyes!" The marine obeyed and began making little jabs at the women, missing by inches, splintering the cutter's woodwork instead.

The happy faces above them just as suddenly vanished under a barrage of cracks and slashing thuds as Sinclair came up from behind with his cob. He glanced over the side himself and casually squirted tobacco juice at the cutter's sail. "Having a spot o' bother, lieutenant?"

"Er, no! Just a certain reluctance to board, that's all!"

Sinclair made a very rare grin. " '*Reluctance*,' eh?"

"You could say so!"

"Not I, *you* say so." Sinclair was tucking the knotted rope under his belt. Then he came over the tumblehome with surprising grace, landed lightly and decked the nearest woman with his knee. The cob set to work, pounding each item up *Alexander*'s side; Sinclair was deaf to their shrieks and dragging chains as he packed them aloft, head to tail. The last woman curtseyed; the cob whizzed overhead, missing her completely; she straightened again and stepped across the grinding wash between cutter and transport.

Sinclair blinked after her, then tucked the rope away and glanced at King's sweaty face. "I'm not allowed to flog yon articles, o' course, since that would be against Commodore Phillips' orders. So what ye've just seen is a 'start,' same as we'd tickle any saucy bint off the Slave Coast. Ye'd agree there's no similarity wi' a flogging, and that no orders have been broken . . . ?"

"Yes. There is quite a difference."

"Good, good, ever happy to oblige an officer and gentleman in difficulties," Sinclair drawled approvingly. "Your humble servant. . . ." He bowed, then sauntered aloft himself, sea boots thudding on the companion's rungs.

The crow flinched, barely a handspan away as they passed, his ear squeezed against *Alexander*'s damp timbers. "Shiiit! What a servin' someone got. . . ."

"What's up, Dan?" Thorpe demanded, crouching close in the darkness, but the family's lookout was still listening to other things, face screwed tight with concentration, trying to interpret the faint squeals, bumps, thuds and rattles. "Dunno, mate. Jus' for the moment it sounded like some cove was strippin' the 'ide off a pack o' morts."

Thorpe translated into Suffolk. "Ar? Women? *'Ere?*"

"What's up, Ben?" Cribb hissed, also crouching.

"Dan'l reckons as there's a parcel o' *women* a-bein' flogged somewhere—"

"Shh!"

The crow and Thorpe fell silent and listened with Cribb: the grating was being thrown back. One of *Alexander*'s mates was coming down into the gloom with his keys. He finished unlocking the starboard cage, coughed and flapped air, then inched aside as the first of the convicted women dragged her pain over the combing, slowed by her wrist irons and the rags of a full skirt. Her bare feet missed the third rung and she slid the rest of the way, dumping on the deck.

The others were more steady and made their own way down the ladder as best they could while almost every man in the hold stampeded, shrieking and howling. Even those too weak to creep a few moments earlier were now hobbling forward. Cribb clawed the bars and squashed face between them, also counting the new arrivals.

The roar of catcalls tumbled away to low growls of appreciation as the eleventh and last mort handed over the tenth's baby, hitched her petticoats and began an unhurried entry down the ladder.

"Gor! Jus' wipe your whiskers round tha' lot!"

"She's got *shoes!*"

"Gorrr. . . ."

The petticoats fell like a theatre curtain as she stepped off the ladder, glorying in her skill, coppery hair piled under a man's black billycock hat with one brim low over the left eye in a jaunty follow-me-lads roll. The green velvet jacket and lilac taffeta skirts were hardly dirty. She was radiant, she was in total command of the situation, and she knew it.

So did nearly two hundred lags as she dimpled at the grinning crewman who had just failed to grope up her linen. "Tch, tch, didn't your mother tell you never to finger the goods till you've paid the bill, honey joy?" she asked with a husky chuckle, part Irish, part genteel English, and all a style of her own as she playfully smacked the offending paw with her fan. The sailor never saw the knee which folded him against the ladder, eyeballs popping from their sockets as she turned away and strolled into the cage, smiling back at the thunder of applause from the men's hold.

Cribb's eyes were also popping. "It's 'er!"

Alexander's second mate kicked the gate shut after the woman. "Bitch!"

"It can't be," Cribb repeated aloud, trying to clear his head. "Not the gen'ral's lady, not *'ere*—"

"What, tosh?" another lag gasped, also crushed against the iron bars.

"She's 'ere," Cribb repeated in a flat voice. "Mrs. Brandon's 'ere."

"Not Kiss an' Kill Kitty?!" the lag hissed. "Not the mort what done that toppin' job on a swell with 'is sword?"

Sweating and confused, Cribb nodded and started tasting breakfast again.

"Hey yous! Kitty Brandon's in there—!"

Cribb surrendered his place at the gate and reeled away, grabbing his shelf for support while his stomach heaved up the burgoo.

Ben Thorpe was shadowing him, protecting and being protected. "Joe! Be you orright? You look like you just seened a ghost!"

"I—I 'ave." His friend wiped mouth with a shaking wrist. "I seen Mrs. Brandon 'erself—"

Thorpe looked baffled. " 'Oo's she then?"

Cribb finished scrubbing the shaky hand around neck and naked chest, battling to get his thoughts under control again. "That's all I needed— them morts, an' *'er*. Now what . . . ?"

"Well, if you asks me, Oi smells nothin' but trouble," Thorpe announced to the world, passing judgment on the day's happenings with a gloomy shake of the head.

"You're not wrong," Cribb grunted, spitting to clean his mouth.

"I seen what 'appens when we not got enough ewes in the yard back 'ome, comes tuppin' time, an' Oi can tell you it's murder wi' them rams," Thorpe went on, still shaking his head. "Tha's what it's a-goin' to be 'ere, Joe, mark my words. Always was bloody murder when there's not enough twat to go round."

Ben Thorpe only seemed gormless when straying outside his very small field of experience. But once safely behind the fence again, the farm boy's mind worked like flint and steel in Cribb's private opinion, slow to get started until the right spark was struck, then it fired up just as brightly as a jar of phosphorus and turpentine.

Cribb said nothing and watched the first of the family brethren come giggling back from the gateway. He cocked an eye at Thorpe's moody frown. "Pecker up. We'll play this the way the cards fall. Stick close and 'ope we get the right deal." Then he turned and tried matching smirks with the others as they gathered round their leader. "What a turn-up, eh? *Now* where do we go . . . ?"

Dipper's answer served for everyone, a huge grin and one finger pumping wildly through his clenched fist. "Muffin, Phoss! Loverly juicey muffin! I ain't 'ad none for two years!"

Cribb said nothing and watched *Alexander*'s fire hose jetting sea water through the grating, swilling men and boys into heaps behind the gate. Ben Thorpe had been right: the women had just brought a whole new parcel of troubles aboard for him. Brother Dipper was feeling his oats. So was Brother Scag, a professional dognapper reprieved to penal servitude for life, and Slyboots, fourteen years transportation for snitching gentlemen's cloaks and sprinting away up dark alleys; both now sniggering and nudging while they shared a wonderful secret. As were Brother Tickler— the family's locksmith—and Crystal Prig, a journeyman glazier who used to smash the gentry's front windows at night with a slingshot before going round to their backdoor tradesmen's entrances the next morning to repair them.

Cribb tugged Pimple's old jacket tighter around his bare shoulders and kept silent. He had never doubted that it was far easier to win power in a hot fight than to hold onto it once the jealous and crafty began their boring and tunnelling—like Dipper—all the while protesting loyalty to the upright. Eyes blank, Cribb went on studying the circle of sweaty, excited faces. Only Thorpe managed to look glum about something. "Pecker up, Ben. You just lost a george and found a farthing?"

The younger man refused to be humoured, even by his only friend. He flicked a dirty look at the women, now visible again since the hose had knocked most of the men off the bars. "Oi don't like it."

"Why's that?" Cribb asked, ignoring Slyboots' snort, winning time to think ahead.

Thorpe's face tightened under its crust of dirt and grease. He knew what the family called him behind his back—Bacon Chewer, Clodhopper, Sheep Shagger—and it was no secret that most of them resented their upright's blood debt to him, a bumpkin outsider. Thorpe also knew that when it came to matching wits against flash city coves he would always run a poor last, but there was obstinate sinew in him. He glowered round at them all. "Oi tell you Oi don't like it!"

There was another mocking titter from Slyboots and Thorpe blushed with fury. "Oi don' mean *that*! Oi'm good to throw up a maid's dress an' green 'er quick as the best! But that aren't all to things by a long shot—!"

Cribb's finger silenced him. Thorpe's voice had been rising steadily: the off-duty marines were only five or six yards away beyond the bulkhead. "Sorry Joe," he mumbled, "but Oi smells trouble, like Oi said."

Cribb nodded for the rest of the family to keep reasonably quiet, too. "I don't quite get what you're trying to tell us, Ben. . . ."

Thorpe took a deeper breath and started again. "Oi seen what 'appens when we not got enough ewes back 'ome comes tuppin' time, an' it's bloody murder!" He glared round at the other scabby faces. "Tha's what it's goin' to be wi' us, bloody murder!"

"Well, I'm gettin' *mine*," Dipper promised, threatening nobody in particular, yet.

"But what about them others?" Thorpe demanded stubbornly. "Ain't they a-goin' to want their bit? An' when they do, where's tha' a-goin' to put us once all them other buggers get their 'eads together? What chance *you* got o' stoppin' ruttin' bulls an' rams then? Oi'll tell you now, fook all! Oi reckons them women's as much good to us as a dose o' the itch, tha's what Oi reckon."

Cribb pulled a face, as if this were a point he had never considered before, and glanced at the others, also hunched shoulder to shoulder in the hold's permanent gloom. "Looks like Brother Ben's got a bene brainbox on 'is shoulders. Like 'e says, that little mill we just seen ain't nothing to the battle we'll 'ave if we don't get *our* 'eads together first. . . ."

Dipper's scowl was deepening. "What you mean, Phoss?"

Cribb shrugged. "I mean there ain't nothin' in the world what says them other buggers 'ave *got* to do things the family way. There's plenty o' coves down 'ere what reckon they could be family too—their family— with *us* jumping on the shovel every time one of them shouts 'Shit!' "

"Yair? An' wha's that got to do with them morts?" Dipper challenged, sensing a sudden gap between leader and led. One quick shove now could topple this cautious redcoat's austere rule once and for always. He grinned round at the rest. "I tell you this, covees, the first what gets them doxies on the job an' workin' for *us*, wins!"

" 'Ere, 'old your 'orses, tosher," Cribb cautioned. "Things like this need thinking through, they need plans."

"Plans!" Dipper sneered. "What's there to plan, eh? I—tell—you: we can sit 'ere on our fannies an' do nothin', or we can get them morts back on the game afore anyone else 'thinks it through'!" He could feel the flood of popular support turning his way. "I mean it, mates! It's so simple a baby could see it with both eyes shut! Once we get the clamps on them morts they're goin' to be our tickets to whole buckets o' grub, an' baccy, an' grog once the tars an' lobsters know what we got to sell 'em. I know, I been on the game since I don't know when! I know all the wrinkles an' it's money for jam, believe me! Bossin' a string o' firecrackers on the streets is better'n findin' the front door key to the Bank o' England! So I say we grab our chances now, while them other silly pricks is still lookin' the other way!" Dipper wound up his election speech on a high note while his exciting word pictures did the rest.

Cribb couldn't offer the family anything so good; besides, he knew that Dipper was right. Putting the hard word on ten whores to set up as their protector was common sense in a floating world of almost three hundred men—free and unfree. That was no problem, but the eleventh woman was going to be a harder safe to crack. His palms were already sticky at the prospect of having to bully a woman who had once fought off wolves with a blackthorn club at the gravepits of Saratoga. He squirmed and began realising what a no-win hand Dipper had just dealt him. Now he must either stride into the cage and brass out the consequences or tamely surrender the family without a struggle; if there was a third way, he had yet to find it.

He wiped palms again, cleared a parched throat and spat to prove to the world that he wasn't frightened. "So that's what Brother Dip' reckons we ought to do, is it? Fair enough, but what's the rest think . . . ?"

"I say we stop lippin' an' start fillin' them morts!" Scragger growled, speaking for an overwhelming bloc of family votes.

"Easier said than done, 'arder done than said," Cribb replied, probing the almost solid front which Dipper had suddenly raised against him. He waited for at least token support from Thorpe, but the countryman had slipped away to a private past—as he often did—leaving Cribb alone to grope for something, anything to slow this headlong charge into the unknown. Every instinct was warning him to tread slowly, but every moment's delay was establishing Dipper's hold over the other men.

"Garn, Phoss! F'shitsake get a move on!"

"Yair! Put the 'ard word on 'em now!"

"Maybe 'e's savin' it up for Chrismuss!" Dipper quipped, winking back at the laughter.

Cribb had been manoeuvred into a corner: there was no way out but to look masterful and nod at the Tickler. "Got your stuff?" The locksmith grinned with everyone else as he fanned a kit of bent nails from the top seam of his ragged breeches. "Let's go and chat with them morts."

Cribb squared shoulders and shoved his way into the central aisle. The whole family marched up the wet deck behind him and stood guard against the other lags while Tickler groped through the gate and tickled its padlocks from outside, shooting their hardened steel tongues as his picks tweezed springs. Cribb checked that the marine sentry had tired of trying to peer into the women's hold and returned to his lonely beat, tramping twenty-four paces aft. Halt. Turn. For'ard again. Cribb nodded a silent command and ghosted through the open gateway with Thorpe and Dipper, Crystal and the Tickler, who just as deftly unpicked the women's lock. "There y'are, Phoss!" he hissed. "Put it to 'em!"

Dipper was sidling past, ready to lead a pack rape even if he couldn't yet lead a family, but Cribb's palm flattened against his chest. A huddle of scared, curious, saucy faces were staring back from almost total darkness; most were naked, mopping each other's welts and bruises. Cribb was still opening his mouth as Kitty Brandon whipped round, hands on hips, skirts blocking the view. "Get out."

"Garn, Phoss! Put the 'ard word on 'er!"

"Yair, tell the bitch who's boss!"

"I said, *get out.*"

Cribb was drenched with sweat, trapped, trying to ignore the woman in front of him. "You lot back there! Listen in! I'm Phossy Cribb! I'm the upright, the number one man down 'ere! Me, Phossy Cribb! All right?" As an opening pitch it was a shocker.

"I know you all been lagged for working the street game! Right? So you all know what 'appens when there's no cove to pimp proper! Right? You do what the family says an' you'll be all right! Right? But step out of line once and there'll be such a bashing you'll never forget what's what!" It was a terrible speech, and Cribb knew it as the giggling morts joined with the men, led by Dipper.

"Bra-a-avo. Hooray. More."

Cribb now had to look Kitty Brandon in the face for the first time. "Uh, what's that, ma'am?"

"Come, come, sir! You've not finished yet, surely?" she asked.

"And what if I 'ave?" he demanded.

"Why, then you may leave. And shut the door behind you. And never come back till I give you permission so to do." The acquired London veneer was flaking away to expose bedrock Dublin Irish.

"Yes, ma'am. Sorry, ma'am. It was just we sort of wanted to 'elp look after you—"

"Look after us? *You?*" And she slowly wagged her head from side to side at the man's breathtaking insolence. "Little chap, little chap, 'tis a great future you have behind you on the stage—playing the arse end of pantomime donkeys—such a natural comedian you are." She stopped him with a stare as he lunged into the cage, fists bunching. "Go on. Hit me then. I shall scream. But not such a scream as ye ever heard before," she went on calmly. " 'Twill be one that will surely bring every *free* man running, just to see whose throat has been cut. Then, 'midst all my anguished tears and sorrow, I shall tell how *you*—Mr. Fester Uptight Crap—broke in to have your lustful way with we poor, defenceless maidens. What will happen then I cannot imagine, nor do I care overmuch, but 'twill be all Drury Lane to a China orange you'll be travelling hard for the rest of this journey. Meantime, we young ladies—of whom I, Mrs. Katharine Brandon in person, have the honour to be governess and chaperone—will have taken our rightful place in the society of this fine ship."

"Y-you can't talk to me like that!"

"I just did."

"B-but I'm the upright man! You need 'elp!"

"If anyone needs help, 'tis not I," she observed neutrally, brushing a speck of dust off her sleeve, "and certainly not while there are sufficient handsome soldiers and fine sea captains upstairs, eager to throw protective arms around we poor, defenceless women travellers." She dimpled. "So, as we say in the theatrical profession, bugger off."

Cribb's mouth dropped open, then snapped shut as Dipper howled with laughter.

In the repertoire of talents which had lifted her from a strolling troupe of Irish street jugglers to the forefront of the English stage, Katharine Brandon really did have a most unusual scream. Cribb collided with Thorpe and just snatched him through the last open gateway before the sentry's boots skidded to a halt overhead. "Who goes there?" he bellowed, musket levelled through the grating.

"Oh, colonel! Dear colonel!" a terrified voice called back from the shadows. "What a fearful fright! A huge rat just ran out of here! Won't you *please* help us? Don't go away, colonel! Be a honey joy and we'll all sleep so much safer with *you* nearby."

" 'A rat jus' run out!' " Dipper mimicked in a quavering falsetto, drawing guffaw after guffaw from the family brethren. "Yuss m'm, no m'm, three bags full m'm!" he replied, voice swooping to a trembly bass as Crystal Prig sagged against Slyboots, helpless with laughter.

18

PHILLIP CRADLED the telescope against *Sirius'* mizzenmast and watched her launch pulling from Portsmouth Observatory. The bright disc of light held it in focus for a few moments longer, then began tracking over Spithead's rolling waves, following *Hyaena's* jolly boat as it rowed away with his orders for her captain and a copy of the port admiral's authority to break moorings and proceed to sea.

Phillip clapped the glass shut and straightened, reading the sun's altitude and checking his flagship's pennant: the easterly wind was holding: there was still a working margin of time before dusk: his ships would clear western Wight on the falling tide. Normally it would have been prudent to wait for the next ebb at dawn tomorrow, but Phillip knew that even in darkness the Portsdown semaphore could relay Admiralty commands by lantern, halting all movement on the anchorage; the next sixteen or seventeen hours could cost him a lifetime's work, a lifetime's ambition.

He turned, mouth parched. "Mr. Hunter?"

Sirius' captain stepped forward. "Sir?"

"Make to all." Phillip hesitated, weighing risks. "Proceed. Line astern. Commodore in the vanguard."

"Aye aye, sir!"

The flagship's gun thudded as red, yellow and black bunting ran up her signal halliards and Phillip paced to windward.

His throat felt like sandpaper: he prayed that he wasn't now hatching a fever caught on one of the transports. He tried distracting this latest fret by looking at the gentle swell of land between Ryde and Bembridge, allowing his telescope to pick its own way between trees, up hillocks and across church spires.

He was still worrying as he focussed again on the much closer waters of St. Helen's roadstead and calculated the sea room needed to manoeuvre between three frigates and a newly arrived sixty-four-gun once *Sirius'* tops'l backed her off the mooring ground.

The glass shut again. Phillip squinted up at the pennant: still east nor'east and steady: from that quarter it ought to hold until his convoy was clear of the Needles tonight. A good wind. A good omen. The wind which had brought him HMS *Hyaena* would soon be putting him safely below the horizon. But the same wind was also gathering the most powerful peacetime fleet Britain had raised in a generation and Phillip feared it: it was now no secret that if the king of France wanted a base for operations in Holland, he would first have to control the Narrow Seas, and to do that his ships would need to sink every man o' war the Royal Navy could throw into action and—

Hunter was touching hatbrim. "Mr. Dawes' compliments, sir. The Observatory has certified our chronometer."

Phillip nodded and turned away from the public to his private worries. Time. The split-second measurement of time. Time. The only treasure man could never hoard; the only blessing given equally to rich man and poor alike; the only enemy neither could ever hope to stop. Phillip's lens focussed again on the gaunt white semaphore arms atop Portsdown hill. At any time in the past week they could have begun their weary wigwagging, racing ahead of an Admiralty courier as he posted down from London with war in his despatch bag. And there was still time for it to happen and return him to the Active List as just another aging post-captain with a junior's seniority.

The telescope's brass tubes swallowed each other with controlled violence and Phillip tilted his chin, reading the pennant again. " 'And thus fair stood the wind to France,' " he muttered, " 'When we our sails advanc'd. . . .' "

"Sir?"

Phillip glanced up at Hunter's profile and snowy hair. "I beg pardon?"

"I thought you spoke, sir."

"No. Just thinking aloud. That's all." Phillip squared shoulders and paced aft, to the taffrail, where he could be alone again. He must break this lonely man's habit of debating problems with himself, it could lead to gossip. But the problem of France and her ambitions could not be broken so easily, or—

He glowered at the cheeky gull which had soared past and then flapped to a landing on the rail by his elbow. "Shoo! Begone!" The bird hopped a couple of paces to the side, then fluffed feathers and settled down to study the world of men through hard yellow eyes. Phillip turned his back on the intruder and searched for a new fret.

He had enough experience of secret diplomacy to know that one paragraph misunderstood by His Grace of Bedford in Paris, or a single comma misplaced in a despatch from M. le Marquis de Salignac in London, and both nations' ambassadors would soon be exchanging boats under a flag of truce in mid-Channel as another seven or eight years of war erupted around them, spilling over into Canada, Spanish America and the Dutch East Indies. And New Holland too, if he ever got that far.

A distant concussion swung his glass at the signal mast above Portsmouth's ramparts; a false alarm, without *Sirius'* hoist number. Phillip's breathing slowed again. Not yet, not quite yet, with her speed and his judgment *Sirius* would soon be cutting a track across the world's least-known waters, years removed from any chance of recall or the cancellation of his commission.

He knew that his own vessel now stood ready, lying into wind, held only by a single bower anchor. The port and starboard watches were manning the braces, facing aft to where Hunter stood ready with his speaking trumpet. The capstan party, too, was ready. And the topmen swayed aloft on the high yards, poised to let the t'gallants belly out and swing *Sirius'* bowsprit as her anchor broke ground and tore free.

The flagship's signal gun thudded again, blowing powder haze across the poop deck, but Phillip no longer noticed, his wrist cradling telescope at *Golden Grove* and *Borrowdale*. Nothing. Not a flicker of movement! And only a trace of half-hearted interest aboard *Alexander* and *Friendship*. The rest of his convoy was laying snugly at anchor, lines of laundry snapping between their shrouds, gulls wheeling around *Scarborough*'s heads where a row of pink bumps were easing themselves over the side, backs turned on their commodore and all his instructions.

The telescope's disc jarred again and another cloud of burned sulphur whipped past Phillip's taut face. "Mr. Hunter!"

"Sir!"

"What the hell's going on out there!"

Sirius' captain ran to a halt, head uncovered. "I'm calling away the launch to investigate, sir!"

"Damned right you are!" Phillip crushed the telescope tubes into each other and turned, breathing much faster. "I shall go below and attend to my papers. You will inform me immediately those—'sailors'—condescend to allow us to proceed to sea!"

The commodore marched past Hunter and trod down to his cabin before a surging temper detonated in public and gave the malicious something to really gossip about. The heavy oak door slammed behind him and its marine guard strained to hear the thuds and crashes of kicked furniture on the other side, but he was disappointed.

Phillip had folded several written sheets and tapped their sand back into the caster before Hunter finally bowed under the door frame and heeled it shut. Phillip sat upright in the cabin chair. "Well?"

Sirius' captain ran fingers through sparse hair and chose his words. "It would seem that the merchant masters are having a little difficulty starting their men today, sir."

"*Difficulty?*" Phillip's eyebrows collided. "Are you saying that my orders are being disobeyed?"

Hunter would never be rushed to judgment. "Not exactly 'disobeyed,' sir, it's more a question of—"

"Are they, or are they not, making sail!"

"Not yet, but—"

"Then they are disobeying a lawful command!" Phillip's fist smashed its quill through the paper as he sprang upright, chair toppling backward, all restraint overturned by nine months of late nights, grinding worries, self-doubt and hard work. "This is mutiny—!"

Hunter held his peace as Phillip's hand pounded the table, scattering papers, books, curses, jerking the sentry to attention behind the door. Hunter checked an impulse which had earned him the affectionate nickname of "Daddy John" throughout the Royal Navy: this was no time to put a comforting arm across his superior officer's shoulders.

Phillip's rage was approaching hurricane force. "Hang them! Flog them! Break them—!"

Hunter nodded sympathetically: thirty years in the king's service, and until quite recently only as a middling warrant officer, had taught him much about rebellious crews and their isolated commanders. Phillip's reaction was utterly predictable, Hunter knew. The only surprise was that his commodore's painfully English courtesy hadn't collapsed long before, once he began burning candles till three in the morning, seven days a week, visible from Hunter's lodgings in Penny Street, just across from the Bower Anchor.

"Those civilian dogs are under Admiralty orders now! They have mutinied! Mutiny is a hanging matter—!"

Hunter nodded at the truth. He also sensed that Phillip's fury was being blown to white heat by wounded pride, the same prickly honour which Hunter suspected behind this small man's careful reserve. Not that it was entirely without reason: Phillip's first order as a convoy commander had been promptly disobeyed, a good tale for every other officer on Spithead to tell. It had not been a promising start.

"Convene a general court-martial! Those whoresons will never treat *me* this way again!"

"Aye aye, sir," Hunter replied with a brisk heel-click. "The ringleaders will be sent ashore under close guard immediately. The merchant masters will also be needed to give testimony before Admiral Muir; I'll make certain they understand their duty. Afore the week's out we shall have broken a few necks and will then be ready to make sail with a new spirit of cheerful obedience to orders."

"A *week*!" Phillip spluttered.

"With respect, sir, I think we'll be able to hurry the process a little. I can probably cut a few corners with our paperwork and assemble a hanging case for the port admiral to judge."

"I want—!"

Hunter's forefinger rose slightly. "With respect, sir, I know exactly what you want. Those mutineers must become an example for everyone else."

"Damned right!"

"And not only aboard our convoy, of course, but for the whole fleet to witness."

"Uh?"

Hunter's softly accented Scots never wavered. "Nothing less than a full court-martial will do. After all," he went on thoughtfully, half to himself, "mutiny cannot be summarily punished by a commander. Mutiny in port requires a board of five flag officers with the port admiral or his delegate as board president. Of course we cannot expect less justice since we shall be killing men who are still technically civilians, though in the king's service." Hunter's plain Edinburgh burr was relentlessly stripping all evasion from words like "execute" and "punish," leaving them as "kill" and "break necks." He looked down at his commodore. "We ought to finish them by, oh, next Saturday?"

Phillip studied a deep graze across one of his knuckles and sucked blood, feeling its throb for the first time. "Too long. I must be halfway to Teneriffe by then."

Hunter nodded. "As you say, sir, but may I respectfully add that a court-martial will cost at least that delay? Possibly more if the ships' owners get wind of it and choose to raise Cain in London. Now," he went on soberly, "I'm not saying that a court-martial is not justified in this case. But it could be that if you cared to review the men's complaints you might find some mitigating detail. . . ."

Phillip had stopped and recovered the fallen chair. He sat down with a bump. "Are you insinuating that there could be mitigating circumstances in this mutiny, Mr. Hunter?"

"That's not for me to say, sir," *Sirius'* captain corrected quietly. "It is just that the crews will not man the yards till they get their back pay and one last visit ashore to spend it."

"Their pay's in arrears?" Phillip scowled.

"Seven clear months." Hunter was laconic. "They need the money to buy their working clothes." He paused, watching Phillip shove away from the table again and walk across to the stern windows.

The commodore turned, shoulders slumped against the panorama of Wight's coastline, now inching backward as a flooding tide aborted any further hopes of getting away before tomorrow morning. "I suppose they are alleging that their masters have deliberately stopped shore pay so that each man will be forced to buy from the skipper's private slop chest once they're at sea?"

"Something of that kind, sir."

Phillip shook head at memories of similar tricks when he was a young sailor in the merchant service. "What utter bastards they all are." He looked up again. "And these are the facts as they have been presented to you?" Hunter nodded. "And these men understand that mutiny is punishable by death?"

"I think it highly likely, sir. The marines had matters firmly under control even before our launch hailed them."

Phillip braced shoulders and moved forward to the table again. "Then my compliments to Mr. Ross for their prompt attention to duty." He sat down and moodily tried straightening the broken quill. "From what you have said it would appear that no sensible person would have intended deliberate mutiny, for that would have been suicidal."

"Entirely, sir."

Phillip gave up trying to repair the quill and tossed it aside. "Therefore it would seem they only intended to register a protest by disobeying their masters' orders to make sail."

"Definitely, sir."

"Such being the case," Phillip concluded, more to himself, "I wonder if a summary punishment might not be as effective as a court-martial, under the circumstances. What do you think?"

Hunter considered the judgment from all sides. "A very sound decision, sir."

Phillip's fingertips drummed table top. "So be it. Make to all affected ships: ringleaders and kits to be sent aboard for punishment and transfer. Meanwhile, rig the grating."

"How many?"

"Two dozen." Phillip began sharpening another quill. "Let each man clearly understand how lucky he is not to be sent ashore for trial. And pipe all hands: nobody must be under any illusions after today: my orders will be obeyed without question."

"Aye aye, sir."

Phillip bowed head over a fresh sheet of paper as *Sirius'* captain clattered up the companion ladder, signalling his first lieutenant. "Mr. Bradley! Make to all ships, ringleaders and kits. Bosun's party to the grating. Pipe all hands."

"Aye aye, sir!"

Hunter returned the salute, twitched his faded fearnaught's collar against the breeze and strode for'ard to attend to other duties as bunting flew and a heavy teak frame was winched upright beside *Sirius'* entry port in the waist. Two of the gunner's boys climbed from the magazine with leather buckets of sand for the deck. The marine detachment marched to its post, weapons clinking the pace. Their drummer boy adjusted his shoulder strap, tightening the drum's parchment by ramming its side rope with his sticks, lightly tapping the skin to get it properly tuned. Then the bosun's pipe called both watches on deck, parading them by divisions under their petty officers in a hollow square round the grating.

The afternoon sun had lost its warmth over the gentle hills of Hampshire when the first launch rowed across from *Scarborough* under marine guard and moored alongside *Sirius*. Two merchant seamen, their hands roped, were jabbed aboard at bayonet point, faces tense as they stared back at the distant curiosity of men who served in the other navy. Lieutenant Bradley gave the command and both were untied. They were initiated shellbacks and wore the tortoiseshell scars of other floggings across their shoulders, buttocks and legs as they stripped naked, rolling shirts and underdrawers together and stowing them where they would not be spattered with blood.

The elder of the two faced the wooden grating and embraced it, waiting for his wrists and knees to be seized tight with cord by the bosun. Meanwhile, two floggers were limbering up with a few practise shots at the mainmast, flicking away splinters with their whips' nine-times-nine knots.

Sirius' surgeon climbed from the orlop with his red baize toolbag and a slate to record the number of lashes served. Bradley turned and marched across to Hunter. "Ready, sir."

Hunter opened his ship's articles of war and read them aloud in a slow, practised voice, reminding everyone present that all orders were lawful, that all orders were to be carried out promptly and cheerfully, that any ideas to the contrary were punishable by death once at sea. Then he closed the book, its leaves fluttering in the chilly wind, and looked at his bosun's impassive face.

"Lay on."

The crucified merchant seaman rolled his chin sideways and bit into his own leather belt as the two bosun's mates took up positions and spat on their palms for a better grip. The marine sergeant barked an order and his drummer boy began rolling a harsh double-double-double, then struck a single blow. The cat of nine thongs hissed, ripping away flesh. Hunter wiped face and moved further to windward as the floggers got into their swing, slashing down on every alternate drum roll, overlapping from left and right—hiss, crack, hiss, crack, hiss, crack—crisscrossing the opening wounds, spraying clots of blood and skin across the sanded deck.

They cut him down after twenty-four strokes and the surgeon dressed his shoulders with coarse pickling salt as the second mutineer embraced the sweaty grating and a launch rowed from *Golden Grove* with her ringleaders.

Phillip moved nearer the cabin's window for a better light and continued a despatch to Lord Howe at the Admiralty, hoping that it would reach London before any exaggerated stories of the transports' disobedience did. He glanced up as his sentry stamped boots outside and Hunter bowed head under the door frame again. "Well?"

"All served a full ration and then transferred into fresh ships."

"Good." Phillip sat back, absentmindedly stroking his chin with the new quill. "Now, concerning our departure. The tide will be ebbing at first light: I intend that we are upon it, regardless. Understand? Another public scandal like today's spectacle and I shall have to take severe measures."

"Aye aye."

"And pass the word that I shall do my utmost to procure all necessary clothing and such other comforts as may be had at Rio de Janeiro. That will be all."

"Sir."

Hunter almost collided with Phillip's manservant as he went up the companionway to the darkening deck. Bryant tapped the door and edged in. "Er, supper's ready, sir." Phillip pushed away his papers and made room for the platter of braised chicken, fresh vegetables and white bread.

Bryant's flint chipped sparks and within a minute or so the cabin's lantern was rocking a soft yellow glow across the cluttered table. "Um. Wine an' cheese, sir?"

"When I call for them."

The door shut behind Bryant. Phillip crumbled bread into the chicken gravy and reached for a book, any book so long as it would divert his imagination from today's loss of face. He cleaned the fork and began to eat while he opened William Rose's copy of *Gulliver's Travels*.

" 'We set sail from Bristol, May 4, 1699, and our voyage at first was very prosperous,' " Phillip lip-read between chews, noting the almost coincidental date eighty-some years earlier. " '. . . In our passage from thence to the East-Indies, we were driven by a violent storm to the northwest of Van Dieman's Land. By an observation we found ourselves in the latitude of 30 degrees 2 minutes south. Twelve of our crew were dead by immoderate labour, and ill food, the rest were in a very weak condition. On the fifth of November, which was the beginning of summer in those parts, the weather being very hazy, the seamen spied a rock, but the wind was so strong, that we were driven directly upon it, and immediately split.' "

The book snapped shut and Phillip tossed it away.

Six-inch Lilliputians were probably intended to be amusing fictions, but a ship's cabin on her last night in home waters was no place to be reminded that her crewmen would soon be killed by overwork, that disease would soon begin creeping atween decks, and that uncharted reefs were laying in wait off unknown coasts; Lieutenant Bligh's "bits of driftwood" were as likely in eastern New Holland as they were on the west coast of Canada. Such adventures might be the stuff of romantic entertainment for bored landmen, Phillip thought, but real flesh-and-blood sailors had to battle them day and night, in arctic gale and tropic storm. He also knew that long before this voyage made its landfall on the far side of the globe, Gulliver's imaginary disaster might easily describe his own convoy and its fifteen hundred souls.

The lantern swung overhead with the creak and running chuckle of water under *Sirius'* stern ports as Phillip wiped fingers on the tablecloth and reached for something less morbid than *Gulliver's Travels* to distract him. Fortunately Sir Joseph Banks had sent down a small chest of texts from the Royal Society's library, including copies of five or six reports of those other voyages to New Holland over the past two centuries. Phillip adjusted his spectacles and picked up the first, recently translated from an account written by one of the Dutchmen who had originally given that shadowy land its name, and returned to his interrupted dinner.

" 'Mijnheeren XVII the High Directors of the Amsterdam East India Company, animated by the lusty profits of five spice ships richly laden, caused eleven more vessels to be fitted out under Commodore Jakob Spex—' " Phillip tried to ignore the ominously similar number, rank and name. " 'Among them was the *Batavia*, commanded by Captain Franz Pelsaert. They sailed out from Texel on twenty-eighth October 1628 and rounded the Cape of Good Hope. On Whit Monday, June fourth the following year, *Batavia*, being separated from the fleet by a violent storm, was driven upon those shoals which lay in the latitude of twenty-eight degrees off the west coast of New Holland. Captain Pelsaert was sick in bed, but feeling his ship strike, ran upon deck. It was night and the sea appeared to be covered with white froth. The captain called up the master who excused himself by saying that, having seen the froth at a distance, he thought it to be the reflection of moonbeams. The captain then asked what was to be done and in what part of the world they were, but the ship's master replied that only God knew, and that *Batavia* was now surely stuck fast on a reef.' "

Phillip's mouth hardened as he dealt with the luckless master and his moonbeams. For several moments he continued forking dinner off the pewter plate while he considered abandoning this book, too, but curiosity won and his lips began silently moving again. " '*Batavia*'s crew threw their cannon overboard, hoping to lighten ship, but while they were thus employed, a most dreadful gale arose of wind and rain, and being surrounded by rocks and shoals, *Batavia* struck once more. The crew then resolved to chop away the mainmast, which they did right speedily, but it became entangled with the rigging and did naught to ease the ship's distress. They could see no land except two islands which were about three leagues off and, it now being about nine in the morning, they sent most of the company on shore to pacify the women, the children, the sick people and those out of their wits with fear, whose cries and noise had rendered the night horrible. They embarked these in their shallop, seeing that *Batavia* was beginning to split apart, but what hindered them most was that the crew had made themselves drunk with spirits.' "

Phillip paused again while he weighed what options he would have if— or when—something like this happened to him during the next eight or nine months. For a long while he brooded over the likely outcome if his cargoes of hand-picked thugs saw a chance to imitate Mijnheer Pelsaert's men in the same distant waters, and the knowledge did nothing to erase the memory of today's disgrace which had happened within five miles of the port admiral's office.

The next of Banks' suggested readings were chosen with greater care: it appeared to be a translation of a recent stock company prospectus offering shares in New Holland, written by a bankrupt Swiss merchant who had briefly managed an indigo plantation on Sumatra. Phillip rang for the wine and cheese while he checked ahead for tales of storm, pestilence, fire, rape,

murder, shipwreck, mutiny, thirst, famine and flood. Reassured, he waited
for Bryant to leave again and tried composing his mind for sleep by reading Pierre Pury's brighter version of the Great South Land's future.

" 'Who knows what there is and whether the land does not count richer
mines of gold and silver than did Peru or Mexico? Why would all the other
countries which are situated around the thirtieth degree of latitude—like
Barbary, Syria, Chaldea, Persia, Mongolistan and China—be good, and
this one alone be worthless?' " Phillip had to agree and flicked away a
cockroach which had lost its footing on the beam overhead.

" 'I beg of my readers to consider this one question, how can one say
that New Holland is of no use to anyone, seeing that nothing is known of
it and that nobody has been there? For is it not true that New Holland is at
least as vast as all Europe? It therefore seems to me that the first thing we
must do is to disembark five or six hundred men, all good soldiers, to spy
out the land. I admit that Christopher Columbus had not so many when he
set out to discover the Americas, but we are situated differently, and we
shall be taking a risk if we imagine that the Indians of New Holland have
less courage than the Indians of America, or if we think they have not the
same intelligence as ourselves.

" 'Why, for instance, should they also not have fortified cities? And, if
we have had the use of gunpowder these last three hundred years, why
should they not also have invented machines of war yet more terrible than
our bombards and cannon? I say rather, as there were before the Deluge,
giants of extraordinary strength and size, why should anyone say there
cannot also be giants in New Holland? Giants not only in stature but in
knowledge too? Giants so prodigious that their like has never been seen in
any other country of the world? Consequently it seems to me that it would
be best to take five or six hundred armed men and go to discover them.' "

Phillip let the book shut itself. Rumours of giant Indians probably belonged with Dr. Gulliver's six-inch Lilliputians, but in all other ways
Pury's vision of New Holland was neither unlikely nor impossible. Phillip
tasted the wine and tried to imagine how seven hundred convicted thieves
and sluts would react to walled cities and secret engines of war more terrible than cannon. Ross' men would die hard, of course, but nobody could
expect London's human cess bucket to face the dangers of Botany Bay
with discipline and courage.

Phillip had once read how Portugal colonised a similar bay on the east
coast of Southern America, almost three centuries earlier. That isolated
garrison and its convict work force had soon angered the Indians and a vicious war had broken out in the jungle, a war in which many of the convicts and some of their guards had been taken alive, tortured to death,
blanched like pigs in boiling water and then ceremonially roasted outside
the small fort of Rio de Janeiro for the rest to see.

Phillip was more troubled than he cared to admit as he stood to trim the lantern's candle. Its warm shadows darted from side to side, swaying across the yellow woodwork as he considered going on deck. Instead, he snuffed the candle and tugged back his cot's blanket: the longest day of his life would start early and it was now only a few hours away.

19

BUT HE COULD only doze, imagining the compass bowl's restless tilt around and around its gimbal rings in the darkness above his face as *Sirius* rode at anchor. Today's humiliation would not be forgotten by the invisible critics who whispered "Phillip? Phillip who . . . ?" True, he had only just taken command of the convoy, and its merchant captains had yet to be brought to heel, but that was not the way it would be read in London, and this killed any hope of an easy night's sleep.

Not that he ever slept well, unless physically exhausted or mildly drunk: the first was almost impossible on *Sirius'* cluttered deck, and the second a last resort he used only when all else failed. So, instead, he began mentally checking the inventories which the fleet commissary had been copying for his signature these last several weeks as he assumed responsibility to the Ordnance Board for stocks of bar metal, forge tools, anvils and bagged charcoal; sledgehammers, rock drills and shovels; spikes, nails, brads, clouts, tacks; shoe leather, woolen caps, linen cloth; wheelbarrows, sieves, rakes, forks, mattocks, pickaxes; soap, styptics, physic, emetics, opiates. Coals for ballast. Scythe blades for next year's harvest. Writing paper and ink powder to give praise and order punishment. Tin lamps, trade hatchets and small grindstones for the Indians—assuming they were not lords of power more terrible than the Incas—and still valued such cheap brummagem frippery. The commissary's lists never ended and, Phillip never doubted, were still incomplete: he had yet to serve aboard any ship in any navy and not find that vital equipment had been wrongly labelled and badly stowed.

The compass bowl rocked and tilted, its dry brass rings squeaking gently, inches above his nose.

Waiting for this last English dawn was proving no easier than waiting for many another on the climb from poor boy's hammock at Greenwich to a governor's tent beyond the edge of the known world. Now, at an age when most other survivors of war and shipwreck were enjoying grandchildren and some easing of life's pace, Arthur Phillip had again asked—had petitioned—for one last chance to share a naval cot with a sack of straw and two government-issue blankets. And to fret about the fifteen hundred strangers who packed crevices aboard his twelve ships, listening to the same suck and thud of waves against their timber homes, waiting for the same dawn to glide across Asia to Europe.

Phillip crooked arm under head and stared back at the clammy darkness: the night must be creeping past for them too. Seven hundred or so were with him only because an unknown magistrate had scrawled a signature on a warrant to get rid of them, but the other half of his expeditionary force—the sailors, the marines, the civilians—had also been drafted by similar marks on similar sheets of paper. The difference between keepers and kept was starting to blur. Both would drown together if their ships foundered; both would go hungry in a French prison if war did break out and they were taken off the Channel mouth; and, assuming they ever arrived in New Holland, gaolers and gaoled would serve out their time under the same sun and under much the same discipline.

Phillip grimaced: the very best and the very worst of modern England had been herded together by chance and would soon be set adrift to fend for themselves. Lagged and free; gently born and gutter rat; clodhopper and city craftsman; officer and private soldier; woman and sailor. The foul, the fastidious. The habitually drunk, the religiously sober. The meek, the violent, the sly, the stupid, the cunning, the mad. Total strangers who never would, most likely never could have spoken to each other in England, were now bound for the same remote unknown.

Phillip yawned and tried stifling all further thought at this point, but he was having no more luck tempting sleep tonight than on many another. Instead, he remained stubbornly awake, blankets to chin, listening to the half-hourly bells being struck by the sentry at each turn of the sandglass. It was useless even trying to sleep—

Phillip punched the pillow and dropped bare legs over the side of his cot. He pulled on stockings and shoes again, flipped off the nightshirt and pulled on a warm waistcoat, then reached for his cloak and gold-laced hat. The sentry came to attention and sleepily watched his commodore stride past and disappear on deck.

It was not yet moonrise. A dank sea fog had spread across Spithead from the mainland, coiling itself round the riding light at *Sirius'* stern. The black guns were soaked with dew, Phillip noted, trailing a finger over their chilly iron as he paced deck from chicken coop to taffrail, then for'ard again to the heads. And the wind had dropped away completely, leaving only a muted creak of ship's timbers and the oily slap of low waves. Another reason to fret: when the wind rose again at dawn it could easily strike from another quarter, embaying the convoy for days, for weeks during which history would cheat him of this one last chance.

Phillip sensed rather than saw the duty officer, muffled between compass binnacle and lee stays. The sentry was also pacing off the night, musket cradled against his chest, hands tucked up opposite sleeves, always crossing to leeward of his commodore as they passed. Phillip halted as he heard the marine's salute behind him, and turned as another dark shape climbed the companion ladder to tread deck.

Sirius' captain joined him at the stern.

"You can't sleep either?" Phillip asked.

Hunter's silhouette shook its head, hands shoved deep inside a seaman's jacket, also watching the moon rise beyond Selsey, full and round as a Spanish dollar.

Phillip eased over, glad to make space by the lantern for this man's warm, dependable presence. Although they were serving their first commission together, the two men had already discovered mutual friends within the Royal Navy's closed circle of professional seamen. In fact, long before meeting him for the first time at an Admiralty conference, Phillip had begun sketching a mental picture of a very unusual subordinate commander—one who was loyal and willing, with the happy knack of staying genial while sharing cramped quarters with tetchy, often fighting-drunk men.

He was unlike Phillip in other ways, too. Nephew to a lord provost of Edinburgh and elder son of a once-prosperous Leith shipmaster on the Norway trade, John Hunter had appeared content to remain a plain ship's master and navigator for almost twenty of his thirty years in the king's service. Phillip had been even more puzzled when he studied the man's confidential records and found that they had both qualified as lieutenants in the same year, but Hunter had continued to be rated as an aging master RN until the closing stages of the next war. Lord Howe had then personally advanced him for distinguished services during the Delaware River campaign, since when his climb through commander to post-captain had been rapid.

And yet this man had never been rated a simpleton by anyone, Phillip also knew, now standing a few feet above a shelf which ran the full length of the captain's cot: a broad plank wedged against the cubby's bulkheads and packed tight with books on astronomy and surveying, philosophy, religion and logic—several in the original Latin and Greek—which he appeared to read for pleasure. True, some of these might be holdovers from Hunter's time at Aberdeen University, studying for the ministry, but whatever their real cause, *Sirius'* elderly captain was proving to be no less of an enigma than many another bound for Botany Bay.

Phillip coughed in the lantern glow. "I would like to thank you."

Hunter chuckled quietly. "That's civil of you sir, but why?"

Phillip tugged his boat cloak much tighter. "For the way you handled this afternoon's disgraceful scenes. Both of them."

Hunter smiled. "They tell me worse things happen at sea. Besides, the ringleaders have been soundly scourged, we shouldn't have any problems getting away on the next tide, I fancy."

"Always assuming our wind doesn't back round again," Phillip nagged, more to himself than the other man.

"It won't." Hunter reached inside his patched jacket's pocket for the stump of a clay pipe which he liked to suck. " 'If the wind be nor'east three days without rain, eight days must go before south again.' We've had no rain for nearly a week," Hunter added with a spit to assure good luck for the old jingle.

"Hn! If only I could be as confident nothing else were lying in wait to scupper us!" Phillip looked ashore at the curtain of darkness which hid Portsdown semaphore, half expecting to see its lanterns cancelling his authority to sail.

Hunter drew on the cold pipe and hunched shoulders under his tarred canvas collar. "We shall glide away tomorrow, sweet and smooth as fresh butter, so you might as well save yourself all these pointless worryings."

"Pointless, are they?" Phillip snapped back. "Is the safety and well-being of my convoy pointless?"

"No-o," Hunter conceded fairmindedly, "but worrying about what might happen, or what ought to happen, or what-could-have-happened-if-only, will make not a scrap of difference now. We are as prepared as we'll ever be. We've victualled, we've taken on water, most of our ships are tolerably dry inside and, certainly, their crews are less frisky than they were this morning. So what more do we need?"

"Wind."

Hunter sucked on his pipe and spat again, rather more to the nor'east than before, then cupped hands and added a low, cautious whistle to strengthen the charm. "There. That'll hurry it down."

Phillip blinked uncertainly. "Such things work?"

"Mostly." Hunter tasted the pipe. "My father always had a Finlander aboard our ships in the Baltic: they control the weather," he added. "One, his name was Paavo something or other, was what they call a sky wizard. Only a dried-up little cork of a thing to look at, but when we needed a following wind he could bring one down as surely as a shepherd brings his dog."

"Hmm."

"It's true," Hunter insisted without taking offence. "I've seen him do it many a time, and what he taught me hardly ever failed us on the Saint Lawrence, where we surely needed it. How else do you think we made it up to Quebec?"

Phillip blinked again, beginning to wonder if this could be some elaborate Scottish leg-pull. "*Quebec?* What on earth has whistling down the wind got to do with that, for heaven's sake?"

"Everything." Hunter was laconic. "Each night for over a week a handful of us went ahead of the fleet, sounding and buoying the channels: we could never have done it without the right winds."

Phillip scratched an ear in the darkness, more puzzled than suspicious now. "I didn't think you'd been rated master in Canada?"

"Nor was I, indeed I was still only a middie, but I've always had a bit of a way with figures, so when *Pembroke*'s master—Jimmy Cook, you'll remember him?—called for volunteers, I was quickly volunteered out o' *Neptune* to help him make the survey."

"How lucky." Phillip smiled at the irony.

"Aye, not that I thought so at the time. Mr. Cook was a hard dominie to learn under, but we had been engaged to do men's work so there was no time for 'if you please' and 'thank you kindly,' by night, in freezing silence, reading the lead line and compass while Mr. Cook marked more rocks and shoals than a cat has fleas. And as if that weren't enough," Hunter went on, "snipers popping away at us from the French bivouacs, aiming between the splash of our oars while their Indians waited at the narrows, promised a gold *louis* for every scalp they took."

"Good Lord, really?"

"The little imps nearly cashed mine once," Hunter said. "It wouldn't fetch sixpence now for cushion stuffing, of course, but that particular night it felt a lot thicker and warmer." He chuckled at the thought.

"Go on. . . ."

"There's not much more to say. We'd just worked between a place called Beaupré and Orleans Island when a dozen or so Mohawks swarmed over the side from their canoe, yelling and warbling as Mr. Cook and I hopped over the other. Hot as hell while it lasted, but at least the river was refreshingly cool," Hunter added with a deprecating shrug. "Not that the monsieurs stopped us then, of course, any more than they'll stop us now. Why, it only needed a handful of men to pilot an entire fleet up the Saint Lawrence under cover of night—and we lost not a single boat or man of the nine thousand–odd General Wolfe needed to finish the job. And why was that? Because *I* made sure the wind was right." Hunter loaded and shot another spit to nor'east. "Ask Bobby Ross, he saw it."

"What? *Major* Ross?"

"The same." Hunter nodded soberly. "Of course he was only a young man then, like the rest, but he was already making his mark as a very capable officer—"

"Hn!"

"And being one of us, so to speak, he was ever glad to join fellow Scots for a dram and a pipe whenever duty allowed."

Phillip's mouth tightened in the darkness. "You make him sound like good company."

"Indeed he was," Hunter agreed simply. "But then, who isn't at sixteen or seventeen when all the world is wide and the grass green?"

Phillip fell silent and pulled his cloak tighter against a chilly breath of wind that was starting to shred the mist. Something heavy rose and splashed on the moon's silvery track across Spithead. "I wonder why he's never mentioned Canada to me . . . ?"

"Beg pardon?"

"I said, I wonder why Major Ross has never cornered me with tales of his exciting adventures in Canada?" Phillip made a gob of his own and spat astern. "I'd like a guinea for every time he's tried to regale me with his rousing exploits at Bunker Hill and his hardships when the French took him prisoner, but never once did I know he'd served at Quebec. Why . . . ?"

Hunter stiffened. "I'm sure I don't know, sir, but of one thing I am very certain, it would be a serious error to underprice Bobby Ross or to doubt his courage." Hunter checked his tongue, realising how it could sound to the other man. He tried softening the effect with a shrug. "I know he's sharp cornered at times, but at heart he's a sound fellow and efficient with his duties."

"I'm glad to hear it," Phillip replied, "but I could only wish he were as good humoured and flexible as you say he is efficient."

Hunter kept quiet for several moments. "May I put it another way? If I were given the choice between some back-slapping boozer and an officer who keeps his troops close-hauled, I know which one I'd want guarding those animals out there." *Sirius'* captain jabbed pipe stem at the moored transports, now dimly outlined by the moon, their bare poles and yards gently rocking against the night breeze. Almost on cue, a gurgling scream rippled back from *Alexander*.

"Point taken," Phillip conceded. "Well, then I must suppose the man has some rough-hewn charm which has escaped my notice thus far. Perhaps he will reveal it to me within the next three or four years, do you think?"

"For everyone's sake, sir, let us hope that he does," Hunter agreed. "But to be frank, I would never expect anyone who was not born a 'guid son o' the kirk' to entirely fathom a man like our Robert Ross. . . ."

Or a man like our John Hunter, Phillip thought as he glanced up sharply. "How do you mean?"

The slightly older man picked his words. "Shall I say that life has always been somewhat less certain north of the border? And that recent events have done nothing to make it any easier for us?"

It was Phillip's turn to fall silent. Hunter, a shrewd and loyal number two, was now buoying and marking one of the most dangerous shoals which could wreck an apparently English governor and his obviously Scottish deputy. It was equally plain to Phillip that Hunter was charting a course for their dealings in the long years ahead.

Although only half native English himself, Phillip had quickly learned which half had brought with it centuries of hatred between London and Edinburgh, centuries in which the northern kingdom had always allied herself with France against the English. Twice within living memory Scots armies had fought their way over the border to unseat the German kings and to restore a Stuart to the throne. Phillip had never forgotten the panic when the last invasion had penetrated to within ninety miles of the English capital, or his eighth birthday treat when his mother paid five shillings to see the Jacobite generals being executed at London Tower, barely a mile from Bread Street.

It was only England's need to rebuild an army that could hold France and Spain on four continents which had relaxed the laws against Highlanders bearing arms. A number of regiments had been raised in Scotland to serve abroad, where the risks were highest and the opportunities for rebellion most remote. But even this trust and goodwill had rebounded once lean, ambitious Scots began competing on equal terms with Englishmen for the limited number of commissions which a colonel had to sell in his regiment.

Matters had gone from worse to worst once a Scot—John Stuart, third earl of Bute—became the present king's prime minister, to conclude peace with Paris and Madrid. At the time it had seemed as if the Scottish aristocrat were selling off cheaply all that had been bought so dearly with others' blood. With the stroke of a pen France regained the wealth of the West Indies and a Spanish viceroy returned in triumph to Havana as if he had never once run for his life. Yet the same peace treaty had broken fifty British regiments of the line, sent squadrons of warships to the wreckers' yards, and thrown many thousands of veteran officers into the streets on half-pay, Phillip among them, while a typical Naval List of new promotions had included eleven Stuarts and four McKenzies.

Phillip coughed. "Thank you, John, I value your counsel. Tell me, is there anything else I ought to understand about Major Ross?"

Hunter nodded. "He leaves a sizeable brood of children behind and not a penny piece in the bank to feed them with except from his pay: I'll let you imagine what he thinks of that prospect."

"Really?" Phillip sounded quite surprised. "I knew he'd enrolled that boy of his for the voyage, of course, but I never suspected he had others at home."

"Aye, several, and no mother to care for them." Hunter was thinking of his own widowed sister and the nephews he was supporting on a few shillings a day, often paid months in arrears by the naval agent, a family trust which had long ago thwarted his own hopes of marriage and children. "He's also concerned about the lack of prize money where we're bound. . . ."

Phillip's frown deepened. "What on earth has that got to do with it?"

"Everything. Like everyone else in our plight he knows that the only sure way to a snug berth in old age is by marrying it young, or by cruising off Gibraltar when the next war breaks: since the first option is no longer open to him, it must be the second. Like the rest of us, Bobby knows that win, lose or draw at the peace treaty, there'll always be rich pickings for the first to get aboard the enemy's homeward-bound Indiamen."

Phillip waited for the sentry to turn and go for'ard again. "Does Major Ross feel that, by being sent to New Holland, he will be denied a share of these, ah, rich pickings?"

"Aye."

Phillip did not dispute the fact. His own cheque from Havana's prize-master had come to a useful two hundred pounds, fifty times more than an able seaman's, of course, but still far short of the quarter of a million with which Admiral Pocock had retired to buy a seat in the country and a seat in the House of Commons. Ross, like today's mutineers, perhaps even like Hunter, had some reason to resent a voyage into the distant Pacific just when fortunes were about to be won much nearer home, off the ports of Brest and Cadiz.

"That might be so," Phillip replied, tapping finger on the taffrail to emphasise his point. "But neither is he likely to be crippled, or blinded, or shredded to dogs' meat at point-blank range. However, I do know what you mean. Look, if ever you get an opportunity to discuss this with him—or anyone else who feels the same way about our voyage—I'd be obliged if you reminded him that we shall be soon in a new world, one every bit as large and unknown as that which the dons conquered—"

"*Oh?*"

Phillip smiled at the other man's sudden interest. "It's true. After all, who can tell what might be waiting for us when we arrive at Botany Bay? Perhaps another Peru or a greater Mexico will be just a few miles inland? And if that is the case, which it so easily could be, just think how much richer the pickings will be then! While everyone else has stayed behind to plod up and down the western approaches in all weathers, we could be filling our knapsacks with emeralds and gold dust."

"Good point, good point," Hunter said, rubbing chin. "I'll wager he's not considered that possibility yet."

Phillip's smile ripened. "Depend upon it, John. I have. Often. And strictly *entre nous,* I wouldn't exchange my governorship of that bay for all the wealth of the Sugar Isles. Brazil's diamond mines could be nothing more than a beggar's pence compared with what we may be discovering in only a few months from now." He paused lightly. "I'd be most obliged if you could bring that thought to Major Ross' attention if you see an opportunity."

"Of course, of course." Hunter had begun stowing his pipe again. "I flatter myself that I can speak with Bobby as freely as any man alive, and perhaps more than most. After all," he added, "we served together when M'Lord Howe first hoisted his flag in the American colonies."

Phillip read another clear warning as the other man casually dropped the first sea lord's name and, with it, a hint of the powerful patronage which had secured a lieutenant governorship for Robert Ross, but he was distracted from asking more questions as the sentry turned his sandglass for the last time and struck eight hesitant bells at midnight, tolling the end of Saturday, May 26, 1787, for landmen, though sea days began and ended at noon.

The messenger boy pattered away and crouched below to rouse the middle watch from their hammocks, getting the usual kicks and snarls for his pains as weary shapes struggled from the fo'c'sle. Hunter and Phillip stood away as the old and new watches mustered below the poop, marines' nailed boots contrasting with the scuffle of sailors' bare feet while they formed to port and starboard. The duty officer could sense the commodore's interest and made a brisk tally of names before dismissing his old watch and handing over the new for the last four hours of the night.

Phillip stifled a yawn. " 'S gettin' later than I thought. We'd better snatch some shut-eye while we can: tomorrow will be a long time passing."

"None longer," Hunter agreed. "And please to observe that our wind is now exactly where you requested it. . . ."

Phillip peered up at the stiffening pennant, visible against the moon among dark ropes and stays, braces and lines. It was his turn to chuckle slightly. "My compliments to your Finnish friend. We could use more happy omens like that."

"Ever our pleasure, sir." Hunter smiled back. "Now, am I to assume that your sailing orders still apply?"

"Yes." Phillip steadied himself against *Sirius'* gentle roll. "Make to all at first light: line astern, commodore in the vanguard."

20

THE SIGNAL GUN jarred *Sirius'* timbers. Phillip's eyes flickered and focussed on the compass overhead: a rich sunrise was spilling through the stern windows, gilding the worn brass rings a few inches above his nose. "Bryant!"

Someone fumbled with the door catch and pushed past. "Sir?"

"Shaving water. And coffee." Phillip was heaving legs over the side of his cot and pulling at the breeches draped across a rope between the two cannon. "Quickly now!"

"Aye aye!" Bryant trotted back to his pantry to check the kettle. Satisfied that it was muttering to itself over the spirit lamp, he measured half a pint of water from the commodore's daily ration, added a splash of hot to the can, then hurried past the sentry. Phillip had finished buttoning into his flannel undervest. He pointed for the shaving water to be set down near a window while he went on stropping his razor and stared out at the sky. Bryant coughed. "Beggin' pardon, sir, but the weather glass is risin' an' the wind's nor' nor'east, jus' strong enough to flap a Dutchman's britches."

"Good." Phillip was lathering his face with quick, precise strokes. "How's that coffee coming along?"

"Drawin' nicely, sir."

"Excellent." Today was unfolding exactly as Hunter had predicted. Even Phillip's chin stayed unbloodied as he clapped his razor shut and tossed it back in the drawer: another good omen. He splashed a handful of tepid water on his face and began towelling himself as Bryant poured the coffee and brushed the nap on his sea coat.

"Superb." Phillip sipped the drink with gusto and sat for a minute while Bryant dressed his hair and tied the queue with a black neck ribbon. Then he stood again, punched both arms into the coat and ran fingers up the brass buttons. Bryant held out his master's sword and cocked hat. Phillip clipped scabbard to belt. The sentry stiffened to attention as he hurried past and clambered up the companion ladder, stepping from *Sirius'* deckhouse, returning her captain's salute.

Hunter stood at the compass binnacle with his copper speaking trumpet. Phillip joined him and shielded eyes, counting the topmen spaced along the yards, ready to cast off their gaskets while, a clear hundred feet below, both watches were mustering at the port and starboard braces, waiting for their orders too.

Lieutenant Bradley hurried aft and touched hatbrim to Hunter. "Boat swayed aboard and secured, sir! Capstan manned!"

Every hand who could be spared from other duties had shipped long hickory bars into the capstan's drumhead and stood to order, feet gripping the deck's wooden cleats for extra purchase. The viol rope was turned round its vertical barrel and run aft, then back again through a block to the capstan in one unbroken loop. The gunner's boys were ready to move in fast with their short, braided cords, to nip the lighter viol to the anchor's cable, hauling it through *Sirius*' hawsehole in the bows.

Phillip nodded at Hunter—their navy's discipline was as firm as ever—and reached for a spare telescope to focus on the merchant transports, still riding at anchor below a cloudless spring sky. But not for much longer. One by one they were obeying their flagship's signal and running up their own reply pennants while crewmen started aloft, like ants climbing slack cotton threads, Phillip thought.

He shut the telescope as Bradley snatched a message from the duty midshipman and relayed it to Hunter, who turned to Phillip. "All acknowledge. They will proceed to sea by line astern, commodore in the vanguard, sir."

Phillip could not keep his face impassive any longer: he fairly beamed: "Execute."

"Aye aye, sir." Hunter hid his own smile inside the trumpet's mouthpiece. "Capstan there!" his voice echoed. "Step lively now!"

The heavy pawl began clanking, walking up the cable's slack. "Heave *ho*! Heave, *ho*! He-eave, *ho*—!" *Sirius*' sailmaker also doubled as her fiddler. He took his timing from the naked shoulders straining past him and struck up a jaunty tune as eighteen men, three across each bar, inched their ship's dead weight into the wind, creeping her ever closer to vertical above the bower anchor. "Eeeve, uh! Eeeve, uh! Eeeve, uh—!" The boys darted forward again and again, nipping the creaking hemp cable. "Anchor aweigh!"

Hunter felt the immediate change in pace as iron flukes broke ground under *Sirius*' cutwater and Wight's hills began drifting across her quarter. He tilted speaking trumpet. "Tops'l sheets there! Cast loose . . . !"

The gaskets slipped, dropping bunched canvas with muffled thunder, sails bellying, filling straining against the top slings, trapping wind power, starting the softly bubbling wake astern.

Hunter cocked head to one side, listening, feeling, imagining, testing every tremor and rumble against a lifetime at sea as he turned, plotting the rise and dip of *Sirius*' bowsprit across the crowded anchorage. The convoy's transports were also breaking their moorings, tan, white, buff and faded grey sails blossoming aloft in line astern behind the flagship.

He completed the slow circle and signalled his shipmaster to step aft. "Mr. Morton. Lay for Calshot. Full and by."

"Aye aye, sir!"

Hunter squared his shoulders: he was now the one whose orders made other men jump smartly: after all the hoping and working, hardship and disappointment, he'd finally done it. *Sirius*' captain snapped back to the present as Ross marched closer, leaning against the deck's heel. He also seemed far more sprightly than normal. "Ah! There you are, Johnny!" The two exchanged courtesies as equals, doffing their hats and smiling. "I was thinking how good it would be if our band played a few airs, to cheer us out to sea as it were!"

Hunter nodded. "An excellent suggestion, Bobby."

The marines' small band formed ranks under the swelling spanker as course after course of canvas boomed aloft, bending the great yards, shouldering *Sirius*' bows through flying spray. Although he had little time for music these days, Phillip began tapping feet in time with Hunter's as Ross ordered the musicians into a shaky version of "Britons Strike Home"; they were improving by "Hearts o' Oak" and really quite steady at "Rule Britannia," drummers rattling along with the fifers' shrill tune.

The sailors were enjoying it too, leaping to their duties with pride. Even Ross was brimming with unusual goodwill for the world, Phillip noted, quietly wondering if Hunter had already planted the hope of a new El Dorado in the mountains of New Holland—why!—they were exchanging courtesies without once mentioning the marines' extra rum ration.

Only the pigs and chickens, the ducks and geese cooped in their covered yards between *Sirius*' haystack and her foremast, only the cook's livestock had no reason to celebrate the future. The marine officers' sow, panicked by the blaring music and sailors' shouts, backed off, then dropped her snout and lurched forward, grunting wildly, crashing the pen's gate, bursting its hasp, exploding across the deck with twelve squealing piglets in tow. The holystoned planks and their steep cant to lee were even more unsettling than the music; legs splayed, trotters scrabbling uphill, the beasts skidded down into the rails and thrashed around the scuppers. A rousing cheer went up as one of the bosun's mates lost the leg of his breeches to the sow's teeth. Ross howled with laughter and almost drove an elbow into Phillip's ribs. "This is better'n a whore's wedding night!"

Phillip smiled bleakly as the small herd of his officers' future sausages and black pudding, pork and crackling, tumbled nearer an open wash port, chased by a pair of marines. They kicked the last piglet back into the yard and wedged its gate shut until the carpenter could cut a stronger hasp. Ross wiped his eyes, face purple with happiness. "M'God! Omigod! Was that not a sight to remember? The silly bugger nigh on lost his *breeks*!"

"Indeed. Most droll." Phillip drew his telescope again and scanned a second sight that was anything but amusing. Even before his convoy had begun altering course about Wight's northern headland, ready to beat sou'west down the Solent, his transports were straggling; *Charlotte* and *Lady Penrhyn* were sailing like bricks; *Friendship* was sulky and the same could be said for every other ship which had taken part in yesterday's mutiny, Phillip realised, beckoning Hunter to step closer. He pointed. "What d'you make of that little pantomime?"

Hunter shaded his eyes, lips moving as he counted, then glanced down at his commodore again. "I would venture to suggest that we have not quite whipped the devil from them yet, sir."

"Agreed. Make to all: close up and hold station in line astern." He began to add something, then changed his mind. "I shall go below for breakfast. Let's see if they can get themselves together in the meantime. Carry on."

Phillip heard the signal gun as he sat down to Bryant's offering—cold potato fritters, cold fried egg, two pieces of smoked fish—neatly arranged on a cold pewter platter. Phillip sighed, the main galley could not have been lit yet, but at least the coffee was warm and the early start on deck had whetted his appetite.

He finished sharpening the knife blade on its fork and tucked into the fritters, generously spiked with brown chop sauce from his own private cellar in the pantry. The fish and egg were also welcome, if a trifle greasy, he thought, polishing his plate clean with a plug of bread. The cabin seemed to be growing stuffy. He loosened cravat. In fact the place seemed—hand clapped to mouth he crouched round the table, knocked open one of the stern lights and puked into *Sirius'* wake. Then he dropped his sweaty forehead on the wooden sill, eyes squeezed shut, and hoped to die. Five years had passed since he had taken HMS *Europa* around the Cape to India: it had been his last active command.

It seemed almost as long before he returned to the quarterdeck, handkerchief balled in one tight fist. Hunter was still near the binnacle with Mr. Morton, finger marking a page in the pilot book while *Sirius'* master hunched over his compass, adjusting its bezel ring and squinting between the wires as Calshot Castle floated across his line of sight. "Bearing! Nor' nor'wes' one 'alf league!"

"Lay wes' sou'west, Mr. Morton."

"Aye aye, sir!" The master straightened, taking his place by the helmsman. "Bosun there! Pipe all 'ands! Man the braces an' prepare to tack!"

"Aye aye!"

Bare feet slapped deck, manning weather and mizzen braces to port and starboard as the pipe shrilled. Lieutenant King was in position, too, timekeeper in one hand, sword in the other. Morton looked back at the helmsman's taut face, arms thrown wide across his wheel, reading the wind pennant at the mainmast truck. "Wes' sou'wes'."

"Wes' sou'wes'!"

The teak spokes began to spin heavily, winding rudder chains, wake boiling under *Sirius'* stern as she ponderously laid onto her last tack before Hurst Castle and the open sea, running down between Wight and Hampshire's forested shoreline as the mainyards were braced over and secured. The helmsman watched his compass card back round its bowl, then settle again. "Wes' sou'wes' it is!"

"Full an' by."

"Full an' by it is!"

Mr. Master Morton wiped the palms of his hands across his jacket and watched Hunter, impassive as the figurehead, pilot book under one arm, alert to everything as it happened, missing nothing, a professional shipmaster himself. "Er. Wes' sou'wes', sir."

Sirius' captain turned and touched hat to the commodore's lonely shape. "On course, sir."

"Thank God someone is." Phillip was watching vessel after vessel stagger round Calshot buoy in his flagship's wake. Sailcloth pounding aback, *Borrowdale* all but rammed *Golden Grove* dead amidships, then somehow hauled away in a drunken zigzag which came within yards of shearing *Prince of Wales'* bowsprit as the leading transport wound down her helm on a converging course—

"Holy Jesus." Hunter was staring at the same pitiful sight. Phillip had never thought he would live to hear this man blaspheme; he could barely keep his own temper under control as he scanned from side to side, hunting up the convoy's two ladies; *Charlotte* and *Penrhyn* were still lumbering away on their original course with *Alexander*, as if to drop anchor off Southampton before noon and forget Botany Bay altogether.

Phillip shut his spyglass with suppressed fury. "Not five miles under our keels and we're already the laughingstock of England!"

Hunter tried making a smile. "They'll shake down in a few days, sir."

"If we're spared that long!" Phillip stuffed the soggy handkerchief in his pocket and paced to windward while the captain and master continued their duties at the binnacle. Elbow on rail, he drew the telescope's tubes again: *Sirius* was coming abeam Lymington, among its meadows at the water's edge.

After some effort, and still blinking against the light, Phillip thought he could see Lyndhurst hill in the far distance, below a pack of white cumulus clouds. "If wooly fleeces bedeck Heaven's way, shepherd be sure no rain will mar your day," the countryman in him recited aloud while focussing the telescope's disc round where Mr. Secretary Rose might now be standing, if he had ridden up from Cuffnells for his morning trot. But the haze from charcoal burners' camps in the forest was too thick and Phillip slowly lost interest as the glass slipped further and further astern, searching for his convoy again.

Borrowdale was still lurching from side to side as if a brace of apes had seized her helm and was fighting for a banana, he noted bitterly, but at least *Alexander* and the two ladies had consented to alter course and wander after their commodore. Meanwhile *Prince of Wales* and *Golden Grove*, *Fishburn* and *Scarborough* were stumbling along behind the government's ships—HMS *Sirius,* HMS *Supply* and their armed sloop HMS *Hyaena*—now readying themselves to fire salutes as they transected Hurst Castle on the beam and began breasting the open Channel. Even as Phillip turned from the rail, his flagship's starboard armament began thumping a broadside, rippling aft from the bows, each cannon roaring its blank charge at five-second intervals by Lieutenant King's watch.

The shore gunners returned the compliment, *Alexander*'s master noted with contempt, steadying his own spyglass on the spectacle at the head of the column. He straightened without hurrying and cocked an eye at his first mate. "Yon bluejackets are no more than a gang o' hooligans on Guy Fawkes' Night wi' their bang, bang, banging!"

"Yoh!" the mate grinned through teeth like mahogany pegs.

"Do ye have any idea what their little game is costing us?" Sinclair went on in the same self-righteous bray. The mate shook his head, as required. "Then I shall inform ye, Mr. Olsen: elevenpence halfpenny! That's the cost o' mealed gunpowder nowadays, elevenpence halfpenny a cartridge! But do our fine gentlemen over yonder care what it costs? O' course not, the public purse will pay the bill! To hear such popping their peashooters, a man would think revenue money fell off bluidy trees like leaves in autumn!"

Sinclair glowered at the scarlet coat of his sentry, by *Alexander*'s brass "murderer," the stubby swivel gun which could sweep a gallon of broken glass, bent nails and pebbles across the waist-deck if ever the ship's cargo dared break hatches without permission. "I'll wager they'd not be so free if they first had to find nearly a shilling piece from their own pockets," he went on. "And I'll wager something else, Mr. Olsen," *Alexander*'s master continued, jabbing a thumb at the chalk cliffs which rose shear from the sea off Wight's western headland. "Afore we're even clear o' the Needles, our fine lords an' masters will start their bang-banging again, flying their pretty flags and tellin' us to close up—! Ye'd think we were bluidy schoolchildren from home the first time." Sinclair's bottom lip pouted, squirting tobacco juice as he launched into his only relaxation, a hearty grumble at anyone's authority but his own. "Yon' Commode Sparrow Legs is all piss and wind, some bluidy turnip farmer they've hauled through a hedge backward to wear you' fine hat." Sinclair scowled at his first mate. "How many voyages d'ye have to Canton, Mr. Olsen . . . ?"

The mate ticked fingertips. "T'ree."

"Exactly. *I've* logged nigh on twice that number o' passages to China, an' that's not includin' untold shipments of niggers to the Barbados, but does our fine English gentleman—?"

Alexander's lookout, perched aloft on her foretop, cupped mouth over the rim. "De-e-eck a-lowww! Signal! On—the—commodore . . . !"

"What did I tell ye, Mr. Olsen?" Sinclair snorted. "One shilling will get ye five that's a slap on the wrist to hurry us along." *Alexander*'s master steadied his glass again and focussed on *Sirius*' halliards, drawing code letters for his mate to copy on the binnacle slate. He shut the glass without haste. "Ye've just lost yourself an easy five shillings, Mr. Olsen: this must be your unlucky day. 'Close up' indeed!" Sinclair chewed another cud of baccy and thought about *Sirius*' command before nodding an order to fly *Alexander*'s red and white answering pennant. "And shake out another reef on the lower main to oblige our fine gentlemen."

"Yoh!" Olsen knuckled his forehead and shoved past the sentry at the spiked barricade gate, whistle in one fist, knotted cob in the other.

Cribb could not hear the mate's yelps and thuds happening on the deck over his shelf. Drenched with sweat, burning with the swamp fever he'd brought home from Virginia, Cribb was now fighting for his life, trying to kill Levi and Thorpe before breaking through the stockade gate at Copper Hill prison camp. The two men could barely pin him down as *Alexander* lunged into another Channel roller, timbers groaning, smashing a wall of green water across her bows. Cribb screamed. All around, stacked like wet logs of wood, almost two hundred men were out of control as a latrine tub broke from its moorings and began tumbling down the main aisle. Another heavy sea burst round the transport's bowsprit, spray dancing on the sunlight, white foam surging aft along the foredeck, swirling over the hatchway's bars.

"Aaaagh—!"

"Oi'm drowdin'!"

"Holy Mary Mother o'—!"

The cascade drained away through bilge gratings and limber holes, sucking down most of the fresh sewage, blending it with yesterday's on the bed of gravel ballast. Then the barque's blunt chin dropped again and she plunged, gathering speed, coming up short at the bottom of her dive, spume flying. The same check heaved back a wall of brown bilge through the gratings, driving a knee-high wave up the aisle, smashing the oak latrine tub against the mainmast, hurling its splinters into the lowest rank of shelves.

Levi sapped Cribb's head, yelling for Thorpe to lie flat across his legs. Not for the first or last time Levi was wondering why he'd ever bothered with this patient while another, detached part of his brain went on fingering the scarred outer face of Cribb's left buttock; gunshot wound, cleaned with a branding iron, good stitching, the fingertips reported back; stitches quite as neat as any they had made while cutting for bladder stone in the market places of Little Russia and Turkey.

Others were less used to life's ups and downs than the Jewish quack doctor. Terrified men were crawling and tumbling for'ard, heaping against the barred gateway, screaming, begging, pleading to be let out. The sentry was also panicking, levelling, aiming back through the hatch, firing over their heads: the lead ball mushroomed in the women's cage and howled into darkness.

"They're murtherin' us all!"

"Save me—!"

The drummer boy was at his post, pounding the general alarm while a sergeant bawled commands and men doubled across the deck, bayonets rattling from their scabbards. "Prepare to advance—!"

Sinclair cuffed the poop sentry from *Alexander*'s swivel gun and lowered the cocked flint before leading a counterattack of his own, rope cob slashing left and right, halting the stunned redcoats. "Sergeant Ramsbottom!" he yelled point-blank into the marine's ear. "What in the name o' bluidy hell d'ye think *my* ship is?!"

"Gen'ral alarm! Them crim'nals is escapin' down there!"

Sinclair's lip curled. "Is that a fact, Sergeant Lamb's Bum? Well! Since I am still nominally in command o' this vessel, perhaps I had better take a look afore ye do anything hasty?" He craned over the hatchway, ignoring its ripe stench while listening to the riot, then straightened again with an exaggerated slowness. "Sergeant Sheep's Arse. When ye've guarded three gross o' jungle niggers tearing at their bars in a hurricane, *then* ye'll know what it means to sound a general alarm. Until ye have, avast there! And belay those bluidy sea sodjers!"

Another white crest was breaking over *Alexander*, swirling between the marines' gaitered legs, thundering into the hold. Sinclair nodded at his first mate. "Rig a tarp. And man the pumps."

Thorpe whimpered in the gathering gloom as Olsen's men jumped in front of his cob and began lacing a tarpaulin over the hatchway. Levi cursed them all: Cribb's arm had slipped from his grip and was now swiping around wildly, beating off the Nightmare. Its phantom pack of wolves was once again slobbering among Saratoga's dead as a billowing cloud of scarlet cloak swept across a frosty moon like the Queen of the Night, Mrs. Brandon's stick whacking left and right, driving the brutes back into the forest behind Schuyler's Farm.

Alexander dived through another roller, timbers rumbling, piling chaos upon confusion below decks. Cribb screamed and Levi swore again, losing his own fight with a terror of drowning as the barque shouldered her way onto the open sea.

Cribb was raving, trying to hurl himself off the narrow shelf, biting and spitting at the packs of urchins who were now darting between the shambling, shuffling, stumbling ghosts inside his skull: London's Pride, the Seventh Fusileers, were coming home from the war. Cribb and a mate were limping through the jeering streets with a third lad, the top of his face buried in a rag, blindly clutching at their sleeves, head bowed against the dog turds which children were scooping up to pelt the returning soldiers.

"*Meshugass!*" Levi knocked him down again, wincing at the skin's heat as Cribb went on babbling crazily. He punched Thorpe's shoulder to get his attention and the two men began lashing Cribb's wrists to the shelf, using most of Levi's hoard of stolen rope.

Cribb jerked rigid, then began fighting as he had never fought before. They were dragging him onto Newgate's scaffold again. Rank upon rank of darkees were already twirling on ropes, gurgling inside their flour bags, red coats and shiny brass buttons flapping, legs kicking in time with Mrs. Brandon as she swirled Tarleton's satanic black cloak at them. The crowd was jeering louder. Cribb gnawed Levi's thumb as an invisible sheriff obeyed the she-devil's orders, lashing his wrists and ankles, snugging the noose around his neck, getting the knot firmly under his chin. Mrs. Brandon was throbbing with laughter at the sight of him, naked and alone on the drop. The crowd cheered as she slowly pulled the lever, plunging him straight through the gallows' floor—

But Cribb had worked one hand free and jammed it under the rope collar, dangling, spinning, wheezing like the traitor he'd been ordered to neck from a shaft pole at Greensboro, in the Carolinas. That had been one execution which Cribb had bungled, and, in every repeat of the Nightmare, the same elderly man had kept jerking his knees to chin, choking to death while barnyard fowl clucked around him in the sunlight. And, like the Rebel spy, Cribb was losing his grip on the rope as it—

"*Got tzu danken!*" Levi felt Cribb collapse into a coma, then relaxed his own grip and flexed the aching thumb. "Ei! What a tartar!"

Thorpe didn't hear; Thorpe didn't care. Abandoned, wretched and alone, he clung to Cribb's spindly legs for support and comfort: his only protector aboard *Alexander* was dying and would soon be heaved over the side! Levi snatched at a stanchion above the shelf as their transport took another sea, then swung a jab at the young man's head. "What you blub'ring for, heh?! Get off your arse, *schlub!*"

"H-he be dying!"

"So what's new in the village?"

"H-he be dying!" Thorpe bawled again, staring up for the first time. "Now what's going to 'appen to me?! Oi never done nothing wrong—!"

"Horsezhit!" Levi sneered, hopping away as another tub broke loose and cannoned past. "When you got the *sumpffieber* like this, your mate got it, then you gone and done something wrong! Till then, shut the face and be a man!"

The second tub had burst apart and it was time for Levi to go, swinging across the clogged aisle to clamber up to his own territory again, high under the deck timbers. But someone from the lower ranks of shelves had sensed a chance to rise in the world when Levi was next called away to a patient. A terrible mistake. The man's forehead smashed into the low timbers as Levi attacked, rolling and dumping him over the other side.

Satisfied that the secret tobacco cache was still intact behind the shelf frame, Levi settled down and made himself comfortable. Contrary as ever, he remained stubbornly immune to seasickness while, all around him, other lags retched and begged for death.

21

LEVI SHRUGGED: *Seekrankheit* kills nobody, but swamp fever is a dog with a harder bite. Today it attacks Mr. Kripp, tomorrow who next? Levi burrowed under his mattress hay, looking for a cabbage stalk from the morning's ration bucket, then settled back for a leisurely chew.

However things ended for Cribb, Levi's problems would not be so easily solved. All the bluster, all the bustling around *Alexander*'s cargo space was nothing more than bluff, the need of an outsider to be needed by insiders. Yet what else had he to trade aboard this floating madhouse? Nothing. Who could pay him to charm a bad tooth? None. And which of these English needed his skill with garden herbs? Nobody. And when would anyone ever do him a favour after he'd turned away the Death Angel, with magic numbers from the cabala? Never.

Levi grimaced and knocked wood at the name. *Margan* and his demons had often passed over the marshland villages of Poland when Abraham Levi was still Red Dov, Samuel Moseiwicz's heartbreak son. His father had broken more sticks on Dov in the house of prayer than he had ever paid coins for the village scribe to chalk pious lies on the door of their hut behind the slaughterhouse, promises to the Death Angel that Hyam and Chaim, Reuven and Rebekkah had now left home to live with relatives in a distant city. But *Margan* had never been fooled for long; one summer he had breathed down the chimney, wrapped Hyam and Rebekkah in burning shrouds of swamp fever and flown them away on the smoke of the cooking fire.

The deaths of an elder brother and sister, lying beside Dov on the same bed of untanned sheepskins, had been among the first of his life's many interesting puzzles. Not that it had ever been any puzzle why his name had been left off the chalked list outside; the entire village would have read it as a good omen if only *he* had flown away up the chimney, but evidently *Margan* hadn't troubled to learn his Hebrew characters any more than Dov had. Or did the Dark Angel also have a streak of dark humour?

Levi shrugged. Whatever the truth of the matter now, a lifelong habit had begun that sultry Polish summer. Others would huddle together for protection indoors, and die; Dov would stride outside, daring the heavens to do their worst, and survive. Not always easily, of course, but in this world even one bite off a crust is better than no bread at all, and when tomorrow comes, who knows what will be in its pocket? For example, how many of the family, of the People, had got thus far?—one half of Levi's agile mind began arguing with the other half—how many, heh? None. So, was this mad journey to Bottommy Bay another curse from Heaven, or was it a blessing disguised, like his red hair?

Levi always enjoyed haggling with the only person he had ever recognised as being worthy of such close attention, himself. "Sinful pride," they had called it, back in the village. "Dangerous arrogance! It will get you into trouble!" And, for once, the elders had been right. "Be humble! Be of service to the almighty Count Czytno or else his servants will surely humble you!"

Levi grimaced at the memory of so many thrashings for his own good before the synagogue lectern, but it is not easy to seem humble when one stands tall, with wide, Tartar cheekbones and shaggy red hair blowing around in the wind. It would have been easier to overlook the fact that he was living proof of an earlier kinswoman's weakness after a gang of soldiers had passed her way; she had failed to do the only decent thing, either drown herself or strangle the little bastard before it could draw breath and be counted as human. But the wretched woman had done neither and her family's tainted blood had again become a scandal with Dov's first breath.

That such a boy would bring endless woes to his parents was obvious to any neighbour with an eye to see and a tongue to gossip. Where was the father who would let *his* son marry the dutiful, the virtuous Rebekkah if there was even the slightest risk that his grandchildren would also look like drunken Cossacks? And which merchant in the provincial capital would ever consider the dutiful, the studious Reuven as a prospective son-in-law if that living disgrace, Dov, also had to be invited to the wedding feast? But in the end *Margan* had solved everyone's problems, as he always does; fever had claimed the hand of Rebekkah before her virtuous poverty could be traded for something better, and tuberculosis had snuffed out Reuven's hopes of a glittering marriage before he finished the years of starvation as a Talmudic scholar, up north in Lithuania. As for the rest of his brethren and kinsmen, Levi never knew how many remained to curse his name after the Russians, and the Prussians, and the Austrians had chopped up the Polish potato with their sabres, but he could guess—none.

Meanwhile, after Poland finally collapsed under the weight of three crowned heads, the unrepentant ne'er-do-well was doing quite well for himself, plodding down the pedlars' tracks to Lublin fair. The teams of Jewish horse traders tested him—deep-chested men in their padded leather coats and tall wolfskin hats, grim fighters with the whip, boot and fist, and Red Dov was no longer travelling alone as he continued southward across Walachia and Bulgaria, following the annual fairs, sharpening his already formidable wits with men of all nations and all colours.

If Lublin had been a new world after the mean and squalid life back in the village, Constantinople had been a new universe to the northern Jew after he'd tramped with his pack across the hillsides of apricot blossom which overlook the strait between Europe and Asia. And the sultan's capital had kept its promise behind the walls of the grand bazaar where four thousand merchants offered everything a man would ever need from blond Circassian slave boys to boxes of rose petal jelly. It had only been a matter of days before a friend of a friend—a money changer in the Street of Sublime Delight—hired the tall foreigner to be his personal bodyguard and debt collector. Then another friend of a friend asked for the services of such a reliable man to escort a caravan of carpets to Latakia, but once on the Mediterranean coast the never-ending road seemed to unroll ahead of Levi like one of the carpets, drawing him onward to Baghdad and Isfahan, to Bokhara and Tashkent.

Years passed and Red Dov was again trudging across Europe, working the market places of Pressburg and Vienna, Berlin and Frankfurt, Trier and Koblenz. To stay one jump ahead of the *Judenhäscher*—municipal bounty hunters who lived off the hundreds of thousands of other unwanted, unwelcome Eastern Jews—Dov hawked his potions and cast spells to cure toothache. He might still have been banging a drum in some market place between Petersburg and Palermo, barking the wonders of Sultan Selim's Syrup: "As drunk in the harems of the mysterious Orient!" Bang. "When royal princes must satisfy the hunger of one hundred passionate virgins in a single night!" Bang, bang. "Every bottle guaranteed to contain the secret essence of an eunuch's former manhood!" Bang, bang, bang—if only he hadn't lost his voice to laryngitis one autumn afternoon in Koblenz. Without warning he was left holding a dozen and a half crates of caramel water, spiked with *nux vomica* and raw schnapps, in a city where masterless Jews and gypsies were regularly broken on the rack if denounced by more than two citizens. It was an uncomfortable situation and Dov had been about to order fresh labels from the printer—"Pharaoh's Wart Killer"—before trading his stock for a bolt of Osnaburg cloth, when a serving man approached him through the crowd and respectfully tugged at the long sleeve of his Turkish robe. It seemed that the man's master was begging the honour of a private audience to discuss a matter of the greatest importance. . . .

Red Dov listened attentively (without a voice this was his best course of action) and followed. But his hopes of selling the elixir at a better profit faded as the servant led him along the muddy lanes of Koblenz' ghetto. Then the man halted in front of a three-storey, brick-built residence with windows—not the usual warped wooden shutters or flattened sheets of cowhorn, but panes of real, bottle-green glass! Dov ran his eye over the property like an auctioneer's tape measure and his spirits soared again as the servant bowed, holding open the street door for him to enter first; if respect and privilege lodged at this address in the Judengasse, then surely money and culture lived under the same roof.

A portly, bewigged man in fashionable mauve silk stockings and blue sateen *culottes* stood waiting in front of the blazing hearth. He smiled and hurried forward to greet his guest in the shabby robe and turban. "I am so honoured that you could come, my dear sir! Pray allow me to introduce myself: I am the Rabbi Mordechai of Lindau. You have heard of me, yes?"

Dov hadn't, but an eventful life had taught him that a polite bow will answer most questions. He was still straightening again when his host suddenly reached for a pair of scissors and, before Dov could move, snipped off a lock of hair.

The older man hurried away to the window, where he began peering through a magnifying lens. Then he dipped the hair into the first of several flasks. Satisfied that its colour remained fixed, he turned again, hands rubbing together. "Forgive my caution, dear sir, one encounters so many frauds and imposters these days. But no matter, I am quite satisfied that you are indeed red, just as my informants tell me that you are truly a Jew. Therefore you are a red Jew, yes?"

Dov began edging toward the window and escape across the roof line before this maniac struck again, meanwhile he played for time with another bow.

"Splendid! You have no idea how long I've been waiting to meet you. All my life I have been waiting for this moment. Then, just when I am beginning to think that I shall never make the journey, along you come! I am so happy!" Dov had already halved the distance to the window. Mordechai frowned after him. "Is there perhaps something the matter with your voice?"

Dov paused and tapped his larynx. "If Your Honour had some warm honey water," he whispered, "with a dash of peppermint oil perhaps . . . ?"

Reb Mordechai understood. He rang for the manservant to climb upstairs again and put a kettle on the fire. Then he beckoned for his hesitant guest to take a seat near the blazing logs. "Now, I imagine that you must be wondering why I requested the privilege of your company today, yes? I shall therefore be brief, for the time is nigh and our age is drawing to its predestined end—"

"*Uh?*"

"Ah hah!" The rabbi chuckled. "I can see that you are surprised anyone could uncover your secret so quickly! But have no fear, you are safe with me. You see, I know where you come from, and I intend returning home with you before I die—"

Dov stopped thumping his chest and slumped in the brocade chair. "You crazy!"

Reb Mordechai slapped his knees at such a capital joke. "Don't think I didn't penetrate your disguise the very moment I heard about you, so let us both stop beating about the bush and get down to business, yes? Item: how much will it cost me to reach Sabation? And how long will it take?"

Dov blinked and, for the first time, a seed of doubt began sprouting in the cultivated soil of the rabbi's imagination. "Sa-ba-tion? The river which flows beyond Babylon. You *are* from the East, aren't you?"

Two things only now made any sense to Dov: the roaring fire and the glass of hot cordial which the manservant was stirring for him. All the rest was madness, but at least it was a comfortable insanity, so what harm would be done by humouring the worthy old gentleman for a short while? Say until the next springtime, after the snow had melted and the roads south had dried out? Surely it would be an uncharitable act to deprive the reverend gentleman of such a simple pleasure as his—Dov's—company in the dark winter months ahead?

Dov could feel the honey and peppermint soothing his throat, and he sighed with relief as if a heavy pack were slipping from his shoulders. "It is plain that I can no longer hide the truth, Your Honour. You are right, I am a red Jew."

"I knew it!" Mordechai clasped his hands with ecstasy. "At last! Oh, tell me, dearest friend, how are things now for our people in Babylon?"

Dov rocked a hand from side to side. "Fine, just fine. Of course, it depends on the exact time of year Your Honour wishes to discuss, but summer is always better than winter."

Reb Mordechai was radiant at the news and it was midnight before he could stop telling and retelling of his lifelong dream to join the ten lost tribes of Israel. Hours earlier, a drowsy Dov had kicked off his boots and watched the servant prepare a second platter of savoury goose dripping on hot toast.

Now, as nearly as the pedlar could follow, once, long ago, others like himself and the rabbi had been thrown into the town gaol at a place called Babylon. The name was familiar, of course; the village slaughterman had nagged his worthless son with it every High Holy Day. However, according to this strange rabbi from Lindau, not all of those earlier exiles had returned home; some, a whole ten tribes, had been trapped behind a river of fire in remotest Asia, the Sabation. Six days every week a wall of flames stopped anyone crossing back and, on the seventh day when the fire died down for the Sabbath, the ten tribes could still not move because of the Law.

However, Reb Mordechai went on, through laughter and tears, the prophets—Isaiah, Jeremiah, Ezekiel—had promised a golden age when the entire Jewish nation would again be reunited and the thousand-year reign of justice begin on earth. Now, at last, all the signs were that the days of exile were drawing to a close, that the end of the world was nigh, and wonders abounded for those who could interpret them. Had not a parchment from Achitov Ben Azariah, king of the ten tribes, fallen from the sky over Jerusalem? And had not a hail of flintstones smitten the ungodly in Bohemia? And in the Holy Land were not the Turkish mosques being swallowed up by the earth? Soon the Jews on the other side of Sabation would come and liberate their western brethren in the final battle of Armageddon! Then would the dead be raised, their bodies transformed to pure spirit, and each day would last a century while the seraphim chanted praise without end—!

The rabbi mopped his brow and rang for the yawning manservant to come up and fill the kettle for more coffee.

So, all the known facts indicated that the thousand-year kingdom was about to begin, it must therefore be possible to cross Sabation, but how? To answer this, one needed a messenger, one of the lost tribesmen who, from time to time, dared to brave the flames and bring witness to his western brethren. But such messengers from the East were nearly always attacked by Satan, who needed to stop them from revealing their precious secret. How, then, could an ordinary mortal recognise one of the lost Jews?

"By our red hair?" Dov queried.

Mordechai clapped his hands again and began to laugh with delight, stopping short with a concerned frown when Dov went on to show the scar above one ear—a battle trophy from the grand bazaar—which explained why his memory had been almost entirely wiped out since a djinn attacked him on the road from Samarkand. Since when, Messenger Dov had been wandering the world, praying that some learned rabbi would teach him the secret of his mission, and, perhaps, if he were willing to risk the journey East, return home to speak with King Achitov. . . .

Thinking back on it now, chained aboard a British slaver and outward bound for God only knew how many other market brawls, Levi remembered that winter in Koblenz as if through a haze of golden sunlight. For the first and only time in his life others had made it their work to feed and clothe him. Meanwhile, Reb Mordechai had made it an honour and a pleasure to restore the messenger's memory by reading aloud from books of commentary on the Egyptian exile, the Babylonian captivity, the destruction of the Temple, and much else that Dov could barely grasp. Most of what the rabbi said made good sense, of course, but some didn't. However, what else could one expect from a man who chose to dress and speak like a high-born *goy?* Anything was possible from a man who never tired of saying how lucky he was to be a Jew under the benevolent protection of such an enlightened ruler as the prince archbishop of Koblenz. The assimilation of cultures, he had once described it, the need to greet our Christian cousins on the level, halfway across the bridge of reason. All that then needed to be done was to extend the cordial right hand of fellowship and it would be only a matter of time before every other German city-state shared the same *Juden Tolerenz* and the world would be ready for the Messiah's return.

Dov had sometimes wondered where the prince archbishop's rack and gibbet fitted into this holy design, but kept such nagging doubts to himself. Not that all the rabbi's ideas were so extreme and, in this life, one learns never to push a girl off the bed while picking fleas from her blanket. Besides, as week followed week, Red Dov Moseiwicz was learning who he was, and the lessons had more to do with a nameless huddle of huts on a Polish noble's estate than with a tribe of legends in a city of jewels beyond the sunrise.

For the first time ever, Dov was learning that Jews—men like himself—had been mighty kings long before the first Count Czytno was even a robber baron. Goose pimples had rippled down to the soles of his feet when Reb Mordechai began chanting of the victory after Joshua ben Nun went up into the hills of Judea with his men of valour to annihilate the Amorites, when even the sun and moon had obeyed the children of Israel and stood still on Beth Horon. A few days later, as a blizzard lashed Koblenz, the study candles had been lit early and Reb Mordechai had begun telling in a sombre voice how Judah Maccabee and his brothers had risen against an empire and died hard on the field of honour rather than eat the bread of slavery.

That night Dov had tossed and turned under his feather quilt, and it was not only the storm howling outside which kept him awake. Now he was having to grapple with uneasy questions about himself. Was it right to continue pretending to know the road to that river of fire? Was it the proper thing to let Reb Mordechai finish selling his property before going East in spring with his messenger? Looked at from any sensible point of view there was no problem; it would be the easiest "mark" in his career to swindle the trusting old man down to his last shirt button once they were travelling alone together, and who else would ever know? Who else would even care?

The trouble was that Dov himself knew. Dov had begun to know and care. This was one deception he could not hide behind a new label, just as nothing would ever hide the fact that Joshua and Judah had remained men of respect, men of honour to the grave and beyond. They still had that eerie power which made others tingle just to hear their names spoken. Compared with such men, what were today's children of Israel? They were little more than dogs, happy to lick any hand which held out a bone or raised a whip.

A few months of easy living had given Dov the leisure to fill his imagination with dangerous new ideas. What the outcome would have been for him, he never found out. One rainy afternoon the rabbi came home chilled to the marrow. That night the community's doctor had hurried upstairs with his jar of leeches and a cupping bowl. By the following noon Reb Mordechai was dying, but it took another two days and a night of opened veins before a chilly sweat settled like dew across his staring face. "Why do you weep, Dovchen?" the old man had whispered. "It is only that a greater Messenger has come first, and—"

After the funeral, Dov began stuffing his few personal belongings into their sack. For a moment he even considered leaving the Turkish robe and old turban on his bed for the ragpickers to squabble over, but common sense triumphed over sentiment and he stowed his working clothes as well. But one thing he did leave behind as he stepped into the slush of the Judengasse for the last time: Red Dov Moseiwicz. From now he would at least try to be a man like those greater men of long ago; he would be "Abraham," the father of his people, and "Levi," the guardian of his faith during the long years of Exodus.

How well he kept that promise since leaving Koblenz was a matter of opinion. Sultan Selim's Syrup had got him out of a tight corner in Antwerp, and there had been that misunderstanding with herbs back in London, but he had never entirely given up trying to act honourably in his personal dealings—and that was a considerable victory, all things considered.

London? Levi grimaced at the name as *Alexander* plodded down Channel away from England. What an upside-down capital of an upside-down people! True, it had been the first European city he had ever entered legally without first paying a *Leibzoll* at the gates, like a pig, or a donkey, or a Jew. The reason had not been hard to find: among a people as peaceful and law-abiding as the English, there were few city gates worth mentioning, unless one counted Newgate. Nor were there soldiers beating drums at curfew while bounty hunters ransacked lodginghouses to find Jews without a decent bribe. To that extent London had been an even more amazing city than Constantinople, every street corner a new horizon, like Reb Mordechai's readings from Leviticus and Joshua. Never in all his days had Levi found himself among such a frenzied nation of hucksters, and gamblers, and mountebanks. The camel traders of Damascus had at least lied with murmuring smiles a man could understand, but these English were like yelling savages in their headlong chase after guineas, and the newcomer had lost no time joining the hunt.

The London Guild of Barbers & Surgeons had a royal charter which gave them the monopoly on cutting for stone, and tooth-pulling was well protected by certain other interests, so Levi had decided to open shop as a fortune teller and herbalist instead. Sitting in the perfumed half-light of Dr. Achmet's Magnetic Consultorium, stroking the palms of masked ladies had taught him that nobody in London yet had the recipe for a discreet remedy such as the women of Smyrna used to get rid of their unwanted family problems. And soon the golden guineas were rolling his way, too.

Then, just as the sun seemed to be shining on him forever—pfft!—that *yukel* Bessie Jarvis had to get his instructions wrong and bleed to death in front of her busybody mistress. But even then these English had lived up to their reputation for standing the world on its head. Did they let the mob rip him apart like any normal citizens would have done elsewhere? Of course not! The sheriff's men had closed ranks round a foreign Jew and convicted murderer, escorting him to prison like a man of title, so that he could be killed later, at the proper time, in the proper way.

Levi preferred to forget the weeks in Newgate's death cell. Toward the end it had been a close race between meeting the hangman and pulling the right strings to bargain for a pardon. But once again the Death Angel had passed over without calling his name, which brought Levi almost full circle from Poland to the English Channel. Once more he was hungry and alone, but with this difference: soon he must begin fighting for respect on the crowded streets of New Holland—wherever in God's name that was! Would this New Dutch be anything like Old German, or something different? What percentage would the street lords expect for their protection and goodwill? Would there be friends of friends waiting with secret handgrips, or what?

Levi sighed: so many problems, so few answers. It would be a bad start to a new life if all his plans for that Kripp and his young friend were to come to nothing just because of a dose of swamp fever. Very well—he shrugged—if the question was that simple, so must be its answer. From now on the rest of his patients aboard *Alexander* would have to take their chances: Mr. Kripp must not die.

22

SLEET OR SUN, every day at sea would begin at four bells of the morning watch after the flagship's carpenter crawled below to inspect her bilge. Every day he would chalk the dipstick's mark on his slate before climbing aloft again to report to her master. Every day her pumps would then be manned and the overnight leakage sucked over the side. Meanwhile, hammocks were being brailed up, divisions inspected by their petty officers, defaulters punished and the decks holystoned. Ross' marines were also paraded in close order and, come sun or sleet, their equipment would gleam before the guard marched aft to the great cabin, and *Sirius'* magazine, and her padlocked water butts.

The crew's breakfast drill was as tightly regulated. Each mess drew lots to send someone to queue outside the galley door with their bucket and jug. Whatever the weather, the same ladles of smiggins—boiled barley and beef water—were doled out, except on Sundays when a kindly cook might serve "tar and maggots," rice stewed in thin molasses. The cook's mate then splashed rations of Scotch coffee—burned biscuit soaked in weak sugar water—and the sailors could return home to the fo'c'sle for the day's first meal.

It was now the second morning at noon. Phillip polished his fried egg off the plate and went on deck, hair blowing, his fearnaught buttoned to the chin. He squinted aloft: the sky was still high and open, the wind nor'easterly; there was no need for him to run for safety in Torbay to ride out a Channel gale. But he was taking no chances as he stood at the windward mizzen brace and trained his glass astern at the merchantmen, still plodding to port and starboard. And still straggling woefully. *Hyaena* and *Charlotte* were, he knew without looking, still lumbering along on the horizon, bringing up the rearguard. Phillip shut his telescope and beckoned for Hunter to step nearer. "Make to all: close up."

"Aye aye, sir." Hunter went forward to pass the order before joining *Sirius'* master and one of his mates as they were about to heave the log. The mate streamed it astern, letting the knotted line run across his palms as the master watched his sandglass. Sixteen fathoms had run out before the glass turned. After a struggle with addition and subtraction on the binnacle slate, Mr. Master Morton announced that his ship now had a forward speed of two sea miles an hour.

"And still those sleepy laggards can't catch us?" Hunter queried, peering over the man's shoulder to check his sums. He straightened. "It is my opinion that we could walk overland to China in half the time it's taking us to sail there. Carry on."

"Aye aye, sir!"

The second day passed, regulated by half-hourly bells and the rhythms of life aboard a man o' war. *Sirius*' sailmaker took the opportunity to bring out his work and to sit cross-legged on deck, stitching and patching her tropical rags. The suit of sails which was taking her down the Channel would be struck at Teneriffe and replaced by a lighter set for the middle passage to Rio, where her third and best suit, her storm canvas, would be rigged for the hardest run of all—across the South Atlantic, past the Cape of Good Hope and almost down to the Antarctic before wearing north again, round Van Dieman's Land to Botany Bay.

HMS *Supply* shepherded the merchantmen into their second night at sea as the flagship's lantern swayed aloft, as much to warn French smugglers to stay clear on their overnight runs to Cornwall as to signal her convoy to hold close stations.

The wind freshened at dawn and the queue at *Sirius*' galley had to secure their breakfast buckets with waist ropes by the time Phillip was ready to climb on deck and turn aft. The sun was glaring fitfully down long streets of cloud. He joined Hunter at the flagstaff and squinted aloft past the ensign. " 'Mackerel skies and mares' tails, warn tall ships to wear short sails.' We could be in for a blow before sundown, John."

Hunter nodded. "The weather glass is unsettled, sir. It might be prudent if we ordered a general muster before clearing Land's End."

"Agreed. Do it."

Phillip returned to his cabin to finish a late despatch as *Sirius* further shortened sail to let the transports overhaul her. He swung round in his seat by the stern windows and watched *Prince of Wales* lead the muster, beating heavily across the wake as her master tossed a list of deficiencies and requests over the side in an empty bottle for *Sirius*' longboat to fish from the sea. Phillip hoped, all experience to the contrary, that nothing of any great importance was now being reported missing and that soon he could crowd on sail to clear Scilly's reefs before the weather broke.

Hunter almost kicked the door shut behind him when he came into the cabin to make his report. Phillip laid the quill aside and quietly folded hands. "Well?"

"No, sir, it is not." *Sirius*' commander fanned a sheaf of creased papers across the table. "We now have seven hundred felons aboard this convoy and not one provost marshal to police them when we get to our destination."

Phillip sat forward. "Say again?"

"Certainly. Our provost marshal changed his mind about boarding *Golden Grove*."

"Good—!"

"One moment, sir, that's only the start," Hunter went on. "Captain Mason informs us that *Prince of Wales* has not a stitch of women's clothing to hide their lewdness from his men, and many were naked when they embarked."

"God. . . ."

"In addition, everyone but *Alexander* says that their cargo manifests and records are still ashore at the factor's office. By my reckoning," Hunter continued, "there are around five hundred items out there of whom we know nothing, why they were convicted, what useful labour they can perform, nor even for how long they are supposed to remain in Botany Bay."

"John—?"

"With respect, sir, let's swallow this medicine in one draught. The guards have only six rounds of ball ammunition apiece. Someone forgot to bring the other ten thousand or so cartridges issued to our battalion."

Phillip looked ill as he sank back into his chair again. "Not a word, understand? If the convicts get wind of this, we're scuppered."

"Agreed, sir. Now, if I—"

A musket crashed overhead and someone fell screaming on the cabin roof. Hunter's sword was drawn as he burst past the sentry and ran aloft. Phillip joined in time to see four marines dragging away a fifth, his leg trailing blood across the scrubbed deck. "You!" Phillip's sword aimed at a sixth redcoat. "What the devil's happening?"

"Dunno, sir!" the man gasped, knees clenched to attention. "Corp'l Stokes was a-showin' us the proper way to ground arms when it sort o' slipped an' went off!"

Phillip kept silent as Ross and his officers also ran on deck, then he turned and beckoned Hunter to follow him down to the cabin again. But *Sirius*' commander was still trying to trace the bullet's path, through the marine's leg, through a harness cask of salt beef for the crew's dinner, and straight through a pair of geese in the officer's farmyard. Hunter picked at the grey metal mushroom which had flattened itself against an iron chain plate, then stood, shaking his head in wonder. "What a freak show."

"I would describe it more as a Punch and Judy tent!" Phillip snapped, leading the way below. The cabin's door slammed behind them both and he resumed his seat by the stern windows. "Indeed, I am amazed that we have managed to get thus far down Channel without sending ourselves straight to the bottom!" Something in Hunter's face made him stop short.

The other man accepted an unspoken invitation to be seated. "That was a matter I had intended mentioning before we were interrupted, sir."

"Go on. . . ."

"Master Morton has given me Chippy's report for today: we're making water."

"Making water? How much?"

"Six inches."

"Good God! But how?"

"Our seams are working."

"There's been no bad weather yet!"

"So much the better for us. I've known this old tub to pull twelve once the seas get up."

"Say again?"

Hunter studied the liver marks on the backs of his hands. "She'll go down twelve inches an hour, easily. I once pumped her all the way home from Kingston; that was while she was still the victualler *Berwick*, of course. Since when, Ordnance has loaded another hundred tons of gun metal atop her timbers. For their part, the dockyard mateys have slapped on a lick of paint to give them some additional strength. . . ."

Phillip watched him glance at the canary yellow walls above the cot. "I—I'm sorry, I don't understand."

Hunter looked back. "There's little more to understand, sir. This sieve was originally laid down for the East India trade, but while she was in the fitting-out basin, the contractor went bankrupt and his creditors sold her to the insurance company by burning her to the waterline. Meanwhile, our lords of the Admiralty sniffed a bargain. They bought what remained, had her rebuilt from the scrap of other hulked vessels and put her on the Caribbean run as *Berwick*. Then, with the prospect of a voyage into the South Seas, they freshened her up with a new name."

"Good God."

"I believe that to be true, sir, despite everything we do to provoke Him," Hunter replied. "Many a night I've lain in that cot with only a sheet of tarpaulin to keep myself dry, but let's not anticipate trouble yet. I've sent a bosun's party to caulk the most accessible seams and, if the worst comes to the worst, I shall pump her out to New Holland, then pump her home again."

"Unbelievable."

Hunter shook his head. "With respect, when one has served the king at sea for as long I have, nothing is beyond belief. Whatever her many faults, *Sirius* will never be as rotten as *Apollo*."

"*Apollo*?"

"Sixty-four guns, Captain Grayden, dismasted by a squall off Nova Scotia while escorting a convoy into Halifax during that winter of 'seventy-nine," Hunter replied. "The commodore ordered us to scuttle her, so our carpenter dropped a couple of eighteen-pound shot through the fo'c'sle hatch. Wet pasteboard would have been stronger than her timbers. She went down within twenty minutes." He stood. "With permission, sir, I'd better see how things are going below our waterline."

Phillip nodded as the other man ducked and went for'ard to the orlop's ladder. Hunter squeezed himself between kegs, bales, casks and cases of officers' furniture to reach six men, fighting to budge a crated pianoforte as sea water dribbled through the seams above it. "Right, m'lads, what's happening?"

The leading hand picked at a plug of pulpy oakum as waves piled against the hull a bare six inches away. Hunter also probed the rotting mess. He straightened. "What can't be endured must be cured. Carry on."

"Aye aye, sir."

Sirius' commander stepped back to give his men room to swing their caulking mallets, and almost collided with the marines' commandant, now crouching aft from the sick bay where he had demoted the former Corporal Stokes.

"That you, Johnny?" Ross asked, peering against the lantern light. "Where's Number One?"

"The poor devil's still working on his despatches—"

"Then he won't mind if I see him right away."

"Bob, I wouldn't—"

Ross continued up the ladder to the gundeck and went aft to the great cabin. Phillip managed an affable nod as his lieutenant governor and one of Lord Howe's Interest clomped in, letting the door bang shut on a rolling swing. "Ah, major, and to what do we owe this unexpected pleasure?"

Ross made himself comfortable on one of the folding chairs. "I've inspected the lunatic who discharged his weapon without permission."

Phillip smiled distantly. "A regrettable accident."

"Damned stupidity if you ask me," Ross snapped back. "He's made the whole regiment appear a laughingstock afore the entire world. I'll flay his hide for boot leather once he can stand upright again."

"That is, of course, your decision to make," Phillip observed, "but what exactly do you want me to do about it now?"

"Nothing."

"Then why tell me?"

Ross' lip jutted. "I've a bone to pick. Item: rum. Will my troops receive their supplementary spirit rations in Botany Bay, or will they not?"

Phillip sneezed and groped for a handkerchief to mop his nose. "Aren't they being a little impatient?"

"Impatient?"

"Premature. Hasty." Phillip folded the soggy piece of rag and tucked it up his jacket sleeve again. "Glance through these windows behind me, please. Do you not observe a dark smudge between the clouds and the horizon?" He waited until the marine officer had peered astern. "It's called England. Or, if you prefer, South Britain. Several months must pass before we are even this close to our destination. Do we really have to begin discussing the finer points of our administration just yet?"

Ross' lip jutted again. "Will they or will they not get their rum?"

Phillip's control was slipping. "No."

"This is prepost'rous! The cream o' the world's fighting men, packed off to the rump end o' nowhere to guard a pack o' English gutter trash! And then be denied their rightful dues!"

Phillip's face was hot with more than flu. "Major Ross. You have ink and paper. Despatch a complaint to London aboard *Hyaena* when she leaves us. Within a year or two we might get a directive which, if favourable to your men's request, I shall execute immediately."

Ross was shaking his head from side to side, rather like a terrier killing a rat. "They'll not like it!"

"Then so much the worse for them," Phillip replied sharply. "Even I cannot conjure extra kegs of grog from thin air!"

"Surely that's easy enough to fix?" Ross glowered. "One hint from you and the purser will stretch their jug with water, and who'll be the wiser? All my men need is the sniff and feel o' an extra measure—"

"I never heard that suggestion," Phillip interrupted. "Now, before I return to my duties, is there another matter you wish to discuss?"

"Aye. Jimmy Campbell."

Phillip mopped his nose again. "What about Captain Campbell?"

Ross was frowning with effort. "Well, you'll recall that I'm to be the judge o' the Vice Admiralty Court in New South Wales?"

"A judge *in,* not the judge *of,*" Phillip corrected. "It is, I understand, a sinecure which comes with your lieutenant governorship."

"Quite so, quite so. Well, just this morning I was thinking to myself that it would not be fitting for a judge's right-hand man to be without at least some legal status in the colony. After all, young Mr. Collins is to be judge advocate general, for some reason. And doubtless you've slated Johnny Hunter to be a justice o' the peace, along with several others o' the quality, so it would be only a pen stroke if Jimmy's name were added to your list, eh? What say?" Unfortunately, Ross had never learned when to stop. "You see, it's not only the fees and emoluments he wants, it's a sign that he's not been overlooked by those in authority when others with less service are given the posts o' honour. And if anyone should think otherwise," he went on, lip jutting again, "let him recall that Captain Campbell is a kinsman o' a certain great interest in the world o' shipping and Parliament. . . ."

Phillip opened his eyes. "Major Ross. Your motives do you credit. Both of your requests have been on behalf of others. Your men's welfare evidently comes first and, naturally, you wish to do something for your deputy. It is an admirable trait which I salute. However," he went on, "I must insist that you recall that we are not yet out of sight of Britain. That New Holland is several months into the future. And that neither of your requests need greatly concern us until—"

"Smooth words never buttered parsnips! Neither my men nor Captain Campbell will be satisfied with only—!"

"Stop interrupting me!" Phillip shouted, infuriated by the other man's assumption that his restraint hid a weakness which could be exploited by a show of bluster. "The satisfaction or otherwise of your troops is your only concern, now or in New Holland! They are, however, but one-third of the many problems which beset me every hour of every day!" His palm slammed the table and the inkwell jumped. "I have surly convicts and no provost marshal to be their taskmaster! I have missing stores! I have a flagship which, even as we sit here exchanging pleasantries, is visibly sinking beneath our feet! And *you* have the gall to come pestering me with trivialities which will concern nobody until next Christmas at the very earliest—!"

"Trivialities?!" Ross shouted back. "I'll have you to know that my men's rum rations are—!"

"Damn your men! Damn their rum!" Phillip roared. "I wish that I had so little to preoccupy me! Barely three days out from home and I have a warship that may be pumping herself to stay afloat when called upon to defend this convoy against a French squadron! I have six transports that couldn't outsail flotsam in a hurricane! I have diseased streetwalkers, failed burglars and incompetent cutthroats to convert to industry, sobriety and thrift! I repeat, the devil take you and your men if all there is to worry about is the certainty of not getting an extra pint of grog per day!"

"The Maritime Regiment o' Foot's the finest body o' men who ever drew breath!" Ross thundered. "The heroes o' Gibraltar! Every man worth ten Frogs and twenty Dagoes—!"

"Who also shoot themselves through the feet and leave all their ammunition on the beach when they go to serve abroad."

"Uh?"

"I said, your 'heroes' can neither handle their weapons in a soldierly manner, nor remember to bring along replacement bullets."

"That's not true."

"It damned well is."

"It's not true!"

"It is!"

"That's a slander o' the finest body o' men—!"

"The hell they are!"

"That's a slander o' the whole Maritime Regiment o' Foot!"

"Which is the only target they can shoot to hit!"

"That's not true!"

"Then challenge your own officers aboard the transports!" Phillip yelled, sweeping up the sheaf of reports and throwing them at Ross' chest. "No more than six rounds of ammunition per weapon now stand between us and a convict uprising! And why? Because *you* cannot oversee the proper supply of basic equipment!"

"What's that?"

"No more than six round of ball per weapon now stand between us and a convict rebellion."

Ross began pounding the table with both fists. "I'll have Campbell's hide for shoes!"

"I don't give a damn if you serve his head on a dish with a roast apple stuffed in his bloody mouth!" Phillip yelled, making the sentry outside flick his ear away from the shut door. "If *this* is the best he can manage while guarding criminals, God only knows what he'd be capable of doing if he were also their magistrate! And major—!" Ross spun round in the cabin doorway. "Your—heroes—will attend very closely to their duties between now and Rio de Janeiro! I have no intention of exposing myself or His Majesty's navy to the ridicule of a past and future enemy by having to beg musket cartridges for idle British soldiers from the Spaniards at Teneriffe. Now, beg off with you and leave me to get on with my own duties!"

23

LAND'S END faded into the dusk astern and, by next morning, the convoy was alone on the green Atlantic rollers, rising and falling, jibs nodding over flung spray. The threatened storm had come to nothing, but every day Phillip hurried aloft to consult the weather glass before taking a few turns round the quarterdeck with Hunter while they planned the day's work.

"Good morning, sir." Hunter saluted and fell into step with his commodore as they began walking for'ard to the main hatchway, then aft again to the taffrail.

"Good morning, John," Phillip replied. "I think this must call for a celebration, don't you?"

"Sir?"

"It's Sunday, one week to the day since we set sail, and still we're afloat. We're even managing to hold formation."

Hunter shaded his eyes. "Amazing."

"Isn't it? Indeed, all things considered, the omens are propitious. I shall order *Hyaena* to escort our rearguard for another two days before releasing her. That will put Brest and Lorient well abeam." He glanced at the masthead pennant. "Not even a French frigate can intercept us from that quarter while this wind holds."

Hunter frowned slightly. "Would they have any reason?"

Phillip grimaced. "Has there ever been a time in history when they haven't had a reason to fight us? For all we know they might be loading for another shot even as we stand here."

"Oh." Hunter was losing interest. "That Dutch business."

"Not entirely," Phillip corrected. "Our destination is no secret to the French embassy, of course."

"Of course."

"Yet, only a few days before our departure, I happened to notice M. de Hérault, their naval attaché, dressed very discreetly in the English style while he strolled around Southsea Common with a Victualling Office clerk, discussing us. Strange companions."

Hunter was becoming interested again. "Why on earth should a Frenchman be bothered to ask the why and wherefore of this floating menagerie?"

"More than you might think." Phillip hesitated, remembering that Lord Howe could be listening indirectly. "Let's just say there's hardly a quill driver in the Ministère de la Marine who could not calculate that, for the money we've spent on fitting out this convoy, it would have been possible to feed every felon in the land with roast beef and pudding? So, whatever we're about, it is not the transportation of seven hundred derelicts to the far ends of the earth as an act of public philanthropy. Quite the reverse. Fairy tales about overcrowded prisons, and threatened epidemics, and the reform of useless rogues by foreign travel may gull our votemongers around Whitehall, but they haven't fooled the French. Paris remains very aware of the possibilities of where we are bound and what we must be going to do with it. If that were not the case, why has Admiral de La Pérouse spent the last two seasons cruising the Pacific?"

"Blowed if I know!" Hunter shook his head. "This is the first time I've even heard of the fellow."

"But not the last, you may be sure." Phillip hesitated again. "Strictly entre nous, convicts are to our purpose as sugar is to a bitter pill, a sweetener to get others to swallow it and not ask too many questions. But the facts of the matter are somewhat different, especially now that France has gained a two-year headstart on the last New World this planet will ever provide."

Hunter was frowning. "And that is the intention of this Mister Pérouse?"

"Yes. The last anyone heard, he was retracing every voyage of exploration to the South Seas, complete with a supply of copper plaques engraved with the royal arms of France which he could nail on prominent trees overlooking vacant harbours. For all we know he is hammering one of the damned things at Botany Bay at this very moment, and we won't know for the next seven or eight months." Phillip grimaced slightly. "The golden lilies are probably flying over Fort Saint Louis, the future capital of *La Nouvelle France,* and there won't be a damned thing I can do to haul them down again, short of declaring war on my own initiative."

"Beg pardon?"

Phillip shrugged. "There won't be a thing I can do. And why? Because *L'Astrolabe* and *La Boussole* will be infinitely better ships at the end of their commission than is our tub now, at the start of hers. You and I must make do with a flagship cobbled together from wreckage. Paris, by contrast, has despatched a pair of sixty-fours straight off the yards at Toulon, copper plated and planked with Corsican oak on Siamese teak frames, and I am expected to believe that such ships have been sent around the world to collect dead butterflies and to sketch naked Indians?! Heaven protect us if ever we get within range of their open gun ports," he concluded. "You and I will be feeding the crabs within minutes if our twenty-four irons start feeding smoke to La Pérouse's one hundred twenty-eight."

"A disagreeable prospect, sir."

"Yes." Phillip began another turn around the quarterdeck, hands clasped behind his back. "However, I suggest we climb that fence when we come to it. Meanwhile, you and I have more immediate matters to consider. Mr. Surgeon White has been speaking to me about the general standard of health and hygiene aboard the transports. There is room for improvement."

"I can imagine."

"So can I," Phillip replied. "As I have stated on many occasions, those boxes of human rubbish must somehow be converted into robust farm hands, or else we shall all go hungry. I therefore propose we begin now, while this weather holds." He glanced up at Hunter as they halted at the taffrail. "Make to all: permission to release prisoners for deck work."

"Aye aye, sir." Hunter beckoned for the duty officer to bend on *Sirius'* signal while Phillip crossed to windward. The cannon banged smoke. Satisfied, Phillip was about to go below for breakfast when Ross began marching aft, black hat jammed low over his face, pigtail stiff above his scarlet collar. The marine officer halted. "Sir! I must lodge the strongest objection!"

Faces flicked round on the crowded poop deck, then just as quickly went back to spinning rope, rigging tackle, buffing brass and whitening planks before the bosun struck. Phillip nodded for Ross to step closer. "What is your problem, major?"

"That!" Ross pointed aloft at the signal hoist. "What kind o' lunacy would order the *release* o' criminals?"

"Actually, mine."

"Then I am indeed protesting to the right person! My men are in constant contact with cannibals and savages; I would no more think o' striking off their fetters than I would think to fling open a cage o' spiders and serpents!"

Phillip considered his reply. "Thank you. I shall see that your protest is logged and drawn to the attention of the authorities at the end of our commission. You may now retire, absolved from all blame if anything unlikely should occur."

"Unlikely?! I consider it a certainty that we'll live to regret this day's madness!"

"Moderate your voice. My orders were, are, and always will be that all deserving items are to be allowed on deck for a minimum of two hours daily, weather permitting. Also that—"

"They'll slit our throats!"

"Nonsense! Any one of your troops could subdue a hundred such specimens, with both eyes shut! God Almighty, isn't that what you train them to do? To kill ten Frogs and twenty Dagoes apiece?"

"Not once they're roaming free again!" Ross snapped. "Once on deck they'll be ripe for devilment! I insist that you recall that order forthwith, or else Lord Howe will—!"

Phillip's sallow face had turned waxy grey. "Major. You and I still have to work together for several years, like it or not." His hand silenced the redcoat. "My orders stand."

"They'll say we've gone soft!"

"What that class of individual says is of no importance." Phillip was very remote now. "All that matters to me is that their physical tone is greatly improved, ready to labour the moment we disembark at Botany Bay. That is the end which justifies any means I choose to adopt, now or in the future."

Ross' lip was jutting. "They'll say we've gone soft!"

Phillip watched the empty horizon. "Major Ross? Why do I get this persistent feeling that one of us is Poor Mad Tom o' Bedlam masquerading as a king's officer?" He glanced back. "Item: every shipmaster has been given strict instructions to encourage informers below decks; plots and mutinous combinations are therefore not possible. I am now offering the 'carrot' of fresh air and healthy labour on deck; in the other fist I am holding the 'stick' of further confinement below. Only the dullest donkey will fail to make the right choice, and behave accordingly."

"They'll say we're gone soft."

Phillip was saved by one of the midshipmen, hurrying from the lee braces to Hunter, who turned and doffed his hat to the commodore. "Mr. King's compliments, sir. *Alexander* still refuses to acknowledge our signal."

"At least someone knows what he's about!"

Phillip ignored Ross. "Thank you, Mr. Hunter. My compliments to Mr. King. A full charge of powder this time. If that fails to clear the wax from Captain Sinclair's ears, put a shot across his bows. Should it also carry away his jib sails, too bad. Carry on."

"Aye aye, sir."

Sirius' signal cannon recoiled to the full length of its tackle as *Alexander's* number broke aloft again.

Sinclair spat tobacco juice as a distant thunderclap rolled past, then casually focussed his glass on the flagship. "Our fine gentlemen are becoming impatient, Mr. Olsen. They really do want us to allow the niggers on deck. . . ."

"Yoh?"

Sinclair shut the glass and reached inside his jacket for a clasp knife to pare his fingernails. The knife bounced as it hit his boot: an iron shot blurred across *Alexander's* heads, kicking water as it skipped away. "The little bugger's serious! Acknowledge!"

"Yoh!" The first mate doubled away, his rope speeding others to their work as he snatched the keys from the deckhouse and roused the guard.

" 'Ullo, soldier boy. . . ." A dark voice hissed from the women's cage as the first marine clambered down the ladder. "Slip us a twist o' baccy. Garn! See what I'll do for it. . . ."

Sergeant Ramsbottom looked confused, then nervous, then stern as he raised his voice for everyone to hear him obeying orders. "You slut! Fancy talkin' that way to 'Is Majesty's uniform!"

The girl relayed his wink to her governess' shelf. Kitty Brandon gave an approving nod and finished braiding her own hair in an almost demure style, then stepped across to the bars as Olsen unlocked the men's hold to her right.

The first mate wrinkled his nose. "So! Is like pig house here? No! You smellings make the pig sick his breakfast! But I got news for you lazies, you going to work, bloody hard!" He waited for someone to object, but the only sound, apart from the thud of water breaking against *Alexander's* timbers, was a tubercular cough from the darkness aft. Olsen flicked his rope at the starboard tier of shelves. "You going topside now. You think you make trouble, you find *I* make good trouble!"

The first shift of deck workers was unbolted from their "goree" ankle irons, supplied to most Campbell slavers, and jabbed up the ladder one by one. It was Cribb's turn. He crept aloft for the first time since embarking off *Retribution* the previous winter. He almost collapsed as the morning sun attacked his eyes like flying grit. He whimpered and clung to the mainmast's fife rail. Others were less fortunate. Those who fainted were revived by the mates.

"They would appear to be out o' sorts, Mr. Olsen," Sinclair commented. "One shilling will get ye five that we'll soon have them full o' beans again." The first mate grinned obediently as his master went on, "They only need a scrub and someone to shear their wool to look as good as new." Cribb staggered out of range as Sinclair sauntered past. "Why, Mr. Olsen, I'm willing to wager a shilling that, under all their dung and nastiness, they could almost be human. Rig the hose and let's see."

Cribb was among the last to be shoved forward by the grinning marines and crushed into the scuppers where *Alexander*'s barricade joined the ship's rail. Cornered, with only the ocean behind him, and still wearing ten pounds of iron chain, he could do nothing more than the other ninety men before him, endure while the pump smashed water against his chest and face. The crew were tiring of their sport and Cribb got only a quick scrub with the heads' brush. Then he was inspected and passed fit to rejoin the rest, now huddling together for warmth amidships.

The women lags, by contrast, were about to start travelling in style. Without waiting to be invited, Kitty Brandon curtsied to an amused Sinclair before completing the introductions. "And this is Miss Molly Pickles. Pay your respects to the gentleman, Molly. Remember what I've taught you." The young laundress frowned with concentration, bobbed a curtsey, and held it until the older woman nodded her approval. "And Miss Sarah Chapman, shirt maker." Another of Kitty Brandon's charges paid her respects to the ship's master. "And last, but not least, Miss Jane Dundas, lady's maid."

Sinclair inspected each of the women in turn—the sly, the squinty, the stupid, the stolid—before inviting their governess to come across the barricade and join him on the poop deck. Then he looked at the first mate. "The rest o' yon rubbish appear to be feeling cold. Exercise them."

"Yoh!"

Alexander's crewmen were glad to hand over their buckets, rags and holystones to the new underclass. Cribb was still fighting off the effects of swamp fever. He shivered with Thorpe at the edge of the crowd. "D-do what I do, B-Ben. Stick close. Look busy. Army style."

But this was the merchant navy. Sinclair went on chatting with Kitty Brandon while they arranged for his personal service, then he began taking an interest in his male lags again, the instincts of a lifetime alert to the troublemakers, that small percentage in any cargo who stand out from the crowd. Two such items were making themselves known. Everyone else out there was still falling around like dying sheep in a butcher's yard, but this pair was starting to appear busy. The shorter, darker one was even daring to address *Alexander*'s chief petty officer. "Mr. Olsen! What's yon lump want?"

"Is wanting a mop!"

"Then we'd better give him one." Sinclair's face was impassive. "Bring him here."

Olsen obeyed, shoving the little man aft and halting him in front of *Alexander*'s master.

"Name?"

"Er, beg pardon?"

"Your bluidy name!"

Captain Gun, terror of Covent Garden, would gain him no room for manoeuvre. Nor would any hint of night raids and massacre in America. Which left only one choice, the oldest, the safest play of all, the Cheerful Dimwit. Cribb grinned vacantly at Sinclair's belt-buckle. "Um. Joe."

"Joe what?"

Cribb let a tear fall. "Not Joe Watt, Joe Cribb, Josh Cribb's little brother."

Sinclair ignored the decoy. Instead, he made a curt gesture. "Give him the mop."

Olsen dropped it on deck, arm-locked the bewildered lag and kicked both knees over the hard, unyielding stick. Cribb almost fainted with pain and would have collapsed if Olsen had let go of his wrists. Sinclair tilted the sweaty face. "Let me hear that name once more. . . ."

"J-Joe Cribb! I never done nothing to 'urt you, mister!"

"It was never my intention that ye should," Sinclair replied, letting the filthy chin drop before wiping his fingers clean. "I've been observing the way ye stay close to yon limb o' Satan." He nodded toward Thorpe, now trying to hide himself behind Crystal Prig. "Any closer and I wouldn't be surprised if ye both started to clap hand and shout hosannah. Why?"

Cribb's tears were genuine now. "If only we could!" he gasped, trying to move his weight from one knee to the other. "If only we could clap 'ands 'osannah again! Ouch!"

Sinclair was testing this man with all his experience of mankind at its most shifty. "Ye would not be one o' those Wesleyan Bible bangers by any chance?"

And Cribb glimpsed a gap in the enemy's lines: he went straight for it. "Only since I seen them silver spoons an' fell to the Tempter! Them spoons saved me!"

Kitty Brandon was standing nearby, watching the improvised performance, one professional judging another's work on the stage of life.

Alexander's master wiggled a fingernail around one ear. "And what of the other one?"

Cribb glanced at Thorpe's sickly stare, then looked back at the patched knees of Sinclair's breeches. "We're as one! Darkest sinners both, working now for the 'Eavenly reward what's promised to all as repents!"

"Uh huh." Sinclair studied the earwax. "Is that why ye have some kind o' hold over him? A ringleadership?"

"*Me,* sir?" Cribb sounded shocked by the very thought.

"Aye. So let's hear what trade ye had afore ye 'fell.' "

Fire raiser, or grave robber, or broken sergeant major would not get Cribb off the broom handle within the next few seconds, but something he'd just overheard, something about shearing heads, jogged a memory of the softest job aboard the transport to Canada. " 'Airdresser!"

Sinclair now had something he could prove or disprove in the little man's story. "Get up." Cribb swayed uncertainly with *Alexander*'s rolling gait. Sinclair nodded across at the other lags, now clustered for safety around Dipper, enjoying their former leader's latest public humiliation. "One o' ye! Step lively!" Ben Thorpe inched closer. Sinclair looked at Cribb again. "Cut *his* hair. . . ."

"Er, yes. An 'aircut for this ge'man?" Cribb darted round the cluttered attic of his mind for another memory of hairdressing in action, but the best he could find was of the rainy afternoon he'd fenced a barrel of soap to a barbershop in Whitehall.

"Lively now! We haven't all day!"

Cribb flashed a brittle smile. "I must 'ave a razor. An' scissors. Must 'ave proper tools to do a proper job."

Sinclair crooked a finger at the sailmaker to bring over his canvas shears, and waited for the next objection. He'd misjudged his man. Cribb's smile never wavered as he tugged Thorpe to the nearest coil of rope, pushed him down, then nearly knocked him over with the wrist chains as he swung the shears at Thorpe's defenceless head. He muttered an apology, looped the manacles round the back of his own neck and began again. The first lock of hair dropped away, nearly followed by a slice of Thorpe's ear as *Alexander* pitched again, and there was a smear of blood on the next strip of hair to fall.

"Enough!" Sinclair stuck both thumbs under his belt and scowled. "If that's the best ye can do, ye'd better practise by scalping the rest o' yon items." He jetted baccy juice at the other ninety-odd lags, still huddled round Dipper but no longer laughing as Sinclair's meaning hit them too.

"*All* of 'em?"

"Why not?" Sinclair replied. "No matter what a hash ye make, they can't look any worse. Lively now!"

"It'll be a regular pleasure. . . ."

Sinclair turned and crossed the barricade as William Balmain climbed from the poop deckhouse. *Alexander*'s naval surgeon straightened into the sunlight. "A good morning to you, captain."

"It is," Sinclair agreed, always ready to spend a few moments chatting with another tenant risen in the world from the duke of Athol's Perthshire fiefdom. "Ye've just missed the fun. I've set one o' yon items to shear our flock o' lost lambs. That ought to keep him under my eye and out o' mischief while he performs a necessary chore."

Balmain nodded. "If I may say so, it's not before time; their quarters are becoming quite yeasty."

"Yeasty? Young man, air is not reckoned to be properly foul until the candle goes out! Remember that while ye have the honour to serve aboard my vessel."

"True," Balmain replied, "but all the same I'd like to take the opportunity to splash some tar oil below while the fine weather holds and there's room to move around."

"It's your time and the government's money." Sinclair shrugged, watching as two marines dragged Dipper to the barber's.

Balmain took this to mean that he now had permission to visit the convict quarters and signalled for Sergeant Ramsbottom to get a couple of extra guards, then he pointed to the iron pan beside his medical bag. The marines slung their muskets and helped the surgeon to carry his equipment for'ard to the open hatch and followed him below.

Balmain lit his safety lamp and began checking each of the vacant starboard shelves. The mattresses were foul, of course, and sprouting pale tendrils where the seeds had germinated inside, but that was the way items of this class preferred to have their beds: rotting hay gave off a pleasant warmth at night. But a general fumigation would do no harm, and some tarwash would kill the white toadstools which flourished between the damp timbers.

The surgeon clicked fingers at one of the guards, ordering him to move closer with the bucket and brush. Balmain peered around for a volunteer helper from the port shelves. One gaunt shape seemed to be more alert than the rest: he'd do. "Here! Look lively now!" Levi shuffled nearer, gripping his shirt. Balmain pointed at a garden of fungi. "Paint that!"

Levi obeyed and started daubing tar wherever Balmain's finger jabbed as they worked aft, shelf by shelf. The ship's surgeon halted: there was a malingerer on one of the shelves. He swung his lantern across a face with even less colour than the toadstools behind it. He frowned. This would not read well in his official journal, where no news was good news for his future career at sea. Irritated, Balmain pulled back the verminous blanket and prodded a belly the texture of lizard skin. "Hmmm. . . ."

Levi watched closely. "What you think, *doktor?*"

The younger man stiffened at the impertinence of a convict who dared to speak without permission. But *doktor* . . . ? Even the outlandish pronunciation could never dull this word's lustre for an apprenticed surgeon, a plain mister. For William Balmain was only a warrant officer, somewhere between *Alexander*'s carpenter and sailmaker, and far below the status of a university-trained physician. So he chose to ignore the question and leave the impertinence unpunished.

Levi shrugged and went on watching closely as the surgeon groped around his toolbag for the apothecaries' kit with its numbered jars; there were also some suggested treatments pasted under the lid, where the clients couldn't see. Balmain squinted at it in the feeble light, then straightened again. "I am prescribing a 'four,' " he announced, unstoppering a jar and rolling out a pill roughly the size and colour of a pistol ball. He wrapped it in a twist of red paper and tossed it for the impudent lag to administer, if he wished. "See that he takes that before dining tonight."

Levi rasped a sceptical thumbnail in the darkness, testing the pill to see if it was the usual calomel—sublimated mercury—or just a harmless knob of clay, sugar syrup and oil of thyme. It was impossible to tell, though in either case a number four was unlikely to cure tuberculosis, Levi already knew.

The private consultation was at an end. Balmain stood and continued ordering that more shelves be drenched with tar before the inspection was complete. Then he pointed for the iron pan to be set at the foot of the hold ladder. Sixteen ounces of gunpowder, lightly damped with vinegar, were heaped in the centre and saltpetre sprinkled like frost. Balmain opened his lantern to light a short match of sulphur cord, then planted it on top like a birthday candle. The roaring belch of hot smoke forced some of the foul air through the open hatchway.

Alexander was now as healthy as she could ever be.

24

A FLOATING TOWNSHIP of eleven neighbourhoods had begun shaping itself as the convoy beat across Biscay into warmer waters. One district—HMS *Sirius*—had the class, set the tone. Others—like *Alexander*—were known to be rough and ready for anything, especially after her marine bugler had sounded "still" at night. While the rest—like the store ship *Borrowdale*—plodded along and minded their own business.

The expeditionary force to Botany Bay was like an English town in many other ways, too, with its ladder of privilege down which a bucket chain of commands was passed to haul up work and obedience from below. Phillip stood on the topmost rung, answerable only to the King and God—in that order—as the mayor and military governor combined. Below him were his bailiffs, stewards and beadles; the ships' captains, masters and petty officers. Below them, in turn, were his guardians of the peace, the marine battalion. Finally, in normal times, there would have been the crewmen at the bottom, carrying everyone else on their scarred shoulders. But no longer. There was now a fifth class of citizen, the government's legal slaves, bound to penal servitude and stripped of everything but the power to endure.

Each morning at first light, regardless of the weather, the transports' head pumps were rigged and batches of convicts shoved aloft to holystone the decks, to buff brasswork, to polish exposed nail heads with brick dust and spit. They had done them yesterday and they would do them again tomorrow; Campbell's ships had never been so trim. Meanwhile the lags' breakfast buckets had been taken for'ard to the galleys for rations of burgoo—boiled oatmeal thickened with chaff or straw—and a gobbet of pickled horse, or mule, or donkey, or dog, or anything else unwise enough to stray into a victualling contractor's slaughter yard.

The official table of rations only regulated their weight—less the traditional purser's thumb on the scales—never their quality. Men who had spent years waiting in the hulks, or Newgate, or a county gaol, were now tormenting themselves with daydreams of fried saveloys, and hot potatoes, and all the delights which a sixpence or shilling had once bought from kindly turnkeys. Thorpe could think of nothing else, though in fact he had less reason than most to complain about his food. Within hours of being appointed *Alexander*'s unpaid barber, Cribb had opened negotiations with the one-legged cook for an occasional snip of beef off the bone for himself and Ben Thorpe: real beef, lean beef, officer-grade beef. Cribb had stretched his smile and his luck to win a spoonful of the meat's tasty slush for their tiles of ration biscuit, but even this luxury scum off the boiler's water could never hide the flavour of the weavils which tunnelled through the bread bags, mining the grey dust which thickened the convicts' breakfast swill.

Of the two hundred–odd convicts aboard *Alexander*, only two others had risen above the grind of daily life. Levi had been quick to promote himself as the personal valet and handy man for the ship's surgeon; Balmain no longer needed to carry his medical bag on the daily rounds which took them to all parts of the vessel, including those off limits to everyone but the officers. Kitty Brandon was also travelling well, sweeping, tidying and rearranging *Alexander*'s great cabin every morning before taking Sinclair's bedding aloft to beat it clean on the mizzen shrouds. If she noticed the wisps of hair which the barber launched her way, she never let it show.

These pinprick attacks were a poor sort of revenge, Cribb knew, but at least they were skirmishes to keep the enemy on the defensive until he was ready to strike. Later, when the moment was right, he would show her who was master, just as surely as he had shown Dipper—now holystoning in the full sun, his blistered head as bald as an egg, one eyebrow shaven off, two tufts of hair over his ears like limp cow horns.

But, for the moment at least, Cribb was content to attack the woman with lumps of dirty hair for Sinclair's bedding and dirty looks for her back whenever she stood tiptoe at the washing line, pinafore and skirts blowing round very neat knees. Cribb hated her. He hated her bright, quick movements beyond the barricade. More than life itself he wanted to rip off that green headscarf and set free her glorious hair before strangling her with it. This daydream had become his only relief from a fever even more agonising than malaria—jealousy.

Regular as the marines' bugle calls it burned him every morning while he opened the barbershop under its canvas sunshade and watched Sinclair's woman walking free, a few yards away in the land of privilege beyond the iron spikes and sentries. Cribb kept his back turned whenever possible and concentrated on trimming heads and beards for the lags, and the crew, and the marine detachment too. By now he and Thorpe were handling a full workload—many an English village had fewer inhabitants than *Alexander*—and his skills were improving fast.

A genuine barber, serving fourteen years for dealing in unlicenced writing paper, had shown Cribb the way to handle scissors and razor in exchange for six inches of tobacco and the vague promise that, one day, he might become Thorpe's assistant lather boy. This brief training, with his own ability to use curling tongs on sergeants' grey horsehair wigs, was all that Cribb needed to scout behind enemy lines by just keeping his ears open. Now, while snipping and combing, he could gossip quietly with any other lag, the ordinary seamen, the marines, the third and second mates too. Only Olsen and Captain Sinclair demanded total silence. In every way it would have been the ideal berth if only that Brandon woman hadn't arranged for better: working at her own pace in the morning, taking her ease on the poop with a sewing basket in the afternoon; ignoring the minor annoyances which Cribb sent her way.

Cribb was in no better mood two mornings later when the convoy drifted past Madeira in a dense fog, damp dripping off every surface aloft and alow. Warning guns had been fired at every turn of the sandglass and all convicts had been ironed in their holds under close guard while the candle flames burned darker and darker with every hour the ventilator scoops were shut. It hastened the inevitable when, shortly after eight bells of the first watch, Balmain's tubercular patient gave up the struggle for breath.

Another day and night drifted past before the hatch cover was thrown off and work parties pushed aloft to resume their holystoning, and buffing, and polishing, and swabbing, and scouring. Balmain hurried down the ladder, whistling a jaunty air, and listened to Levi's report. He stopped whistling and crouched after his handy man. Olsen was also ducking below for a quick inspection. His nose wrinkled. "All you making the pig sick up breakfast bowl!" He stopped his normal greeting and looked at the blotched cadaver, stretched on the deck between Levi and Balmain.

Olsen prodded it around with his boot cap to make certain someone wasn't trying to get off work, then ordered Levi to take both heels and drag the corpse to the gate while a line was rove through a running block and the noose dropped below. Olsen hitched the puffy mauve ankles together with the line and gave a shout which swayed his latest casualty through the hatch, dangling upside down, wrists and chains swaying.

The Reverend Mr. Johnson had taken advantage of the convoy's slow headway and the improving weather to have himself rowed across from *Golden Grove* to recover one of his books, accidentally left behind when he and Mary transferred to more roomy cupboard on the other merchantman. The past two weeks at sea had sharpened his reflexes as he jumped from the longboat and climbed *Alexander*'s tumblehome, clerical black flapping behind him. Olsen was standing at the entry port and escorted the clergyman aft, through kneeling lines of holystoners. Sinclair was also waiting, behind the barricade. He squirted a web of tobacco juice to leeward. "I trust the new quarters are more to your satisfaction, Mr. Johnson?"

"Oh, yes," the young man replied with a quick smile, "much better. Thank you."

"Uh huh," Sinclair replied. "Ye ought to've kept wi' us; we've room to spare. . . ." He jabbed a thumb at the dead man, rolled in the scuppers under a piece of sailcloth now that his chains had been struck off and returned to stores. "It's fortunate ye chanced along today. O' course, the law says I can do it myself, but seeing as yon item would have been one o' your parishioners in New Holland, so to speak, I think it would be a suitable gesture if ye turned him off in style."

The chaplain swallowed. He had been ordained only a few weeks before embarking and this incident threatened to be his first funeral service as an officiating priest. "Er. Isn't it—isn't it supposed to be sewn up in a tarpaulin jacket or something?"

"D'ye think my ship's a floating tailor shop?"

Johnson groped for another valid objection. "Well, isn't there supposed to be a—a cannonball at the departed's feet?"

"Not at one shilling tenpence apiece."

"Then what about scrap iron?"

"Young man," Sinclair said, head shaking, "there is no such thing as 'scrap iron' in Canton. Every last shoe tack has its price in Chinee."

"A piece of rock then?"

"Aboard a ship wi' gravel ballast?"

"But surely we can't just throw him over the side!"

"And why not? Better men than he will go the same way afore Judgment Day, as ye should know, Mr. Johnson. Why, even ye might as ye stroll the deck in the southern latitudes, head up in the clouds, chatting wi' the angels, not paying attention to what matters back on earth when— whoosh—a braw greenie breaks over the bows. And when it's gone, so has Mr. Johnson, to talk wi' the angelic hosts in person. . . ." Sinclair grinned as the clergyman winced. "Come, come! What odds if the seagulls get him and the crabs miss dinner for once? It's all the same over the long haul."

Defeated, Johnson patted his pockets for the prayer book which he felt certain Mary had put there, found it under some copies of *Exhortations to Chastity,* and sorted the fluttering pages until he had the right one. Meanwhile, Olsen had picked four volunteers from the convict work parties to come aft and pick up the corpse.

Johnson cleared his throat. " 'We brought nothing into this world, and it is certain we can carry nothing out!' "

A group of lagged women, cranking a twine mill for Sinclair, making money from old rope, glanced over their shoulders without slowing the pace. Heartened by their interest, Johnson went on, "The Lord gave and the Lord hath taken away; blessed be the name of the Lord. 'Man that is born of a woman hath but a short time to live, and is full of misery. He cometh up, and is cut down, like a flower; he fleeth as it were a shadow, and never continueth in one stay. In the midst of life we are in death.' "

The chaplain could feel the shipmaster's impatience and skipped the next few verses. " 'Forasmuch as it hath pleased Almighty God of his great mercy to take unto himself the soul of—' Of?" Johnson realised that he had no idea whom he was burying. "Er, Captain Sinclair? The departed? What was his name?"

"How should I know?"

"Oh. Very well, 'Of our dear brother here departed, we commit his body to the deep, to be—' "

"Heave away!"

The four volunteers strained with their puny strength and unevenly tumbled another partner over the side, leaving him to bob astern as *Alexander*'s wake creamed past.

Johnson shut his prayer book. His very first burial had just been robbed of all dignity, of all purpose, and he had done nothing to stop it. Jettisoned slops would have been a more uplifting lesson for the other fallen brethren who had been listening. Johnson's cheeks burned with shame. Only one of the convict barbers, scissors respectfully silent, seemed to understand. The chaplain impulsively pulled a leaflet from his pocket and pressed it into other man's grimy palm before crossing the barricade and going below to collect his copy of Bishop Leakey's *New Hope for Sinners*.

Cribb pocketed the freshly printed pages to repair his shoe, later. The second mate was coming for his daily shave. Thorpe shook out an improvised towel and prepared to tuck it round his neck. The petty officer sprawled in the shade and snapped his fingers for service, feet outstretched against the barque's roll, eyes shut while one of the silent lags whisked lather and the other began stropping steel on an old belt.

Olsen and the carpenter were also wandering across to the welcome patch of shade; they hitched themselves against the barricade which formed one wall of the barbershop. It had become their favourite place to take a short break from duties while still keeping an eye on the lines of swabbers and spinners and stoners. Olsen spat, watching the wind fly it like gossamer to the other side of the deck. The carpenter, older and more wily, gobbed higher, lobbing his into the entry port at extreme range. "*That's* the way it's done, Erik me ol' pal!" He paused as Johnson went for'ard to the waist again, black gown flapping like a crow's wings behind him. "That was a rum go, though. . . ."

Olsen sharpened a splinter of wood and started picking his teeth. "What's rum go, Chippy?"

"*That*," the carpenter replied, watching the clergyman back out of sight into the longboat. "An' the way number one razzed 'im today. . . ."

Olsen stopped picking his teeth. "The buryings?"

"What else?"

Olsen's face relaxed again. "Ach, was nothing."

The carpenter shook his head. "It weren't right, stirrin' up trouble with a parson."

"Ach, you know what he like." Olsen shrugged. "Don't mean nothing bad. Was just bit o' fun."

Alexander's carpenter began whittling a toothpick for himself. "Somethin' else I don't like about that business, Erik. It weren't proper. . . ."

"What not proper?"

"Stirrin' up trouble with a parson," the carpenter brooded aloud. "When 'e was sayin' the words for a dead 'un. An' us just flippin' the poor bleeder over the side like a bucket o' shit when we got a proper God guesser aboard."

"Why that stiff different from others we feeding the shark fish?" Olsen contradicted. "All smelling same way."

The carpenter shook his head. "Maybe, but they're not all the same. Not *this* time. We 'ad a proper parson on board to do the job, an' number one 'as to go an' make trouble. . . ."

Olsen fell silent and watched the first gulls he'd noticed since leaving the English Channel, seven graceful birds, tacking across the southern light as *Alexander*'s bows chinned the dazzling white foam. This was no day to feel a sudden creeping of the scalp. Olsen shook himself together. "Ach, Chippy, you always farting through the teeths!"

His friend was not smiling. " 'Ave it your own way, but others 'ave laughed at things like *that,* an' it never done them no good."

Olsen's smile wobbled. "What you meaning?"

"I'm meaning Old Vanderdecken, that's what," the carpenter muttered uneasily. "Remember, 'e also got on the wrong side o' a parson what was tryin' to do the right thing. Said as what '*e* was number one on board an' no man alive would ever tell 'im what to do. Look where it fished 'im, an' the whole crew—poor bastards."

Olsen's smile died. "Old Vanderdecken" was the only way to mention the Flying Dutchman without speaking the terrible name aloud and so attracting his bad luck to *Alexander* as surely as a knife blade attracts a compass needle. There was hardly a crew afloat which did not have at least one hand who had seen, or who knew someone who'd seen, the ghostly black shape of a Dutch East Indiaman of the previous century, still battling to get home to Holland from Batavia, with never a soul manning her yards or wheel. And all because her captain, Van der Decken, had cursed God for the gale which had kept his ship from rounding the Cape of Good Hope. A *predikant* of the Reformed Church had been praying for better weather and Van der Decken had cursed him too. Since when, captain and ship had been condemned to sail the desolate seas until Judgment Day, when they would finally dock in Hoorn, draped with green weed, sails in rags, a crew of skeletons at their posts as a warning to all blasphemous sailormen and their masters.

Olsen tried to shrug. "Ach, all that happening years ago! Can't happen now, can it?"

" 'Then laughed the merman. . . .' "

Olsen felt sick. "Where you hear that?"

"Same place as you, I wouldn't wonder," the older man replied, hacking at a stick of scrap wood with his knife. "On the Norway trade. An' it's true."

"What's true, chief?" the second mate interrupted, following this yarn while he waited for the lag to finish stropping the razor.

Olsen shrugged nervously. "The Iceland merman. Is nothing."

"Uh?"

"Is old story," Olsen muttered. "I don't like it. Ask Chippy."

"Gor! What a pair of rotten ol' rumbleguts!" The young man laughed. "Ask a straight question, get a crooked answer!"

"The merman's not for laughin' at!" the carpenter snapped. "Like ol'

Vanderdecken, there's a power o' wisdom in 'is story, if only them what ought takes the trouble to listen to them what knows."

The second mate was still grinning. He crossed his arms. "I'm listenin'."

"About time too." The carpenter flung his mangled piece of wood over the side, then cleared his throat and spat for luck. "It 'appened this way. A young fisherman o' Reykjavik Town was out fishin' for cod when 'e nets a merman. Just like a proper man it was, but with brown seaweed for 'air, an' long green arms with flippers on the ends. 'Why!' says 'e, 'this'll sell for its weight in gold!' So straightway 'e claps on full sail for 'ome.

"Now, waitin' on the beach was the fisherman's wife. You should've seen 'er! Just like number one's fancy, she was. . . . Anyway," the carpenter went on, "just as 'e stepped ashore she ran forward to kiss 'im, but at the same time the fisherman kicked away 'is dog what was rubbin' against 'is leg. An' then laughed the merman. An' the young fisherman asked why he done that, an' the merman said, 'I laugh at folly!' "

Alexander's carpenter accepted a gnaw of Olsen's twist tobacco and settled down for a regular sea yarn. "Well—" chew—"the young fisherman started draggin' this big net filled with merman, but as 'e plodded up the beach 'e stumbled over a little lump in the ground, so 'e cursed it, and then laughed the merman, sayin', 'Unwise man. . . .'

"Now, this really got the fisherman, so straightway 'e banged the fishy monster into the kitchen coal box till it mended its manners! Now, that very same night, along come some pedlars—Jooz, an' gypsies, an' suchlike—to show 'im their stuff. So the fisherman let 'em put out their things on the kitchen table, right close to where the merman was, 'is dirty green face shoved against the bars like them other sons o' Satan alow us now," he added, cocking his eye toward the hatchway.

"Well, they showed some nice new sea boots, but straightway 'e chucked 'em back, sayin' as what the soles was too thin an' would soon wear out. Then the merman laughed a third time an' said, 'Many a fool thinks 'isself wise. . . .' " The carpenter shook his head. "*That* did it! The young fisherman was just like Number One after a night on the bottle, but it didn't do no good.

"An' then laughed the merman for the last time. Said as what 'e wouldn't say another word till 'e was took out to the fishin' bank where 'e was netted. There 'e would squat on the oar blade an' answer all the fisherman's questions. So, out they go at first light till the boat's over the right spot, an' the merman gets 'isself comfortable at the end o' the oar. Then the fisherman asks whose folly it is when 'e kicked the dog. 'Yours!' says the merman. 'For the dog loves you like its own life, but your missis wants you stinkin' dead so's she can marry your brother.'

"That shook the fisherman, so 'e asks what 'ad been unwise when 'e tripped over that mound o' dirt. At which the merman replies, 'You were! For under it is gold enough for a thousand lifetimes.'

"Then the fisherman asks who was the fool what thought 'isself so wise? An' the merman says, 'You again! Them sea boots you thought was so thin will outlast you by many a long month. Look over there an' you'll see the squall comin' what'll make you a drownded man! An' for the way you treated me, no other sea animal will so much as take a bite o' your flesh, but you'll float forever, a stinkin' lost corpse!' An' with that the merman laughed a last time an' slipped off the oar blade to vanish under them terrible waves. . . ."

Nobody said a word. *Alexander*'s shrouds throbbed in the wind. The second mate finally broke the silence. "That true, chief?"

"Yoh. I hear it of a man in Bergen. He was big friend of the fisherman's granddaughter. It all true."

The barber leaned forward and tilted the mate's chin to begin shaving it. How anyone could ever know what was said in a two-man boat after one drowned and the other escaped to live under the sea again was beyond Cribb. But for the moment it was enough to know that these ships' officers lacked the cunning of a four-year-old gypsy off on his first job. Interesting.

25

CRIBB WAS STILL wondering how to use this chance insight when the supper buckets were served and all hatches padlocked till next morning. The tension eased. Day belonged to the dark drudgery of deck work, but darkness brought back life and light to the unfree as they whispered in small groups, chains chinking, making trade. Like the banknote forger who now sold clay pipes squeezed from damp biscuit crumb and dried whitewash; smoked carefully, they gave a good nine or ten puffs before crumbling into dust again. And the reprieved deserter who had once supplemented his army rations by snaring rats with braided shirt thread; now he skinned them whole to make useful purses and pouches before auctioning their delicate pink flesh for the inches of tobacco, the playing cards and the coat buttons which were the pounds, shillings and pence of *Alexander*'s underground economy.

Cribb kept to himself, taking turns with Thorpe to defend their shelves. Two young lads had tried winning a place in the new family after Dipper's rise to power and had begun crowding the fallen upright at the breakfast bucket. One now had pus dribbling from his ears; the crash of Cribb's cupped hands had been the last thing he would ever hear. And the other was still learning to eat without teeth. Since when Cribb had been left alone, or nervously flattered by those who sensed that his mauling by Dipper and Kitty Brandon might not be quite the end of the matter.

Fortune's wheel was rolling them further and further from England, lifting some, dropping others, crushing the rest. Cribb's fall from power ought to have been permanent. Instead, by the standards of *Alexander*'s underclass, he was becoming a man of means: it was a rare day which didn't earn him and Thorpe a sly twist of baccy or some biscuit, tipped by crewmen and marines who knew that the barbers could butcher them with a dry razor, or make it glide sweetly through soap bubbles.

All lags spooned the same basic ration from their bowls, but only the privileged few—like the barbers—could linger at night over an extra biscuit or two, spread with cheese crumbs and Cooky's slush. But not the tobacco, that was too valuable to smoke. Instead, hardly an evening passed without some less-provident lag applying for a loan at the Tobacco Barons' Trading Bank. No agreements were signed, of course, and none were needed. Every loan was lodged inside Cribb's memory with its repayment plan, and if any cove then thought he could default on the barons, the terms were renegotiated for Thorpe to deliver, slapping and bashing until Cribb judged that the debt was properly understood.

The only other large-scale tobacco dealer could have been Levi, who collected his tips from Balmain's patients during the daily round, but he preferred to roll his own Turkish papirosi—plug tobacco grated with a rusty nail, then rolled inside paper cadged from the surgeon—and stay aloof on his shelf. He was wise. Without a knuckle man like Thorpe to service his debts, Levi would have had even more problems to cope with, and there were enough already, beginning with Dipper.

The current upright's rise had been well planned, in Levi's opinion, but Cribb's revenge had been brilliant. Dipper's ridiculous haircut had done much to undermine his authority. But Dipper was game. Head swathed in a stolen shirt, potblack eyebrows smudged in place, he had bullied, chivvied and cajoled his wavering mates to stay behind him and not to split off with Mangler, the family's enforcer. But for Crystal Prig, Slyboots and the rest to stay loyal to him, he now had to find another target, someone weak and isolated. Cribb no longer fitted this bill, which made Levi the obvious choice—redheaded, foreign, a Yid. There had been several scuffles in the aisle whenever Levi pushed past the family's corner.

He sighed, pinched out his half-smoked papirosa and eased over the side of his shelf to go visiting. Mangler saw a chance to score off Dipper. Nudging and winking, he waited till Levi had almost passed the family's table, then shouted another move in the old street game of Jew baiting: "Snipcock!"

The results were disappointing. Levi didn't seem to hear as he squeezed past Thorpe's shelf, just in time to spoil Cribb's best fantasy so far—listening to Kitty Brandon's screams as his men roped her and Sinclair to a cartload of Rebel ammunition. Eyes shut, Cribb had laid a powder train to the cart and was about to show the weeping, abject, broken woman the pistol he would fire to light the fuze, when—

"What you looking so bad for, Fozzy?"

Cribb kept both eyes shut, hoping to save the dream. "Bugger off."

"Not yet. I asking myself, what you looking so bad for? Is *this* the face of the man who was beating at Death's door, wanting to go inside?"

Cribb opened one eye, furious at losing his fantasy so near its climax. "Bugger off!"

"That's better, now you listening." Levi smiled. "Two questions, please. One: what has a cove who travels so easy as you, with extra baccy and food, got to have a face like a boot?"

The eye snapped shut. "None of your business."

Levi shrugged. "Only days ago you was still my business, but memories are short. No longer is it 'help me, Leafy!' but just 'bugger off.' I understand. . . ."

"And the second question?!"

"Good, you are still with us, for one moment I was thinking you preferred the company of Mrs. Brandon—"

Both eyes shot open. "What d'you know?"

Levi smiled blandly. "Most coves only talking in their sleep. But when Fozzy has the swamp fever, he screams his dreams! Tsk, tsk, you have a dirty mind."

"Watch it!"

"Why? Is untrue? *Ei*, the things you want with that lady even a Turk would blush. What she done to you?"

"Bugger off!"

"So you keep telling, but I ask, what she done to you that you want her so much?"

"I *don't* want 'er!" Cribb had abandoned the voluptuous tingle of sending up Kitty Brandon and the Bulldog on a fireball of exploding musket cartridges. "All I want is to get even, right? Now, for the last time, bugger off!"

"Soon. But first the second question. When are we getting to Bottommy Bay? How much time we got?"

Cribb wearily rolled over and propped his head on one elbow. "And 'ow the buggery should I know?"

"You always talking with sailors, they must be telling you when we stop again."

Cribb sighed irritably. "Why do you want to know? What's your corner?"

"Everything. Nothing. Something." Levi smiled. "No, what I want to know is how many days we got left to get ready. Will not be easy starting in New Holland."

"Hm, s'pose so," Cribb was forced to admit as he chased an itch under his arm. "Well, if it'll make you any 'appier, Chippy's mate reckons we're going to be on land soon. Teneriffe."

Levi frowned. "Is part of Bottommy Bay?"

"Search me, but whatever it is I can't get there quick enough," Cribb replied. "Now, for the 'undredth time o' asking, *please* bugger off an' let a cove get some shut-eye."

Levi crouched away into the shadows, but Cribb's fond dream of blowing up Kitty Brandon had itself blown up and was scattered beyond recall. Bored and awake, Cribb even considered leaning across to Thorpe's shelf to share a grumble, but he decided against it; the young man had only one topic of conversation, which was his baffling arrest, the puzzling trial which followed a few months later, and this confusing journey to nowhere. Cribb knew it all by heart.

Ben Thorpe's story always began at Tattingstone, the bleak Suffolk village whose squire had ordered his steward and young Ben the gravedigger's boy to walk a flock to London, where there were said to be better prices for mutton than at nearby Ipswich. "Five 'undred 'ead there was, and nigh on a 'undred mile to drove 'em, Joe."

That hundred-mile walk was almost certainly the greatest distance any Thorpe had ever moved from home since the first one embarked in North Germany at a time beyond memory, sailing west in a Saxon longboat to probe the defences of Roman Britain. *Ceorls* they became, digging tiny fields from the sandy heaths of their new-found land, giving back their dung and blood to the poor soil as Viking raiders, Norman overlords and the North Sea winters snuffed out their short lives; but ever loyal, stubborn, as enduring as the barley and rye they harvested for others. *Ceorls,* serfs, bondmen, labourers, lags, there was no practical difference between the latest Thorpe to go wandering and the first.

After his safe delivery of five-and-twenty-score sheep to Smithfield market, Thorpe's wages had been paid with a pewter five-shilling piece. He had protested to his master's steward, who cuffed him into the lanes of St. Giles to find one of the middlemen who bought duds at a discount for refacing and reissue. Ben Thorpe had still been trying to match his wits against one of these street pirates when the City Watch made one of its occasional raids, and the countryman was grabbed holding ten shillings' worth of pot-metal pennies as well as the bad crown. The trial judge had been in a mellow mood when he listened to the bewildered yokel's tale and had sentenced him to transportation for the term of his natural life; normally he would have swung at Newgate wall.

It was a dull story in Cribb's opinion, and he had frequently offered to add more colour and drama, but Thorpe obstinately stuck to the truth.

Still bored, still with nothing better to do, Cribb stifled a yawn and pretended to doze as Dipper scuttled back from the now almost empty women's cage. One of Cribb's eyes opened; the eager-to-impress leader was showing something excitingly secret to his less-than-eager followers. Something the size and colour of an English florin in the lantern light. . . .

Cribb patted another yawn and dangled both legs over the side of his shelf. Dipper had gone into a huddle with the family, Cribb noted, strolling past until he reached the gate where Tickler was guarding the opened padlock. "Nice 'aircut?" Cribb asked, pausing for a chat.

"Er, yuss. Thanks, Phoss. Real nice." Tickler winked and smoothed a hand over his head, glad now that he had stayed quiet during Dipper's push for power.

" 'Appy to oblige." Cribb smiled back. "By the way, is Tommo on the game again?"

Tickler looked uneasy. "Well, yuss. Sort of."

"Then 'e won't mind if I pop inside for a moment to see if 'e needs any 'elp."

"Look, mate, it's not—!"

Cribb sauntered past the sentry and stepped into the women's cage, his first visit since the scene with Kitty Brandon. Luckily the governess had moved into the great cabin with Sinclair and the cage was now needed only for rest and repair by the exhausted women. Two were slumped on their shelves as he crouched past them and looked down at the deck. The straw had been scraped to one side, the latrine bucket lifted from its stall and a section of planking lifted to make a trapdoor into the space below.

Cribb had stolen the saw which had made this hiding place on the Thames the previous winter, when there were still only men in the cage. The saw, and protection, had been the family's percentage in Thomas Barrett's mint; an investment in the future once it was known that *Alexander* would soon be sailing for parts so foreign that English duds would surely be taken as genuine silver.

"Going all right, Tommo . . . ?"

Barrett wriggled backward between the ballast and the deck timbers, then blinked into the weak lantern light. "Oh. 'Ullo, Phoss. What's new?"

"Not much." Cribb yawned, bracing himself as the transport continued her rolling and pitching into the night. "Bulldog was speaking to 'is mates today. They reckon we're going to be in Bottommy soon. . . ."

Barrett was glad to take a short rest after his work among the suck and surge of raw bilge. He perched on the edge of the hole with Cribb and accepted a small chew of baccy. "Ta, mate, that's what I 'eard too. Dipper reckons we're goin' to be in 'Olland soon."

"The Bulldog's words exactly," Cribb replied. "I s'pose that's why 'e told you to open the mint again . . . ?"

Barrett shrugged. "A cove's got to be ready. I mean, there's not much time left, is there?"

"So they say," Cribb agreed, starting to lose interest in the subject. "Still, take my tip, a cove can't be too careful."

Barrett stopped chewing. "What you mean, Phoss?" Cribb silently jabbed a thumb at the women, sitting above them on the shelves and both listening hard. Barrett's worries eased. "They been took care of. Dipper told 'em what'd 'appen if they squealed."

Cribb kept quiet. The last time anyone had threatened a woman in this cage, that someone had been taken care of. The new upright was either more persuasive than the old, or more simple-minded. "Well, mate, the best of luck," Cribb said after a few moments. "Talking of other things, you still making ace deucers?"

"Not 'alf!"

"Mind if I take a squint?"

"Sure!"

Barrett was always glad of a chance to show off his skill as a coiner. Cribb squeezed after him through the trap hole and crouched on a small island of gravel where a wooden box had been packed with ballast and raised above the splash line. Four holystones had been keyed together with nails and a small fire built under a cook's ladle, also stolen, to melt some musket balls and one of Sinclair's old shoe buckles.

Barrett went back to pumping a pig's bladder which served as his bellows, snorting the telltale smoke and fumes underwater, through a flue of hollow bones from the officers' beef ration. Cribb watched closely as the other man cast a fresh batch of two shilling pieces in a biscuit dough mold, then ran a thumbnail over King George's profile on a coin from an earlier pour.

"Not bad, eh?" Barrett asked with a confident wink.

"Bloody brilliant," Cribb conceded. "But even so, I'd go easy showing them around too much. Know what I mean?"

Barrett gave another cheery wink. "Mum's the word, quiet as the grave."

Cribb knocked wood at such an unlucky word, then leaned closer to the other man's ear. "Take a tip, don't let them morts see too much. One word from them to Pig's Breakfast an' *you'll* be the next one we tip over the side, with your neck twisted and your eyeballs popped."

Barrett winced. "Oh, the morts are orright, Phoss, Dipper's put the 'ard word on 'em."

"Lucky for *you* 'e did, eh?" Cribb whispered, starting to lay an imaginary powder train from this hole in the deck, aft to *Alexander's* great cabin. "*I'd* watch my step, I would. *I'd* be very careful. . . ."

Barrett's hand topped him straightening into the women's cage again. "What you tellin' me, Phoss?"

Cribb shook his head and tried shaking away the other man's hand. "Nothing. Nobody's supposed to know—"

"To know *what?*"

"Nothing."

"F'Chrissakes, Phoss!"

Cribb shook harder. "I can't! It's a secret. Bulldog would 'ave my balls if 'e thought we knew—"

"Jesus, mate! Knew what?"

Cribb sank back into the hole. "Promise not to breathe a word?"

"Cross me 'eart an' 'ope to die!"

Cribb knocked wood again. "All right, it's like this. The ship's jinxed—"

"*Jinxed?!*" Barrett's yelp carried to the far corners of the women's cage.

"Shhh!"

"B-but 'ow?"

Cribb raised his voice slightly. "It's Scragger, what we chucked over the side this afternoon—"

"Uh?"

"You must've seen all the officers go to the back of the ship before we was sent down for the night?"

"Yair!"

Cribb wiped his face and, in his imagination, cocked the pistol. "Well, the lookout 'ad just seen old Scrag swimming after us, all slimy green like a fish, long brown seaweed for 'air, a floating curse on them what chucked 'im over the side without the parson ever finishing *the proper words*—!"

One of the listening women muffled her scream with a sackcloth pinafore as Cribb straightened again. "Yet we 'ad a proper God guesser to say the proper words over Scrag, didn't we? So Bulldog went an' chucked 'im over the side like a bucket of shit." Cribb paused ominously. "That's why I'd watch my step tonight, mate. Scrag's still out there, swimming along behind us, watching for 'is chance to creep aboard again and strangle some poor cove. . . ."

The two women clutched each other for support as Cribb slipped away into the darkness.

26

"YOU BE FEELING right, Joe?" Thorpe asked as he helped rig the sunshade next morning.

"Like a thousand guineas."

Which was more than anyone else could say aboard *Alexander* as the day wore on. Cribb began humming a march in time with his scissors as Sinclair ordered a boy seaman to be seized up to the ratlines after sighting a corpse swimming astern. "It was a dolphin!" the master shouted between each crack of his lash. "A dolphin! A dolphin—!"

Sirius' signal gun had been quiet for several days. Now it began thudding again, ordering *Alexander* to shake out another reef and keep up with the convoy; even *Charlotte* was outsailing the barque.

A second flogging did nothing to lift her men's morale and it was a sullen crew which gathered for the noon muster, bare feet shuffling as they muttered and whispered. Duncan Sinclair hitched his belt and marched for'ard to address them. From now on they would belay all gossip about ghosts and unhallowed corpses or risk the certainty of becoming both under *Alexander*'s yardarm before sundown. Not a man or a boy present doubted that he meant every word, or that their master had every power to execute summary justice upon them. And yet, as *Alexander* ploughed through shoals of flying fish, her crew was becoming more rather than less surly and frightened.

"Mr. Olsen!"

"Yoh?"

"What the bluidy hell's got into them?"

The first mate looked uneasy. "Is the one we feeding to the shark fish yesterday—"

"Belay!"

"Yoh."

Sinclair finished taking a turn round the poop deck to control his anger. "A good dozen or two have pitched over the side, Mr. Olsen, and nobody gave a thought for them! Now they're acting like a lot o' bluidy old women!"

Olsen tried again. "The men saying we got God guesser this time—"

Alexander's master spun, fist bunched. He stopped. Two of the lags had also begun shouting at each other. One of the swabbers, a burly item, was pointing to an overturned bucket and waving his mop at a second convict, lanky and redheaded.

"Mr. Olsen! Secure them!"

The two lags were hauled aft on the double and halted at the master's shadow. "And what was the first lesson I taught ye aboard my ship?" Sinclair thundered. "Was it not the rule o' silence?!"

"Ja, Excellenz, but—"

"Silence!" Sinclair glared back at his first mate. "Two dozen apiece!"

"Excellenz! First hear what happen!"

Sinclair blinked at the taller lag's nerve. "Very well, Mr. Olsen, make that three dozen—after we hear what happened."

The evidence was brief. The swabber—Mangler—claimed to have been toiling away when Levi passed by and deliberately kicked over the bucket to get the other lag into trouble with the petty officers. Levi contradicted him and claimed that he had been taking a message to Balmain when, without provocation, Mangler had kicked over his own bucket and then attacked him with the mop handle.

" 'Umbly beggin' your pardons, ge'men?" Mangler interrupted, his head bobbing at the master and first mate. "Permission to talk?"

"Aye. . . ."

Mangler was taking no chances. He kept his head down and only spoke to the master's shadow. "Beggin' pardon, but this is the real way o' it. This shonky sod's been givin' us a lot o' lip down below, been causin' a lot o' bad blood. Says as what 'e's so thick with Capting Balmain that 'e—the Jew boy, that is—can do what 'e likes an' get away with it. Then, last night, 'e got too big for 'is boots an' I 'ad to tell 'im to button 'is lip."

"Oh, aye?"

Mangler bobbed his head again. "But 'e knew as what I'd been in the fight game once, so 'e starts tryin' to needle me, sayin' as what one smart snipcock can always knock the stuffin' from a proper Christian."

"Go on."

"Well, I couldn't do nothin', I just 'ad to swallow it. I was still ready to forgive an' forget this mornin', but Ikey Moe still thought 'e could get away with it, seein' 'e's so thick with Capting Balmain." Mangler looked up for the first time. "I—I'm sorry I almost lost me temper, but creepin' Moses 'as been fishin' for trouble since we left England. I—I'd like nothin' better than to knock 'im down a peg or two, it's what 'e needs. Then we can all get on with our work." And Mangler would have outpointed Dipper in their personal battle for leadership below decks.

"An interesting tale." Sinclair's face was impassive. "Ye claim to have been in the pugilistic profession?"

"Guv?"

"A pug! Bruiser! Fisticuffs!"

"Yussir! None better'n me, once. I—I done for Toby Kemp, on Epsom Downs." Mangler suddenly faced the deck again. "That's why I'm 'ere now. . . ."

"Oh, aye?"

"Yussir. It was me what croaked Toby," the ex-boxer whispered. "Murder they calls it, but I knows it was only an accident."

"Oh, aye."

"Yuss. I—I promised I'd never lay another finger on nobody so long as I lived, so 'elp me God." The family's enforcer was looking up again. "But this kike's gone too far this time!"

Sinclair glanced at Levi. "Well?"

"Lies," Levi replied quietly. "As God is my witness, what have I to get by fishing for trouble? Am I needing more?"

Sinclair hitched thumbs under his belt and prepared to deliver judgment. A sound flogging? He'd promised it, but he had already had a couple today. The devil's broomstick ride, then? Both lags pitted in a dead man's race, the first to collapse winning a week to recover in the galley coal box? Some light entertainment would get his crew's minds off floating corpses. Sinclair looked up at the full spread of canvas, filling easily, driving *Alexander* across the sun track. All hands could be spared for a short while and a rest would be a tonic for everyone.

He glanced down and got Mangler's attention by hitting the crown of his bowed head with a gob of tobacco juice. "Ye claim to've been a fighter?"

"Yussir!"

"And ye say yon Ikey has been causing trouble aboard my ship?"

"Yussir. Lots o' trouble."

"Then there's only one thing to be done about it." Sinclair began smiling. "Mr. Olsen? Pipe all hands and clear the decks. Our two gamecocks are about to give an exhibition o' the noble art o' self-defence."

"Yoh!"

The ship's hands swarmed aloft with more energy than anyone had shown all day, settling themselves along the ratlines and across the galley roof, facing inward over the waist deck while the second mate traced a rough square on deck with the sailmaker's chalk. Sergeant Ramsbottom brought his gyve spanner and released the two convicts in the centre.

Mangler grinned as he strode back to his corner, where most of the lags were waiting for him, as eager as anyone else to see the fun. Dipper was quick to snatch back the initiative. He began slapping the pug's bare shoulders as he stripped off, managing Mangler with confident directions for the others to see and hear.

Levi stood alone.

Cribb glanced at Thorpe under their sunshade. "Don't look right, some'ow, Ben."

"But what can we do?"

" 'Elp."

A crewman, perched on the rigging overhead, tried getting long odds on this uneven fight. There were some takers. Olsen began walking around with binnacle slate and chalk, making a book. The crew's tobacco and small coins started filling his hat. Nobody was betting on Levi, of course, but it was possible to make side wagers on how long the fight would run.

Most of the lags were not so well organised. Officially, none of them had any tobacco to bet, and it was unlikely that any of the free men would stake a farthing against the grubby playing cards which circulated after dark. Barrett was one of the few with ready coin. He struck a bargain with two of the younger marines and covered it with the best of last night's dud deucers, certain that soon they would be back inside his pocket, together with a fistful of legal silver.

Cribb had closed the barbershop. He nodded at Thorpe and they trod over to where Levi was knotting his shirt round the top of his drawers, copying the pug in the opposite corner. "G'day, mate."

Levi stared ahead. "Bugger off."

"Bugger off yourself," Cribb replied without heat. "Mangler's got the whole world and 'is brother; you've got nobody."

"I got Joshua. I got Judah!"

Cribb ignored him. "Sorry, you've got to 'ave seconds."

"What's seconds?"

Cribb almost said that, in his opinion, this would be all the distance such a fight could go, but thought better of it; Leafy was going to need all the heart he could get just to walk into the ring and take a bashing. "Seconds, mates, somebody to tidy you up between rounds, to give you a shout and a shove, that sort of thing. Ben and me are now your seconds."

"Bugger off! I don't need you bastards!"

"Not allowed," Cribb replied. "A fight's not proper legal without seconds."

"Always it got to be 'proper legal'! First was Newgate, now this! What next you Englishers thinking of?"

Cribb pointed to Thorpe to drag out the barbers' seat and a wooden kid of water they used for shaving, then tapped Levi's bony shoulder to make him turn around. "Sit down. They're going to do it proper, so there'll be a bit of argy-bargy to start. Now, this is what'll 'appen," Cribb went on, squatting on his heels and facing Levi. "Bulldog's going to be time-keeper—" Sinclair was winding his pocket watch and shaking it close to one ear—"what means you'll get three minutes in the ring with one off. Now—pay attention when I talk, soldier! Now, this ain't the first time Mangler's been in a mill. 'E's murder with 'is maulies. So take the tip from a cove what knows a thing or two about the fight game, get a quick 'un into 'is brisket, and then go down to stay down. Right? Bulldog will count up to ten and you'll be in the clear, no bones broke. But if you don't, if you try standing up to 'im, there's not going to be enough of you left to bury—"

"He say 'shonky,' he say 'Jew boy.' "

Cribb was not impressed. "I been called worse, tons o' times, but I'm still 'ere. Make sure you can say as much in a few minutes. Look, I *seen* Mangler go fifty-seven rounds with Gerry Sullivan for a purse of ninety georges, just after I got 'ome from Americky, and 'e plastered poor Gerry all over the wall to make sure 'e got 'em."

"He call me 'creeping Moses.' "

Cribb rolled his eyes to Heaven, but it was too late, Sinclair had got his watch going and was stepping into the ring. *Alexander*'s master peered round at the happy faces of her crew; they were changed men since the noon muster. "Belay there! These two items—" he gestured at Levi and Mangler—"have bad blood between them! I'll have no ill will aboard my ship, so may the best man win!"

He looked at Mangler's crowd of supporters, then at the man crouched in the opposite corner. "I shall call three-minute rounds wi' one minute rest! There will be no biting, kicking, gouging, spitting or butting wi' the head! Everywhere above the belt is fair, the rest is foul! Two fouls is a disqualification and a count o' ten is out! Ye hear me there?"

Both fighters nodded.

"Then clear the ring and be ready to fight when ye hear the bell!" Sinclair turned and went aft to the binnacle, where his steersman had slipped rope beckets over the wheel spokes to keep *Alexander* on course while he stood atop her cabin skylight for a better view.

Cribb had stopped trying to talk sense into Levi and was now hurrying to finish tying the other man's hair back with a piece of twine while Thorpe knotted strips of rag around his bare knuckles. Sinclair gave the ship's bell a jerk. The two fighters stood: Mangler, squat, well muscled even on a lag's diet; Levi, taller, skinny.

Cribb shut his eyes and ears against the slow handclaps and whistles. "Tell me when it's over, Ben."

The catcalls turned to a sudden roar. Cribb's eyes snapped open. Mangler had squared off like the prize fighter he was, toe to toe, fists up, and fired a mighty right at Levi's face. The human bonebag wavered as the punch hissed past, then steadied to dot a sharp 'un on the pug's nose as he glided out of range, almost skipping. Mangler got his guard well up and set off after Levi. "Stand your ground!"

"Why?" Levi panted back, both fists bunched against his chin, hopping forward like a French dancing master to biff Mangler's left ear.

The crowd was turning ugly. If Sinclair hadn't been there to see fair play they would have been pelting Levi by now. Cribb's own fists were bunching and twitching as he followed every twist and turn. The fight was into its second minute and Levi had yet to be peeled off the deck, indeed Levi had yet to collect anything more serious than a graze on the arm. Mangler wasn't hurt, of course, but that drip from one nostril wasn't making him look so flash. Another bunch of Levi's knuckles stung the pug into a flurry of punches which would have flattened a brick wall, had there been one nearby, or killed Levi—if he had still been in range.

"Ben . . . ?"

"Ar?"

"Nip off and see what odds you can get on Leafy to win." Cribb's lips barely moved, his voice pitched very low. "You'll get twenty, thirty to one, dead cert. I'll look after 'im."

"You're backin' Leafy to *win?*" Thorpe whispered back, unsure when he was supposed to laugh.

"Too right." Cribb was mentally counting the bits of chewing tobacco in his secret cache, then converting them into "fingers." Without any official weights or measures the lags had made their own. Now five fingers made one "hand" and two hands made one "leg" of navy twist, the tobacco standard which regulated the exchange rate between playing cards and buttons. Cribb added his funds invested with others, then looked back at Thorpe. "Put five legs on Leafy. And do yourself a favour as well."

"You're barmy," Thorpe said flatly.

Cribb tapped the countryman's shoulder and turned him round to face the ring again. "Ever seen a cove mill that way, all jiggy-jig like a pair of tits on 'orseback?"

"No, Oi—"

"I 'aver Dan Mendoza, 'the Jerusalem Lion.' I seen 'im go forty with Breaker Leach at Mile End. Dan beat the livin' shit from poor ol' Breaker with all that fal-lal footwork."

"Be you sure, Joe? Oi reckon—"

"Move!" Cribb gave Thorpe a hard shove as the bell struck. Both fighters dropped their guards. Mangler tried getting in a last punch, but Levi was elusive as ever. The crew and lags were yelling abuse as he sat on the barbers' keg. Cribb began sponging a wad of oakum and sea water over the other man's heaving chest and shoulders. He winked. "Nice work! I only seen one other cove mill like you; young Danny Mendoza."

Levi's eyes opened with effort. "Also Jew."

"That where you learned the trick?"

"No." Levi was gathering himself again as Sinclair raised his hand to start the second round. The bell struck. Both men went into the ring. Mangler had been rubbed over with grog—courtesy of Olsen—and his mouth sweetened with the rum. Dipper had also smeared him with slush—courtesy of the cook—to skid off Levi's annoying taps.

Cribb watched the two men start circling each other. Mangler had decided against killing Levi yet; he would hoard his power while grinding down the weaker man; play with him a bit before giving the crowd what they wanted. Levi was just as careful to keep out of range while staying inside the chalk square. The time to score easy *klops* on Mangler had passed, from now on the other man's better condition must become decisive. Both men were half-starved, but Mangler's was recent hunger, not the legacy of boiled potatoes and salt fish behind a Polish slaughterhouse.

The second round ran its course without any more than a handful of serious punches between the fighters. The crowd was restive again as Levi walked back to the keg and slumped down for a quick sponge from Thorpe while Cribb began slapping and kneading his chest. "That's the stuff! Let 'im run out of puff, then dish 'im like young Dan, eh?"

Levi forced his eyes open. "How long—you think I go—like this? Forty rounds?"

Cribb chewed his lip. "Right-o, let's shut 'is peepers. Go for the brisket, make 'im drop 'is guard, then get in with this—" Cribb was shielding his own fist from everyone else, clenching it with the thumbnail jutting like a chisel blade.

"Will blind him."

"I should 'ope so! If not, if we don't stoush 'im soon, wait till you see what 'e's got for you!" Cribb stopped as the bell struck and the third round began.

Mangler was starting to look the fresher of the two, his mouth sweetened with more rum, his skin glossy with fresh lard as he ripped off some very close left-right-lefts. Levi backed away, still bobbing, still guarding his chin, but no longer the novelty he'd been in the first round. The crowd had settled down again, content to await the inevitable. Levi was sweating harder as the deck tilted and rolled under his scuffing feet. The bell struck, not one moment too soon. Three minutes had never seemed so long, and a minute would never be shorter as he sagged onto the keg and let Cribb slosh water over his bowed head.

"Go for 'is peepers . . . !"

Sinclair opened the fourth round and tested his crew's new mood; a fleet of corpses could have been swimming astern of *Alexander* and not one of her sailors would have known or cared. The fight was becoming critical. Levi was losing wind, going flat, no longer the duellist able to keep his distance with rapier thrusts; Mangler's British beef had soaked up the best he could fire and still the man came back for more, like a company of grenadiers. The bell struck.

"Go for 'is *peepers*!"

The fifth round. Levi dragged himself upright, sweat and sea water streaming off his face. Mangler was aging, too. The grog had sweetened his mouth and made him feel ten feet tall, but on top of an empty belly it was affecting his ring craft. Levi even managed to sneak in a couple of stingers which closed his other nostril and got the claret pouring again. True, Mangler had speared Levi with a right which dumped him for the count of seven, but he was back on his feet by eight. "Stan' ground!" Mangler panted, brows knotted, trying to crowd Levi into a corner where he could begin the long overdue slaughter. "Jew pig—!"

Levi stopped moving backward. His fists began rapping just above Mangler's belt. The pug grunted and launched a swipe at the other man's head, but Levi seemed to float away, then come back again, mouth agape, breath sawing in and out, dotting Mangler's stomach muscles. The fifth round could not end too soon for the other man.

Mangler trod back to his corner and collapsed on the cook's armchair while Dipper, Slyboots and Crystal Prig crowded round with good advice. He shoved their pannikin of grog aside and tried snorting his nose clear. Dipper emptied a bucket of water over him and crouched in the puddle, staring up at Mangler's puffy face. "You listenin', shitbrain? You been tellin' us 'ow good you was when you croaked Toby Kemp, yet this fuckin' Yid's startin' to make us look stupid!" The bell tolled. "Get out there! Kill 'im!"

Dipper gave his enforcer the shove which sent him into the sixth round, but Levi was waiting, bouncing up and down, never still for a moment, using his longer reach to snake past the pug's guard. Levi's punches were starting to tell. Mangler was finding it harder to breathe. The plugs of rag up his nose were driving back the blood, not stopping it, and every time he swallowed he had to miss a breath. His bellows weren't pumping too well, now that Levi was firing everything at the same complex of muscles below the ribs.

Not that the fight was really going Levi's way. He finished the last thirty seconds on raw courage alone. His throat was ablaze with thirst, his legs were jelly as Cribb steered him back to the corner and went to work with the sponge again. *"Go for 'is peepers!"* Levi's head wobbled from side to side, rejecting the plan. "But it's our only chance!" Cribb almost sobbed. "Christ, you've already gone more'n anybody thought possible! You're an 'ero—!"

Sinclair had struck the seventh round. The crowd strained forward as the two fighters clashed. Dipper had offered Mangler two options: either destroy Levi this round, or have the family attend to him after the bugler sounded tonight. The enforcer's future was now in his own hands. Guard up, lips flaring back, Mangler was firing salvoes of punches straight through the other man's crumbling defences, crowding him into the blind corner between the galley and the coal box—

"G'vald mir, Jud-a-ah!" Levi fired his last shots straight into the other

man's belly. The pug wheezed, dropped his guard to swat them aside, and left his neck open for a splinter of time. Levi went straight over the fists like a matador, crushing a single punch into the man's windpipe. Mangler jerked upward to cover his choking throat as Levi crashed into him, banging left-right-left point-blank into the defenceless gut. Mangler's guard dropped again and something seemed to blow up between his chest and chin. A whirlpool of dark red sparks was sucking him under. The Mangler was drowning in dry air, nostrils blocked, gullet clogged with blood and spit, his windpipe collapsed. Eyeballs rolling, arms windmilling, Mangler was rocking away as a screaming Levi swarmed over him, ripping *klop* after *klop* into the same two inches of neck—

Sinclair grabbed for the bell. The pug's knees were buckling, bouncing as he hit a rising deck, then rolled over. And over. And over to his corner in the lee scuppers. The crew was going wild, yelling, hats off, pummelling each other with delight. Cribb was running across the ring, yards ahead of the other lags who were also coming to pay homage. He jumped round, shoving the crowd back to a respectful distance. "Make way! Make way for Mr. Leafy Levi! Make way there—!"

The crowd was also making way for Kitty Brandon as she ran from the barricade, her face radiant. She brushed Cribb aside and landed two hard kisses on Levi's astonished face, then grabbed both fists to kiss them as well. "And wasn't that the grandest Donnybrook of them all?!" she shouted for everyone to hear, close to tears herself as she hugged the foul, unshaven, wonderful man.

Not even the lookout's hurried "Land ho-o!" could stop the seamen, the marines, and the lags struggling to follow Kitty Brandon and touch a bit of Levi's luck for themselves. Sinclair was not sure he approved of her conduct, but he was happy enough to let his men off the leash a while longer as he peered aloft. "Where awa-ay?"

"Two points astarboard!"

Alexander's master slung his telescope on its braided marline and began clambering aloft to the foremast toproyal slings. Puffing, he wrapped his legs round the yard and steadied himself against the mast while his glass searched for Teide, Teneriffe's peak, far to the south among packs of white cloud. The first leg of his latest voyage to China was almost ended.

Sinclair climbed down again as Olsen started the swabbers to clean away the chalk marks and bloodstains. William Balmain was having less luck restarting Mangler as he pressed one ear to the fallen man's chest. He glanced up as Sinclair's shadow fell across him. "Not responding to treatment."

"Oh, aye?" Sinclair queried. "What d'ye think might've happened?" The ship's master was now asking for an official cause of death, should a Board of Trade inspector ever ask for *Alexander*'s log.

Balmain slowly got to his feet. "It is apparent that the *defunctus* is suffering from extensive contusions to the upper process of the thorax and lower thyrodic cartilage. Moreover, both the sternomastoid and sternohydroid musculatures are grossly disrupted—"

"Ye would not be telling me that he could have been, ah, skylarking aloft where he had no right to be in the first place, then slipped off?"

Balmain hesitated. "The injuries are consistent with such an accident, yes."

"Uh huh." Sinclair started looking around for the other fighter.

Levi was still recovering on the keg while Cribb and Thorpe kept the last of the crew and marine detachment at a respectful distance. They also felt Sinclair's shadow and scattered back to their duties: the afternoon's break was over. The master halted, thumbs hitched under his belt again, and stared down his nose at the three lags. "An interesting display. What's your name?"

The seated lag stood unsteadily. "Abraham Levi."

Sinclair nodded at something. "Well, Mr. Levi, ye would seem to have a natural aptitude for the noble art. Ye also cost me five shillings: I wagered yon English fairy would knock ye cold inside the first round. It seems I was wrong. Tell me, which land do ye hail from . . . ?"

"Er. Po Land."

"Oh, aye? Not Danzig by any chance?" Sinclair queried, remembering his own tormented years as an apprentice on the Baltic trade.

"No, a bit more the other way." Levi gestured, as if directing Sinclair down a country road.

"Interesting, interesting. Sawbones says ye also have a certain aptitude for matters medical. . . ."

"Only what I pick up here, pick up there, is nothing."

"Oh, aye? That's not his opinion, but I'll let it pass. Ye must be in need o' rest after this afternoon's exertions, Mr. Levi?"

"Some? A little, perhaps."

Sinclair nodded again. "As ye wish. I shall order yon Ram's Bum not to be in any hurry to restore the fetters; ye may yet have to defend yourself against other trash o' a similar stripe."

The ship's master turned away and paced aft as his crew began shortening sail, preparing *Alexander* for another night of convoy sailing before entering port.

Cribb watched him go, then turned and slowly put out his hand. "The name's Joe, to my special mates."

"And Oi'm Ben!"

Levi finished peeling off his strips of rag before returning the two grips. "Abe will do, I think."

27

PHILLIP HURRIED on deck at first light, still buttoning his white flannel waistcoat, but Hunter was already squinting as the sun rose out of Africa and gilded Teide's cone. Phillip joined him at the port rail and also shaded his eyes. *"That's* what I'd call a welcome sight, John. Now for Rio, then the Cape, then . . . ?"

Hunter smiled at the other man's impatience: he was content to enjoy every moment of this southern dawn as *Sirius'* head pumps were rigged for the crew's morning wash. "Do you know what I chanced upon in my copy of Herodotus just afore turning in last night?" Phillip shook his head. "I found that it was Teneriffe, no less, which the ancient Greeks rated as the Gardens of the Hesperides, the Isles of the Blessed. . . ."

Phillip smiled back, no longer unsettled by Hunter's many surprising turns of mind—though this was the first time he could remember shipping with a classical scholar in tarred sailcloth jacket and patched galligaskins of a cut which had been going out of fashion a generation ago—and went on focussing his glass on the mountain snows ahead.

The snows of Mount Teide would always hold a special place in the secret world of Phillip's imagination. They had watched him sail down the long years, first as a merchantman's poor boy, then as a young noncommissioned master, later as the greying commander of a man o' war, and now they were watching him again, fixed as the stars in their courses. Teide's dazzling peak had become a personal sundial marking the steady passage of Phillip's hours from morning, through noon, into the gathering shadows of night, just as it had timed countless other mariners gone before him onto distant waters.

Across the centuries, traders and whalers, privateers and slavers, viceroys and bishops had all come together at Santa Cruz de Teneriffe, victualling and taking on water before laying their separate tracks for the horizon. Some—a few—had found wealth and glory beyond the edge of the world. Many had vanished. The survivors had limped home, derelict and lonely men.

Phillip disciplined his imagination and swung the telescope downslope to find the familiar Horse's Head, Teneriffe's northwest cape, as *Sirius* continued beating closer on a light easterly, holding the other island—Gran Canaria—on the windward quarter. Distances were deceptive in this southern light: only if the wind held would the convoy be able to anchor before nightfall, otherwise Phillip would have to ride it out till tomorrow morning. The thought irritated him. He shut the spyglass, nodded to Hunter and went below for breakfast before completing his despatch bag to sign over to the Admiralty agent in Santa Cruz.

There were other reasons for his irritation. It was annoying to be in overall command of a world as complex as this expeditionary force and yet to have no specific duty as it slowly made port. His quill dipped ink and went on squeaking across regulation light blue paper. For the first time in his life at sea Phillip was a passenger, free to watch and note, to punish and praise, but only in an extreme crisis allowed to interfere personally.

The sun was westering as *Sirius* drew abeam Santa Cruz' outer guard— a dismasted three-decker, still wearing the crimson and gold colours of Spain. The British man o' war shortened sail, dipped her ensign and ran up a single yellow jack to announce that she was without fever and requested free pratique.

Hunter took the short pause to duck below again. He stripped off the baggy petticoat breeches and jacket of a working sailor, then, as quickly, buttoned into the blue and white serge of a naval officer. Satisfied that his best—his only—black silk ribbon was a credit to the king's service and neatly tied around his pigtail, he crouched to unhook his sword from its nails in the beam overhead and went aloft to rejoin Mr. Master Morton and Mr. Surgeon White at the binnacle.

A small cutter was on her way from the blockship to *Sirius*, water creaming under her stern as she came alongside. "Someone's in a damned hurry," Morton grumbled, snapping his glass shut. "Let's hope they've not quarantined the bloody place. Idle buggers."

White grimaced and gave a brisk slap to the canvas bag under his arm. "Well, at least we know how to run a clean ship."

"Hn! And what about that lot?" Morton asked, jabbing a thumb astern at the transports, still being shepherded along by the sloop *Supply*, still hoping to make port before night fell.

"Those?" White replied. "Perfect bills of health. Fit as fiddles, every one."

"Perfect, eh? That's the ticket!" Morton said. "Now, let's see if the dagoes will buy it from us." *Sirius'* master stopped speaking and began strolling forward to greet the health officer and his interpreter as they puffed aboard and doffed their hats to the quarterdeck.

The interpreter flashed a row of chipped teeth at Morton. "My dear sir. Further to your communication of the yellow one above, I have the honour to address you for the part of the distinguished mister, Don Pablo Morales y Velasco, of this province, the medicine!" Don Pablo's interpreter had learned his English by copying letters in a trading post. "The distinguished medicine begs the favour of enquiring if this vessel is without the fluxies and contages?"

Morton tilted his chin. "You may tell Mr. Velasco that is the reason I gave orders for our yellow flag to be flown, and why I now request free pratique—as is my right."

The interpreter told Dr. Morales y Velasco nothing of the sort. Instead, he began another paragraph. "Further to your communication informing us of this joyful event, I now respectfully beg leave to sight all *documentación* referenced above, forthwith."

Morton glanced at White. "The papers."

White unbuckled his bag and handed over a bound volume of health certificates and edited reports from the rest of the convoy. The interpreter took it and looked around for somewhere out of the wind, somewhere he could not be overheard by anyone else on the quarterdeck, and took a few paces aft to the deckhouse. He allowed the health officer to riffle a page, then firmly shut the volume on his master's fingers and looked at White again. "The distinguished Don Pablo begs leave to enquire if this certification pertains to the other noble vessels of your honour's *flota*?"

"Yes."

"And all are without the contages, the poxies and the flux?"

"Yes."

The teeth flashed again. "I cordially salute you upon your good fortune, but further to this happy intelligence I must beg leave to be informed of the nature of their cargoment?"

White hesitated. The distinguished Don Pablo might not be so casual if he knew that seven hundred pieces of diseased riffraff were now asking permission to anchor only half a mile from his home. It would be well within his powers to order a general quarantine of the British convoy until every man, woman and child aboard had been inspected and certified clean: an unlikely prospect. White's reports from the other surgeons showed that fully one-tenth of all prisoners aboard the transports were now suffering from intermittent fever, were grossly debilitated and, officially at least, on convalescent rations of meat and wine. A further eight convicts had died, mostly aboard *Alexander,* who had just launched her twenty-first since embarking two hundred at Blackwall. The plain truth was that every transport was little more than a floating pesthouse, but the surgeon was ready for all emergencies. He bowed to the Spanish doctor, one man of honour to another of equal rank, and smiled. "All-o cargo is-o *colonos.*"

Both Spaniards were politely surprised at his gift of tongues. The interpreter fell silent while he composed his next paragraph. "*Colonos* there are of many categories, some free, others not free. Of which pertain these of yours now?"

"Freeborn Englishmen, every one," White replied without blinking.

"Ah, freeborns?" The next paragraph had been written many times before. "Regulations governing *colonos* are very abundant and complexed. All, proceeding from outside the realms of His Hispanic Majesty Carlos III, must suffer the inspection of strict rigour."

It was now the two Englishmen's turn to exchange glances as Hunter joined them, foot tapping impatiently. "We're losing the day! What the hell's holding us up?"

"An inspection, sir," White replied.

"Then get on with it!" Hunter turned and left his two senior warrant officers to strike whatever bargain they could in the shortest time possible. Meanwhile, the interpreter was assembling a mournful smile. "Unhappily the certifications of *colonos* is of elongated labour. Alas, it is my anguished duty to inform you that soon it will be the fiesta of the Carmen Virgin, when all tasks must end for many, many days."

"This is preposterous!" White snapped, his own foot stamping now. "You surely cannot mean that we will not obtain pratique till your bloody fiesta is over!"

The next paragraph was mercifully brief: "Yes." Then, as a helpful postscript, "Unless, of course, your honoured *colonos* prepare to contribute to the municipal health taxing . . . ?"

Morton was a more experienced traveller than the younger White. He looked at the two health inspectors. "How much?"

"Five and twenty *monedas de guinea.*"

"Done."

"Addition a ten for the interpretings fee."

"Done."

"Supplement a five for the boat tax."

"God damn your eyes! Done."

The interpreter chose to ignore the Englishman's bad manners and silently passed the bound documents for Don Pablo to design an ornate signature inside its fretwork of loops and curlicues—bought for forty guineas from *Sirius'* discretionary funds it was virtually an original work of art— then returned the free pratique to Morton with a bow as he pocketed a draft on the Admiralty's account with Messrs. Callogan & Company of Santa Cruz.

There was no risk of default. If the paper was not honoured within hours, an epidemic of regulations would keep the British convoy in port while the price of victuals doubled and fresh drinking water became a luxury few could afford. A forty-guinea bribe to allow eleven ships to pass uninspected was, Morton knew, a bargain, as his voice echoed from its speaking trumpet and *Sirius* got under way again.

Aloft, the ship's aristocrats—her topmen—were stepping along the yards, all canvas but the tops'l and jib sheets clewed up. Below, seamen and marines steadied at the braces, facing aft, silent. *Sirius'* bowsprit slowly dipped and rose again across the sun track.

"For'ard there!" Morton shouted. "Ready to sound!"

"Ready aye ready to sound!"

"Heave away, then!"

"Watch there, watch!" the leadman called to his number two, heaving the seven-pound plummet so that its line would be sheer below *Sirius'* keel as she passed over.

"How does it read?" Hunter demanded, never far away.

"By the mark thirty, sir," Morton said.

Hunter waited till the line was coiled again, then scooped the plug of soft tallow from the lead's cup and rubbed it on his palm, reading the sea bottom by feel and colour. "Hmm. Shell, pea gravel, black mud. How says the pilot book, Mr. Morton?"

The master had fingered the right page, waiting to be consulted. "Shell on the nor'eastern bank, sir. 'Soft black mud and jettisoned ballast on the anchoring ground atween fifty and twenty fathoms.' "

Hunter studied all the other shipping moored ahead as his command continued picking her way into Santa Cruz harbour, steering west by south, almost parallel with a range of steep, barren foothills which ran down from Teide's peak. "Sound again, Mr. Morton. Prepare to let go at five and twenty fathoms."

"Aye aye, sir." Morton clapped the book shut and hurried aft to his post at the bearing compass while the leadman coiled his wet line and heaved once more. "By the mark, seven an' twenty-y!"

The lead plummetted again. "By the mark, five an' twenty-y!"

Hunter nodded at Morton. "Helm."

"Helm it is, sir."

The remaining canvas began slapping aback as *Sirius* ponderously turned into wind and lost headway over the anchoring ground.

"Let go."

"For'ard there!" the speaking trumpet echoed. "Let go!"

"Letting go!" Mallets swung, driving out the shackle pins, plunging both bower anchors together, cables smoking after them through the hawseholes. Water splashed inboard on the rebound. The ship's timbers rumbled and shook as she came to rest for the first time since leaving Portsmouth.

Hunter finished another sweep of the harbour, then shut his glass. "Mr. King? My compliments to Mr. Ross. Have him step aft."

"Aye aye, sir."

The senior marine officer marched onto *Sirius'* poop deck a few moments later. "Good to smell the land again, eh, Johnny?!"

Hunter nodded, distracted by other things. "I've given strict orders for our 'colonists' to be battened down for the duration of our stay. However," he went on curtly, "I would not put it past them to try stirring a pot of trouble when they also smell land."

Ross' eyes twinkled. "We know how to handle such nonsense—"

"Not while we're on foreign territory you won't," Hunter contradicted. "Your men will be conspicuous by their absence. I require shirt-sleeve order only aboard the transports during day hours: there'll be not a scrap of scarlet to be seen by anyone ashore, understand? Their firelocks' primers will be drawn till we make sail again: if you have to settle anyone's hash, use cold steel, not gunfire."

Ross puffed his cheeks and shook his head. "I don't like it, Johnny."

"Liking or not liking an order is no part of being a king's officer," Hunter said. "Pass the word." Phillip was writing in his cabin: he glanced up as Hunter ducked under the door frame, head bared. "Permission to rig for the night, sir?"

"Permission granted. Oh, and would you remind Mr. Ross to keep his redcoats out of sight, except aboard the man o' war?"

"I've already done so."

"Good. Then let us both get an early night's rest. Tomorrow we shall pay our respects on the civil authorities and make all haste with victualling. Never forget, John, speed remains the very essence of our contract. I have no doubt that the French resident will be rowing around at first light, fishing for useful scraps of intelligence about our cargo and its destination: I would."

But he wasn't. By the time Phillip had breakfasted and let Bryant tie his hair after taking out the papers which had set a paste curl over each ear, the French commercial secretary in the Canaries was only thinking about sending his Spanish valet down to the quay to ask the bumboat owners for some gossip to spice his monthly return to the Ministère de la Marine, an elegantly written report which helped pay for the endless leisure of Santa Cruz.

Even the Reverend Mr. Johnson was more alert as he said goodbye to his wife, then shut their cupboard door and asked for a boat to take him over to *Sirius*. Still beaming around at the sunny day and the fact of this, his first landfall anywhere outside England, Johnson clambered up the tumblehome like a veteran sea dog and almost collided with Phillip at the head of the poop ladder. "Good morning, good morning! What a wonderful day for it!"

The commodore slept alone, whenever he slept at all, and most of his previous night had been spent over secret despatches for the Admiralty, Rose and the Home Office. He was in no humour for riddles as he began pacing the deck. "Wonderful? For whom? Why?"

Johnson peered down at the smaller man and fell into step with him. "But today is the fourth of June."

"So?"

"The fourth of June," Johnson insisted, watching Phillip for something more than an irritated scowl. "His Majesty's birthday . . . ?"

"Oh, that." Phillip checked the fit of his white kid gloves and his plain sword. He had wanted to wear his Rio Plata prize, but had reluctantly put it back inside its wooden case: one Spanish grandee might not approve of seeing another's sword being worn as a trophy of war. He glanced up again. "Then I suppose that is something else I shall have to square with the civil authorities. Thank you for bringing it to my attention. Now, is that all?"

Johnson was happy again. "Well, I was rather wondering if I could gather all our people together, on shore, to celebrate this joyous occasion in the style authorised by the Book of Common Prayer. Don't you think that would be a good idea?"

Phillip kneaded an aching forehead. "No. I do not."

"I beg pardon?"

"Mr. Johnson, I do not think it would be a good idea if you took anyone ashore to celebrate *anything* in the style of a Protestant prayer book. So, please, don't go stretching the considerable limits of Spanish hospitality by an ill-considered enthusiasm to see your, ah, parishioners. . . ."

Phillip turned away as Hunter trod deck, also in the sober blue of a Royal Navy officer: his frayed cuffs and collar had been trimmed by Bryant, who had sponged the patches of mildew with neat vinegar and buffed his tarnished gold lace with one of Phillip's old handkerchiefs: Bryant served both masters impartially. The two men exchanged salutes and prepared to be piped over the side when Phillip, on impulse, turned and beckoned the clergyman. "Coming ashore, Mr. Johnson?"

"Who, me? Oh. Yes, please!"

The three men climbed down into *Sirius*' longboat and joined Major Ross, now in full scarlet regimentals, his silver gorget plate a polished half-moon on its chain over a starched linen cravat, his best grey wig curled and powdered under its hard black tricorne. He glowered at the civilian cleric, but inched over to make room between King, Phillip's flag lieutenant; Captain Tench, Ross' young aide; and Lieutenant Dawes, going to test the chronometer at Santa Cruz observatory. Phillip settled in the stern sheets and nodded at the coxswain. "When you're ready, Evans."

"Aye aye, sir!" The petty officer was also rigged in full review order, brass anchor buttons freshly polished on their canvas jacket, tarpaulin hat sloped forward at a jaunty angle with *Sirius* painted in bold white letters around the crown, baggy breeches flapping over red stockings and buckled shoes. The scrubbed blades swung together, making the spray fly to the creak of bare muscles, starting to outpace several other boats which were also rowing to the pier to buy water for their ships. Phillip approved. A proper show of spirit by his seamen would not be lost on the local authorities at a time when Madrid was preparing to ally herself again with Paris. In the present climate of European diplomacy even a leaky two-decker like *Sirius,* anchored in a sensitive base like Santa Cruz de Teneriffe, could tilt the balance in London's favour, Phillip was reminded as he crouched to go ashore when the boat spanked alongside the sea stairs and shipped oars.

He jumped, steadying himself for a moment by grabbing one of the leather hoses which hung from the pier's water cistern, then led his officers to the roadway on top as Spanish wharfers and stevedores eyed the latest newcomers. A four-wheel gig had been tethered by the line of hollow tree trunks which zigzagged down Teide on several miles of trestles to pipe ice water to the world's shipping at five shillings a ton. A tall man in plain grey worsted straightened from the gig's shade. "Cap'n Phillips?"

"Phillip, no 's,' " the short naval officer corrected, touching his own hat in reply. "And whom have I the honour to address?"

"Ezra Adams, master mariner and agent general for Messrs. Callogan & Sons of Liverpool," the elderly man announced with an unmistakeable Connecticut accent, slyly enjoying the shades of shock among the British officers halted behind Phillip. "We received your communication of yesterday evening," he went on in the same level tone. "All formalities have been completed to see His Excellency, so step this way, if you please, gentlemen."

"Thank you, Captain Adam," Phillip replied with a short bow, following the man's gesture and climbing up to the wheel spokes to board the gig. Adams followed the other officers, then jabbed a finger into the driver. *"Póngalo en marcha! Al presidio! Pronto!"*

After a brief thrashing, the team of four donkeys leaned into their ropes and began plodding shoreward along the pier's uneven stonework, clopping between piles of baskets, fishing nets and tar pots. Adams gripped the central handrail to stop himself being pitched backward over the side and looked at Phillip. "I trust you had a pleasant voyage, sir?"

"Yes. Thank you. Very." Phillip's teeth were snapping together like castanets at every crater on the cobbled track, biting off words and ideas with unusual abruptness. "Tell me. Captain. Adam. Are there any. Despatches?"

"Yes, sir, per HMS *Gloucester,* outward bound for Grenada this week past," the American replied with sober courtesy. "I have them under lock and key in our countinghouse, where they await your signature and convenience."

A scowl was rarely far from Ross' face these days. He glared at Adams again. "You—are not the Admiralty's agent?"

Adams inclined his head. "I also have that honour, sir."

"But you are—a damned Yankee Doodler! 'Pon my word—what's the world coming to?!"

Phillip coughed drily. "I am quite sure Captain Adam must have given satisfaction. I am equally certain he faithfully represents our interests in the Canaries. Or else he would not be here today."

"But for yon idiots in London to entrust the *despatch bag* to a Rebel!"

Phillip's smile was strained. "As I recall, Mr. Ross, that particular incident is closed. Moreover," he added through clenched teeth as the gig lurched along Santa Cruz' packed quayside, "not a few remained loyal. Is that not so, captain?"

"Not a few were," the American replied neutrally.

"But were *you* one?" Ross demanded, chin jutting, ready to march on Concord again, singlehanded.

Phillip had enough problems already without anyone's raking over the embers of recent history for more: he gestured for his deputy to sit back and be silent. "Captain Adam's past opinions are of no concern. His knowledge of current affairs most certainly is." Phillip looked back at the Admiralty agent. "Captain Adam?"

"Adams, sir, with an 's.' "

"Quite so. Tell me, I do not see any French vessels in port. Isn't that rather unusual?"

"Not for this time of the year, sir," Adams replied, guessing the Englishman's real question. "The last to victual was *Hermione*, a seventy-four outward bound with a battery of artillery for the Mauritius garrison—"

"When?"

"Twenty-one days ago."

Phillip fell silent while he calculated the rival commander's likely track and speed around the Cape of Good Hope, ahead of the British convoy. "Hm. Is there anything else I ought to know?"

"No, sir."

"Hn!"

Phillip's back remained turned to Ross. "Captain Adam, when is His Excellency the governor's levee?"

"At ten." Adams checked his pocket watch and gave the driver another sharp jab in the ribs.

"And who is he these days?" Phillip went on.

Adams shut his watch lid and tucked it inside his grey waistcoat. "The Marqués de Branciforte."

"We have not met. What's he like?"

"A gentleman," Adams answered, "much as one would expect of a Sicilian noble."

"True," Phillip agreed. "When we leave our homes to serve under another's flag, we are doubly conscious of our native country's honour and good reputation. Isn't that so, captain?"

Their awkward conversation was mercifully brought to an end as the donkey team shambled to a halt outside what might have been a prosperous inn, facing the city's *plaza mayor*: only the eagle of Spain above a low archway, splotched with lichen and guarded by a detachment of local conscripts, boasted that here was the governor's court, the garrison headquarters, Teneriffe's palace of justice, its main gaol, the post office and Madrid's empty treasury, too.

Ross was the first to dismount. Sword hilt clenched, heel irons grinding the pavement slabs, he marched over to inspect the bewildered Spanish sentries. He fingered their filthy yellow and blue tunics, then looked down at the broken straw sandals on otherwise bare legs. "What a sorry apology for fighting men," he rumbled aloud to nobody in particular. "Any one o' *my* men could kick the tripes from—"

"Major Ross! Kindly remember whose guests we now are!" Phillip checked his tongue as a platoon of similar conscripts scuffed through the gateway, parading the regimental and national colours. The two flags dipped unevenly. Adams was stunned by the compliment, usually reserved for only the most distinguished visitors to the *presidio*. Phillip gravely removed his hat, bowed over the flags and gathered up their hems to kiss each one in turn. The watching crowd broke into spontaneous claps and whistles at such a rare attention to local custom as the foreigners were escorted out of the heat by a governor's aide.

The sudden drop in temperature and noise level was welcome behind the gateway, where a large courtyard had been flanked by orange trees in wooden tubs. Cooling water was being raised by a convict treadmill down in the dungeons, then trickled over the mossy stonework.

His Excellency the captain general and governor of the Canary Islands, Don Luigi, marqués de Branciforte, remained seated under his canopy of state at the far end of the *audiencia general*. Of middle years and grown rather stout since his master—Don Carlos, king of Naples—had mounted the Spanish throne, the governor watched carefully from under his wig fringe while the Englishmen shuffled into line and took their time from Phillip as he led the bows. Branciforte bobbed chins to acknowledge their homage and waited for Captain Adams to begin the usual wearisome introductions. But this time it was the senior naval officer who paced forward and bowed again with rather more polish than most men of his country managed on such occasions.

The little man straightened up again. "By personal command of His

Britannic Majesty, Jorge III, I am instructed to most cordially greet Your Excellency," Phillip began in serviceable Spanish, though with a heavy Portuguese inflection, Branciforte noted. "Your Excellency's name and honour have long been held in the highest regard at the court of His Britannic Majesty."

Branciforte beamed. He didn't believe a single word, of course, but what matter? At least this Englishman made a refreshing change from the blue-coated lumps who normally slunk into the *audiencia* for his approval. It would simplify his work now that he could speak directly with the man named in Madrid's latest secret instructions to this strategic outpost of the empire.

The governor inclined his head a fraction. "You may convey our cordial salutations to His Britannic Majesty and assure him of our warmest regard for the traditional friendship which has flourished between our two great nations for so many years past." Branciforte's brown eyes sparkled: Phillip was clearly not believing a single word, either. Reassured, now that they understood each other so well, Branciforte went on: "The fact that His Majesty of England would have instructed none other than the illustrious Commodore Admiral Don Arturo Felipe, *gobernador y capitán general de la Nueva Holanda*, to present his felicitations, only underlines the strongest bonds of fraternal regard which unite our masters, His Hispanic Majesty Carlos III and His Britannic Majesty Jorge III, in their quest for peace, stability, and the prosperity of their two great nations."

The deliberate use of Phillip's future titles also underlined far more than empty ceremony: someone, somewhere was taking a close interest in his convoy's progress to the Pacific. "Your Excellency is too kind. . . ."

"On the contrary." Branciforte smiled back. "It is Your Excellency who honours our humble audience. Would you now favour us by presenting your staff officers?" the governor added, struggling to stand upright beneath the canopy and catching his breath again before crossing the marble floor to the reception line.

Phillip bowed. "May I have the honour of first presenting Captain John Hunter, Royal Navy? With three citations for distinguished conduct in the American colonies, Canada and India, Captain Hunter is my senior navigator and mathematician. He also studied moral law and philosophy at one of Britain's oldest universities and is highly regarded by many as a classical scholar."

Branciforte was amused by Phillip's distortion of the facts, for whatever hidden purpose, as he exchanged glances with this rather shabby old man.

"Major Robert Ross," Phillip went on, delighted with his ascendancy over the redcoat as quick-fire Spanish whizzed past the man's irritated ears like canister shot. "Seven citations: seven wounds: captured in battle by the French. A veteran of the Quebec campaign and the siege of Louisburg, also of numerous engagements in the West Indies and the American colonies. Major Ross is one of His Majesty's senior officers in years of service. He is also my marine commandant," Phillip added as an afterthought.

The Sicilian was a shrewd judge of human nature. Phillip may have been presenting Hunter as something he clearly was not, but there was no mistaking Ross' type. Here was the authentic fighting man. Branciforte had met a few others from the same mould during his own service against the Ottoman Turks in Albania.

"Lieutenant King?" Phillip went on. "A veteran of the American colonies and India. My naval secretary." Branciforte nodded. "Captain Tench? Another veteran of the American colonies where he was held prisoner before being exchanged." Branciforte nodded. "Lieutenant Dawes? One citation for gallantry at the Battle of Chesapeake. One wound. Lieutenant Dawes is highly regarded by the astronomer royal and can anticipate a distinguished career in His Majesty's service." Branciforte nodded. "And, finally, Mr. Richard Johnson? A graduate of the University of Cambridge. Mr. Johnson's intellect is respected by many of His Majesty's leading counsellors of state. . . ."

Branciforte glanced at the black-coated civilian and then beamed at everyone alike. "Be—welcome!" Then he lapsed into softly accented Spanish again. "Don Arturo. It is our pleasure to extend the hospitality of His Hispanic Majesty to you and your convoy for so long as you need the unworthy facilities of Santa Cruz. Your wish is now our command."

Phillip inclined his head. "There is one small request—"

"Yes?"

"It is His Britannic Majesty's birthday. Today, wherever loyal Britons may be gathering, we all unite to wish our noble sovereign a long, peaceful and prosperous reign—"

"You want to fire a salute?"

"Yes."

Branciforte's eyes twinkled again. "Then may we hope you are better able to use your guns than you were last night?"

Phillip's smile never wavered. "It was my intention to apologise profoundly for the discourtesy in not addressing your defences with the customary number."

"Why not?"

Phillip's smile warmed. "There were certain essential stores which had to be moved onto the gundecks—" In truth *Sirius* had begun taking two feet of water an hour and her pumps were losing the race against more rotten seams: Hunter had been on the point of ordering his bosun to demolish the piano with boarding axes and then jettison it with the other officers' furniture while his men fought to stop the flagship from sinking under them in calm weather. The recoil of nineteen cannon, even with reduced charges, would have given the Spaniards something to marvel at for years to come. "In the confined space below, recoiling batteries of ordnance would have only endangered the lives and limbs of His Majesty's loyal subjects," Phillip concluded with another bow.

Branciforte snapped fingers at a waiting secretary. "Sovereign's salute, twenty-one guns, taking their time from the English warship."

"*Sí, excelencia!*"

Branciforte's smile slipped into place again. "Don Arturo? Your presence today can only reinforce the fraternal relations which forever unite our royal masters. Perhaps you and your staff would be our guests in a simple *vino de honor* . . . ?"

The despatch bag in Messrs. Callogan's strong room would have to wait. Phillip bowed, then glanced at the fleet chaplain. "Mr. Johnson? Be so kind as to return immediately to *Sirius*. Instruct Mr. Morton to dress her overall and prepare to fire a royal salute at noon. Half a pint of grog to all hands and light duties for the rest of the day. Understand?"

"Er, yes, I think so."

"What are you to tell Mr. Morton?"

"Oh. A royal salute at noon? Extra beverage for the sailors? Light duties?"

"And dress *Sirius* overall."

"And dress *Sirius* overall."

"Good. You may now leave. But don't forget to face His Excellency till you reach the door: it is most impolite to turn the back on a grandee."

Phillip watched to see that Johnson did as he'd been told before leading his staff officers after Branciforte, through another pair of ornately carved doors and up a broad flight of stairs between trophies of ancient wars—crossed pikes, rusted bucklers, medieval broadswords.

"Don Arturo?" Branciforte asked with another warm smile. "One so rarely has the pleasure of conversing with your countrymen in a civilised tongue. Tell me, where did you learn to speak Castilian so fluently?"

Phillip shrugged. "Force of circumstances, nothing more. The merest chance."

"Ah. Not that merest chance which just happened to lay your *Nossa Senhora do Pilar* alongside our *San Agostino* off Buenos Aires?"

Phillip smiled and said nothing as Branciforte led the way under an arbour on the flat roof where flowering pomegranates were arranged in tubs as windbreaks while, overhead, vines had been trained across trelliswork to block the sun. Small earthenware pots of chirping cicadas were hidden among the leaves which threw a dappled shade over the Spaniards' simple, informal lunch.

A polished table, longer than *Sirius'* gig, had been rebuilt on the roof so that today's guests could dine at leisure while enjoying the view over Teneriffe and Gran Canaria, now only a mauve smudge between Santa Cruz and Africa. Platters of broiled mountain goat, grilled lamb cutlets, roast veal, fried swordfish, smoked squid and fresh mussels had been arranged with bowls of saffron rice, sweet corn, beans and baskets of fruit. A silver wine cooler, the size of a battleship's galley boiler, had been winched onto the roof and loaded with blocks of ice. The rest of that morning's consignment, by donkey train from Teide's summit, had been crushed and spiked with liqueurs to make sherbet.

"I'd like a guinea for every time I've called at this port," Hunter whispered, pausing alongside Phillip, "but this is the first time anyone's so much as thrown a ration biscuit at me."

Phillip nodded. "Same with me, John. I wonder what our hosts intend?"

"To see us all thoroughly pickled?" Hunter replied, watching the decanters of spirits which more footmen were setting along the table. Meanwhile, Branciforte's private orchestra—two mandolins, two fiddles, one oboe—were being ordered into a corner with the garrison buglers to await further commands. Five Spanish officers had also presented themselves and were pairing off with the British visitors while their respective chiefs sat together.

Branciforte beamed around with an expansive sweep of the hand. "Be—welcome!"

They needed no further encouragement to roll up tunic cuffs and begin. The governor sipped mineral water and smiled at his guest again. "Don Arturo? May we hope that, when you return from the Pacific, you will gratify us with the pleasure of your company once again? Speaking of which," Branciforte went on, as if the idea had just occurred to him, "when *do* you anticipate returning from New Holland . . . ?"

Phillip made an honest shrug. "Frankly, Your Excellency, I don't know. Three years? Four, perhaps? Five? Never?"

"Three or four years! We are consumed by curiosity, Don Arturo! But what exactly *is* it you hope to discover in such distant parts?"

Phillip beckoned a footman to add more *agua mineral* to his small glass of claret while he tried to find a convincing answer for the unseen watchers in Madrid. He could either tell them that he hoped to find giants with frightening new engines of war, or armies of little men no taller than his fist, or dense jungles which might hide cities of gold. On the other hand he could simply admit that neither he nor anyone else in Britain had any idea what lay behind a few hundred yards of beach, last visited half a lifetime ago. The problem was, neither reply would do anything for London's diplomatic offensive in Madrid, so Phillip chose the third alternative: he put his glass aside and smiled again. "Your Excellency. May I answer in this manner? Long ago, perhaps in the very place where we are now seated, your illustrious predecessor in the Canaries also entertained the commodore of a *flota* outward bound for distant waters. It is highly likely that he asked the same question and, when he did, that Don Cristóbal Colón replied, 'I do not know, but I can hope!' "

There was a murmur of surprised approval from the Spanish officers as they stopped making sign-talk with the other guests. Phillip's smile included them, now. "Gentlemen: where would the world be if so many sons of Spain had waited until they knew where and upon what their ships would make landfall? Can we imagine Don Francisco Pizarro, or Don Hernando de Soto, or the immortal Cortés hesitating for one moment to strike into the unknown for the greater glory of God and the Fatherland?" Phillip's voice was strengthening as he warmed to the theme and left Branciforte's original question far behind.

Hunter eased back in his seat, flanked by Adams and an aged gunnery officer on one side, Ross on the other, and watched the scene develop, eyes half-shut, while Adams continued whispering a parallel translation of Phillip's speech as it unrolled before the delighted Spaniards.

Hunter had begun to suspect some of the passions which his commodore tried to hide behind that urbane, English manner. Physically one of the shortest men at the table, Phillip was showing all the animation of a small man demanding respect in a tall man's world: Hunter, a head and shoulders taller, sympathised and guessed much else as he compared Phillip's dusky, aquiline face with that of an Andalusian infantry officer sitting opposite. It was a timely insight. *Sirius'* captain had already seen that Phillip's tolerance could be stretched so far, then, without warning, collapse. Now he understood why. Emotion, the grand gesture, a prickly sense of personal honour, all the foreigner's insecurity and longing to belong were Phillip's mainsprings. The bland self-control was not an inborn gift but only the product of constant struggle and discipline, and most likely on hair trigger. Let anyone or anything touch that trigger and Phillip would as surely detonate as he had when the transports' crewmen refused to man the yards back in Portsmouth.

Hunter sighed and began working a whalebone toothpick around his mouth: the next few years of colonial service in Britain's most isolated outpost were going to be difficult enough even if every officer in the garrison had the patience of Job, and was a cold sober patriot with never a tincture of personal ambition. But they weren't. On the one hand Botany Bay would soon have a governor who could be provoked into volcanic tempers, and on the other hand a lieutenant governor like Ross. And in the meantime there was himself, John Hunter, with the dormant commission which ordered him—not Ross—to take command of the colony if Phillip were killed or died, either of which was quite likely to happen.

Hunter sighed again: he was going to need all his talent as a peacemaker to buffer these two men and to stop their garrison splitting into factions when it might also be fighting off Indian attacks and a French blockade.

"—Therefore I say, as Don Cristóbal declared in this very place, I do not yet know but I have faith that, with God's grace and willing hands, we shall yet plant the banner of civilisation on barbarian shores!" Adams concluded, finishing the translation as Phillip sat back, wiping his brow.

The Spanish officers' applause almost drowned Ross' acid whisper into Hunter's other ear. "Does it not make you want to *spew*—?"

"It's called 'diplomacy,' Bob," Hunter replied.

"Pshaw! The man's a whited sepulchre, a dago hi'self!"

Hunter was saved from beginning his peace mission now, in Teneriffe, as Branciforte stood and lightly rested his paunch on the edge of the table. "Today it is our pleasure to welcome one whose reputation travels before him, heralding his arrival! *Caballeros!* You will join us in toasting our distinguished guest and his royal master: may eternal peace and prosperity crown their labours!" Branciforte raised his glass and saluted Phillip as the Spanish officers stood to honour the men seated on their right. The orchestra also stood and began strumming "God Save the King."

Phillip's smile was relaxed and generous as he straightened up and rested fingers on the table. "On behalf of my officers and myself, I thank you all from the bottom of my heart for the hospitality and goodwill which forever adorn the reputation of Spain and of His Hispanic Majesty, whom we also respectfully salute today." Phillip's smile embraced everyone, even Ross.

"A few moments ago I spoke of that first admiral of the ocean sea and viceroy of the Indies whose courage and vision launched Spain upon her course to glory: his example stands before my nation, too. Perhaps he also sat on this very rooftop and looked upon his ocean sea as we do today? Certainly his *flota* also lay in this harbour, awaiting the command to go forth upon the unknown. Surely then, a bright golden thread binds us together across the years, uniting our nations' achievements . . . ?"

Phillip waited for the applause to fade away, then gestured over the low parapet at the forest of masts and spars on Santa Cruz roadstead. "Too soon my ships must also depart. No less than *Santa María*, *Niña* and *Pinta*, we are bound for the unknown. What dangers await us there, nobody can say. Yet of one thing we can be sure, in those years when we shall be beyond the edge of the known world, isolated from all that is nearest and dearest to our hearts, it will be the example of Spain which will give us the courage to dare all, to endure everything, to conquer everywhere! Gentlemen," he continued, returning to English for the moment, "I ask you to join me in a toast to His Hispanic Majesty, Carlos III, His Excellency Don Luigi de Branciforte, and the gallant officers of his garrison."

Dawes, Tench and King scrambled to their feet. Hunter had to kick Ross under the table before the marine pulled himself upright, glass slopping from side to side. Adams braced one elbow, Hunter the other as Phillip led the loyal toast and, by a happy accident of timing, *Sirius'* guns began thudding restrained puffs of brown smoke in the harbour below.

28

SINCLAIR SQUIRTED tobacco juice again as the flagship thumped her last salute and the shore batteries began making reply. "Mr. Olsen? That firework display for the dagoes has just cost the Treasury twenty shillings and tenpence."

The first mate grinned obediently and finished wiping his own hands after scolding two crewmen for gossiping about ghosts, then knotted the towel round his neck and peered up at the noonday sun, now almost directly overhead as tar oozed between *Alexander*'s planks.

The king's navy might have money and leisure to decorate their ships and then declare a half-holiday for the men, but aboard the rest of Phillip's convoy, June fourth was just another page in the logbook between London and Canton, tea and dividends. There would never be any idle hands aboard the merchantmen. Since dawn, work parties had been clambering aloft to bend on lightweight tropical canvas, ready for the easy trade winds of the middle passage to South America, while others dangled free under the yards, tarpots and brushes swaying with them, daubing the hempen rigging. *Alexander*'s launch had continued ferrying empty water barrels to the pier where the second mate kept the tally and bumboats splashed past, shouting and whistling, shaking live chickens and piglets, hands of bananas and lucky charms at the weary sailors.

The scuffle of bare feet and the squeal of livestock were never more than a few inches above Cribb's face, eyes squeezed shut against the heat, too exhausted to even daydream about murdering Kate Brandon as he waited to disembark at Tenner Iff, Bottommy Bay. But first, he knew, there would be the inevitable inspection and confusion: however, the later in the day they went ashore, the less chance of a heavy search through their kits by the ship's officers, so in the end it would all even out. Besides, later meant cooler.

It had been cool when Cribb landed in Canada about ten years earlier. A springtime blizzard was howling up the St. Lawrence, blotting out Quebec's ramparts above them as the Seventh Fusileers paraded on their transports and merchant officers went on a rampage to get back some of their ship's rations from the plundering redcoats. Cribb had lost the square of new sailcloth which he'd made into a gypsy *benda*—a lightweight tent—but he had still marched ashore with three pounds of trade tobacco rammed down his musket barrel. That wouldn't work now, of course, so most of the last month's earnings had been sewn inside his fearnaught's lining and the rest twisted into the rag belt which now held up his breeches.

Ben Thorpe, panting and sweating on the next shelf, had copied the idea and made himself a belt before trading the rest of his baccy for the buttons which now outnumbered all the holes in his shirt. Levi had shrewdly kept his options open: some of the stick tobacco was being kept back for smoking, some for an almost complete pack of cards which would equip his next street-corner casino, and the remainder had been pounded flat then bandaged round his bruised arm.

Up and down the hold, almost two hundred diseased and unwashed men begged sips from shared water pannikins, and waited for that moment when the hatch would crash open and Pig's Breakfast came down to order them ashore.

Olsen's eyes stung with ammonia fumes as he clambered down the ladder. A feeble cheer met him at the bottom. He coughed, flapping a hand at the putrid darkness and rattled keys in the gate's padlock. The lantern's flame faded to a dull yellow as he stooped inside the hold and began picking faces at random. Cribb was chosen.

Seven or eight other lags were jabbed up the ladder after him. Cribb covered his eyes against the blinding sunlight this time, not snow, but Tenner Iff looked like Quebec in most other ways: high ground and a fortress, plenty of streets, plenty of ships anchored on Bottommy Bay—

Olsen bashed the last of his volunteer labourers into line, too warm for hot words; besides it was time the regular deck workers enjoyed their siesta in the galley's shade while the passengers continued stowing water for them.

The sailors had clubbed a few coppers together and bought a basket of apricots from a donkey cart on the pier: now they were free to gorge themselves on the sweet yellow fruit. Apricot pips are quite smooth and slippery: it was only a matter of time before someone learned to pinch them between finger and thumb, skimming shots across the deck at *Alexander*'s entry port. It was fun and it needed some skill, but the lags were an even more challenging target as they began shuffling across the crew's field of fire, pairs of chained men with capstan bars across their shoulders, kegs slung on rope strops between them. Cribb grunted as a flying pip clipped his cheek and spun over the side.

Sniping fire began to harass the lags as they stumbled into range from the winch, going backward and forward to the canvas chute which drained fresh water into the empty tuns below. One of the sailors yawned and spat out a bit of overripe fruit, then lobbed what remained at the nearest item. Dipper squeaked as wet pulp splashed the nape of his neck. The sailor grinned and threw a whole apricot this time, getting Dipper straight in the eye. "Owww!"

Sinclair hooted with laughter and gripped the barricade's spikes to steady himself as the rest of his crew joined in with a rolling barrage of pips, jeering as they pelted the convicts backward and forward. The other man of Cribb's pair suddenly lurched, his bare sole skidded on a splash of pulp and he was down, dragging Cribb after him, dropping a hundred-weight keg across one ankle. The bung popped and fresh water began sloshing across the deck—

Sinclair was no longer laughing; he vaulted the barricade, cob cracking left and right. Cribb escaped with a welt across the shoulders, but his other half was less nimble on only one good leg. Sinclair's hatred of ungodly be-haviour in general, sinners in particular and the English especially stoked his fury as he began kicking the screaming lag up and down the scuppers: "Thruppence a load that costs me! Thruppence! Thruppence—!" After a while the master's flogging arm tired and he sagged against the gunwale, breath roaring, wig askew. *Alexander* resumed her watering. The uncon-scious man was bundled out of sight into the hold and reinforcements sent aloft to scrape the deck clean—again—while the regular watch went back to the siesta and the apricots.

The sun had lost its heat behind Mount Teide and dusk was filling the harbour by the time the jolly boat had rowed from the pier with the last kegs of water and tied alongside, ready to begin again at dawn. Olsen straightened from his coil of rope, yawned and scratched, then jabbed his work force back to the main hatchway. Crossbars dropped, padlocks clacked, day was done.

"What you see, Joe?" Levi hissed, wriggling onto the other man's shelf.

"Whoa, 'old your 'orses." Cribb winced, easing out of his shirt and rolling over with some difficulty. "Give us a bit of a rub—there!" he added, biting his lip as Levi's fingers began kneading where the capstan bar and Sinclair's cob had raised another bruise.

"*Nu*, what you seen up there? Why we not landing today? What's happening?"

"Abe, one at a time!" Cribb grunted, face down on his rolled fear-naught jacket. "This Tenner Iff's a lot bigger'n any place *you*'ve ever seen," he went on, determined to outdo Levi's tales from Aleppo, and Smyrna, and Damascus, and other places which were nothing compared with Montreal, and Ticonderoga, and—

"*You* tell me what it's like, *I* will then tell where I seen it," Levi replied, giving an extra hard squeeze of Cribb's shoulder muscle to shut him up. "First, the town, is big or small?"

"Ouch! Big, I suppose—!"

"And the harbour? Bottommy Bay?"

"Stuffed full o' ships, what else?"

"And the houses, what are they like?"

"Oh, sort o' white and squarish—"

"Tripoli!" Levi concluded with another triumphant slap at his patient's naked back. "I gaff in Tripoli, once. Wonderful place, wonderful time, too bad it had to end. But this time? *Ei!* Perfect, I tell you—"

"And I tell you that 'urts!" Cribb snapped, wriggling under Levi's massage. "I don't know nothing about Tripoli, but I do know a cushy billet when I see one, and I tell you this Tenner Iff's got all the makings of a snug season's work."

"Why?"

"Ow! Steady on, matc!"

"Why?"

"Simple," Cribb replied between gritted teeth. "There's all them boats on the bay. Where there's boats, there's sailors, right? And where there's a sailor, there's a pocket with a george or two fighting to get out. If you and me and Ben can't feed off suchlike, then it's time we packed up, got back 'ome and called it quits."

Levi nodded, his fingers spreading and closing over Cribb's neck muscles. "What else you see?"

"Well, there's a whole lot of big 'ouses up the mountain, back of the docks, so there's flash living to be 'ad with sirs, and ge'men, and suchlike. Right? Now, I've seen a thing or two," Cribb went on, warming to his lecture. "Where there's sirs there's sporting 'ouses to protect, debts to squeeze and coves what need topping off on the sly. But that's only for starters. Them flash bastards get careless and start leaving papers around—reckoning as we don't know what's what—and pretty soon a cove's got the fangs in and we're set for life. I reckon, if we stick together, we'll be living on custard and cream before twelvemonth's out, and that's a fact."

"Uh huh. And what about the other coves what's already squeezing debts and protecting sport houses?" Levi enquired, kneading away. "They going to stand aside and say, 'After *you,* my dear sir. Here, eat my custard and cream'?"

"Not bloody likely," Cribb murmured, eyes shutting as he relaxed under Levi's probing fingers. "They'll 'ave knucklemen, of course. So I'll pick out a crew what's not doing too good. I chuck our metal behind 'em to clean up the others, then we give the first lot a biff between the ears and the street's ours. I must've worked it a 'undred times on the resurrection game. 'Tactics' is what officers call it, so we'll tactic any bugger what gets in our way."

"And what if the Tenner Iffers won't be tack-ticked?" Levi persisted amiably, digging rhythmically up and down Cribb's spine. "What if there is already another Fozzy Kripp waiting for us to come ashore?"

His patient almost smiled into the rolled fearnaught jacket which served for a pillow. "Then we're going to 'ave some fun."

"But let's say we don't have fun, for once. What you going to do then?"

" 'Ead for the 'ills and regroup," Cribb replied with a dreamy sigh. "I'll put out scouts. We'll take a short breather. Then—"

"There hills in Tenner Iff?"

"There's a whole bloody mountain!" Cribb said. "That means there's got to be forest and lakes and rivers and suchlike behind it. So if things get too warm for us in town, we can nab three nags and take to the woods. Once there, with me up front, you've got no worries. None. We'll be living like gamecocks, picking off supply waggons like ripe apples. 'Ere, talking about apples, did I ever tell you about the scrap we 'ad north of Charley's Town that summer—?"

"Later," Levi commanded. "Now, this Tenner Iff, this summer, it has a market place?"

Cribb frowned, trying to sort out the jumbled impressions he'd collected of Teneriffe around a swaying water barrel. "Oh, I suppose so. I mean, what's a town without a market?"

"Quite," Levi agreed drily. "So what the hell are we doing stealing horses? What are we, *Kossaken* making plunder with waggons? Why aren't we warm in bed, like gentlemen? Tell me that!"

"Uh?"

"Joe," Levi went on simply, "there is much of you I need, there are even things I could like one day, but sometimes I wonder what you got inside this head!" He gave the neck an extra hard pinch. "So, when we get ashore tomorrow, we don't steal no horses, nor do I want to hear no more that *shtarker* talk, right? No. First we going to sit down quietly in the market, and then what are we going to do?"

"Go 'ungry, that's what we're going to do," Thorpe grumbled, listening to the older men beginning yet another of their endless, bickering disputes. "Oi reckon we'd better follow them morts of Mrs. B.'s and wait till some ge'man's on the job, then pinch 'is coat and britches and sell 'em. That's what Oi reckon."

Smithfield, Newgate, the hulks and now a month at sea understudying Cribb had put a certain polish on the peasant who had trudged away from Tattingstone behind a flock of sheep. Levi nodded his approval. "Is a good idea, Ben, I like it. But first we got to know where is the best price for britches, and that takes time. Like you say, we go hungry unless we go to work directly, so, no britches yet. Instead, I think we begin with the rajah's pocket watch *shvindel*."

"Ur?"

Cribb's massage was at an end. Levi wiped his hands on the other man's shirt and sat back. "First, we going to need a good, honest, stupid sailorman to gaff for us. That's you, Ben."

"Right-o!" Thorpe almost hugged himself at the prospect of being included in a swindle run by these two flash men.

"Always you just come from distant parts: a little walnut juice fix that. Hendrik, my gaff in Amsterdam, always was come from Batavia or Kaap de Goede Hoop—where in God's creation they are! But to continue. Next we need a gold-dipped watch that costs a guilder but looks like one hundred.

"Now we got to the market place, you and me, where Joe is waiting. You kick my arse. I roll around and spit at you, weeping real bad: the gaff is in. Everyone is looking and having good time at our fight. And how they will cheer when you shout that no way in all the world will you ever sell such a fine watch to such as me! I scream again. You kick again.

"Now you turn to our mark—Joe will have fingered the right one—and you will tell him that as a poor sailorman come home, your cruel captain has cheated you of your wages: is a normal story. However, you still have this elegant, wonderful, extra superfine, filled with rubies and diamonds gold watch. It is the present of a great rajah whose life you save at sea in a bad storm. You treasure it like nothing else, you say, unwrapping your sailor's neckerchief just enough for him to see the watch round your neck on a string.

"You wanted your grandson to have it one day to remember him of his brave grandfather, you say, hiding it again, for the world is so full of cheats and robbers—who can say what the cruel captain will do if he knows you have such a watch? Why, the king of China offered you two hundred fifty guilders for such a watch! But no, you wanted it for your grandson. But now you must sell it to help your little girl, who is dying. At this point, let the tears fall like winter rain—"

"Oi will!"

"Good." Levi smiled. "Is now my turn again. I whisper to our mark that if only *he* buys it from you for seventy-five guilders, then meets me later, I will give him one hundred, cash! Very, very carefully—so nobody else know what we plan—I show him a leather bag that makes beautiful noises when I shake it. Joe, all this time, is keeping the crowd happy by rolling drunk and singing songs at it. Our mark is more serious stuff. He is only interested in the music that leather bag is making as it vanishes under my coat again. One hundred guilders? *Ei!* That is a clear five and twenty *prozent* for ten minutes' work.

"So, away he goes to haggle with you. You argue back and walk away, but not too far. Now the mark needs that wonderful watch more than life itself. Joe is keeping the crowd moving around us as, finally, you sell that noble watch for about eighty, and if you cannot blub hot tears at this point, let Joe teach you, he has the gift."

"But you're not there to buy it later, eh?" Thorpe asked slyly.

"Of course not! You, me, Joe, we all eating like lords someplace else."

"Oi can't wait to get started!"

Levi smiled encouragement at his latest pupil. "It will be a pleasure, but we waste time. Tomorrow we got to be ready for Bottommy Bay, so, what first you got to do with our watch . . . ?"

29

THE REVEREND MR. JOHNSON coughed and asked one of *Golden Grove*'s sailors if it would be possible to go ashore on the next victualling trip: the convoy had almost finished watering at Teneriffe and, unless he took the plunge and went ashore with his wife today, they might never have another chance to peep inside a papist place of worship. The sailor palmed Johnson's shilling like a conjurer and helped the civilian couple to clamber into the waiting jolly boat. Mary Johnson hitched up her skirts and led the way while her husband passed down the parcel of beef and biscuit which she had put together for their excursion into Santa Cruz. She stowed it between her feet, together with the wicker jug of *Golden Grove*'s English water, the only sort one can trust in foreign parts, and really quite palatable after a few runs through the Johnsons' personal dripstone to filter out the algae.

Richard followed her, dressed up for the holiday in his brown coat, brown shirt, brown linen cravat, brown breeches and brown kersey stockings: however, his shoes were a sober clerical black. He sat down with a satisfied bump and smiled at his wife as the sailors bent to their oars. "What a lovely day to be sure! I am so looking forward to showing you the sights." Johnson's hour with Phillip had made him quite an authority on Santa Cruz. "There is an intriguing church, if one may so describe a place of Romish worship, and a market place with a stake in the centre where they must have burned many witnesses to God's truth, don't you think?"

Mary smiled back at her husband while she smoothed skirts to save the nearest sailor from losing his stroke at the oars as he tried staring up her rather good legs. "Let us hope they won't do anything so disagreeable today." She frowned at the grinning sailor, then looked at her husband again. "By the way, did you see any potted flowers for sale? It would be rather pleasant to have something cheerful in our cabin, would it not?"

"Er, I really cannot say, my dear."

"Then we shall look." Mary was getting ready to stand as their boat shipped oars under the watering hose. She led the way up the steps, Johnson carrying the picnic, and leaned against the cistern wall for several moments while the earth seemed to rock around them.

"What an extraordinary sensation!"

"Isn't it?" Mary replied. "Almost as if one were on a swing at Saint Bartholomew's Fair."

Johnson was not sure if he approved of such a comparison with the English capital's annual debauch, but he decided against chiding her for the moment. Besides, he secretly treasured these madcap flashes of wit in their otherwise earnest debates on slavery, and consubstantiation of the Host, and martyrs, and—

His wife had straightened into the sunlight and was tying her straw bonnet against the stiff breeze. "Shall we walk?"

Johnson made sure his own tricorne was jammed about his ears, then tucked the parcel of food under one arm and let the wicker jug swing lightheartedly on his finger as Mary led the way ashore between drying nets, lobster pots and piles of cordage. Faces like dried apples with gold earrings returned the visitors' stares at naked toes which gripped the nets for repair. "How ingenious! Who do you think taught them to do that?"

Mary kept a straight face. "Perhaps they have a school for such things?"

"Oh. Do you really think so? Wouldn't it be a wonderful sight to see them at their lessons?" Johnson replied with a frank smile at the whole world in general, and his very own wife in particular. "It would be almost as wonderful as that moment recorded by the Apostle Matthew—remember?—'And going on from thence he saw two other brethren, James the son of Zebedee, and John his brother, in a ship with Zebedee their father, mending their nets; and he called them.'" Johnson sighed and shook his head. "And to think that we unworthy servants have now been chosen to take that same call to New Holland."

He was still collecting other word pictures for his next sermon when they stepped off the pier and stood for a moment on Santa Cruz' narrow quay side. Behind them, on the roadstead, was moored the shipping of half the world's nations. In front of them, across the roadway, were the taverns and brothels, crimping houses and shoddy stores, pawnbrokers and fortune tellers through which half the world's sailors appeared to be reeling, and swapping punches, and falling over drunk. Mary took her husband's arm and firmly led him away from all *that*, a city girl's instincts guiding her straight for the market place, where she intended buying one of the red flowering plants which seemed to grow on every balcony in this country.

"Hey! Mistah! Missis!" Mary halted as the first of three urchins tangled with her legs and clutched at Richard's parcel. Her husband was quicker than she was this time. "Be off with you! Shoo! I shall call the Watch!"

"I rather think they wish to be of some small service to us," she interrupted with a slight frown. "If we allow one to carry the picnic, the other to carry our beverage, and the third to carry the pot of flowers—when I buy them—then we shall not be troubled any further."

"But what if they run off with our things?"

Mary Johnson pretended that she hadn't heard the question. Instead, she undid the plain etui clipped to her wrist and took out a penny which she held for the urchins to inspect. "Now," she began in a slow, measured voice, "you shall each have one when we finish our shopping, but not before. Understand?" The young Spaniards flashed smiles and understood as Mary shut her purse again.

Her husband had wandered away a few paces, fascinated by the market's displays of bonito and octopus, squid and albacore arranged on stone slabs while the fishwives fanned away the flies. One large tuna had been put inside a picture frame of fresh mussels with a small shoal of sardines. Johnson was entranced. The fishwife was delighted and began wrapping up about fifty pounds of food for the milord to buy and take home. Mary's smile never wavered. "Not today, thank you." She gripped her husband's arm again and headed toward the flower market, ablaze with carnations and hyacinths, gladioli and mimosa. "One of those, please." She pointed at an earthenware pot of scarlet geraniums, signalling the third urchin to collect it while she began holding up fingers at the stall holder.

He raised five: she countered with three. The man rolled his eyes to Heaven, then held up four: Mary held up three. He shook four fingers under her nose: she motioned for the urchin to put the flowerpot back. Trumped, the stall holder graciously accepted the threepence which Mrs. Johnson had been holding all the time in her other hand. She pointed for the urchin to collect the plant again, and nodded at her husband. "There. Just what we needed."

Richard Johnson was bemused by women's thinking in general and this one's in particular. "As you say, my dear, I'm sure it will look very well in our cabin. Now, let us proceed to the church; I think I saw it near here when I was with Captain Phillips." It was now his turn to push and jostle between stalls and carts, aiming for the flat tower with its ornate hoops of wrought ironwork where a single bell hung outside in all weathers, not inside a proper steeple like English bells. Johnson was also looking around for another glimpse of the stake—identical to the ones he had often seen in Foxe's *Book of Martyrs,* with its woodcuts of exquisite rackings and roastings—and he found it on a low scaffold about ten or twelve paces from the municipal fountain. "Ah, here we are—!"

Mary and the three young porters followed in their own time as he hurried to get to the garrotting post and began searching the cobblestones for any human cinders which could be sent home in a letter to Mr. Wilberforce. But the Spaniards seemed to be unusually tidy in this respect, though their market place was hock-deep with everything else imaginable. "Do you think they, um, throw the martyr's ashes into the river, rather like Joan of Arc's?" he asked Mary.

"Perhaps they burn them elsewhere?" she replied, pausing for a moment with her husband to look across the eye-level stage where those convicted of capital crimes were strangled with a twisted cord and stick. "That would appear to be very old timber and quite untouched by flame of any kind."

"Oh." Johnson could not believe it was that simple as he began walking round the scaffold, trying to decide how to burn a martyr without, at the same time, burning the stake. Perhaps it was a sign of Divine Grace, like Moses' burning bush? Or did the cunning inquisitors first heap sand on the platform and use replaceable stakes? Or—?

"Hey, mistah! Missis! You go jiggy-jig on gee-gees! Ver' good, ver' cheap!" The eldest of the urchins tore at Johnson's coat, urging him to meet a very small man in a very large hat who was dragging a line of mules across the plaza from a narrow side street. The muleteer nodded in time with his boy, "*Sí, señor!* You go jiggy-jig up Teide!"

For once in his life Johnson was lost for words, then he recovered himself. "What?"

"You go up Teide! Ver' good gee-gee!" the leading urchin commanded, poking these latest tourists toward the mules.

Johnson's face went red. "Confound you all! My wife and I have absolutely no intention of going anywhere!" he spluttered, trying to shove the boy away.

"No, no! You go La Laguna!"

"Get away from me, you horrid boy! Shoo, be off! I'll tell your mother! My wife and I have no intention of—!"

"Your humble servant, sir, ma'am."

Johnson's face went white. That had to be Captain Sinclair, no two men could possibly have the same accent: this brief holiday was about to become a total disaster. Johnson turned, preparing for the worst as the convoy's marine commandant clicked heels and bowed, hat off to Mrs. Johnson, the other hand gripping the shoulder of a sandy haired boy, also in a patched red tunic with plain horn buttons and no badges of rank, the nearest to mufti which father and son could afford to wear ashore. "Ross, Robert, major, the Maritime Regiment o' Foot. Permit me to present my boy."

"Oh. Um. Delighted, I'm sure."

"Present yourself to the gentry," Ross prompted with gruff pride. The young lad clicked heels and bowed. "Ross, John, gentleman volunteer, the Maritime Regiment o' Foot!"

"Good, good," the father murmured, then looked at Johnson again. "I observed you to be having some altercations with yon dagoes."

"Um, yes, but only a little one," Johnson replied cautiously. "They don't seem to understand English very well."

Ross nodded soberly. "I know the breed, sir." He fixed the muleteer with an unblinking glare. "*Voo!* How much?"

The delighted man held up ten fingers: Ross held up five. The Spaniard began explaining how costly such superb mounts were to buy and maintain, then held up eight fingers. Ross' face was impassive as he tweaked three and rolled them backward into their own palm, very hard. "I said *five,* you fornicating limb o' Satan, and when I say five I mean five, not six, or seven, or eight." Ross was rather enjoying this little haggle while he continued educating his son in the ways of the world on foreign service.

The muleteer sucked fingers and watched Ross count out two silver *reales* from his purse and then add five Dutch *stuivers,* small copper trading tokens which the soldier valued at ten to the *real.* He then glanced at Johnson. "Give him a couple o' shillings with sixpence to call it quits, then we can be on our way up the hill."

Johnson took a deep breath. "Thank you very much for all your trouble on our behalf, but my wife and I do now wish to go up the hill. We intend—"

"Stuff and nonsense, sir! Of course you want to go up the hill, there's no other thing in Santa Cruz worth a damn." Ross bowed to Mrs. Johnson again. "Allow me the honour o' picking a mount suitable for a lady."

Mrs. Johnson smiled warmly. "Why, thank you, major. Am I to assume that you have ascended Mount Teide before?"

"Yes, ma'am. As often as can be."

"Then tell me, is it true when they say there is a fine prospect to be had from the summit?"

"Yes, ma'am, though reaching it across the snowfield is a task not to be undertaken lightly," Ross replied with another heel click. "These reptiles will try taking us to La Laguna: we shall go to Santa Ursula instead. The one is a fleabitten burgh with nothing to recommend it but the fact that the tavern keeper pays yon spawn o' Satan a small commission to bring in more victims for his cooking while they bring up his rations. The other is a small croft with a fine view over the harbour to Barbary in Africa."

Mary Johnson turned quickly. "Did you hear that? Would it not be pleasant—and educational—if we saw Africa while we had the opportunity?"

Her husband shrugged and watched Ross begin marching down the line of mules while he slapped and prodded without mercy, lecturing his son on the finer points of requisitioning animals from the natives. He picked the most docile one for Mrs. Johnson and waited till she had paid the three-pence to her young porters, then cupped hands for her to step up and sit on one side of the pannier harness, counterbalanced by tarred goatskins of wine. She held the flowerpot firmly in her lap and smiled down at him. "Thank you, major." Young John Ross was swinging legs over the next mule up the line, then his father took the lead animal. The Reverend Mr. Johnson finished sorting the English shillings in his pocket, found that he had no small change and, flustered, gave three instead of the two and six-pence. The muleteer gave him a hand onto the mule behind his wife, then gave the mule a hearty kick in the tail to get it moving.

The line of animals plodded out of the *plaza* and started uphill between overhanging balconies and lines of washing which strung from house to house: Johnson had to duck his head several times to avoid a scandal with this or that item of female underwear, draped provocatively low in the narrow lanes. Nor was it easy to stay on a mule, despite the Biblical quotations which this adventure was bringing to mind. Fortunately the houses were thinning out as the muletrain stumbled upward between clumps of wild aloe and sisal cactus on the grey, cindery hillside.

Ross smiled up at the distant skyline, humming a brisk tune, proud to be leading this patrol between boulders tufted with aromatic sage and wild thyme. He reined his mount and fell back to pace his son's. "Have a care in this sort o' country," he warned, resuming the lad's military education. "I well recall the day we marched from Boston Town to nip that rebellion in the bud. Not halfway to Concord Green and they were getting our range from behind cover such as we pass through now, but had we stopped to flush 'em out, why, we'd still be there. So we had to take our losses like men."

"Yes, sir."

"Remember: the profession o' arms was never meant to be easy. It calls for a special kind o' man, plain-spoken and loyal, since fancy words and fal-lals count for less and less the nearer you get to the front. But it's a life of compensations, as I well recall——"

Ross was distracted from continuing his lecture as another line of mules staggered downhill, piled high with faggots of brushwood for the bakers' ovens in Santa Cruz, rather like a line of porcupines on the march—he thought—pulling over to let them pass while looking astern to see how the rest of his patrol was coping. The parson's wife was built from the right timber, head up and alert as she enjoyed the sparkling Atlantic, the distant smudge of Gran Canaria and the leathery haze of Africa. Ross returned her smile. "Now ma'am, is that not a prospect worth the ascent?"

"Indeed it is!"

He chuckled. "Then wait till we reach Santa Ursula. I promise you one such as you'll remember till the day you die." Her husband was starting to look as if that might not be delayed much longer in his case, slumped in the saddle, listless and uncaring. Ross frowned. "Mr. Johnson, sir! Front and centre!"

"Uh?"

"Up here! Lively now, before we move on!"

Johnson stirred his animal and plodded nearer this eccentric soldier. "Yes?"

Ross' frown had not eased. "Do you know the name o' yonder tree? Up five hundred, left twenty yards?"

Johnson sighed with irritation but obediently squinted into the mountain sunlight until he'd found the single tree, spikey and gnarled. "What of it?"

"That's the dragon tree, sir, the source o' the dragons' blood styptic which surgeons use to staunch our wounds."

"Oh."

" 'And there was war in Heaven: Michael and his angels fought against the dragon; and the dragon fought and his angels. And prevailed not; neither was their place found any more in Heaven. And the great dragon was cast out, that old serpent, called the Devil, and Satan, which deceiveth the whole world: he was cast out into the earth, and his angels were cast out wi' him.' "

Johnson was dumbfounded. "Goodness gracious!"

"That must be quite a 'Revelation,' eh?" Ross drawled.

"Indeed it is! But, tell me, wherever did you find the time to learn?" Johnson asked, starting to come back to life.

"The Good Book was all we had at *my* academy, sir," Ross explained with a steady frown. "Happily it is the only one a man needs to master the rules o' grammar, syntax, figurative imagery and prepositional analysis."

"Er, yes, of course!"

Ross felt more secure now that he had shown off his learning, and booted his mule into a shambling trot as the firewood convoy passed. "There are many who think that the more books a man has gathering dust inside his chamber, the more brains he has inside his head," Ross continued, curtly beckoning for Johnson to keep up. "The Reverend Archibald McMurdo, M.A. o' Saint Andrews University—you've met him?—was of a contrary opinion. A mortal lifetime studying John Calvin's lessons through the *Book o' Discipline* and Holy Scripture would barely suffice to comprehend the merest outline of the Lord Jehovah's mighty purpose for us, was his opinion—"

"How very true!"

"To which end my father, the Ross o' Rothesay, summoned the Reverend Archibald from Edinboro' to lodge at our country residence as his sons' dominie, but *not* to clutter our minds with Greek and suchlike gew-gaws, o' course."

It was all lies, all the more sad because it was all so unnecessary: the plain truth would have reflected greater credit on Ross. The middle son of Auld Bobby, servant cattleman on Lord Bute's Argyle estates, Young Bobby might also have drudged out his short life in the fields to rent a bare croft of two dirt-floor rooms, one hearth, one door, one-quarter of an acre of turnips, kale and oats to feed his family, burying babies almost as soon as they got themselves born—but he didn't.

Something about the lad's face caught the attention of the Reverend McMurdo at the manse, where he drilled the third earl's illegitimate sons in Greek and Latin, theology and mathematick; McMurdo was also do-minie to the small day school, where his leather strap flogged accurate spelling, fair-hand writing and simple reckoning into young memories. Only the most promising of the estate's boys won a place on his school bench; only the best of these dared hope to earn a scholarship to one of Scotland's four outstanding universities; and of that ambitious few, only those summa cum laude graduated to begin another generation of grim, tough-minded Calvinist schoolmasters.

Robert Ross had applied himself to self-improvement with a stubborn rage at poverty, forcing himself to memorise enough grammar and arith-metic to earn a place as a sub-factor in the earl's estate office, copying let-ters and keeping the rent rolls. He was the first of his line ever to rise above crofting, and so he might have lived out his days in peace if only M'Lord Bute, down south in London on the king's business, hadn't won a wad of blank army commissions in a winning run at whist with the queen.

Most, in fashionable English cavalry and infantry regiments, he'd pawned or traded for political favours round Parliament; the rest he used to repay family obligations in Scotland. One cousin had put his hand into Bute's hat and drawn out a lieutenancy in the Maritime Regiment of Foot, and with it the right to take along a gentleman volunteer. Young Robert had somehow raised the necessary five pounds—two shillings here, half a crown there—against his future prize money and bought himself into the marines as Lachlan Gurr's servant. He had then sailed for the West Indies to make his fortune with his only asset, courage.

Thirty years of unrelenting pain and frequent hunger had seen him ad-vance through the ranks until he was now a private stock company, re-turning an annual dividend from his eight shillings and twopence a day to those who advanced him the price of his commission. He had also become a widower and father of five surviving children, four of whom now lodged with his wife's relatives while the most promising, John, embarked for New Holland to learn the family trade. Ross knew that he had done ex-ceptionally well for a landless crofter's son; he also knew that *his* son would do infinitely better with a father who would soon be acclaimed the governor of El Dorado.

They had reached the dragon tree and the muleteer was already taking the lower fork in the track. "Halt, damn your eyes!" Ross shouted, kicking after the startled man and blocking his way. "Where the hell d'you think we're bound for, heh?"

"*Sí, señor!* We go—La Laguna—!"

"The devil we are not!" Ross replied, wrenching the lead animal around and thrusting it up the higher track. "*Nix* La Laguna, Santa Ursula *toot sweet!*"

The well of Saint Ursula could be approached only along a narrow scar of Teide's flanks, doubling and redoubling across ancient lava fields until the track dipped into a shallow valley where an underground spring watered the plot of garden for a tumbledown adobe farmhouse. Mary Johnson was enchanted by everything as the mules plodded between rows of tobacco and maize, melons and pumpkin vines, before shambling to a halt in the corral where chickens scratched everyone's dunghill for worms and maggots.

Her husband got both legs over the same side of his animal and fell off. Mary dismounted and aimed straight for a domed bread oven between the kitchen wall and a terraced slope planted with clumps of cochineal cactus. Johnson limped after her and sank into a cushion of twiggy firewood while Mary peered around the oven's black mouth. "How primitive," she said, voice echoing, "but I suppose it must serve well or they would have changed it. Tell me, do you think they'll have similar stoves at Botany Bay, or do you think they'll provide our brick ones with the iron tops?" she went on, head and shoulders still inside the oven.

Johnson wasn't paying attention. Young John Ross was marching across the farmyard, that absurd red jacket buttoned to the chin, tiny black hat on, spine stiff. In any decent, normal society such a boy would be working hard at his school lessons, not being traipsed around the world, playing soldiers, Johnson thought as the lad halted, heels clicking, head bobbing. "Major Ross begs leave to present his compliments, sir! A repast is being spread if yourself and Mrs. Johnson would kindly step this way with me."

"Much obliged, I'm sure."

Mary Johnson had straightened away from the oven and was now dusting her hands clean. She smiled down at the boy. "Thank you, John. Or is it 'Mr. Ross'?"

The young lad almost blushed at such rare concern for his feelings. "Well, ma'am, while I'm on duty it must always be Mr. Ross, o' course."

"Of course," she said, nodding. "I shall remember that whenever we meet again and you are on duty. However, today none of us are on duty, are we?"

The nine-year-old gentleman volunteer covered his confusion by clicking his heels again. "As you say, ma'am. This way, if you please."

Mary Johnson took her husband's arm and allowed him to escort her to the farmhouse. He grazed his scalp quite badly on the door frame as they ducked inside a single room which served as a stable for the animals, an eating place for everyone, and a bedroom for the family—most of whom were away herding goats along the snow line. Only the mother and the latest baby were at home. The woman was pounding something in an iron pot while she kept looking over her shoulder at the uninvited guests who were now emptying knapsacks across the table, her only working surface other than the floor.

The major's servant aboard *Sirius* had packed a ration of meat, cheese and biscuit around his master's lunch bottle to protect it from breakage. Ross pulled out the quart of naval spirits, then tugged open a clasp knife to saw off the generous collop of ammunition beef which he shoved at the Spanish woman. She smiled timidly and hid the surprise gift as Ross took out a dented tin mug, half-filled it with rum and added a measure of water. "To your good health, sir, ma'am." He toasted his guests before shutting eyes and up-ending the mug in one straight, painkilling draught.

Young John had unbuckled his own field kit and taken out a much newer tin pannikin. His father chopped a fresh lemon in half and squeezed it, using the knife blade to flick away the pips, then measured a similar ration of water from his canteen. "There, get around that, boy. And stay off the grog for as long as you can," he lectured, watching the boy quench his thirst with bitter lemonade.

"What eminently sensible advice," Johnson commented, looking at his handkerchief before starting to pat his scalp again.

Ross stiffened. "Am I to interpret your tone as indicating that you would now like to add, 'So why don't you take your own eminently sensible advice, major?' "

Johnson damped lips. "Actually, I wasn't. But now that you raise the matter, why don't you? Strong drink is injurious to health and wealth: you ought to strive to set a better example to others."

"A *better* example, eh?" Ross drawled. "I must remember that. As for the matter you allude to, you'll have to smell your own uniform burn with others' gunpowder before you'll understand the need for such medicine. However, as I don't ever recall hearing your name on the field o' honour, I doubt you'll know what I refer to. As for the young lad, thank God he's still sound in wind and limb; there's no need for the strong liquor yet."

Mary Johnson had been listening intently; now she smiled and leaned forward. "You must have led such a fascinating life, major; I'd dearly love to hear more."

Ross frowned. "Another time."

The Spanish woman had set an earthenware bowl of dried figs and *gofio*—thistle seeds pounded with bread crumbs and olive oil—on the table. Mary Johnson untied the small gingham cloth in which she had wrapped the picnic of biscuit and beef from *Golden Grove*'s quartermaster, together with a jar of pickled onions from the Johnsons' personal chop-box. Her husband folded his handkerchief and pursed his lips. "Grace?"

"Of course, dear, just as soon as everyone is ready."

Johnson waited a few moments, checked that Mary's eyes were shut and her hands folded, then closed his own. "For what we are about to receive, may the Lord make us truly thankful. Amen."

Ross nodded at his son. "The words o' life."

Young John stood to attention like his father and commanding officer, eyes uplifted beyond the low ceiling of agave cactus stems wadded with straw and dirt. "O Dread God Jehovah, hearken unto Thy unworthy servants as we prepare to partake o' Thy bountiful blessings. Humble wretches we are, yet we, yet we—"

"Yet we beg," Ross prompted.

"Yet we beg Ye will ever keep vigilant watch over us that we may be blessed always. Amen."

"Amen," Ross echoed, pulling up a stool and sitting down to eat.

Mary Johnson cut the waxed paper which closed the jar and held it open. "Major . . . ?"

"Why, thank you kindly, ma'am." Ross' frown eased at her peace offering. "I must confess a partiality to such dainties," he added with ponderous dignity, stabbing the topmost onion with his knife to lift it out.

Johnson had left the conversation. A gecko lizard was hunting dinner above the table. Even as he stared at it, a large spider rushed a cockroach and was itself rushed by the gecko: something spiralled down from the ceiling and landed near the tiles of ration bread. Johnson shuddered.

Ross glanced up, then looked down again. "You appear to be discomfited by our surroundings, reverend sir. . . ."

"Certainly not. It's just that I am unaccustomed to dining in company such as *this*," Johnson replied, pointing at the hairy spider leg.

Ross sniffed. "Many's the tenant on my father's estate would have thought himself fortunate to live so well."

"Happily *I* am better situated in the world!"

Mary Johnson was leaning forward again. She brushed away the leg and smiled at the elderly marine officer. "May I enquire where that might be, major?"

"Ma'am?"

"Your estate. May I ask where it is located?"

Ross hesitated. "Rothesay." In imagination, the Earl of Bute's land on the Clyde had suddenly acquired a new laird.

"And do you propose retiring there after your duties are done in New Holland?" she persisted.

Ross studied his chunk of pickled beef. "No, ma'am."

"Oh . . . ?"

He shifted uneasily in his seat. "It has passed from my branch o' the family."

"Oh."

"An involved legal matter. I'd rather say no more."

"Of course."

Ross didn't look up from the table as he began mixing another draught of painkiller. Young John was still watching. Ross drained the mug and returned his son's blank look. "Your grandfather was an honourable gentleman! Those who s-say otherwise are liars!"

"Yes, sir."

Ross wiped his mouth along the back of his wrist. "He never intended that his last will and testament would still, would still be afore the procurator fiscal, in Edinboro'."

"Yes, sir."

Ross squared his shoulders. "But where we're bound, *I'll* be the law!"

"I beg your pardon?" Johnson asked, primly folding his handkerchief and rejoining the conversation.

Ross aimed an unsteady finger at the clergyman. "It's going to be my name on the k-king's commission. *Me,* the lieutenant governor o' New South Wales, and when I'm the law in Eld'rado, there'll be no lawyer talk, to twist the truth."

Johnson blinked. "I'm not sure I quite understand?"

Ross had braced his elbows on the table and was chipping flint over his tinderbox. He breathed the spark to flame, tweezed it over the bowl of his clay cutty while he drew smoke and savoured the bite. Then he leaned back, his pipe at a jaunty angle while the grog continued mellowing his many hurts. "You know the first thing I'll buy, with the prize money? A house. A big house. In the country. And all the gentry will pay calls upon us, in their carriages, like they do in the Sugar Isles." He fondled that image for several moments.

"And the next thing?" he went on. "A seat in Parliament. Not that I'll sit in the Commons m'self, being a peer o' the realm, but that's no reason why my boy shouldn't take it." Ross' eyes were dreamy. "With me pulling strings in the Lords, it'll be no time before they acclaim him the finest orator o' the age. Then, Cabinet." He caressed the word, then whiffed smoke and looked at his son's taut face. "Never forget, Mr. Pitt's grandfather was only a pipsqueak Company quilldriver, but when *he* returned from foreign parts he was a nabob worth millions!"

"Yes, sir."

Ross slashed the air between them with his pipe stem. "And that's the way it's going to be for *you*, with the conqueror o' El Dorado for a father."

"Yes, sir."

30

"WEATHER GLASS 'igh and steady sir. Wind nor'easterly and backing."

Phillip opened gummy eyelids and peered at the compass overhead. Satisfied by *Sirius'* heading, he swung his legs over the side of his cot and groped around for a working shirt and breeches while his manservant laid the razor, strop, soap mug and coffeepot alongside the sealed packet of despatches.

Bryant reamed the pair of wax stumps from their sockets for recasting as new candles while Phillip finished buttoning his shirt and sipped the hot drink. "Aaah." His eyes opened again. "My compliments to Mr. Hunter and Mr. King: have them step aft. And bring another brace of cups."

"Aye aye, sir."

Phillip was pouring a refill and spooning sugar by the light of the sunrise astern when Hunter crouched into the great cabin, faded black hat under a tarpaulin sleeve, soaked with dew. "Good morning, sir."

" 'Morning, John." Phillip turned away from the windows with a relaxed smile, spoon clicking round his cup. "Like one?"

"Thank you."

Phillip poured another and nudged it across the chart table. "All squared away?"

"Yes. We're as ready to go as this floating colander ever will be," *Sirius'* captain replied, cupping both hands round the drink for warmth. "Chippy's down the well, sounding last night's leakage. After all the caulking we've hammered below the waterline we ought to be as dry as an old bone: I expect it'll be leaking three or four inches an hour."

Phillip frowned. "That's not good enough, John. Dammit all, we still have to make the middle passage to Rio, and then the Cape, before weathering the latitudes south of Van Dieman's Land."

Hunter pulled a long face and sucked coffee. "Well, that's all a matter of opinion, sir. *Berwick* or *Sirius,* this old tub will still weep like a widow at every seam, and there's not a damned thing you or I can do about it. So, as they say, what can't be cured must be endured."

Phillip fell silent, his imagination probing the dark, rarely visited parts of a ship's carcass where decay flourished unseen, where teredo worms feasted and slapdash carpentry was hidden under a lick of tar. His convoy's only fighting escort, apart from the 170-ton brig *Supply,* had not covered one-tenth of her track to New Holland and was already being pumped at every watch just to stay afloat.

Phillip sipped more coffee and tried to ignore Lieutenant Bligh's bleak pictures of the Antarctic, still months into the future, when *Sirius'* spongy timbers would have already withstood the south Atlantic's gales. Heaven help them all if he then had to engage La Pérouse's two frigates at the end of such a voyage: the first British shots would most likely be the last as *Sirius'* armament recoiled, ripped the eyebolts clean from her frame, careered across the gundeck and smashed through the opposite side. It had happened before. Admiral Kempenfelt's hundred-gun *Royal George* had gone to the bottom off Spithead with all hands when her timbers collapsed only three or four years earlier.

Lieutenant King stepped past the saluting sentry. "Good morning, sir!"

"I hope you're right," the commodore observed. "Like a cup of coffee?"

"Yes, please."

Phillip waited till the younger man had poured himself a share, then cleared his own throat. "Speed remains the essence of our contract. I propose to lay for Rio without further delay. High water will be one hour before noon. We go out on the ebb. Mr. King? My compliments to Mr. Adam: he will secure these despatches until they can be forwarded to London. You will then go directly to the *presidio* and request His Excellency's formal permission to depart." Phillip turned slightly. "Mr. Hunter? Make to all: the convoy will proceed by single division, commodore in the vanguard. Thank you, gentlemen."

They saluted and the door swung shut behind them. Phillip was still buttoning into his own salt-stained coat as the signal gun thumped overhead and more yellow paint flaked from the cabin wall near his cot. He chose not to notice. Instead, he scooped his hat off its shelf in the coffin-cupboard and strode along the companionway.

The morning tasted better as he climbed through the deckhouse and turned aft to join Hunter at the lee rail while bunting tore and snapped on the halliards. *Sirius'* commander had trained his telescope at the nearest transport, watching a stir of interest as someone in authority noticed the flagship's signal. He lowered the glass and looked at Phillip. "I'd say it was unlikely if one man in ten over there would know if his bum was on fire at this moment. After the events of the past month or so you'd have thought they would have learned something."

"And frogs might fly," Phillip answered, shielding his eyes to watch the rest of his convoy snoozing at anchor. The cannon had to fire two more charges before *Alexander* jerkily hoisted her answering pennant and began the quickening rhythm of making ready for sea.

King's gig was the last boat to be winched aboard and secured after he'd come alongside and climbed through the entry port. *Sirius'* topmen obeyed their bosun's whistle, racing each other aloft while both watches—marines and sailors—manned the braces far below. Lieutenant Bradley marched aft and touched hatbrim to Hunter. "Boat swayed in and secured, sir. Capstan manned. All vessels will proceed by single division, commodore in the vanguard."

Hunter looked at Phillip. "Ready, sir."

"Execute."

"Aye aye, sir."

The iron pawls began clanking in time with the fiddler as sweating, grunting, heaving, cursing men dragged their ship along the creaking cable. "Anchor aweigh—!"

Santa Cruz' white houses and Teide's ash grey slopes were already starting to cross *Sirius'* bowsprit as the breeze payed her off the mooring ground. Hunter tilted his trumpet and squinted into the morning sun. "Tops'l sheets there! Cast loose!"

Gasket lines slipped, shaking out their patched canvas with grumbling thuds and shudders, bellying onto the light air, bubbling a creamy wake across Teneriffe's crowded roadstead.

"Mr. Bradley!"

"Sir!"

"Clear the starboard battery: nineteen guns as we draw abeam the fortress. Lively now!"

"Aye aye, sir!"

Hunter returned the salute and stepped aft to where Phillip stood alone by the taffrail, also watching the transports get under way, their grey and tan, buff and white tropical canvas billowing against the summer sky. *Sirius'* commander briefly touched his hat. "Compliments will be paid to the governor as directed."

"Thank you, John." Phillip hesitated, then added with a wry smile, "One soon learns to appreciate these small courtesies in a position where there are usually more kicks to be had than handshakes."

Hunter smiled politely. "Beg pardon, sir?"

Phillip shrugged. "I rather fancy that His Excellency is human enough to hunger for a little pomp and ceremonial, now and again. It must make the gossip and backbiting a little less—bitter." Phillip hesitated. "God knows there'll be few enough perks to sweeten the pill when finally we take possession of New South Wales and I move to the top of the totem pole, as well." He tried another smile to soften the effect of his words. "Indeed, the right to order your own public fireworks display is something *you* might yet enjoy if our sailmaker parcels me up for the fishes: it'll probably be the only fun you'll ever get as governor," he added with a lame attempt at humour.

Hunter's face stayed as impassive as *Sirius'* figurehead. "Then may I hope such a thing never comes to pass, sir? A change in command would be unfortunate, especially while Mr. Ross labours under the illusion that, as lieutenant governor designate, he automatically becomes number one the moment you splash over the side."

Phillip's smile faded. "Does he now? How awkward."

"Indeed, very awkward if he tries to honour some of the promises he's made to certain of his officers."

"Promises?" Phillip's eyebrows had become a single dark line. "What manner of promises?"

"Several," Hunter replied. "Lieutenant Collins remains judge advocate general, but virtually every other appointment will be refilled entirely by military personnel. His young lad gets an ensign's commission, while Jimmy Campbell goes up to major, gets command of the marines and becomes a justice of the peace. However, as recognition of the navy's part in this expeditionary force, I've been offered the lieutenant governorship—"

"He—has—*what*?!"

"He's promised me the number two roost when he climbs onto the top perch—"

"You corrected him, of course!"

Hunter quietly shook his head. "No. It would not have made one scrap of difference while he was carrying such a skinful under his belt."

"But surely the man was informed of his commission's limitations when first he received it?"

"Surely he was," Hunter agreed, pausing as the first gun fired, breathing hot sulphur along *Sirius'* upper deck. "Not that it matters a tinker's damn what anyone told him in London, it's what he believes now that encourages him to promise plantations, and trading licences, and grants of slaves to his cronies. And to remind the rest of us that plain Major Bobby Clive eventually became Robert, first Baron Clive of Plassey, a nabob worth a cool half million sterling once his particular handful of trained soldiers had 'booted the Frogs and Dagoes from Bengal. . . .' "

Phillip was still groping for a coherent reply when the second gun banged its salute at the Spanish governor of the Canaries and the British ships began passing in review, breaking out their colours on the freshening breeze. It ought to have been a proud moment for the convoy's commodore but, suddenly, he had lost all appetite for the trappings of power now that his innocent remark about a possible, a *possible* El Dorado in New Holland had been so deliberately distorted by Ross. "If, if only the fool had the wits of a weavil, he would have, would have—!"

"Would have still been pushing a pen for M'Lord Bute instead of seeking his fortune with a regiment in the Indies?" Hunter suggested neutrally.

"Of course not! But the man ought to have spoken with me first before letting his mouth gallop away with his brains! I intend having this matter out with our Mr. Ross, once and for all!"

"As you direct, sir," Hunter replied. "But may I ask one question before you do?"

"Well?"

"You are aware of the Oriental's notion of 'face'?"

"I served in India."

Hunter nodded. "I thought I'd heard mention of it, sir, for which reason I respectfully draw your attention to the word again. I have also observed that our dusky allies of Madras are—like your North Britons—somewhat touchy on matters which affect their private honour and their public face." Hunter could have been discussing the state of the weather.

Phillip had been given quite enough time to regain control of himself. He looked up from the desk. "What is it you're really telling me, John?"

Hunter still chose his words with care. "I fancy that, when a stranger observes Major Ross, he sees only a very choleric and none-too-sober deputy, a threadbare old redcoat whose only qualification for the task is Mr. Pitt's belief that our military guard ought to have some say in running a colony which it may soon be defending against the Indians, or the French, or both together.

"By contrast, whenever I look at Bobby Ross I catch fleeting glimpses of a young boy who led his men up the cliffs of Quebec to fight for England with bomb metal in both legs till he dropped, still shouting defiance at the queen's grenadiers of France. For which reason, no matter how much I may disapprove, I find it hard to condemn his intemperate use of the bottle: one only has to suffer toothache a few times to understand any man whose body has given him pain every waking moment of the past thirty years."

"Hm."

"But there is yet a third Mr. Ross," Hunter continued, "and he is the one who concerns us now."

"Oh?"

Hunter nodded. "It's the face he grooms in the mirror every morning and which he wants his son to see. It's the face he wants us all to see, and admire as much as he sees and admires it."

"*Oh?*"

"It's the face of Major General the Lord Ross, first nabob of New Holland, the darling of London society, the wonder of Parliament when they vote him a mansion in the country and a pension on the Civil List. It's the face some earl or duke will recognise in a few years' time when their two heirs are betrothed; as such it is always lean, and manly, and masterful. As such it is never splotched with strong liquor nor soured with envy for that promotion which will never come his way while other, better-connected officers climb over his shoulders. English officers like young Mr. Dawes, tucked under the protective wing of the astronomer royal." Hunter fell silent.

Phillip squirmed at the truth of Hunter's homily. *Sirius'* last gun fired and it was now the turn of the Spanish battery to thump out its reply, but the convoy's commodore was no longer listening. He coughed painfully instead. "What action do you suggest I take, John?"

Hunter had been studying the distant puffs of powder smoke as they squirted from the fortress' embrasures. He glanced down at Phillip again. "Well, sir, and this is only a suggestion, but I would never contemplate anything which touched that third Major Ross, never, no matter what the provocation."

"Why?"

"Because, in my experience, we all need our dreams," Hunter went on soberly, "no matter how futile and silly they may appear to everyone else around us. Often such dreams are all that make this vale of tears endurable and, if another should prick the bubble before it bursts of its own accord, then often a mere nuisance becomes a sworn enemy for life in less time than it takes to blow out a candle."

"All that may be so," Phillip said, beginning to scowl at the mild sermon, "but I cannot permit a subordinate officer to make promises which he simply does not have the power to deliver."

Hunter was not put out by the sharp edge in his commander's voice. "Does it matter, sir?"

"Of course it damned well matters!"

"Then I must beg leave to disagree with you."

"Uh?"

"I must disagree with you, for while you remain alive and well, all else is pipe smoke up the chimney. And if—God forbid—it comes to a slanging match between Bobby Ross and myself at Botany Bay once he remembers that I have the dormant commission to be your successor, not he, then it will mean you have already slung your hammock in the next world. Either way there is nothing to be gained by you now challenging his illusions." Hunter was well aware of the risks he ran by deliberately putting himself between two men of such prickly honour and fragile temper, but still he went on: "Meanwhile, if ever I saw an opportunity of sharing a dish with him in the great cabin, just now and again, then I would, for it would give the lie to gossip that neither he nor his officers have received any mark of favour from our side of the king's service."

Phillip glanced up wearily from the deck. "The fellow must be out of his mind to envy anyone this job."

"Sir?"

"I said, the man must be stark raving mad to wish himself the next governor of anywhere." Phillip hesitated. "Oh, I know how it feels to imagine myself an admiral of the ocean sea, to fly my broad pennant for men to salute, to wear gold lace and to play God when I hope nobody else is looking." He made a lopsided smile. "There was once a pastry cook's shop across the street from our lodgings when I was young. Every morning, as I went down to fetch the water, I used to squash my nose against the windowpane and stare at all the custard tarts inside. Anyhow, one day, one of my father's pupils gave me a penny for running an errand. But instead of passing it to my mother for housekeeping—as I ought—I hid the penny. Can you guess what happened next?"

Hunter smiled. "Which tart did you buy?"

"The biggest and stickiest in the shop, the one nearest the window." Phillip paused. "I'm sure the sparrows ate more than I. You see, the ones at the back of the tray were freshest, but I wasn't to know that at the time. And so it is with being captain commodore of this expeditionary force, my friend.

"I'm ashamed to admit that, until a few months ago, I would have cheated, lied, perjured my soul to win a commission as a colonial governor—perhaps I did?—for you may be sure that ambition can turn heads far stronger than Mr. Ross'. But the last few weeks have taught me that my latest prize was only on display because nobody else wanted it.

"Frankly, if I could honourably bestow this burden upon Major General the Lord Ross and return to being plain Mr. Arthur Phillip, gentleman and farmer of Lyndhurst in the county of Hampshire, you would not see my heels for dust. But it's never that easy, is it? *Befehl ist Befehl,* a command is a command, and that's an end to the matter."

"I'm not quite sure I follow you, sir . . . ?"

Phillip tried hard to smile. "You would if you wore my shoes, John, you'd understand. Perhaps you will wear them one day? Then you'll know what I mean. Remember this if ever you take over from me in New South Wales: you'll be damned when you're right, damned when you're not right, and damned when you do nothing at all—and often by the same people.

"Believe me, you'll have earned every trifling perk which comes with this thankless office. The fireworks and the flags are not really much consolation for what I must face every day, and will have to face again if I live to present my journals of account to a parliamentary committee of scrutiny, a gang of drunken votemongering civilians who will not know the difference between their arse and their nose, let alone know how to decide the most prudent course of action off an unknown coastline." Phillip paused. "In addition you will need the wisdom of Solomon and the hide of an elephant if ever you are to walk free again with your sanity and your honour intact." Phillip tried to soften the effect with another smile, but failed. "Please convey those sentiments to Major Ross with my best wishes if ever a suitable opportunity arises."

"Aye aye, sir," Hunter said. "And now, if I may be excused, I observe that we are about to tack and lay for Point Rojas."

Phillip nodded a dismissal, but continued watching his transports as they also breasted the Atlantic swell, putting over onto a southerly track down Teneriffe's coastline before starting the long run to Rio, three thousand miles southwest. Teide's snowfields had never seemed more inviting or more remote as their almost perfect cone drew abeam and then started falling astern.

Sirius was ghosting along on a light nor'esterly, shoals of flying fish skipping under her bows, slicing through the glassy blue waters, herded by a pod of sperm whales which blew their feathery spouts and sounded again, continuing their migration to the calving grounds of Gomera—now visible in the haze off Teneriffe's southernmost cape—where the harpooners of San Sebastián were lying in wait with their longboats and lances.

Phillip watched them go and then went below to resume work on his papers until the ships cleared Teide's wind shadow and some semblance of discipline could be restored to his convoy. Not that anyone else appeared to be worried much as the breeze continued dropping and the transports barely made headway under full sail. Sinclair, for example, was quite happy to see the convict women pick oakum for him, and began taking another leisurely turn around the waist deck before going below for his noonday nip and nap.

"A brief word with you, captain?"

Sinclair turned. "Mr. Balmain?"

The younger man shifted his instrument bag from hand to hand. "We've just lost another."

"Oh?"

"He'd been rather poorly, recently, but this morning he just seemed to give up trying."

"Ah."

"Indeed, he seems to have been in rather low spirits since dropping a water barrel on his leg the first day we were in port."

"Oh?"

"I did not witness the incident, of course, but I can tell that he fell rather heavily," Balmain went on, choosing his words with care. "The barrel not only appeared to have fractured the fibula, it also seems to have affected the internal organs somewhat, inducing hemorrhage from kidneys, spleen, etcetera."

"Ah."

"It is not possible to be more precise without first performing an examination, *post mortem*."

"Oh?"

"But since the accident did not happen ashore under another's jurisdiction, a coroner's verdict is not strictly required. The master's signature in my journal is considered sufficient should anyone ever enquire after the *defunctus*."

Sinclair had been nodding in time with his surgeon's explanation. "I understand your natural concern for prompt and proper action, Mr. Balmain, most commendable. Ye have the book handy?" He took the journal. "And what might be the cause o' death for which I am signing?"

"Dropsy."

"Dropsy, eh? A most likely end for someone who dropped so far in the world, then dropped into eternity after dropping a keg on hi'self!" Sinclair took the surgeon's pencil and printed a laboured signature on the fluttering page. "There. We thank ye, Mr. Balmain, keep up the good work."

"There remains one last detail to be settled. . . ."

"Oh?"

"The disposal."

Sinclair's lip curled. "Heave the useless—!" Then *Alexander*'s master stopped short. "Correction: tell the sailmaker to do the full honours, Mr. Balmain, we can afford a block o' holystone for the sinker. And tell Mr. Olsen to step aft."

Within minutes *Alexander*'s signal gun had been primed, run out and fired as *Golden Grove*'s number jerked aloft and flapped limply on the halliards. Meanwhile the second mate had cleared the jolly boat and begun rowing across to pick up a visitor.

Neither ship had made any headway against the current which flowed between the twin islands of Gomera and Teneriffe by the time the convoy's chaplain had tugged on a fresh shirt and clean breeches, rolled his clerical gown and prayer book together, and clambered down to the waiting boat. Johnson had reason to feel uneasy at this sudden call to duty: his last visit to *Alexander* had been unforgettable. He composed himself in the stern sheets and frowned at the second mate: "Well, my man? And what would appear to be your trouble this time?"

The mate squirted tobacco juice as his men leaned into their sweeps and the jolly boat returned home. Sinclair was rather more suave than his petty officer, waiting at the entry port while the small boat rolled alongside on the swell. He parked his quid inside one cheek and extended a hand to help the Englishman climb the last two rungs. "Welcome aboard, Mr. Johnson, sir. I trust you were not otherwise engaged . . . ?"

"Not at all," Johnson replied stiffly. "To what do I owe this pleasure?"

" 'Tis no pleasure, sir." Sinclair's head shook under its load of grief. "Another of your future parishioners is now numbered among the Blessed. I would esteem it a singular favour if ye could perform the last rites. . . ."

Johnson wondered if either Sinclair or himself had been touched by the sun, especially when he saw the long bundle sewn in new sailcloth, laid on a grating in the scuppers with the Union Flag folded alongside. "Last rites?"

"I knew ye would, sir," Sinclair nodded. "But first, would ye care to step into my humble cabin to fortify yourself wi' a small dram?" He bowed unsteadlly toward the hatchway as Mrs. Brandon came aloft.

"No, thank you." Johnson shook out his gown and tried plunging both arms into its black sleeves.

Sinclair volunteered to be his valet and waited until Johnson's finger had found the right page of his Book of Common Prayer. "Are ye ready, sir?"

"Yes."

Sinclair turned. "Mr. Olsen! All hands!"

"Yoh! *Alexander*'s mate snatched at his whistle lanyard and began limbering up to speed laggards with his cob.

Bare feet pounded over the convicts' hold, where most of them had been chained since *Alexander* dropped anchor the week before. Only the few on essential duties—like the women, the barbers and Balmain's assistant—were on deck while the crew and marine guard jostled into a hollow square, facing Johnson, the master, the bundle.

Sinclair checked the sun's angle, now slanting down between almost slack sails, glaring straight at his men's eyes or roasting the backs of their exposed necks. The caulking was also unpleasantly tacky beneath his sea boots. Content that everything was properly staged and that his own patch of shade was secure and cool, Sinclair looked at the convoy's chaplain again. "When ye are ready, sir."

The parson edged into some shade as well. " 'We brought nothing into this world, and it is certain we can carry nothing out.' " The women spinners slowed and the two convict barbers in the back row swapped blank looks. " 'The Lord gave and the Lord hath taken away; blessed be the name of the Lord.

" 'Man that is born of a woman hath but a short time to live, and is full of misery. He cometh up, and is cut down, like a flower; he fleeth as it were a shadow, and never continueth in one stay.

" 'In the midst of life we are in death.' " Johnson's careful enunciation slowed, ready for Sinclair's impatience to boil over as it had during the previous funeral service aboard *Alexander,* but this time the master had both eyes shut, chin on breast: Duncan Sinclair had even stopped chewing baccy as a sign of his respect. Far from convinced by this conversion to sober good manners, Johnson returned to his prayer book. " 'Forasmuch as it hath pleased Almighty God of his great mercy to take unto himself the soul of—' "

"Pascoe, George," Sinclair prompted from the corner of his mouth.

" 'The soul of our dear brother here departed, Pascoe George, we therefore commit his body to the deep, to be turned into corruption—' "

Sinclair's chin jerked a command at his first mate. Four crewmen were volunteered forward while Olsen shook out the flag, knotting its upper corners to the grating to save Mr. Contractor Campbell the cost of a re- placement. The four sailors bent and heaved their awkward load to the gunwale. Olsen got ready to give the bundle a shove with a mop handle in case it stuck when the grating tilted. Sinclair glanced at his clergyman. "Ready. Sir."

Johnson damped lips. " 'Looking for the resurrection of the body, (when the sea shall give up her dead,) and the life of the world to come, through our Lord Jesus Christ.' "

The grating heaved upward and suddenly its flag was fluttering free while something splashed out of sight. The crewmen dropped their load and moved off briskly as Johnson snapped his book shut and prepared to do much the same. But Sinclair was far from done. "Mr. Johnson, that was a credit if I may venture to say so." He also ventured a near smile. "It seems to me that we so rarely have the comfort o' a minister's presence aboard, now would be the ideal time for a few words suitable for the occa- sion." He held the smile in place and raised his voice for every man on deck to hear him clearly. "Words that will, as it were, embrace *all* the dear departeds who haven't enjoyed the consolation o' Holy Scripture!" Sinclair looked at his crew's troubled faces as the westering sun lanced into them, checked that none of the sails needed trimming yet, then looked back at Johnson. "Take your time, sir, we're in no hurry to see ye go."

Johnson frowned slightly. "Do you mean a sermon?"

"Precisely so, a sermon."

"One based on *The Book of Discipline* perhaps? One outlining the duties of master and servant in the face of death . . . ?"

"The very same." Sinclair nodded with some surprise. "But not one o' yon thirty-minute snacks o' the New Testament. What my men need is a hearty plateful o' the bread o' life, a feast o' God's word to revive their fallen spirits and, as it were—" Sinclair pitched his voice for everyone to hear again—"to remind *everyone* o' the need to be subordinate to his mas- ter's will and to obey his commands at all times!"

Johnson heard the undertone of malicious irony and felt a sudden chill in his belly. "So be it, Mr. Sinclair, so be it. I shall indeed remind *everyone* of our Master's will and the need to obey His commands, at all times." Johnson didn't allow himself further time to lose his nerve. Mouth set, he stepped from the sail's shadow and stood forth to face the blinky, sullen crewmen. "Today we shall consider the inward meaning of Saint Paul when he wrote in his Epistle to the Colossians, 'Servants, obey in all things your masters according to the flesh. . . .' "

Cribb inched further into the awning's shadow and glanced at Thorpe, lips barely parted. "No good."

The younger lag twitched an eyebrow in reply. "Nah."

Johnson had finished a sweeping gesture with the black gown and was now aiming his finger at the sweaty, fidgeting crew. "Consider your duty to our Master in the face of death, such as we have seen today! Remember, when a man dies of old age we regard it as coming in the common course of things. But when a young man, such as we have just committed to the boundless deep, when a young man dies then we understand that not one among us may reckon upon a long day of life! In a single heartbeat our sun may be set forever ere it is yet life's full noon—!"

"Not a bit of good," Cribb muttered again, more to himself as he stifled a yawn and wondered if anyone would mind if he sat down on the barber's keg for a short kip till the show was over. Probably not, but at least while he stood he could still glare across the barricade and watch that—that Mrs. La-de-dah Brandon resting easy on her laundry basket until the service had ended. Hn! He'd been patient quite long enough with her, some coves would say he'd been too patient, but that's what comes from being a decent bloke. Any other cove would've bashed her in the beginning, but he'd been a decent bloke—and look where it'd got him!

Cribb glared harder, hoping that she would take notice of him and turn his way, if only for a moment, but she never did. Stuck-up bitch. Still, there was no denying that she looked good enough to eat, with all that long, coppery hair a-shining in the sun, all combed back like a lady's under that headscarf. . . . And he wouldn't mind betting that the hands, folded out of sight in her lap, were just as washed, and scrubbed, and clean, and things.

Not that she was his style, not her! Not in a hundred years. He preferred 'em darker, like the saucy young mollishers he used to battle for behind hidden gypsy encampments. Dark and saucy. Mrs. B. might suit generals and captains and such, but a regular cove needs something better, something with more shine, not so stuck-up. Cribb grimaced. Even if he did bother to take her across the river to Vauxhall Gardens, there wouldn't be enough food in the kitchen to start filling her out in all the right places: it'd cost him pounds to get her back into shape. But, he mused, wouldn't it be worth trying . . . ?

Johnson's voice rose as a swaying seaman in the front row keeled over with heat exhaustion. "We all have a clear conviction that others will die, but as to ourselves, we put far from us that evil day! Fools that we are—!"

Thorpe shifted from one foot to another, bored by the heat and inactivity. "Oi reckon 'e ought've been learned by Rev'rent Collins, back 'ome, that's what Oi reckon, Joe."

"Bene devil driver?"

"Not 'alf 'e were—" Thorpe chuckled, also lost in memories of happier days—" 'specially after a Saturday night on the grog with squire and the rest of the gentry."

"That's the ticket," Cribb murmured absentmindedly.

"Brethren!" Johnson announced, sleeves flapping urgently. "Solemn reflection upon the shortness of life and the certainty of death will prove to be the most important moment in your earthly career if only it be allowed to work as leaven upon the hard lumps of your sinful hearts!"

"Amen," Sinclair said as another of his crewmen crashed onto the hot planks: it would be many a long day's sailing before any more floating ghosts troubled the good ship *Alexander*.

"But," Johnson went on, "what can be said of the *master*'s duty to his servant in the face of death? What lesson is to be learned from Pascoe George's timely example to us today? Is it not that, no matter how low or high we may be, God's unseen hand can sweep all of us off the table of life in the twinkling of an eye . . . ?"

Sinclair's complacent yawn snapped shut as Johnson's voice dipped to an almost conversational tone. "Yes, brethren, death can, death *will* happen to everyone, be he felon, or sailor, or shipmaster even. Any one of us could be walking on this very deck in a southern latitude, perhaps with our minds distracted by other things when—without warning!—a 'braw greenie' sweeps up from the deep and, when it has drained away, no more felon. No more sailor. No more shipmaster. Gone. Utterly gone, as totally and completely as our late brother in Christ, Pascoe George, who now rests content beneath the rolling waves till that last Great Assize when all will be judged, be they felon or sailor. Or shipmaster," Johnson added, glancing at Sinclair again. "Thank you, captain."

Sinclair ground his teeth. "Mr. Olsen! Starboard watch alow! Hand the forebraces! Trim the yards!" His boot landed in the nearest unconscious body. "Start these lazy buggers aloft!"

Johnson strolled away to the entry port as Olsen's cob cracked and Sinclair marched for'ard to check on dinner in *Alexander*'s farmyard by the bowsprit. The marline spinners and oakum pickers hurried back to work, and Kitty Brandon stood to untwist the washing line and nip the tails of Sinclair's shirts.

Levi stepped from his patch of shadow near the barbers and approached the barricade with a bundle of his own under one arm. "Lady . . . ?"

She paused, then turned and smiled. "Why, Mr. Levi. And what may I do for you?"

"For me? Nothing. But for the Dr. Balmain? Much. He sends compliments. Is possible for one of your young ladies to—how can I say—to wash these nasties?" Levi sighed and opened the bundle to show a mess of foul rags, recovered from the latest patient to die aboard *Alexander*.

"Of course. I shall see it's done personally."

Levi frowned. "You will personally?"

She was amused by his concern for her finer feelings. "Mr. Levi, I have seen and handled far worse, and, God willing, I'll live to do it again. You seem surprised?"

Levi shook his head. "With you, no things surprise me."

"Then I must be falling down somewhere in the act," she replied, lifting his bundle of washing across the spikes.

"No, what I mean is often I am hearing such good things what you do at the *schlog* of Tzara-Togo," Levi insisted, artlessly dropping the name.

Kitty Brandon's smile died. "And what would a foreign gentleman like yourself know of a filthy slaughter like Saratoga, I wonder?"

"God forbid was me!" Levi laughed politely. "No, is a friend, a mate, one who is long speaking of what you done there for him."

Her smile thawed into spring again, warm and full of ripe promise. "Doesn't that beat the band? Here we are, halfway between God-knows-what and God-knows-where, passing the time of day with yourself, and it turns out that once you had a friend who was one of the poor lads we so shamefully left behind in the Colonies. Ah, well, 'tis a strange life we've been told to enjoy."

"*Have* a friend," Levi corrected. "Here. We are all in the same boat."

"I'll bet we are," she replied drily. "And what might his name be, I wonder?"

"Kripp. Josef Kripp."

"*Cribb?* That insolent little organ grinder's monkey!" Kitty Brandon glared across the barricade at the ship's barber, now brushing out Sergeant Ramsbottom's grey horsehair wig. "My dear Mr. Levi, 'tis you who surprise *me* if that is the best company you can keep!"

Levi stepped sideways, blocking the view. "Always we must speak as we find, and I find Joe—how you say?—upright cove. Oh, like you, first I think, 'What kind of *klotz* is this?' But now, I think different. Anyhow, is not important. You will return me the wrappings for Dr. Balmain when they are clean, yes?" He bowed slightly, sensing Sinclair's sea boots tramping nearer, and went about his business.

Alexander's master crossed the barricade between the sentry and the brass swivel gun. "What did Ikey Mo' want?"

"Just a small favour for Dr. Balmain," she replied brightly, opening the parcel of bandages for him to look inside. "Miss Dundas will see that one of the girls takes care of it."

Sinclair sniffed and lost interest. "Aye, well, yon Ikey's sound enough, but ye are to keep a proper distance from the English flotsam. I'll not have ye mixing wi' such idle trash."

"There is no risk of me doing *that,*" she agreed, eyeing Cribb with contempt as he turned his back on her and began cropping the sergeant's head.

"Mind ye do. Now, lay the meal. I'll be down presently."

Kate Brandon collected the wicker basket which she'd made her badge of office, hitched her skirts and climbed below, edging aft along the companionway between the petty officers' cupboards. She went into the great cabin and leaned against the door, holding it shut from inside while she enjoyed one of her rare moments of privacy. She looked around.

God alone knew it was little enough to be proud of, but at least and at last it was starting to smell clean. Indeed, the tiny box of a room was becoming quite homely now that the sailmaker had finished the curtains for Duncan's cot and *Alexander*'s stern lights. The master had predictably grumbled and rumbled at all the expense and frippery, but later on she'd caught him out, shyly running a hand over the design which she had inked on the plain canvas: a grim King Neptune with his trident, riding a sea monster, both copied from one of the Dutch charts which were now stowed in alphabetical order under the table—where they ought to have been all the time.

She straightened away from the door and finished stowing her basket with the needlework and darning which filled the long afternoons while Duncan Sinclair snored and whimpered at the teeming rats of his apprentice years in the Baltic. Kitty Brandon had made it her business to learn all about them and, to an extent, sympathise. It had not been difficult. She had also begun making her way in the world as soon as she could walk: in his case it had been sink or swim as a cabin boy on a timber schooner, in hers it had been sing or starve around the taverns of Dublin.

She started polishing two knives, two forks, two spoons, one rummer and one wineglass, using the tablecloth—another refinement since she'd taken *Alexander*'s master in hand. It would soon be time for his noon nip and nap. Luckily, after twenty-odd years working the playhouses of Ireland, and England, and the Americas, there were few things which could shock, or surprise, or unsettle her—not even the sight of a drunken slaver trying to claw up the cabin walls to escape phantom rats the size of cats.

Was it really twenty-odd years? She grimaced at herself in the cabin's misty dressing mirror, twenty *odd* years more likely! She stared back at what she saw, a stage bluff which had worked well enough on others in the past, but she could no longer bluff herself, these days. Every year which passed was leaving deeper lines between those eyes and under that chin, and devil a thing there was she could do to slow the tide of time.

Very deliberately she tilted her reflection, trying to stay detached while she valued the one property which had once seemed such a guarantee of success, of a climb to her rightful place in society. Then, in those days, men of title, men of breeding, men of quality had acclaimed it a damned good face, well shaped, full of spirit and, in the right light, with a flawless complexion. And it still was a damned good face, better by a mile than the tragic teapot of a mug which Sally Siddons was trading on, with or without the longer nose which had won her Lady Teazel in *School for Scandal*, the very part which—as everyone who was anyone knew damned well—had been written with *her* in mind!

This was only partially untrue, like much else she needed the world to think about her, but it is quite likely that Richard Sheridan did have Katharine Brandon in mind as he wrote line after line of invective into the vindictive young bitch he'd married to the elderly Sir Peter Teazel for his latest stage triumph. As such it had been exquisite revenge by Drury Lane's manager on the illegitimate half-sister who had erupted from nowhere to blackmail him for work while he was fighting to enter Parliament, and still living down the scandal of his elopement with Elizabeth Linley.

La Belle Brandon's entries were, as he was to learn to his cost over the next few years, rarely less than perfectly timed and never less than breathstopping. There had never been any doubt that the woman was all she claimed to be, an utter bastard, combining the unmistakeable Sheridan sparkle and charm—inherited from their common father, Thomas—with the frightening rages of her natural mother, the young dowager Countess Brandon.

There would have been no problem if the love child had been a boy, as the countess rather hoped: some member of the family could always have adopted the little chap until he was old enough to seduce an heiress, or buy a commission in the army, or take up a living in the church. But it had been a girl, a girl without any prospect of inheriting the dowry that would make seduction or elopement worthwhile, so the wretch was put out to care and visited by her "uncle" every payday.

It had been a sentimental weakness which the legitimate heir, Richard, lived to curse. Frequently. Somehow the child survived Dublin's annual epidemics of smallpox, cholera, meningitis, diphtheria, typhoid, whooping cough and spotted fever. She survived, she thrived among the open sewers which poured into the Liffey. Somehow she even learned to hold a tune in her head and jig for halfpence while juggling old beer corks.

The shadowy uncle—Thomas Sheridan—was permanently stumped for fresh acts to put on with his performing dogs, singing pigs, fire-eaters and slack ropedancers at Dublin's Smock Lane Theatre. For lack of anyone better, he billed the young girl as Cupid in Madam Rinaldo's aerial troupe and was relieved when she packed off to England, there to sink into decent obscurity. That was his second misjudgment. Charming, witty, talented girls rarely needed to sink into anything deeper than a gentleman's feather bed, but that was not the elder Sheridan's last mistake: the same network of theatrical gossip and scandal flourished on both sides of the Irish Sea. It wasn't long before a casual question in this playhouse, an unguarded answer in that barn, and broad hints everywhere began shading in the young actress' empty background. Uncle Tom, she had already guessed, was not just the kindly old family friend which he'd claimed to be on the infrequent visits to Mrs. O'Flanagan's baby farm and training brothel. It had taken rather more persistence to uncover her blood relationship with the late Catherine Marie Devlin, Lady Brandon—

"What's to eat, woman?"

She turned away from the mirror with a bright, welcoming smile and gave Duncan Sinclair a peck on the cheek. "Only good, wholesome, plain food, you may be sure."

"Aye, good, good," he winced, lowering himself into the captain's chair.

"Is that back troubling you again?" she asked with genuine concern.

"Ah! Ye can rub it. After we feed," Sinclair muttered, jerking the bell wire which alerted his steward and signalled no more idle chatter until lunch was done.

31

"AND WHAT WAS *you* doing with Lady Lardy Dah again?" Cribb sneered as Levi joined Thorpe and himself for the evening's ration. "I saw you at it!" he added, working biscuit crumb and cheese between his palms, crushing it like glaziers' putty.

"So?" Levi replied, also starting to mash his dinner.

"Don't give me none of that 'so?' malarkey!" Cribb warned, finger stabbing across the puddle of candlelight as *Alexander* pitched and yawed into the night. "I saw you!"

"So?" Levi repeated, nibbling at the greasy wad in his fist. "Tell me, Joe, why you think Cooky don't stick all this zhit in a big pot and warm it like pie for once?"

"Oi reckon," Thorpe agreed moodily, licking each finger to stretch dinner time.

Cribb's scowl hardened. "I saw—!"

"What you saw, Joe? Tonight I see you are not feeling good."

"I'm feeling fine!"

"Then how must you look when you feeling bad?"

"Piss off!"

Levi smiled dreamily. "How much I wish I could, back to Warszawa. There I know a girl who—"

"I'll bet she does!" Cribb snarled. "I'll bet you know tons of girls what does!"

"Tons, eh?" Levi's smile never wavered. "*Ei!* What a heavenly way to die. . . ."

"Huh!"

"Something biting you, Joe?" Thorpe asked, getting worried.

"Chrissakes! Not you now!" Cribb spluttered, ramming the last crumbs of biscuit and cheese together.

"Mr. Kripp?" Levi interrupted politely. "Why do I have this feeling there is something not good with you tonight?"

"I saw you buttering up 'er ladyship!"

" 'Butrinkup'?"

"Arse 'ole crawling!" Cribb was spoiling for a fight with someone, anyone.

Levi frowned as he translated the unfamiliar phrase. "Such ugly words for such a lovely woman. Don't—"

"See! There you go again!"

"Mr. Kripp, silence! Many things I take from you, but never this *meshuggeh* horsezhit! So, straight up, what's biting you?"

"I saw you with Lady Muck!"

"Mrs. Brandon," Levi corrected. "And that is the three time you tell me what you seen today. I am getting tired of waiting for you to see something new. At this speed we shall all be in Bottommy Bay before you do." He paused. "So, you don't like I talk to her?"

"She needs taking down a peg!" Cribb glowered, fists bunching. "Stuck-up bitch!"

"No joke?" Levi commented. "Well, of course I must respect your opinion, but I think different. So you respect mine."

"She needs 'er teeth bashed in," Cribb replied, gritting his own.

"Why?"

"Because, that's why!"

"Sorry, 'because' is no answer." Levi smiled distantly. "I seen one more like you, in Lvov. There was him, and there was this girl—"

"Hh!"

"All the time he talking dirty of her, just like you. Told me he wanted to cut her up for dog, that sort of talk. You know what happened?"

" 'E did."

"Nuh huh. Last I seen, they have three boys and a girl. Was all fart talk. Deep down was different inside—"

"Not with me it isn't!" Cribb screamed, making the other families of lags jerk around at dinner to see where the latest punch-up would explode. "I'm going to get even with that, that bitch for what she done!"

"And what she done?" Levi asked mildly.

"She's done nothing but make trouble since she set foot on this boat, that's what!"

"Shh, coves is looking at you."

"Balls!"

"Yours, not mine," Levi replied, getting ready to move back to his own shelf until Cribb's ill-humour had blown over. "Mine I save for that Warszawa girl. You want to hurt Mrs. Brandon? Fine by me. But what you waiting for? A letter from God?"

"Uh?"

"Tomorrow. Wait till she walks past the barbery and—zzzt!—chop her with the razor. Go for the neck," he advised, tapping his own throat. "Is messy, but quick."

"*What?*"

"For you, will be messy but slow," Levi continued. "The Bulldog will not like what you done to his lady. But at last you will be happy. Mrs. Brandon will be *kaput,* you will be *kaput,* no more problem. Ben and me will be happy. Tomorrow we eat your dinner. Thank you, Joe."

"Are you, you serious?"

"If you are," Levi replied, standing to full height between the deck beams. "But, one way or other, do something." Suddenly, he crouched again. "Wake up, prick! How much time we got to be ready for Bottommy Bay? Forever?" He paused, face hard and angry. "Soon we are there; I hear sailors talking, too. About you I don't care nothing, but about me I care everything. When I get to New Holland will not be like when I get to Old Holland. This time is *me* what shouts hep! hep! hep!"

"All right, all right," Cribb muttered, backing away.

"The next time I'm going to be number one! Or else why do I teach you the rajah's pocket watch, heh?"

"So's we can all get a slice of cake." Cribb scowled. "Rio or Tenner Iff, it's all the same to me, nothing's changed with us."

"Once more wrong, *shlanger*!" Levi controlled his voice to a hoarse whisper as his finger began stubbing Cribb's forehead. "Think, *think* what a crew we will be with me, with you, with Ben, with Mrs. B. as well!"

Cribb flinched from the relentless finger. "You joking? 'Er ladyship, crew up with *us*?"

"Why not?" Levi enquired coolly. "The boat does not go forever. Soon it stop when we get to land, then bye-bye Bulldog, hello new friend. . . ."

Cribb was certain that Levi was ill. "Mate, you've just got to look at the way she looks at us, never a kind word for a poor bloke these days, the stuck-up bitch."

"Tch, tch, that so? And when you last give her a kind word then?"

"What?"

"How many times you talk with her? Ten? Five maybe? Three? Two? None?"

Cribb squirmed. "Don't know. Must be dozens."

"Horsezhit, you don't talk with her in Americas. She was high general's lady, and you was a *mamzer* fusilman, so all that horsezhit, too." Levi's mouth curled as Cribb seemed to shrink by inches. "But one time you talk with her, on this boat you talk with her, and how you talk! And now you surprised she looks like dirt at you? Feh! You smell like dirt! I smell like dirt! We all smell like dirt! But for me, I know there is no good looking and talking like dirt!"

" 'Ere! Steady on!"

Levi ignored him. "You know what a man teach me? He say in this world are two kinds of animals, the wolf and the sheep, the diner and the dinner. So, when I look at Mrs. Brandon, you know what I see? I see she is one of us, a diner. You don't believe? Open your eyes, *draikop*! See the way she travels? Others work and work like donkeys, she washes a shirt and bosses number one. *Ei!* What brains, what spirit, what style! What a future!"

"Not with us, she's not," Cribb muttered.

"Wrong. Is why so much depend on what we do now, before we land in Rio. Futures, like luck, is what we make!"

The convoy was still drifting within sight of Teide, sails fitfully banging, the ships rolling heavily on a waxy green sea as the sun came up from Africa.

Levi nodded as he passed the two barbers, rigging their awning, getting ready for another day of light duties while almost every other lag aboard *Alexander* rocked dumbly over a holystone or buffed brightwork. Thorpe winked and nodded back. Cribb just looked busy and looked the other way until Balmain's odd-job man had gone below on some errand. Then he turned, took a deep breath, and plunked himself down on the keg. "Let's get started, *toot sweet.*"

"Ur?"

"A close crop, same as you seen me give Sheep's Arse. And a shave."

"You all right, Joe?"

"Never felt better." Cribb tilted his chin. "Blaze away. Short. Regimental short."

Thorpe scratched himself while he puzzled out the best line of attack. He decided to make a start on the familiar latherwork. Cribb sat bolt upright while grimy waves of bristle peeled round the razor and were wiped into the wet plug of oakum. Then it was his hair's turn, blowing away among the ranks of scrubbers as Thorpe gnawed at the dense black mat with his scissors.

"Look better?" Cribb demanded as the other man stood back for a last time, head cocked on one side, eyeing his handiwork. "Look the same as that other sergeant's?"

"More or less. . . ."

"It'd better be *more*," Cribb warned, shoulders squared as he stood to brush himself off. "I don't take less of nothing."

Teide's snowfields had sunk almost below the horizon by next morning. During the night a light breeze had set in and begun filling the convoy's standing canvas, not much yet, but enough to bring out the navigators' traverse boards and log lines.

Levi stepped round Olsen as the mate streamed *Alexander*'s log, and nodded at the barbers as he passed their pitch. Cribb was starting to look quite dapper after trading some tobacco for a sailor's red neckerchief, and cobbling together the holes in his shirt with sailmakers' twine. In fact he no longer looked like a wild animal, Levi thought, as Thorpe finished giving him his second shave in two days.

The chief barber's chin was up, scissors clicking smartly, when Kitty Brandon also came on deck a few minutes later. " 'Morning, ma'am."

The horizon was as empty as a lag's dinner bowl as the convoy rode on into a sparkling dawn, running easily under full sail. Lifting. Dipping. Lifting again as lines of whitecaps marched past on the nor'easterly trade wind.

Levi was humming a jaunty air as he came on deck and nodded at the barbers. "Good morning, Ben. Good morning, Joe. What weather! Is always like this in Bottommy Bay, you think? Well, soon we find out," he concluded affably, sensing that Mrs. Brandon must have appeared behind the barricade, to judge from the sudden tilt of Cribb's chin.

Levi nodded again and, still humming, strolled away to find a patch of shade to spend the morning, slowly rolling and rerolling the same bandages for Balmain.

Kitty Brandon had indeed come on deck. Cribb's scissors were clicking harder. " 'Morning, ma'am." But she didn't notice his greeting. More interested in pinning out the Bulldog's nightshirt, drawers and stockings on the nearby rigging. Pretty as a twenty-pound note, though, no denying the fact. Standing tippy-toe, wind tossing her skirts, making it tricky to get Bulldog's things in order without scattering them over the side and into the sea.

She was intensely annoyed by his impudent stares. Kitty Brandon tried smoothing her skirts down, lost her grip on one towel and swore roundly as it whirled away, tumbling end over end for the gunwale. Cribb's face flicked up, he saw the rag spinning past and, without thinking, he bayonetted it midair with his scissors, bringing it down in a heap on the marine Thorpe was shaving. "Sorry, colonel," Cribb muttered. He took his time folding the threadbare strip of cloth before putting it flat.

Kitty Brandon was waiting impassively as he halted on the other side of the spikes and handed over Sinclair's towel. "Thank you, Mr. . . . ?"

"Cribb, ma'am. Joe Cribb. The Seventh Fusileers, attached to the Sixty-second Foot, Gen'ral Burgoyne's Army of Canada," he added crisply, hoping for some flicker of interest as she turned back to the washing line.

The Botany Bay expeditionary force was settling into the timeless routines of life at sea; the steady toll of watch bells; the easy creak of cordage; the melancholy shrill of bosuns' whistles as the convoy plodded down its latitudes for the equator. These were the days, the weeks which men would remember as they were called on deck to face the icy darkness of the graveyard watch, ordered aloft before dawn, through driven snow and sleet to master the pounding canvas. But not yet, and the seasoned crewman made the most of this trade sailing to get his duffel in order for the storms ahead, sewing, patching, daubing hot tar on his jacket and britches, husbanding his strength.

These were the nights they would remember on the trackless wastes of the Southern Ocean; steering into the red eye of tropical sunsets while, all around, the trade wind clouds glowed like a goldsmith's furnace and the ships' navigators raised their hands to the North Star, bringing them down over their compass cards to check the needles' accuracy with a pilot's blessing.

HMS *Sirius* persisted in trying to set a lonely example of discipline and traditional values for the other floating neighbourhoods to follow. Every Sunday morning her marines were drilled in their best scarlet, belts pipeclayed, weapons sharp and bright for church parade on the waist deck. It was no longer possible to hail the Reverend Mr. Johnson now that each ship was booming along under a full spread of sail across several miles of open seaway, so the two senior commanders aboard *Sirius*—Captain Hunter for the navy, Major Ross for the military—took turns at doing the clergyman's duty.

It was Ross' week to read the Sunday prayers, which he delivered like court-martial verdicts. Satisfied, he snapped the book shut and ordered his musicians into a marching "Oh God, Our Help in Ages Past" while he shouted the pace and noted any soldier who failed to pull his weight with the verses. Phillip had chosen to keep himself rather to one side of the tiny congregation, neither leading nor following; gold-laced hat under one arm; white gloves folded round the pommel of his Rio de la Plata prize; setting a proper standard of attention to discipline and traditional values.

He stopped admiring his red and white commodore's pennant as Ross finished reading Psalm Twenty—"The Lord hear thee in the day of trouble"—and handed over to Captain Campbell for the troops to be dismissed to their regular duties. Phillip smiled briefly and returned Ross' salute as they both replaced hats. "Handsomely done, major, your men are a credit to the king's service."

"We thank you, sir."

"Indeed," Phillip continued, smile fixed in place, "I was just thinking to myself what a singular pleasure it would be if you and Captain Campbell were to share luncheon with me."

Ross blinked, rather taken aback by the abrupt invitation. "Today?"

"Yes, why not? Unless you have some other more pressing engagement, of course. In fact, why don't we dispense with formality on this day of rest and step below for an immediate refreshment?"

"Oh. Well. That's uncommon civil o' you, sir." Ross turned smartly, heels crashing together. "Mr. Campbell!"

"Sah!" the other veteran marine officer shouted back, boots whacking deck planks, sword hilt clenched.

"Follow me!"

"Sah!"

Phillip beckoned Hunter and led the way below, along the short companionway and into *Sirius'* great cabin, where Bryant had been kept busy during the church service. The chart table had been rigged and a cold buffet laid inside rope quoits to stop the crockery skidding through the open stern lights as following seas rolled under the flagship. The cook had prepared a dish of hardboiled eggs in mustard, a cheese pie, and a dish of jellied ration beef garnished with cress grown on a damp blanket—never a difficult salad to sprout aboard a man o' war. Two bottles of Rhenish, two of Madeira, and one of Mr. Pitt's clarets had been unpacked from the empty cartridge bags which had kept them safe while chilling overnight down the iron throat of an eighteen-pounder.

Phillip stowed his hat inside its tin box, wrapped his sword and hung his dress coat inside the coffin-cupboard. He turned, slackening his cravat as he gestured for his guests to also make themselves comfortable. Hunter stripped down to his white flannel waistcoat; Ross peeled off his faded red tunic and rolled it around his sword before tossing the bundle at Phillip's cot; Campbell firmly put on his hat and opened every second one of his coat buttons.

Phillip rang for Bryant to bring in the glasses and to start drawing the corks. Meanwhile, to help maintain the fragile mood of good fellowship, Phillip stepped across to the stern lights and hauled up a hemp line which was trawling a small grapnel astern. Ross and Campbell edged nearer to see what he was doing as the hook swung inboard with a fathom or so of seaweed snagged on the prongs.

Phillip searched among the brownish leaves. "I find these to be fasci nating creatures under a magnifying lens," he commented to nobody in particular as he straightened again, a sizeable shrimp twitching and kicking between his fingertips. "Almost like having a sea garden at one's doorstep, isn't it? Oh, you wish to examine it, captain—?"

"Sah!"

Phillip was happy to establish an interest of any kind with Ross' deputy and gladly handed over his marine specimen for examination. Campbell peered at the almost colourless shrimp for several moments, then bit it in two and swallowed both halves.

Phillip popped the next specimen inside the wooden bucket which he'd rigged as an aquarium on his window ledge. As there didn't seem to be much point in any further scientific discussion, he threw back the grapnel and waited for Bryant to finish filling the first round of glasses with Mr. Pitt's claret. The cabin door shut behind the steward and Phillip cut himself a wedge of the cold cheese pie. "Well, gentlemen, as I was remarking to Mr. Ross only a few minutes ago, we all have every reason for satisfaction with our progress thus far. Our, ah, passage to the Canaries was without undue incident and a good omen for our run down to Rio.

"There may, of course, be some dissatisfaction among our cargoes as we pass through the Doldrums since none of them will have strayed thus far from whatever hutch or hovel used to be their abode, and neither will they be familiar with the need for strict water rationing. Tropical heat, the boredom of waiting for a wind, and all the minor discomforts of shipboard life—to which we are accustomed—may prove unsettling." Phillip looked at Ross again. "I would suggest you alert your guard units to the possibility of disturbances for the next week or two."

"Sir."

"Now," Phillip went on, "two or three weeks thereafter we ought to make landfall off Rio de Janeiro, our nation's only ally in the Americas when next we go to war—assuming that has not happened already. There will be no need to remind anyone how vitally important it is for us to maintain correct and cordial relations with the Portuguese viceroy and his garrison. Fortunately I have some experience of those waters, which ought to stand us in good stead and put us on course for the Cape in the absolute minimum of time. Thereafter, bearing in mind that Admiral de La Pérouse is also busy in the Pacific, we crowd on sail for New Holland and whatever fate has in store—"

"Payrooz?" Ross was suddenly alert. "He's not a Frog?"

"Er, yes, the Count de La Pérouse does happen to be a French officer, among other things."

"Hn! We'll soon put *him* down for the count, eh, Jimmy?" Ross told his deputy. He glanced back at Phillip. "Do you think he'll have his fortifications dug before we're ready to strike?"

"I rather hope not," Phillip replied warily, "but who can say what is happening—at this very moment—half the world away? My information on the French flotilla's movements is rather limited, just as it is on the entire subject of New Holland." Phillip paused to sip wine. "I cannot stress that fact too much, gentlemen. We really know nothing about our ultimate destination, except its vital importance to the empire, and the fact that Sir Joseph Banks once spent a few days botanising there some seventeen or eighteen years ago. Since when, it might as well have been the dark side of the moon—"

"What's that?" Ross interrupted, eyes narrowing.

"I said, nobody knows anything about Botany Bay, except its geographic location, the existence of adequate water and a sound anchorage."

"*Nothing?*"

"That's right, major."

"Then it's prepost'rous!"

"Not really," Phillip corrected mildly. "You see, it has been our good fortune to be chosen to found the empire's eastern outpost, our new Gibraltar, therefore—"

"Good fortune!"

"So I believe," Phillip insisted quietly. "It is seldom that anyone is given such a chance to begin anew, free from the errors and mishaps of past generations. With such a fertile soil, a kindly climate and willing hands, we shall, I'm sure, convert Botany Bay into a veritable botanical garden."

Ross whipped round and gave Campbell a hard jab in the belly to get his attention. "You hear that, Jimmy? London's packing us off to some flyspeck on the map that nobody's seen in a hundred years! Jesus alive, this is prepost'rous!"

"Sah!"

Ross' finger swung and aimed at Phillip. "What o' the plantations, then?"

"I was about to come to those, major."

"*Sugar . . . ?*"

"I suppose there could be," Phillip conceded. "The latitude would seem to favour its cultivation. Also indigo, a very profitable dyestuff, you'll agree? And tobacco. Wines, olives and silkworms have also been suggested, though, at the moment, our government is mainly concerned with the cultivation of flax for our new dockyards."

"Uh huh, and what about El Dorado?"

Phillip considered both of Ross' questions, the spoken and the unspoken. "Shall we say there is no reason to think that New Holland is less endowed with riches and opportunities than was New Spain and Peru? But—and here again I must stress the point—until *my* commission is proclaimed and I formally take possession of the colony as your governor, all else is pipe smoke up the chimney. I repeat: all else is pipe smoke up the chimney until I order otherwise. Now, gentlemen, what refreshments can I offer you . . . ?"

32

EVERY NIGHT the pilot's blessing became shorter and shorter as Polaris sank over the northern horizon: every noon the sun stood higher and higher above the sagging pennants. The trade winds had finally blown themselves out and the convoy was now wandering among the sultry calms of the Doldrums.

Tempers flared as shipmasters ordered their men to trim and retrim the yards, hunting and trapping every passing breath of air to make seaway by any means possible—and some impossible. Captain Sever of *Lady Penrhyn* lived up to his name and reputation when he ordered his four youngest apprentices to be stripped naked during one noon muster while the first mate roped their left wrists together to make the spokes of a wind-wheel. Then each boy was made to take a bosun's cob and lash the shoulders of the boy in front, but still the barque's sails hung slack on the air as she ghosted along.

The sea had changed. No longer was it a bright, lively blue. Now the convoy was adrift on an oily slick under steamy grey skies where dry lightning fizzed and glared between towering thunderheads. Below decks, cloth and leather sprouted the delicate green whiskers of mildew; haybag mattresses rotted; journal pages fell out as glue and thread dissolved in the moist heat. Ticks and bedbugs, fleas and cockroaches, lice and body crabs swarmed among the toadstools and fungus of the hold.

Cribb was listlessly trimming Sinclair's chin late one morning when, without a sound, one of the scrubbers got up. Holystone under one arm, fetters under the other, he marched past stiff-legged and toppled into the sea. Sinclair opened an eye and glanced at Olsen, also idling under the barbers' sunshade. "Rig the boarding nets. He could start a fashion."

"Yoh."

The day wore on. *Alexander* drifted along with the rest of the convoy, creeping under the clammy shade of a mountainous anvil cloud. Cribb snipped, Thorpe lathered, lags scrubbed. The crewmen yawned and yarned quietly while making up cordage from the marline which sweaty convict women were spinning out in hanks on their hand wheels. Sinclair now lay in a shallow doze on his hammock, slung athwart the mizzen's shade, his fingers twitching over a pair of pistols, a bag of bullets, a flask of powder.

Almost everyone aboard the ship had adjusted to the sporadic whoof! whoof! of their master's gunnery throughout the endless days of drifting. Sometimes his target was a scrap of firewood chucked over the side, sometimes it was an imaginary rat escaping along the taffrail, sometimes it was a bottle dangling below the main course. Cribb and Thorpe flinched every time a random ball from the Bulldog's barkers howled, cracked or moaned through the air. Cold sober, Sinclair was an average shot, but after his noonday nips the captain's eye never managed to swing in time with the latest empty to sway a yard or so above the barbers' shop.

The first icy splat of rain hit *Alexander*'s decks between two rows of lags bowing over their holystones. Then another landed. A sulky pause. Then a sprinkling of hail the size of dried peas. Another moody silence. Then the cloud burst, dumping curtains of grey water across the convoy, blotting out the ships, sky, sea in one roaring onslaught.

Kitty Brandon had been walking back from the ship's heads. Without thinking, she grabbed up her skirts again and sprinted for the nearest cover as lags, guards and crewmen milled around the waist deck. She dived under the barbers' awning, shaking water from her ears and eyes. Thorpe edged away from her to make room under the sunshade, now bagging with the rain and hailstones which bounced, whirred and ricocheted off the spars, masts and rigging. Cribb promptly shook out the square of old sailcloth which he tucked round his customers' necks, and moved closer to the woman, tucking it round her shoulders instead.

There was no other sound possible but the roar of falling water as the thunderhead drifted across the convoy. Lags and landmen huddled where best they could while a silently yelling Olsen ordered his watch to rig a tarpaulin over the main hatchway. Sinclair was also pantomiming commands right and left as other men struggled to winch a scoop and hose over *Alexander*'s water butts. Nobody had to order the starboard watch aloft. Seamen were now running past the gunwales below the boarding nets, bolting down the washports to stop the rain getting away. Others were stripping off, pounding their foul, tacky, salt-pickled duds as the deck flooded around them: one inch, two inches, three, more.

Abruptly, the rain stopped. Grown men went on capering about like naked urchins in a street puddle, whooping and splashing at each other with the sheer joy of washing their salt sores in unlimited sweet water. Cribb would not have minded joining them, but his chains made it impossible to undress without permission from the corporal of the guard. So, instead, he coughed nervously and glanced at Kitty Brandon's haughty profile. "Nasty weather, ma'am." There was not a flicker of interest on her face as she continued staring the other way. "Not as bad as it was round old Schuyler's Farm, though. . . ."

Abruptly, the skies split open again and the tropical deluge dropped like ramrods. The ship's crew never noticed, still scrubbing each other's bellies and backs; holding their faces to the skies, eyes shut, mouths agape; trampling their clothes over and over the shallow lake which now sloshed between *Alexander*'s gunwales. Cribb, Thorpe and the woman were standing ankle-deep in the water which Sinclair was ordering into the scoops to replenish his stock below. The rain tapered off and stopped. Kitty Brandon took her time folding the barbers' cloth and patted it reasonably flat before handing it back. "The Sixty-second Foot, did you not say, Cribb?"

"Yes, ma'am."

She frowned distantly. "You cannot be aware of the fact, but General Burgoyne himself could scarce hide his emotion when you formed ranks. To march up Bemis Heights that last time."

"No, ma'am?"

She nodded impersonally at both men and waded back to the forbidden territory beyond *Alexander*'s barricade. Thorpe stopped scratching himself and looked baffled instead. "What she mean by all that, Joe?"

Cribb swallowed hard. "Nothing. Nothing you'd know if you lived a 'undred years. Come on, let's pack up and get some grub."

It was Cribb's turn to serve dinner, watched closely by Thorpe and Levi as they hunched around their stolen candle: not one crumb too many fell into any of the three wooden bowls.

" 'Ere's 'ealth," Cribb whispered, toasting his messmates before sipping a vintage blend of Thames water, Teide's runoff and today's cloudburst.

"Down the drain."

"*Mazel tov.*"

Cribb had always taken pride in mastering his belly. This was another skill which had served him well in the dank tunnels of Copper Hill prison camp where hunger had always been a cove's worst enemy; a moment's weakness, the rations vanished, and rumbleguts was back grumbling for more.

He finished dividing the tile of biscuit and settled down to enjoy to-night's episode in the lags' ongoing, imaginary feast. "Know what I'm going to do once I get back 'ome . . . ?"

"Stuff your gob with that there fried sausage, and mash, and blue ruin at that there Saracen's 'Ead thing," Thorpe muttered, bored silly by the other man's unchanging fantasy, month after month.

"Wrong." His mate smiled dreamily, setting the scene in his imagination. "Tonight I reckon it's time we took a trot over to Vauxhall Gardens. I know someone there, someone *very* special. . . ."

"They got good grub?"

"Not bad."

"Not bad? Well, Oi reckon that's not good enough. Oi reckon—"

Cribb sighed. "Mate. You ain't lived till you been to the gardens. They got *more* than just grub. They got all them fountains, with pretty lights, just like fireflies on a swamp. And they got bands playing music, free. And they got ropedancers, the real sort."

"Well, Oi reckon—"

"And that's only for starters," Cribb hissed, warming to his story. "There's jugglers, and fire-eaters, and places you can get your fortune told. You ever 'ad your fortune told?"

"No, Oi—"

"You should," Cribb advised. "I mean, 'ow else is a cove to know what good luck's coming? I've 'ad mine told tons of times. I'm going to croak in a regular bed, like a gent, with a bag of georges under the pillow. I mean, that's good luck, eh?"

"Oi—"

"But the best thing in the gardens, top apple off the tree, is what they call the Pavilion," Cribb went on with another sigh. "Me and a mate went there after we got back from Americky, only *this* time it'll be real good. This time I'm going to talk in as bold as brass and sit right at the front where they got all the music and a big row of lamps to show you what's 'appening."

"Ur?" Thorpe queried, starting to lose himself in this tale from fairy-land.

"Right-o. Look over them lamps and there's this great big curtain thing, with pictures of ladies and ge'men painted on it, in colours. Sort of rude in places, with only a bit of stuff 'ere, and a bunch of flowers there—"

"Gor!"

Cribb grinned. "And there's pies so good the 'ot gravy just drips off a cove's chin. And there's custards. And there's oysters. And—"

"Gor!"

"And then up strikes the band. And the curtain just sort of floats away. And there, right behind, is more pictures, yards 'igh, of palaces and such like, all in colours. But that's still not 'alf the story."

"*Ur?*"

Cribb chuckled, eyes shut as he fondled the memory. "And then the music sort of changes, and there she is!"

" 'Oo is?"

"Mrs. B. . . ."

"What?"

Cribb's chuckle ripened. " 'Er ladyship, in person, she's on tonight. Surprised?"

Levi grimaced as he finished rolling a fresh papirosa. "With your imagination, nothing surprise me. But is better you doing this than all those Turk things to her. Please continue."

"Well, Oi reckon it's time we got more grub," Thorpe grunted, sipping his water ration before he chased another itch.

"Later," Cribb promised, clinging to his memory of Kitty Brandon in flowered muslin skirts, dressed like a shepherdess as she advanced to the theatre footlights for her first number.

"Now, Oi'm 'ungry," Thorpe announced, crushing something between his thumbnails. He looked up again. "Oi reckon the best grub Oi ever et was when Dad and 'is mates bagged a load o' rabbits up at the Grange that Christmas, that's what Oi reckon."

"Rabbits! What's *rabbits* alongside them pies, and sausages, and oysters, and—?"

Thorpe ignored him. He stared into the wavering candle flame. "Dad got back while it were still snowin' so's the squire's men couldn't follow— regular crafty, my old dad. And Mum done them bunnies in the big pot with spuds and stuff and there was a bit o' meat for all us kids and—"

"You dozy bastard!" Cribb snarled as the beloved image faded in his mind's eye. "I've snitched more bloody rabbits than you've 'ad 'ot dinners, and let me tell you, I'd swap the bleeding lot for another squint at 'er ladyship doing 'er stuff on that stage—!"

"What's this I hear?" Levi murmured, leaning forward to suck fire off the candle. He eased back on the shelf, trickling smoke. "You must be feeling better. Soon I shall hear you saying, 'Kiss your hand, Doktor Abe, never I forget what you do for me. . . .' "

"Watch it!"

"Why? Is not true?" Levi queried innocently. He patted a yawn. "But is plenty of time for thanks when we get to Bottommy Town. Will be just like when I get to Bokhara. *Ei!* So many days and nights and days again across that bad land they call Kara Kum, not far from Sabation River I tell you of, remember?"

Cribb wasn't rising to the lure of another yarn from distant parts. Instead, he glowered at his bare toes. "None of you coves deserves a good feed. First it's bloody rabbits, now it's more slogging after them bastard camel things."

"Sure," Levi agreed amiably. "Things got to be bad before they can get good. Is like that for us now, and was for me the same then, but once I got to Bokhara, did I get good grub!"

"Like what?" Cribb sniffed.

"*Kefta,*" Levi replied with a dreamy sigh. "Bits of sheep meat, all chopped with onion and fried. And *tadjin,* bits of sheep with fruit and vegetable in a big pie. And—"

"Oi bet it were never so good as them rabbits," Thorpe interrupted gloomily, still staring into the flame, his shoulders slumped.

"Or seeing 'er ladyship when she gets up and sings, and things."

"Phu!" Levi blew smoke at the roof rafters. "Still you want rabbit when you can get *khali* and *kebabs?* Still you want song when you can get much, much more in Bottommy Town? Tch, tch, tch, you coves don't deserve good luck." Levi studied the tip of his papirosa. "But I understand; once I was the same as you. Then, Bokhara. Like a king I lived in Bokhara. Everything all so green and cool, with figs, and grapes, and lemons, and things I don't know the name, in that garden. . . ."

"Vauxhall's tons better."

Levi shook his head and drew smoke again, eyelids drooping. "Soon we see who's right when we get the other side of Kara Kum and reach Bottommy. Palaces? More than we have fingers to count. Grub? More than we can eat. And girls? *Ei* . . . !"

33

" 'MORNING, MA'AM."

"Good morning, Cribb." Kitty Brandon nodded to both barbers as she came on deck with Sinclair's bucket. Cribb's scissors slowed to a halt as she went for'ard to the ship's heads. Indeed it was a good morning, a very good morning, like yesterday, and the day before. And the one before that.

Every dawn since crossing the equator, *Alexander* had been returning to life, butting through seas streaked with dazzling foam, rolling down the miles to Rio. And now the convoy was riding from another sunrise, running sweetly under main royals and skysails, bowsprits lifting easily and dipping again, like the glossy black dolphins which ran alongside, tumbling and frisking in the bow waves.

Life was worth living again as the sou'easterly trades droned through standing rig and the duty crewmen jumped to their bosuns' whistles. Life was even worthwhile for the lags, most of whom aboard *Alexander* had just found a chunk of shark flesh in their ladle of breakfast burgoo.

Olsen had jagged an eleven-foot mako with his bait the previous evening. Two other men had swung between the starboard cat-head and bowsprit shrouds, up to their waists in the sea while they harpooned the shark and ran a line over the forecourse yardarm to sway it aboard. The holystoners and brass buffers had scattered as a biting, threshing monster skidded toward them. The crew had jeered, then cheered as Olsen massacred the fish with a capstan bar before poking out both eyes with a boat hook and ritually chopping off the fins with a boarding axe, nailing them to the bowsprit for good luck.

Any useable bits of skin which survived Olsen's attack were flayed to make shagreen trinket boxes or corn rasps for the sailors' own leathery feet. That night there had been a banquet in the fo'c'sle mess where Cooky laid on a feast of hot sea pie for his mates—fish, onions, biscuit and water—and the leftovers had been scraped into the galley copper for the lags' morning meal.

Cribb was still burping rich and wonderful flavours for his second, and third, and fourth breakfasts when Kitty Brandon came back with the empty bucket and went below.

The Bulldog had not been on deck for several days. Everyone missed him, lags and crewmen alike, and a book had been opened on the exact day and time he would be splashed over the side. Olsen, *Alexander*'s next in command, now walked his cob round her decks with a spring in his step and a cocky glint in his eye, but Cribb had first checked with Balmain's unofficial shadow before getting too excited. Levi had given an expressive shrug: "I seen better men die, I seen worse live. . . ."

Cribb dipped another wink at Levi as the ship's surgeon and his odd-job man began this morning's rounds by crossing the barricade and climbing down to the great cabin. "Good morning, captain," Balmain announced with a brisk smile, "and how are we feeling today . . . ?"

Kitty Brandon hoped that Sinclair felt better than he looked, propped up on his cot, nightcap crumpled on his balding poll, eyes glazed and dull whenever he opened them. King Neptune's curtains had been drawn back and a stern light opened for ventilation. She had also borrowed the barber's razor at the end of work the previous day and given Sinclair a shave. He still looked terrible.

Balmain gently pressed around his patient's chest, watching the grim face flinch at every stab of pain. "Good, good," he concluded, sitting on the edge of the cot for a moment.

"How is he, doctor?"

Balmain glanced up at the master's woman and smiled professionally. "Well, ma'am, everything appears to be localising as per indication. Unless there are any setbacks, I think we shall soon see him up and about again."

"Thank you."

"No, ma'am, thank *you*," Balmain insisted with sober gallantry. "Indeed, if I may be so bold, Captain Sinclair has been singularly fortunate in the care he receives at your hands. But, as I was saying, I see no reason to change our present course of medication." He stood, head bowed under the cabin roof as Levi passed him the bag. Balmain took out a quart earthenware bottle and refilled a blue vial on the chart table. "*Mist tussis*, ma'am, a sovereign remedy."

He spoke the truth. Malingering sailors and lags might get a number four or two sevens if they dared to report sick, but men of Duncan Sinclair's rank deserved only the most powerful drugs known to medicine: ammonium bromide and belladonna in camphorated oil and sweetened alcohol—in other words, cough mixture.

Levi shut the bag and prepared to follow the leader. Balmain stood and gave the elderly shipmaster a reassuring squeeze on the wrist. "Chin up. You'll soon be as fit as a fiddle again."

Kitty Brandon watched as Levi shut the door behind them, then she turned and stowed the vial on the shelf with Sinclair's sextant case until it was time for another spoonful. She sat down on the cot herself and tried to smile. "I'm sure the doctor's right, Duncan. Now, time for your gruel: remember strength goes in at the mouth. Open wide, there's a good—" She caught the dribble of boiled oats and kindly poked it back. Sinclair mumbled but swallowed, eyes shut, face slack and unfeeling.

She looked up from her workbasket by the stern lights as Levi knocked and entered again, some minutes later. He ducked through the doorway and peered around. "The Dr. Balmain's compliment. Is a little bottle here?"

She shook her head. "I don't think so."

"But you permit me looking?"

"Of course."

Levi began peering under the table and around the darker corners. After a few moments he palmed an empty number three bottle from inside his shirt and stood again with a relieved smile. "Was under the bed!"

She smiled back. "Then I am happy for both of you that it's been found, for 'tis a long walk to the next apothecary's shop."

Levi slowed his short walk back to the door and turned. "Soon we are in Rio and there are *apotheken* on every street. Tell me," he added, perhaps a shade too casually, "when will that be, you think?"

Kitty Brandon pulled a face and laid her sewing aside for the moment, glad of an opportunity to chat with one of the few like minds she had met since that fatal evening in Winchester the previous year. "I cannot say for certain, Mr. Levi, but of one thing I am sure—it can't be soon enough."

Levi sighed. "Is true. Rio, Bottommy Bay, let it be soon. Tell me, was so long a sailing when you go to Americas?"

She considered the question, trying to remember that other convoy to a new beginning, over a decade ago. She smiled sadly. "It probably seemed so at the time, but I am thinking that Botany Bay is much, much further."

The tall, interesting man had moved closer to the cot and was studying Sinclair, head to one side. She frowned slightly. "And now what is it you're looking for?"

Levi glanced up. "I was thinking, on deck he is one man, but down here, he is so different. Is often so, I find. We see someone and think, 'Feh! What a dirty!' Then, later, we think again, 'Hmm, maybe not so bad. . . .' " He shrugged. "So it is with you and Captain Sink Lair, also with me and my mates. On deck Joe and Ben are so hard looking, but down under they are different men. Like them, I think your Bulldog is a good man, one God will listen to."

Kitty Brandon wasn't sure if the hearing would be on earth or at another port of call, but she had to agree with Levi's sincerity. "Well, I'm hoping you're right, for I have found Mr. Sinclair to be a man of some generous impulses and 'twould be a thousand pities if he were to leave us just yet."

Sinclair's eyes flickered as Levi went out and shut the door quietly. "What? Was? That?"

"Only Dr. Balmain's assistant," she reassured him, squeezing his wrist. "He says you'll soon be on the mend, but he has such a comical way of speaking, he's as good as a play. Now, back to sleep."

Indeed, Mr. Levi *had* been as good as many a play. Why, with a bit of coaching he could have earned himself a respectable place in the profession, she judged, making herself comfortable at the workbasket again. But returning for a "lost" bottle? God save us all! Had she not spoken almost exactly the same lines when she revived *A Covent Garden Tragedy* at Bath? After the Fair Kissinda—herself, who else?—returns unexpectedly to find Old Mother Fuddle and Captain Bilkum about to "Seal a deal, a devilish steal, from the Garden's delicious stores, of bullies, bawds, sots, rakes and whores . . ."? But well done, as Mr. Levi had just done it, why, 'twas well done. And finding a laugh aboard this dismal disgrace was surely as hard as finding a guinea in the manager's purse on opening night. So what odds if Mr. Levi was a bloody sheeny? On the boards one soon learns to hobnob with all sorts or go under, and many a good Christian gentle-man has run off with the week's takings, which must prove something. And another matter: Mr. Levi's was the only name which came even within hailing distance of her reputation among England's print sellers and ballad singers. Which was only natural, of course, coming so soon upon the kicking heels of Fagin Zellick and his cutthroat gang, so 'twould be a wonder indeed if the public had let Leafy Levi leap into Eternity with not so much as an adieu and damn you too. And by all accounts, hadn't his trial been a marvel? With dragoons on the streets, and cannon, and all the trimmings? So naturally everyone had talked about him. Though, just as naturally, she would still be talked about long after others had taken Mr. Levi's place in the public's affection, which was only to be expected and reflected no discredit on his performance, just the simple truth, plain and unvarnished. For what was helping a poor girl with a half-crown packet of stuff compared with *her* final appearance at Winchester? Nothing. Indeed, she would be a wealthy woman if she could but collect one shilling from every moll in the land who had found herself out of luck and in the Cherry Club. But giving Boy Hardwicke his comeuppance with a yard o' steel—straight through the giblets!—had that not been an act in a class all of its own? It had. And if she had to quit the English theatre, which must hap-pen to all sooner or later—though later rather than sooner, thank you—then she'd had the satisfaction of quitting at the very top of her form, while her public was shouting "More!" not "Get off!" But concerning Mr. Levi, had he not also got off? Got off a necking charge? And if in-formed rumour were to be credited—which is generally the case—then had he not even got onto Jack Ketch's rumbler, but had got off even be-fore he got on, as it were? Such being the facts of the matter, and all the evidence suggested it was so, then would he not also need rather more than charm and a lot of what the cat licks her arse with, to get off? For, no doubt at all, Mr. Leafy had been booked to do the Newgate hop before a capacity audience, but he had not, which is surely as good as a nod and a wink to the informed? Because when many a good Christian whistles through the sheriff's hempen keyhole and a Mr. Levi does not, what does that say? Surely it says that he was far deeper with the Interest than many another, less provident? And such being the case, what in the name of all the saints was he up to now, playing silly buggers with an empty pill bottle . . . ?

" 'Morning, ma'am."

"Good morning, Cribb."

"Still on the mend, I 'ope?"

"Oh yes, thank you, Mr. Sinclair will soon be as fit as a fiddle."

"That's the ticket: they can't keep a good man down."

"Indeed they can't."

Cribb's scissors clicked along merrily as he watched her go for'ard to the heads: pretty as a crisp fifty-pound note, she was, a regular treat for sore eyes.

So was the increasing number of gulls and frigate birds, soaring against the sun and diving again as the convoy ploughed south, laying almost parallel with the coast of Brazil, forty or so leagues further west.

Every sunset, since drawing abeam off Pernambuco and beginning the long run past Bahia to Cabo Frio, ramparts of cloud had stacked themselves above the jungle-clad coastal ranges, washing out to sea the mud, the branches, the entire trees—many still in leaf with vines trailing—which would slowly roll and broach across the ships' way a few days later. Mary Johnson had stopped borrowing a telescope from *Golden Grove*'s binnacle since one thick raft of vegetation had drifted past, half awash, with a terrified monkey just above the breaking waves. There had been no hope of stopping the ship or turning back for a rescue, she knew, steadying her lens against a ratline as the tiny castaway dwindled into nothingness. "God moves in a mysterious way, His wonders to perform," Richard had reminded her at supper when she'd told him of her feelings. "He plants His footsteps on the sea and rides upon the storm. . . ."

It was now almost time for luncheon some days later, as they sat together in a pleasant patch of shade and the sailors went about their tasks. Richard Johnson was deep in a book, pencil jotting comments in the margins, while Mary tried her hand at finishing a watercolour sketch of *Golden Grove* to include in their letter home when they berthed in Rio, tomorrow or the day after. He paused a moment, smiling at his wife's efforts while she laboured to improve her mind. "You need more blue on that sky, dearest. And your horizon is too close."

She glanced up at her husband, still jiggling the brush around a tin cup to rinse off the last trace of aquamarine. "How is Captain Phillips' book coming along?"

Johnson eased back in the canvas chair to consider her question at length, absentmindedly strumming the pencil across his knuckles, another habit he'd picked up from his tutor at Magdalene College.

While the expeditionary force had still been drifting from the Doldrums, Phillip had taken the opportunity to send over *Sirius'* longboat with a sealed packet and a note asking for a scholar's frank comments on the enclosed journal. Immensely flattered by the request, Johnson had set to work correcting and improving Phillip's terse intelligence reports on the Portuguese colonial empire, ten years earlier. Which meant that, by now, the convoy's Protestant chaplain was better informed about the history, the customs and the religion of Brazil than he would have been before Phillip's tutoring.

The pencil slowed and stopped. "Did you know that *Rio de Janeiro* translates as 'River of January'? Apparently it was discovered in January and they thought it was the mouth of a river."

"Really?" Mary was choosing between burnt umber and raw sienna for *Golden Grove*'s deck. "Isn't it?"

"No." Johnson peered over his wife's shoulder. "That is the wrong brown, dear."

"Why didn't they change the name once they found they'd made a mistake?" she asked, licking the brush to a fine point.

"Oh. Well, apparently they did. For a while it was called *La France Antarctique* by the French—that translates as 'Antarctic France'—when they took it from the Portuguese and used it as a base to collect slaves. But the local Indians, Captain Phillips calls them 'Guanabaras,' were cannibals and ate them all up, the French, that is—"

"Good."

"So the Portuguese took it back and have been ruling there ever since."

Mary frowned hard as the buffeting wind made her hand wobble while she tried dotting some belaying pins into the painting. "Do you think we shall meet any cannibals when we're ashore?"

"I—I really don't know. Captain Phillips doesn't seem to mention them in his observations of life in the Brazils, nowadays."

Mary Johnson considered her handiwork for a moment. "Well, does he say *anything* about Rio, nowadays?"

"Mm!"

She rinsed the brush and rested. "Which money do the shopkeepers prefer us to offer?"

Johnson began searching through his commodore's journal. "Ah, here we are! He says: 'The basic unit of currency is an imaginary copper coin, the *ree,* of which one hundred sixty equal one *vintim,* which should be worth about one shilling in honest money. In addition there are Spanish dollars, ducats and gold johannas which circulate widely. But take care, false coin abounds and its use is punishable by death at the stake.' "

"Oh, dear," Mary sighed, "not another lot of people who go around burning each other. . . ."

34

" 'Morning, ma'am."

"Good morning, Cribb."

"A regular treat to see 'im back on deck again." The barber winked cheerily at Sinclair's hammock as it swung from side to side in the mizzen's shade.

"Indeed it is. A regular treat." Kitty Brandon nodded distantly and continued past the sentries on *Alexander*'s small farmyard, rolling up her sleeves and getting ready to kill the captain's dinner. And hers.

Cribb grinned admiringly: pretty as a——! His scissors jerked, making the man on the keg yelp as another pistol bullet coughed past them both, two yards below the swinging bottle. Either the Bulldog was starting his noonday nip earlier than usual or his cartridges were damp, and either way he deserved seven days stable duties, not fried chicken for dinner, the barber thought, opening his eyes again.

Pig's Breakfast wasn't looking so chipper any more as his cob enforced the rule of silence where a line of off-duty sailors was making cordage opposite a knot of women picking oakum. Luckily it was still a bene day out there, with birds, and fishes, and bits of tree floating past all the time now, and Bottommy Bay just over the hill. Soon there would be no more Bulldog to humour, no more Pig's Breakfast to avoid, no more sailors to chat up. He bent forward over the man on the keg, mouth ajar. "Reckon we'll be in Rio soon . . . ?"

The young sailor nodded slightly, still watching the first mate pace the deck—looking for someone to bash, to take out his disappointment at Sinclair's continued recovery.

"Been there before?"

"Nah."

Cribb straightened suddenly and squinted into the sun: Leafy was onto something hot with Mrs. B. . . .

Levi had been whisking the mildew off Balmain's going-ashore clothes before spending the rest of the morning in the shade, pressing them and sewing the buttons on, over and over again. He looked up as Mrs. Brandon sharply called his name, obediently rolled the surgeon's clothes in a bundle to reserve his place on the deck, and walked past the dozing marine sentries. The master's woman had sat herself on a low bulwark between *Alexander*'s haystore, the empty pigpen and the almost empty chicken coop. "How can I do for you, lady?"

She winked. " 'Tis the devil's own work I'm having to make this confounded bird do what it ought! Stand there a while and hold its legs: I shall try another way!" Her voice dropped back to its normal, pleasant pitch now that she had explained Levi's co-operation to everyone else on deck. "I have been thinking about you, Mr. Levi."

"Thank you." He held the dead bird's claws and made himself comfortable against the tarpaulin windbreaker. "Why?"

"You are an interesting man," she replied, "and interesting men are rare, particularly the way we happen to find ourselves travelling at the moment."

Levi smiled politely. "Thank you."

"We have much in common," she continued, starting to pull out the chicken's pin feathers one by one.

"Is true?"

"Oh, 'tis true enough, and there is never any point in denying the truth with me," she advised, wiping her fingers clean before starting on another feather. "Consider the facts. We are both recent arrivals upon the London scene—in short, we are both damned foreigners—and yet we both score a resounding success in our respective manners."

Levi smiled modestly. "I was not knowing you heard of me."

"Of course," she replied. "Now, let us return to the present moment and consider what I chance to see every morning, when I come on deck."

"What you see?" Levi asked, his dark eyes wide with innocence as yet another feather whipped away downwind.

"Why, I observe that the great majority of men—at sea as well as on land—must slave from dawn to dusk as if the devil himself were at their shoulder, which in a sense he most certainly is. I also notice that we ladies are being kept usefully occupied. But, I see other things as well. . . ."

"No!"

"Yes." Another feather flipped away. "For instance, I see that your Mr. Cribb never, ever lifts anything heavier than a comb and scissors from breakfast to suppertime. I can also see that his shadow, Mr. Thorpe, exerts himself manfully by stirring a mug of soap bubbles. And as if that were not enough, both keep themselves cool and refreshed on even the hottest of days." Kitty Brandon let go with a handful of fluff this time, to prove to any watchers that the captain's dinner was being hurried along. "And I say to myself, for I have no one else with whom I can share this piquant observation, I say: 'Now, *there* go two individuals who've learned the way o' the world. But who could have taught them?'"

"Amazing."

"Isn't it?" She plucked another feather. "So, I begin looking around to see who that mysterious third person could be. But he is not hard to discover once I see him also working so hard at looking busy. And I enquire of this and that other person if he might not be the celebrated Mr. Leafy Levi himself, that same public performer who was on everybody's lips just two seasons ago, and in a flash the mystery is solved."

"Mystery?"

"The mystery of who might represent a certain Interest aboard this floating rat trap."

"Interests?"

"You heard me," she replied, letting another handful of feathers spray downwind. " 'Tis the first law of nature that, wherever and whenever you find more than one man and his shadow, there you will find a leader—and a follower. Aboard this tub, on the streets, in the theatre, someone has to do the shoving—and someone else has to tell him how—or else the whole damn' production falls flat bang on its arse." She paused, smiling. "You are that person vis-à-vis our busy barbers."

"Me!" Levi squirmed with embarrassment as she continued looking straight at him. "I—I am a harmless nothing! I am poor *karabelnik*—Jew pedlar man—what they tell is terrible lies!"

"Rubbish," she contradicted, tweaking breast feathers. "Harmless? You're forgetting I saw the way ye served that knuckle noodle and a sweeter little mill I never saw in all me days. Glory! If only I'd had a thousand on ye to win—!" She stopped short; her tongue was forgetting itself. "As for being poor, I do not doubt that you also know the meaning of the word, but you could not have been so poor when it was your turn to front up for the big prize in Lord Luck's legal lottery."

"Please—!"

"Be quiet, I can't stand here all days peeling this damned fowl; unlike Mr. Balmain's coat buttons, feathers won't stick on again. But, as I was saying, you were certainly not a poor man by the time it became necessary to decline the leading part in a certain dramatic spectacle outside Newgate wall. And if you think to convince me otherwise, kindly recall that you are now speaking with a lady who was also asked if she would take a cart ride to another gallows, in another market place, but who gave up her seat to another less fortunate."

"Please—!"

"However, all that is stale news. Sufficient it is for the moment that I know who's who and what's what."

"*Please.* Listen. I don't know what you hear about me at Winchester, but you are wrong."

"The hell I am."

"Joe, and Ben, and your humble servant too, we are just mates. That is all."

"The hell it is."

"No, word of honour, we are just mates. I don't tell Joe what to do."

"Twaddle. Every man and his brother must tell a bootface soldier what to do: without it the whole damned army would also fall flat on its arse and never get up again. I know."

Levi's mouth twitched, delighted to meet another with the same low opinion of soldiers in general. "Yes, you are right. No, you are wrong. If Joe is such a bootface, *ei!* What an army it must be."

" 'Tis you who are wrong, Mr. Levi." Kitty Brandon began ripping out tail feathers. "I saw what happened to those poor lads when they went into the prison camps and waited, and waited, and waited so many years to be set free again." She looked up. "I also saw them come home. It would have brought tears to the eyes of King George on the back of a copper penny. Boys, men too, hurling turds at them in the streets."

Levi nodded quietly. "I know. Often Joe tell me what it was like."

Kitty Brandon shrugged. "So now you know why a broken soldier will never again amount to anything. Nothing can put the heart back once it's broken. Something dies inside, and though the outside husk may look manly enough, where it counts there is nothing left." She ripped another handful of feathers. "That is why I know someone else had to put him up to that barbering job, though I'll admit he put on a fine enough performance for himself when Captain Sinclair gave him the broomstick ride. Suffice to say, I know that someone must be you, Mr. Levi, for you're the only brain in the whole lot."

He kept silent while she turned the bird over and began twitching off the last patch of down. Then he cleared his throat. "Interesting. I must think. But one thing you are wrong. Joe is no bootface. Ask him about Americas, you'll see. Only two, three times I meet another like him, a bit of gypsy man, a bit of something else, and all were like eagles in the sky. One day, with luck and mates, Joe will be king—"

"I beg your pardon?"

"Is true, word of honour. Joe will be number one in Bottommy."

Kitty Brandon could barely control her irritation as she tore off the last wisp of chicken fluff. "And what of yourself? Which string will you be pulling when King Cribb reigns supreme?"

Levi made a baffled smile. He glanced over one shoulder, then back at her again. "Please? I go. Pig's Breakfast will think I am not working."

" 'Morning, ma'am."

"Good morning, Cribb. A delightful day, to be sure."

He nodded. "And they reckon we'll soon be snug at Rio."

"Yes, that will be pleasant. However, I can't stand here all day while there is work to be done." Kitty Brandon unwrapped a pair of scissors, then raised her voice. "These are Captain Sinclair's and they need sharpening. You have the things to do it?"

"Hmm." Cribb ran a thumbnail along their bright, clean edges. "It'll take us a minute or two."

"Very well, then I shall just have to wait, but don't take long."

"Scissors is tricky things to get just right, ma'am," Cribb cautioned, opening his tool pouch. "Impossible to 'urry scissors," he added, starting to touch up the blades with a small lump of holystone.

Kitty Brandon shaded her eyes and began watching a lone pelican glide between the ship and the forested headland of Cabo Frio. "I've been thinking about you, Cribb. Tell me about yourself."

"Not much to say," Cribb replied, sighting along both blades and making an imaginary correction while Olsen was looking his way.

"But were you not at Saratoga?"

"There must be many 'undred others could say as much." He began whetting the blade with his thumb, to give the impression of work.

She watched the Brazilian *sertão,* a dense mantle of trees and cloud shadow beyond the distant surf. "The Sixty-second Regiment, you said. Whose company?"

"Mr. Travers."

"What as?"

"Scout. Me and a mate come over from the Seventh Fusileers in Canada."

That at least tallied with the facts, as far as she could remember them. "So what did you think of captivity?"

"Not much."

"But surely, after the first few years, it becomes tolerable? Waiting for a war to end?"

"You could be right," Cribb agreed, working on the scissors, "only I never planned to find out."

For the first time she looked his way. "And what do you mean by that, I wonder . . . ?"

He glanced up. "Me and the mate bolted, once we 'eard they wasn't sending us 'ome like they promised."

"What happened then?"

Cribb hesitated. "The Indians got 'im; I got nabbed again."

It was her turn to hesitate. "Then what . . . ?"

Cribb spat on his piece of belt leather and he began sweetening the scissors' cutting edge. "Case of second time lucky: I legged it to New Ork."

"To rejoin the Fusileers?"

"No way!"

"Oh . . . ?"

Cribb's hand slowed and he rested for a moment. "I'd promised myself the next time I 'ad to feed smoke to the Doodle Dandies it would be off the back of an 'orse, like a gent. I'd walked enough."

"They let such as *you* into the cavalry?"

"Why not?"

"Whose regiment then?"

"The Rangers."

Kitty Brandon's head came round as if he'd just slapped her. "Colonel Tarleton's?"

"The same."

A barefaced lie. "That's impossible!"

Cribb's face froze. "Lady, there's nothing I can't do."

"But—!"

"No 'buts' with me, this is Mr. Joe Cribb. Sergeant Major. Two wounds. Seven battle honours. . . ."

She gripped the scissors. "Enough of that!"

" 'Mr. Cribb.' "

The scissors wouldn't budge from his fingers. "Let! Go!"

" 'Please let go, Mr. Cribb.' "

She stamped her foot with rage. "Let go, Mr. Cribb!"

"A regular pleasure. Good morning, ma'am. . . ."

35

"Coffee, sir?"

"Later, Bryant." Phillip was finishing a late luncheon, buffing the plate with a plug of pancake. He stood, still chewing, and slipped into his deck coat while Bryant cleared the table. Hunter was waiting at the binnacle, a stiff breeze riffling the pages of his pilot book. Phillip halted. "How do we go, John?"

"Full and bye, sir."

Phillip nodded, eyes shaded, scanning the last mile or so before *Sirius'* convoy joined the other foreign merchantmen under the guns of Forte São João, Rio's outer anchorage. How effectively this quarantine of non-Portuguese shipping controlled the invisible export of contraband diamonds, gold dust and tobacco he could not even guess; not that it was strictly any concern of his, just for the moment it was enough to be coming home again.

Phillip began pacing the deck as the sun inched behind the forests of Serra da Carioca. Falling away to starboard, the brooding foothills of Niterói: to port, the long, slow, creamy Atlantic combers still burst up the lonely beach of Forte Copacabana: and two points astarboard off the bow, the Sugar Loaf still guarded the gate to Guanabara Bay.

He distanced himself another pace or two from Hunter and Morton at the binnacle, and watched *Sirius'* helmsman watching her wind pennant. His flagship's bosun piped and her topmen began racing each other aloft. Home, again. Home? Why not? The bustling frontier settlement of Rio de Janeiro could so easily have been home, with a wife, and children, and a gentle decay into an honoured old age for Almirante, Dom Arturo Felip.

He drew his telescope as the starboard battery began thumping cautious blanks and *Sirius* came abeam of Forte de Imbui, the other gatepost which guarded the riches of Brazil. He steadied the lens, framing the Portuguese batteries, half-expecting to see roundshot skipping across the waves.

The last time they had replied to one of his salutes, during his command of HMS *Europa* on her way to India, live shell had splashed around the British man o' war. It had been a careless mistake, as much of a mistake as his later scene with the *fidalgo* who had replaced his old patron—Dom Fernando, marquéz de Lavradio—as viceroy of Brazil. Phillip's own temper had been on short fuse after a trying voyage from Portsmouth in the closing stages of the American war. The new viceroy—Dom Luis, Cónde de Vasconcellos e Sousa—had also been ready for a fight that day in the *audiencia.* The result had been predictable. Two short, dark, hook-nosed gamecocks had defended the honour of their respective flags in what was, Phillip realised now, at worst a trifling diplomatic squabble. But, at the time, it had blown up out of all proportion and there had been hard words between the Crown of Britain and the Crown of Portugal over the training of gunners when handling live ammunition. It had been a dismal final curtain over the happy years he had known at Rio. But now the curtain was about to lift again, briefly, and Arthur Phillip sincerely promised himself to watch his tongue with Vasconcellos' successor.

Sirius' port battery was starting to thump burnt powder smoke along her decks as she drew abeam São João on the Sugar Loaf's seaward promontory and her jack broke at the masthead, requesting free pratique. Morton tilted his speaking trumpet. "For'ard there! Ready to sound!"

"Ready aye ready!"

"Heave away!"

Hunter crouched at the bearing compass, one eye shut, squinting between its wires as his command led the way onto the sheltered waters of Botofogo Bay.

"By the mark! One an' twenty!"

The topmen were stepping along their high yards, clewing up the main course and fore t'gallant, showing the other foreign vessels the proper, the only, the Royal Navy way.

"Ten an' eight!"

Hunter straightened as Corcovado's cone transited his bearing. "Helm, Mr. Morton."

"Helm it is, sir!"

The canvas aloft began pounding full-aback as the frigate came up into wind, losing headway over the anchoring ground.

"Let go."

"For'ard there!" the trumpet echoed. "Let go!"

Mallets swung, shackle pins shot free, cables plunged after their anchors into the surging splash. *Sirius'* rigging shuddered and rumbled as she overran, snubbed her bitts and slowed to a halt.

The signal gun banged. Phillip scowled as more flakes of yellow paint sifted across his bunk, then dipped his quill in a bottle of clear liquid and went back to printing the cypher grille—random squares clipped from a current calendar, matching the 1786 card in Rose's cabinet at Cuffnells—hurrying to close the despatch bag and get it aboard a whaler, homeward bound for London.

Phillip blew the paper dry, corked the bottle and pushed back his wire-framed spectacles. He managed to squeeze another cup from the coffeepot and stood to stretch his legs in front of the open stern lights. Now, at last, he could begin to relax and enjoy the spicy fragrance of the forest around the Sugar Loaf, about three cables astern.

Forte São João's granite walls and gun embrasures were all that now remained of Rio's first settlement where a generation of Portuguese convicts had cracked rock and hewn timber to build an empire from the Brazilian wilderness. All else had fallen into ruin over the past two hundred years and the *sertão* had reclaimed its own after the capital had been moved further inland, to a better defensive position against the French corsairs—and after smallpox had run its course through the native tribes.

Phillip sipped coffee and wondered if, in the end, this would be the story of his colony, too: hostile Indians prowling the forests, the French probing his seaward defences, and Ross' marines spoiling for a fight with everyone. The Indians and French he could cope with, given time and goodwill on both sides, but Major Robert Ross and his redcoats were threatening to become a more persistent problem.

There was a sharp rap at the cabin door. Phillip turned. "Come in!"

Hunter bent under the door frame and straightened again. "All merchant skippers assembled as instructed, sir. When will you be ready to receive them?"

"Almost immediately, John. Thank you." The commodore locked away his cyphers and seated himself at the head of the table as his convoy's commanders began filing into the great cabin. Phillip waited for them to make themselves comfortable on whatever came to hand—his sea chest, the two cannon, the folding stools—then nodded impersonally. "Good morning, gentlemen, I shall be brief. First: my congratulations. You have made excellent time and running these past months. However, as we all know from experience, from Rio onward we shall be sailing into less welcoming seas, but that must not prevent us from establishing ourselves at Botany well before the southern winter sets in. Speed, therefore, is of the utmost importance in the success of our plans, speed and hard work. I am allowing you a week, ten days at most, to revictual and be ready for sea again."

Duncan Sinclair was readying himself for a grumble but the rest seemed to be in broad agreement with the implied need to reach Canton before the next monsoon. "Turning now to an equally important matter, gentlemen, we must never forget that Portugal—and this includes Brazil—is our nation's oldest ally. Indeed, for all practical purposes, the Portuguese are now our only allies in the Americas. No effort must be spared to create a positive impression with our hosts, for I can assure you that every move we make will be noted and commented upon in Lisbon and London. Impress this fact upon your men by whatever means you like, and make certain that the devil finds no work for idle hands to do in Rio." Phillip looked more than ever like an angry kestrel. "Any questions?"

"Aye!" Sinclair rumbled, eyes opening for the first time. "Yon lagged trash. Are they to show their face above decks this time, or what . . . ?"

Phillip considered the question. "I see no reason why not, in moderation. Rig boarding nets, double the guard and alert your informants below decks. I think that will suffice. Any further questions? Very well, let speed and urgency be our watchwords for the next week. Good day, gentlemen."

He stood and followed them out, grateful to be free from paperwork, free to enjoy his first morning home. He saluted civilly as each of the masters went over the side and rowed back to their own vessels, also riding snugly at anchor on Botofogo Bay, also surrounded since dawn by bumboats offering the marines and crewmen fruit and mounted butterflies, carved wooden curios and caged monkeys, gaudy parrots and much else.

Phillip smiled indulgently at the cheerful, sunny confusion alongside, and readied himself to begin haggling for a couple of live fowl. He turned, still smiling, as Hunter's shadow fell across the rail. "You're dining with me tonight, John, something very special; chicken in shrimp sauce and—"

Sirius' commander had halted, hat cocked against the sun's warmth, face grim. "Thank you, sir, I only wish I could be as glad to hear Chippy's news."

"Beg pardon?"

"He's been working a gimlet under that new copper sheathing we had put on the bowsprit strakes."

"And?"

"Rotten."

"*Rotten?*"

" 'Like cheese.' "

Phillip began to swear, then pulled himself together. "The man's sure?"

"Absolutely. I've checked it myself. The first decent blow and our forestays rip clean away, the masts tumble, and she'll be under."

"Good God." Phillip was struggling to control his fury. "And those worthless, idle sons of whores in England knew before they sheathed it? They *knew* it would cost our standing tackle and lives—?"

"So it would seem, but fortunately it has cost us neither, yet. If we can dock here a while, Chippy and his mate will oversee the necessary repair work—"

"But that will take weeks!"

"Better weeks here than the rest of forever out there," Hunter contradicted, nodding beyond the Sugar Loaf.

Phillip was beyond coherent speech. The problem would not stop after they'd sawn out a few spongy timbers or stepped a new spar, he knew. The entire bow section would need to be pulled down, framing and knees would have to be sawn, planked anew and caulked to withstand the punishing gales of the next three or four years—five thousand miles from the nearest dockyard, in Java. It would be *Sirius'* one repair that could not be hurried or slapdashed with tar if she was to return home from the Pacific. Phillip felt ill: every additional day at Rio was a day lost in his race against La Pérouse and the unknown southern winter.

He squared shoulders. "Thank you. I shall arrange the necessary clearance and payments. See that our carpenters are ready to work as they have never before worked, once we dock."

"Aye aye, sir." Hunter touched his hatbrim and prepared to turn away, then stopped: a black gundalo with high curved bows and a raked lateen sail was slicing across the green waters, coming from the settlement near Ilha das Cobras.

Phillip said nothing as the small craft luffed under *Sirius'* stern and came alongside on sweeps. The gundalo's coxswain took up a mooring on *Sirius'* boom while a dark-suited official and his secretary climbed aboard the man o' war. Lagging behind them, being prodded up the tumblehome with a boat hook, was one of the mulatto bumboat owners.

The official brusquely doffed his tricorne to the British quarterdeck, then rapped something at his secretary. The younger man bobbed chins and nervously scanned the deck, trying to sort out the clusters of scarlet and navy blue uniforms, hoping to find an officer with more gold lace than the rest. "Ah. By command, the *condestable mayor,* of captain generalcy Brazils, who are you?"

A short, dark, angry man in shirt-sleeves marched forward and halted.

"Eu sou Dom Arturo Felip, contra-almirante de armada reál británnica. Que significa isto?"

The *condestable mayor,* Rio's law officer for crimes not directly handled by the inquisitors of the Holy Office, was visibly taken aback. He bowed slightly, abandoned his secretary's fumbling English, and got straight to the point. Ross, standing alongside Hunter, tried to follow the gist of this conference as two matched men impatiently shrugged and sighed at each other with words like, *"Por ordem de. . . . Severo. . . . Falsificacão. . . ."*

"What the hell is yon' dago trying to pull over us now?"

"Blowed if I know, Bob," Hunter muttered back, "but from the look on the old man's face I'd say we're in for squally weather."

Phillip's foot tapped furiously, "Senhor! If, as you claim, a person under my command has passed false coin, then he will be punished severely. However, first there must be witnesses, there must be evidence!"

The law officer bowed. "Regard my witness! Consider his evidence!"

The unhappy mulatto was nudged forward and began to reply to the *condestable*'s questions in an uneasy monotone: Phillip had the feeling he was seeing a rehearsed performance.

Q. "Tell what happened!"

A. "At the time of two church services earlier than now, I approach the English ship to offer my oranges."

Q. "What happened then?"

A. "A soldier lowers a rope with a large basket, in the bottom of which is this English quarter dollar."

The Brazilian official flourished a newly minted two-shilling piece and showed it to Phillip.

Q. "Did you get any other such coin from an English?"

A. "No."

Q. "Just this one?"

A. "Yes."

Q. "Of this ship?"

A. "Yes."

Q. "What happened?"

A. "On the way up the harbour I count my take. This quarter feels strange. I scratch it with my knife: it is not silver but lead! A poor man, I am cheated, for all my labour I am given this *dinheiro inutil*! I appeal to the authority and beg for justice! They bring me here."

The mulatto squirmed as Phillip began to question him, too. "There are on my ship over thirty soldiers, and you claim that *one* gave you this coin. Even if it were true, how do I find him? Answer!"

"By the stick used under his arm, for a leg."

Phillip stopped short. One of Ross' marines still hobbled around with a crutch after accidentally shooting himself through the leg some months earlier: the wretched bumboat owner's story might not be so easy to sink after all. Phillip glanced past Hunter: "Mr. Ross? The name of that man with the limp?"

Ross considered the question for several moments. "Ex-corporal Stokes. Sir."

"Kindly tell him to step aft."

"Why?"

Phillip's mouth tightened. "There are serious accusations which need to be smoothed over without delay. Have him step aft."

"Serious accusations? By yon jackanapes? Against a *marine*?!"

Phillip was already pale. "Get that damned man aft!"

Ross passed the word. A few minutes elapsed before Marine Stokes hopped into sight and halted in front of his commanding officer to await further orders. Ross took his time issuing them. "The commodore wishes to ask you a question."

"Sir?"

"Answer it."

"Sir!"

Phillip's fingers snapped, making the man face his way. "Have you bought any fruit from anyone today?"

"Er? Sir! Me an' a few mates, that is."

"What sort of fruit?"

"Um. Oranges, mostly, I think. Sir!"

"Did you pay for them?"

"Oh, er, um, I think so. Sir!"

"What with . . . ?"

"Oo, can't remember exactly, it all sort o' 'appened in an 'urry."

Phillip smiled apologetically at the *condestable*. "You must forgive me. The soldier whom you seek has been seriously injured on the field of honour, as you can clearly see, but, as you cannot see, it has affected his mind. Poor fellow, he is to be repatriated to England at the earliest opportunity."

The Portuguese law officer bowed at such sad news. "I am desolated for him and his family, *senhor,* please accept my condolences."

"*Obrigado,*" Phillip murmured.

"However," the other man went on, as if he had never heard the Englishman's thanks, "there still remains the matter of justice for my poor man and his family. . . ."

Phillip nodded with deep understanding of life's many woes. "Yes, your poor man and his family must have justice. However, my poor man is not responsible for his actions, nor has he been for many, many weeks. Yet it is my sincere desire to be fair to everyone."

"*Senhor?*"

Phillip smiled. "In the more enlightened parts of the globe there is always—how shall we say?—a fund which helps those less fortunate. It will be an honour to put in five guineas for this unfortunate man, and another ten for your trouble today—"

The law officer sadly shook his head. "Alas, no."

"Seven, with a clear fifteen for yourself?"

"No."

Phillip's smile was getting strained. "I fail to comprehend your reasoning, *senhor*. This fellow complains to you for lack of a couple of *vintim* in his change, from the nobility of my heart I offer five pieces of gold, and you refuse? Permit me to observe that the value of your currency must have multiplied many times since I had the honour to serve Her Majesty of Portugal in a high appointment!"

The law officer drew himself up to full height. "In matters of national honour, no price is too great to pay for justice and retribution."

"Retribution?"

"Yes. I am empowered by the law to arrest and detain any man for questioning in connexion with *crimem* committed within the jurisdiction of the captaincy general of Rio de Janeiro and—"

"This is absurd. Pray step below to my cabin, where we shall discuss how best to resolve this unfortunate misunderstanding."

"No. It is not permitted. This soldier must return with me and give an account of himself before the authority."

"Eh?" Ross was elbowing between the two smaller men, glowering left and right at both faces.

Phillip silently counted up to five, then opened his eyes and beckoned the marines' commanding officer to step leeward on the quarterdeck, where they could whisper without being overheard. "Mr. Ross, attend me closely and do not interrupt. There is something going on here which I do not understand—"

"I'll bet there is!"

"It would appear that a soldier of ours has passed a dud two-bob bit. I've tried greasing palms but there is far more to this matter than meets the eye—"

"Hn!"

"Rio's master-at-arms refuses to be squared and is insisting on his right of arrest and detention."

"That dago's trying to arrest one o' *my* men?"

"Yes."

"Over my dead body!"

Phillip's patience had worn out. "Let us hope that will not be necessary,

Mr. Ross, but the final decision must be yours. In the meantime I am faced with no practical option but to release the man to the local authorities while seeking an immediate audience with the governor."

"You've the impudence to suggest that one o' *my* men is to be sent ashore wi' yon grinning monkey?!"

Phillip marched back to where the marine stood, nibbling a fingernail. His commodore halted. "Pay attention. In a few minutes you will gather your kit together and go ashore with this Portuguese gentleman, there to answer certain questions concerning the florin you spent this morning to buy fruit."

"Sir?"

"You will deny everything and demand that one of your officers, myself, speak for you. I shall do my utmost to see you are released as soon as possible. However, all will depend upon how honestly you now answer my questions."

"Sir."

"You knew that money was false?"

"Sir."

"Very well. Now my second question: have you any more in your kit?"

Stokes was sweating, eyes darting from side to side. "Yussir."

"How many?"

" 'Bout four or five, sir."

"Where did you get them?"

Stokes gnawed his lip. "A mate o' mine. On *Alexander*. In Tenner Iff. We didn't mean no—"

"His name?"

"Marine 'Odge, sir. Jack 'Odge."

Phillip turned as the marines' commanding officer stepped closer. "Mr. Ross? You will question a Marine Hodge aboard *Alexander* and get to the bottom of this miserable business. Meanwhile, detach a corporal and two men with rations for twenty-four hours to accompany this man and stay with him ashore. Don't argue! I shall be seeing what can be done elsewhere."

Phillip swung back to the Portuguese law officer. "*Senhor*. Because of the tradition of friendship between our two great nations, I accede gladly to your request. The soldier Stokes is now a guest of the Crown of Portugal; as such you will be held responsible in Lisbon for anything which may befall him in Rio."

Phillip clicked fingers at his flag lieutenant. "Mr. King? Sway out the boat. Alert the crew. I see the governor this afternoon. You will accompany me."

"Aye aye, sir!"

* * *

Phillip checked that his Rio de la Plata sword was secure, then backed over *Sirius'* side as pipes shrilled and King made room in the stern sheets below. "When you're ready, Evans."

"Ready aye ready, sir!" The coxswain put up his helm and watched the swelling lug sail draw them away.

Phillip tucked his white gloves inside his coat and composed himself to wait while *Sirius'* gig tacked up Guanabara Bay to the settlement. "D'you remember the last time we made landfall at Rio, in *Europa*?" King nodded, gloomily. "So do I," Phillip continued. "And that scene with the last viceroy, Vasconcellos. A bad business. And now look at the pretty pickle we're in: a flagship that needs docking, and a sea soldier who needs a sound thrashing. Sometimes I'm damned if I know which way to turn, Pip." The commodore fell silent.

The gig downed sail between the fortified arsenal on Ilha das Cobras, and the main settlement, then started a cautious sweep inshore to the Praça do Palácio, Rio's waterfront square, which had once reminded Phillip of Venice. Now it was just a promise of more trouble, he thought, climbing the sea stairs. Fronting his left was the tumbledown Treasury building which still doubled as the municipal gaol and viceregal palace for the richest province in the Portuguese crown. Straight ahead were the ornate bell tower and facade of the Carmelite convent. And, to Phillip's right, the fish wharf.

His nose wrinkled; nothing had changed. He ought to have been exhilarated as he began crossing the square, surrounded by the familiar shouts of negro water sellers and the plod of bullock teams dragging sledgeloads of sugar and hides to the warehouses. A *fidalgo*'s carriage clattered past as he halted at the Treasury gate and returned the captain of the guards' offhand salute. Phillip opened his notecase and took out a card. "You will present this to His Excellency's secretary with my compliments. You will inform him that I require an immediate audience."

The infantry officer toyed with the small piece of pasteboard. Hardly a day passed without some irate foreigner demanding to see the captain general because of this or that imagined grievance: they made a welcome break in the otherwise endless yawn of colonial garrison duties. Less frequent, however, was a foreigner who could put the unmistakeable whipcrack of authority into an accurate burst of Portuguese. To be on the safe side, the guard commander clapped his gaiters together and flicked a finger.

The two Englishmen followed him between sleepy sentries, under an archway and into a bare room which probably doubled as an interrogation cell and occasional lock-up, King thought, reading the stains and splotches around the wall. Two privates wandered behind with a pair of wooden chairs, dropped them on the floor and shuffled away again. Peasants, conscripted for life, shipped beyond the seas, allowed a few coppers a month by the regimental paymaster, neither man had any reason to do more than the barest minimum of anything for anyone.

Phillip sat down and worked each finger into his gloves, then began smoothing their creases up his wrists. King sat opposite, waiting for something, anything to happen. He sniffed. Somewhere, someone was boiling a cauldron of cabbage and salt cod for the troops' and prisoners' dinner. The stench leaked through an open window, overlooking an inner courtyard which ventilated the city gaol and the viceregal palace. Rio's blowflies were just as free with their favours. King whacked another to the floor with his hat as the guard commander marched back with more energy. His boot heels clicked this time. "You were expected, Dom Arturo. . . ."

Phillip stood, sword hilt clenched, and fell into step with the infantryman. They tramped down a colonnade lined with open rooms and cubbyholes, most with a torpid clerk seated between pairs of negroes, rearranging the papers which slept under lumps of brick to prevent the slaves' fans disturbing them. The viceroy's principal secretary was waiting in front of two plain doors. He straightened from his bow. "This way, if you please, *cavalleiros*."

King shared a puzzled look with Phillip as one of the doors swung open and they were ushered into the governor's private cabinet and archive. Phillip caught his breath: Dom Luis, Conde de Vasconcellos e Sousa, still ruled the Brazils.

"Welcome back, Dom Arturo," the *fidalgo* murmured from his writing table. "If my memory serves me right, your aide is the Lieutenant King? I seem to remember you introduced him when last you and I discussed certain aspects of artillery. To what do I owe the honour of your visit today?"

Phillip felt ill. "Your Excellency's memory is, as ever, a model for the rest of us."

"Thank you."

"Indeed, I well recall my old friend and patron, Dom Fernando, informing me how delighted he was to learn that you would be his successor and—"

"Dom Arturo, it is a hot afternoon and I am tired. Shall we get straight to the 'milk in the coconut' as they say?"

"Excellency?"

"Item: unless I am misinformed, one of your soldiers has been arrested for passing false coin. Currently he is lodged in the Forte Santiago, a considerable privilege, he could be in the gaol next door. And now you have come to ask me to free him."

"Your Excellency is, as ever, a man of the greatest perception and clarity of mind," Phillip said.

"True. However, my clarity of mind is one matter, another's alacrity of action is something else." Vasconcellos eased back in his seat. "Dom Arturo, tell me, why do you think that, even if I sign a release for your miserable soldier, it will end as you wish?"

Phillip made a tactful smile. "Your Excellency, a command from you is like a command from Her Majesty, and must be obeyed by all loyal subjects on pain of death."

"Do you really believe that?"

"Of course."

Vasconcellos sighed and shook his head in wonder. "May I hope that, when it is your turn to rule a distant province—which they tell me is the case—your subjects will regard your every word as coming directly from the throne and so above question or doubt?" He smiled quizzically. "Perhaps you English are more docile than we Portuguese; perhaps recent events in your American colonies are only the exception which proves this rule. Unfortunately, for me, things are less tranquil at the moment; call it our Carioca temperament, if you wish.

"I suppose that, when an outsider looks at Brazil, he is dazzled by the chests of diamonds, the bars of gold, the mountains of sugar and tobacco we send home year after year. I suppose he thinks: how fortunate must be the man who rules over such countless wealth! Why, with a single stroke of his pen he can create a million *cruzados* in cash, he can award a plantation of a thousand slaves to each of his friends, he can free one careless English soldier. After all, Her Majesty is God's regent upon earth, and the viceroy is Her Majesty's regent in the Brazils, I am but two paces removed from the Almighty. . . ." Vasconcellos' smile faded. "Such is the theory of our rank and privilege, Dom Arturo. Shall we now consider the practical aspects of our work?"

"As Your Excellency pleases," Phillip murmured, alert to every nuance.

"Item: a royal governor is nothing more than the head bookkeeper for masters who may be two, three, four thousand leagues from his palace. Viewed from Lisbon, whatever happens on this side of the world is of no consequence while the Royal Fifth is regularly paid to whichever banker currently holds our empire in pawn." Vasconcellos sighed quietly. "I see you do not like my image. Very well, I shall rephrase it. Let us say that we royal governors are no better than cowherds who have to feed and water the brutes, keep them alive and obedient by the cheapest means, all the while sending quantities of butter and cream to the owners—whoever and wherever *they* may be."

"Excellency?" Phillip was beginning to wonder if his command of the language was slipping.

"It therefore follows that every day I must balance three conflicting interests," Vasconcellos went on. "First: I must do nothing that will disturb the cow and interrupt her flow of milk. Secondly: I must skim the cream without her noticing. Thirdly: I must ensure that enough remains around the rim of the jug for my own finger to scrape out a portion, or else why ever did I leave my estates at Lourinhã and come to this godforsaken hole?

"So much for the honour, the power and the glory of being a captain general and viceroy, and I wish you better luck of it in Novo Gales do Sul. Who knows? Maybe the English Crown is more lavish than mine and you will not have to share your palace with a gaol, full to overflowing with failed thieves, and a Treasury packed to capacity with more successful robbers. But to continue: you are doubtless asking yourself what any of this has to do with releasing your soldier."

"Yes, I am."

Vasconcellos made a grimace of resignation. "Dom Arturo. When one or another of us finally punishes that stupid fellow, it will *not* be because he could not tell the difference between a piece of lead and a piece of silver. No. It will be because he so quickly blundered into the trap which had been set for us."

"Trap?"

"Correct. You see," the viceroy went on, "ever since a certain nation's thirteen colonies decided they would rather spend their Royal Fifth upon themselves, the rest of us in this hemisphere have been living on a volcano. True, only a few puffs of steam and an occasional whiff of sulphur have escaped so far and, God willing, things will go back to sleep. However, for the moment at least, I sense a spirit of insubordination among our merchant princes. Encouraged by certain powerful interests in Paris, certain leading families have begun questioning the natural order of government. Now, while they content themselves with reading forbidden books and thinking forbidden thoughts, I really could not care less what they do. But when they and their French masters begin digging pits for me to fall into, then I become concerned. I am concerned now."

"Beg pardon?"

Vasconcellos nodded. "I am concerned by the matter of your stupid soldier. Let us consider the facts. The world's richest colony is awash with counterfeit money, some of it shipped in by foreigners, such as yourselves, hoping to smuggle out our sound bullion. The rest, a considerable part, made much nearer home. What can I do? Someone is watering the cow's milk! At times I can see the bottom of the jug when it is filled to the brim! *Deus,* making bricks without straw is nothing compared to making butter without cream! So, naturally, I invoke the severest penalties for the law: in the past two months alone I have condemned twenty-six or -seven men and women to the flames for dealing in base coin, but still more crowd behind, trying their luck. It is all so unpleasant, Dom Arturo, for nobody likes the sight and smell of such things.

"But to continue. At this precise moment, along blunders your booby of a soldier with his putty dollar and gives it to one of our traders. The man loudly demands justice and public retribution instead of the bribe you must surely have offered him to shut his mouth. You notice something strange, perhaps? Meanwhile, your soldier is arrested and must soon face a tribunal. At which point I have but two choices open to me: either free one heretic while continuing to burn good local Christians out there in the Praça, or toss your worthless man on the next bonfire to satisfy local passion, and so bring down the wrath of Heaven upon my head when Lisbon and London hear of it! But what of the French, you say? Simple: whichever card I choose to play, they win the trick. Free the heretic and I give Rio's would-be Lord Washingtons something else to plot about: burn the soldier and I endanger the alliance between our two nations at a time when we need each other more than ever before. Elegant, mm?"

Phillip eventually cleared his throat. "We do seem to have rather a problem, don't we?"

Vasconcellos politely shook his head. "Not so, Dom Arturo. *You* have a problem: I have two. Mine you may forget, just tell me about yours."

Phillip tiredly puffed cheeks. "There are not enough hours in the day for me to do that. Instead, and with Your Excellency's permission, I intend asking your frank advice." Vasconcellos nodded permission for the other man to proceed. "Let us imagine that you had served some modest distinction in the Royal Navy," Phillip went on, fingering his sword "Then, after a few years' absence, you return to London and, on the first day, one of your Portuguese sailors falls foul of the English law. What would be your next step?"

The viceroy smiled. "I am not surprised that my predecessor wanted you to stay in our navy, Dom Arturo. Very well, let me answer by addressing your present problem. First: I would spare no effort to create a favourable impression among my people, to neutralise some of the French influence. It will not be easy. Too many of your countrymen are cold and unfeeling, openly critical of the True Faith and our customs. By contrast, I've always found that the Carioca temperament responds to displays of warmth and emotion. Secondly: I would hope that the local authorities could delay your soldier's case until other novelties had captured the public's imagination and we could arrange for a discreet exchange, early one morning, when even Rio must sleep. Mm?"

Phillip inclined his head. "Your Excellency is too kind."

"Yes." Vasconcellos was losing interest. "The afternoon grows late: is there anything else you wish to ask me?"

"Just one item," Phillip replied warily. "It seems that my flagship needs refitting in some trifling way before she is completely seaworthy."

"And you need her to come up to the Ilha das Cobras?"

"If at all possible, Your Excellency, yes."

Vasconcellos thought. Allowing a foreign man o' war to berth at the very heart of the Portuguese colonial empire was not easily done. On the other hand, with the present drift toward another European crisis, it would do no harm to Portugal's interests in America if a British expeditionary force were seen riding at anchor off the Praça. And it would do no harm if the local revolutionaries were reminded that Her Majesty in Lisbon could mobilise powerful allies in London. . . .

Vasconcellos clicked a finger at his principal secretary, somewhere among the folios of correspondence to dead viceroys. "Memorandum to the superintendent of Royal Dockyards: copy to Lisbon. Authorise Almirante Dom Arturo Felip and his fleet to make all necessary repairs, settled by cash drafts drawn upon the English Treasury."

Phillip went aloft to the twittering of pipes and doffed hat to *Sirius'* quarterdeck. Night was falling fast. "Mr. Hunter!"

"Sir?"

"We are to be tugged to Snake Island on tomorrow's tide. Alert the carpenters to begin the moment we berth. Speed and action."

"Sir."

"And Mr. Ross? Has he yet returned from his tour of inspection aboard *Alexander*?"

"He has."

"Present my compliments: have him step aft to the cabin."

"Sir."

Phillip was still folding away his coat in the coffin-cupboard when someone accidentally kicked open the cabin door. " 'Lo. Sir."

It was probably too late in the day to expect the marines' commanding officer to be cold sober, but surely it was still too early in the evening to find him warmish drunk? Phillip thought, easing into his chair of state behind the chart table. "I observe that you have seen Captain Sinclair's guest. Did you also find an opportunity to mention the matter of false money circulating aboard his ship?"

Ross found himself a chair and dropped into it. "I did."

"And?"

Ross rummaged around his pockets and spilled a handful of musketball florins across the table.

Phillip trapped a couple as they trundled toward the edge. "Anything else?"

"It—seems one o' the lags—made himself a manufactory—for such."

"Don't be absurd, nobody could have made these while we've been at sea."

"And why not?" Ross replied with heavy dignity. "It's no more dif'cult—than casting bullets on a campfire."

"Except that—that *those* items are not supposed to have access to campfires!" Phillip snapped back.

"Hn! Try tellin' that to this 'un."

"I certainly shall! What is his name?"

"George Pascoe."

"Very well, send him aboard for questioning first thing tomorrow morning: this outrage must be stopped!"

"You'll have to fight the fishes first!" Ross hiccuped happily. "The idle sod was chucked over the side, off Teneriffe!"

"Then who else knows, or knew, or has known, or might have known what was happening?"

"What odds?" Ross grunted. "We've got all the coin he ever made. And Sinclair's mice squeaked where the moulds were hid, so there's an end to the matter."

It had been a long, hard day for Phillip, and it was not over yet. His palm slammed the table, making the duds clunk together. "On the contrary, this matter has hardly begun! How many more of your men are going to try their luck and my patience once we let them loose on the bright lights of Rio? And how many more are going to run the risk of becoming a bright light, on top of a bonfire outside the municipal gaol?"

"Uh?"

"You heard! Passing base coin is as much a capital offence in Brazil as it is in Britain! Twenty-odd offenders have already been burned at the stake this month! There is every sort of incentive to add your idiot to the list!"

"O'er my dead body you will!" Ross was lurching upright again. "I-I'll burn the bloody place to the ground before a dago lays a finger on one o' my men! I'll—!"

"You'll do as you're told!" Phillip shouted back, all restraint collapsing under the pressures of command. "The only marines who are going ashore in Rio will be your musicians and a colour party! Beating the retreat! Every evening—!"

36

VASCONCELLOS WAS a man of his word. Two days after Phillip's audience with the viceroy, the British force took up new moorings off Rio's dockyard and HMS *Sirius* warped alongside a pontoon crane to begin a rebuild of her bows.

A floating village of bumboats now jostled around the convoy while faces of all shades of coffee brown jigged and whistled for attention, shook live fowls and dead fish, tossed pineapples and guavas, oranges and limes at the grinning crewmen and guards. Other white faces peered through the draped nets which secured the transports, pale faces, as remote from the cheery scene as the cinder grey ones which stared from cages aboard two Angola brigs, waiting for clearance to discharge their cargoes into the Valongo—Brazil's wholesale slave depot.

Kitty Brandon came on deck again as the sun sank behind forested peaks and cones at the head of Guanabara Bay. The mate's personal woman was hurrying aft to meet her. Kitty Brandon put down the laundry basket and waited. Jane Dundas curtsied and straightened again. "It's as you thought, ma'am. Jill Harper's a good two months gone—"

"Damn."

The other, older woman had been taught to keep her tongue and her place, working in service as a lady's maid until she was found copying her mistress' signature on a promissory note. She waited until Kitty Brandon recovered her composure.

"She *is* certain?"

"Yes, ma'am."

The women's governess breathed out, slowly. "Did I not tell her? Did I not *show* her how to satisfy her duties without, at the same time, getting stuck in the club?"

Jane Dundas folded both hands across her pinafore. "Yes, ma'am."

Kitty Brandon finished scowling at the crewmen as they secured their barque for the night, then looked back at the plain, stolid, reliable maid. "I don't suppose she knows who put her in it?"

"I asked her that, ma'am, and she thinks it was the one they call Jim M'Ginnis."

"*Thinks?* If she were able to think she wouldn't now be making little arms and legs to further complicate our existence!" Kitty Brandon controlled her annoyance. "Thank you for informing me, Jane, I need to know these things. I shall speak with Captain Sinclair and see what can be done to make the best of a bad job. Meanwhile, is there anything else the young ladies require? Are they getting their proper rest periods, as I arranged?"

"Yes, ma'am."

"Good. Tell them that, while we are in port and fresh water is freely available, they must make every effort to use it. It won't harm them. Employed with plenty of soap, it is the universal cure for grime, pimples and sour odours, none of which I tolerate in any company I direct."

"Yes, ma'am."

"For although we may seem to have been abandoned by the world at large, and cast adrift upon a course to God alone knows what destination, experience has taught me that Lord Luck may appear at any moment—and we must be ready to greet him. Clean fingernails, an upright posture and a cheerful countenance are often all that we ladies have to ascend his golden staircase to higher realms. Sometimes, we need nothing more."

"Yes, ma'am."

"Very well, away with you, and see that they understand. I shall be along later to have a word with everyone. We can't afford another mistake, can we?"

"No, ma'am."

Kitty Brandon watched her deputy go for'ard again, then began pinning out Sinclair's shirts in time with the "British Grenadiers," now being played by the marine band. She listened critically. That band was definitely improving, getting better every time it banged and tootled the retreat, marching and countermarching across the town's main square through crowds of clapping Portugees.

She shaded her eyes against the afternoon glare and watched the flash of scarlet and the glitter of steel as an officer swept his sword in salute to the local garrison commander, so close to *Alexander*'s moorings that he would not have been the distance across St. Stephen's Green, had she still been home in Dublin.

Instead, she was penned aboard this floating brothel, struggling to maintain some semblance of sanity in the world of men. Men? She grimaced. God damn them all to fry in hell forever. It was not right, it was not proper. But for the luck of the draw *she* would have been born to wear free-striding breeches, not be hobbled by petticoats, and by God would not the world have known it by now!

At twenty-six, going on twenty-seven, she could easily have been the colonel of her own regiment, for had not her mother's great-grandfather been such a one when he followed King James into French exile at much the same age, after the Boyne? And had he not been struck down at the head of his immortal Brigade d'Irlande as he led it against the English and Dutch armies on the field of Oudenaarde? And had not his last surviving son, the younger James Devlin, been killed in the very moment of glory at the siege of Antwerp, where he had commanded King Louis' infantry division? So what might not his grandchild have become if only his sole daughter—the wilful and dazzling Catherine Marie—had been content to take her chances and marry up in the velvet French aristocracy, instead of down into the threadbare linen Irish? And if only *her* child had been a duke's legitimate son, not a theatrical hack's bastard daughter, 'twas but common sense there would now have been a future marshal of France in the family!

She abandoned Sinclair's laundry with loathing and began bracing her spirits with one of life's necessary daydreams—the image of herself mounted on a thoroughbred, a map rolled in one fist like a baton, a spyglass in the other while she studied the thunder of a cannonade from a hilltop. Around her, aides-de-camp waited for her order to turn loose the cavalry, sweeping across the valley at a gallop, sabres flashing, bugles braying, colours streaming in the wind! Time after time, in the colonies, she could have done it, if only—! If only she had not been a mere woman, little more than a high-class camp follower.

She glared over the washing line at the nearest specimen of those arrogant lords of creation who had kept her in her "proper place," *Alexander*'s tame barber, meekly snipping and snapping his scissors. Fah! Such a sorry object would never understand the depth of her contempt. He was only a bloody-backed mule, a dumb item of equipment to be ordered and counterordered, marched and countermarched, like the sea soldiers ashore at this very moment.

Or was he? What if there was just a mite of truth in his tale? What if he had indeed ridden behind Colonel Tarleton to one of those great victories which had set all London agog just to read of them?

The absurd image of the ship's barber once bestriding a war horse, charging with Tarleton's cavalry as it smashed the Rebels again and again, made her snort. With only half an eye anyone could see that he was as foul-mouthed a little tinker as it had ever been her ill fortune to curse. And so glib with it! "Sergeant major. Two wounds. Seven battle honours." What nonsense!

But was it not said that such lying and idle gypsies often had cunning skills as horse quacks and leeches? So perhaps, just maybe, that was the part he had played? Most likely he had been an ostler or sutler, holding the horses' heads while the true men mounted for action. Then, with the passage of time, he had promoted himself off the ground and safely into the saddle until, in his imagination at least, he really *had* been Banastre Tarleton's senior noncommissioned officer, the lynch pin between the gentlemen with the sword, and the boots with the bayonet. . . .

Much happier now that she had got to the bottom of this irritating puzzle, Kitty Brandon decided to put it to the test without delay. She would expose the shabby fraud for what it was. She took the scissors from her apron pocket and strolled past the sentry as the barber brushed off his last client for the day. "A good afternoon to you, Cribb."

The man glanced round, back to the setting sun, face in shadow. " 'Mr. Cribb,' remember?"

"Oh." She'd been ready to cope with his usual fawning leer, not this curt cut-down. "I see. That's to be the way of it. Very well, *Mister* Cribb, I shall be obliged if you will sharpen these scissors again."

The man flicked a thumbnail along both blades. "Not needed."

She blinked, she scowled, she stamped her foot. "When I wish for a second opinion on the matter to hand, 'Mister Cribb,' I shall ask you for it! Meantime, get back to work and I'll be the one who tells you when to stop!"

The man didn't move. And Kitty Brandon shivered. Then, very quietly, he opened the scissors and began stroking steel. "That's better!" She backed off another pace. "Now, as I recall, when last we spoke, you claimed to have had some experience of Colonel Tarleton?"

"So?"

She folded her arms. "I am curious, that's all. There were so many stories about him at the time, which should one believe now? That he was the greatest battle commander in the king's army? Or that he was a drunken, cruel, lecherous tyrant who should have been hanged? What is your opinion? After all, you claim to have known him. . . ."

Cribb signalled Thorpe to take away their tools and hide them below. He turned again "When we drunk, the colonel drunk. When we et, the colonel et. That was enough."

This was not the answer she had been angling for. She frowned impatiently. "But do they not say he was hot-headed and very quick to anger with his inferiors? Surely, as his sergeant major you'd have known that much . . . ?"

Cribb shrugged, distracted by other things. " 'E was all right. As for what other coves say about 'im, so what? 'E wouldn't 'ave been in this trap for more'n two ticks. Up and off and fifty miles away, that's the way we done things in the Rangers."

This chance opinion would probably have passed unnoticed by any other person aboard *Alexander*, but Cribb had forgotten Levi's opinion of this formidable woman's intellect and insight. Kitty Brandon began to smile. "Is that a fact? What a fascinating man he must've been in the colonies, to be sure. You must've shared many exciting adventures, Mr. Cribb, I'd dearly love to hear more."

Cribb looked back at her from eyes like caves. He returned the scissors. He made sure his sunshade was brailed up for the night—level with the top of the boarding net—and went below.

* * *

Cribb licked his dinner bowl and stowed it under his jacket-pillow. Then he traded half a page of *Cautions Against Swearing* from Levi on the next shelf and began grating tobacco with a rusted nail to make himself a papirosa. Ben Thorpe had borrowed their candle to finish cobbling the one remaining sleeve on his shirt. Cribb rolled the paper tube, tucked in both ends and leaned across to the Suffolk lad, winking as he sucked heat off the flame. Then he eased back, arm under neck, trickling smoke at the foetid darkness. This was the best time of day, grub time. Up and down the hold, busy as dung beetles, other lags were chuckling and chaffing again after Bulldog's rampage for the mint.

Cribb felt mellow. It had been months since he'd treated himself to a decent smoke: normally he reinvested his tobacco in others' habits. Humming off-key, he began beating time with the glowing tip. "Oh, there once was a girl of fame and renown, a ge'man's daughter from out the next town. As she rode by the barracks, this juicy young maid, she stood on 'er coach to see the dragoons on parade." He tugged smoke and held it for the count of five. "Oh, we was all dressed like ge'men's sons, with our bright shiny sabres and our carabine guns, when quick as a flash I—"

"Going somewhere?" Levi murmured, trapping Cribb's wrist while he took a light for himself.

Cribb eyed the other red dot, now only a few inches away. "Why you say that?"

A soft chuckle. "My friend, I say nothing, you telling me everything." The tip glowed hot, then cooled again. "One. All day long you looking happy, except when Mrs. B. is talking with you. *Ei!* For so long it was the other way about. Two. Ben looks unhappy all day and says nothing, but still he is getting that shirt ready for something. Three. Never have I seen you smoke this much *tabak* before. But, I think, it makes less to carry, yes? So, what are you planning this time, Joe?"

Cribb trickled smoke. "I'm off. Ben too."

"No zhit?"

"We're bolting. Are you game to try, this time?"

Levi's tip smouldered to a dull red. He coughed. "So, once more we are back to making like *Kossaken* with waggons in the trees."

"You're not wrong," Cribb replied, taking a hard pull at his papirosa. "I've been talking with the lobsters. They reckon this New 'Olland place is right off the end of the world, and there's nothing there when we get there. They also reckon they've been sent for another go at the Frogs, and that we've been drafted along to dig the trenches. I've done that before, so I'm off now, *toot sweet.*"

"Sure, sure," Levi soothed. "I am hearing that fart talk all the time. But what do they know about what really happening, heh?"

"More than you or me," Cribb replied unemotionally. "I'm off."

"So you keep telling, but how are we getting ashore? Walk on water?"

"It's fixed."

"Fixed . . . ?"

"*Fixed.*"

Levi fell silent and eased back to share Cribb's pillow. He blew a thrifty jet of smoke at the same darkness. "One. Sadly is true this Rio is not yet Bottommy. Why? I not know. Like you, I want to get back to grifting work. Like you, this *chazzerei* is not the perfect living. But, and here our difference is, my friend, I need the right way off. For you, is always burning waggons and riding horse to look the big *macher* with girls. But me? When I ride a wooden rocking horse, it kicks me, like I tell you many times before."

"And like I told you before, it's dead easy once you got the knack," Cribb insisted, also blowing smoke.

"I think not, but we waste time." Levi shrugged. "Do you think because we cannot yet run a *shvindel* we will never grift one in Bottommy? Of course not! Have faith! For how long was Moses in the desert with the People? Thirty, forty years—?"

"You got to be joking!"

"But in the end all was made good again," Levi continued. "So will it be for us, I promise, word of honour. And why? Because all your lobster sea soldiers are not such *feinshmecker* clever dicks! Answer me this: how will a boat sail to the end of the world where there is nothing? It will hit the sky once it gets to the edge, so they are wrong."

"Hmm."

"And as for making another *shlacht* with the Frogs, so what? Let them all go bang their stupid heads together, is no business of you and me what they do. When they finished, we can start with the winners, and sell them the rajah's pocket watch, like we plan." Levi shrugged again. "After the *shlacht* of Braslov I know a man who buy all the soldier bones to whiten bread, and he say to me—"

"I'm sorry you're not game to bolt with us, Abe," Cribb mused. "We'll miss you."

"Did I say that?" Levi asked sharply. "When I go bolt, it will be straight to a featherbed with a full plate on the table every time I want it, not when—pam!—you shot dead some waggon driver!" He stopped short and reached out for Cribb's arm in the darkness. "Look, what's the hurry? Wait a day, wait two, I need time to think."

Cribb's papirosa cooled. "Take all the time you like. Think. Just remember, one morning soon you're going to 'ave to scoff two more issues of swill—Ben's and mine—and it'll be too late to change your mind then."

37

OLSEN HALTED at the barbers' sunshade next morning and jerked his thumb aft. Cribb and Thorpe obeyed, and left the marine bugler to wipe his own face dry as they followed their keeper onto the poop deck, down the hatch and into the great cabin where Sinclair sat among the debris of breakfast. His woman was sponging mildew off his going-ashore suit of nankeen breeches and white cotton shirt. He peered at the two lags, then tilted back in his chair. "The usual." And, as usual, Olsen kept watch from behind while guarding *Alexander*'s arms locker.

Kitty Brandon was also watching, wondering if the older of the barbers would glance her way so that she could ignore him, but Mr. Cribb was proving to be even more infuriating than usual. Yet, plainly, he was getting ready to bolt this latest prison to hold him; every movement, every gesture proclaimed the fact, once his silence was broken, so to speak. Mr. Cribb might fool *Alexander*'s master by poncing around with that wig—damping the horsehair with flour paste before twisting the curlers—but since last night she had known better than anyone else who had mastered whom. And wasn't he a natural-born actor with it? Playing the pint-sized gypsy jockey to perfection. Blazes, had he not taken her in for a while? And wasn't she as fine a judge of human nature as had ever read herself into a part?

She smiled. For the past several months, Bloody Tarleton's right-hand man had been swishing a blade around many a fine throat, and not one of them had suspected the piquant truth of the matter. Why should they? Dressed in those wretched hand-me-downs, Mr. Cribb was just another lump with no past to speak of, and little enough future to look forward to. But what a fine, commanding figure of a man he must've cut on horseback, with the silver shoulder knots of a sergeant major on his forest green tunic. When such as *he* gave the orders there'd be no mistaking the authority in his voice as the cannon roared and the muskets crackled and the king's men cheered and the enemy fled and he was looking at her now—!

She smiled back, but Cribb's face remained a blank, the same two dark eyes calculating, measuring, memorising the stored weapons as Sinclair tugged on his wig again. Olsen jerked his thumb at the open doorway. The barbers packed their tools and meekly followed while Sinclair laced the breeches over his stockings. Then Kitty Brandon gave him the brown tricorne hat with a matching cockade, adding a modern touch to the jumble of styles—some dating back to the reign of Queen Anne—which packed the depths of Sinclair's sea chest. He preened himself in front of the cabin's piece of mirror, then looked at his woman again. "Now, is there anything else ye'll be needing while I'm ashore?"

She was ready with a long shopping list of improvements, including half-gross lots of bone and brass buttons in assorted sizes. He lip-read her uncertain spelling and looked back at her. "What do we need wi' so many fastenings? Did I not buy ye two guineas' worth in Santa Cruz?"

"Indeed you did," she replied. "However, 'tis high time we went through your wardrobe and decided what a gentleman like yourself ought to be seen wearing in public. I have a lot of tailoring ahead of me, for which we shall need more buttons." And more trading tokens for her hardworking young ladies to invest on *Alexander*'s thriving black market where lags, crew and guards haggled over rum, tobacco and special favours.

Sinclair blinked. "And what—may I ask!—is wrong wi' the way I choose to dress myself?"

The man had yet to be born who could outstare Kitty Brandon. "Wrong, captain dear? Why, nothing at all, while you choose to play the simple sailorman upon life's grander stage."

"And what's wrong wi' that?"

"Everything. A sailor? Maybe. But *simple*? By God, nobody ever says that about my men! Deuce take it, 'tis a figure of power and authority you are in the world, or would Mr. Campbell have named you master of this barque?" she demanded, hands on hips. "There's many a fine London gentleman would think himself King Midas in person had *he* been commissioned to bring home eighty thousand pounds' worth of silk and tea!" Her finger silenced Sinclair. "I am shocked, sir, at your lack of proper spirit."

"Aye, well—!"

"And another matter, while we are speaking plainly," Kitty Brandon went on, starting to frown. "You have an able seaman James M'Ginnis on the books at sevenpence a day, less off-reckonings of one penny for clothing, comforts and rations. Halve the difference and his child will be better off by threepence a day."

"*Child?*"

"The one he forced upon one of my young ladies."

"Uh?"

Kitty Brandon's frown was hardening. "Seaman M'Ginnis had his lewd, lustful, drunken way with Miss Jill Harper some two or three months ago. She is my responsibility; he is yours. I am offering him an honourable alternative to marriage which, under the circumstances, would not be easy—or prudent. It seems to me that a deduction of threepence a day, payable to mother and child when they are discharged at Bottommy, and your man will have got off lightly."

"Tuppence!"

"Threepence. Now, away with you, and don't forget to buy everything on my list so that I can make a wardrobe more suitable for a man in your station of life—!"

Alexander's master was shooed from his cabin and up the companionway ladder to the waiting jolly boat. What else he would also bring aboard after dark, Kitty Brandon could only guess at the moment. In time she would learn to the nearest ounce how much contraband gold dust and how many uncut gem stones were being carried on private account for sale in Canton.

She stood by the stern window and listened to the creak of oars as Sinclair's boat hauled away for one of the Angola brigs, commanded by an old colleague in the slave trade and his new contact with Brazil's thriving underground market. Now and for the next several hours she would be her own mistress, free to come and go as she pleased while tidying the master's quarters. Still smiling, she made a start by flicking the crumbs off Sinclair's place by the chart table, then made herself comfortable in the captain's chair.

If there was any better way of travelling to Chinaland, she had yet to hear of it, and once again she had landed on her feet when others had thought she was knocked down for the count. But that was to be expected, for was it not written on her palm that she was destined to become a woman of great power and wealth in a distant land? Sure, nypping shirt buttons aboard this tub might seem a comedown after her previous achievements on the world's stage, but what odds? None at all. For does it matter how far a person might seem to slip, just so long as she is game to get up and rise again? Of course not.

By midmorning Kitty Brandon had draped Sinclair's blankets in the sunlight aloft and had filled a basket with two dozen empties from the darker corners of his cabin. Then she knotted a headscarf to save her complexion from the curse of more freckles, and went on deck to find a buyer for the bottles.

"Hoi! Missee!"

He'd do for starters, one of many bumboats which were cruising around the British convoy, as alert as anyone aboard the ships to strike a bargain. Oranges were, she knew, fetching sixpence the score: the Portugees must have a forest of bushes to produce fruit so cheaply: devil a chance she'd ever had of buying one at Drury Lane for under sixpence the piece.

Keeping her other bottles out of sight, she hoisted one on a piece of marline and tossed it over the side for the mulatto to fish out and price. He held up ten fingers. She tweaked the bottle free and let it dangle, just out of reach. Another ten fingers and the old bottle slowly fell back into the man's grasp.

Now, if one of these was worth twenty oranges, there'd be the equivalent of four hundred and eighty oranges in that basket, or say twelve shillings. Swapped for chewing tobacco and added to the buttons, then put to work by the girls at five percent per week, that made—

"Mizzis Brandon?"

She stopped calculating her profits and turned away from the ship's rail. "Why, if it isn't Mr. Levi himself, come to visit me. And how are you this smiling morn?"

Mr. Levi felt terrible this smiling morn: it had not been possible to sleep with all the problems which now crowded his head. "Thank you, good."

Kitty Brandon finished hauling up a woven palm bag of fruit on the marline and bit one of the oranges in half, then held out both pieces. Levi took the slightly smaller one and watched her wipe her mouth on the back of her wrist. "Delicious! And so cheap. Now, to what do I owe the pleasure of this visit?"

Levi was unsure. Fortunately the orange had given him an opening. He finished his half and smiled back. "Wonderful. Just like they selling in Smyrna. You were in Turk Land, too?" he added innocently.

She shook her head. "I'm afraid you have the advantage over me there, Mr. Levi. Do tell me what it's like."

He shrugged. "Sometimes is good, sometimes is not good. Like they say, with enough gold one can buy a cool drink in hell."

"And without it, go damned hungry in Heaven."

He nodded. "Just between us, now, I wonder if it will be the same in Bottommy Bay? One moment some cove says, big town! Next moment another cove says, little village! And next another says, nothing there! What a mishmash, heh?" He skimmed the orange peel over the side. "Tell me, from what you are hearing the Bull—er—Captain Sink Lair talking, which cove is right, when we get there?"

When *you* get there, Kitty Brandon thought, knowing that her own stay in New Holland would be mercifully brief before she completed her journey to Canton in style and comfort. Too bad they could not take Mr. Levi along with them. He would also land on his feet, no matter where they hit ground. It would have been a pleasure to confabulate with such an unusual man whenever she grew tired of speaking Chinee, but that's life.

She grimaced. "I fear there is little enough on the map after the place they call the Cape, our next stop after this, so I'm told. Indeed, listening to Captain Sinclair and his officers, one is left with the distinct impression that not a living soul has ever seen this bay of which they speak, which further complicates our tale." She sighed. "How they'll sort out the third act before the curtain drops, I cannot say, for 'tis quite beyond me to make rhyme or reason of the plot thus far."

Levi could have wept. Instead, he took the second orange she was holding out for him, and began dropping it from hand to hand. "Nothing? Just this Cape, then Bottommy, is that what you saying?"

"Not I, Mr. Levi, but Captain Sinclair himself. To hear him discuss such matters one would be excused to think that the inmates of Bedlam had broken their chains, pirated a fleet and escaped to the furthermost ends of the world. Speaking of which, and quite beside the point, I am anxious about your friend, Mr. Cribb. He seems—how can I put it?—he seems strangely preoccupied. He is not at all his normal cheerful self. I do hope he is not sickening?"

And Levi glimpsed the opening he had been working for, the one compelling reason which could stop Cribb from galloping off to live the short, the lonely, the unhappy existence of a Cossack robber in Rio when, with help, he could begin to enjoy a full and long life in Bottommy Town.

It was Levi's turn to sigh. "Then you are also seeing how Joe is in such bad trouble?"

"Trouble, Mr. Levi?"

He nodded wearily. "It worries me sick to see such a strong man, such a good man, hurting inside." Levi leaned closer. "Between us, I think something bad happen to him in Americas—"

"*Bad?*"

He nodded again. "At night, I am listening when he sleeping. All the time such weeping! Such swearing! Such shouting about the *shreklich* things what happen at Tzara-Togo. Night after night, always the same. Is terrible."

He stopped. It would only spoil the effect if he tried any harder. Levi had often put bread on his table by reading palms, which is only another way of reading faces, and he could read from this woman's that the gaff was in. One day they would both bless him for today's work, but what else were friends for? Without a matchmaker, how many lucky couples would never have met in the first place? Besides, wasn't it a *mitzvah* to make happiness for others?

"Mr. Levi!" Her voice could be very sharp. "I asked, how long has this matter been troubling him?"

The apprentice marriage broker fell back to earth with a bump. "Long? Oh, for a long time, but it was never so bad as it is now." He glanced over one shoulder at *Alexander*'s waist deck, as if someone just called his name, then looked back at Kitty Brandon. "I talk later, yes? The Dr. Balmain is going to land, he needs to speak with me first. Oh, one more orange, please?" Levi helped himself from the bag and hurried away to help the ship's surgeon prepare to move ashore to lodgings for the duration of their stay in Rio.

Balmain's portmanteau was packed and ready to be swayed over the side when *Alexander*'s boat returned from ferrying Sinclair to the Praça do Palácio. Happily, there were still plenty of busy tasks which the surgeon's odd-job man had saved up for such dangerously slack moments: Levi could never see any point in helping the ship's water carriers, or depriving the bilge scrubbers of a job. His talents lay on a far higher plane, sitting in the shade, counting the ship's stock of pills and repacking their jars. And with any reasonable luck he would still be chalking meaningless tallies on the surgeon's slate when the transport got ready to sail again.

The heartwarming glow from today's *mitzvah* for Joe and Kitty—such lucky names!—had faded by the time he'd displayed Balmain's pharmacy on the piece of sailcloth, arranging the coloured pills in little heaps, rather like the walnut sellers of Bokhara's *suq*. Last night's worries had not vanished. Now they were being joined by the certainty that Bottommy's fabled city was still a long, long way around the huge ocean which encircles this world's big flat dish.

He began rearranging the pills, to prove to everyone that he was indeed very, very busy.

Levi's geography was as well ordered as his salesmanship, and it always hurt him whenever some know-all *feinshmecker* failed to grasp its symmetry and logic. First, in the middle of everywhere, stood Jerusalem: everyone knew that. Next came all the mountains and lakes and deserts and towns and things, protecting the Holy City. Then came the big concentric belt of sea water. And, finally, came the tall sky which held everything together, rather like a huge glass bottle for God to look through. The sun was his lamp and night was his shadow as he walked around, keeping an eye on business inside the bottle. And whenever God wept, which was quite often, it rained.

So why was life getting so complicated? Levi tallied more pills as the first mate's shadow idled past, making for the ship's heads. Nothing made sense any more. Teneriffe? Rio? The Cape? For what purpose was all this blundering about? Surely it was not the start of another forty years in the wilderness? That would be too much! Besides, it was impossible to imagine a Promised Land sufficiently dreadful for all these little tribes of robbers to inherit. No, it had to be something else, something bigger, something deeper. . . .

Levi was remembering a chance remark he'd recently overheard. At the time it had made no sense, but what if the Dr. Balmain had been guessing right for once—or had been let into the secret by Sparrow Legs—when he mentioned that Bottommy was halfway around the world? Not a quarter way, but *half* the way round the big flat plate. And what if even the name told more than it said, Bottom being the opposite of Top? And if—?

Levi's fingers clicked. The facts of the matter were as plain as God's lamp up there in the sky! Consider them. The English, ever with their keen nose for business, were sending this expensive flock of boats to visit a city which had never been seen by a living soul: that was what Mrs. Brandon had said, and she would know from what the Bulldog said, and he would know from what Sparrow Legs said.

Now, if one added what Reb Mordechai had said, there *was* such a city, exactly halfway round the world, the city of gold, and marble, and jewels and green gardens! It was the capital city of the ten lost tribes who were destined to bridge that river of fire and return to glory. Now, what if the cunning milords of London Town also knew that? And what if they had discovered that by sending their boats halfway round the ocean, they must come to the other side, behind Sabation, and sidestep the flames which had stopped every other nation . . . ?

Levi almost hugged himself at the sudden illumination. And it didn't stop there! The next question was as logical as the first: why were the English sending all their expensive ships and soldiers and things? Answer: to make allies with the powerful Red Jews, against the French. But what evidence was there that this was London's secret plan for the world? Answer: Sparrow Legs.

Levi polished a pill bottle as Pig's Breakfast sauntered back, still buckling his belt. So, it was Sparrow Legs—Herr Phillip—who was the vital link in this chain of evidence. Everyone else had missed it, of course, but not he. From the very first moment, when he had dared ask for more green rations, Levi had suspected that the sallow little man in English uniform was far more than he pretended to be: he was Jewish. So what were all the fine, the pink-faced, the big lords of England doing when they sent such a man exactly halfway around the world, if not to be their secret ambassador to those other Jews, the lords magician of hidden powers?

Levi was dizzy at the breathtaking sweep of his discoveries. No other man aboard this *Alexander* could have made them in a thousand years. Not Ben Thorpe, not Joe Cribb, not even Mrs. Brandon. None of them could have uncovered England's secret plan as he had just done. Levi rubbed his hands together. Wait until tonight when he explained it—well, some of it—to Joe! What was running away to rob a village like Rio? *Meshuggeneh!* Soon they would all be living like kings in the greatest, the biggest, the finest, the richest city in the world.

Red Dov ran his fingers through his hair, giving it an extra hard tug for luck. At last, after so many false starts, after so many heartbreaks, he knew where he was going. He was going home, and it felt good.

38

LATE THE previous afternoon, young John Ross had climbed the narrow stairs to the Johnsons' lodgings. He had clicked his heels as the chaplain's wife opened the door. "Major Ross begs leave to present his compliments, ma'am! He will esteem it a singular honour if you will join him on another excursion, to survey Mount Carica!"

Mary Johnson had smiled down at the boy and begun declining his invitation before her husband recovered from his siesta, but the door knock had spoiled that hope. The Reverend Richard had rolled over, a copy of Canon Tovey's *Five Steps to Salvation* had fallen off his face, and he was awake. Still yawning, he had accepted Ross' invitation to ride the next morning.

He had then contradicted his wife's excuses in front of the young boy. After all, this would most likely be the last such expedition they could make in Rio. During the past three weeks, *Sirius'* rotten planking had been cut to the waterline, a new bowsprit stepped and sound timber pegged to her rebuilt frame. The convoy's flagship now needed only a coat of hot pitch to be serviceable for the last half of her voyage into the Pacific, which meant that time had almost run out for everyone to stretch their legs on terra firma. Surely his wife could comprehend something that simple?

Reluctantly, Mary Johnson had gone downstairs and told the mistress of the house in which Captain Phillips had found a room for them that she and her husband would not be home for lunch the following day. It had not been as difficult as it seemed. Mary's common sense had been helped along by the scraps of English which Senhora de Freitas—the widow of a Portuguese naval officer, fallen on hard times—remembered from happier days.

A negro padded into the Johnsons' chamber shortly after first light and put down the usual cups of chocolate. The Reverend Richard had given up looking for marks of hot pincers or the lash whenever the slave served breakfast. Indeed, there had even been moments when he had taken the poor creature to task, and once he had just stopped himself from treating the servant as if he were English, with a sharp box to the ears. But he hadn't. Instead, Johnson had done the sensible, the human, the only thing under the circumstances and adjusted to life in the tropics like a seasoned traveller. But he was still unsure what Mr. Wilberforce would have said to such a moral compromise as he took today's cup and strolled onto the bed-chamber balcony.

Captain Phillips had been very lucky to find this spot for their stay in Rio, Johnson thought, sipping warm chocolate and looking across the street at a patch of farmland behind the walls of a Benedictine monastery. It was Friday; Brother Otto would soon be off to the fish market. Johnson stirred another spoonful of sugar. Within a few days of coming ashore to lodge, he had begun responding to a harmless little game with the limping German monk—seeing who could wave first whenever they saw each other across the street.

A delightful fellow, though a bit of a rough diamond, of course. How or why he came to be in Brazil, Johnson had no idea, but to guess from his peculiar English he might once have served in the king's Hanoverian Legion, or something. But no matter; Brother Otto had more or less adopted the young couple for the duration of their stay in Rio.

He had made it his duty not only to show the Reverend Richard around the monastery buildings, but to lead Mary Johnson over its gardens at every opportunity. By now she knew how to tell when a melon is ripe before picking it—the monk had presented her with a huge packet of seeds to experiment with in New Holland—and how to grow seedlings from orange pips. She had also been taught how to graft the best fruiters onto others' root stocks and how to pollinate pumpkins by hand.

Johnson put down his cup and leaned over the balcony as a string of mules clattered into sight, Ross in the lead, cursing a slave-drawn sledge laden with tobacco barrels, which was slowing his advance. "Good morning, major!"

" 'Morning, sir!" the marine officer shouted back. "Ma'am!"

Mary didn't answer. She left the balcony to finish dressing in the privacy of their chamber. She had grown quite fond of the solemn little John Ross in his grey wig and scarlet tunic. She had even begun to tolerate Captain Campbell's odd ways: it must have been quite upsetting to find oneself the sole survivor after HMS *Galatea* blew up and sank off Trinidad. But, since landing in Brazil, she had learned to loathe Major Ross. And the more he tried ingratiating himself, the more hearty her dislike of the man.

Mary Johnson had returned with blazing headaches from every one of their outings to this or that hilltop around Rio. Had there been just herself and Ross to consider, there would have been high words between them by now, especially over his public behaviour, and the manner in which, over and over again, he boasted about "his" colony!

Her husband's opinion of the man had also changed since their excursion in the Canaries. Now Richard was eager to sit anywhere, any time, while Ross lectured him. There had been several occasions during the past three weeks when Mary Johnson had been most vexed by the way the marine officer had assumed that her husband was one of his followers, one of his men.

She was also extremely irritated by the way that Richard liked to tell and retell Major Ross' wearisome war stories at every opportunity. The attack on Bunker Hill, as experienced by Ross and then imagined by her husband, had led to the first serious quarrel of their married life. And now she was faced with the prospect of spending one of her last days ashore in that dreadful man's company. It was too much for anyone to ask, even for the sake of family peace.

She turned, fingers squeezing her brow. "Dearest?"

"Mm?" Richard was tilting his hat over one eye, getting it at a rakish angle. Her husband had taken to copying Ross in other ways. He now carried his walking cane under one arm, as if reviewing a parade of soldiers. And if he stayed much longer in Rio he might even pluck up enough courage to buy one of those flashy swords which hung in bundles outside every ironmonger's shop in this country. Indeed, he had already played with several on their evening strolls, and had once laughingly tried one on—then quickly put it back when he saw that she was not amused.

"Dearest?" she repeated. "Would you mind if I didn't come out with you today?"

"Not come out?" He had begun to notice her.

"I am feeling fatigued. It must be the heat."

"Oh."

"You're sure you don't mind?"

"No. Of course not. But do take good care of yourself," he added, heading for the door.

His wife stood on the balcony, watching Johnson and Ross exchange manly laughs. Then the chaplain walked down the line of waiting animals until he reached the mount which had been left for him. He stepped astride its wooden saddle and glanced up at the balcony, rather like a boy caught in a neighbour's apple tree. Mary watched the little convoy set off, led by Ross and Campbell, then young John and the mule driver. And then her husband, at the rear.

She turned and trod downstairs to explain why she would now be lunching at home, alone. Senhora de Freitas nodded sympathetically and offered the *ingléza* a sunshade and a slave to carry it, but Mary declined, saying that she would be just going across the road to the monastery garden for a change of scene. For a change of company.

Brother Otto had just finished drilling his latest intake of mulatto novices—showing them the only, the precise, the German way to plant rows of onions—and the young children were hurrying away to their reading lesson. He turned, straw hat on head, hoe gripped to the side, coarse woolen habit tucked around his bare legs. "Ah! Mis' Johnson. Good."

"Good morning," she replied with a warm smile for the older man. "And how are your gardeners doing today?"

The monk grimaced. "Slow. When I their age was, still learning the man to be, hup! First time I learn or with the sandbag and musket I parade all day. But not these youngs. For them is a life of bread and butter. Come. I show you something." He turned on his heel and began marching along one of the paths which divided the garden into equal plots.

He halted, toes gripping the soil. "At home, is the same as growing here?"

Mary Johnson controlled her smile at his invariable catechism. "No, it is not."

"Why?"

"The sun is much stronger."

"Happens next?"

"The plants wither, and die."

"So?"

"We must always remember to shade and water them, every day, without fail."

He nodded, satisfied with her answers. "But what if the plants too high are for shade?"

"I beg pardon?"

It was his turn for a slight smile. "Indian corn, Mis' Johnson, is not onion or potato. Is high. So what you must do in New Holland?"

"I—I don't know. Yet."

"Watch." He turned and pointed at the nearest garden plot, now ankle-deep in old stable straw and rich green shoots. "In America was many, many times we hungry men were. Cold and hungry. Will be the same for you if you not growing corn to eat." He tapped the hoe handle at his side. "*This* more than all guns and such. Now, I show you. . . ."

Mary Johnson was still on her knees beside the monk, weeding and listening, when the Benedictine's abbot and a guest strolled past a nearby grove of citron trees. Arthur Phillip did not see his chaplain's wife as he halted in the cloisters' shade and Fray Raimundo took leave of him.

"*Muito obrigado*, Dom Arturo. As always, your wishes reflect only the greatest nobility of sentiment and delicacy of feeling," the abbot said, tucking an envelope up the sleeve of his robes. "Ten masses for the repose of her soul? And the remainder as bread for the poor? I shall personally see that everything is done as you command."

Phillip returned the bow and continued walking alone toward a part of the grounds behind the monastery chapel where dark cypress trees had been planted during the previous century. The iron gate squealed open, then squealed shut behind him. It always had; and if, against the odds, he lived to return to Rio, its bone-dry hinges would complain the next time as well.

He paused in the shade of the archway. Nothing had changed. The same path of worn quartz pebbles still led around the cemetery's four long walls where the colony's quality were bricked up, six deep, row upon row until the Last Judgment, or until their names died out and others, better connected, needed to rent a space for their coffins. But at least her family was still managing to hold its own, Phillip saw as he began pacing under the trees.

He halted at the end of the path and removed his hat. Then he made room for his posy beside a withered wreath. It was not a good sign. Who else would remember her when he stopped? Some frail aunt might continue burning candles every All Souls' Night until her own light was snuffed out. Then, one day, the masons would smash down this marble slab, and whatever remained of her would be raked onto a cart to make room for another generation of flowers, and candles, and memories.

She would be shovelled into the communal fosse with even less ceremony than he was going to get when diplomacy failed and *Sirius* had to defend Britain's honour against two French men o' war. Outgunned, outclassed, the little frigate would as surely become his final resting place among the silent weeds and corals of Botany Bay.

Phillip was listening to the pulse in his ear, hoping that somehow, somewhere, she was still understanding, still supporting him. He sighed and returned to the present as the gate squealed again.

Mary Johnson stood in the archway, brushing her hands clean and looking around for something. Phillip hoped that, after she'd found it, she would go away and leave him in peace. But she didn't. Instead, she stood there, quietly feeling the echoes of his silence. He waited a moment longer, then removed his hat again. "Your servant, ma'am."

She curtseyed. "Captain."

The formalities completed, he expected that the wife of Ross' latest ally would now scurry away with some new gossip about him. But she didn't. He marvelled at the woman's lack of tact. "You are, perhaps, searching for something?"

"No." She paused. "I saw you pass. I took the liberty of following."

"Oh." Phillip shook out a handkerchief and crumpled it before slowly wiping the sweatband inside his hat. "There is some favour you wish me to grant? Perhaps you and your husband would like more spacious quarters after sampling those of *Golden Grove* and *Alexander*?"

She shook her head. "Thank you, no. Everyone is really most attentive to our needs. We wish for nothing more."

Phillip folded the handkerchief and replaced his hat, tilting it against the sun's heat. "I see. Well, I shall convey your sentiments to Captain Sharp. However, apart from doing that, I am not sure I can be of any further assistance." The confounded woman still would not take a hint. He waited. Then, wearily, "Is there something else troubling you?"

There were many things troubling Mary Johnson after her first eight months of marriage, but she knew that it was not proper to discuss them with anyone. At the moment, more than anything in the world, she needed the secure, the dependable company of a man who did not almost buy a sword, who did not ride the last donkey, who did not echo every hiccup which popped from Ross' mouth. "I—I rather hoped I might ask your advice, captain."

Phillip inclined his head. "Your servant, ma'am."

Reassured, she went on. "You very kindly asked Mrs. de Freitas to look after us, and I thank you for it. However, soon we shall be on our way again and I do not wish to leave her without expressing our gratitude in the style of the country, whatever that may be."

"Ma'am?"

"You see," she continued, "although we have paid her seventeen shillings and ninepence a week for board and lodging, she has given us far more in return."

Phillip frowned: what such a perceptive and sensible woman could ever have seen in Richard Johnson was beyond him to fathom. Then Phillip began to smile for the first time that morning, perhaps for the first time since Marine Stokes' arrest. "I think I understand, ma'am. Openhanded generosity is ever the Carioca way. And now you wish to thank her in the same manner?"

"Yes." Mary Johnson hesitated. "No doubt an extra guinea or so would be most welcome, yet somehow it does not seem the right thing to do." She looked up from the path. "You have much more experience of these people than I. What ought I to do?"

A few moments earlier and he would have suggested that she leave him alone, to let him spend the rest of the morning with his memories; but no longer. She had just presented him with an opportunity to make contact with someone inside Ross' camp, and he would not have to dress up as Herr Doktor Mahler to cross enemy lines.

Phillip beckoned her to a bench under the trees. He shook out his handkerchef again and spread it for her to sit on while he sat at the correct distance. "I am very touched by what you have just said, and very grateful. You see, despite my best endeavours these past weeks—the music, the fireworks, the dinners and so on—there are still many in this beautiful city who think that we English are a stiff and cold race, forever disdainful of others' customs and traditions."

"*No!*"

"I am afraid so," Phillip replied soberly. "And, *entre nous*, I don't altogether blame them."

"I—I beg your pardon?"

Phillip chose to ignore the question. "Just for a moment, ma'am, let us imagine that His Excellency of Brazil were to visit one of our seaports with a fleet of Portuguese ships, and that some of his—how shall we say?—popish crewmen created a nuisance ashore, near some of our public buildings and monuments. What might the average Englishman do and say then, do you think?"

Mary Johnson hesitated again. "I imagine there would be words. The foreigners would not be made welcome."

"Quite so," Phillip agreed. "There would be bad feelings. So what would the Portuguese commander have to do during his stay in England?"

She thought hard. "I cannot say, not being a man or a commander. But surely it would be best if he somehow counteracted the impression, would it not?"

Phillip nodded again. "A most perceptive judgment, ma'am. He would indeed have to counteract the bad impression made by his men, for when we travel abroad we are all ambassadors of our country, and our good name is its good name."

He eased back in the seat and began poking gravel with the tip of his sword scabbard. "Thus it is with me in Rio. Sailors will be sailors the world over. Once ashore they make a beeline for the nearest pot house and are not content till every penny is gone. It is a disagreeable fact of naval life, and most of the locals make some allowance for it. However, it is less easy for them to forgive bad manners when our gentlemen make excursions to points of interest—like hilltops, every one of which is crowned by a church or convent—there to criticise what they have come voluntarily to see. . . ."

Mary Johnson blushed. Five days earlier, outside the Rosário dos Pretos, Major Ross had begun to lecture her husband in a voice even louder than normal, and one of the nearby seminarians had understood English. She would prefer to forget the scene which followed.

"Let us now return to your original question," Phillip went on. "Senhora de Freitas is a lady of good family, one who would rather give than receive. She is also a lady who, while her gallant husband was still alive, would never have entertained the notion of lodging strangers as if her home were a common inn. You are therefore right to think that, when you leave her house for the last time, you must not toss a half crown on the table as a tip: she would lose caste and we would lose a good friend where, God knows, we have few enough."

Phillip was picking his words with greater care, now. "Mrs. Johnson, what I am about to suggest may not meet with your husband's complete approval, for he has often given me his opinions on the subject of popery. However, when in Rio we ought to try and do as the Romans do."

She smiled at his play on words. "And what might that be?"

Phillip glanced back from the niche in the opposite wall. "If you sincerely wish to thank Senhora de Freitas for her kindness, allow me to approach the abbot on your behalf. He will see that a mass is said for all the dead children and grandchildren whom, I know, she will have told you about." His hand stopped the Reverend Johnson's wife from commenting yet. "Oh, I know what you are going to say, that such things are a superstitious blasphemy, and no doubt your husband is right.

"However, let us view matters through the eyes of the lady whom we are trying to please. The guinea or two which I shall donate in your name will be read out before her neighbours next Sunday; you can judge how she will feel about that. But it won't stop there. Your thank-offering will not only buy her a psalm, a candle and a puff of incense; it will also buy some bread for the poor, some clothes for the naked slave, some shelter for the orphan. Thus you will not have been disloyal to your husband or his principles."

Mary Johnson considered the older man's kindly suggestion. Then she looked up. "I can only give you six shillings now, but—"

Phillip stopped her from opening the purse. "Repay me by growing a melon for my table if—correction, when—we eventually settle New Holland." He eased back in the seat. "Brother Otto has been keeping me informed. He says you are a willing pupil: high praise indeed from such a stern drillmaster! And welcome news for me. Ah, if only I had more with your foresight, ma'am."

Phillip returned to tracing patterns in the dust with his scabbard. "You see, our destination may have been called Botany Bay, but I'll wager the hour will come when we would be overjoyed to find a simple cabbage or a humble turnip growing among the many vegetable wonders which Sir Joseph Banks has promised me."

Mary Johnson was frowning. "But surely New Holland lies on about the same line of latitude as, well, Rio? And we have found here such a profusion of fruits and other produce. Is it not reasonable to assume—?"

Phillip's hand stopped her. "Ma'am. Experience has taught me the dangers of ever assuming that anything will be as we hope. New Holland may indeed be a land of milk and honey—not that Mr. Cook mentioned either food in his journals, but then he was only there for one week. I, however, will remain open-minded upon the subject until I can see for myself. Oh, I have also heard what some of our gentlemen are saying about finding plantations of sugar and tobacco awaiting their pleasure, but they seem to overlook the fact that what they've seen here in Rio is the result of two hundred years of toil. Abundance there may be now, but I doubt if it was the case when the first captain general landed over there, by the Sugar Loaf, and began discharging *his* assorted misfits from Lisbon's gaols."

"But—?"

Phillip raised his finger again. "To continue. It must have been many a long year before conditions in Rio even approximated those in Portugal. There must have been many times when the infant colony almost died after attacks by the French, and the Indians, and pestilence, and famine. Yet in the end it survived, and, in time, thrived. Do you know why?"

Mary Johnson considered the question. "They placed their faith in God."

"Ye-es. And they also learned to haul together," Phillip said. "In the end they subordinated their private ambitions to the general good. And then the colony flourished. Tell me, ma'am, was it not the Apostle Matthew who wrote: 'Every city or house divided against itself shall not stand'?"

"Yes."

"Now," Phillip went on, "I do not anticipate we shall ever encounter cannibals as fierce as the Guanabaras were, not do I hope for any disagreement with the French after we arrive at our destination; but I would be less than frank if I did not warn you that our first years could be uncomfortable. It will not always be easy for us in New Holland. There will be grumbling. No, please, allow me to finish. There will be rumours. There will be rumours of rumours. There will be gossip, there will be slander, there will be libel. And, knowing the temper of our gentlemen, not a few will come to blows over trifles."

Phillip wearily shook his head. "However, at such dark moments, all will need to remind themselves that there is room in the colony for only one authority, just as there is place on the quarterdeck for only one captain. Those entrusted with offices of great responsibility—like, for example, a chaplain—will owe it to themselves and their families to support and obey that authority. Never forget, order and counterorder invariably lead to disorder, and, under the circumstances which I describe, *that* leads straight to disaster. You understand?"

"Yes. I do." She hesitated awkwardly. "Brother Otto has told me what happened to his comrades in arms, in the Colonies, after they went into their winter barracks, and how low spirits carried off more soldiers than even hunger and privation. I—I wonder if it could ever come to that, for us, in New Holland?"

Phillip patted her wrist. "Not while we have men of your husband's calibre, ma'am. He is, I know, highly thought of as a scholar by discerning judges of such matters. And for the past several months I have been forming my own opinion of him as a man of honour. You are fortunate to have wed him."

"I—I am?"

"Most certainly. He takes his duties seriously and, I do not doubt, is destined to become one of the mainstays in our infant community, a man of consequence and respect. I am confident that, when he sits upon the Bench as a justice of the peace, he will indeed bring the gift of peace to the often thankless task of doing justice."

"You—you really think so?"

"Yes."

Mary Johnson tried to hide her blush. She looked down at the pathway again. "Not everyone has understood Richard that well. It is never easy to heed God's word among the babble of worldly distractions, and then to obey it."

Phillip smiled kindly. "I do not doubt that his task was made all the easier by his wise choice of a helpmate, ma'am. If a young man is blessed by a loyal and loving wife, why, nothing remains beyond his grasp in the happy years which lay before him. You are both very fortunate. Very fortunate indeed."

Phillip had pushed himself upright. He leaned on his sword for a moment, almost as if it were a walking stick. "Please give my compliments to Mr. Johnson when he returns from his latest excursion with Major Ross. You might even suggest that he consider choosing Matthew twelve, verse twenty-five for his next sermon. Now, if I may be excused," Phillip concluded, raising his hat again, "there are private matters I must consider. Alone."

Mary Johnson curtsied. "Thank you, captain."

"Thank you, ma'am."

39

"AND A VERY good morning to you, Mr. Cribb," Kitty Brandon smiled. The smile cooled. "Mr. Cribb?"

"Oh. 'Morning."

"Indeed," she went on, "as I was saying to myself only a moment ago, what a wondrous fine day it is to be off on our travels again." She had stopped by the barbers' shop to display the new straw hat which Sinclair had bought for her on his last day ashore, but its green silk ribbon and bow were wasted on Cribb; his heart was lost to the hills and peaks of Brazil, slowly falling astern as a gundalo tugged *Alexander* to the Sugar Loaf where *Sirius* was already breasting an Atlantic swell.

It was too late now. There was no way to change his mind now, to go back, to bolt. There'd still been a chance last night, but no longer. Not any more. Too late. He was stuck with Leafy's promises of the mates waiting for them in Bottommy Town. They'd better be prime, and Leafy had better be right.

Kitty Brandon approved of the determination on his face, of the manly frown, what a devil daunter he was! And why not? Was that not always the daringest way? Indeed it was. No nets to climb, every man jack busy with other work, just a hop, step and jump over the side as they passed the Sugar Stick. She sighed, picturing the scene within the next few minutes as Cribb vanished forever into the forests of America, there to pick up his life where he and Colonel Tarleton had left off in Virginia. . . .

A month of easy living in Rio had given her many opportunities to chat with the ship's barber about his dashing victories at Lenew's Ferry and Waxhaws, Catawba Fords and Blackstock Hill, Allemance Creek and Charlottesville. Fine colonial names, ablaze with the stab of gunfire as yelling Rangers spurred to deathless glory behind the swinging sabres of herself and Cribb. And Tarleton too. Not that Mr. Cribb had ever told it that way, of course, being an unexpectedly modest man about his many adventures in the Colonies, but she had filled in the gaps from her own memories and imagination.

Mr. Cribb had turned out to be many unexpected things during their conversations over blunt scissors. For one, he had all the gypsy's quicksilver wit, capping rhymes and riddles with the delicious ease of a born trouper. And for two—unlike the common ruck of tinkers—there was a quality of pride, of power in the way he held himself, even when plaiting some boozy old tar's topknot. In a word, Mr. Cribb was a stimulating change from the woebegone items which otherwise infested *Alexander*, not worth tuppence the lot as dog's meat in a year of hunger.

Too bad he had decided to leave the ship to seek his fortune in a new land, but each to his own; Mr. Cribb would doubtless do very well for himself in the Americas, just as she would in Chinaland. She sighed, determined not to stand in his way when the moment came for him to cast aside his fetters and leap for freedom, his trim body slicing the water like a sword, outpacing the boat they would launch to recapture him. Kitty Brandon approved; it was his style. But how was he going to close the act? Would he turn at the water's edge and shake his fist in defiance? Or would he make one last, sad, sweet, secret salute in her direction before vanishing from her life forever?

Alexander had drawn abeam the Sugar Loaf and was casting off her tug's line while Olsen's whistle sent the topmen aloft at the double. Cribb eyed the granite peak and fortress as it swung within musket range. Not a hope in hell of making it, even if he could ditch the iron darbies. He'd sink like a shot duck unless he could also jump with a plank of wood to paddle himself Romany style—

"Mr. Cribb. The land is starting to recede."

He turned. "What?"

Her frown hardened slightly. "I said, the land is receding. If you have the courage to jump ship, then jump now before 'tis too late."

Cribb steadied his balance as *Alexander* began to roll under increasing sail. "Who? *Me?* Bolt? *Now?*"

"Yes! It's your only chance!"

"*Uh?*"

"Go!" She struck a pose. "Break for liberty!"

Cribb had cocked his head to one side. He smiled uncertainly. "You feeling all right?"

Kitty Brandon stiffened, hurled one of the glares which Lady Lucinda Lively had once reserved for such base cowards, and turned on her heel.

Brazil was low on the horizon by the time the officers' steward brought luncheon from the galley boiler to the Johnsons' wind shelter. Though only a few hours from land, the convoy had picked up a bright northwesterly and was now driving headlong into blue foam for the Cape of Good Hope, four thousand miles across the South Atlantic.

Mary Johnson laid her paintbox aside and rinsed the brush before starting to ladle two bowls of mutton broth from the open bucket. "Are you ready?"

Her husband glanced up from his journal. "Mm? Oh. Yes. Thank you. I am rather peckish." He took the bowl. "For what we are about to receive may the Lord make us truly thankful, amen."

"Amen." Mary broke bread. "I have been thinking about New Holland."

Richard Johnson's spoon stopped, halfway to his mouth. He had learned to interpret that tone of voice: his wife disapproved of something. Or someone. "You have? So, I imagine, has everyone else aboard this ship. However, I am afraid that it is now too late for us to reconsider our choice of parish."

She was not amused. "This is neither the time nor the place for levity. The matter is serious."

"Of course." He finished the spoonful of broth. "Have I ever indicated otherwise, either by word or by deed?"

She frowned. "By word? No. But it is apparent to me that you have not given sufficient thought to what lies before us once we land at Botany Bay."

"I haven't?" Johnson queried drily. "I seem to recall that we have brought two hundred copies of *Faith Abounding,* and—"

She ignored the excuse. "I have been thinking of little else. It is quite plain to me that conditions will not be easy when first we arrive at our destination. There could be difficulties and scarcity, and such things always breed complaints. I do not doubt there will be several gentlemen who will feel that they can manage our colony better than those set in authority over us."

Johnson began to smile indulgently. "Need we concern ourselves with such matters, just yet? Why, I was speaking with Major Ross only yesterday, and he assured me that we still have many months of travelling ahead of us. Come now, sup your broth, it's getting cold."

She put down her spoon. "I do not care for the opinions of Major Ross."

Johnson put down his spoon. "Which is something else you have made abundantly clear. I, however, consider Major Ross to be not only a very experienced officer, but also a future leader of our colony. He is a man whom I highly regard and who, I believe, reciprocates my respect. I must therefore ask you to be more civil when speaking of him in my presence. I do not expect to have to rebuke you again on this matter."

Mary Johnson's face had gone grey. "Is that all?"

"Yes."

"Very well, before I leave, recall that *you* are also a 'future leader,' *if* you trouble to exert yourself!"

"Uh?"

She controlled herself. "I said that, as the sole representative of the church, you are also one of the foremost men in our colony, *if* you avail yourself of the opportunity. Why else does that, that individual persist in seeking out your company if not to detach you from your family's interests before attaching you to his?"

"Major Ross is a loyal—!"

She leaned forward sharply. "Your loyal Mr. Ross is setting himself up in opposition to our colony's governor."

Johnson blinked. "In a manner of speaking he *is* the governor. Isn't he?"

"Not while Captain Phillips remains alive!" she snapped. "Even I can see that! I can also see that, unless you learn to be more careful with whom you mix in public, you will find yourself on the wrong side of a very serious quarrel between Captain Phillips and Mr. Ross. . . ."

Johnson blinked again. Too much foreign travel was starting to disagree with his wife, it was changing her. Then he remembered who was the head of this household. "Enough! You are not to concern yourself with such matters!"

Mary Johnson flicked the crumbs off her lap and stood. "We shall see. My only hope is that your admiration for that insufferable creature has not blinded you to other, far better opportunities for advancement after we reach our destination."

"But—?"

"I am going below. I do not wish to be disturbed. By anyone."

Phillip had hunched over the table by the cabin's windows since early afternoon, buttoned inside his fearnaught, a red woolen cap on his head, trying to bring his accumulated paperwork under control again. A difficult task. The past days of surly weather and half-storms had made it almost impossible to pen a single line on the growing stack of pursers' accounts, quartermasters' lists, gunners' inventories, carpenters' reports, signal duplicates, deck journal entries, letters in, documents out, and all the other memoranda without which no warship of the Royal Navy was operationally at sea.

In theory he could have tossed the lot into his flag lieutenant's lap. In practise, while still only a barefoot able seaman aboard HMS *Buckingham* in the Mediterranean, Phillip had seen what happens to commanders—like the Honourable John Byng—who grow too grand for simple clerk's work. Perhaps, if Byng's daily records and signals had been kept in better order, the admiral would not have been shot by firing squad on his own quarterdeck for failing to beat the French off Minorca. Perhaps not. It no longer mattered. Thirty years after his commander in chief's execution, Arthur Phillip was not about to slip into the same dangerous habits. If anything he would err on the side of caution, fretting over pilfered sailcloth and evaporated rum in case a parliamentary committee of enquiry ever used such trivial details to sharpen its claws for him, too. It could happen so easily. Perhaps it already had?

Worried, Phillip reached for George Rose's private note—written *en clair* in vanishing ink on the back of Billy's latest letter per the Admiralty agent in Rio—and adjusted his spectacles.

My Dear Arthur,

   I would be doing less than my duty if I did not warn you that events are not going well for us. Wherever I turn to view our endeavours, at home and abroad, I am dismayed by the number of obstacles in our path.

   Mr. Pitt, assisted by myself and My Lord Sydney, are hard pressed by His Majesty's disloyal opposition, whipped on from the shadows by His Majesty's heir and successor. Indeed, as I write, I doubt our ability to survive in government another fortnight.

   By the time you read this you may well be serving a new king and a new administration at Westminster, and both are implacably hostile to everything you and I have laboured for so long to bring about. When you are re-called to give an account of yourself in New Holland, do not expect the re-ception you so justly merit. You are, I know, too honourable a man to lick the boots of Messrs. Sheridan and Burgoyne, so be prepared for those same boots to kick you.

All this is in addition to affairs in the Netherlands, which are worsening by the hour. This morning's mail from Harwich brought news of the *stad-houder*'s overthrow and of his wife's imprisonment by the mob. What this will mean I can only conjecture, but the fact that the Princess of Orange is—as you know—sister to His Majesty of Prussia puts the gravest com-plexion on the crisis. We shall have to intervene to restore legitimate rule, and France will have to intervene to safeguard her interests in the Low-lands, and the outcome must be a resumption of the war.

If only I could find some item of good news to send you, but I cannot. The best I can manage at the moment is to wish you good luck and God-speed.

Your afft. friend, Geo. Rose

And that letter had been dated July 1, almost three months ago, Phillip was reminded as he felt around his jacket pocket for a pair of knitted gloves. He tugged them on and began slapping his palms to get the blood moving again.

Although it was still too early in the transit to Africa to be into the Benguela Current, the south Atlantic was earning its reputation for grim sailing, even when the sun shone—which was less and less as day followed day. With every noon sight off the quarterdeck, the sun's disc was dipping further north toward the equator, and with every degree the convoy ploughed south, their daylit hours dwindled down. What they would be into once they were running a further thousand miles south and another eight thousand east, off the capes of Van Dieman's Land, Heaven alone knew.

Someone tapped on the cabin door. Phillip glanced up. "Enter!"

Bryant crouched through. "Beggin' pardon, sir, but will you be wantin' me to light up yet?"

Phillip looked astern at the sullen following seas, then back at his man-servant. "Yes."

Bryant dug last night's stump from the lantern and took a spare candle from his jacket, chipped fire into his tinderbox and lit the fresh wick. "There we are!" He looked down from the yellow glow behind its sooty glass. "Dinner, sir?"

"When Mr. Hunter has completed his rounds."

"Aye aye." Bryant turned and collided with *Sirius*' commander in the doorway. He stood back as Hunter ducked through, hat under one arm, collar pulled up to his ears and tied with a woolen muffler. "Rigged for the night, sir. All snug aloft and alow."

"Thank you, John," Phillip replied, capping his inkwell and starting to lock away the papers until tomorrow morning. "You'll find a bottle and glasses over there."

Hunter unlocked the pipkin, a small naval powder keg which *Sirius'* carpenter had sawn down the middle and then hinged to make a safe stowage. The ship's commander steadied his wrist against her incessant pitching and yawing and managed to tilt two pegs of rich brown Funchal wine before handing one across the table. Then he pulled up his usual chair and sat down to thaw out after a day on deck, worrying over the frigate's bowsprit repair.

So far the Portuguese workmanship was standing up well enough, but there was no way of telling what they had done to save themselves a shilling while Chippy's back was turned. As it was, the former *Berwick's* tired old seams were up to their usual tricks. The crew was steadily wearing out over her pump handles as sea followed sea, pounding her stem and quarters, day after week after month. Even the old man had taken to sleeping under a sheet of tarpaulin as yellow paint peeled off the wall above his cot. Nothing had changed for the better. Nothing ever would, neither the sea nor the slovenly rubbish good men were supposed to work until it killed them.

Hunter swished the brandied liquor between his teeth and swallowed it. Thank God for grog. Without the prospect of a stiff dram at the end of a wet watch, there was twice nothing in the whole world for Jack Tar to live for. Blue Lighters ashore could preach until they were blue in the face about the huge quantities of rum shipped aboard His Majesty's men o' war, but let one of *them* sign up for a lifetime of salt scab and rheumatism and earache and—

"John?" Phillip was speaking again. "I said that I especially wished to speak with you this evening."

Hunter hauled himself back to the present. "Sorry. I was just consigning a pack of landgoing busybodies to a life of living hell."

Phillip's eyes crinkled slightly as he folded his spectacles and put them away. "That's another emotion I am becoming familiar with. However, as I was saying, I am now being troubled by persons rather closer to home."

"Sir?"

Phillip took his wine. "Strictly *entre nous,* I am by no means convinced that Major Ross yet understands the nature of his commission. In a nutshell, he is still granting plantations which do not exist and promising advancements which he will be unable to deliver—even if his fondest dream comes true and the Death Angel calls my name tonight." Phillip drained his wineglass. "Would you have another word with him, please? Whenever I allude to the matter we either raise our voices or I might as well be speaking—if that's the right word—with Captain Campbell."

Hunter remained silent, then nodded. "I'll do my best, sir, though God knows I've tried enough times already."

"I know and I appreciate your efforts," Phillip replied, "but I have been giving this matter a lot of attention. After all, with every passing day we are that much closer to New Holland. It could be unnecessarily difficult for everyone if we arrive and he discovers that Botany Bay is not the El Dorado he's been promising his henchmen. We must clear up this misunderstanding. It is plain to me that, if we persist in divided loyalties, then we shall have a very hard row to hoe once we establish our colony. However, if soldiers and sailors can be taught to haul together as they are meant to, I see no reason why things should not go well."

Hunter raised his glass in salute— "Good luck—" and emptied it.

Phillip gripped the arm of his chair as *Sirius* took another heavy sea. "John? Tell me straight. Do I speak English clearly? Or do I have some impediment of speech, some incomprehensible accent?"

"I beg your pardon?"

Phillip's fingers had not relaxed even though the ship was riding easily again. "I'm serious. I need to know if I am making sense to anyone out there. Whenever I must deal with Major Ross I have this feeling that whatever I tell him is gibberish, but that he is being too polite—or too dense—to mention the matter to my face. Even when I went to all that trouble of buying him ten thousand musket cartridges from the Portuguese, to replace the ones he left behind at Portsmouth, there was not the slightest indication of comprehension or gratitude. It was just the same when I obtained the release of that stupid soldier of his: not a single word of thanks."

Hunter said nothing.

Phillip shrugged. "I understand Captain Campbell's affliction, of course, but what of our Mr. Ross? Short of ordering Chippy to drill a large hole in the man's skull, through which I can then insert a funnel to pour my words into his brainbox, I am quite at my wits' end."

Hunter still said nothing.

"You see, John," Phillip went on, "there can be no question of our expedition succeeding, any more than a cart can hope to be drawn by two horses pulling in opposite directions, while we remain divided into redcoats and bluejackets. Surely *you* can see the logic of that?"

Hunter had taken the two empty glasses and was refilling them at the pipkin. He turned and sat down again. "Surely I can, while I wear a blue jacket myself. But if it were red, all this might appear somewhat different." He hesitated. "I can only promise that I'll do my best to get Bobby to lower his sights. Oh, I know how stubborn he can appear at times, but isn't that the very quality which has raised him to where he is today?"

Phillip took a good pull from his glass and studied the candle's reflection. "Let's hope you succeed. However, and still *entre nous,* I'm starting to wonder if we might not be aiming at the wrong bird in that little flock."

"How do you mean?"

Phillip finished the rest of his wine. "It could be that someone else is stiffening our Mr. Ross in his resolve to become the first nabob of New Holland, the fount of all land grants, slave parcels and positions of power."

"I'm not sure I entirely understand you," Hunter said warily.

"I mean Captain James Campbell," Phillip replied. "There's more between that couple than meets the eye, mark my word. Ross is his nominal superior and commanding officer, yet often I sense that it is the other way around. But, as we all know to our cost, Captain Campbell is mostly 'elsewhere' even when he's supposed to be on duty, so what's his magic?"

"He was on *Galatea.* . . ."

"I don't give a ha'penny damn if he was on Mount Aetna when *that* blew up!" Phillip snapped. "It is irrelevant to the issue under discussion, namely his continued suitability as an officer in this expeditionary force."

"Sir?"

Phillip scowled. "The moment we arrive at the Cape I shall begin proceedings which will return Captain Campbell to England for an honourable discharge from the service. I fancy we shall then see a marked improvement in our dealings with Mr. Ross."

Hunter was saved from having to comment as Bryant elbowed the door open and swayed through with a wooden box, packed with bedding straw to keep the dinner warm and dry on its run from the galley. Phillip reached for his fork as the manservant uncovered a stew made from the last of the Rio chickens. "Delicious!"

"None better," Hunter agreed, also serving himself from the earthenware crock.

"Wine, ge'men?"

The commodore signalled Bryant to draw the claret's cork and then to leave them alone. The door shut. Phillip topped up Hunter's glass too. "Now, where were we?"

"You were about to heave Jimmy Campbell over the side," the other man replied, gnawing a leg bone.

"Not exactly heave," Phillip corrected. "It just seems logical to me that, after some thirty-odd years in the service, and so obviously disabled, that it's high time he called it a day and retired to enjoy the fruits of leisure."

Hunter nearly asked, "What fruits? What leisure?" but thought better of it. Instead, he sat back and wiped his mouth. "Describe it how you like, sir, the result will be much the same for him: three bob a day, six months in arrears. He won't like it."

"John, none of us *like* it, but such are the facts of life. Sooner or later the time must come for everyone to be put out to pasture. The only marvel is that Captain Campbell has contrived to stay in harness for rather longer than most. I'm sorry for him, of course, but someone in authority has to bite the bullet and muster him off the payroll before we're stuck with his peculiar company for another four or five years. He'd never last the distance in New Holland. It's a kindness really," Phillip went on, spooning gravy over his ration biscuits. "Can you imagine the poor old chap having to campaign against the French and Indians under the sort of conditions we'll be encountering?"

Hunter considered the question, then replied with one of his own. "And can you imagine how your action is going to be viewed in London, sir?"

"What on earth has *that* got to do with it?"

"Everything." Hunter helped himself to a boiled onion. "You'd better consider Mr. Contractor Campbell's lively displeasure."

"Surely they're not kinsmen?"

Hunter nodded.

"You're not *serious* . . . ?"

Hunter nodded again.

"Oh. I see. It's one of those arrangements."

"Yes."

Phillip reached for his glass. "Then let us hope that the change of climate revitalises our Mr. Campbell: someone has to get lucky, sooner or later." He began pouring a refill. "So far all the cards seem to be running Major Ross' way, don't they? First he gets his war, now he gets his crony back. Happy days," Phillip added, emptying the glass with a flourish.

"War?"

"Yes. Major Ross enjoys wars: he told me so himself; it's another thing we fail to agree upon." Phillip had begun rolling the drawn cork between his palms. "I imagine he'll get his fill of battles before the next truce is signed."

Hunter had leaned forward. "Since when have we commenced hostilities with anyone?"

"Since about two and a half months ago, I'd say," Phillip replied, looking up from the cork. "It was something else I intended discussing with you tonight. The Dutch business has boiled over, there's every likelihood we'll be made unwelcome at the Cape."

"How?"

"Apparently the republicans in The Hague have arrested their king and queen; it's in those cyphers from George Rose." Phillip flicked the cork at his locked desk. "Parliament has voted another million off the tea revenue, we've mobilised the fleet, and the duke of Brunswick is about to lead the Prussian army into Holland to put his sister-in-law's husband back on the throne. In a word, my friend, the Continental fat is well and truly in the global fire, again."

"And what of the French position?"

Phillip grimaced. "They've been working for this opportunity since Yorktown; they'll have jumped at it. The Rhine ports are theirs for the taking, a counterblockade on the Channel which frees them to support the Dutch garrisons at the Cape and the Malacca Straits. We've been put in check."

"Good God."

"I hope you're right, for we're going to need all the divine help we can muster," Phillip replied, reaching out to cut a fresh slice of cheese. "However, it is no part of my brief to fret over grand strategy, not while I have enough troubles closer to hand."

"Sir?"

Phillip nodded. "Long before we clear for action against M. de La Pérouse in the Pacific, we'll have had to give the slip to his fellow countrymen off the Cape. The next week or so could prove interesting, so we'd better start planning our response now. . . ."

40

IT WAS THORPE'S turn to serve dinner. He knelt on Levi's shelf, doling out the spoons of skilly into three wooden bowls as *Alexander* rumbled and groaned through the night. There had been no barbers' work and no tips since a week after Rio. Now the three men were on official rations—less the purser's thumb on his scales, less the cook's perks, less Sinclair's percentage, less Olsen's cut, less spoilage, spillage and theft.

"*Mazel tov.*"

" 'Appy days."

"Huh."

And dinner was over.

Cribb finished licking his bowl, then stretched out on the shelf: it was his turn to lie in the middle and be kept warm by the other two men.

"What about Americky, Joe?" Thorpe whispered from his side of the bed, in the mood for another story about the hams, and corn bread, and cream, and eggs, and peach brandy, and cider and beer which Tarleton's Rangers had gorged on during the sack of Mr. Jefferson's palace in Virginia.

But Cribb was more concerned with the future. He tugged the blanket up to his chin and glanced at Levi instead. "You sure there's really all that stuff? In Bottommy?"

Levi wriggled closer to save warmth. "Sure I'm sure. Wait. Soon you will see what Reb Mordechai promise is true. Right?"

" 'Ow much bloody longer we got to wait?" Cribb grumbled, trying to get himself comfortable on the rotten haybag.

"Who knows?" Levi shrugged in the darkness. "Perhaps tomorrow? Perhaps day after?"

"And per'aps never."

"Is not the way, Joe," Levi cautioned. "You got to believe."

"First I got to eat and get warm," Cribb muttered.

"All that coming, believe me," Levi insisted.

"I did. In Rio. When I could've bolted. Like a mug I didn't. 'Rivers o' fire'? Horseshit."

"Joe, you are wrong!"

"Is that a fact?" Cribb had given up trying to half-inch some of Thorpe's space for himself. He rolled over to face the other man's breath. "Well, let me tell you something, mate. If I'm wrong, you'd better be bloody right!"

Levi was about to accept the invitation to a fresh row, but someone else was trying to interrupt the family squabble. "Phoss!" an urgent little voice whispered from the other side of darkness. "It's me! Sly!"

"Piss off."

"Shhh! Not so loud!" Slyboots pleaded. "We need a word with you!"

" 'We'?"

"Crystal's 'ere as well."

Cribb ignored Thorpe's grumbling and eased back to the other shoulder again. "Why?"

"Shh! 'Op down, there's a mate."

" 'Mate,' eh?"

"*Phoss!*" a second whisper pleaded. "We got to talk with you!"

Cribb considered their proposition, balancing it against the loss of warmth on his share of the bedding. "All right. But one foot wrong and I'll bash you."

"Cross my 'eart an' 'ope to die," Slyboots promised fervently.

"And I'd bet on that."

Cribb climbed over Levi and swung off the shelf. The three shapes eased forward to a patch of neutral territory near the main grating, as far from others' ears as they could get, then hunkered down, faces touching.

"It's like this," Slyboots began. "There's something 'appening what we don't like."

"Lucky you. There's lots o' things 'appen I don't like. What makes yours so special?"

Sly bit his lip. "Phoss, this is no joke. Dipper's up to 'is neck in some lurk with Matty Zennor's crew, an' we being dragged into it!"

Cribb said nothing. From their first day together on the Thames, as *Retribution*'s hard cases were herded aboard the transport at gunpoint, Mathew Zennor and his handful of Cornishmen had seized one corner of the hold and dared everyone else to overthrow their claim. It had been the one challenge to his authority—until Kitty Brandon's entrance—which Cribb had declined.

These men were all who remained of the fishers and tin miners who had stormed Penzance Custom House with their own artillery to liberate the ten thousand gallons of French brandy captured by King George's excise officers. The tin miners had then rolled fuzed kegs of blasting powder into the fortress and blown it to rubble on top of the Preventative Service garrison.

Wild men, even by the standards of a county which thrived on free trade and wrecking, they had been captured only after the Royal Navy put a battalion of troops ashore with orders to crush Cornwall's resistance to the rest of the United Kingdom. Those who escaped an immediate bayonet, or a later stretch of rope at Bodmin Assizes, had been taken in chains to English gaols to await transportation beyond the seas for life.

Cribb had begun to smile in the darkness. "Poor ol' Dipper. . . ."

"Yeah, we reckon," Crystal hurried to agree. "And some o' us don't like it."

"I don't suppose you do," Cribb murmured. "So what 'appens next?"

Sly left his lip alone. "They saying as what they going to nick the ship."

"They're going to *what*?!"

"Shh! Not so loud!"

"They're going to what?" Cribb repeated.

"Nick the ship. Then croak Bulldog an' Pig's Breakfast. Then sail 'ome after we nabbed some boats to get the treasure."

Cribb said nothing.

"Er, Phoss?" Crystal prompted timidly. "What you reckon we ought to do?"

Cribb took his time. "When's all this supposed to 'appen?"

"Soon."

" 'Ow soon?"

"Soon soon."

Cribb shook his head. "Muzzle toff."

"Wha's that?"

"Good luck. The sort you're going to need in cartloads once Mad Matt tries on a caper this big. Still, thanks for the nod; I'll know when to keep small."

"Phoss, listen! Bygones is bygones, we coves need your 'elp!"

"That a fact? All right. Let's say you some'ow stoush the guards. Then you grab the gun and croak Bulldog. What next?"

"Well, Matty's got all these coves what reckon they know about ships and things. And the crew's so pissed off with Bulldog they'll work the boat for just 'alf the treasure and a free trip 'ome with us."

"They'll *what?*"

"Shh! The crew's in it. It's fixed."

Cribb's breath trickled away. This was no longer an impulsive daydream by confused and hungry men. Dipper and Zennor, Sly and Crystal Prig were marching in lockstep toward a drumhead court-martial and firing squad, whether they knew it or not. This was mutiny.

"Fixed, eh?"

"Yeah, fixed."

"Not doing things by 'alf measures, are we? All right, question number two. Is this your idea, or did Dip send you across to deal me in?" The two shapes wriggled uncomfortably on their heels. "So you've switched sides again. Why?"

Sly stopped squirming and inched closer. "Look, mate, remember what you always used to nag us about? About thinkin' ahead before we moved? Well, me and Crystal an' a few others, we sort o' been thinkin' ahead."

"Don't strain yourselfs."

"Phoss, *listen!* We been thinkin' real 'ard. An' what we been thinkin' is Dip's all right in 'is way, an' Matty's not so bad once you get to know 'im better, but sometimes they both sort o' need someone like you to get their brains straight. Right?"

Cribb stood. "Muzzle toff."

"Phoss—!"

"Who be that, Joe?" Thorpe mumbled as Cribb climbed into bed again.

"Just a couple of mice puffing themselves up as rats," Cribb replied as he dragged the blanket over his head, suddenly much warmer and at peace with the world. The would-be mutineers evidently didn't suspect that Cooky's two little helpers might be earning their right to lick the spoon clean, but then Dipper had never had to survive a New England winter inside a prison camp. Cribb smiled at the darkness. If the mutiny went off right, then he'd have been wrong about Bulldog having weasels below decks, and Dipper would have to be given the shove by other means. But if he was right, then Dipper's reign was about to end even more abruptly than it had begun.

The family's sentry crouched away from *Alexander*'s timbers and winked: the cook's paddle was starting to thump against the copper boiler as it stirred breakfast in the galley overhead. Dipper winked at the Cornish corner: a minute or two longer and their food buckets would start passing up and down the ladder, no different from any other morning of the past nine or ten months since embarking at Blackwall Reach. But today was going to be different.

Today was different. The hatchway crashed open and Sergeant Ramsbottom tumbled over the combing in battle order, followed by six privates with drawn boarding cutlasses. Olsen slid down behind them with his keys. The gate heaved open and the marines stormed past, booting and cuffing, straight up the aisle.

A sudden, stunned silence. Someone was darkening the hatchway, tramping down rung by rung into the hold. Sinclair's cloak sparkled with melting sleet as he stepped off the ladder and paced through the open gate. "Are these the items, Mr. Olsen?"

"Yoh!"

The shipmaster inspected Dipper and Zennor, now gripped between guards. "And what do they call ye?"

"Ma'ew Zenn'r," the tin miner answered without a blink of fear.

"Uh huh. English?"

The Cornishman spat.

Sinclair wiped his face dry and glanced at the next item on his spies' list. "Name?"

"Sam Spillet, your honourship, but my mates always calls me Dipper."

Sinclair began to smile. "English?"

"Er, yussir. London Town."

The smile ripened. "That must make ye a very happy man." Sinclair loosened the brass throat chain and slipped his cloak for Sergeant Ramsbottom to catch. "London's a very agreeable city to reside in, Mr. Spillet."

"Um. Yussir."

"So agreeable that ye would rather *Alexander* now put about and sailed back?"

Dipper began to look unwell.

"Come, Mr. Spillet! At least have the courage of your convictions—in your case penal servitude for life—and speak up like a man!"

Dipper began to faint. The master's fingers revived him, gripping one ear, almost ripping it off. "Mr. Spillet. I am not in the habit o' speaking wi' myself. Now, do I have the honour to address the upstanding hero who is about to replace me in command o' *Alexander* before sailing home to the delights o' London?"

"Ahh!"

"It is hardly an original notion, Mr. Spillet, but every attempt at mutiny must be judged on its individual merits, ye agree?" The fingers ripped again. "Ye agree, Mr. Spillet?"

"Ahh!"

"However, a man o' your experience must understand how curious I am to learn the method by which ye propose murdering me. . . ."

"Eeee!"

"Come Mr. Spillet, ye'll have no need o' a silly old buffer like me to annoy ye once everyone's set up as bold, brave buccaneers! Of course ye'll have to murder me. Mr. Olsen too, and doubtless a few others. So, what's it to be? A dirk between the shoulders?"

"Guv! Pleeeease!"

"No? Well, unless ye plan to tickle me to death wi' a feather duster, ye'll have no alternative but to use these." Sinclair pulled the pistols from his belt. He clicked the hammers to full-cock. "This has been your lucky day, Mr. Spillet: I'm about to give ye a fine pair o' loaded weapons to do wi' as ye wish."

"No!"

"Hands out—"

Olsen snatched each wrist.

Sinclair took aim and tugged the triggers, snapping hammer flints across both thumbnails—

Cribb winced at the back of the crowd of staring lags. He'd interrogated spies and turncoats in America: he'd seen what happened once thumbs were crushed by musket locks. And Dipper had just copped a double dose.

Alexander's master shook his head as the lag panted and mewed against the two guards, pistols dangling from each bleeding hand. "Did you ever see such manners, Mr. Olsen? I offer him what he wants, and he can't even say thank you. Whatever is the world coming to?" Sinclair paused. "It must be time for his bell rope."

"Yoh!"

The first mate looped a coil of hemp around the lantern hook in a beam overhead. Dipper's arms were wrenched behind his back, the pistols were returned to Sinclair's belt, and both wrists were lashed together. Dipper began to die as both heels cleared the deck, swaying in time with *Alexander*'s plod toward Southern Africa, swinging from side to side like a demented bell clapper, his arms pulling from shoulder sockets.

Sinclair looked at the marine sergeant. "Time for their chain."

"Sah!"

A hundred feet of chain was tipped from a sack and run aft through the rings welded to each set of manacles, around an eyebolt in the after bulkhead, then for'ard again. Every man and boy was now bound shoulder to shoulder on a single loop which began and ended at the mainmast foot.

Sinclair glanced at Olsen again. "Mutineers? *Pirates?* Hoo!" Still chuckling, he collected his cloak from the sergeant and climbed on deck while the privates poked Mathew Zennor up the ladder and mounted a sentry on the gate to watch over Dipper.

Alexander's crew had been mustered on the waist, facing inward while red-coated marines held strongpoints fore and aft. A curtain of rain squalled up from the Antarctic, drumming against the taut brown canvas aloft. Sinclair checked that his brass swivel gun's hammer was down, then trod past its sentry into the hollow square of seamen. "Belay there!"

The bare feet stopped shuffling.

"At six bells o' this morning watch, the eighth day o' October, seventeen hundred and eighty-seven, it was brought to my attention that certain elements in the cargo had conjoined wi' disaffected members o' my crew wi' intention to commit mutiny and murder most foul.

"Acting upon information received, I have dealt with the former. I shall now punish the latter. Under Article Thirty-four o' the relevant Act o' Parliament, a shipmaster may, upon due notice o' impending mutiny and insurrection, take whatsoever steps he deems necessary to restore good order and discipline to his command. The act does not exclude summary execution by hanging." Only the keening of the wind broke the absolute silence. "Seaman M'Ginnis, stand forth!"

Alexander's bosun seized the marked man and kneed him to a halt in front of the master. Sinclair peered down his nose from a great distance. "Seaman M'Ginnis, ye have been named the prime instigator o' this unnatural crime against your superiors."

"No!"

"From evidence given, I judge ye guilty o' attempted mutiny and murder."

"No—!"

"I therefore sentence ye to one hundred cobs and to one full watch at the heads every day o' the next seven. Pay and rations will be deducted for such time ye are noneffective."

The seaman was clubbed to his knees while a broomstick was laid under them. Two marines then stretched his arms over the carpenter's sawhorse while *Alexander*'s bosun pulled down the man's ragged britches.

"Lay on."

The knotted rope hissed.

Balmain was watching from the sidelines. The seaman was vomiting by the fortieth stroke and unconscious by the fifty-seventh.

"Captain Sinclair? A word wi' ye!"

Alexander's master ignored the surgeon and glared at the sweating bosun instead. "Avast the butterfly kisses! He'd have cut your bluidy throat too!"

Ninety-eight.

Ninety-nine.

One hundred.

Sinclair looked at the rest of his crew. "Dismiss."

Olsen saw that the sailor was dragged for'ard to where icy seas burst over *Alexander*'s bows. The mutineer was about to be shackled to the capstan and repeatedly brought to the point of death, four hours every twenty-four, the next seven days.

Sinclair turned. "Ye wished for a word wi' me, Mr. Balmain?"

"Aye! Well. Yon man could drown."

The master considered this opinion. "I suppose he could. On the other hand he could have been jerked to Glory at the yardarm. Now the choice o' living or dying is his."

"But captain—!"

"Enough. How many tears d'ye think they would have shed over us had they gained the upper hand this morning?"

"But—!"

"Good day to ye, Mr. Balmain."

Sergeant Ramsbottom clapped his gaiters together. "Beggin' leave to speak, sir! What's to be done with this item?" He gave Zennor a sharp kick.

Sinclair peered down his nose and inspected the defiant lag. "Ye would not be from Falmouth by any chance?"

Zennor stared back. "I be from Marazion nigh Penzance I be."

"Near enough." Sinclair clicked fingers at his second mate. "Make to *Sirius*: mutiny suppressed. Ringleader being transferred forthwith. Acknowledge."

"Aye aye!"

41

TABLE MOUNTAIN stopped moving across *Alexander*'s stern windows as the barque snubbed her moorings. Outside, gulls screeched, treading the high, bright sky, fighting over the cooks' slops as they floated away on a falling tide. It was a southern spring day on Table Bay, but inside *Alexander*'s cabin the climate was frigid as Thorpe finished whisking his soap and got ready to lather Sinclair with quick, nervous dabs.

His hand shook, but the master's was steady. Only the cocked pistols in his lap moved slightly, in time with his breath, aimed point-blank at the convict's belly: there would be no more talk of mutiny and murder aboard this transport. Then it was Cribb's turn to step into the line of fire and finish the close shave while Kitty Brandon kept her back turned and busied herself with Sinclair's new suit.

The master gestured and Olsen stepped forward to prod the two lags aloft while Sinclair began checking himself in the mirror. Kitty Brandon heard the door shut and turned again. She smiled and held out the master's shirt and breeches, his blue stockings and the bottle green coat which she had turned into a dashing *frac* with brass-buttoned cuffs.

"Bluidy fal-lals," Sinclair grumbled from force of habit, and knotted his freshly ironed cravat.

"On the contrary, 'tis the very picture of a successful gentleman of affairs which you now present to the world," she corrected. "Why, I'll wager a guinea to a groat that, when the Chinees clap eyes upon us, they'll declare that a duke and duchess have come to visit the king."

"Hn! I had no such frippery before, and the Chows gave *me* no cheek—"

"Times change and we must learn to change with them, or get left behind in the rush. Speaking of which," Kitty Brandon went on, "I happened to notice that the late seaman M'Ginnis still has three pounds, two shillings and sixpence against his name on the books. Now, it seems to me—"

"Enough!" Sinclair's hand abruptly silenced her. "The law demands that his effects are forfeit to the ship's account! Ye can't wheedle around me this time!"

Kitty Brandon stroked her hand across his lapel and straightened a button. "You are quite right, I should never have raised the matter."

"I'm not listening!"

She didn't look up. "I was so proud of the way you acted—"

"Enough!"

"Indeed, it is the mark of a gentleman that he *can* be strong when the occasion demands," she went on, gently twisting the button this way and that on its thread. "But when the problem has been resolved to his satisfaction, why, then he can become a gentle-man again, without losing the world's respect. In fact, he gains honour and good opinion by a show of magnanimity." She patted the button in place and glanced up, smiling. "Now, after you've finished with the commodore, please continue ashore and buy these few necessities for the luckless girl who was also cruelly betrayed by that unspeakable wretch. . . ."

Sinclair found himself folding a lengthy shopping list into his pocket while he went aloft. His gig was waiting at the entry port. He was still muttering under his breath as he backed over the side and arranged his coat tails on the thwart. "*Sirius*!"

As always, he was the last of the merchant skippers to pull into the shadow of the flagship. *Lady Penrhyn*'s master made a rare grin as Sinclair puffed aboard and joined his colleagues on the waist deck. "Bloody 'ell, Duncan, you'll be settin' up as lord mayor next!"

Alexander's master flicked his coat sleeve. "Not bad, eh? I'll wager that, when the Chows see me, they'll say it's a—"

"This way, if you please." Lieutenant King made a curt bow and began shepherding the civilians below.

Phillip had a list of pencilled notes on the table in front of him: he blinked at Sinclair's finery as the convoy's captains found room to attend him. "Good morning," he said. "I congratulate you on the generally uneventful crossing we have just enjoyed: I consider it a happy omen for the last leg of our voyage. We shall need it. Meanwhile, you are to start making all possible haste with the watering and revictualling. Now, more than ever before, speed is of the essence for our business, but I shall return to that point in a few moments.

"An additional problem will be the embarcation of livestock and feed. I know it will be difficult, but that can't be helped. You will bear in mind that such animals will be vital for our colony until herds of native cows, horses and sheep can be domesticated. You will therefore make every effort to accommodate them aboard your vessels. If, as a consequence, your human cargoes suffer some discomfort, so be it, *these* beasts must survive. I repeat, if it is a question of humouring ten persons or one pig, the pig wins. Understand?"

His captains nodded. Their commodore did tend to dwell on the obvious; besides, as was not the case with the human cargoes, there would be a cash bonus paid for every live animal landed at Botany Bay.

Phillip's pencil had ticked that item off the agenda. "Let us now turn our attention to the situation which awaits us in this, our last port of call before New Holland." There was a stir of interest, and even Sinclair's eyes were open again as Phillip went on. "I regret to inform you that the Cape is neither Santa Cruz nor Rio de Janeiro. The Dutchmen owe us few thanks for anything. It was, after all, Commodore Johnstone's squadron which captured their fleet of East Indiamen here, back in 'eighty-one. When I called a year or two later, on my way home from India, our flag was most unpopular and our uniforms were spat upon. I do not doubt that matters are much the same, so you must expect to drive a hard bargain for every *rixthaler* the locals demand for their produce."

His captains nodded again as Phillip eased back and began polishing his spectacles. "There is one final complication." He squinted through one of the lenses and went on polishing. "Our nations are now at war in Europe."

"Good God! I most strongly—!"

"Later, Mr. Sinclair, if you please." Phillip breathed on the other lens and gave it a rub with the square of wash leather. "My latest despatches from London were written just after a republican rabble seized power in The Hague to overthrow the crown of Holland."

"Bloody 'ell. . . ."

"Exactly, Mr. Sever," Phillip agreed. "However, it does not follow that the present governor of the Cape is sympathetic to his new masters in the Netherlands; quite the reverse, I'd imagine. Therefore we are, technically at least, on neutral territory until the French can send out a fleet with a replacement governor. By the time they do so, it is my intention that we are well on our way into the Pacific." Phillip settled the spectacles on his nose. "The utmost speed and urgency are now our watchwords. Good day, gentlemen."

Cribb snapped his fingers for the next lag to step up and sit down. One of the cook's helpers sidled under the sunshade and squatted while Thorpe began grating soap with a strip of sharkskin. Cribb started whacking the razor on its leather strop a few inches from the lag's ear. "Nice weather, Ratbag. Too bad Dipper 'ad to miss it."

"Yuss. Too bad."

"Rough way to croak, I reckon," Cribb observed, testing the razor's edge. "Still, who'd 'av thought Dip would take so long to cough? Game cove."

"Yeah. Game."

Thorpe began whisking lather in his mug. Cribb moved further round the front to let Ratbag watch him sweeten the blade. "Rummy lurk that." Whack, whack, whack. "Reminds me of something else I seen once." Whack, whack, whack. "Over There, in Yankee Land, Copper 'Ill camp." Whack, whack, whack. "Me and some mates was planning to bolt when, one dark night—squeak! squeak! —a little weasel begun whispering to the screws." Ratbag's eyes were staring over his mask of soap bubbles. Cribb sighed. "Weasel was dobbing 'is mates to them Yankee bastards for a lick of grub." The razor whacked again. "Nasty."

Ratbag found that he couldn't strain backward any more, now that Thorpe was pressing forward. He whimpered as Cribb delicately stroked the cold steel across his windpipe, then, suddenly, gripped his nose and twisted the head right back, poised for a swift, short slash. "Only our little squealer, Over There, didn't go as game as Dipper, because dirty little shit'ouse rats don't know 'ow!" Cribb hissed, crushing the nose between finger and thumb.

"Phoss!"

The barber squeezed harder. "Dipper 'ad mates. They been asking questions, like 'ow Bulldog knew. The real quick thinkers are starting to say that someone on the chain dobbed 'im in for a lick of Cooky's spoon—"

"N-no!"

"Don't give me that crap!" Cribb snarled, now only inches from the other man's face. *"You* blew the bugle! Dipper was no mate of mine, but 'e was one of *us*! And you dobbed 'im in! Ratbag? Shitbag!"

"Phossss—!"

"Shut up! Bulldog's keeping you now, but what 'appens once we get to Bottommy Town?" Cribb suddenly let the nose snap into shape again. Ratbag drew a shuddering breath, his eyes crossing as they searched for the razor under his chin. Cribb nodded. "Take a tip: get a family. Quick."

"Family?"

"Like me. And Leafy. And Ben." Cribb eased the razor's weight on the other man's taut throat. "We're your only chance, but it'll cost you—"

"Sure!"

"You 'aven't got the bill yet," Cribb cautioned. "From now on you're telling me what you've been telling Cooky to tell the Bulldog, only you're telling *me* first. Because if you don't, you can bet your balls you're going to get run up an alley in Bottommy—"

"P-please!"

"And get jobbed with a chunk of lead pipe."

Cribb ripped the bristle off Ratbag's face and shoved the cook's helper from the patch of shade while he looked around for the next client. Levi was wandering past, still uncertain on his feet after a recent bout of the flux, still gripping his busywork bag of empty medicine bottles. "Like a fresh up, Abe? You'll feel tons better."

Levi lifted a weary finger and shuffled along the line of grumbling lags who were still waiting a turn. He sank onto the keg and shut his eyes.

"Still not bene?" Cribb asked, starting to click his scissors.

One dark eye opened a fraction. "I feel like a cat sicking me up."

Cribb trimmed around Levi's ear. "That means you're getting better. A cove's always got to feel crook before 'e can feel better. Stands to reason. I mean, look at this trip we're on. Rough, right? But the next stop, Bottommy, with all your mates taking us 'ome to dinner." He chuckled quietly. "Today it's skilly, but tomorrow's going to be more grub than we can stuff in a box. Right?"

Levi smiled wanly. "Joe. Never again we going to eat food like that. The lost tribes don't live that way. There, every man is like a prince. Reb Mordechai promise it many times. *Ei!* He so wanted to come to Bottommy."

"Too bad, but that's life." Cribb was clipping round Levi's neckline now. "The important thing is you're on the mend, and soon we'll all be riding in carriages up the sunny side of the street." He dipped a wink at Thorpe. "It'll be just the way that old 'Gyptian woman used to tell me: when I croak, it'll be in a bed, like a proper ge'man. . . ."

42

"AH, COME IN, Pip. Sit down." King accepted the offered chair as Phillip finished sprinkling sand over his daybook. "Any luck yet with His Excellency?"

"Yes. At last."

Phillip blew the page clean. "When do I see him?"

"This afternoon. At three."

Phillip shut the book. "What's his name?"

"Van der Graaf. A baron, I think."

"What's he like?"

King shrugged. "Oldish, stoutish, liverish and much given to shouting at his interpreter. In a word, he's no gentleman."

"Sounds more like a nobleman to me," Phillip commented, starting to peer at the list of points he needed to discuss with the governor of de Kaap.

King grimaced. "I had a strong urge to put my shoe where it would have done some good."

"I'm so glad you resisted the temptation." Phillip didn't look up. *"M'sieur le baron* is going to require rather more deft handling than that if he is to give us everything we require before his replacement takes over."

"Give? Frankly, sir, I don't think he would give an Englishman the time of day!"

Phillip folded his spectacles and put them away. "Why do you say that?"

"Well, it's the damned fellow's arrogance. And, well, everything. He's a typical cheesemongering Hollander, if you ask me."

"Really?" Phillip sighed. "Still, let's be charitable to our host, he must have some redeeming feature. The typical anything never became governor of anywhere."

"I'm damned if I can see what it may be." King shrugged. "The fellow's a typical mallet-headed cheesemonger—"

"So you keep telling me," Phillip interrupted mildly. "But we must never forget that behind the man stands what he represents."

"And what might that be?" King sniffed. "Apart from boorish manners?"

"No, not those particularly. I am thinking more of the United Provinces of the Netherlands," Phillip replied. "An interesting cluster of towns and cities, well worth the trouble of making a visit. I suppose you knew that, while hardly more than a sandbank across the mouth of the Rhine, our united cheesemongers were sending their convoys around Africa to the Indies, and China, and Japan?"

King was always annoyed whenever his commander put on this schoolmaster pose. "Yes. I did."

Phillip nodded. "I thought so. However, I'll wager that none of their navigators had only *Gulliver's Travels* to get 'em there."

"I beg pardon, sir?"

Phillip's finger began rapping the table. "With the exception of a few hundred words in Mr. Cook's journal, Dr. Gulliver's myths are all I have to guide us across an ocean which the Dutch charted almost two hundred years ago."

"Sir?"

"Pip. Surely to God I am not the only officer on this expedition who has noticed that we are bound for New *Holland*? And that every landfall of any value has already been named Kaap Leeuwin, or Pieter Nuytsland, or Van Dieman's Land, or something similar?"

"Oh."

Phillip sat forward abruptly, elbows on the table. "The Dutch have almost certainly forgotten more about this benighted end of the globe than we shall ever know: it is my duty to make good that deficiency by every means possible."

"Make good?" King smiled uncertainly. "How?"

"Mijnheer Van der Graaf is going to want to help me. He is going to give me the information I seek."

"He won't give you the drips off his nose."

"Indeed, I rather hope he doesn't," Phillip replied. "All I need from him at the moment is permission to leaf through the old pilot books in his archives. That done, we may have the tides and currents which will allow me to steer the most direct course between Africa and Botany Bay without, at the same time, piling our convoy onto Vlaminck's Head, or Houtman's Archipelago, or God knows what else."

King began to frown harder. "He won't do it, sir."

"He will."

"He won't. I've seen the man. I tell you, we'll be damned lucky to buy water at twice the listed price."

Phillip was thumbing the lid on his pocket watch. "Three o'clock, did you say? Then we'd better put our best foot forward." He glanced up. "My compliments to the coxswain: sway out the launch and make ready for my courtesy call on His Excellency."

The commodore went over the side to the trill of pipes and settled himself on the thwart between his flag lieutenant and Hunter, and faced the marine commandant in his scarlet regimentals. "When you're ready, Evans."

"Aye aye, sir!" The helm went over. "Lively now, lads! Heave away!"

Phillip smiled impersonally at Ross. "This is your first call at the Cape, is it not, major?"

"Aye."

"Sound folk. I'm sure you will get along splendidly with them."

"Aye."

Phillip's smile never altered. "You and Captain Campbell will have to lodge ashore; we'll be here a little longer than I'd planned. Captain Hunter informs me that our flagship is sinking again. Distressing, isn't it? That means my bluejackets will be making rather a lot of noise with their caulking irons. No doubt you would prefer to recover from your exertions in more tranquil surroundings."

"Aye."

The conversation lapsed as *Sirius'* launch came alongside a jetty which sold water and fresh vegetables at monopoly prices to the world's shipping. A harsh, dry wind blew off the slopes of Table Mountain, whipping dust and grit across an uneven, tussocky parade ground. Phillip clamped hand on hat until the wind dropped and he could look up again.

Nothing had changed. The settlement still sheltered from the bitter southeasterlies by facing north across Table Bay, its back turned on Tamboerskloof. To his right were the thatched and gabled houses of Greenmarket, crouched around the town pump and the Burgher Watch House. Ahead, directly across the Parade, were the Dutch East India Company's gardens and their slave lodge. And to his left was the squat pentagon of Good Hope Castle, the settlement's bulwark against seaborne attack. Beyond that sprawled less and less of anything except rough tracks and bits of pasture which petered away into coastal scrubland.

Phillip knew that, for all practical purposes, a century and a half of civilisation began at this jetty and stopped five hundred yards inland. The next patch of light on the map of Africa was the equally remote town of Luanda, two thousand miles north, where he had once embarked Ndango workers for the Brazilian canefields during his service with the Portuguese navy. And yet, compared with the outpost he or the French would soon be planting on the shores of the Pacific, Atlantic toeholds like the Cape and Luanda were thriving cities the equal of Paris or London. It was a sobering thought for the man who had orders to establish a similar tavern of the seas in months, not centuries.

The wind fell and Phillip looked around again: Governor Van der Graaf had not had the common civility to send even a native boy, let alone provide a saddle animal or cart for his visitors. Phillip shrugged it off; the brisk walk would make a change after his cramped quarters aboard *Sirius*. The watch lid snapped shut. "Twenty minutes, gentlemen. Let's not keep His Excellency waiting."

The British officers fell in behind their leader and set off along the track of Zee Straat, moving over to one side as a couple of Malay slaves ambled closer, droving a flock of sheep from the outlying pastures. Phillip glanced at Hunter. "We'd better buy some of those for our table, John. What do you think they cost nowadays?"

"Four or five times their true value, if we're lucky."

Phillip nodded and began moving again, trudging on in his best blue uniform and white stockings, aiming for the castle's main entrance between the Buren and Leerdam bastions. And between its well-hung gallows. "Major Ross! I haven't all day to waste while others admire the view!"

A squad of East India Company musketeers blocked the moat crossing at its forward redoubt, keeping it shut against the British uniforms. Phillip gripped his tricorne against a fresh dust cloud and waited until an officer could be found to escort them under the bell tower and onto the *wapenplaats*.

He had not only studied *Gulliver's Travels* recently, there had also been confidential notes from Rose on the Verenigde Oost Indische Compagnie—the Cape's overlord—whose ownership was emblazoned above the gateway with the arms of the Amsterdam and Rotterdam, the Delft and Zeeland, the Hoorn and Enkhuizen chambers of commerce. A brave and imposing sight, once, but the great trading company had not returned a penny in dividends to its shareholders since Commodore Johnstone's raid. Governor Van der Graaf's troops had not had a pay parade since 1781, and it was unlikely that the Cape garrison would get a copper *stuiver* until the home government had devised some way to underwrite its bankrupt assets. Meanwhile, the best that could be done was to bluff the world from a position of fearful weakness and hope for the best.

"*Kom!*"

Phillip followed the shabby old junior officer under the bell tower and onto the cobbled inner courtyard where someone's slave woman was flogging his wet shirt against the fountain's stonework. Rusting cones of cannon balls poked above the weeds around her, waiting to serve a battery of twenty-four-pounders on the curtain wall overhead. Phillip judged that the casualties would probably be heavy once they began continuous firing and their worn barrels split, decimating the gun crews. Meanwhile, dinner had been tethered to a post and was being whipped to make the meat tender. The bullock was lowing and bellowing as two kaffir boys swung their lashes and the regimental butcher sharpened his knives on a grindstone.

"*Kom!*"

Phillip led his officers onto the administration block's *stoep* behind new wrought iron railings. A company stonemason was chipping an ornamental fanlight from the wall above the door. An aimed chunk of rubble narrowly

missed Hunter's cocked hat and bounced harmlessly into the courtyard.
"*Kom!*"

The antechamber to the governor's quarters lay to the right of the entrance hall.

"Wait!"

The moments began dragging into minutes, but at last the butcher stopped the bullock's groans outside the window. King sighed and leaned against a wall—there were no chairs, of course—and searched his pockets for the book he had already finished, twice, waiting in his room for Van der Graaf to notice him. Phillip smoothed his white gloves again and checked the time, again. A blowfly tried to join the others feasting on a puddle of blood outside the window pane. Ross gripped his sword hilt. Hunter yawned.

"*Kom!*"

The second door stood ajar. Phillip took his time flicking the dust from his sleeves. Then, hat under arm, he led the British officers into the company's audience chamber. It was half past four and His Excellency was now ready to receive them, lounging on the seat of justice, a bulky man in sober greys, his hair pulled back and tied at the nape. Phillip halted, waited for his officers to form a single line, then led their bows.

Van der Graaf finished cleaning his fingernails with a penknife. He admired the effect, then barked something at his interpreter.

"By command—Hizzonuh guvnor—what you wanting?" the clerk repeated mechanically.

Phillip ignored the fellow. "*M'sieur le baron?* I thank you from the bottom of my heart for the cordial honour you bestow upon us by your presence today. You ask, what do we want? I reply that, in every way, I am well satisfied with what I already have. Oh, naturally there may be certain details which I shall consider purchasing for my convoy, but they can await a more opportune moment. For the present I am content to experience— how can one say?—the profoundest sense of admiration."

Van der Graaf's mouth had dropped open as the little Englishman spoke to him fluently and directly in French, Europe's only tongue for civilised men. "Admiration?"

"But of course." Phillip seemed politely surprised. "The boundless courage and achievements of Holland's noble sons shine like the sun across the centuries, beckoning those of us less endowed by Heaven." The Royal Navy commodore straightened from another bow. "Name what you will and where you like, a Dutchman will have been there already, and triumphed. It is an undeniable fact of history, as I was reminded only a few moments ago, when I passed under the coats of arms on your magnificent gateway. Where else on the face of the entire globe could one find such vivid evidence of the financial genius for which your nation is so justly renowned?"

Van der Graaf had recovered his poise. He was sitting much straighter. He inclined his head. "The Netherlands lead. The rest follow."

"My sentiments exactly." Phillip inclined his head. "If I may be permitted the honour of speaking personally, it is a matter of the deepest sorrow to me whenever two great nations, such as the United Kingdom and the United Provinces, find themselves in disagreement over issues which ought to be resolved at the conference table—as among friends and brothers—rather than on the field of conflict, where even the winner must lose something . . . ."

Van der Graaf nodded stiffly.

"Still speaking for myself, *m'sieur le baron,*" Phillip went on with a sad smile, "I regard such a *contretemps* between Briton and Netherlander as nothing less than civil war. Why, was not our late majesty, William III, also *stadhouder*? And are not many of our great families blood cousins? I can assure you that His Majesty's government in London regards the present *impasse* between your sovereign and the so-called Patriot Party with the utmost disquiet. . . ."

"Dogs."

"Our opinion, too," Phillip replied. "You may be assured that His Britannic Majesty, whom I have the honour to serve, is doing everything possible to restore legitimate rule and order in Holland. And when he does, all true patriots will be advanced with every mark of distinction and royal favour. . . ."

"Of course." The governor of the Cape made another terse nod. "In the name of the United Provinces. Refresh your ships and men."

"Your Excellency is ever the model of courtesy and consideration."

Van der Graaf's face was starting to hurt with the strain of not scowling. "Orders will be given to make you welcome. Goodbye."

Phillip led the British officers' bows and took the customary three paces to the rear before leading the way from the audience chamber. Through the entrance hall. Across the *wapenplaats*. And onto the wasteland beyond the castle gate.

Ross relaxed the grip on his sword hilt. "Damned jackanapes! If it'd been *me,* I'd have taught him respect for the king's uniform!"

"Perhaps you'll have an opportunity of doing so later?" Phillip replied, taking off the white gloves and stowing them inside his coat.

"Later!"

"Of course. I have only just begun. Mr. King—?"

"Sir!"

"You will return tomorrow morning with my compliments and an invitation to dine aboard *Sirius*. The rest of us, gentlemen, will make it our duty to see that His Excellency and his officers revise their opinion of our nation. Why not? I imagine that life in such a remote and barbarous land must dull the memory of happier days." Phillip made a brief, impersonal smile. "Our Dutch friends are about to rediscover the delights of good cooking, sound wine and civilised conversation—major."

43

MARY JOHNSON shaded her eyes as she studied the slave women grouped around Greenmarket fountain with their brass water pots, and made haste to get them on paper before the next span of oxen ruined her composition, but she was still too slow. The next laden waggon was rumbling into her picture, its master riding ahead while his dogs guarded the flanks and a Hottentot boy plodded behind in the dust, steering the dozen yoked beasts.

Four other families had already outspanned on the Tuingrond after ruining the scene with their yells and whipcracks; however, the traders of Rijger Street did not share Mrs. Johnson's irritation. These native-born farmers might seem an embarrassment—rough, unlettered Afrikaners who barely spoke the same language now as the urbane Hollanders out from home on company contracts—but their money was always acceptable on these annual visits to the Cape, where they bargained their hides and tallow, wax and ivory, for gunpowder and bullet lead, salt and sugar. Besides, they rarely stayed in town for longer than necessary. Soon enough they would inspan again and lumber away to the Komsburg Frontier, two hundred miles upcountry, where others like them were guarding the herds against Xhosa war parties.

Mary Johnson began putting away her pencils; by now she knew what to expect from such Boer cattle drovers. Mrs. Botsma, the Johnsons' landlady in nearby Olifant Street, had a brother whose tenth son was married to a half-cousin out at Franshoek, who had an elder nephew on the Hex River, who was uncle to—at which point Mary Johnson had stopped trying to unravel a tribal network which could have migrated straight from the Old Testament. It was sufficient for her that Cousin Jacobus, one of the little land convoy's forward scouts, had appeared at Aunt Botsma's the previous lunchtime, just as the Johnsons were about to say Grace.

A burly shape had ducked under the open doorway with a muzzle loader in one fist, a woven reed hat in the other. The patina of body sweat, animal fat and tobacco smoke on his beard and clothes had made Mary Johnson's eyes smart, and even Mrs. Botsma had felt uncomfortable at her relative's surprise visit until he had tied rawhide shoes to his feet so that he was respectably dressed to greet the visiting foreigners.

Lunch had been an ordeal. Cousin Jacobus had gone through his bowl of mutton broth as if an attack were due at any moment. Between mouthfuls he had roundly cursed the scoundrel dogs of the Oost Indische Compagnie for the monopoly prices their clerks extorted from decent, peaceable, God-fearing farming folk; the swine of a *smous,* a wandering Jewish pedlar, who had pulled a bad tooth—the jaw was held open for everyone around the table to look into its crater—and left a botched job which Cousin Jacobus had finished for himself with a red hot nail; and thieving Bantu in general. Common courtesy had made him drop the English from today's list of grievances.

Later, after he had gone to feed his pack of dogs in the yard outside, Mrs. Botsma had apologised to Mrs. Johnson for these stubborn patriarchs who were forever uprooting their families, heaping everything aboard the waggon before marching deeper into the veldt, distancing themselves from the company's tax-gatherers and a degenerate world where folk wore shoes and weakened their bodies by washing away the natural grease which God had ordained for a purpose.

Mary Johnson sighed with irritation and turned, her sketchbook under one arm, ready to go back to yet another lunch of boiled mutton, when she saw a familiar figure in brown mufti walking across the market place. "Captain Phillips—!"

He turned her way and doffed his hat. "Your servant, ma'am."

She joined him. "Is it not a beautiful day? They do say that when it does that—" she pointed at the cap of cloud across Table Mountain—"we shall have three more of equally fine weather."

"A happy omen." He smiled. "Tell me, how are your drawings coming along?"

"Still not as well as I would like."

"Allow me to judge. May I see?"

"Of course." She opened the sketchpad. "This one is of a waggon."

"So I see," Phillip observed. "The wheels are good, but moving animals are never so easy to portray, are they?" He took the next sheet of paper from her. "Ah hah! *Now* we're showing promise."

Mary Johnson almost blushed. "Thank you, captain, but I feel that I need a lot more practise, especially with this sort of subject."

"Really? And why do you say that?"

She hesitated. "I can't say, exactly, but there is always something wrong with the light. It conspires to make everything look so different, so grey and ugly. And yet the sun shines more strongly than it does at home in England. You'd think it would be more cheerful, but it isn't. It's almost like the people one sees here."

"A perceptive comment," Phillip said, examining the third drawing. "It is indeed a different land. Nor are the people the same."

Mary Johnson shivered. "I—I hate them."

"Because they are so unlike the English?"

"Yes. No. I don't know." She hid her confusion by looking around at the hobbled oxen, the smoking campfires, the jabbering farmers leaning on their whip handles. "They're so—different. So wrong."

Phillip handed back the last sketch and leaned on his walking cane. "You could be right, ma'am, but we must prepare ourselves to cope with something rather similar at Botany Bay."

Mary Johnson frowned. "Do you mean, our home could be like this?"

"Indeed, very easily," Phillip replied. "It is known to be south of the equator and it is roughly on the same line of latitude as the Cape. It follows that the sun will also shine from the north, not the south as we are accustomed to, and we'll probably find the landscape just as unsettling."

"But the *people*? They're all so backward, so uncouth, so dirty! And everything they attempt is so roughly finished and decrepit," Mary Johnson persisted, groping for words to describe what she felt so strongly.

Phillip hesitated and poked at the dust with the tip of his cane. "Nothing can alter the fact that we must prepare ourselves to make considerable allowances for our new homeland, ma'am. Every single one of us, regardless of our birth and origins, must be ready to change or be changed. For if we don't—"

"Yes?"

Phillip glanced up. "It will destroy us. If the mountain won't come to Mahomet, Mahomet must learn to swallow his pride and start walking toward the mountain, or else nothing will ever happen." He studied her vexed frown. "Oh, I know what many of our officers and gentlemen are saying about the simple conditions which these rustic Dutchmen seem to enjoy, but let us stop and consider for a moment. Aren't we mocking a century of dogged effort by a sober, thrifty, industrious folk who are used to working miracles every day by the sweat of their brows?"

"I—I don't understand you."

Phillip waited until another waggon had rolled past in a cloud of grit, shouting men and yelping dogs. "If you will permit a tinge of blasphemy, ma'am, 'God made the world, but the Dutch made Holland.' They also made this Cape of Good Hope which seems to us to be the very end of that world, in every sense."

"Yes?"

Phillip sighed quietly. "Ma'am. It will soon be my duty to lead our convoy upon an ocean where hardly anyone before me has dared to go, and eight thousand miles later to begin building a New Holland with citizens whose only skills are theft and murder. Frankly, I shall be astonished if—a century from now, by its own unaided efforts—our little tavern of the seas at Botany has bred a single cow or filled one cask of beef for any passing ship to buy from us. Indeed, the prospect of our reluctant colonists even being able to grow their own daily bread is beginning to worry me more than it ought—" Phillip was feeling inside his waistcoat pocket. He took out his watch, thumbed back the lid and peered long-sightedly at the time. "However, standing idle never improved a bad case. If you'll excuse me, I have an appointment to keep with His Excellency, and you know what demons for punctuality these Dutch can be."

"Of course."

"Your servant, ma'am." Phillip replaced his hat and continued walking across Greenmarket to Zee Straat.

It was dark by the time Phillip and Van der Graaf had finished a very pleasant dinner and the officer of the guard had been called to escort the British visitor back to his lodgings.

Phillip watched the picquet's lantern march away, and then turned, letting himself into the room where Lieutenant King had been busy throughout the afternoon: a fresh pile of papers lay on Phillip's bedside table, weighted with a piece of roof tile against the eddying draughts. For a moment the convoy's commodore wondered about lighting another candle, but, instead, he peeled off his shirt and breeches, huffed out the single flame and collapsed moments after his head hit the straw bolster.

Click.

Phillip skimmed from sleep into midnight, alert to the patient gnawing mice at the kitchen cupboard in the next room. And the restless clicker-tik of his watch, by the papers, on the table, near the bed. He thumped the straw and tried plumping a fresh pillow before the last shreds of sleep blew away like mist. With any luck—

Clicker-tik, clicker-tik, clicker-tik.

Gnaw. Rustle. Scamper.

Clicker-tik, clicker-tik, clicker-tik.

Scritch. Scratch.

Clicker-tik, clicker-tik, clicker-tik.

Squeak!

With any luck he might still get some sleep. Please God. Sleep? Phillip hunched over on his other shoulder and punched the lonely pillow again. "Oh, hell!"

Clicker-tik, clicker-tik, clicker-tik.

Time. The one gift shared equally by rich man and poor, the one treasure which can never be hoarded. So what's to be done with it now? Fight to get back to sleep? Or get that other candle and go to work on the inventories? No, it would be better to deal with the watch lists first, they haven't been checked for a week. And the livestock muster. And the pay-rolls. And the daily journals. Damned daily journals. Pack of bloody lies. The Admiralty only makes such a fetish of them so that a board of nit-picking land lawyers can find fault with sailors, years after the event, and pin the blame. Keep them brief, keep 'em noncommittal, keep on doctor-ing the journals so that they'll be acceptable to whichever gang rules the roost in Westminster when we get back.

Phillip hunched over again. "Empires rise, kingdoms fall, but a govern-ment paper will outlast them all." Who first said that? Don't know, but he was right. Tougher than rope, a bit of bum fodder will kill a man just as quickly. Hadn't they slipped a sheet of government blue paper into HMS *Culloden*'s logbook so that they could then convict Byng? Outright forg-ery, of course, but what odds? What was it we said at the time? "The admi-ral had to be shot because the prime minister deserved to be hanged." Damned right. And what was it George Rose once said about such com-mittees of political reptiles? "Searching for a sacrificial lamb to slaughter on the altar of Public Good."

Poor old George. He knew their slimy tricks better than most. Kicked from office again. He'd be managing his estates now that the Sheridans and Burgoynes were plundering Treasury to muckrake patronage over the Prince of Wales' other cronies. But in the end someone would have to be found to foot their bill, someone without connexion. Connexion? What use had *that* been when John Byng went before the firing squad? If a safe seat in the House of Commons and a father in the Lords hadn't stopped the venomous gnomes of Westminster from destroying him, what hope was there going to be for a total nobody with cousins who still picked rags along the Judengasse?

"Oh, God."

Phillip sagged flat on his back and dragged the blanket over his face. The entire weight of responsibility for failing at Botany Bay would fall upon him, upon him alone, not upon anyone else. Not upon his successor, Hunter. Not upon his deputy, Ross. The blame, the disgrace, the punish-ment would be his. He was going too slow to stop the French admiral: New Holland was now *La Nouvelle France*. Not one hack pamphlet writer in all England would even pause to consider that Jean François Galaup, Count de La Pérouse, Knight of St. Louis and hereditary *grand seigneur*, had been given two new warships to sail into the Pacific and make it French. Public opinion would only remember that Arthur Phillip, Esq., had failed to beat the enemy after limping halfway around the globe in a sinking frigate.

"Oh, God!"

Phillip knew what would await him when he returned to England with his bedraggled little fleet after failing to take Botany Bay. A court-martial.

And in the shadows, behind the admirals who would judge him, would be men of immense power and connexion, whispering orders to their creatures and placemen to make sure that he bore the blame for the scandalous state of the Royal Navy, just as Byng had in his day. Arthur Phillip would be condemned to death, for if he was not shot, then great names would be proven guilty—and that must never be allowed to happen.

Arthur Phillip was no longer dreaming of a star and ribbon and a fashionable address in London; Arthur Phillip was fighting for his life.

A side party of marines saluted him aboard *Sirius* as the dew was evaporating from her guns. Hunter paced forward, hat off. "Good morning, sir. I trust that was another fruitful meeting with His Excellency . . . ?"

" 'Morning. All squared away?"

"Mostly," Hunter replied, falling into step as the corporal dismissed his men behind them.

"See that it is. We embark the livestock. Mr. King has written the lists for each vessel."

"It'll be a tight fit."

"Noah knew worse." Phillip was grim. "I shall have four sheep and a dozen ducks sharing my quarters. Others can make an equivalent sacrifice."

Hunter was following his commodore down the companionway ladder. "May I ask who my companions are to be?"

Phillip slowed and opened the captain's cupboard door while he glanced inside. He looked back. "The rabbits?"

Hunter pulled a face as he tried imagining their cage among his books and spare clothing. "Aye, well, if we're that pressed for space, I'll do my bit, of course."

"Of course." The great cabin's door slammed shut and Phillip sat at the table, fingers locked, elbows at his side. "It will be pointless stowing them among the crew; they'd be eaten before we cleared the harbour mouth. It is of paramount importance that we not only embark the greatest number of livestock, but disembark them, too."

Hunter began studying the roof beams. "Yes, sir."

"The very future of our colony will depend upon us landing every animal possible until we can domesticate the native ones."

"Yes, sir."

Phillip began fiddling with a quill near his inkwell. "There is no telling when our crops will prosper once we land. Even now the Dutchmen are unsure of the seasons in these latitudes, yet, until our first harvest is safely in, the natural increase of livestock will be the only thing we can count upon to supplement our casked rations."

"Yes, sir."

"It will be then that one pig will count for fifty of the wretched items we have penned aboard those transports," Phillip went on, glowering at the stern windows. He frowned. A launch was stroking alongside the flagship. "Someone's in a damned hurry. That's the trouble with people. They're always in such a damned hurry. They forget that Rome wasn't built in a day."

"Yes, sir."

A marine sentry saluted someone on deck and, moments later, Lieutenant King strode into the great cabin. "Good morning, sir."

" 'Morning, Pip. All squared away?"

Hunter coughed discreetly. "If you'll excuse me, gentlemen, there are matters aloft which I must attend to."

"Of course, of course." Phillip waited until the door shut, then he looked back at King. "Well? Everyone ready to get their stock aboard?"

"No, sir. Not everyone. There is considerable resistance to the quotas we have assigned, and—"

Phillip hunched back in his seat. "Let me guess: Captain Sinclair is once more standing upon his dignity?"

"Captain Sharp as well."

"Hn! What's biting *him* now?"

"It's the horses," King replied, slumping onto one of the ammunition trunks. "He maintains that *Golden Grove* won't hold them."

"Of course it'll damned well hold them!"

"My words exactly." King pinched the bridge of his nose and squeezed both eyes shut.

"You offered the bonus?"

"Yes."

"And?"

"Flat refusal."

Phillip scowled. "What about the other one? Sinclair?"

"He's furious."

"Tell me something new."

"He refuses point-blank to handle sheep *and* pigs."

"Why?"

"He claims that, with two hundred lagged items—"

"One hundred and eighty-one."

"He's operating at maximum capacity."

"Rubbish."

"Sir, I'm only repeating his words," King insisted quietly.

"Don't." Phillip's chin was now on his chest. "Of all the conceited, arrogant, insufferable, opinionated, stubborn, mule-brained men I have ever met—" Someone knocked on the cabin door. Phillip's chin flicked up. "Come in, damn you! Oh. Sorry, John."

Hunter smiled. "When you're free for a moment, step aloft, sir. There's a vessel approaching her moorings; she might be of interest. . . ."

Phillip pushed himself from the chair and reached for his hat. He glanced down at King. "Keep hounding the other commanders. I shall make it my pleasure to negotiate directly with Messrs. Sinclair and Sharp unless they resolve their difficulties quickly."

"The best of British luck, sir."

"Hn!" Phillip turned and followed Hunter on deck. *Sirius'* commander had his own telescope; Phillip took another from the binnacle locker and joined him at the weather rail. Hunter was focussing his glass on a three-masted stranger, picking her way across the anchorage. He glanced sideways. "What do you reckon?"

Phillip squinted against the brittle light. "A whale fisher. Her lower courses are as black as a kettle."

"And . . . ?"

"And what?"

"Where do you think she hails from?"

Phillip squinted harder. "Bremen. No, wrong lines. She's not London built, either. Could she be off your Leith or Aberdeen yards, perhaps?"

Hunter shook his head while he waited for the stranger's nameboard to swing into view. "Not when she's built like a butterbox, with six chasers and two trypots stowed like that. I'd bet my hat she's homeward bound for New England."

"Hm." Phillip continued studying the laden ship.

"Strange," Hunter went on, more to himself now, "we don't usually find New Englanders this far south. Besides, I thought the war had finished the whale fishery for them."

"So where the hell's she been?" Phillip asked, still watching the whaler through his telescope as she got ready to put up her helm. "Brazil? The Horn?"

"I don't think so," Hunter said, wiping his eyepiece with his sleeve before trying again. "By the look of the wear on her hull I'd say she's been East, to the Sunda Straits or the China Sea, or even up to that Russky outpost in the Aleutians which everyone was talking about only a few years back." Hunter slowly lowered his glass. "Come to think about it, long before we left, Sam Enderby told me he was going to send out a fleet to fish off Java. It's just possible, I suppose, that our mysterious neighbour heard about it and jumped the gun first?"

Phillip wasn't listening. "Bugger."

"Sir?"

"There goes her Rebel duster." Phillip lowered his glass, too. "She's a Yankee after all. That's all I bloody needed today."

Hunter was steadying his telescope on the flag's red and white bars as the whaler's anchors shot and she ponderously ran to a halt on their cables. "I see what you mean. A sharp customer indeed. But what else can we expect from the master of an *Enoch and Judith Hayes*—" He finished decyphering the weathered paintwork. "From Nantucket?"

The morning had begun badly for Phillip; it was becoming worse. He rammed the telescope tubes together. "And for this you called me aloft?"

Hunter shut his glass. "Yes, because Rebel or not, her master has been far and seen much."

"Like the China Sea? Or Petri-whatsisname?"

"Yes, Petropavlovsk." Hunter shrugged. "He may even have crossed tracks with a certain French gentleman and his confounded flotilla. . . ."

"Hm." Phillip considered the thought for several moments. "Very well, damned Rebel or not, just as soon as it is decently possible, make to her master and invite him aboard. Let's pump him."

"Aye aye, sir."

"And whip some ginger into those bosun's mates. They're supposed to be *lifting* that sheep aboard, not hanging it at the yardarm. And another matter—" Phillip stopped. Two more launches were stroking hard for the flagship, racing each other to get there first.

Sinclair won by a whisker and Phillip was braced to receive him as *Alexander*'s master thumped through the entry port. "This is bluidy prepost'rous!"

"Compliments to the quarterdeck," Phillip snapped back.

Sinclair bobbed his head and kept on coming. "Yon Mr. King o' yours has had the audacity to assign three dozen ewes and five pigs to *my* vessel!"

"Lieutenant King has had the good sense to obey *my* orders," Phillip replied stiffly.

"Then I have indeed come to the right person!"

"So, it seems, has Captain Sharp," Phillip observed. "Shall we go below, gentlemen? We'll be able to speak more freely in my quarters."

Sinclair glowered and Sharp sniffed, but both men followed their commodore along the companionway and past the sentry. The door slammed shut. Phillip sat down. "Now. What appears to be your problem?"

"Yon bluidy sheep and pigs, *that's* my problem—!"

"An' them two 'orses on top of everything else I got!" Sharp added, wagging his finger.

Phillip said nothing. Then, "Before nightfall I shall have four sheep and twelve ducks sharing this cabin with me. In addition there will be fourteen bags of barley meal—roughly where you are standing, Mr. Sharp—and six sheaves of hay where you are sitting, Mr. Sinclair."

"But I've got pigs!"

"In addition to which," Phillip went on very quietly, "I am expected to supervise all eleven vessels of our convoy and eventually to bring you to safe landfall after sailing an ocean route which has only been navigated three times in recorded history—"

"What about them 'orses!"

"God damn your horses." Phillip had begun to rise. "God damn your pigs. God damn your petty, scheming, snivelling complaints!" Phillip's inkwell was jumping across the chart table in time with his pounding fists. "Get out! Get out the lot of you! Get out! Get out—!"

The sentry's ear flicked away from the door as the two merchant masters trudged past and climbed on deck again. Sharp pulled a long face. "I didn't think 'e 'ad it in 'im."

"Hot words never buttered parsnips, or stowed those bluidy animals," Sinclair replied, reaching under his jacket and pulling out a fresh stick of tobacco. He gnawed one end and passed the rest to *Golden Grove*'s skipper. "So he can't be bluffed into taking them off our hands. Now what?"

Sharp had negotiated with Sinclair before. He sadly shook his head. "Search me. What d'*you* reckon?"

Alexander's master let both shoulders sag. "That's a very difficult question, Walter."

"Desperate 'ard, Duncan."

The two men chewed along in silence while the second of *Sirius*' flock was winched aboard and booted into a temporary holding pen amidships. Somewhere upwind the convoy's chaplain was finding it difficult to start a hymn among his congregation; it had been *Alexander*'s turn for an open-air service today. Sinclair gobbed downwind.

"The truth of the matter is, it's like this," Sharp went on simply. "It's not them 'orses. 'Orses is nothing—we must've shifted tons of 'orses to Yankee Land during the war, money for old rope—it's their feed. See? They eat too much."

"Aye, and pigs stink too much."

"Not all that much," Sharp disagreed amiably, also gobbing to leeward. "Besides, Sparrow Legs is offering another couple of quid on top for every bugger you land. I mean to say, that'll be an extra ten quid, straight in the pocket, just for feeding the little sods. Money for jam. . . ."

Sinclair had to nod at this fair description of his usual business dealings. "Look, Walter, why don't we both put our cards on the table?"

"Good idea, Duncan."

"I think I can see a way to get us both off the hook."

"I reckoned you might."

"How about ye take the pigs—and the extra ten pounds, cash—and I take back your two passengers? It'll work like this," Sinclair went on modestly. "Mr. and Mrs. Johnson are not the most happy souls to have aboard, as I well recall from the start of this fool's errand, and in addition they've been filling that enormous space you have abaft the spirit locker. Right?"

"I wouldn't 'ave said it was all *that* big."

"It'll hold two horses, not to mention five pigs," Sinclair announced briskly. "That way ye get—let me see—twenty pounds for the horses, plus ten for the pigs. Why, that's close on one hundred in bonus payments, once all the loose ends are tied up! And it doesn't stop there—!"

"Oh, but it does stop there," Sharp interrupted with a melancholy sigh. "I mean, there's the question of the passage money what the devil driver and 'is missis paid. It's on the ship's books now. Desperate 'ard juggling owners' accounts, as you would know. Won't look good for me when I get back to London and they go through the books, and they count the cash-box, and they find it don't tally."

"I see your point, Walter."

"I thought you might, Duncan."

Sinclair's fingers suddenly clicked. "Look, how about I chuck in half a dozen sheep—they're worth a clear thirty shillings apiece—and we'll call it evens for the Reverend's passage money after you write a chit on the *Ko-Hong*'s agent in Canton? That way it doesn't have to go through the books."

Sharp's fingers also snapped. "I got a better idea. *You* keep the sheep—and their thirty bob apiece—and the pigs, too. I give you the devil driver and missis, and I take the 'orses. Right?"

"Walter," Sinclair rumbled gently, "ye already have the horses. What ye now need is space to put 'em in, and I am the only one who can provide that. . . ."

"Duncan," the other shipmaster replied with a wondering shake of the head, *"you* got them pigs. Now, speaking for m'self, I don't mind pigs. So if I take a couple off your 'ands, you get the devil driver, I keep the accounts straight, and nobody gets a chit on the *Ko-Hong.*"

"Walter, ye are a hard man to please."

"That's what mum used to tell me."

"Look," Sinclair insisted reasonably, "I'll take the Johnsons while ye take the pigs and six of the sheep."

"Straight swap."

"No way. Two passengers, five pigs, six sheep or the deal's off."

Sharp shook his head. "Two passengers, two pigs, no sheep, and I keep the baggage."

"Oh, aye?" Sinclair began stroking his chin. "What might your slice o' that cake be, I wonder?"

"Books, 'undreds of books, full of paper. There's a bloke I know in Greenmarket will take any amount to make cartridges and such."

Sinclair aimed his finger. "Two passengers, five pigs, no sheep, and keep the baggage."

"Four pigs."

"Five!"

"Four."

Sinclair grinned. "Done. And I'll let ye take two o' the sheep as a special favour."

44

JOHNSON PAUSED for breath and tried smiling again at today's congrega tion on *Alexander*'s waist deck. "Thus, as was written by the prophet Isaiah: 'Come now, and let us reason together, saith the Lord: though your sins be as scarlet, they shall be as white as snow; though they be red like crimson, they shall be as wool—' "

But many of the lags still scratched themselves; and most of the crewmen still dozed; and all of the marines still stood rigidly to attention, watching their commandant's back while being watched by their sergeant at the back.

The convoy's chaplain suddenly flung both arms to Heaven, his gown and white Geneva bands flapping in the wind. " 'But if ye refuse and rebel, ye shall be devoured with the sword: for the mouth of the Lord hath spoken it!' Amen."

Johnson's arms fell to his side. The lags stopped scratching The crew woke up. Ross turned. "Sarn't Ramsbottom!"

"Sah!"

"Carry on!"

"Sah!"

The marine commandant turned again, his heels clicking smartly. " 'But if ye refuse and rebel, ye shall be devoured with the sword'? I like it, Mr. Johnson."

The weary chaplain began packing away. "Thank you, major. I am happy someone does. But as for the rest of our brethren, who can ever tell what they are thinking?"

"Thinking?" Ross almost smiled.

Johnson glanced up. "Yes, thinking. Though they may fidget, and yawn, and resemble blocks of wood, they remain sentient human beings, capable of expressing some thought and emotion. But what thoughts? And which emotions?" He shook his head and finished wrapping the black gown around the chalice, the unopened flask of wine and the intact box of consecrated wafers.

Ross smiled indulgently at the much younger man. "I'd never bother myself on that account. They're not worth it."

Johnson looked up sharply. "But you are wrong, they *are* worth it. And it does trouble me to find myself so incapable of reaching those most in need." He hesitated. "They move and they articulate words. They have human faculties and functions. And yet they remain as impervious to reasoned argument as the man on the moon." He hesitated again. "I know what to think of them, but who knows what they think of us?"

"Think?" Ross laughed outright. "Since when have items of that stripe been expected to *think*? That's what we've been told to do, to think for 'em!"

"Major, I did not—"

Ross was shaking his head from side to side. "The average private soldier is the most pathetic item of equipment we use, unable to tell his right foot from his left. He is dirty, he is stupid, he is forever grumbling. And yet, show him enough stick, and he performs well enough." Ross pointed at the four ranks of redcoats, now marching on the spot while they fixed bayonets to the staccato yelps of their sergeant.

"I am not qualified to comment—"

"Quite."

"However, I was not referring to your troops."

"Uh?"

Johnson hefted his bag and frowned. "My duty embraces our fallen brethren as well, most of whom might indeed be enslaved Africans for all that we understand of their ways." He hesitated, frowning more to himself now. "There could be darker continents, much closer to us than we have hitherto imagined. But, as I have already said, even these prisoners were once born sentient humans, amenable to the Gospel's truth—"

Ross clenched his sword grip. " 'Servants, be subject to your masters with all fear; not only to the good and gentle, but also to the froward.' First Peter, chapter two, verse eighteen."

"The devil can always cite Scripture for his own purpose, major."

"I—I resent that imputation, sir!"

"Why? Is it not true?"

Ross' face went mauve. "I'll be damned if I—!"

Johnson's face went pale. "You'll be damned if you continue using such language? That is, I fear, ordained by Scripture." He turned. One of the convicted labourers was standing only a few feet away, listening intently. "Yes?"

"Er, begging pardon, ge'men." Cribb forgot himself and stiffened to attention for a moment. "One of them?" He pointed at the wad of pamphlets which the chaplain had intended distributing to his congregation.

"You would like one to read?"

"A couple, if it's all the same, yes. Er, me and a couple of mates like to put our 'eads together and, well, sort of look at 'em when we get the chance." Cribb's lip suddenly trembled as his voice choked on a tear. "We reckon it's the only way, us being lagged, like. Some of us is—is regular bad lots." He blinked down at the deck, then up again, smiling manfully. "But they goes quiet as little lambs when we tell 'em stories, about Bible things and such. Does 'em the power of good, it does. Us too."

Johnson smiled compassionately. "May God's blessings be upon you, my son."

Cribb bobbed his head and took the top three pamphlets, then turned on his heel and strode away like a man with a renewed mission.

Johnson met Ross' glare. "That is your answer, major. Dirty and stupid they may be, but the Gospel's leaven still has the power to work upon even their stunted, brutish hearts. Good day."

The chaplain almost collided with Sinclair at the entry port as the older man puffed aboard. "And a good day to you, captain."

"Aye." *Alexander*'s master watched the civilian climb out of sight, then turned and cocked an eye at Ross. "What's up wi' him? Been giving ye cheek?"

" 'The devil can quote Scripture for his own purpose'? By God, let him wait till I command the colony!" Ross' boots slammed the deck planks as he spun around. "Sarn't Ramsbottom!"

"Sah!"

"Seven days parade order kit inspection!"

"Sah!"

It was Levi's turn to host dinner. Not one crumb too many fell into any of the three wooden bowls. Cribb licked his clean and burped with contentment as he stretched out on the other man's shelf for a yarn. "Raspberry Nose was in a regular shitty today. 'Ere, chuck us the doings—"

Levi passed over one of the new pamphlets.

Cribb ripped the title page in half and began grating a knuckle of tobacco into the folded paper. "Of course, Colonel Tarleton 'ad tons more class, but even 'e was a prime shitfire when things wasn't done right, first time," he went on fairmindedly, tipping the dark brown chips into his palm to rub them. "I reckon that's why 'im and me got along so good, once we begun pumping lead into the Doodlers, Over There. And I reckon that's 'alf Raspberry's trouble; what 'e needs is a proper sergeant. Poor ol' Ram's Bum wouldn't know 'is arse from 'is elbow once Jacky Reb' jumped 'im with an 'ot ambush." Cribb licked the paper tube and tucked in the ends. " 'Elpless bloody sea soldier."

"The devil driver wasn't so bad today," Levi commented, also ripping a square of paper to roll a papirosa.

"I seen worse," Cribb was forced to agree, leaning over the candle and sucking at the concealed flame. He eased back, whiffing smoke at the timber overhead. "Abe?"

"Uh huh?"

"Straight up, mate, you reckon all that Bible stuff works?"

"Sure it works. Did it not get us more doings when you gaffed for it?"

"No, straight up, serious. You reckon all that 'sins white as snow' stuff works?"

Levi leaned across the candle, one eye on the gate at the far end of the hold where a bored sentry lounged, two hours on, four off, whenever the convoy was in harbour. He shrugged, the smouldering tobacco hidden inside his cupped palm. "Joe, if praying was any good, we would have to buy it years ago. So why you think the devil driver is still trying to give it away?"

"Hmm. Good point."

"Well, Oi reckon Raspberry was on the grog, that's what Oi reckon," Thorpe announced, rejoining the conversation. He grinned happily and tapped something bundled under his arm. "What say we join 'im?"

"That's the ticket!"

"Sure!"

The other two men wriggled closer as Thorpe reverently unwrapped a stoneware half gallon of homebrew—mashed biscuit, sour oatmeal and dried fruit pinched by Ratbag from the officers' pudding mix just before Cooky sank it in the galley boiler. Stirred with water, it had been aging for several days inside an empty laudanum bottle—borrowed by Levi from Balmain's stock while the surgeon was attending to other things—and kept warm inside one of the new haybag mattresses tossed aboard at the Cape.

Cribb let Thorpe draw the stopper, a plug of old bandage which had let the gas escape while most of the fermenting liquor stayed behind. He had concocted similar cordials in the prison camps and this latest one had been his idea; he had also supplied some of the biscuit as well as putting the hard word on Ratbag for raisins and dried apple. "Smell all right, Ben?"

"Oi reckon!"

" 'Ere, let's see." Cribb sniffed the bouquet, then cautiously rolled a sip around his palate, eyes shut, and swallowed. "She'll do."

Thorpe almost hugged himself, hurrying to help while Levi decanted the murky liquid through another piece of bandage and Cribb held the first bowl steady.

"Muzzle toff. . . ."

Levi winked back.

Thorpe gave a dreamy sigh and joined the warm, friendly silence as the opening round of drinks went down.

"Ahhh. . . ."

"Ah hah."

"Good drop o' belch that, Oi reckon!"

Cribb licked his bowl and rolled onto one elbow to relight the stub of his papirosa. "I've 'ad worse." Puff. "But I've 'ad better. In Vauxhall Gardens. . . ."

Levi raised an eyebrow at Thorpe, but Cribb didn't notice. He trickled smoke. "They've got all them pretty lights, just like fireflies they are. And they've got bands, with tons of tunes, free. And they've got—"

"A special lady what you cannot stop thinking of, heh?"

Cribb stroked the memory. "You're not wrong, mate. She's special all right, top apple on the tree. You should've seen 'er, Over There. . . ."

"No." Levi was still smiling as he filtered another round of homebrew. "I am happy just to see her with us here. The rest you can keep."

Cribb blew smoke and glanced sideways. "Abe? You noticed something odd about 'er ladyship?"

"What?"

"She's different. She 'asn't looked the same since we got to this Cape place." He sighed and shook his head. "For a while, back there in Rio, I reckoned we was getting along like an 'ouse on fire. No more, though. I 'ope the Bulldog's treating 'er right. Still, once we get to Bottommy Town, I'll see she gets fed tons of grub."

"Sure."

Cribb drew smoke. "Straight up, I'll croak the first bastard what so much as thinks of laying finger on 'er—"

"*Mazel tov.*"

"Ta." Cribb took the drink and raised it to Levi and Thorpe in turn. " 'Appy days."

45

KITTY BRANDON sauntered past as the barbers began packing away for the day. She slowed and turned. "You spoke, Cribb?"

"You bloody well know I did! That's the second time I've said good night!"

"Is that a fact? And here was I thinking you were saying goodbye."

"What's *that* supposed to mean!"

She struck an elegant pose and swept one hand across Table Bay, from Zout River to Signal Hill. "I would have imagined that a person of your alleged daring would long since have bolted, for was that not what you promised me you were going to do in Rio?" She folded her arms. "We must therefore conclude that you have found this floating farmyard more to your taste than the Copper Hill prison of which you so often boasted, or surely you would not still be with us?"

"Why! I'll—!"

"One step more and I shall scream."

"You—"

"Indeed I am not," she replied. "Once, I almost believed that twaddle about your adventures in the colonies with Bloody Tarleton, sergeant-with-seven-battle-honours." She shrugged. "Well, if nothing else, it has proved that you are not only an outright coward, but a natural born gypsy liar as well."

"You bitch."

"Flattery will get you nowhere." She unfolded her arms. "Good night, Mr. Thorpe."

The barber's assistant scratched his ear. "Oi reckon that's not being fair, that's what Oi reckon."

"I—I'll kill 'er."

Thorpe stopped scratching. "Then Bulldog'll get you, then what?"

"Chrissakes, not 'ere, stupid."

"Oh, where then?"

"Bottommy."

"Well, Oi reckon—" Thorpe shut his mouth. Sinclair was on deck again, pacing for'ard as *Golden Grove*'s launch closed over the last ten or fifteen yards. It bumped alongside. Sinclair looked up at a passing gull as Richard Johnson came aboard and stamped his foot. "This is an absolute outrage! My wife and I have just been evicted from our quarters without so much as a—!"

Sinclair looked down. "Good evening, sir. Ma'am. I trust ye both had a dry crossing?"

Mary Johnson was no less furious than her husband, but her temper was under better control. "Mr. Sinclair. Would you have the kindness to explain *why* our quarters have been taken back at such short notice?"

"Commodore's orders," Sinclair replied simply. "The horses will be required in the colony."

"While I suppose we are not!" Johnson snapped.

"That is entirely a matter of opinion, sir. Now, if you will accompany me, I'll show you to your place—"

"Captain Sinclair," Mary Johnson interrupted, "our cabin was hardly adequate six or seven months ago."

"It won't be the cabin, ma'am."

"Good!"

"Ye will find the geese and most of the poultry feed in there now."

"I—I beg pardon?"

"But Mr. Olsen has volunteered to share his bunk with ye, Mr. Johnson—"

"No!"

"While ye, ma'am, will share the chart table."

"No! No! No!" Richard Johnson was starting to quake. "This is an—an—an—!"

"Of course," Sinclair mused, "if ye would prefer, I can pack ye ashore now so that a passing vessel will take ye back to England."

Mary Johnson suddenly groped for her husband's arm, clutched at his coat and pressed her face into his shirt front. Sinclair pointed at the passengers' two bags. A sailor picked them up and waited for orders while the master tapped Mrs. Johnson on the back. "Come, come, worse things happen at sea. My woman has cooked something tasty for ye both."

Her husband found a handkerchief and Mary Johnson blew her nose; then, with her still leaning on his arm, they followed Sinclair aft and down to the great cabin. Richard Johnson squeezed to one side and let his wife go first. Two hammocks stuffed with green fodder swung between the roof beams, and a basket of chickens was adjusting to life on top of the arms locker.

Kitty Brandon had put on a fresh pinafore to mark the occasion. She inclined her head as if acknowledging applause, and moved forward a pace. "Good evening."

Johnson shut the door once he'd squashed into the cabin, then nodded at the self-assured young woman. "Ah. Good evening. Er. . . ?"

"My name is Brandon, Mrs. Katharine Brandon, actress."

"Oh." Her national reputation had not penetrated the stone walls of Magdalene College, Cambridge; the name and the profession meant nothing to him. "Good evening, Mrs. Brandon."

"Delightful weather, is it not?"

"Yes. Isn't it?"

"When you are both ready, I shall start dinner."

"Oh. Yes. Of course." Johnson wriggled one of the chairs away from the table so that his wife could sit. Then he joined her while the master took his place at the head of the chart table. Kitty Brandon did the honours with pot and ladle. She lifted the lid, dipped a generous serving of mutton stew and poured it into the master's bowl. Then Richard Johnson's. Then his wife's. Then her own.

Mary Johnson was in control of her face again. "Thank you, Mrs.—?"

"Brandon."

"Grace?" Johnson prompted. "For what we are about to receive may the Lord make us truly thankful. Amen."

Mary Johnson said nothing. She poked her spoon at the chunks of meat awash with broth. Kitty Brandon swapped glances with Sinclair across the table while she cut herself a slice of bread. "Would you like some too, Mrs. Johnson?"

"Thank you, no. Mrs.—?"

"*Brandon.*"

The conversation lapsed as Sinclair tucked into his dinner. "This is wholesome good!" He frowned at the Johnsons. "Eat up. A month from now, when it's salt junk and biscuit, ye'll be glad ye did."

Richard Johnson put down his spoon. "My wife and I have adequate provisions of our own, thank you."

"Oh, aye?" Sinclair nodded approvingly. "Where?"

"They will be coming across from *Golden Grove*, in due course."

"I fancy they'll be staying where they are, wherever that may now be."

"I don't understand you?"

"Room, Mr. Johnson, room," Sinclair replied, blowing across his spoon to cool it. "First the livestock, then their food, then the rest o' us. Commodore's orders."

"But this is a—!"

"I've no doubt it is," Sinclair agreed, sucking the spoon dry. "Let's just say that when next ye view your baggage, it will come as something of a surprise? As for any extra dainties, they'll be something to look forward to in Botany Bay. Meanwhile, if I were ye, I'd eat up or else it's hungry to bed. . . ."

Johnson looked at his wife's set face, then back at Sinclair. "This is not of our choosing. First thing in the morning I shall protest—in person—to Captain Phillips. Therefore you must understand that we will only be staying the night. Now, am I to understand that Mr. Olsen will be giving his bunk to me?"

"He will be sharing it wi' ye."

"And my wife?"

"She gets a berth under the table."

Johnson laughed unsteadily. "Table?"

"That's what they're called in Scotland."

Johnson glanced between his knees at the floor, then up again. "But there is not enough room there for one person."

"True," Sinclair agreed, nodding for Kitty Brandon to cut him more bread, "but it'll take two at a pinch."

"*Two!*"

Sinclair squashed some crumbs into a ball and thriftily popped it into his mouth. "My woman has to rest somewhere. They'll be quite cosy together."

Mary Johnson's eyes opened, shut, opened again. "Are you saying that I—I must sleep with that—*that* woman!"

Sinclair scratched his chin whiskers. "Aye. It's that, or take your chances in the fo'c'sle."

"No! No, no, no!" Mary Johnson could feel her control slipping fast. "Never! Not with—with that woman!"

Sinclair looked at Kitty Brandon's impersonal smile for a moment, then looked back at the other young woman. "She suits me well enough. Why, there's many a duke would think himself lucky to have found as good. What's the problem?"

"She—she is—she is that Brandon woman."

Richard Johnson gripped his wife's wrist. "Control yourself in public! Which Brandon woman?"

"She. She k-killed. Her lover."

"More bread, Mr. Johnson?" Kitty Brandon enquired, holding out the knife.

"No! Thank you." He was trying to push from the table. "This has been a very upsetting day for my wife. The fresh air on deck will do her good. If you will excuse us—"

"Of course," the master's woman replied, "take all the time you need. I'll have the mattress ready when she comes back."

Dinner was served. Cribb biffed Tickler aside and helped himself at the bucket of beef water and greens, then held a place for Thorpe and Levi, before letting the rest of the hold inch forward and feed.

Levi sat cross-legged on Thorpe's shelf. "What's this Ben saying about you and Mrs. B.?"

Cribb glanced up unemotionally. "She's put on a dead man's shirt. Chuck us the mouse mirror."

Levi obliged by passing a hard, flat tile of ration bread. "Why?"

Cribb drank over the rim of his bowl. "None of your business."

Levi ignored the tone. "What she say?"

"None of your business."

"So when you going to croak her?"

"None of your business."

"One of my mates is to cut Bulldog woman's throat and is none of my business?"

"Uh huh."

"Joe, please, what she do?"

"None of your business."

Levi peered across the candle's glow. "What she do, Ben?"

Thorpe grimaced uneasily. "Reckoned Joe were a coward. And things."

Levi looked back at Cribb, now leaning against the curved hull timbers while he rolled an after-dinner smoke. "That what she say?"

"Uh huh."

"Why?"

Cribb picked up the candle and sucked his tobacco alight. "None of your business."

Levi began rolling himself a papirosa. "Joe? Once, long away, I have another good mate. Was also half gypsy man. Like that we were, yes?" He crossed his fingers. "Then, one day, some *loch* call him a bad name. Out with the knife—zzzt!" Levi shrugged. "You know why they burn him? Not for doing knife job. No. Was for having what you have, my friend, too much pride."

"You was thinking that when you croaked Mangler?" Cribb queried, studying the tip of his own papirosa.

"Puf! Was different."

"Sure, sure."

Levi borrowed the candle and lit up. "Coward? What's Mrs. B. know? She is a clever woman, but she is still only woman. For your own good, forget it."

Cribb snorted smoke down his nostrils. "She reckons I never been in Americky."

Levi shrugged again. "What she know about that?"

"She was there. Remember?"

"Oh."

Cribb took another pull at his papirosa. "She reckons I never 'eld rank. She reckons I never done them seven battles."

Levi had begun to frown with a shared concern. "Joe? I understand. She hurt you? Sure, is natural what you feel. Maybe I had been a fusilman I would feel the same. But is this reason to chuck everything we working for? Think of Bottommy Town!"

"She reckons I'm, I'm a gypsy liar."

Levi pinched his smoke cold and stowed the butt for remakes. "Joe, tell me what you got in there for brains? Old shoes? Think! Soon we are going to be more lucky than any cove in the world! Reb Mordechai promise it, remember? But our Joe wants only to chuck it away because what a woman say. *Ei!*"

Cribb folded a second page in one of Johnson's pamphlets and ripped it down the middle. "Did I ever tell you what was so special about being Over There?"

"They give you money for killing."

"Sometimes," Cribb agreed, rasping his tobacco stick onto the paper. "But there was more."

"Like what?"

Cribb hesitated. "You ever 'ad some swell cove set 'is dogs on you?"

"Sure."

"When you was only a nypper *that* big?" Cribb asked, lifting his hand waist high.

"No-o. I was little older."

"You ever watch your grandma get whipped?"

"No."

"You ever 'ad some flash bastard try selling you the coat some other poor bugger's got the pox in, so's you'll catch it and croak, too?"

"No."

"Then you not even started to know what it means to be called a gypsy."

"I been called worse."

"No way." Cribb shook his head. "So now you know what was special about being Over There."

Levi changed his mind about not rolling another smoke. He took the other half of Cribb's paper and borrowed the tobacco grater. "What you mean?"

"I mean there's no sod sets dogs on the king's uniform, not when a cove's got an 'orse and a yard of steel in 'is fist." Cribb's voice was flat. "I mean nobody gives lip to a sergeant major. I mean them bullets don't ask who your grandma was, because when they're pouring in, the only thing that counts is what a cove is." Cribb hissed smoke between clenched teeth. "And long before it ended, Over There, I counted for plenty."

"And for this you will now kill Mrs Brandon?"

"Yes."

Levi sighed and leaned across to the candle. "You are so much like my mate, the one they burn for the knife job. Like him, you have much to learn yet." He glanced sideways, sucking heat. "Be like little grass, Joe, not big tree. Bend."

"So's some other shit can wipe 'is boots on me? No thanks! I've 'ad that."

Levi sighed again. "Once there was a Jew pedlar man watching two fine gentlemen with pistols on such a grass. Was also 'honour affair' with bad names, the whole *shmeer.* Someone drop a handkerchief. Up with the pistols, pam-pam! The two gentlemen they put in boxes and carry away. The pedlar man walk away. Crazy."

"That so?"

"Yes."

It was Cribb's turn to draw smoke. "Once there was a *didikai* watched another cove stand up with nothing but 'is bare maulers to square a regular pug. That stoush 'ad bad names as well. I never seen a mill like it. The bloke should've been pasted flat by the pug, but 'e wasn't, and 'e didn't bend. Game? I reckon they don't come no better than what 'e was that day. Crazy? Not on your life. 'E done the right thing, 'e croaked the bastard."

Levi frowned earnestly. "All that Mangler stuff is different, Joe. We *need* Mrs. Brandon to grift with us in Bottommy. Remember?"

"You do, I don't." Cribb reached for his end of the blanket. "Wake me up when it starts raining gold spoons."

Levi ripped the blanket off Cribb's face. "Listen to me, *putz*! All my life I work for this! I eat zhit for this! For this I say, 'Yes, your honour! No, your honour! Up your arse, your honour!' And why?! Because one day I'm going to be a number one! You think being gypsy is bad?! Try being Jew! Try—!"

Cribb snatched the blanket. "Shut your bleeding gob!"

"No! You think I sell rajah watches all my life, *shmuck*! Not with that lady I not! With that lady we have class! With that lady we have future!" Levi's breath rasped as he stopped. "And now little Joe wants to kill her? All because she call him a bad name? Tch, tch, tch. . . ."

"Listen you—!"

"No. You listen. Lay one finger on Mrs. Brandon and I fix you good." Cribb's face was cinder grey. "Don't give me no more lip."

"And Oi reckon you both got enough of that there blanket!" Thorpe snarled, dragging it all his way. "This be *my* place! And if you don't like it, bugger off back to your own! Go on! Bugger off!"

46

RICHARD JOHNSON had to cool his heels on deck until Phillip finished breakfast and had his hair set. Then, a quarter of an hour later, the commodore was ready to step out in full dress, gold braid buffed, buttons gleaming, breeches pipe-clayed.

"Captain Phillips! One moment, if you please."

"Yes?"

"There has been a most dreadful mistake."

"Mistake?" Phillip was genuinely puzzled.

"Some would call it another thing, but I shall forbear." Johnson paused. "Yesterday afternoon, without so much as a by-your-leave, Captain Sharp put us aboard a rowing boat and sent us back to *Alexander*. Since when my wife has had to sleep with a murderess, and I—? Well, it has been most unsatisfactory."

"Let me get this straight. Captain Sharp transferred you back to Captain Sinclair's command?"

"Correct. Most unsatisfactory."

"I wondered how they would swing it," Phillip commented. "Tell me, did you see any horses?"

"Horses? Oh, well, yes, I did. Going into our cabin."

"Splendid." Phillip began pulling on his white gloves.

"Captain? You don't seem to understand," Johnson insisted, falling into step with the dapper naval officer. "Where are my wife and I going to sleep tonight?"

"Where did you sleep last night?" Phillip asked, glancing through the entry port to check that his gig was ready.

"Well, actually, she with this—murderess. And I, with a sailor."

"And you were both still intact this morning?"

"Yes, but—"

"What a lucky omen for our enterprise. Think of the sermons you'll be able to compose now." Phillip briefly touched his hatbrim. "My compliments to Mrs. Johnson when you return to *Alexander*."

"But—!" But the chaplain was speaking to himself.

Phillip finished arranging his coat tails and nodded at the coxswain. "The American."

"Aye aye, sir! Lively now. Heave away!"

The stench had been terrible downwind from *Enoch and Judith Hayes,* and it grew worse as the Royal Navy gig stroked closer. And closer. Years of flensing and boiling hot blubber on deck had pickled the entire vessel in rancid oil and fat. Phillip stopped trying to hold his breath as the coxswain reached for a mooring line and his men shipped oars.

There were, of course, no ceremonial side parties to pipe him aboard this or any other American merchantman he might have chosen to visit. Indeed, there was nobody on deck to greet him except for a few negroes and Polynesians, lascars and Greenlanders at their duties; whaling skippers kept themselves in command by keeping their crews divided.

The officer of the watch ambled from a patch of shade by the bricked cauldrons abaft the mainmast and eyed this latest visitor from the British flagship. "You that Cap'n Phillips they been talkin' about?" He was a Londoner, almost certainly a deserter or prisoner gone over to the enemy during the recent war, and clearly enjoying every moment of the meeting, as he had when Lieutenant King was snubbed the previous day.

"Phillip. No 's,' if you please. Captain Brown is expecting me."

"You reckon?"

The visitor did not reply but, instead, ducked after him down the hatch. They straightened in the harpooners' quarters—hardly less spacious and comfortable than the master's, further aft—Phillip judged, waiting at the cabin door while the mate knocked and stood aside for him to squeeze past.

Captain Amos Brown did not look up. Wire-framed spectacles on long nose, grey hair plaited in a pigtail, homespun sleeves rolled over his wrists to save the ledger from smudging as his quill looped and dotted across the page.

Phillip composed himself to wait, and watch, and learn. He was not offended by his reception. The trader captains of New Bedford and Newport, Martha's Vineyard and Nantucket had been ruined after the Royal Navy bombarded their home ports. However, to judge from the weight of polished brass and varnished mahogany built into *Enoch and Judith*'s great cabin, Amos Brown must have run several good cargoes of contraband through the blockade off Long Island, because few admirals could afford to keep the same state when they were at sea. No cannon were lashed to this polished deck, no ammunition chest stood where the horsehair sofa rested, and here was one ship's officer who didn't need to sleep under a sheet of tarpaulin whenever a mild chop squirted water between the rotten planks over his ear.

The ledger shut. The inkwell shut. The spectacles shut. Amos Brown's face shut as he looked up. "Well?"

"May I sit down?"

"Only if you must."

"Thank you." Phillip chose the sofa, loosened his blue frock coat and made himself easy, ankles crossed. His smile never wavered. "May I say how much I regret that you were unable to accept my invitation to dine aboard *Sirius* last night? However, had you done so, I would've been deprived of the pleasure of accepting your kind invitation to luncheon today."

"Uh?"

"You see," Phillip went on, "I have to entrust a small but profitable commission to a prompt, to an honourable, to a dependable sailing master." He shrugged. "I saw your flag, I read your ship's lines, and I knew that my search was at an end. Assuming, of course, that you are open to my offer. . . ."

Amos Brown eased back in his chair and read the lines of this hooknosed little Brit: a whole peck of pride must've been swallowed before such as he would invite himself aboard an American vessel. He needed something. "Offer?"

Phillip smiled. "Yes. There are some despatches which must reach London without delay. I estimate from your ship's appearance that you are now homeward bound from the Java Straits? The China Sea? Petropavlovsk? Anyhow, such being the case you'll need to water at Rio, which means you'll be able to deliver my papers to the Admiralty agent for onward transmission."

Brown tested each word as if it were a trade dollar. "And what makes you figure I'd take 'em? Or, if I did, that your 'Admiralty agent' would ever get 'em?"

Phillip looked puzzled. "Then I would have been much mistaken in my judgment of you. Oh, I know what you are alluding to. I also realise that the pain of recent events cannot be mopped up like spilled wine. Indeed, it would be a pity if it were, for then both parties might be tempted to repeat the same errors.

"Speaking now as a private citizen, not as a king's officer, it is a matter of the deepest concern to me when two great nations—such as the United Kingdom and the United States—find themselves disagreeing over issues which ought to be resolved amicably at the conference table." Phillip sighed. "The past cannot be remade, much as we might like to rebuild it, but happily we are still the masters of our futures. . . ."

"Still don't tell me why I should be an unpaid postrider for Farmer George."

Phillip's eyebrows shot up. "Did I say unpaid? Great heavens. I shall, of course, be including a draft for twenty guineas, payable in local specie, London credit notes or gold at Rio." He shrugged. "I regret that this is all I'm allowed to offer by way of a mail bounty; however, I'm sure our men in Brazil will direct you to another parcel or packet, for an appropriate fee, of course."

Phillip rested. This could have been a friendly game of whist beside the fire at Cuffnells, partnering Theodora Rose at sixpence a point, as he waited to see which card Brown would now play on the universal trump—money. King George might still blaze in effigy on American village greens every June fourth, or July fifth, or whatever, but Phillip doubted if one in a thousand true patriots would object to carrying His Majesty's effigy in their pockets any other day of the year.

Amos Brown cleared his throat. "Let all know that my vessel proudly flies the colours of the free Republic of the United States of America and, as such, will always abide by the rules of neutrality. Therefore I, the captain, sailing master and principal shareholder in the *Enoch and Judith Hayes* of Nantucket, the Commonwealth of Massachusetts, must be assured and convinced that no package, envelope, paper or document entrusted to my care for forward delivery in any way infringes, contravenes or interferes with the sovereign rights and neutrality of the aforesaid Commonwealth and/or Republic of the United States."

Phillip marvelled at the lung power which drove such voices on and on. "You have my word of honour, captain."

Amos Brown knew all about British words of honour: unlike guinea gold pieces their value was negotiable. But the necessary legalities had been observed, now to business. He reached into a locker under the chair and brought out a cut-glass decanter and two large rummers. "Madeira, Mr. Phillips?"

"Thank you, Mr. Brown."

The whaling skipper filled both glasses to the brim and studied his for a moment. "During those 'recent events' of which you spoke, one of our officers was sent across to parley with your side, and, while behind the British lines, he was entertained to dinner. However, instead of the customary toast, you gave him 'General Washington, dead or alive. . . .' " Brown studied his guest. "To what shall we drink today?"

Phillip considered the question. "Actually, I heard that your colonel first drank to General Washington, then proposed a toast to 'the Prince of Wales, drunk or sober.' However, today I would prefer it if we saluted 'Concord, noun or place-name.' "

Brown chuckled. "To Concord."

"To concord."

The American lowered his glass. "Tell me, Mr. Phillips, why is it so imperative that you send these despatches to London? Why can't they await the arrival of a British ship, homeward bound from India or China?"

Phillip rested his glass and selected the best card to take this trick as well. "I wish that I could, Mr. Brown. However, I am under the strictest orders to proceed with all haste to our, ah, destination. I simply cannot afford to delay any longer."

Brown nodded sympathetically. "May I be so bold as to enquire where that destination might be?"

"There's no need to be cautious with me," Phillip replied with another disarming smile. "Actually, I've been given orders to establish a convict depot and outpost at Botany Bay, on the east coast of New Holland. That's all."

"New Holland, eh?" The American eyed his cabin roof. "A long way from home, Mr. Phillips, a *very* long way indeed. Convicts, you say?" He sipped wine and judged this novel plan. "My! The benevolence of the British government never ceases to amaze. Let me see: six transports hired at two dollars per ton per month, add rations and a back cargo from Canton, add the cost of two warships for escort duties. Yes sir, Mr. Phillips, I reckon we chose a bad time to opt from the empire if your least-regarded subject can now count on free travel to the delights of the South Seas for his punishment."

Phillip frowned. "It may seem that way to you, but in matters of public health and safety no price is too high to pay."

Long experience had taught Amos Brown that only one other merchant had as sharp a nose for opportunity as a New Englander, and that was an Old Englander, and it had been his good fortune to meet a convoy of them outward bound for some trading venture thinly disguised as philanthropy. He leaned forward. "D'you reckon you'll be staying in New Holland?"

"I don't see why not," Phillip replied cautiously. "Why?"

"Then I might just be of service."

"Really?"

Brown was pushing back his seat. "It seems to me that, in two or three years' time when we meet again, you'll be starting to need replacement tools and utensils, dress materials and so forth."

Phillip could read the other man like one of those newly illuminated shop windows in the Strand. "I'm terribly sorry, but we already have plans to send out more convoys to New Holland, many more convoys. These will keep our colonies supplied with everything we need."

"*Colonies,* eh?" The American was stooping upright, a good head and shoulders taller than Phillip, with or without cork inserts in his shoe heels. "Then we do indeed have something to discuss—"

He was reaching for one of several cupboard doors which lined the ship's cabin. It swung down like a store counter. It *was* a store counter. Amos Brown, captain and sailing master of a whaling vessel, was also the proprietor and manager of a cruising emporium, open seven days a week whenever and wherever at anchor.

"And if you will inspect closely, you will observe that I can supply the ladies with an unequalled range of ribbons, lace, pins and fancy notions at prices which are guaranteed to astonish and delight!"

Phillip hadn't the heart to tell him that not one of New Holland's future womenfolk, except Mary Johnson, was in a position to buy laces or fancy notions at any price. He raised both hands in mild protest. "Not so quickly, please. First things first. Allow me to say how much I value and esteem this chance meeting of ours. I am confident that, if my colony establishes itself and I am still in possession of New Holland when you return to southern waters, then we shall indeed have much—"

"If?"

Caught out, Phillip let both hands fall into his lap. "Ah, well, that's another matter. You see, nobody can promise which language you will find being spoken at Botany Bay when you begin trading there. Naturally, I hope it's English. However, we must face facts, it could just as easily be French. . . ."

Amos Brown knew which one he preferred to speak. King Louis may have paid for the artillery which shelled Yorktown, and France might have bought the boots and uniforms in which the Continental Army marched to victory, but all that was politics. It was also in the past. The future was beckoning as the American leaned forward again, elbows on desk. "Admiral P'rouse . . . ?"

"Then you *have* heard of him?"

"We've spoken."

"When?"

"Five months ago."

"Where?"

"The Aleutians."

"And?"

"He's bound south."

"How far?"

"The Marianas. The Solomons. New Holland."

"You're *certain*?"

"Positive."

The Royal Navy officer was also crouching across the table, his fingers clicking impatiently. "Your charts, if you please, captain."

Phillip finished lunch with Amos Brown and then ordered *Sirius'* gig to row him to the watering jetty nearest Good Hope Castle. He did not return to his flagship till last light. He saluted the quarterdeck. "Mr. Bradley! My compliments to Mr. Hunter. Have him step aft directly."

"Aye aye, sir!"

The commodore had unrolled his own chart of the South Seas and weighted its corners flat by the time *Sirius'* captain bent into the great cabin. "Sir?"

Phillip glanced up. "The Frogs are going to winter at Botany. They have a clear twenty weeks' start."

"Hell."

Phillip looked back at his chart. "M. de La Pérouse spoke with Captain Brown at Kamchatka; there is no doubt in my mind that he means to beat me. Only one thing can stop him now." Phillip's finger swept an arc across the virtual blank between Southern Africa and South America, seventy million square miles of opportunity for the first Great Power to grasp it. *"La Boussole* and *L'Astrolabe* are steering past tropic islands. Every new one they sight and name will be another temptation to dawdle while some savant writes about it. I, on the other hand, am going this way." The finger rapped empty white paper below the broken outline of Pieter Nuytsland. "Due south. It's the most punishing run of them all, but it is also the fastest. We have that on the best authority."

"Bill Bligh's?"

"No, His Excellency's. This afternoon he finally relented and granted me permission to see the pilot books."

Hunter blinked. The handwritten *rutters* for the Indian and Southern oceans had been Holland's commercial secrets for two centuries; few foreigners had even seen them, hardly any had ever studied their pages. "But—how?"

Phillip shrugged. "His Excellency supports the legitimate *stadhouder,* not that gutter rabble which Paris has bought. I explained the situation to him and he now agrees that it will be best for his nation's interests if we protect New Holland for a while, rather than have it permanently annexed by the French. . . ."

Hunter whistled tunelessly. "With respect, I've never heard the like before."

"I don't suppose you have," Phillip replied, "and you wouldn't now if I hadn't trusted your absolute silence. As it is, I've gone far beyond the terms of my commission. Not a word, understand?"

"Of course."

Phillip's pencil was starting to move across the almost blank chart, filling in two centuries of exploration and accidental landfalls, relying on the memory developed while Herr Doktor Mahler collected jars of beetles around Toulon dockyard.

He began calculating the seasonal winds and possible ocean currents in the High Forties—memorised from Abel Tasman's notes, written in Low German a century and a half before—and checked against Mr. Cook's recent observations of the Antarctic.

Hunter peered over his commodore's shoulder. "What did the pilot books tell you, sir?"

Phillip didn't look up from his work. "Something rather odd: the shortest track from the Cape to Botany is only short on paper. If we steer too direct a course we'll be trapped by the Variables of Capricorn, here, round Cape Leeuwin. The Dutch convoys to Java have, several times, but we won't fall into the same trap."

"Why?"

"I'm going south, forty-five, fifty degrees if necessary. There we shall be into this probable belt of winds, here, which will sweep us north again past Van Dieman's Land. Here."

"Hm. Longer distance, subtract faster sailing, equals shorter time elapsed?"

"Correct." Phillip had stepped off the distances on the chart with his brass dividers, now he was pencilling sums down the margin.

Sirius' captain uneasily shifted his weight to the other foot. "May I urge caution?"

"Why?"

"Because, in my opinion, we'll be taking a most fearful risk if we were to take that course of action."

"Risk?"

"With respect, sir, I served my apprenticeship on the Norway and Greenland trades. I have seen the power of such an ocean."

"So?"

Hunter damped his lips. "Sir. In the name of reason, please reconsider. The northern route, here, may indeed be slower, but it will also be safer, and it is far better to be safe than sorry in such waters. What is another week or two on the slower passage if, in the end, we reach our destination intact?"

"I cannot afford to lose a single day now. Speed is everything."

"Aye, everything! Yet the plain fact of the matter is that this old tub's not up to battling such gales any more! Our bowsprit's fit only to hang the contractor who supplied it!"

"We sail south."

Hunter wiped his neck and began again. "With sincere respect, sir, I cannot, I must not agree with you. Half our vessels were sinking at Spithead before we even set sail, since when they've put nigh on another ten thousand miles under their worthless keels. Now the other half are in no better shape. No, let me finish. *Borrowdale* is an absolute disgrace, and *Charlotte* is worse. Even in a moderate blow we are bound to lose one or both."

Hunter raised his hand again to silence Phillip's objection. "It will be the height of folly to expose such vessels to such an unknown, to such an untried route. Now, sir, if I read your figures right, once we were into this belt of gales—here—there could be no turning back to Africa when we suffered damage, and there would be no turning aside to Java when the going became too hard?"

"Correct."

Sirius' captain shook his head at the prospect. "We would be committed to whatever lay before us until—or if—we bore north again round Van Dieman's Land. It won't do."

"It must."

Hunter went on shaking his head. " 'Must' and 'can' are not the same words, sir. Full many's the ship I've seen put to sea from Leith to hunt the whale upon waters very similar to the ones you are now proposing. So few returned."

"I know."

"I wonder if you do?" Hunter was listening to the creak of timber and cordage. He glanced down again. "I would not have been above eight years of age when my first ship was driven upon the Isles of the Lofoten, in much the same latitudes of which you speak. It is a cruel sea."

Phillip went on walking his dividers across the empty chart, the Cape to Botany Bay, Botany Bay back to the Cape. "I'm afraid there is no alternative, John. If La Pérouse gains even one day on us now, we lose everything. Everything."

Hunter wasn't listening. "You see, it's no longer the Atlantic any more, up there, between Iceland and the Faeroes."

The dividers stopped. "How do you mean?"

Hunter shrugged helplessly. "Often the sky was black with snow. It was then we felt as if we had sailed off this world and out of this life. It is more lonely than you can ever imagine. And cold."

Phillip looked at the bare paper in front of him. "Yes."

"Then you will reconsider?"

"No."

"But surely—?"

The other man looked up. "My orders are to occupy Botany Bay. Whatever the cost."

"But—?"

The dividers snapped shut. "We sail south."

"But—!"

The commodore drew himself erect. "Your objections will be logged, Mr. Hunter. The court of enquiry will clear your name, whatever may befall us. I shall do my duty. Do yours." He frowned. "Make to all at first light: prepare for sea, immediately."

"Aye aye. Sir."

47

MARY JOHNSON lay rigid and stared at the unplaned, unfinished underside of the chart table. His duty done, the ship's rooster was now shaking his feathers in the basket which swayed near Sinclair's empty cot. All around the plodding convoy, similar birds in similar cages were doubtless making a similar din and, no doubt, somewhere her husband was still making comparisons with Noah and his ark. Not that Richard Johnson had been so wide of the mark when the eleven laden ships began standing out from Table Bay, straw blowing, sheep bleating, pigs squealing, cows mooing, bosuns shouting, sailors cursing.

Mary Johnson winced and tried getting the table leg into a more comfortable part of her back without, at the same time, actually touching her unwelcome bedmate. For her part, Kitty Brandon could not have cared less. Her stockinged feet were resting on the other young woman's bolster, and she was dozing top to tail with most of the mattress still to herself.

Sleeping this way had been the second abrupt turn around in Mary Johnson's world; the first had been the discovery that, close up, so notorious a felon could be so normal, so much like anyone else. It was rather disappointing. Richard Johnson had been interrogating his wife every day since their embarcation to learn more about the Brandon woman's habits, but so far there had not been one single scrap of remorse for the terrible deed which had brought her so low, nor was there any evidence yet of the balm of conscience at work upon her tormented soul.

Mary Johnson was more than disgusted, she was fascinated. And confused. There was something profoundly wrong with a situation which permitted a convicted murderess—a woman who should have been hanged in public a year ago—to stroll freely about the ship, as if she had every right to take such liberties. And that was not all; there was the way she spoke to Captain Sinclair, almost as if *she* were in command. And never once had she been rebuked for her impudence. And that was not all; there was the way she addressed Richard Johnson—and herself, a clergyman's wife—as if she were born an equal, sometimes as if she were rather more. Mary Johnson gritted her teeth and shoved the Irishwoman's feet several inches to the left while she rolled over and reclaimed a little of the mattress for herself.

Those in authority would have much to answer for in the months and years ahead as a normal, decent English town established itself among the palm trees of Botany Bay. There would have to be some very firm snubbing of the servant class before it was taught its station in life and the proper order was restored. Mary Johnson had begun to realise why men like Major Ross were so dissatisfied with Captain Phillip's rule; he would have no one but himself to blame when there was trouble. Her husband had been politely insistent when he went to speak about getting suitable quarters, but instead of a redress of justice, he had been fobbed off with a joke about horses!

And that was not all. There were the clothes, or, rather, there was the lack of clothes. Almost everything the Johnsons had to their name was still aboard *Golden Grove,* while they were expected to maintain proper standards in peasant squalor, among pigs, and goats, and sheep, and dogs! True, the Brandon woman had—in her irritatingly superior manner—offered to loan a flannel petticoat to keep out the chill, but, of course, the offer had been declined. Firmly.

Mary Johnson shivered and tried inching herself upright under the table so that she could use the toilet bucket in private, but even that reasonable need was thwarted as the Brandon woman also awoke, yawned and leaned against the opposite table leg. "Good morning, Mrs. Johnson. I trust you slept better?"

"No. I did not."

The other woman shook her head. "I wonder how you'd have done under an ammunition waggon, in the Colonies? Go ahead, I'm not looking. I doubt you've anything I haven't seen a thousand times. . . ." After a while, Mary Johnson stood and adjusted her dress. Kitty Brandon nodded toward the door. "Oh, while you're up, put the kettle on. I left it filled last night."

"No. I shall not! That is your task."

Kitty Brandon sighed. She pulled herself from under the table and wearily ran fingers through her hair before getting the spirit lamp alight on its bed of damp sand. She turned, gripping the nearest hammock of fodder as *Alexander* slid off a wavecrest. "Mrs. Johnson. This is the third morning I have made a very reasonable request. Your invariable response is starting to lack novelty, just as I am starting to lose patience. In a word, it bores me."

"You impertinent—!"

"Mrs. Johnson. Whatever you may say, I have no intention of standing upon my dignity. As we say in the profession, since our costumes have now been thrown into the same basket, squabbling can only tangle them more."

"I resent your tone!"

"Mrs. Johnson. I have been giving this matter some thought. A little tête-à-tête is long overdue. Why don't we both sit down until tea is ready? We can speak frankly, Captain Sinclair won't be down for his breakfast until the watches change over."

"No. I shall not."

"Suit yourself." Kitty Brandon pulled out a chair and sat down. "Item: you are making it abundantly plain that you object to sharing this cabin with me—"

"Yes. And my husband is no better served. It is daylight robbery. We paid our fare and we were *promised* a cabin of our own!"

"Now there's a horse sleeping on your bed and there's no room at the inn, is that it?"

"Yes! No. How do you mean?"

Kitty Brandon steepled her fingertips and studied the other woman, perhaps no more than eighteen months her junior. "Mrs. Johnson. If anyone has had reason to complain to the management, surely 'tis I? For was I not here long before you were? And are not the modest comforts we now both enjoy—those curtains, for instance—the products of my labour?"

"I refuse to be spoken to like this by a—by a—!"

"Murderess?"

"Exactly!"

Kitty Brandon nodded. "Go ahead, say whatever else comes into your mind, I promise that I shan't take umbrage."

"You trollop!"

" 'Harlot' carries better. I used it with stunning effect when we opened at Cheltenham with *Clarissa's Revenge, or Lust Laid Low.*"

"You, you—!"

" 'Crimson whore'? That brings 'em running! I chose it to revive *Each Servant His Master, or The World at Odds.*"

Mary Johnson's voice was shaking as she stamped her foot a third time. "I've had enough of this!"

"So have I," Kitty Brandon agreed. "Not that I entirely dismiss your alarms as being groundless, Mrs. Johnson, for 'tis not every night one as innocent as yourself must surrender to the arms of sleep while, reposing in the very same bed, lurks a human monster whose hands have dripped with gore. . . ."

Mary Johnson shuddered.

Kitty Brandon shrugged. "I am sorry to disillusion you, but, in truth, we murderers are a pretty tame lot—until someone gives us reason to kill him."

The clergyman's wife blinked.

Kitty Brandon nodded. " 'Tis true. Did you ever hear how I did it?"

"It was all over London. I saw some pictures. Ugh."

"So did I. One hundred guineas would not have printed a finer set of bills. But, of course, they told only part of the story."

"I beg your pardon?"

Kitty Brandon smiled demurely. "I mean, do I seem to be the sort of lady who could bear to pick up Boy's head, even if it had come off at the shoulders, as they allege?"

"What?"

Kitty Brandon paused to hear if the kettle was ready yet. She glanced back at the other woman. "The plain, the unvarnished truth of the matter is that I was trying my damnedest to do the very reverse. I was struggling heroically to prevent myself from being touched by him."

"Touched?"

"Touched." Kitty Brandon paused eloquently. "Mrs. Johnson. If I may venture to ask, what was your manner of living before you wed?"

"I—I lived with my father."

"And what is his occupation?"

"He imports tea. And sugar and spices. From the Colonies."

"He's a grocer, I see. Well, such being the case 'tis plain to me that your experience of mankind has been somewhat restricted—not that you've missed much, generally speaking," Kitty Brandon added. "Now, try imagining that you are about to step onto the stage of life when, suddenly, from out the shadows there lurches a man! Worse for drink. . . ."

"I cannot."

"Try harder. In your fist there is a sword! He is swaying closer, and closer! His foul breath is upon your face as he begins undressing you in public! What would you do?"

"I cannot say!"

"I can. Unless you're a complete ninny, which I doubt, you would immediately hit him with the nearest thing to hand. In my case it happened to be the sword." Kitty Brandon paused. "Now, perhaps you would have hit him somewhere else upon the body, but my experience of life in the Colonies—which did not include sugar and spice and all things nice—my experience led me to essay a left parry thrust and withdraw from the upper quarter. But, in the heat of the moment, I quite forgot how it was done, and so I began hacking away like a cavalryman with a sabre. And—would you believe?—it worked!"

Mary Johnson reached for a chair and sat down. "It did?"

"Sure, like a dream, for why else would they want to hang me?"

"And, afterward, while you were in the condemned cell, did you feel no—remorse?"

"*Remorse*? For topping Boy Hardwicke? Hardly!"

"Was he . . . was he that objectionable?"

Kitty Brandon considered the question fairly. "I've met worse—any officers' mess on a Saturday night can reveal some rare wonders of nature —but the Honourable Mr. Hardwicke simply had no sense of place or timing. I mean, before or after a performance is one thing, but when a lady is about to give of her best to the paying public? Tch!"

Mary Johnson shaped her next question very carefully. "But surely there was the matter of conscience . . . ?"

"Whose? His or mine?" Kitty Brandon stood and went over to the singing kettle. She glanced over one shoulder. "Since he is no longer with us to give an account of his, I can only say that I sleep well enough at night."

"You do?"

"Of course." Kitty Brandon set the two servings of stewed tea on the table and sat down again. "The Honourable Boy had it coming to him, if not from me, then from someone else. It was just his luck that I got in the first kick."

Mary Johnson studied the wavering reflection inside her mug. Less and less of what she had seen and heard since leaving the Cape of Good Hope was making sense. It was almost as if one had to quite deliberately forget the lessons of the past and take each new moment as it came, upon its own terms, no matter what they were or how they might have seemed in England.

After a while she looked up again. "But what did Mr. Brandon say to—to all this?"

"Nothing. There never was any Mr. Brandon."

Mary Johnson smiled uncertainly. "I don't understand you."

" 'Tis very simple really," Kitty Brandon replied. "In our profession, when a lady outgrows juvenile parts, the courtesy is for her to be billed as 'Mrs. Whatsisname,' rather like 'Madam Thingummyjig' in that other ancient profession. . . ."

The quip was wasted. Mary Johnson made an earnest frown and leaned forward, trying hard to remember these answers for Richard when next they met. "But, surely, who looks after you?"

Kitty Brandon studied her fingernails. "Do they not say that God looks after those who look after themselves?"

"Oh."

"Of course, there are many days when Himself is busy with other things, 'tis then we are expected to take matters into our own hands. For example, consider the manner in which I am travelling now."

"You mean, with Captain Sinclair?"

"Exactly so. I am his campaign wife." The young woman sipped tea with genteel relish. "As Mr. Levi would say—what, you haven't been introduced yet? I'll see you are—'In the world of wolves, howl or get eaten.' This is but plain common sense, as you would agree."

"I would?"

"Of course." Kitty Brandon sat back and considered the other woman. "If you didn't agree, how come you chose to wed Mr. Johnson? He's a man of learning and authority, and, I do not doubt, connexion. He was a fine catch."

Mary Johnson tried to hide her blush. "Do you really think so?"

"Indeed I do. A man of his obvious calibre is bound to rise far in the world. Why, there's many a lady of title would think herself lucky to be in your place. You did well for yourself."

Mary Johnson sipped tea with equal restraint and breeding. "Not everyone understands him that well. It is not easy when a man hears God's word and then obeys that call."

Kitty Brandon nodded. "Evidently he is also a man of courage and conviction: I approve. But speaking of calls, in a few moments we are going to get one from Captain Sinclair, demanding to know where his breakfast might be. Now, while I attend to that, you can straighten the table and we'll all be able to sit down in civilised decency."

Mary Johnson went on deck with her husband after helping to put away the cabin's pewter dining service. The sea was still bottle green but closer to the boat it was a greasy black. The air was damper than yesterday, though less cloudy, with occasional shafts of sunlight breaking through from the north. The two passengers stood at *Alexander*'s taffrail, where they were least likely to get in anyone's way, and watched the wake swirling astern, long ropes of bubbles braiding together, then falling apart as the barque ploughed on in convoy.

Mary Johnson leaned against the trembling woodwork, and against the wind as it came over the stern. After a long while she glanced at her husband. "I have spoken with the Brandon woman."

"Yoh? Er, yes?" He began paying attention. "And what have you learned?"

"She is not as she appears to be."

"How do you mean?"

"I mean that her answers, while making complete sense, are utter nonsense. . . ."

Johnson pursed his lips slightly. "Explain yourself."

His wife hesitated. "I wish that I could, but so much of what one now sees and hears is plainly wrong. And yet everyone seems to behave as if it were right. I am becoming rather confused."

Johnson began to frown. "You must always endeavour to express yourself clearly and simply. Now, what do you mean?"

She took a deep breath. "I have spent the last few days sharing a bed with someone who can make cold-blooded murder seem as natural as eating or drinking. I observe that, far from being punished by conscience, she is supremely at ease with herself. Furthermore, instead of being chained below with those, those others, she walks around as freely as you and I." Mary Johnson searched for the right words. "Yet, in a month or so from now, we shall have to subordinate these same persons to their place while we labour to build a proper society. It is not going to be easy once they have enjoyed so much familiarity with us."

Johnson's frown deepened. "Does she repent her sin?"

"No. Not in the least."

"Then I shall have to speak with her."

"Please do. I shall be interested to hear your opinion of the woman."

Richard Johnson nodded, then, suddenly, pointed. "There! Another petrel."

"Where?"

"Over there. See?" He glanced at his wife for a moment. "Do you know why they bear that name?"

"No. I do not."

" 'Petrelo' is the diminutive of Peter, and commemorates the occasion when Saint Peter walked on the water with Our Lord. Look! There it goes again! You see how they flutter their feathers and seem to walk on water, too?"

"I am going below to write my journal."

48

OLSEN TRAINED his telescope on *Sirius* and waited for the noon hoist while Sinclair set the sun filters on the sextant.

"And I say Sparrow Legs must be pissing himself to be in such a pretty pickle," the master observed happily, bracing against *Alexander*'s roll while he began bringing down the sun and averaging his watery horizon. "The old woman's got this bee in his bonnet about yon Frog admiral—"

"Mark!"

Sirius' gun thudded in the distance, sharing her chronometer's reading with the rest of the convoy. Sinclair squinted through the ebony eyepiece while he completed the sight. Satisfied, he lowered the sextant to correct its index error before making a rough estimate of their position at sea. He looked up triumphantly. "Mr. Olsen? Nine days out from Cape Town and we're still sailing backward! At this rate o' progress he'll have us all in Buenos Aires before the month is done."

"Yoh?"

"Aye! Bluidy old woman."

For the past week there had not been a sailing master in the convoy who had not sensed that—though his ship seemed to be pressing into the south Indian Ocean under taut canvas—she was in fact being thrust backward into the Atlantic, gripped by the immense whorl of the Benguela Current as it swept up from the south pole. It had not helped matters when the weather turned sour almost before the last merchantman cleared Point Mouille. A scant hundred miles away the warm Mozambique current had been pouring into the frigid waters off Aghulas, brewing up a devil's cauldron of freezing rain and cloud. Now, on the first day when the sky had cleared enough for a solar shot, the masters were being proven right.

Kitty Brandon cleared some more space for him in the great cabin as Sinclair shut his Admiralty tables with a glad thump and began crossing this noon's latitude with the morning's sun shot to get *Alexander*'s corrected fix. He then bent over the grubby chart to reduce a long division sum which, if true, meant that he was now three hundred miles further from New Holland than when the convoy had left Table Bay the previous week.

His chin flicked up as Olsen knocked and stooped through the doorway. "The Sparrow Legs' got our number flag. 'Muster aboard for conference.'"

"Hn! What the hell does he think this is? The drawing room o' some bluidy admiral's country mansion?" Sinclair let the chart spring tight.

Through the stern windows he could see the flagship as she lay to on a queasy green swell. "He's got to be out o' his mind!"

Sirius' gun squirted more smoke. Sinclair gnawed his lip and weighed the options. "Very well. I'll soon get to the bottom o' this. Acknowledge and sway out the launch."

"Yoh!"

Alexander's answering pennant broke on its halliards, streaming on the icy wind, but Sinclair saw no point in wasting eleven pennyworth of gunpowder for a supporting bang. Instead, wrapped in his tarred jacket, woolen cap knotted under chin, he jumped for the rising boat and settled himself between the rowers. "Haul away!"

It was a wet crossing, sliding into foam-streaked valleys, climbing their peaks again to sight the convoy under a fitful sun, then sliding away once more. Sinclair's were the only free hands in the open boat and, by the time it stroked alongside the flagship, he was bailing steadily. *Sirius'* own launch was fending off while a bosun's party payed rope, lowering a sea chest over the side.

John Hunter was waiting on deck, snugged inside his old fearnaught, looking the way a sailor should, not bedizened with useless gold frippery and fal-lals, Sinclair thought as he grunted through the entry port. *Sirius'* captain stepped forward. "The old man wants a word with you."

"Hn!"

"I'd go easy, if I were you," Hunter continued, turning to lead the way. "It's not been an easy week."

"Since when was life meant to be easy?" Sinclair replied, falling into step. "Now, if only he'd listened to reason back there, we'd be—"

"I said hold your peace!" Hunter commanded, crouching below and stumbling aft between the officers' cupboard bunks. The sentry stiffened to attention as the two men passed, and the door swung shut behind them.

Phillip was waiting, buttoned to the chin in a fearnaught and canvas hood, wearing mittens and sea boots. He bared one hand and extended it to the visitor as he squeezed round the sheep pen. "Thank you for attending so promptly, captain."

Sinclair gripped the surprisingly tough little fingers for a moment, then let go. "Aye, well, if only ye'd listened—"

Phillip ignored the comment and avoided Hunter's eye. "There has been a slight change of plan." He unrolled one of his charts and beckoned the merchant master to come closer and share it with him. "You must be aware that we are making little headway? I thought so. Well, to be frank, we are not making any. It should not come as a surprise to either of us," Phillip went on. "No doubt, on previous voyages to the east, you've encountered some difficulty while doubling the Cape of Good Hope? I have."

"Hm." Sinclair was forced to nod. The waters around Southern Africa were notorious for their fickle weather and dangerous currents. But once abeam Madagascar and drawing away to the north, he had generally picked up a good trade wind on the last leg of his runs to Bengal and Canton.

"Unfortunately," Phillip continued, "this time neither of us is bound for a familiar port, which means we must be prepared to adopt unfamiliar means if we are to reach our destination in time." His fingers tapped empty white paper. "The Dutchmen have logged a belt of strong westerlies, down here, at fifty degrees south. Almost without exception they have made their best passages to the Indies by taking this apparently longer route before steering up the west coast of New Holland to reach Java. We, by contrast, have usually rammed our heads against the wall of variable winds below Mauritius before catching a trade."

"Hm."

"I therefore propose that we follow the Dutchmen's example," Phillip concluded. "I can see no reason why these westerlies, here, do not extend well past Cape Leeuwin, here, in which case we can round Van Dieman's Land—here—and make a swift run north for Botany Bay. Here."

"Hm."

Phillip paused to test the other man's reactions so far. "Let us now return to the present, captain. It is my misfortune that not every ship in this convoy is as well found as your *Alexander*. She is a credit to you and to Mr. Campbell, and I shall say so in my report to London. All others may be willing to try, but not every hull is equal to such a hard run. They will have to drag behind, contenting themselves by taking the higher, the slower route into the Pacific." He straightened from the chart table. "Captain Hunter has agreed to escort them in *Sirius* while I transfer my flag to *Supply* before sailing ahead to reconnoitre our landing place." And to prove to the court of enquiry that Commodore Arthur Phillip had done his utmost to prevent the French occupation of New Holland.

Sinclair's face was like granite. "Ye must be mad. I would never venture upon such waters in yon cockleshell."

"Needs must when the devil drives," Phillip replied, shutting his case of mathematical instruments and putting them in the same waterproof bag as his sextant. "The more desperate the ill, the more drastic the cure." He tugged the drawstring tight. "I cannot say that I am looking forward to the run, but the stakes are now very high. If it has to be done alone in *Supply*, then so be it, I shall. But, between ourselves, captain, I could wish there were an experienced shipmaster pacing me there. Someone with the courage to steer into the teeth of a gale and right down its throat. Someone like you. . . ."

"Me?"

"Yes. Will you come?"

"Bluidy hell!"

Phillip ignored the comment. "I know that I could order you to follow by Act of Parliament. I also know that we'd still be arguing here till Judgment Day if I did, and neither of us has that measure of time to waste. Which is why I'm asking you to escort *Supply*." His finger silenced Sinclair. "We have rarely agreed on anything, I know, but never once have I doubted your personal courage or your skill as a shipmaster. Therefore, if you feel that you cannot comply with my request, it will not be marked against your name when I sail on alone."

"Ye must be mad."

"No."

"I say ye are."

"No."

"I say ye are," Sinclair repeated flatly. "I served my time on the Norway trade, Mr. Phillip, and long afore I'd earned my first command I'd been taught what seas like those can do to even the best-found ship. I judge your proposed course of action to be imprudent. I can think of no reason in the world why anyone, knowing what I do about those northern seas, would ever venture upon their equal in the southern hemisphere."

Phillip breathed out quietly. "I can think of several reasons, captain, but one will suffice for the moment: it must be done."

"Why?"

"Reasons of state."

"Hn! If ye swept every bluidy politician into a heap, the whole lot wouldn't be worth five minutes on such an ocean as that!" He stabbed at the white emptiness below Pieter Nuytsland.

"I disagree."

"Name one!"

Phillip hesitated. "George Rose."

Sinclair frowned. "He from the manse at Pitlochry? Who went south to London? And now heads the Treasury . . . ?"

"Yes." Phillip hesitated again. "Mr. Secretary Rose is my neighbour. We both served afloat during the Quiberon campaign. Later, he honoured me by asking if I would become godfather to his son, William."

"Hmmm." Sinclair began glowering at the sheet of paper, now pinned flat between his clenched fists.

Hunter was still studying the ragged green ranges which rolled under *Sirius'* stern windows, soon to be his own private view of the world again, once he'd moved his damp blankets back to the empty cot.

Phillip waited.

Sinclair's fingernails drummed the chart table. "Fifty south, ye say?"

"Yes."

"Then east for Van Dieman's Land afore bearing north to Bottommy?"

"Yes."

Alexander's master went back to adding and subtracting, dividing and multiplying risks against certainties for Mr. Contractor Campbell.

Phillip waited.

Hunter watched the wilderness of water, three yards away.

Finally, Sinclair shook his head. "It's impossible."

Phillip shook his head. "Mr. Cook went further than ever I shall. And before him, Captain Tasman. All returned safely."

"Aye, because those who failed were never heard of again!"

"I do not propose to fail."

"Hn!" The merchant master went back to his mental arithmetic, fingernails drumming unevenly.

Phillip waited.

Hunter steadied himself by gripping the hammock of sheep fodder as *Sirius* came off a roller.

At last, Sinclair straightened, his mind made up. "On one condition."

"Yes?"

"If I am to be the first transport onto yon bay, I shall be the first out once my cargo is discharged. First in, first away, first to Canton, or ye sail alone."

Phillip put out his hand again. "Thank you."

They gripped hands on it and Sinclair pulled on his glove. "I'll away to bide directions."

The three men climbed aloft to the deckhouse. The sky was darkening. An iron grey sea was starting to run. A sideparty had been brought to attention, marines' red greatcoats facing the sailors' blue jackets. King was officer of the watch. He drew his sword. A pipe trilled, falling, falling as the commodore's pennant was struck for the first time since leaving Portsmouth half a year ago, almost half the world away. Phillip returned the salute and accepted his tattered St. George's cross, bound and folded, ready to be broken at *Supply*'s peak when she became the flagship in a few minutes' time. He turned. Hunter snapped his fingers to brow and all the pipes shrilled together as Phillip backed over the side.

Ross stood easy again, watching the launch dip and slide away into the weather. "The man's mad."

Captain Campbell shook his head. "Yes."

"But I suppose it's his funeral," Ross continued. "That's what generally comes when we ignore good advice. However, it's an ill wind, etcetera, etcetera." The marine commandant turned on his heel and marched aft. He bent below and tramped down the companionway to inspect the sentry before rapping at the great cabin's door.

"Enter!"

Ross let the door swing shut behind him as Hunter went on tucking a blanket around the wet haybag. "Ah, there you are, Johnny. It's time we had a few words."

Hunter straightened. "Oh . . . ?"

"Aye." Ross had taken one of the folding seats. He pushed it open and sat down with a contented grunt. "He's as mad as a tick. Imagine! Dashing away on his own in a shoebox like *Supply*."

"Duncan Sinclair is going to tag him," Hunter replied, moving round the sheep and taking the captain's chair. "As for *Supply*'s size, I agree that she could be a bit more beamy, but our lords of the Admiralty think she's quite adequate for the task. Besides," Hunter concluded, "many's the fisher lad I've seen set sail in a herring smack that would make our brig look like a three decker. Mostly they got home again. I don't see why we should be any less lucky."

Ross shook his head. "The man's mad. It's bad tactics to divide a command at this stage o' an attack. He'd never do in the regiment. Never."

Hunter eased forward in the chair. "Possibly not, but as a naval officer myself, I have to consider his judgment to be sound."

"Come off it!" Ross stuck out his boot to brace himself as *Sirius* got under way again. "Who d'you think you're talking to? The man's made a fatal error of judgment, you know it, I know it, we've all known it since the moment he scrambled out of Table Bay in such a shambles. How long does he think this 'faster route' is going to take, eh?"

Hunter shrugged irritably. "Six weeks. Seven. Who knows?"

"Quite! Who knows? Nobody does! But does a piddling detail like that stop him from running away? O' course not! Meanwhile, the rest of us are left to fend for ourselves while *he* chases after moonbeams. Hn!"

Hunter said nothing. Then, slowly, "We have been rather preoccupied with the question of Admiral de La Pérouse and his present intentions."

"Oh, aye? The Frog prince!" Ross laced fingers across his belly. "I'll settle his hash when the time is ripe, you'll see."

Hunter ignored the remark. "It is the old man's opinion that we do everything in our power to forestall an occupation of Botany Bay by the French Pacific squadron. It is an opinion with which I must concur. It may not seem tactically sound to divide our expeditionary force at this point, but strategically it is of the utmost importance that we confirm Mr. Cook's claim to New South Wales before it is considered to have lapsed in law, becoming null and void."

"Piffle. Now, if you want *my* opinion, it'll be the best thing in the world if the Frogs do get there first, then we can rip into 'em without any legal fal-lals. Indeed, since nobody's going to see *him* again," Ross went on, pointing past Hunter's shoulder at the stern window where *Supply* and *Alexander* were drawing away from the main convoy, "it's high time I told you our next move. Now, this is what you're going to need—"

"One moment." Hunter was shaking his head. "Not so fast. I have already been given my instructions. They are very thorough, they are very explicit, and they do not include any provision for me to open any hostilities against Admiral de La Pérouse. Quite the reverse."

"Pff! Yon shoebox is going to sink with the first real blow, all hands, mark my word. And when she does—which is bound to happen—I shall have stepped up from lieutenant governor to the full command." Hunter began to say something, but Ross brushed him aside. "Therefore, since there is little if any chance of us seeing your old man again, it is proper that we now discuss my future course of action for the colony."

Hunter held his breath, then released it very slowly. "Your future course of action in the colony will be to carry out your duties as lieutenant governor, at all times consulting with the *next* governor of New South Wales—me."

"Uh?"

"I hold the dormant commission."

"B-but I'm already the lieutenant governor! I'm the next in the chain of command! This is an affront to the king's uniform—!"

"Which I also have the honour to wear," Hunter reminded him quietly.

"That has nothing to do with it!" Ross snapped back. "A dormant commission means—means just that! It's dormant! But I'm already an active lieutenant governor! It's *my* colony!"

"It's *my* commission."

"I'm the lieutenant governor!"

"Nobody is disputing that," Hunter said, trying hard to smile. "You are indeed the lieutenant governor—designate—of our future colony. You will remain in that office while Mr. Phillip remains in authority over us. If, sadly, he should die at his post while we are abroad, my lords commissioner of the Admiralty have thought fit to nominate me as his successor. That is all."

"But—!"

"Bob? This is hardly the first time we've discussed this very point, is it?" Hunter tried another smile. "Nobody is taking away your title. Nobody is diminishing your honour by a single inch. You are, and you will remain, number two—"

"Aye! Number two! The regiment's second to none! It's *our* blood on the field o' battle when the Indians and Frogs attack!"

"For God's sake talk sense."

"Sense!" Ross banged his head on the roof as he planted both fists on the table and glared down at Hunter. "I'll give you sense. When a governor steps aside, his deputy steps up. That's sense, that's law, I'm that deputy."

Hunter also stood. "The law, Mr. Ross, is that we must obey our superior officers at all times. Commodore Phillip has—"

"We can forget him!"

"Commodore Phillip has given me my orders," Hunter continued. "If I arrive at Botany Bay after sailing the slower, northern route, and find that he is not here, I am to implement the instructions given to me by M'Lord Howe, which are that I immediately assume the governorship of New South Wales."

"Is that a fact?" Ross drawled, leaning harder on his knuckles. "Here's another. I have two hundred bayonets under my command. How many have you got?"

"What?"

Ross smiled. "I command four companies of infantry. They are aboard every vessel of this convoy, including your own. Indeed, you might even have noticed that *we* decide who may enter or leave this fine cabin. What price a 'dormant commission' now . . . ?"

Hunter sat down very slowly. "I never heard that remark, Mr. Ross."

"Then I'd better repeat it. I said that, in the likely event of us reaching New Holland only to find that your Mr. Phillip has paid the price for his rash conduct, then his lieutenant governor will immediately assume command of this expeditionary force." Ross turned sharply. "Marine Tucker!"

The door flew open. Boots slammed boards. "Sah!"

"Henceforth you will be especially vigilant in your duties at this door. Understand?"

"Sah!"

"Dismiss."

"Sah!"

The door slammed shut and Ross turned again. "Is there anything you would like to add, Mr. Hunter?"

"I shall never allow you to do it."

"You won't have any choice in the matter." Ross picked up his hat, smoothed the crown and set it on his head. He clicked heels. "Good day."

49

FIRST LIGHT. Phillip tried squinting at the inverted compass bowl, still jolting, rocking, swaying and tilting above his borrowed cot. *Supply* seemed to be holding her course a thousand miles southeast of Africa, riding the gales which swept round the Antarctic, from Cape Horn to Cape

Horn. James Cook had ridden them eleven years earlier, the first commander in history to circumnavigate this desolation of storms. And now it was Arthur Phillip's turn. He glanced sideways as someone knocked at the door. "Enter!"

Bryant ducked through from the galley with a pannikin of warmed coffee slopping over one hand, some cheese and biscuit clenched in the other. " 'Morning, sir. Weather glass don't look no worse today." His master rolled under the leaky roof planks, gripped the hand rope to clamber from bed and shoved both legs down the waiting pair of sea boots. He was dressed for breakfast. Bryant coughed. "Like me to 'ave a go at 'eating some water for a shave?"

Phillip shook his head and the cabin door shut, leaving him alone. He fingered the ten days of stubble which had sprouted since they had left the convoy, but decided against changing his mind: the cup of ration water could be put to better use with a tot of rum, or stewed with oatmeal for dinner. And the sooner he grew a full beard, the sooner his face would be safe against frostbite. Besides, where could he shave down here without slashing himself to shreds?

In finer weather and kindlier seas he could have done what *Supply*'s commander—Lieutenant Henry Ball—had often done in this box of a cabin, swing back the skylight and stand up in the square hole while he propped his shaving mirror on the poop deck. But the weather was now rarely fine and the seas were never kindly, and the skylight remained shut against the wash which swept aft every time the brig's tiny bows smashed through a roller.

Phillip glanced up again. "Enter!"

Supply's commander crouched through and saluted. "Good morning, sir."

" 'Morning, Mr. Ball."

"Permission to use the table, sir?"

"Go on, go on." Phillip rapped his biscuit on the chart table and brushed away the weavils as he made room for the younger man. "Did you get a good solar?"

Ball nodded and weighted his chart flat before laying out the parallel rule and pencil.

Phillip sucked tepid coffee and moved closer to peer over the other man's shoulder. "Still a long way to go."

"Yes, sir." Ball didn't look up from his calculations.

"Still, untried route or not, at least we're making headway," Phillip went on, double-checking the commander's arithmetic. "So much for the doomsayers who hoped it couldn't be done."

Ball struck off his last set of figures and tried again, without Phillip breathing down his neck, he hoped. But he was out of luck. The commodore hadn't finished. "I said to myself, if the Dutchmen could do it and survive, and since these winds appear to be constant, we're bound to do it as well."

Ball put his pencil down. "With respect, sir, do what?"

Phillip frowned. "Why, reach Botany Bay first. Before M. de La Pérouse."

"I know all that, sir, but what is there in New Holland that we need it so badly?"

Phillip blinked. For once he was speechless. Quite abruptly the secret interests of a world power, the hidden directives, everything collapsed before one simple, direct question: what exactly *did* everyone want from New Holland?

Mr. Pitt wanted to found a new empire in the Pacific while Parliament's back was turned; the lord mayor was hoping to export some of London's murder and pillage; and George Rose was planning to stop Herr Rothschild foreclosing on the nation's mortgage.

No closer to reality, Major Ross was dreaming of plundering El Dorado and then being given a peerage for his trouble; Mrs. Johnson was fancying herself as the lady wife of a missionary bishop with a diocese the size of Europe; and most of the military officers were riding to hounds across the broad green acres of their imaginary plantations.

What of himself? More than anything else, Arthur Phillip wanted to wake up tomorrow morning in his bedchamber at Vernalls. Instead, he now had to content himself by sharing a confidential smile with Ball. "It's best not to ask those sorts of questions. Affairs of state. . . ."

Ball understood. He finished his calculations and went back on deck. Phillip followed him a few minutes later, snug inside his oilskin jacket against the driving wind. "At least the weather seems better today." Phillip wiped the spray from his face. An albatross was soaring over the liquid mountain ranges which rose astern, gliding after *Supply*'s track down the foothills, snapping at cuttlefish in her wake. Phillip peered around. "Where's *Alexander*?"

"Still there, sir. Pegging along like a confounded dog with a bone between its teeth. He won't let go."

Phillip drew his telescope as the brig rode another wave. The larger barque was five points abaft the port beam, running before the same westerly under a good press of canvas. Even as he watched, small dots began swaying aloft between snow showers to slip another reef. "Mr. Ball? I am starting to think that our Captain Sinclair might know a trick or two!" Phillip stowed his glass as *Supply* rumbled down another long valley and lost sight of her escort.

Ball said nothing. High-ranking passengers might have the leisure to compliment a rival, he had not. Old habits die hard. Within hours of *Supply* and *Alexander* crowding on sail, the privately owned barque had begun to overhaul the naval brig in an undeclared race, as if Botany Bay were now Canton on the Pearl River, with a cash bonus for the first skipper to get his ship into port. *Supply*'s commander had called up his master to discuss tactics, then slipped a reef off the topsail to block Sinclair's threat. Since when, through driving rain and sleet, across shafts of wintry daylight, into squally darkness, three masts had battled two for the lead, and two had fought to wrest it back.

Phillip approved. He would not be ungenerous in his report to the Admiralty if the brig showed *Alexander* a clean pair of heels as a prelude to beating the French. This was no longer an impossible hope: *La Boussole* and *L'Astrolabe* were not being thrashed along on the wings of a polar wind. After two years or more of tropical cruising, the enemy frigates would be foul with weed and barnacles. Every atoll they passed would be a temptation to stop, to water, to scrape and refit. Every hour which Phillip gained, sweeping along the old Dutchmen's latitudes, was one less for his rival to clap on sail for New Holland.

Sinclair also approved. A hard-fought race toned up a jaded crew during the man-killing weeks and months of hauling rope at sea. Even the most dull item off the docks of Glasgow had to feel some austere pride in his craft whenever *Alexander* nosed ahead of the nimble little warship, her tan storm canvas bellying, her spars groaning against their slings, her stays as taut as fiddler's catgut.

Sinclair's glass tracked the brig as *Alexander*'s hands finished laying along her main yard. "Mr. Olsen."

"Yoh?"

"Yon Sparrow Legs and his boy captain might know more than we credit them with."

The master stowed his telescope as Kitty Brandon came on deck, his boat cloak buttoned to her chin. She gripped the nearest line to steady herself as she relished the dash of wind and spray on her face. "Good morning to you, Mr. Olsen."

The first mate came to attention. " 'Morning, m'm!"

She glanced at the master. "Mr. Sinclair. Sometimes I have to wonder about you. There's a fine hot breakfast waiting below, and here you are, getting yourself wet on an empty stomach." She shook her head. "You will have nobody to blame but yourself when it brings on another lumbago. I shall wait two minutes, then we serve without you."

Sinclair muttered under his breath as Kitty Brandon went below again.

He squinted up at the weather pennant, stiff and black against the scudding cloud. Almost a summer's day, off Iceland. Plenty of time yet to trim *Supply*'s lead before the next attack of sleet, or hail, or snow, or all together. "Mr. Olsen? Reef off the t'gallants!"

The mate's whistle shrilled as Sinclair turned and went down to breakfast. The watch left theirs and turned out again, tramping the frozen ratlines to wrestle with sailcloth like rolled metal, antarctic blasts plastering them against the yard, slop shirts blowing under armpits, bare fists beating out the canvas as—

One of the topmen turned, staring over his shoulder. A wave was starting to rise astern. Like the hump of a titanic whale. Slowed by its own monstrous bulk. Higher. And closer. And closer. Straightening into a sheer wall of glass green streaked with foam. Crouching forward, paws of spume flying off the crest as the wave of all the waves reared up and the wind dropped to a bubbling whisper—

Kitty Brandon was about to serve hot buttered pancakes with honeycomb. Mary Johnson was reaching out to help—

It was Thorpe's day to lie in the middle, Levi clutching the blanket one side, Cribb gripping the other—

As the freak wave exploded across *Alexander*'s open poop with a gurgling whine, thundering for'ard, sweeping away her sheep, the haystack, the tarpaulin cover and one of the spare boats.

The pewter plate clanged across the cabin roof.

Thorpe screamed as Cribb landed on top of him and Levi sprawled up the side of the barque with almost one hundred and eighty other lags.

"Good morning to you, Mr. Johnson." Kitty Brandon pulled her cloak tighter. "I trust you are recovered?"

Richard Johnson sighed with resignation and fingered his turban of bandages. "Thank you, I am, somewhat. By the grace of God no bones were broken, but they could so easily have been. Did you *ever* see such a manifestation of the Almighty's power?"

"Not often."

"Not often! Why, days after the event, my head is still throbbing with the crash." The chaplain took his suffering very seriously.

Kitty Brandon ignored it. She gripped the nearest handline and looked around for a change of topic, but the Southern Ocean had lost its strength during the night. An uneasy groundswell was now stooping over itself, round-shouldered and weary, with hardly a crest to be seen. The sky was dismal and hangdog, with sagging curtains of grey rain draped a mile or so to starboard.

Johnson touched his bandages again. "I *still* maintain that, but for the fact that Captain Phillips has insisted that we attempt this insane route, nobody in the whole world would ever have seen such an enormous wave." Noah's Ark had been supplanted in the chaplain's conversation by the Wave.

The Brandon woman looked at him. "Then try imagining yourself in the Atlantic. In winter."

"Oh. Why?"

"Because it would give you something fresh to talk about." Kitty Brandon turned to go below again.

But Johnson was not letting her escape that easily now that he had a chance to examine her. "Have you ever seen a wave that big? In the Atlantic?"

"Yes. Now, I must be about my business."

He blinked. "What on earth were you thinking of to expose yourself to such danger?"

She stopped, and turned. "At the time I was on water."

"Oh. Why?"

"Because one cannot drive a carriage to the Colonies, and I did so wish to get there."

Johnson made an uncertain frown. "Why?"

Kitty Brandon sighed with irritation. "There was a war going on at the time, and the gentleman with whom I was connected was in the army."

"He was a soldier?"

"Alas, no, just a common or garden general. I was his campaign wife."

"Ah hah, then you *were* married."

"Mr. Johnson." There was more than a tinge of severity in her tone now. "You have a professional interest in weddings—likewise funerals—so I shall indulge your curiosity this once." She paused. "To be the campaign wife of a serving officer is to know a hard, often dangerous world, one which rarely includes those tender moments which, I am sure, you are now imagining so fondly. On the contrary, at the end of most days' march, the height of voluptuous abandonment is a pannikin of stew and a dry blanket on the floor of a tent. More often it is a biscuit, a bale of straw and a waggon for the night. But it is a life of compensations." She eyed the heavily built chaplain. "One meets all sorts and conditions of men on the field of honour, and they are not always what they seem. For instance, there's the unlettered little tinker with not an ounce of spare meat on his bones, yet he'll bite the bullet like a hero when they sew him up. And there's the beefy great booby who complains every time his boot pinches. . . ." She paused reflectively. " 'Tis a rare education."

"One moment! Don't go yet." Johnson took a couple of paces forward. "I've never, um, met anyone like you before."

" 'Twould be a surprise if you had," she replied. "Now, if you will excuse me, there is work to be done for my current campaign husband, Captain Sinclair."

"No, please, let me finish." Johnson was becoming flustered. "Why did you do it?"

"Surely you don't expect *me* to travel down *there*?" Her foot tapped the deck above *Alexander*'s hold.

"Yes. I mean no. I meant earlier, in the American colonies. Why did you do it?"

Kitty Brandon understood Johnson's question better than Johnson himself did. She smiled distantly. "What an inquisitive fellow you are. Still, you must have a tremendous load of learning to unlearn. Very well, let us say that, at the time of which we speak, Jack Burgoyne was still deuced well preserved. In brief, he cut a commanding figure upon the world's stage, which is the way we ladies prefer our men to be—ask Mrs. Johnson. General Burgoyne was not only a man of arms, in my arms, but also a man of letters. Frankly, it flattered me when he especially wrote a comedy with myself in the title role, which, when one is all of sixteen or seventeen summers, is heady stuff indeed."

"And for this you . . . ?" Johnson didn't know the correct word.

"And for *that* I bossed his servants and made damned sure the sutlers never overcharged us. In addition, I fetched, I carried, I fixed, I arranged, while at all times presenting him with a cheerful countenance." She paused. "It did not come easily, particularly the latter, once he surrendered his sword and we went into captivity. Devil a thing there was to smile about then, but what cannot be cured must be endured as cheerfully as possible. Speaking of which, how *is* your head after it took such a nasty bump?"

Johnson touched the bandages. "Much better, thank you."

"That's the spirit! Now, if you will excuse me—"

"Please, just one more question." He took another couple of paces forward. "You say you went into captivity? Does that mean you were in prison even then?"

Kitty Brandon frowned impatiently. "There was a war on. We had a battle. We lost."

"Yes?"

"Mr. Johnson. Losing a battle is not like losing one's hat. One does not then go to the Public Office to post a reward of five shillings for the person who brings it back. When a battle is lost, not a few lose their lives, others their limbs, yet others their wits, and the rest their liberty."

"I've never seen a battle."

"Then you were born fortunate indeed."

"What's it like?"

"A very good day to you, Mr. Johnson." She turned. "And to you,

Mrs. Johnson. Pleasant weather we're having, though I'm not sure I care for the look of those clouds. We could be in for another squall before day is done."

Mary Johnson watched the trim, self-assured young woman go below, that striking hair and complexion framed by the cloak's dark collar. She joined her husband at the rail. "Did you find her conscience?"

"Oh. Um. We were just getting to that."

"I see. But she has begun to repent?"

Richard Johnson frowned. "It's rather too early to say yet. She is a disturbing person."

"Really?"

"Yes. A *very* stubborn sinner."

Mary Johnson studied the advancing rain cloud. "Well, if you did not discuss repentance or the pangs of conscience, what did you talk about?"

"She wanted to know how I was feeling."

"Oh."

"Then we talked about the big wave. Then she told me something quite extraordinary."

"Yes?"

"It seems she was once a sort of wife to a general in the Colonies, but they had a battle and were all put in prison."

"And you believed her?"

"Well, sort of. Why not?"

His wife turned slowly. "The woman is *Irish*. She is also a notorious murderess."

"Oh. I hadn't thought of it that way."

"*You* haven't been forced to share the same bed with her, night after night—I am happy to say—which does give me a certain advantage when evaluating her truthfulness, or lack of it." Mary Johnson shrugged. "You are still too trusting. It blinds you to the fact that not everyone is as we are. If you persist in repeating tales of generals and battles from a woman of that class, you are going to injure your public standing in the colony. Need I say more?"

"No, of course not."

"Be on your guard. She is a liar."

"Yes, of course."

His wife glanced at the weather, then tapped him on the arm. "We must hurry and get under shelter."

The advancing rain was raising welts on the swell. The milky green of the water had faded, the white veins of foam had become subdued. The sea was old, pock-marked and grey as rain flailed across *Alexander*'s deck.

* * *

Sinclair and Olsen wore their hats to lunch, which stopped most of the drips from falling down their necks. Kitty Brandon had pulled a shawl over her head. Richard Johnson had the rag turban. His wife had left her indoor bonnet with their other things aboard *Golden Grove.*

One of the sick hens had died during the night and become a welcome addition to the broth which Kitty Brandon was now serving round the table. Sinclair waited. Then, "Grace, Reverend. . . ."

Johnson came back to the present with a jolt. "Oh, yes, of course. For what we are about to receive, may the Lord make us truly thankful, amen."

Sinclair reached for one of Kitty Brandon's oatcakes and looked at his first mate. "Mr. Olsen? I have noticed a certain moodiness among the men. I trust that we are not about to enjoy a repeat performance of the late Mr. Spillet's little pantomime."

Olsen finished drinking lunch over the side of his bowl, and licked the lentils off his moustache. "Don't t'ink so, Cap'n. All buggers the same."

"Ye may be right, but ye could be wrong. Order Cooky to keep his little ears and eyes on their toes, so to speak. I am always uneasy when there's nothing new to report from you-know-where. And tell Sergeant Ram's Bum to alert his men: at the first sign of unrest, get stuck in."

"Yoh."

Sinclair eased back in his seat. "Neither do I wish for any rumours about you-know-who, Mr. Olsen. Situated as we are, with conditions bound to become worse as we persist upon this course, we will not be able to divert the men with another bout o' fisticuffs."

"Yoh."

Sinclair crumbled the oatcake into his bowl and began stirring with his spoon. "Imagination is best left ashore, it overexcites the crew."

"Yoh?"

"Aye. There'll be no more tales o' ghoulies and ghosties aboard my vessel, Mr. Olsen."

"Yoh."

"Ghosts, captain?" Johnson enquired, leaning forward to join the conversation.

Sinclair considered the passenger's eager face. "As I recall, ye had not the good fortune to be aboard *Alexander* when the crew began circulating idle untruths. For a while their minds were not on their work. We became a sloppy ship. At the time it was annoying, nothing else. However, if a similar rumour were to grip them as we steer ever further from the world, just to flatter Commodore Phillip's vanity, the outcome might not be as we wish. Do I make myself clear?"

"Not exactly, no. Would you mind explaining that, please?"

Sinclair swapped glances with his first mate, then looked back. "Mr. Johnson. The average crew is rubbish. If, like rubbish, it is then thrown into a heap and kept wet, it begins to get hot and give off strange odours which it sees as spooks and hobgoblins. In a word it is rotten ripe for mutiny. You seem surprised? Don't be, it happens all the time." Sinclair tried his broth, then put the spoon down again. "Ye have observed that I keep a firm grip on my men? It's the only way. The whip hand is ever the upper hand. Your lady wife has probably told you that my attitude would never do ashore, and she is right, ashore. But once at sea everything changes, and we must change wi' it or suffer the penalty."

Johnson's meal was going cold. "We must?"

Sinclair ignored the query. He dipped his spoon and sipped broth. "The sea has been changing these past days. I've seen it afore, as we went into the ice, off Greenland. We may be heading south, but the colour's the same."

Johnson smiled uncertainly. "What colour?"

Sinclair broke another oatcake. "And there's the same smell in the air. As if the further we steer, the nearer we must get to an edge beyond which is nothing."

"*Now* who's not left his imagination ashore!" Kitty Brandon laughed. "Mr. Sinclair, sir, I am astonished to hear such words from a gentleman of your standing."

"Aye? Well, it's only a manner o' speaking—!"

"No." Kitty Brandon shook her head. "I won't accept that excuse. Why, 'tis plain to me that what you have just described is nothing more serious than a mild dose of the Montreal miseries. Sure, it happens every year without fail," she announced to the table at large. "We got them quite badly after going into winter bivouac before the march on New York."

Mary Johnson lifted an expressive eyebrow at her husband as the Brandon woman went on with her tale. "You see, it also gets darker and colder up there, in Canada. By Christmas Day you're wondering if the sun hasn't fallen into a ditch and broken his neck. All around the huts is snow and ice as far as the eye can see, and the local gentry put runners on their carriages so that they can go for drives up and down the river."

She snapped her fingers. "Then the grumbling starts! And the gossip begins, and the complaints shoot up like mushrooms. Everybody loses their spark, and what was once a fine body of troops seems hell-bent on destroying itself long before the enemy can have the honour." Kitty Brandon chuckled. "There are some stories I could tell about *that*. . . ."

"Please do!" Johnson exclaimed before his wife's foot could reach under the table.

"Well, it happened this way." Kitty Brandon smiled, handling her audience of four with all the flair that had filled many a playhouse. "King George really had two armies, not one, on that campaign. There were our lads, of course, brisk and bold as crickets in their light infantry scarlet; and there were the Hessians, and Brunswickers, and God knows what else, plodding along in their heavy infantry blacks and greens. Heavy, did I say? Poor souls, they wouldn't have known if their britches were on fire half the time. Strong as bullocks they seemed alongside our little whippets, but once we went into winter quarters, they just sat down on their hunks, and died."

Sinclair was leaning forward now. "Died, ye say?"

Kitty Brandon snapped her fingers again. "Like that. Did I not see it happen with my own eyes? And not only once. I recall one of their 'felt wobblers'—that means sergeant in the German tongue—who'd been feeling poorly for a few days. He looked up at me, said that he was going to die, and, by Jings, he did!" Kitty Brandon controlled a belly laugh. "Then d'you know what his comrades did next?"

Mary Johnson kicked her husband and made another I-told-you-so shrug, which left an opportunity for Olsen to seize. "What they do nex'?"

"Why, they sat him outdoors in the snow, with his cap on his head and his pipe in his mouth, for all the world like he was taking it easy. By evening he was as stiff as a plank, so they picked him up and popped him into a shed with all the others of his regiment. Row upon row of them there were, white with frost, smoking their pipes, playing cards, even a few reading books—"

"That's absurd!" Mary Johnson glared at her husband.

"It is?" Kitty Brandon seemed to be noticing the other woman for the first time. " 'Pon my word, it saddens me to hear you say so, ma'am. However, I understand. Your experience of the world is still very limited. You have yet to travel to lands where the soil is frozen solid for months of the year, or live in towns where a barrel of gunpowder would not dig a single grave in midwinter. . . ."

Kitty Brandon paused for comment, then looked back at the head of the table. "The Brunswickers were keeping their corpses till the thaw, but we had a better idea, we kept our men alive throughout the dreary months of waiting. We did that by keeping them busy, which is what I notice you do with yours, Mr. Sinclair."

Alexander's master nodded at the compliment. "Aye. The devil finds no idle hands to do his work aboard my command."

"It's the only way," Kitty Brandon concluded, glancing round the table. "Mind you, it helped that our lads had pluck and spunk to begin with. They still had more dash, at the end of our march south, than those sour-crouch eaters had before we started." She stopped momentarily. "Indeed, 'twould have brought tears of pride to the eyes on a copper penny. To see rank upon rank of scarlet advancing up that hill. Into the guns. Such trim and proper men. Even—" She stood, smiling brightly. "Excuse me. There is something I must tell the cook."

50

"ICE ALEE. . . ." The lookout's warning floated past on tendrils of fog.

Sinclair bit his lip. "Mr. Olsen. Helm aport. Hold the luff."

"Yoh."

The helmsman began spoking his wheel, arm over arm over arm, steering away from the invisible cake of brash ice. Sinclair dug under his jacket. He gnawed the quid of tobacco and worried at the lee rail, squinting under his tarred cowl, waiting for the floe. Somewhere. Out there.

From sky to water, the world around him seemed to be frozen curds and whey. Iceberg weather. Dank clots of fog menaced him, drifting apart as the barque ghosted through, silent, listening for the first whisper of waves on an ice shelf. Somewhere. Out there.

He peered aloft, but the wind pennant had vanished once the thermometer began to slip, and a lichen of frost started growing up the stays and lines. A big one was in the offing. Somewhere. Out there.

Bowed by the weight of his years, Sinclair paced back to the binnacle. The helmsman's messenger was turning the sandglass. He tolled five bells of the afternoon watch. Sinclair nodded. "The gun, Mr. Olsen."

Alexander's cannon punched a hole in the fog. The bang rolled away across an ominously quiet sea. A long, flat pause. *Supply*'s gun thumped in the distance. The naval brig was still proceeding. Two thuds and a red firepot at her peak would have signalled what was going to happen if that floe shattered *Alexander*'s bows. She would sink. Scarce half the crew and marine guard would fill her remaining gig and launch. The rest would have to take their chances on spars and gratings in water one point above freezing.

"Hold that luff, Mr. Olsen."

The master turned heavily, about to go below to where his woman would have another hot grog waiting for him, when—sudden, shrill—"Ice!"

Sinclair spun.

The fog was shredding.

Alexander was gliding into sunlight.

The mother iceberg lay dead ahead on the white silence, a mile from cape to glittering cape—

"All hands!"

The barque's helm was coming up, yards shaking, groping to windward, the off-duty watch was tumbling aloft, running to trim the spanker, to overhaul the jib sheets, to brace the—

"Brace! *Brace,* damn ye!"

The canvas was thudding aback, Olsen was kicking turns off the belaying pins, sending frozen ropes flying through their blocks in a blur of ice dust, every man—carpenter, sailmaker, cook—tailing harder on the weather brace, straining to heave the outstretched yard.

Alexander was barely under way, rocking stiffly, uncertain. A low surf was growling along the floating shoreline, its peaks bleached with snow, its plains crusted with sea spray, its cliffs spilling meltwater across the ship's deck.

"Fore tops'l there!"

The barque was not responding.

Olsen's nails dug into his palms. He had hunted the great blue whale. He had seen icebergs calving, off Greenland's glaciers. He had followed them across the Atlantic with their herds of floes. This one was no different. Polar gales and sunlight were feasting on her as she climbed the latitudes to warmer seas. She was breaking up, giving birth. He stared. A crag creaked. Cracked, crashed in a collapsing roar—

Alexander was gathering way as the surge struck from her stern, heaving the barque up and over its crest, sails slatting, masts flexing like whipsticks as it rolled under her keel.

Thorpe screamed as Levi fell on top of Cribb, who was falling on top of him. The lags sprawled across the icy planks, clutching and kicking each other. Cribb grabbed a stanchion with one fist, Levi with the other, but Thorpe escaped. He had not stopped screaming. Eyeballs popping, he was charging, hurling himself against the locked gate, attacking it with bare fists, smashing his fetters against the bars, splintering wood and iron. Cribb had seen this twice before, once on Bemis Heights and once aboard *Retribution.* Thorpe had gone berserk and it was spreading like a religious ecstasy. Others were starting to follow. Cold, hungry, lost men were sensing that here, at last, was someone with an answer.

The hatch flung open. Cribb heard the hoarse shouts, saw the muskets jostling into line as he sprinted for the gateway himself. Thorpe's head snapped back as his mate sapped it with a chunk of wood, felling him before the row of muzzles crashed their flame and smoke.

"Abe! The other leg!"

Levi stumbled and grabbed the other ankle. He began dragging Thorpe clear of a stampede which was now fleeing in the opposite direction. They heaved Thorpe's dead weight onto his shelf.

"You poor dumb bastard!" Cribb howled, tears splashing off his beard as he tried punching the man awake. "Abe! 'E's croaked it! Jesus, Ben, mate—!"

Levi shoved him aside and knelt, shoulders hunched against the ship's rocking, probing the sticky red thatch of Thorpe's hair.

"I croaked 'im! I croaked 'im! I—!"

"*Naar.*" Levi sat back on his haunches and wiped a hand on Thorpe's shirt. "Maybe with an anvil. Never with a bit of wood."

"What?"

Levi shrugged. "Once, in Hamburg, I see a woman break axe on husband like Ben. Was nothing."

Cribb wiped his nose along his jacket sleeve. "Silly prick," he sniffed miserably. " 'E could've got 'imself 'urt."

"So he didn't?" Levi replied, checking the pulse in Thorpe's neck as others helped their mates by the grating. "Brr! Let's get warm again. Is like Po Land when piss freeze back." Cribb dragged their collection of rags over his shoulders and shared them with Levi. They snuggled together, one each side of the dozing Thorpe, as *Alexander* swayed onto an even keel and drew away from the iceberg. "Now, what am I talking of?"

"That mollisher in Warsaw."

A soft chuckle in the near darkness. "Warm? *Ei!* Hot as hell, she was."

"Bene mort?"

"Better."

"Lucky sod."

"Sure, but she too." Levi fell silent while they shared another daydream of long ago and far away. After a while he wriggled himself comfortable on the other hip. "So, what about you?"

Cribb shrugged modestly. "I always done all right."

"Go on. . . ."

Cribb checked his store of memories. "Well, there was this time we pitched camp down the road from a place they call Norwich, or something. Quiet and dark it is, so's none of the nobs will know they got visitors. There's tons of grub running around on four legs, and tons of firewood, and tons of—"

"Muffin?" Levi prompted.

"Later," Cribb promised. "So, there we are, all snug and secret, when Dad gives me another clip and tells me to fetch the water. So, off I trot, round the bushes, and there she is. . . ."

"Who is?"

"One of the morts. Oh, I'd seen 'er before, tons of times, but always with 'er stuff on."

"And?"

Cribb sighed. "In the nick. Not a stitch. Washing."

"Yes?"

"Like nothing you seen in Po Land—"

"Hh! What colour the hair then?"

"Sort of brown. Like fried sausages."

"And her—things?"

"Like juicy pears. . . ."

"And then you—?"

" 'Ardly! I didn't need another bash on the conk from Dad. No, we done it after dark."

"Good?"

"Like warm custard. . . ."

Both men fell silent. After a long while Levi came back to the present. "One day it will be every day like that in Bottommy Town."

"That what Reb Mordy promised us?"

"Sure. In Bottommy they got everything."

Cribb also fondled memories of good times past, better times to come. "I 'ope 'e's right. We've been on this bloody boat for bloody years. There's no end to it. We're going round and round in bloody circles."

"Sure. God build the world that way."

Cribb was pushing himself up on one elbow. "I'm not joking. This trip's years longer than to Americky!"

"And it ended? So will this. You see."

Cribb subsided. "Well, I 'ope you're right. I don't know 'ow much more I can take of this before I go like Ben. Going round and round in bloody circles, getting nowhere, that's where we're going. It's worse'n the infantry, that's what it is."

"No zhit?" Levi patted a yawn. "I bet you got plenty of muffin, Over There."

Cribb had made himself comfortable again. "Now and then, yes, I s'pose so. But generally we was kept busy, doing other things, not too much time for 'anky panky in the trees. But, yes, we done all right."

"Uh huh. Many with brown hair?"

Cribb searched his memories. "Come to think of it, there *was* a couple. One 'appened after I got back to the place they call New Ork. I got five georges for it, and she 'elped me spend 'em. The next was at—"

"Joe?" the other man interrupted dreamily. "All my life there is one mort I never have."

Cribb rolled over and began taking interest again. "What's that?"

Levi sighed. "One with hair like new copper groschen, and with those little things on the face like the sun been kissing her too. *That's* class."

"You're not wrong," Cribb was forced to agree, twitching the blankets to see if he could inch some more for himself.

Levi nodded in the freezing gloom. "And you know what else special?

Eyes. Green eyes, like cats. Never two heartbeats the same. Always—how you say it?—playing the game with a cove. That's *real* class."

"You're still not wrong," Cribb agreed wistfully.

"Joe? Why are we doing this to each other?" Levi grumbled, rolling over to get the other flank warm. "Let's change subject. You know one thing else I never had?"

"What?"

"A *schlacht,* a real—pam! pam!—all mates together battle."

"You missed nothing."

"No zhit? And you done eight, Over There?"

"Seven," Cribb grunted. "The sort they put a cove's name in General Orders if 'e done all right. The others, well, forget 'em."

"Must be hard."

"Uh."

Levi paused. Then, quietly, "Joe? You mind I ask question?"

"Blaze away."

"The first one you do. The first battle. Is like the first time you do a woman? Special?"

Cribb said nothing.

Levi persisted. "Well?"

"Sort of."

"Go on. . . ."

"That's it."

"No, please, tell me. Is something I don't know."

Cribb said nothing.

Levi persisted. "*Please?*"

Very, very reluctantly, Cribb eased over to face Levi again. "Right-o. But first you got to remember I wasn't more'n a nypper then, and things was different. At the time it seems like wearing the king's uniform was the best way to, get away. From things."

"Yes?"

Cribb hesitated. "They said I wasn't big enough to join, but the fusileers was going to fight in Americky, and they reckoned a square meal would give me another couple of inches." He hesitated again. "They weren't wrong. First time ever I et so good. Then the boat stopped at the place they call Kay Beck and they started sorting for little blokes like me. Strewth, I was the right size after all! 'Scouts,' they called us. They told us to go out front and clear the track, and if we could pop off any Rebel officers, so much the better. Worth another tuppence a day, and no drill, like every day was Sunday."

"And your first battle?" Levi prompted artlessly.

Cribb pulled a face. "That was a bit slow coming. First we 'ad to build the road for the guns and things."

Levi's fingers clicked. "I remember now. You tell me once how there are coaches and officer women and such. Or was that other one?"

"No. That's the one. Shitwits 'ad 'alf London dragging along behind us," Cribb grunted. "If it 'ad been left to me, we could've pissed through them Rebels with our eyes shut. But, no, first we 'ad to build a proper road. And to build a proper road we 'ad to chop down bloody great trees. And to chop them down we 'ad to—"

"Brr!" Levi shuddered. "So then you attack? With cold steel."

"Not yet. Then we come to the end of the road. And it's getting to be next winter. And we're up to our bollocks in mud. And them Yankees 'ave got the 'igh ground. And they've got the grub and new boots."

"And . . . ?"

Cribb said nothing.

"*And?*"

Cribb gnawed his lip in the darkness. "We can't go back. We can't stand still. We fix bayonets."

"And?"

Cribb hesitated. "Four times."

"What four times?"

"Into them guns."

"And?"

Cribb said nothing.

"*And?*"

"I c-copped one. In the bum."

"And?"

Cribb dumbly shook his head.

"Joe. Listen. You must tell. What happen next?"

"G-got p-put in a, in a b-barn."

"And?"

Cribb's shoulders were quaking faster under the blankets.

"*And?!*"

"Sh-she c-c-come."

"*Who* come?"

"M-M-Mrs., uh-uh-uh—!"

"Brandon."

"Uh-uh-uh—!"

Levi was groping across Thorpe and stroking Cribb's face. "Is all right, Joe, is all right now."

51

"DOCTOR BALMAIN! Quickly now!" Kitty Brandon stood back as the bunk's flap swung up and *Alexander*'s surgeon rolled off, still rubbing his own bruises. "Mr. Johnson's hurt himself!"

"That would not be difficult, under the present—"

"Badly. He was knocked off balance. He put out his arm. It's broken."

"One moment." Balmain turned and reached inside the bunk for his toolbag, then followed the captain's woman aft and crouched into the great cabin.

Mary Johnson was trying to support her husband's weight amidst the shambles of loose hay, fallen books, split barley bags and hysterical chickens. Richard Johnson's face was a sweaty white and his left arm was dangling at an odd angle from the elbow.

"Clear the table." Balmain pointed. Kitty Brandon swept the charts into a heap on the floor. "Get him up." Mary Johnson began trying to coax her husband nearer the table, but Balmain shoved an impatient hand under each armpit while the captain's woman gripped Johnson's ankles and helped swing him horizontal. The chaplain gasped and almost fainted.

"It's not going to be pleasant, Mr. Johnson, sir," Balmain promised, uncorking a stoneware jug and measuring half a cup of dark brown liquid. "Better get this down you first."

"What—is it?"

"Best Jamaica rum, a sovereign remedy for all pains."

"No—spirituous liquors—thank you."

Balmain frowned. "I would strongly recommend you did."

"No."

"In which case you'll have to grit your teeth and bear it."

Kitty Brandon had unbuckled Richard Johnson's breeches. She tugged their belt free and folded the leather strap to make a gag. "He'll be needing this, Mrs. Johnson."

"What for?"

"To save his tongue. Wedge it between his jaws: that's the way. Now, grip the other hand as tight as you can," Kitty Brandon advised, standing between Johnson's legs, ready to pin them flat. Balmain took out a heavy pair of tailor's shears and chewed them up the chaplain's sleeve to bare the arm. Kitty Brandon looked down at the gagged man as Balmain peeled off his own coat and got ready to manipulate the broken bones. "Well, you were wanting to know what a battle felt like. . . ."

"Guh! Gheee!"

"Steady, Mr. Johnson, sir!" The surgeon pushed his patient's head flat and began again, grating the fracture into shape.

"Guhhh—!"

"Isn't it time you showed your wife what a man's made of?" Kitty Brandon asked, bearing down harder on his trembling knees.

"Gg."

"That's the spirit."

Johnson said nothing more. Drenched with sweat, he stared up at the roof timbers until Balmain had taken a splint from his bag and bound it in place with strips of rag. Then Mary Johnson prised the wet leather from between her husband's jaws. He shut his mouth with difficulty, and tried smiling at her. "Thank you. Don't seem to be having much luck—with waves—recently."

Kitty Brandon watched the surgeon putting away his tools. "Dr. Balmain? I'm thinking Mr. Johnson will find it hard to climb into a bunk with that arm in a sling. Might it not be better if he and his wife shared these quarters down here? I'll make myself at home somewhere else."

"Good point, ma'am," Balmain replied, snapping his bag shut. "He's going to be out of action for quite a while yet."

Mary Johnson waited until the Brandon woman and Captain Sinclair had finished dinner and left to go on deck, then she unhooked the lantern to look at her husband under the table. "More soup, dearest?"

"Please."

She knelt and began spooning it into his mouth, scraping it off his whiskers whenever the ship pitched. Finally, he shook his head and she put the bowl with the others. She smiled uncertainly. "Feeling better now?"

"Yes. Thank you. It is still very cold, though."

She nodded. "Yes, but they do say we are starting to sail north, to get away from it. That means we'll soon be seeing the palm trees of Botany. That will be good, won't it?"

"Mm."

"Botany will be our first parish, and we are going to be the first to serve it. It will be a—a new beginning. I shall help you in everything you do. I shall plant the garden and look after it. I shall visit the sick, and supervise the servants, and copy your sermons, and bake your communion bread." She pulled back the blankets and eased under the table beside her husband, being careful not to touch his arm. "Richard . . . ?"

"Mm?"

She hesitated shyly. "You were very brave today."

"I was?"

"You were. And you adhered to your promise never to imbibe spirituous liquor. I am *very* proud of that."

"Thank you." He fell silent. After a while he cleared his throat and glanced her way again. "She was right, you know. If having a broken arm is anything like being in a battle, I'm fortunate to have been chosen for the more peaceable vocation." He stopped, puzzled. "Mary? What is it—?"

"Nothing!"

Kitty Brandon stood by Sinclair as the barque shortened sail for the brief hours of southern twilight. The aurora australis was still groping blindly across the empty horizon. She shivered and pulled the cloak tighter. "Dead men's fingers."

"Yon lights?"

She nodded. "We saw them almost every night, that winter, and God knows the men's spirits were low enough already."

"Yon Brunswickers? In Canada?"

She shook her head. "The year after. In the camps."

"Aye. . . ." Sinclair found a piece of tobacco inside his pocket and began chewing. "Well, there's no risk o' these items being upset by lights o' any kind." He stamped his boot on the deck above *Alexander*'s hold.

She nodded again. "I'm surprised by the way they've been able to keep up their pluck this last—what is it now, a year?—without giving up the ghost. They're a poor-looking lot, to be sure, but I'm thinking they could've given the king's German legion a lesson or two. . . ."

"Now then, woman, don't start getting any fanciful ideas," Sinclair cautioned, politely spitting to leeward. "Yon items are still in prime condition because o' the manner I treat 'em. Now, had they been darkies bound for the Barbados, we might have a different tale to tell. But as it is, Mr. Campbell's feeding them on the fat o' the land. They'll be as fit as fighting cocks when I discharge them to labour at Bottommy. Mark my words."

"Duncan . . . ?"

"Aye?"

"There was precious little of Mr. Campbell's fat in the cook's boiler this morning."

"So?"

"A word from you would surely put more heart into them, and meat into their rations. And another thing, I'm sure that their clothing was sufficient when it was thought we'd be travelling through tropical seas, but of late we haven't, have we?"

"What d'ye expect me to do about it?" Sinclair grumbled, starting to wish that he had never begun this conversation.

"Well, now that you ask, there *is* something." She smiled. "I happened to notice that we are carrying one dozen bundles of blanket cloth, on government account, for issue to the labourers upon their arrival in New Holland. Now, it seems to me that, if they were given their blankets now —when they would surely be grateful for them—the government would be saved a chore and we could then move some of that fodder from the cabin into the hold, where it belongs. . . ."

"Hm."

She squeezed his arm lightly and smiled again. "I knew you would."

"Can't be Christmas yet, can it, Joe?" Thorpe asked, looking at the shreds of beef gristle which had somehow found their way into his breakfast bowl. "And all them new bed things, too."

"Blankets. They're called blankets," Cribb replied, still marvelling at the thickness of today's boiled barley. "In the king's service a cove learns to sit on 'em before they grow legs and run away."

"Oh." Thorpe twitched his two yards of coarse grey cloth much closer and sat on top. "Then you reckon it's Christmas, then?"

Cribb chased another itch. "Search me. What you reckon, Abe?"

Levi shrugged. "What am I knowing about Christmas? One thing only I know, today I eat, today I get warm." He finished licking his bowl and hid it under the mattress before borrowing Cribb's razor to slit the blanket. He poked his head through and knotted the corners together. "There. Too bad is not longer, but half cold is better than all cold."

"Bene idea." Cribb took back the razor and slit his blanket as well, then Thorpe's. A small queue was forming along the aisle, new blankets draped over heads and shoulders, waiting to rent the razor. Some tried their luck with rusty nails and broken bottle glass, but most preferred to wait their turn to get a better cut.

When everyone had finished outfitting himself, Cribb counted the knuckles of tobacco—the smallest unit of currency aboard *Alexander*— and split them three ways with the other two men. He glanced at Levi. " 'Ow much longer till we can spend 'em in Bottommy?"

Levi reached up to feel the deep scratches above their shelf, one for each breakfast bucket since leaving Cape Town. "Eight and twenty. Nine and twenty. Thirty! A lucky number for our lucky day, Joe. First we get more grub, then warm bed things, and now a lucky thirty!"

"Ar?"

"You don't think so, Ben?" Levi was hurt that anyone could doubt his word. "Thirty is a very lucky number. Half of sixty, what is—er—three twenties, the number of fingers on hand and foots."

"*Ar?*"

"I prove. Put middle three fingers over middle three fingers and we have *four* little holes. So! Now, four is the number of eyes a man and woman have when—"

Cribb coughed drily. "I said, 'ow much longer to Bottommy?"

"Soon," Levi predicted with utter conviction. "Joe? I ever tell you of the time in Bokhara—?"

" 'Ow soon?"

"How soon? Is difficult to say *exact* number, but Reb Mordechai tell me—"

"It's bloody lucky 'e croaked it or I'd be shoving these three fingers right up 'is nose and ripping 'is bloody face off!" Cribb was crouching forward, shaking his fist under Levi's chin. "There is no bleeding Bottommy! There never was, there's never going to be! We're going round and round in bloody circles, going nowhere, that's where we're going!"

Levi slapped the fist aside. "Sure there is Bottommy Town! Sparrow Legs say so!"

"Horseshit!"

"*Putz!*"

"Oi reckon—!"

"Round and round in bloody circles!" Cribb snarled, slumping into another of his increasingly sullen moods. "Going nowhere, that's where we're going. Worse'n the bloody army."

52

HMS *SUPPLY* had been running through snow showers all day, one reef on her lower main, two jibs set. Only a solitary petrel now dipped across her wake, snapping squid from the foam, but the migrating pod of whales was still keeping the brig company into warmer, northern waters. Or, rather, they had been until a few hours ago. Ball frowned, realising that he hadn't seen their feathery spouts since the noon muster. Now, as the next watch changed over, he went aft to the dog box which served for his deckhouse. He crouched to tap the weather glass and squint at the figures behind their pipe of quicksilver.

Phillip was still working at his chart board when the ship's commander stooped into her cabin. He glanced up. "Ah, Mr. Ball. Well, assuming that your calculations are correct, and assuming that the Lilliput legend has some foundation upon fact, we soon ought to be seeing something to show for our forty days in the wilderness." He rubbed chilblained fingers. "George Rose's lad, William, does so want me—" Phillip stopped. "Is something troubling you, Mr. Ball?"

The younger man stopped scratching under his beard. "The glass is acting strangely, sir."

"Strangely?"

"Er, yes. Almost as if the mercury's leaking."

"As if the barometric pressure were falling too fast, perhaps?"

"Er, yes. Something like that, sir."

"Then we'd better take a look." Phillip ducked his head under the roof beams as Ball led the way up to the deckhouse, where they could squat out of the spray. Phillip gave the weather glass a flick and peered long-sightedly at the black figures on their ivory card, then looked at the other man again. "Have you ever been stationed in the West Indies, Mr. Ball?"

"Er, no, sir. But at the end of the war I did go out to the Med' with Admiral Parker's squadron."

"Hm. Then you can't have experienced a hurricane-force wind."

"I beg pardon, sir?"

Phillip ignored the question. "Mr. Ball. Whenever there's a conflict of opinion between our fallible human judgment and an instrument's imper-sonal prediction, play safe. God allows us only one chance to guess His mind at sea, and then get the wrong answer." The older man hunched his shoulders. "Either the laws of physics have been stood on their heads, and a falling glass no longer means what it used to, or we're in for a bit of a blow." He hesitated. "I once saw something like this off Florida. Coming home from Cuba in 'sixty-two. Usually they're tropical. Off Madras they're called cyclones. The Chinamen call them typhoons. But since we're practically the first to experience one off Van Dieman's Land, we'll have to devise a suitably infernal name once we have a few moments to spare."

Ball said nothing. He only lacked operational experience, not imagina-tion. Older captains and commanders, bosuns and seamen had taught him that a hurricane was not just a gale with rising waves and rolling crests. It was not even a full storm with mounting seas and flying foam. A hurricane was a trial by ordeal.

Phillip tapped the barometer a second time, and then looked back at the other man. "Well, my young friend, at least I have the satisfaction of knowing that the future of my colony is in good hands—yours and Mr. Blackburn's. Now, I suppose I'd better rig myself. You're going to need every man you can muster once things start happening."

"Yes, sir. Thank you, sir."

Phillip went below to the cabin and unlatched his sea chest. The yellow oilskins were under the lid where he'd stowed them in his bedchamber at Vernalls, a lifetime ago. The legs and sleeves were still dusted with pow-dered oyster shell to stop their tacky fabric from cementing itself into one lump. He kicked off his boots and stepped into the stiff trousers, then hitched their leather braces over his fearnaught.

The smell of linseed varnish was heavy with memories of the South Atlantic, commanding his cruiser off Luanda, blockading Montevideo, battling home to Rio again. Now, at an age when the survivors of his generation were starting to enjoy their estates and grandchildren in peace, he was once more buttoning himself into a storm suit.

His fingers slowed. Before nightfall this parchment yellow cloth would have become his shroud, as countless other sets of oilskins had buoyed drowned sailors into eternity, because, admiral or swabber, duke's heir or Jakob Philipp's, the sea accepted all as equals.

His fingers started buttoning again. It would be for the best. There would be no star and sash waiting for him in England, but neither would there be a firing squad on the quarterdeck. Arthur Phillip's memorial was going to be an honourable "overdue" when an Admiralty clerk ruled his name off the captain's list, his accounts paid, his duty done.

Ball coughed louder. "May I step inside for a few moments, sir?"

"What's that?" Phillip looked round sharply. "Yes. Of course. Come in, come in."

Supply's commander ducked under the door frame, his own oilskins draped over both arms. "There's not much room outside, and it's starting to blow a bit on deck."

"Yes? Now, concerning that business of mine off Havana," Phillip said. "I was also damp behind the ears, just another newly made lieutenant. They'd given me the *Infanta*—a Spanish brig even smaller than yours—to sail home. However, as luck would have it, they'd also given me an old shipmaster to be my number two, a real heart of oak, you know the sort?

"Anyhow, I don't mind admitting that I was starting to get a bit jumpy as that hurricane bore down on the fleet, and remember, we were trapped between Grand Bahama and the Florida Keys, not with a thousand miles of clear water under our lee, like you have." Phillip tried smiling. "My master, Mr. Nichol, had forty years under his hat. You know what he suggested we do?"

Ball was watching the older man pull on his sou'wester, rather like a bearded Mr. Punch. "No, sir. I don't."

"One: we agreed that a ship like ours was unlikely to founder if she was securely battened down, for whoever heard of a cork sinking? Great men o' war may break their backs in a storm, but nimble little brigs can always skip between the waves.

"Two: we agreed that our only danger would be if a following sea pooped us. Or, if we hadn't taken off enough sail, that she'd pitchpole arse over elbows. You see, the knack is to run before the wind under jib and trysail while everything else is snugged down.

"That done, you wait until the wind eases—as it will, just before the big snorter—then up with the helm. Coax her around—she'll be shipping it green and heavy, but that can't be helped—till she's lying about six points off the wind. Meanwhile, set your storm spanker and lash down the wheel so that the seas hit under your weather shoulder." Phillip was no longer a Mr. Punch; Phillip was a working sailor. "Hove-to she'll take water over the rail, but if your top hamper holds and your hull is tight, she'll ride out any amount of punishment this side of the Last Trump. You'll also find that a length of coir rope makes a most excellent sea anchor. And I would strongly urge that you—"

"Beggin' pardon, ge'men, but it's a bit o' a squeeze out 'ere."

"Come in, Mr. Blackburn." Phillip nodded affably. "You'll find it much easier to dress in here. As I was saying to Mr. Ball only a moment ago, I'm glad to be aboard such a tight little brig as yours, on a day such as this."

Supply's master began lacing into his storm suit. He nodded back. "What I always say is, who ever seen a cork sink yet?"

Who had ever seen a cork which leaked on a flat calm, or which now had both pumps manned just to stay afloat? But *Supply*'s commander kept these doubts to himself as two more of his crew struggled into the great cabin to bolt oak deadlights across the stern windows.

Phillip let the brig's working officers go ahead, and followed them on deck. He snatched at the fife rail to steady himself as sleet rattled off the helmsmen's coats. Overhead, his pennant streamed like a weathervane. Astern, the ensign stood taut from its halliards. Prudence and economy might have struck the colours by now, but the Royal Navy's pride in tradition would keep the flag flying until it blew to shreds. Or until HMS *Supply* went under.

Phillip squinted against the rising gale. Somewhere out there, *Alexander* must be battening down, for surely an old hand like Captain Sinclair would know the ropes by now?

Alexander's captain had been learning about rope since his fifth birthday, off the Shetlands. The next four decades of tempest and battle, fire and shipwreck had continued his education. "Mr. Olsen! Furl the main!"

The first mate cupped both hands to his mouth. "Furl! Main!"

The watch stumbled back to their posts through surging water and slackened the sheet before starting to haul down on the buntlines, bunching the sailcloth along its spar. Injury and sickness had left Olsen with eight sleepwalkers to drive aloft and secure it, tilting backward over the spindrift, crawling forward again on hands and knees as the mast swung over vertical and dropped away. Feet kicking ratlines glazed with ice, bare fingers clawing, the watch began laying along and over the main yard. Shoulder to shoulder to windward, battling to pass the gasket lines, subduing the canvas while their barque ploughed through smothering seas.

Alexander was now running under stripped poles except for her jib and trysail, her shrouds twanging like harp strings, her stays booming, her wash doors slamming open and shut.

The sea was charcoal grey under a rampart of cloud. Night was falling early. High cloud was thrusting across the sunset, sweeping into an immense, invisible whirlpool of air. The wind was stiffening with every gust. Foam streaked the waves, like cracks in a black mirror.

"Mr. Olsen! Take the deck! Call me up when it's time to go about!"

"Yoh!"

Sinclair fell off the ladder and lurched along the companionway. The officers' pantry had been built between the door and Olsen's bunk, where Kitty Brandon now slept. For the past few weeks the first mate had been doubling with the second, a yard or so away. Kitty Brandon was still up, bracing herself against the bulkhead, trying to chop a leg of pickled beef by the light of an oil lamp.

"For me!"

"For everyone!" she replied. "Devil a chance we'll have to eat again until this lot blows over!"

Sinclair stuffed his pockets with meat and biscuit before swaying into the cabin and groping to find his cot. The stern windows had been boarded over, and, somewhere in the darkness, Mary Johnson was probably still under the table, trying to cushion her husband's broken arm.

The second mate's lantern swung closer. "Ready to go about!"

Sinclair was as fed and rested for the night's work as he would ever be. Boots skidding, he stumbled along the companionway and climbed on deck. The eye of the storm was upon him. The cloud was thinning. A quarter moon was struggling to break through. The wind was falling back.

"Mr. Olsen! All hands!"

"All—hands!"

The marines swayed up, down, up, down on their pump handles as the barque's crewmen waded past.

"Helm alee!"

Four shapes at the binnacle began spoking their wheel, arm over arm over arm, fighting *Alexander* into the weather, shipping great seas as she came about. Bows shuddering. Falling. Heaving. Bursting free before the next roller piled atop the last.

"Helm's alee!"

"Stream the cable!"

Thirty fathoms of coir had been made ready for the sea anchor. Over their waists in black foam, *Alexander*'s men began paying it across her bows as she hove to.

"Cable's streamed!"

The barque was now as secure as she could ever be. While she had an open seaway, while her seams held, while her pumps sucked, she would survive. The eye of the storm was passing. The moon was going out. The wind was rising. Hissing sheets of water were slicing across the flattened crests.

Someone was hauling himself up the handline, gasping to a stop in the flow of the binnacle lamp. "Number two's out, chief!"

Olsen swore and spun around. "Kaptijn—!"

"I heard ye!" Sinclair's hood crowded closer to his mate's and the carpenter's. "Fix it! Get Ram's Bum here on the double!"

"Yoh!"

The marine sergeant dragged himself along the line, greatcoat plastered to chest and back. "Sah!"

"Number two pump's out! All hands on number one!"

"Sah!"

The topgallant had been furled at noon. Now, unseen in the gale, a small puff of canvas was blowing out. A gasket broke. The pouch of sailcloth was a sudden bag, ballooning, bursting with a thundering bang as the next and the next ties split. *Alexander* lurched. Olsen didn't wait for orders. "Lay aloft! Lay aloft there!"

The sail was already half set, thrashing, whipsawing the mast slings. Moments after they snapped, the rest of the barque would be heeling over, filling up, going down.

Eight shapes crawled away from the deck. Swaying backward, pitching forward, clawing the ratlines. Rain turned to sleet again. The pounding yard rebounded as the first topman faced the spar, groping for the footrope, and seven men dragged themselves shoulder to shoulder to windward. Flung across the yard. Fisting the canvas to a furl. Cursing as it burst free. Again. And again. And again. Passing the first turn of a new gasket line by feel. Then the second. And the third.

They came off the shrouds.

Olsen stared at Sinclair across the binnacle lamp. "Made—fast!"

"Not afore time!" the master yelled back. "Ginger yon chippy or it'll count for naught!"

Daybreak. The sky was a low ceiling of dirty plaster. Overnight the wind had flogged the groundswell into regiments of marching crests and valleys, their flanks the colour of dull slate. Now and again one broke ranks and surged ahead of the rest before the gale crushed it back.

Alexander's net guard, stretched taut across her forepeak, was a mad organ, keening, howling, groaning, vanishing as rollers slammed over the barque's bows; groaning, howling, keening again as they rumbled clear, pennants of water streaming from the net, blown to shreds in the great wind.

Number one pump was repaired and manned. The marines were swaying up, down, up, down on number two. While leather clack valves opened and shut in the bilge wells below the orlop deck, and while human muscles powered the iron rods aloft, *Alexander* would not founder.

Richard Johnson could still move his broken arm a little, wedged across the sodden mattress under the chart table, but his sound arm had been numb since midnight, since his wife had clutched him even tighter, since they had begun praying together. She was still shivering. "It's getting worse!"

He kissed her forehead, but said nothing. The time for saying anything more had passed. Now there was only time for feeling. Feeling her weight, feeling her terror, feeling the timber shell around them flex and tremble. Feeling strangely calm. The leaven of change was working and he was no longer afraid. He had faced agony on this table, and now he was sharing fear under it, and both were proving to be nothing more than shadows on childhood's bedchamber wall, when the wind blows and the candle flame rocks.

Daybreak. The ocean had vanished. All that remained was a grey snow-scape, the storm stripping a blizzard of spume from its mountains, dark crevasses splitting this way and that. The air was a fog of flying salt, burning the eyes, stiffening the hands, tearing like grapeshot as the marines manned both pumps again while crewmen hacked away at the trailing mizzenmast.

Alexander shuddered on the peak of a comber as the axes chopped the last rope and the raft of broken timber and sailcloth began its roaring, downhill slide, bare yards ahead of the barque. The men grabbed their handlines. A second cliff of water was dropping into the valley, flinging spars and cordage over its shoulder as it burst along the upper deck.

Sinclair was red-eyed. The deckhouse door slammed shut behind him and he staggered below. He was no longer the man he had once been. Twenty years a shipmaster to the East, he had mastered cyclones and typhoons, but this nameless southern gale was starting to try him sorely.

Kitty Brandon was at her post in the pantry, waiting for him, his breakfast ready. Sinclair snatched the door frame. Inky green water foamed past the glass skylight and drenched him through gaping seams. Wearily, he lifted his head again. "Ye're a good woman."

She watched him fumble a sticky mash of oatmeal and raisins, sugar and rum into his mouth. She had seen that face on many other men, in other battles against worsening odds.

Levi had shared his hoard of rope with Cribb and Thorpe. Now all three were lashed to the same shelf, days beyond fear or feeling. Icy bilge was surging across the gratings below them, tumbling the splintered tubs, the sodden bedding, the lags now too feeble to cling to support.

Levi watched without seeing as grey light leaked around the skylight's bars. Another day was breaking on his long, lonely road from a Polish noble's estate. Was it for this he had trudged through marshes and mountains, deserts and forests, little villages and great towns? Was it for this he had cheated and lied his way off the English gallows? But there is never any escape from God's justice. Better had he been killed on his feet, facing the enemy, like Joshua, like Judah, than drown like a dog, like *this*.

He would never reach the Promised Land. He would never greet other red Jews. Born alone, after a life alone, he would end alone.

Cribb punched his shoulder again and Levi stirred. "What?"

"Sorry!"

"Sorry?"

Cribb shifted closer to the other man. "I shouldn't 'ave said them things. About Reb Mordy. And about Bottommy." He gnawed his lip. "Wasn't fair."

Levi shrugged apathetically. "Fair? Where it say God got to be fair?"

Alexander slid off another roller and pancaked, her timbers groaning under the thunder of wind and water.

Cribb's chest tightened. His breath was quicker, shallower. "Abe? You're one of the best. We'd 'ave done it good. On the rajah's watch caper."

Levi shut his eyes. "No. No more capers. No more *shvindels*. Is all ended."

53

DAYBREAK. *Alexander* was no longer riding high against her sea anchor's drag. Now, low waves were breaking along the orlop's roof timbers and washing across the great cabin's deck above them. Someone, somewhere, was bawling muffled orders while axes and crowbars smashed through another cargo bulkhead. Much closer, other men were screaming, struggling with their chains as sea water broke over the lowest shelves.

Richard Johnson began to hurry, tugging the one sound arm from under his wife. Sick, hungry, confused, the chaplain half rolled, half fell off the chart table and staggered toward the door. He tried pushing, but the heavy planks would not budge. They were jammed, the boat was sinking, he was trapped! "Let me out!" His one fist was pounding harder and faster. "Let me out—!"

He fell backward as the door swung easily against his chest. "Wha's up? 'Alt! Who goes there? Come out you bleeders! 'Vance an' be rec'nised!" a marine shouted, clutching his musket and glaring into the darkened hole.

"It is I! And what is the meaning of this?" Johnson replied with as much dignity as he could muster, crawling forward on his knees until he could reach the doorpost for support.

"Oh." The sentry grounded his firelock and peered over one shoulder at a second, older marine inside the officers' pantry. "It's only the devil driver, Bert!"

Johnson was dragging himself upright again. He scowled at the first man's slurred, saucy tone of voice. "And who, pray, gave you orders to bar our cabin!"

"Nobody, see? We're guardin' the grog. They don't want it to go to waste, see? So piss off!"

Instead, Johnson edged closer and tried sniffing the man's foul breath. "You've been imbibing spirituous liquor!"

The older sentry lurched from the pantry, an opened bottle in one fist, the other one bunched, ready to fight any civilian who dared challenge him for it.

Johnson took a full pace backward. "This is utterly disgraceful! Your indiscipline will be reported to the authorities!"

"Ar, bugger off."

The chaplain stared at these two grinning, bleary men, then at their weapons, and followed the handline for'ard, along the companionway. Unsteady on his feet, uncertain of himself, he climbed the ladder one rung at a time and clutched the coaming at the top to get his balance again.

The gale had eased to a sullen wet hiss and the horizon had blown itself clear during the night. Only an occasional crest broke ranks along the high swell which now appeared to be standing still, like a field of grain swaying in the wind.

"Lively now! Chuck that junk over the side!" one of the mates shouted down the main hatch. Johnson got out of the way as another bale of government cargo was winched aloft to lighten the drifting barque. Exhausted marines and crewmen were still sagging up, down, up on their handles, but *Alexander* was settling faster than anyone could now shift water from her hold. Johnson forgot about reporting the sentries to Captain Sinclair, and started picking his way to the nearest pump to begin pushing down, up, down with his one arm.

Sinclair let go of the binnacle's support as his ship's carpenter hurried aft. "Well?"

"Four feet an' still gaining on us!"

"Bluidy hell. Mr. Olsen!"

"Yoh!"

"Ready or not, yon fothering mat's got to work now!"

"But she needing all hands off pumps, kaptijn!"

Alexander's main course had been cut down and wadded with oakum while the sailmaker finished lacing hog lines to its corners. But only if enough skilled hands could be driven to haul the canvas mat under her bows to stop the worst leaks would there be a chance for *Alexander*'s pumps to gain on the flooding hold.

"Bluidy hell. . . ." Sinclair wiped his face and neck while he weighed the few remaining options. "We'll have to risk it and set the idlers to work. Follow me, Mr. Olsen."

The two ship's officers shoved past Kitty Brandon and the cook, still battling to light the wrecked galley's boiler. A sack of nails and six sheaves of spade handles were swinging through the hatchway. Sinclair paused until they had also been heaved over the lee rail, then slid down the ladder to stand thigh deep at the bottom with the second mate's gang, their axes broaching another tier of government cargo bound for Botany Bay.

Olsen fumbled with the padlock and *Alexander*'s master turned to wade past, into the lags' cage, cheeks sunken under his beard, dark green rings under his eyes. Frightened shapes stared back at him, huddled above the waterline, stacked together under their rags and bedding. Sinclair's cob bashed the nearest face. "Aloft! Man the pumps, damn ye—!"

Ratbag screamed.

Levi grabbed at Cribb's shirt. "What you doing, Joe!"

"Bulldog's got cannon fever! 'E'll croak us all unless someone gets a grip on 'im!"

"Joe! Wait—!"

But Cribb was wriggling over Thorpe's chest and dropping off the other side of their shelf. Chains dragging through the floating rubbish, he surged between Sinclair and the howling convict. " 'Alt!"

Sinclair's fist stopped midstroke. "What's that ye say?!"

"Get a grip on y'self, soldier!"

"Why! Ye impudent—!"

Cribb never flinched. This could have been the moment when his bugler had sounded and Tarleton's cavalry stormed up Blackstock Hill to sabre the Rebel guns. "Flogging a dead 'orse never made it run yet! Rat's 'ad it, you've 'ad it, we've all 'ad it!"

"Seize this item, Mr. Olsen!"

"What'll that prove?" Cribb snarled. "Go on, try croaking me! 'Alf your lot's going to cough it, too!"

"Steady, Mr. Olsen!"

"Because now you've only got a couple of lifeboats! Who gets a seat?

None of us poor buggers, nor the other 'alf of your blokes! They're going to pile into the one you want, and it'll tip arse over ears, the same as it done coming 'ome from Americky!"

Olsen stopped the lag from dropping.

Cribb numbly shook his head clear. "What's that prove? Your men's finished but my coves still fresh enough to work, what's why you need 'em so bad—"

Olsen caught the lag again.

Cribb wiped blood. "So what's it worth? For us to work them pumps, eh?"

Sinclair was almost speechless. "Ye presume to bargain, wi' *me?*"

"What's there for *me* to lose?" Cribb countered. "You've still got this boat, and all the stuff in it for Chinaland. I'd reckon it's worth at least that much."

"Bluidy hell."

Cribb was shoving out his manacled wrists. "Chuck the darbies. A cove don't work good in irons."

"What if I do? What then?"

"Grub. 'Ot grub. Enough when we start, enough when we stop."

"Impossible!"

"Why?"

"The galley's washed out!"

"Then get it lit. Till then, we'll settle for officer beef and a gill of grog."

"What if I won't agree?"

"You croak too."

"Hn!" Sinclair hitched his thumbs and peered from a great distance at this nondescript little item. "Who says ye can deliver?"

"Try me."

"Not I! Ye'll have to prove ye can, first!"

"No grub, no start. No start, no work."

Sinclair had begun stroking his chin. "Which part o' the realm did ye say ye hailed from, Mr. . . . ?"

"Cribb. Sergeant major. Two wounds. Seven battle honours."

Sinclair arched sandy eyebrows in mild surprise. "I se-ee, then ye *did* have a hold over yon items after all? Hm." *Alexander*'s master considered the terms of his agreement with this dark, indestructible man. Then, cautiously, he nodded. "Done."

Cribb shoved out his wrists again. Sinclair nodded at his first mate. "The spanner."

"Yoh!"

Cribb turned as Olsen waded away to the ladder, stepped over a forge and anvil which were also being jettisoned, and scrambled aloft. Shelves of wild, shaggy faces stared back at their upright man as he squared his shoulders. "Listen in! There's grog! There's grub! And the first ten coves 'elp me eat it!" His finger stabbed. "Abe! Ben! Sly!"

Most of the shelves had emptied long before Olsen came below again with the spanner and began unbolting fetters. Sinclair urged the first batch of volunteer workers aloft, leaning against the heel of her deck as *Alexander* continued drifting downwind, out of control.

"Get yon bluidy fother in place, Mr. Olsen!" The master turned to Cribb again. "Man the pumps! Lively now!"

"Grub first."

"Mr. Olsen! Rations. . . ."

Cribb wolfed his share of the beef and biscuit before dividing the squad of men between Levi and Thorpe. "That's your pump, Abe. This one's yours, Ben. Ready? Up. Down. Up! Down! That's the ticket." He faced Sinclair. "Buckets."

"Why?"

The lags' upright man aimed his finger at the open hatch as more cargo swung aloft and was dumped over the side. "I still got blokes down there what can work for grub."

"Buckets, Mr. Olsen!"

"Yoh!"

Cribb shinned down the ladder with two looped over each arm. He waded through the gateway. "You, over there! You, you and you. Front and centre. Listen in. Bucket chain, right? You start 'ere, you chuck it over the top. The rest 'elp. Fifty loads and I'll get the grub coming your way. Move!"

He scrambled on deck again as feeble, frightened men strained to lift half-full buckets after him, passing back the empties into the hold.

" 'Ow's that fire coming along?"

The cook leaned over his galley door. "Terrible slow, Phoss. The wood's wet."

"Blow 'arder."

"Fair goes! I only got—!"

Cribb wasn't listening. He was reaching into the galley and elbowing the woman aside to snatch another bread bag.

Kitty Brandon kneaded her bruise and watched him stride for'ard to fuel his men with more ration biscuits. "Well, it seems he might be a devil daunter after all."

"Wh'sat, ma'am?"

She faced the cook. "Did you not hear what he said? Bestir yourself! I shall crush the beans, you will chop the onions!" She glanced over the galley door. "You too, Mrs. Johnson! Fan the fire! 'Tis still a fighting chance we have while those lads are kept at their labours—!"

Mary Johnson hesitated, bewildered by the wreckage and confusion on

Alexander's main deck, where Olsen's men were awkwardly trying to drag the sailcloth mat under their barque. But weeks of hunger and cold had disheartened them; they were slowing to a halt, staring aft as one of the marine sentries staggered on deck behind the barricade, embracing a cask from the spirit locker, Brazilian *aguardente* sloshing from the open bung. "G-grog up! C-come an' get it!"

"Bluidy hell! Sarn't Ramsbottom—!"

The elderly sergeant was already staring around for reinforcements to lead, but his marines, the seamen and lags from the pumps were starting to trample over each other to get past the barricade gate first.

Cribb could move even faster. Shoulders hunched, he sprinted across the flank, vaulted the spikes near his barbershop and head-butted the drunken sentry. The second marine had been weaving aloft behind him, bayonet jabbing at phantom enemies as he flopped over the poop deck's coaming. Cribb wrenched the musket from his grip and kicked the man's face down the ladder again, then twisted at the crouch and straightened into a smoothly disciplined stab, tug, club.

"Aaagh!" The first of *Alexander*'s crewmen to reach the poop jack-knifed, clutching his belly, tangling with the crowd pressing behind him as the musket butt continued its swing and stove in the cask, flooding ten gallons of raw spirit across the deck and into the scuppers.

"Follo' th' fusileers!" Marines, seamen, lags were trampling over each other to escape as Cribb charged, eyes slit, teeth bared, herding the mob for Sinclair, Olsen and Ramsbottom to flog back to work.

Kitty Brandon had dragged Mary Johnson behind cover and armed the woman with one of the cook's knives while she snatched his meat cleaver, but their help wasn't needed: *Alexander*'s master and the marine sergeant seemed to have matters under control again.

Sinclair tucked his cob under his belt and reached for a fresh chew of baccy. "D'ye indulge the habit, sergeant major?" The lags' upright man grounded his musket and took a bite. "I'll wager that wasn't the first time ye've had to master such scum?" Sinclair went on, nodding casually as Balmain tried staunching the dying seaman's bayonet gash.

Cribb said nothing. Instead, he chose a short oak belaying pin to replace the longer, heavier firelock. He hefted it in one hand, getting the balance. "I'd better see 'ow that grub's coming along."

Jane Dundas had roused four more of the convict women and pushed them on deck to help by the time the first shift of men was ready to be released from the pumps. Kitty Brandon ladled five pots of tepid broth and sent them out with the women to put some heart into the surly crew. Then she knotted her shawl and took the sixth ration into the weather herself. "Quite like old times, is it not, Mr. Cribb? No two minutes ever the same. . . ."

"Abe! Nosh up! One cove off your gang, one off yours, Ben!"

"Indeed," she went on, speaking to his back, "as I was reminding myself only a few moments ago, 'tis quite as eventful a time we've just experienced as ever we knew Over There."

"That's your lot!" Cribb shoved the men back to work. "Next!"

"Why," Kitty Brandon continued with a bright smile, "I clearly recall that matters were almost as inclement one particular night at Schuyler's Farm. . . ."

Cribb tried scowling at the smiling woman, but too much had happened since they last exchanged angry words on Table Bay. The most he could now summon up against her was a terse sniff. "It never was that wet. Not at the farm."

"No-o? Then certainly it was as cold and cheerless."

Against almost every instinct, against his will, Cribb found himself picking some boiled beans from the side of the pot she was holding out. "Long time."

"Ten whole years."

"Lot's 'appened."

"Indeed." She smiled sadly. "A great deal has happened to us both. Who would ever have thought, Over There, that we could find ourselves—here." She grimaced around at the wilderness of grey water. "Lord Luck surely has the oddest way of bestowing his favours, don't you think?"

Cribb glanced up uncertainly. "Um. Ma'am?"

"Yes?"

"Phoss!" The ship's carpenter had been reading his sounding rod on the waist deck. "We're starting to 'old it! Shove more coves on the job, quick!"

"Right-o!"

Kitty Brandon politely moved aside to let the lags' leader stride back to his duties. "Thank you, Mr. Cribb."

54

SUPPLY HAD ridden out the storm, more like a waterlogged barrel than a buoyant cork. Now, slowly, uncertainly, she was making headway again after two new yards and a foresail had been sent aloft. Her deadlights were off and the great cabin's skylight had been unbolted. Phillip was free to stand in the middle of the hatchway, head and shoulders above the poop deck, wincing at a small mirror as he shaved two months of dirty white beard. Another eight or nine weeks and he would have passed his half-century, but the seamed face which stared back at him was far older. He had embarked at Portsmouth a brisk, ambitious, middle-aged flag officer. Weather and *Supply*'s leaks permitting, that wizened stranger in the mirror must soon disembark on an unknown landscape to drink the cup of honour, or disgrace.

Phillip shivered. He shut the razor and stepped down off the stool, pulled on his mildewed watch coat and bent on deck. " 'Morning, Mr. Ball."

"Good morning, sir."

Phillip turned and walked to the taffrail. He stood alone by the tattered ensign and stared out at the marching waves. So this was the Pacific? Assuming that *Alexander* had gone down in the gale, and assuming that *La Boussole* and *L'Astrolabe* had—with any luck—hit a reef coming south, then HM Brig *Supply* was about to present Mr. Pitt with seventy million square miles of what?

Increasingly irritable, Phillip passed the rest of the morning alone, watching porpoises gambol in the brig's wake as she continued limping northward. The noon sun sight gave him something else to fret about on the chart board as he rechecked Ball's arithmetic, but there were no errors, which only made matters worse. Now, unless the wind backed, *Supply* would be off the eastern approaches to Botany Bay in about twenty-four hours' time. Say fourteen hundred and forty minutes. Or eighty-six thousand, four hundred seconds—

Phillip's pencil stopped scratching figures and he stooped back on deck to share his worries with the carefree porpoises. He pulled his telescope at the distant shoreline, still nothing more than a green smudge along the western horizon with, here and there, a few puffs of summer cloud to break the monotony. So that was New Holland? The goal of so much work and worry, Britain's new empire in the Pacific. Assuming that *Alexander* had sunk, and hoping that *La Boussole* and *L'Astrolabe* had followed her to the bottom, then *Supply* was only a few thousand seconds away from presenting His Majesty with yet more loyal and grateful subjects, like Incas. Or giants. Or midgets. Or cannibals. Or what?

Phillip kept to himself on the poop deck, which suited Ball better than he would have dared to admit, as he brought the brig inshore on a long tack to windward, closing with the smoke which had been visible for much of the day, soaring above a wildfire along the coastal ranges.

Phillip watched it glumly through his glass, almost hearing tall trees explode into fireballs as the flames advanced on a miles-long front, fanned by a stiff southeasterly. It was not the most auspicious welcome to *terra australis incognita,* he realised, trying hard to recall how it would feel to be incognito again, snug beside his fire at Vernalls while a winter gale buffeted the farmhouse chimney. Instead, here he was—

"Deck there! Sail ho . . . !"

Phillip's stomach lurched. The French were coming.

Ball cupped his mouth aloft. "Where awa-ay?"

"Three points—abaft the starboard—beam!"

Phillip breathed out. It couldn't be La Pérouse's flotilla from that quarter. Somehow *Alexander* must have weathered the storm off Van Dieman's Land, and was now making up for lost ground. He steadied his glass astern. A barque's royals, set with skysails, were just visible above the southerly bend of the ocean.

"Mr. Ball?"

"Sir?"

"Shorten sail. We shall keep company with Captain Sinclair until we make landfall. A modest show of strength might have some effect on any French interlopers as we stand into the bay."

"Aye aye, sir."

The smoke cloud was also visible from *Alexander*'s deck. Lags and marine guard were starting to snatch a few moments from their work at the pumps to nudge each other and peer northward. Levi, in particular, was muttering to himself and standing tiptoe whenever he had a chance to watch the pillar of fire and smoke.

"Deck there! Sail ho . . . !"

Sinclair cupped his mouth at the lookout. "Where awa-ay?"

"Four points! On the port bow!"

Sinclair glanced down. "Mr. Olsen? Shake out another reef."

The mate grinned back. His whistle shrilled at the deck watch. "Lay aloft! Lay aloft there! Show them navies how is the sailing!"

For once, his men needed no urging to overhaul the naval brig. Soon all padlocks would be off the scuttlebutts and water rationing ended. Soon New Holland's bumboats would start swarming across the harbour with fresh fruit and vegetables, chickens and ducks, sugarcane and coconuts. Soon, laughing, golden-skinned girls in grass skirts and crowns of flowers would begin flirting with Jack Tar while palm trees swayed in the breeze.

The barque had drawn abeam the bushfire by the time evening had turned bright orange, then dull red, and faded behind the haze of flame-streaked smoke. There was no longer a man or woman aboard the transport who could not taste, who could not smell, who could not talk about the pungent, the exciting, the wonderful scent of land.

Levi shoved away his dinner, untouched. Cribb tipped it into his own bowl and went on chewing. "You feeling all right, Abe?"

Levi's eyes were wet with happiness. "Is true. All Reb Mordechai promise is true."

"Sure." Cribb leaned over and took Levi's ration of bread as well.

The other man wiped his eyes. "The River of Fire, Sabation, *is* true."

He clasped both hands, his face transformed. *"Gott tzu danken,* tomorrow we begin living lives of lords in Bottommy Town!"

Thorpe's mouth dropped open. "Ar?"

Levi smiled through his tears. "As was in Holy Book, so is now. To-morrow you see."

The Suffolk farm boy grinned uncertainly. "You reckon them red mates will've got a place for the likes of me? Tell 'em Oi don't mind 'ard work if the grub's right!"

Levi gripped the younger man's shoulder. "Ben. Word of honour. No mate of mine will ever again hungry to bed. *Ei!* What lurks and capers we will make together!"

"Wha's up with Ikey?" a nearby lag muttered to another as they jostled round the food tub.

A third man, two places back, leaned forward. " 'E reckons we getting in Bottommy tomorrow. There's a whole town, see?"

"With free grub!" another voice cut in.

"Garn!"

"Bible truth! Every bleeder there lives like a lord. That's why we been sent, see?"

"Gor!" He spun round. "Oy! Moss Face! You 'eard what's 'appening tomorrow?"

Something alien was starting to infect the cargo of bewildered, hungry, ignorant men, cut off from Outside since embarking on the Thames a year earlier: hope. Every cockney's winter daydream was at last going to become gloriously true. Tomorrow morning they were going to start new lives of ease in a sun-drenched Land of Cockaigne, where rivers flow with beer, hot sausages grow like peas on a vine and roast pigeons fall from the sky.

"And so Reb Mordechai tell me, after they break from Babylon gaol, not all go home," Levi continued, rocking from side to side.

"They wasn't paying escape bounties that year?" Cribb asked, wriggling closer with Thorpe.

Levi tried to remember that wonderful winter in Koblenz. "I don't think he say. But no matter, ten big families get over Sabation River, to the land of milk and honey—"

"And gold?"

"Pfft! They use to make roofs."

"And grub!" Thorpe laughed.

"How much you want?"

Thorpe fumbled for words. "Enough!"

"Then enough you shall have, my friend."

"What about grog?" Cribb demanded, shouldering Thorpe aside.

"One barrel? Two?"

"Three." Cribb grinned back. "Er, you sure you got the right lingo?"

"Sure I'm sure!"

"Then the first round's on me. Two ticks after we land, I'll order a slap-up feed you'll never forget. Just like they serve ge'men at Vauxhall Gardens." Cribb was pulling apart the rags of his shirt to show the body belt of tobacco and ha'pence knotted round his chest.

"More, Mr. Johnson?"

"Er, thank you, no, Mrs. Brandon. I've had a most excellent sufficiency."

Kitty Brandon looked across the swaying pool of lantern light. "Mrs. Johnson?"

"No. Thank you."

Sinclair leaned forward. "I'll not see good food go begging." Kitty Brandon heaped his platter with more of the cook's celebration dinner—a duff of broken biscuit, dried fruit and molasses—and Sinclair eased back in his seat again, one ear cocked for the steady whumph, whumph, whumph of pump rods vibrating through his ship's frame. He picked up the mug of rum. "Land."

Kitty Brandon raised her wineglass. "To land."

Richard Johnson was still lifting a beaker of lemon water with his one sound arm when Sinclair put the mug down again. He wiped his mouth along the back of his wrist. "Tell me, Reverend, what are your intentions now that we have concluded our passage to New Holland?"

"My wife and I will go directly ashore and give thanks to God."

"Uh huh. Then what?"

"Why, I shall take up my appointment as the colonial chaplain and, as soon as may be, start my studies of the Indian tongue."

Sinclair had been nodding in time with the young man's words. "Then may I say how heartened I am to hear that one person in authority has some notion of what he's about?"

Johnson smiled and eased back in his chair, too. "Captain Sinclair, you sound as if you doubt such a thing were possible."

The older man went on forking food from his platter. "Let's just say that I have some experience o' this world and its affairs, as ye have o' the next and its. We both know how rarely they jibe."

Johnson was still smiling. "If ever I thought they did, once, these last months would surely have changed my way of thinking."

"I've no doubt they have," the shipmaster replied, more to himself, as he glanced up from the table and finished chewing. "Mr. Johnson. We have not always seen eye to eye, but never have I doubted your sincerity of purpose or Christian endeavour. Both are excellent precepts and I wish ye well." He paused; he almost hesitated. "But don't build your hopes too high. Live each day as it comes and ye'll make the distance yet."

"Thank you," Johnson replied, "but what is it you are really telling me?"

Sinclair pondered his answer. "This. Ye may find that we've been travelling around the globe wi' a blacker tribe o' heathens than ever ye'll find over yonder, when we land. There might come a day when the Indians, whose tongue ye wish to learn, will seem as angels o' light alongside the Christians ye'll be ministering to."

Mary Johnson sat forward abruptly. "Surely the fact that my husband is——?"

Sinclair's hand silenced her. "I have no wish to dispute points o' doctrine wi' ye, ma'am. It is sufficient to draw his attention to the fact that not all his parishioners and neighbours will be as high-minded and charitable as ye both are." He paused again, his face troubled. "I've had to lead a rough and tumble life. In my calling we have to deal wi' all conditions o' men, in all manner o' ports. Their womenfolk too. That's why I can promise ye thieves, and fornicators, and unregenerate murderers aplenty in New Holland, alongside which any honest black cannibal will seem as one o' the heavenly host."

"Thank you, captain," Mary Johnson replied, staring directly across the table, "but we have already made that discovery for ourselves."

55

PHILLIP WAS on deck long before daybreak, watching the bushfire's dull glow astern. Somewhere, a few miles to the north, smaller fires would now be glowing beside the sea, under the breakfast kettles of a French garrison. Exhausted with worry and self-doubt, he turned from the lee rail as someone trod the deck behind him. *Supply*'s commander was having no better luck with his sleep. He stifled a yawn. " 'Morning, sir."

" 'Morning."

The two men fell silent, listening to the running slap of waves as the brig continued steering her way across black water, into dark grey, onto a sad green swell. Far to the east a furnace mouth was opening in the gap between skyline and low clouds as fiery snakes squirmed across the Pacific. Arthur Phillip shivered. Long before the sun set, he would be either a future nabob or the ridicule of Britain. No other option was left for him. And not for the first time in his life he felt wretchedly alone as he went below to whatever sort of breakfast his manservant could warm on a spirit lamp.

He was still brooding over a pannikin of cold coffee when Ball crouched into the cabin and saluted. "Cape Solander, sir."

Phillip looked up, his eyes red. "You're sure?"

"Unless Mr. Cook's survey is in error, yes."

"And the French?"

"No sighting yet."

"Proceed."

"Aye aye, sir."

Phillip stood, more like one of the condemned at Newgate than a king's officer, and reached for his coat. He followed *Supply*'s commander on deck. Now Holland was very close now, running under the lee at a distance of perhaps two miles as the brig and her escort reduced sail. Four points off the port bow lay a low, wooded headland—Cape Solander, named by Sir Joseph Banks for his Swedish assistant—behind which HMS *Endeavour* had once sheltered for a week.

Mr. Master Blackburn had begun swaying out the pilot boat in which he was going to row ahead with sounding line and compass. Phillip watched the crew's disciplined haste with envy: no matter what happened in the next few minutes, nobody in higher authority would order their execution for being too slow.

Phillip turned his back on them. He slung his telescope on its lanyard. He trod forward to the foremast shrouds. He started aloft up the ratlines—passing the topmen, out along their yard—and clambered onto the empty crosstree. There was still one option. He looked at it, a clear drop of sixty feet to the deck.

Phillip steadied his breath and drew the telescope's tubes, resting them against the rough pine pole. *Supply*'s pilot boat was now a full cable length ahead, its oars dipping the shallows like a beetle on a pond. Tapering away into the distance, far to the south, half moons of surf were breaking along an empty coastline. The telescope's disc crept inland over an unbroken carpet of treetops, tracking a low range of hills, shimmering in the summer heat, as impenetrable as the Brazilian *sertão*.

Cape Solander had inched abeam the brig, slowly opening the narrow strait between its timber and the low scrub of Cape Banks on the opposite shore. Rocking on the swell, bowsprit nodding, *Supply* was feeling her way onto the last thousand yards of a sixteen-thousand-mile voyage.

Phillip was sweating. The glass wouldn't stay in focus. His hands shook. He pressed the telescope barrel flat against the splintery mast. He could smell its creosote in the sun. He wiped the warm salt from his eyes. He tried again, holding his breath as the brig crept round the cape under short canvas. *"Gott sei dank. . . ."* The mast trembled against Phillip's face as

Supply's bower anchors plunged, shattering the tropical peace. Botany Bay was empty. New South Wales was his. New Holland was his. Honour and respect were his.

Alexander's rails and rigging were stacked to the crosstrees with anxious, murmuring men as the barque continued her middle passage between the two headlands. Cribb stood under the sunshade with Thorpe, alert for the first glimpse of Bottommy's crowded docks and warehouses, its gilded palaces and busy streets. He was sweating hard. The body belt was heavy with copper coins and lumps of tobacco.

He wiped his neck. The first thing he must get, once they got ashore, was three beers. And three for Abe. And three for Ben. And they were going to be cool, smooth, brown, with thick, creamy rings of foam round the top of each jug. And they were going to stand them in a line on a table under a shady tree and listen to the band play. And when it got dark, and when everybody was busy looking up at the fireworks, Ben, and Abe, and himself were going to float through the crowd and free some pockets before ordering the best, slap-up feed ever.

Mary Johnson gripped her husband's arm. Very soon now they would see their first Indian canoe, and a native village of grass huts, and all those other curiosities which they were going to announce to the world in long letters home. And there were going to be pagan idols and customs to describe in a book, when, eventually, her husband was invited back to England to be enthroned at a higher bishopric after illuminating the antipodes with the radiant torch of faith. In the meantime, there was going to be so much to achieve in the life of service and duty which was beckoning them both. She gripped Richard harder. "Thank you."

Kitty Brandon kept her distance on the poop deck. She shaded her eyes. So this was Bottommy Bay? Rock bottommy, more like, but what odds that it was as bare as a manager's moneybox two minutes after the show closed? It was going to be a rare treat just to rinse her things in fresh water and pin them on a bush to dry while she strolled along the beach. Then, once *Alexander*'s carpenter and crew had cobbled together the ship's planks again, they'd be off on the last leg of their journey to Chinaland.

A flock of parakeets screeched overhead from the scrub as *Alexander* ghosted on. Two pelicans floated past to touch down near a mangrove swamp. Somewhere a fish splashed. Cribb swapped a puzzled look with Thorpe, then with Levi, now only a few feet away. "Abe? They got it wrong. This ain't Bottommy."

Sinclair was standing close behind, catching some of the shade for himself. He squirted tobacco juice over the side, into the sparkling shallows. "One shilling will get ye five it is."

"You'd lose," Cribb replied. "Bottommy's got everything. What's this dump got?"

"Still don't change the fact that it's written 'Botany Bay' on my charts," Sinclair said, distracted by other problems as *Alexander* came up into the wind.

"You're joking!"

"If I were, it would be the first time the likes o' ye had ever heard me jest," the shipmaster concluded, moving away to watch the helmsman.

Levi was still staring fixedly at the forest as Cribb edged closer and tapped him on the shoulder. " 'Ere. Abe. Bulldog reckons this is Bottommy."

Levi damped his lips. "Is wrong."

Cribb was starting to feel uneasy about something. "Well, mate, I bloody well 'ope you're right."

Alexander's anchors plunged, shattering the silence, their echoes swallowed up by the twisted trees and spiky undergrowth which crowded down to the high water mark. And then the silence crept back. And waited.

A NOTE ON THE TYPE

This book was set in a modern adaptation of a type designed by the first William Caslon (1692–1766), greatest of English letter founders. The Caslon face, an artistic, easily read type, has had two centuries of ever-increasing popularity in our own country—it is of interest to note that the first copies of the Declaration of Independence and the first paper currency distributed to the citizens of the newborn nation were printed in this type face.

Composed by American–Stratford Graphic Services, Brattleboro, Vermont

Printed and bound by Fairfield Graphics, Fairfield, Pennsylvania

Typography and binding design by Dorothy Schmiderer

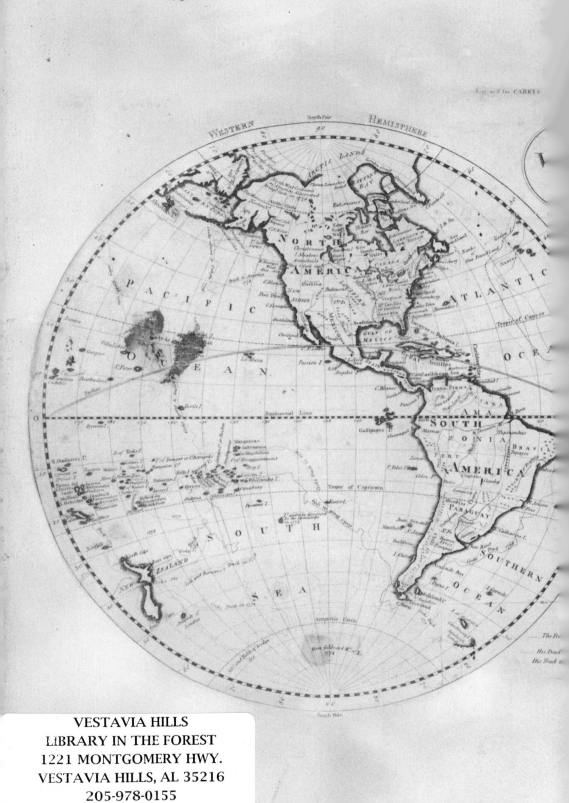